THE YEAR'S BEST

Fantasy & Horror

THE YEAR S BEST

Fantasy & Horror

TWELFTH ANNUAL COLLECTION

Edited by

Ellen Datlow & Terri Windling

St. Martin's Griffin ⚓ New York

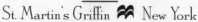

FOR VIC & PEG, WITH LOVE.
—T.W.

THIS ONE'S FOR LUCIUS SHEPARD AND PAT CADIGAN.
—E.D.

Contents

Acknowledgments

A volume like this is made possible with the input and cooperation of a number of people. I'd like to thank the publishers, editors, writers, and readers who send material and make suggestions every year. This year I'd particularly like to thank Linda Marotta, Bill Congreve, C. S. Fuqua, Jo Fletcher, Stephen Jones, Gardner Dozois, Gordon Van Gelder, Sheila Williams, Jamie Blackman, Mardelle and Richard Kunz, and John Klima.

Thanks go to Jim Frenkel, our packager, and his assistants Kristopher O'Higgins and Seth Johnson; to our in-house editor Gordon Van Gelder and his assistants Corin See and Bryan Cholfin; and to Tom Canty for creating a beautiful package for our words.

And a special thanks to my co-editor Terri Windling, who makes the job slightly less daunting just by my knowing she's going through the same thing—particularly at deadline time.

I'd like to acknowledge the following magazines and catalogs for invaluable information and descriptions of material I was unable to get hold of: *Locus* magazine, *Publishers Weekly*, *Washington Post Book World*, *The New York Times Book Review*, the DreamHaven catalog, Mark V. Ziesing's catalog, PDW Books catalog, The Overlook Connection catalog, *Necrofile*, *Hellnotes*, the *DarkEcho Newsletter*, *The Heliocentric Network*, and *The Gila Queen's Guide to Markets*.

—E. D.

I would like to thank all the book and music publishers, publicists, editors, and writers who sent us 1998 material for review. Charles N. Brown's *Locus* magazine and amazon.com were invaluable reference sources, as were *Publishers Weekly*, the *New York* and *London Times* book reviews, *The Women's Review of Books*, *The Hungry Mind Review* and *Folk Roots*. The fantasy half of this volume would not be possible without the Endicott Studio staff in Tucson: assistant editors Richard and Mardelle Kunz, and our amazing research assistant Bill Murphy. Submission information for next year's volume, as well as other Endicott Studio news, can be found on the World Wide Web at: www.endicott-studio.com.

Many thanks also to Jim Frenkel, who created this series and keeps it running, along with his assistants Kristopher O'Higgins and Seth Johnson. And to our St. Martin's editor, Gordon Van Gelder, his assistant Corin See, and my partners-in-crime: co-editor Ellen Datlow and artist Tom Canty. The following folks also have my gratitude for various kinds of assistance: Charles de Lint, Ellen Kushner, Delia Sherman, Ellen Steiber, Jane Yolen, Joe Monti, Andy Heidel, Jo Fletcher, Andy Duncan, Lisa Goldstein, Patrick Nielsen Hayden, Gardner Dozois, and Peter Brough.

T. W.

As packager of this series, I depend on all those thanked above, especially my uberstaff, Mssrs. O'Higgins and Johnson. Also invaluable are interns: Sarah Kleinman, Emily Burchfield, Melanie Orpen, and Emese Gaal. The University of Wisconsin's Memorial Library Reference Desk has been an invaluable resource. Thanks to Jessica Frenkel for brainstorming the jacket concept, and to Copy-Nation for timely faxing in a pinch.

—J. F.

Summation 1998: Fantasy

Terri Windling

Readers familiar with the field of fantasy literature, and with these *Year's Best Fantasy and Horror* volumes, need no introduction to the series—you may want to skip right down to the lists of recommendations that follow. But for readers new to either, an explanation is in order.

The mandate for this annual anthology is to gather together the very best fantasy and horror short fiction published in the previous year. The term "fantasy" is a confusing one, however. Once upon a time fantasy literature was not considered an oxymoron. Shakespeare, Spenser, Goethe, Pope, Rossetti, Morris, Wilde, Yeats, Tolstoy, Chesterton, Thurber and many others penned works with magical elements drawn from folklore, myths, and national epics (Arthurian legends, the Ring of the Nibelungs, etc.). In the 1970s, after the enormous success of J. R. R. Tolkien's *The Lord of the Rings*, fantasy became a publishing category (commonly paired with science fiction) and the term today generally evokes images of Tolkien clones: 900-page volumes and their endless sequels, filled with dragons, wizards, swordsmen, and a singing elf or two.

Yet as the modern fantasy genre grew, despite the commercial popularity of Tolkienesque sagas, the genre also became a home for a group of fine modern writers inspired by the older, pre-Tolkien tradition of fantastic literature. As a result, the fantasy genre today is a lively, topical, extremely diverse area of publishing—ranging from the sword-and-dragon books at one end of the field (which make no claim to literary greatness, and yet can be quite entertaining) to serious works of mythic and magic realist fiction at the other. Readers in the 1990s seem to hunger for both kinds of work, judging by the healthy sales fantasy books enjoy (at least compared to other genres). In addition, there's a great deal of fantasy to be found outside the genre as well, over on the mainstream shelves. Here we rarely find "imaginary world" type fantasy (Michael Ende's *The Neverending Story* is one of the few exceptions), but mythic fiction (contemporary tales infused with myths, folklore and fairy tales) and magic realism (popularized by Latin-American writers) can be found in abundance in the works of such authors as Angela Carter, A. S. Byatt, Joyce Carol Oates, Margaret Atwood, Robert Coover, Steven Millhauser, Sara Maitland, Marina Warner, Alice Hoffman, and a host of others. It is no accident that so many of the aforementioned writers are women—which is also true in the fantasy genre. The roots of fantastic literature run deep into the oral folk tradition, which has been an important venue for women's stories since the dawn of time. In ages past, such stories were dismissed as "just old wives' tales"—today they can be dismissed as "just fantasy." But as many talented writers (both male and female) working nowadays have discovered, a mix of realist and nonrealist imagery makes for powerful fiction, echoing ancient themes yet relevent to our modern lives.

In this anthology, we like to look at the broader field of fantastic literature, which includes, but is not limited to, the modern fantasy genre. Horror fiction is a sister genre with roots in the same soil of oral narrative—so we've chosen to bring these works together into one volume: stories both dark and bright, as well as all the shades that lie between. The fiction in *The Year's Best Fantasy and Horror* is reprinted from genre anthologies and magazines, and also from mainstream collections, literary journals, and foreign works in translation. If you prefer fantasy to horror fiction, look for my initials on the story introduction; if you prefer the opposite, look for Ellen Datlow's. (Stories that fall between the two carry both our initials, with the acquiring editor listed first.) Yet we encourage you to try both forms whatever your usual preference might be, for we strongly believe the two fields enrich each other when viewed side by side.

I am also a great believer in the idea that genre fantasy and mainstream fantasy can easily be read together and have much to offer each other. Genre readers (and writers) who never venture outside the field are creating a ghetto cut off from participation in the evolution of English language literature, with all its riches. Mainstream writers who disdain genre fiction are losing out as well—for genre writers (including SF and mystery writers) have much to teach the mainstream about the building blocks of good storytelling: pacing, plotting, and narrative drive. One thing I've noticed while reviewing books for this year's annual is that we are seeing a whole crop of young writers whose books are gorgeously descriptive, yet never *go* anywhere. It's not such a problem in short fiction, since the brief form of a short story nicely accommodates the "slice of life" approach, a snapshot moment illuminated by the flash of the writer's attention. But a novel moves; it's more like a journey in which the author is our guide—and too many young mainstream writers are turning out books that simply stand still. It's one thing when a master storyteller chooses to subvert the traditional narrative process (as in Robert Coover's brilliant *Briar Rose*) . . . but in too many lesser books, one is left with the impression that young writers are avoiding plotting and pacing because they simply don't know how to do it. (The equivalent in art is all those art students who gravitate to abstract expressionism because they don't know how to draw—unlike Jackson Pollack, who did.) Genre fantasists, on the other hand, excel in the mechanics of storytelling, which is no surprise since we are the "old wives" (men and women alike) of our modern age.

If I could make a wish, I'd like to see genre suspicion of mainstream books, and mainstream disdain for genre books, swept away like the useless chaff it is. I'd like to see all these books sit side by side on a shelf marked "Fiction." *The Year's Best Fantasy and Horror* will continue to provide a forum for both, exploring the myriad ways modern writers use the tools of surrealism, myth, and magic.

Moving on to the fiction itself, the books listed below are ones that made 1998 another good year for lovers of the fantastic. Trends? Well, there is some great Native American fiction out there this year, making beautiful use of mythic and magical elements. Two of the books in the Top Twenty list are by Native authors, and a third draws upon Native folklore. For readers interested in American fantasy, as opposed to the quasi-Celtic, quasi-medieval sort, you can't get more American than this. Another trend is that Imaginary World fantasy is an area that has come back to life, attracting some of the best authors in the genre—which is a real turnaround from just a few years ago. There were fewer end-of-the-millenium books than you'd expect. Maybe they're all in the science fiction field. And there are more gentle books with a turn-of-the-century flavor (the last century, that is), works inspired by the likes of Lord Dunsany and Hope Mirrlees, which is a welcome trend indeed.

My tireless assistant editors, Richard and Mardelle Kunz, collected more than five hundred books for review last year. Here's the best of what came across my desk in 1998:

Top Twenty

Here are the "Must Read" novels of 1998 (in alphabetical order by author). An extended reading list of novels, short stories, art books and nonfiction follows.

Flanders by Patricia Anthony (Berkley): Anthony's new novel is a visceral work of historical fantasy about the life of an American soldier in a British unit during World War I. Set in 1916, the story is told through letters between Travis Lee, a sharpshooter, and his brother back home in Texas. Nothing in Anthony's previous work—strong though it is—prepared me for this astonishing book. The author vividly re-creates nerve-wracking days in the muddy trenches, haunted nights in no-man's-land, and one man's struggle to retain his soul as he walks through hell on earth. Compelling, almost hypnotic, this one belongs on the shelves beside Sebastian Faulks and Pat Barker, which is high praise indeed.

I Was a Teenage Fairy by Francesca Lia Block (HarperCollins): Block is one of the pioneers of "urban fantasy" fiction, bringing myth and magic to modern city streets peopled with sharply contemporary characters—in this case, a troubled Valley Girl and a fiesty little fairy named Mab. Block's books are published for teenagers (among whom they have a cult following), but her work is hard-hitting, with a sharp, dark edge to satisfy adult readers. This one takes on the L.A. modeling world, stage mothers, and pedophiles—as well as love in all of its manifestations, both dark and bright.

Heartfire by Orson Scott Card (Tor): At a time when so many magical sagas use medieval epics or Celtic myths for inspiration, Card has created a truly American fantasy drawn from our own landscape, steeped in the myths and folkways of early settlers, slaves, and native peoples. In volume five of his "Alvin Maker" series, Alvin's wife Margaret (who can read the future in the "heartfires" of others) becomes involved with the redundant abolition movement in the southern states. As always, Card tells his tale with clean, clear prose, rigorous scholarship, and a bone-deep knowledge of American history, folklore, and human nature.

Lambs of God by Marele Day (Putnam): This oddly captivating book was one of my favorite finds of the year. The novel was a bestseller in Australia—and you gotta love that country, since how often do books about nuns, selkies, and sheep hit our bestseller lists? The story takes place in a crumbling abbey on an island that has been forgotten by time. Three rather earthy nuns live there, spinning fairy tales and the wool from their flock, until a young priest stumbles into their garden of Eden from the World Outside. He's come to the island with development schemes to turn it into a wealthy resort. What happens next is too strange to reveal. You must read it for yourself.

This Body by Laurel Marian Doud (Little, Brown): Doud's first novel begins with the death of its protagonist, Katherine Ashly, a middle-aged housewife and mother of two. She wakes up a year later in the body of a rich, thin younger woman in L.A.—not the worst of fates perhaps, but there's a catch. Thisby, whose body and identity she has assumed, is a drug-addicted mess. And Katherine's own family up north seem to be doing just fine without her. This isn't a perfect book—the plot relies on too much coincidence, and the ease with which Katherine enters the L.A. art world requires even more credulity than the body-switching premise. It's not even an original idea—*Trader* and other novels have used it before. So why am I listing it in the Top Twenty? Because, despite its flaws, Doud's novel is highly entertaining, saved by the author's gift for creating fresh, compelling characters—particularly Katherine's Shakespeare-spouting, completely dysfunctional new family.

Someplace to Be Flying by Charles de Lint (Tor): This is the first of three excellent novels making use of Native American myth. It's the latest book in de Lint's "Newford" series, and easily the best one to date. Set in Newford, a contemporary city somewhere in North America, it is the story of the First People (the animal people), legendary figures who appear in the tales and creation myths of numerous indigenous tribal groups. In de Lint's story, these ancient First People still hold the fate of our world in their hands—but now Coyote, Raven, Fox, and others (including the delightfully punky Crow Girls) have taken on modern coloration. They walk among us, recognized by only a few for what they really are. Those few include artists, dreamers, and outcasts: typical de Lint characters, brought vividly to life. This Canadian author is considered one of the very best storytellers in the field of mythic fiction, and his unusual, deeply magical new novel demonstrates why.

The Antelope Wife by Louise Erdrich (HarperFlamingo): When I finished this book, I had tears in my eyes—not because the ending is sad, but because it's a novel so beautifully crafted, so rich in color and character, that it moved me to the core with its sheer power of language and story. Set in modern Minneapolis, it's a tale of "urban Indians," family, and the many faces of love: from selfless and redemptive passions to soul-destroying obsessions. Myths, legends, and history are all mixed into the contemporary story, stitched into patterns as bright and intricate as Indian beadwork (a recurrent image in the text). Erdrich (a mixed-blood Chippewa) has always been a gifted author, creating interesting tales in collaboration with the late writer Michael Dorris; but with this tour de force of mythic fiction she has come into her own. The slight chill in her previous work is entirely absent here. *The Antelope Wife* is a warm-blooded, passionate book, and as fine as they come.

Stardust by Neil Gaiman (Avon Books): British writer Neil Gaiman has already proven amply that he's one of the most talented and versatile writers working in the modern fantasy field, so it should come as no surprise that when he strays into the realm of Faerie he conjures pure enchantment there—despite the fact that this magical landscape lies rather far afield from the edgy dark fantasy and horror tales that are Gaiman's trademark. The story is set in mid-Victorian England, in the woodland town of Wall, named for the rock barrier that skirts its eastern edge. The realm of Faerie lies on the other side, and the wall may not be breached—except for a few days every nine years, when human and faerie folk mingle in a vast, exotic outdoor market. Gaiman draws upon British folk tales, as well as classic fantasy literature by George MacDonald, Christina Rossetti, William Morris, William Hope Hodgeson, Lord Dunsany, and others, to create a sparkling new story with all the magic of the old ones. *Stardust* began as a graphic novel created in collaboration with artist Charles Vess, and thus is also available in illustrated form. Whichever way you choose to enter Faerie, through the novel or the collaborative version, you'll find a land of wonders there, and a story for readers of all ages destined to be a classic in its own right.

Strandloper by Alan Garner (Harvill Press): Garner is the author of *Elidor, The Owl Service, The Weirdstone of Bringamen* and other British fantasy novels, now considered classics, that have strongly influenced our field. Despite a subtle and sophisticated sensibility, these works were published as children's fiction. Now he has published an unusual novel specifically for adult readers—a deeply mythic tale unlike anything else you will have read before. Set in the 18th century, it was inspired by the true story of an Englishman named Will Buckley who was arrested for performing an ancient fertility rite in a rural village. Charged with "lewdness and popery," he's transported to a prison camp in Australia—at which point history loses sight of him, while Garner's novel continues. In Garner's story, Buckley escapes and is taken in by Aboriginals, where he undergoes an extraordinary transformation among the rites and tales of the Dreamtime. The novel is told in lyric prose, steeped in the folklore of two lands that are worlds apart . . . yet not so different in spirit. This challenging work of mythic fiction won't be to every reader's taste, but it's a brilliant book, at the cutting edge of the field, filled with genuine magic.

Power by Linda Hogan (W. W. Norton): In a year in which we have an embarrassment of riches when it comes to tales based on Native-American myths, the latest novel by this Chickasaw writer is a real treasure nonetheless. Set in the swamps of Florida, it's the story of a Native girl whose aunt has ritually hunted and killed an endangered species of panther. The novel is partly a mystery (why would her aunt kill a beautiful creature with whom she has a strong mystical connection?), partly a courtroom drama (pitting Native rights activists and environmental activists against each other), and partly the coming-of-age story of a teenager discovering her own identity, history, and power. The writing absolutely shimmers and Hogan's plot is highly suspenseful, making for another fine work of mythic fiction that I can't recommend too highly.

Sailing to Sarantium by Guy Gavriel Kay (HarperPrism): Kay's new novel (the first half of a two-volume work) would be historical fiction if it weren't for the fact that his tale unfolds in a landscape that doesn't exist. Sarantium is a city of multilayered complexity, a place where "everything on earth was to be found, from death to the heart's desire." The main protagonist is a mosaic artist, whose

journey to Sarantium leads him into the dark woods both physically and metaphorically. Again, to quote the author: "To say of a man that he was sailing to
Sarantium was to say that his life was on the cusp of change: poised for emergent
greatness, brilliance, fortune—or else at the very precipice of a final and absolute
fall. . . ." Indeed, here we have the theme of Kay's powerful story in a nutshell.
Kay is a literate, fiercely intelligent writer, and he brings all his considerable
imaginative powers to the creation of a fully realized world, a brilliantly nuanced
set of characters, and a Byzantine plot that draws you in and leaves you wanting
more.

The Vintner's Luck by Elizabeth Knox (Farrar, Straus & Giroux): Sometimes
you stumble across a book that you immediately have to give to all your friends—
and for me, this astonishing novel (by a writer better known in New Zealand)
was one of them. Set in rural France at the very beginning of the nineteenth
century, it's the story of Sobran Jodeau, the scion of a wine-making family, and
his relationship with a beautiful male angel named Xas. The novel follows Sobran
from youth to manhood, from marriage to old age and death, shadowed by a
creature who has been marked by both God and Lucifer. Initially meeting just
once each year, the angel slowly moves into Sobran's life, his heart, and eventually his bed. It's an amazing story about friendship, family, faith, rural village
life, sensual pleasures, and fine French wine. It will leave you breathless.

A Clash of Kings by George R. R. Martin (Bantam): We listed Martin's last
novel, *The Game of Thrones*, as one of the Top Twenty books of 1996; now
Martin has given us a sequel to that volume, and it's a winner too. If all those
dreary, derivitive sagas that crowd the bookstore shelves these days made you
swear off traditional fantasy (and multi-book epics in particular), here's one that
will change your mind. Like Guy Gavriel Kay, Martin is a skillful, intelligent
writer breathing new life into the tropes of the genre. It's the story of a land
ravaged by politics, war, and wizardry—but Martin subverts these potential clichés to create a taut, ingenious tale, filled with real people, not cartoons. Give
this one a try. Your faith in fantasy will be restored.

The Ballad of Frankie Silver by Sharyn McCrumb (Dutton): This is the fifth
book in McCrumb's best-selling "Ballad" series, contemporary murder mysteries
imbued with the folk tales, music, and magic of American-Appalachian culture.
Her latest follows two plot lines: the true 19th-century story of the first woman
in North Carolina to be executed for murder, and a contemporary tale of a young
sheriff whose testimony sent a man to death row. McCrumb weaves these tales
together, along with glittering nuggets of mountain country history and lore. If
you haven't yet discovered McCrumb's fine "Ballad" series, then I think it's only
fair to warn you that you're likely to be hooked.

Song for the Basilisk by Patricia A. McKillip (Ace): *Booklist* calls McKillip "one
of the least-publicized American masters of fantasy," and I agree. This writer
should be winning awards left and right and appearing on the bestsellers lists;
instead, she quietly turns out one exquisite book after another—without fanfare,
yet avidly snatched up by discerning readers. Here's yet another McKillip gem:
the story of musicians in a wind-swept land and a walled city with a Renaissance
feel. The protagonists are an enigmatic poet/harpist and his headstrong grown-
up son, searching for memories and identity in the ashes of the past. The narrative is poetic and elegant, yet there's real human warmth here, too, and

characters who win your heart. On one level, it's a traditional quest story—on another, the book and its wise author have deeper issues to explore about the relationship between making history, community, and music.

The Innamorati by Midori Snyder (Tor): If you had to pick only one Imaginary World fantasy novel to read this year, this would be the one. Like Patricia Anthony, Snyder's previous work does not prepare you for the power and scope of her ambitious new novel, which has been garnering acclaim from both genre and mainstream reviewers here and in Italy. The world of *The Innamorati* resembles that of the Italian Renaissance, but one in which myths, mazes, masks, and magic are brought to life. Borrowing from early Roman myth, Boccacio, Dante, Italian folk tales, and the Commedia dell'Arte, Snyder's story involves a vast cast of characters on pilgrimage to Labirinto, a city with a mysterious labyrinth at its heart where curses may be lifted. The bawdy exuberance of Snyder's language and plot are arrested only by moments of breathtaking enchantment: a Siren who sings a city into coral; masks that take on a life of their own; Bacchian revelers, monsters, centaurs, and ghosts touched by the madness of the gods. Snyder spent a year in Italy preparing to write this magnificent book, and her love for the land, its history, art, and myths, shines in every line.

Mockingbird by Sean Stewart (Ace): Antoinette Beauchamp, corporate actuary, has no interest in the magic that ruled her mother's life, alternately gifting and tormenting her. So on the day of her mother's funeral, she is dismayed to discover that it is she (not her clairvoyant sister) who has inherited her mother's gifts—specifically, the Riders, a set of six eerie handmade dolls kept in a wooden chifforobe, each with a powerful character capable of riding or possessing their keeper. Once the Riders enter Toni's life, it promptly falls apart—and the novel is the story of how she rebuilds it. The magic here, a wholly original blend of New Orleans-style voodoo and the Mexican supernatural, colors a loving portrait of contemporary Houston, with its lush gardens, gleaming skyscrapers, cutthroat commodities traders, trailer parks, ghosts, and "spirit cars" (lowriders capable of driving into alternate realities). It's a simpler story than Stewart's last novel, *Nightwatch*, yet even more memorable—a story about families, their secrets and betrayals, and the love that heals the wounds of the past.

The High House by James Stoddard (Warner): Many of the readers and writers who came into the fantasy field from the mid-1970s onward did so because of the "Sign of the Unicorn" series (edited by Lin Carter), which published classic fantasy works by past masters like William Morris, E. R. Eddison, Mervyn Peake, Lord Dunsany, James Branch Cabell, et al. Stoddard's marvelous novel is a loving homage to these classic tales, and evokes a particular sense of wonder I haven't experienced in years. It's the story of a magical house so vast it has its own weather system, and of a man summoned to be Steward of the house after his father's death. There's peril, of course, and magical characters, creatures, and objects with a life of their own. It's a glittering tale, with a few small faults (the narrative is somewhat episodic), but then it's a first novel, and as such pretty darn confidently told. *The High House* is a book to remind us of what attracted most of us to this field, a literary magic too often obscured by all the Tolkien-redux books. Thank you, Mr. Stoddard.

The Compass of the Soul by Sean Russell (DAW): This is the second half of a two-volume story beginning with *Beneath the Vaulted Hills*. I recommend reading them together. Set in an imaginary land where magic is on the wane, this is a traditional quest fantasy of the very best sort: where the quests are spiritual and personal in nature as well as heroic. The focus of this volume is a young woman in training to be a mage—much to the displeasure of the last true mage, who has visions of an apocalypse to come if the practice of magic does not cease. Russell's characters (and moral outlook) are mature, multilayered, and fluid; there are no clear-cut heroes and villains here, but real people making history the way real people do: groping in the dark, doing the best they can, guided by conflicting systems of belief. The story transports you into a fully-realized secondary world, beautifully rendered, filled with a cast of characters so real it seems that you must say goodbye to friends when the tale is done. Book by book, Russell is emerging as one of the best fantasists of his generation.

The One-Armed Queen by Jane Yolen (Tor): While many fantasy writers seem to need an endless number of 900-page tomes to create a convincing secondary world, master storyteller Jane Yolen brings an entire culture to life—along with its folklore, folk ballads, and ancient history—in just a trio of slender volumes, of which this is the third. The story is set in the Dales, an enchanted land ruled by a magical queen, a warrior with a mystical second self: her "dark sister." The story concerns the queen of the Dales, her adopted daughter and heir, and a foreign king determined to sow dissent among her sons. Yolen, a folklore scholar, is celebrated for a narrative voice that makes her fiction read like stories that have been passed down through the generations. This one is a beauty.

Also Recommended

Those of us who put together annual "best of the year" reading lists are always afraid we'll miss something great—and last year most of us did. Jeffrey Ford's *The Physiognomy* (Avon) snuck past me, and then won the World Fantasy Award. Mea culpa! If you also missed Ford's impressive first novel, it's now available in a paperback edition. The protagonist is a sardonic, drug-addicted practitioner of physiognomy (a "science" popularized in the 19th century in which character is determined through the study of head and body shapes), investigating the theft of a fruit that may confer immortality. It's a strange and marvelous work of interstitial fiction, falling somewhere in the shadowland between fantasy, mystery, science fiction, and allegory.

First Novels

While 1998 didn't produce the bumper crop of debut novels of the previous year, there are still some excellent additions to the fantasy field worth noting. The best first novels published in genre are James Stoddard's *The High House* (described previously) and the highly iconoclastic *King Rat* by China Miéville (Pan, UK). Miéville's interstitial novel winds through the streets of London council estates, raves, and jungle music clubs to reveal a clever twist on the old Pied Piper of Hamelin folk tale. The plot involves a standard young hero who does not know he is heir to a kingdom, but nothing else about this dark, atmospheric book is standard in the least.

I'm also intrigued by Mark Anthony's debut novel *Beyond the Pale* (Bantam), which is fantasy of the Stephen Donaldson sort about a Colorado drifter and an ER doctor who fall into a secondary world. The story is suspenseful, confidently told, and entertaining. *Silk* by Caitlin R. Kiernan (Roc) is more horrific than magical, but is likely to appeal to fans of urban fantasy. It's a dark tale of fallen angels, rock musicians, street people, and kids with attitude, from a writer who has already made a name for herself in the short fiction field. Other notable genre debuts: *The Witches of Eileanan*, a sprightly quest fantasy by Kate Forsyth (Roc); *Daughter of the Blood*, a sensual and dark novel by Anne Bishop (Roc); *Wit'ch Fire* by James Clemens (Del Rey), a well-crafted quest fantasy despite all the annoying apostrophes; and *The Blood Jaguar* by Michael H. Payne (Tor), a surprisingly captivating animal saga set in North America and *The Last Dragonlord* by Joanne Batin (Tor), a sparkling tale that is both magical and romantic.

In mainstream fiction, there are strong debuts by Laurel Marian Doud (listed previously), and by Mia Yun with a gentle coming-of-age story titled *House of the Winds* (Interlink). Yun's novel is a lyrical re-creation of her childhood in South Korea, in a house filled with weeping ghosts, ancestral spirits, stories, and folklore. Reminiscent of Heinz Insu Fenkl's *Memories of My Ghost Brother* (although not as polished as that beautiful volume), this realist novel with magic at its core is worth seeking out. I also recommend *The Priest Fainted* by Catherine Temma Davidson (Henry Holt), another autobiographical novel—this one about a Greek-American woman who returns to the land of her ancestors. It suffers from mainstream art-novel-itis (a weak plot structure and lack of narrative drive), yet Davidson does a fine job weaving strands of myth into contemporary life. Her feminist recasting of Greek mythology is occasionally heavy-handed, but at her best (particularly in the first half of the book), Davidson's ideas and prose are equally luminous.

Contemporary and Urban Fantasy

This category consists of contemporary tales in real-world settings infused with magic—sometimes differing from mainstream "magic realism" only by the fantasy label on the cover. Francesca Lia Block, Charles de Lint, and Sean Stewart all produced strong novels of this sort this year (listed previously); in addition I particularly recommend new offerings by Pamela Dean and Marina Fitch: *Juniper, Gentian and Rosemary* by Pamela Dean (Tor) is a sparkling novel about three sisters and the mysterious young man in the house next door, a spellbinding tale steeped in English folk ballads and Shakespeare's *Twelfth Night*. Dean's plot sneaks up on you, and the book is darker than it first appears. *The Border* by Marina Fitch (Ace) is the touching story of a family split by the Mexican-American border: one sister raised in the U.S. by her father, the other in Mexico by her mother. Although it stumbles in a few places, overall this is a lovely little book involving spirits, saints, chupacabras, and the cruel realities of immigrant life.

Also of note: *The Tooth Fairy* by Graham Joyce (Tor) is a *tour de force* of dark fantasy about three boys growing up in the British midlands—a harrowing modern fairy tale that is definitely not for children. We listed this as a Top Twenty book in the year of its original publication in England; now this British Fantasy Award winner is available in an American edition. *Irrational Fears* by William Browning Spencer (Borealis/White Wolf) is a sharply comic novel involving time travel, New Age lunatics, and Alcoholics Anonymous. Spencer is a writer whose skill is apparent even though I have a blind spot for his brand of humor, so I'll quote reviewer Elizabeth Hand instead: "Think of an H. P. Lovecraft tale adapted by Philip K. Dick, filmed by David Lynch and produced by Brian Wilson." *Changer* by Jane Lindskold (Avon Books) gathers a variety of figures from world mythology and plunks them down in modern New Mexico. Loki, Lilith, Merlin, and Elvis share the stage with assorted selkies, yeti, tengu, and tricksters in a droll tale of family dysfunction among the immortals. *Iron Shadows* by Steven Barnes (Tor) is a magical mystery about two detectives infiltrating a mystic New Age cult. Suspenseful, fascinating, this is the best one yet from this versatile author. *Dangerous Angels* by Francesca Lia Block (HarperCollins) is a omnibus volume of her "Weetzie Bat" books—urban fantasy set in a magical, hip-hop version of L.A. This edition comes packaged with a fabulous photographic cover by Suza Scalora.

Imaginary World Novels

Just when we were beginning to think that Imaginary World fantasy (a.k.a. "Tolkienesque," "Traditional," or "High" fantasy) was running out of steam, a remarkable number of fresh, new novels blew into the field like an invigorating wind. The best of them this year are the Gaiman, Kay, Martin, McKillip, Stoddard, Snyder, Russell, and Yolen works listed previously. In addition, three writers in particular have published new works you should take a look at: Elizabeth Lynn, C. J. Cherryh, and Robin Hobb. *Dragon's Winter* by Elizabeth Lynn (Berkley) is a welcome return to the fantasy field by a writer who has been silent for too long. Lynn, a martial arts expert, excels in creating stories that are muscular and adventurous, yet also transgressive and thought provoking. Using the same tropes as countless lesser tales (warriors, dragons, magical amulets), Lynn creates a gender-bending, character-driven story, inspired by a vigorous mix of Eastern and Western mythology. *Fortress of Eagles* by C. J. Cherryh (HarperPrism), the sequel to *Fortress in the Eye of Time*, is another novel about politics and warfare in a stark, enchanted land. Like Lynn, Cherryh is an intelligent writer who fills an action-adventure plot with morally complex characters, mature themes, and passages of lyric beauty. Anything by Cherryh is worth taking a look at, and this is one of her best. *Ship of Magic* by Robin Hobb (Bantam), is the first book in a lively new series of magical aventures set aboard sentient ships made of "wizardwood"—the fantasy equivalent of Patrick O'Brian sagas. If you know someone who is hooked on bad bestseller fantasy, give them this to read instead. It's fat, action-packed and entertaining, yet skillfully written and original. Megan Lindholm writing under the Hobb pseudonym just goes from strength to strength.

In addition, I recommend: *Dragon* by Steven Brust (Tor) is an acerbic swashbuckling fantasy in the Roger Zelazny tradition, following the further adventures of a charismatic assassin-for-hire. Brust is doing interesting, even subversive things with character development, so don't mistake his "Vlad Taltos" series as generic fantasy adventure. *The King and Queen of Swords* by Tom Arden (Gollancz), on the other hand, doesn't stray far from the traditional fantasy formula, yet is seeded with engagingly quirky touches. Arden is a writer to keep an eye on. *The Shadow Eater* by Adam Lee (Avon Books), sequel to *The Dark Shore*, is by A. A. Attanasio writing under a pseudonym. As Adam Lee, he reins in his imagination and sticks to generic fantasy tropes: dragons, witches, trolls, magical assassins, etc., but he's too fine a writer not to bring fresh inventiveness to this material. *Death of the Necromancer* by Martha Wells (Avon Books), the sequel to *The Element of Fire*, is an intricately plotted tale of opium-addicted sorcerers, thieves, theater people, and other ne'er-do-wells in a magical cityscape. It's unusual, with a nice dark edge. *The Book of Knights* by Yves Meynard (Tor) is the first English-language publication by a popular French Canadian author. Meynard's story about a young foundling in a medieval land has a fairy-tale quality without being overly light or fey, and can be enjoyed equally by young and adult readers.

If you're in the market for page-turners that won't insult your intelligence, try: *The Gilded Chain* by Dave Duncan (Avon Books), *Icefalcon's Quest* by Barbara Hambly (Del Rey), *Otherland: River of Blue Fire* (sequel to *City of Golden Shadow*) by Tad Williams (DAW), *The Painter Knight* (sequel to *The Stone Prince*) by Fiona Patton (DAW), *Prince of Dogs* by Kate Elliot (DAW), *Fire Angels* (sequel to *Mage Heart*) by Jane Routley (Avon Books), *A Cavern of Black Ice* by J. V. Jones (Warner Aspect), and *The Tower of the King's Daughter* by Chaz Brenchley (Orbit, U.K). Also of note: Ballantine has published a handsome 25th anniversary edition of William Goldman's *The Princess Bride: S. Morgenstern's Classic Tale of True Love and High Adventure*, with a new introduction by Goldman and the first chapter of the "long lost sequel," *Buttercup's Baby*. If you've seen the movie but haven't read the book, you don't know what you're missing.

Historical Fantasy

Historical fantasy novels published in 1998 range from India to America to the front lines of World War I. The very best of them is *Flanders* by Patricia Anthony (listed previously), but I also particularly recommend new novels by J. Gregory Keyes, Kara Dalkey, and Parke Godwin. *Newton's Cannon* by J. Gregory Keyes (Del Rey) is an unusual alternate-history novel, set in the 17th century, drawing Louis XIV, Ben Franklin, and Sir Isaac Newton into an erudite plot about revolutionary politics, mathematics, and alchemy. With three strong novels under his belt, Keyes has emerged as a major talent. *Bhagavati* by Kara Dalkey (Tor) is the third book in a series set in 16th-century India. Like its predecessors, this one is impeccably researched, sensual, and exotic. *Lord of Sunset* by Parke Godwin (Avon Books) is based on the life of England's King Harold. There are no fantastical elements here, but the novel is a "prequel" of sorts to Godwin's wonderful Robin Hood tales: *Sherwood* and *Robin the King*. This 11th-century story is romantic, tragic, and absorbing.

Other notable works: *Apacheria* by Jake Page (Del Rey) proposes an alternate version of American history in which the Apache nation successfully forms an independent country. Page is also a scholar of Native-American history and legend, so it's no surprise that this thought-provoking tale rests on sound historical conjecture. *American Woman* by R. Garcia y Robertson (Forge) is a historical novel with a mystical edge, envisioning the Battle of Little Big Horn from the point of view of a former missionary married to a Cheyenne warrior. *Jericho Moon* by Matthew Woodring Stover (Roc) is the sequel to *Iron Dawn*, a dark, muscular story set in the years after the Trojan War. *The Lady in the Loch* by Elizabeth Ann Scarborough (Ace) is a light but charming "whodunit" set in nineteenth-century Scotland, casting the writer/folklorist Walter Scott as the sheriff of Edinburgh in a plot peppered with Scottish legends and gypsy lore. *Darker Angels* by S. P. Somtow (Tor) could be called either dark fantasy or horror. The tale is set in an alternate version of 19th-century America, mixing Abraham Lincoln, Walt Whitman, and Lord Byron with werewolves, shamans, and zombies . . . in other words, it's pure Somtow.

On the mainstream shelves, I recommend Andrea Barrett's brilliant epic *The Voyage of the Narwhal* (W. W. Norton). This is gripping, old-fashioned adventure set in 1855, about a crew of men in the Arctic looking for traces of Lord Franklin's expedition. (The mythic elements arise in the sections of the book concerned with the Arctic's native people.) Barrett delves deeply into Victorian attitudes toward science, exploration, and conquest while also telling a rousing good story. If you love Victorian fiction, as well as fiction about the period, this one is a must. *Selene of the Spirits* by Melissa Pritchard (Ontario Review) is another memorable tale set in the nineteenth century. Inspired by the true history of a vastly popular young psychic, the novel re-creates the heated world of spiritualism in Victorian England. *The Son of Light, The Eternal Temple, The Battle of Kadesh, The Lady of Abu Simbel,* and *Under the Western Acacia* are all part of the "Ramses" series by Christian Jacq, translated from the French by Mary Feeney (Warner)—an epic of ancient Egypt that has been enormously popular in France and is now available here. *Stone Tables* by Orson Scott Card (Deseret Books) is a biblical/historical novel, but will be of interest to Card's many readers in the fantasy field. The novel paints a dramatic portrait of the brothers Moses and Aaron.

Arthurian Fiction

For fans of Arthurian fiction, there are a number of good volumes to chose from this year. My own favorite is the most unusual: *The Royal Changeling* by John Whitbourn (Earthlight, U.K.). This wily novel mixes Arthurian themes into a story about the British Reformation, throwing in Dr. Johnson, Pepys, elves, and the kitchen sink for good measure. In lesser hands it would be a mess, but Whitbourn is a clever writer who knows exactly what he's doing. I also highly recommend *The Wolf and the Crown* by A. A. Attanasio (HarperPrism), the third volume in this author's iconoclastic retelling of Arthurian myth. Beautifully written, completely fresh, the book is full of surprises.

Also of note: *The Saxon Shore* by Jack Whyte (Forge) is the fourth volume in a series that has become an international bestseller. Here, young Arthur is adopted by his cousin Caius Merlyn Britannicus, and groomed to be the leader who will unify Britain against Saxon invasion. *Excalibur* by Bernard Cornwell (St. Martin's Press) is the third and final volume in a Dark Age version of the Arthurian mythos—a page-turner from an author better known for his best-selling "Sharpe" series. *The Enchantress* by Vera Chapman (Gollancz, U.K.) is a limpid novel about Arthur's "three half sisters": Morgan, Morgause, and Vivien. The manuscript was unfinished at the time of Chapman's death and has been completed by Mike Ashley. *Guinevere Evermore* by Sharan Newman (Tor) is the final book of a pleasantly romantic trilogy, following *Guinevere* and *The Chessboard Queen*. *Into the Path of Gods* by Kathleen Cunningham Guler (Bardsong Press) is an odd romantic saga by a Celtic historian, imagining the life of a Welsh spy master in the period leading up to Arthur's reign.

Three of the best Arthurian novels of the year were published in the Young Adult field but are recommended to adult readers. *The Fires of Merlin* by T. A. Barron (Philomel) is the third book in Barron's "Merlin" series (now projected to run to five volumes). Drenched in myth and magic, permeated with a subtle spirituality, this one will leave you spellbound. *I am Mordred* by Nancy Springer (Philomel) is a thoroughly engrossing story from the point of view of Arthur's bastard son (born to his half sister Morgause). It's a moving tale of a tragic young man who can't escape destiny. *Parzival: The Quest of the Grail Knight* is a gorgeous retelling of the Wolfram von Eschenbach original by Katherine Paterson (Lodestar). The author gears her tale to young readers, but her translucent text has an ageless quality. The edition concludes with Paterson's informative notes on the original story.

Other Arthurian publications to look for: *The Mammoth Book of Arthurian Legends* edited by Mike Ashley (Carroll & Graf) collects forty short stories inspired by the legends of Camelot, ranging from works by John Steinbeck and P. G. Wodehouse to those of Tanith Lee, Brian Stableford and Jane Yolen. Editor Mike Ashley has done an outstanding job, as usual. *Camelot Fantastic* edited by Lawrence Schimel and Martin H. Greenberg (DAW) is less ambitious in scope, but it's worth picking up for good new tales by Brian Stableford and Rosemary Edghill. *Isaac Asimov's Camelot* edited by Gardner Dozois and Sheila Williams (Ace) is a reprint volume collecting stories first published in *Asimov's Science Fiction* magazine. This is a very strong collection with fine stories from an A-list of authors: Tanith Lee, Megan Lindholm, Jane Yolen, Michael Swanwick, Esther Friesner, Roger Zelazny, and many more.

Other Mythic Fiction

1998 was another good year for fiction inspired by myths, ancient epics, fairy tales, folklore and folk ballads. The best novels in this field are the Day, de Lint, Erdrich, Garner, Hogan, McCrumb, and Snyder books listed above, as well as the folkloric first novels by Yun and Davidson. In addition, I highly recommend *Ka* by Roberto Calasso, translated from the Italian by Tim Parks (Knopf). It's hard to describe what exactly *Ka* is: part fiction, part philosophical memoir, and part mythic exploration of the Joseph Campbell sort. You may remember Calasso as the author of the brilliant *Cadmus and Harmony*, a meditation on Greco-Roman myths; now he's let his imagination loose on Indian mythology and stories from the Indian spiritual tradition. It's a book that stretches your mind and heart, and is surely going to be a classic. I also strongly recommend *The Lake Dreams the Sky* by Swain Wolfe (Cliff Street Books), a wonderful work of mythic fiction set in the mountains of Montana. Wolfe combines a piquant love story about a drifter and a local waitress in the years after World War II with the contemporary tale of a real estate analyst returning to Montana from Boston on a journey of self-discovery. It's enriched by vivid characters, folklore, mysticism, and magic, and was one of my personal favorites of the year. If you like the fiction of Alice Hoffman, Susan Power, or Charles de Lint, then go and find it.

Other recommendations: *The Last Paradise* by James D. Houston (University of Oklahoma Press) is a mystical mystery tale about an insurance investigator on a job in Hawaii. His encounters with an old lover (a mixed-blood Native woman) draw him close to the living myths of the land and Pele the fire goddess. It's a suspenseful, romantic novel about about myth and spirit in the ground below. *The Giant O'Brian* by Hilary Mantel (Henry Holt) is the tale of an Irish giant and storyteller of the 18th century who flees to England hoping to make a living as a sideshow exhibit—where he attracts the attention of a surgeon obsessed with dissecting his dead body. This is very dark fantasy, chock full of folk and fairy tales, beautifully written, incredibly grim, deepened by meditations on science, history, and art. *Darkest Desire* by Anthony Schmidt (Ecco Press) is an odd, amusing novella from the point of view of the Big Bad Wolf in German folk tales. Filled with angst, ashamed of his compelling desire to devour children, the Wolf is befriended by the Brothers Grimm . . . or so he thinks. It's a wicked look at the nature of fairy tales, and of desire. *Little Red Riding Hood* by Manlio Argueta, translated from the Spanish by Edward Waters Hood (Curbstone Press) is a hard-hitting book by one of the most important writers to come out of El Salvador, mixing fairy tales and poetry into the story of two young lovers in a war-ravaged country. Argueta's novel is brilliant and touching, but not for the faint of heart.

The Mermaids Singing by Lisa Carey (Avon Bard) is a book I fully expected to love, and was disappointed. Carey's first novel is the story of three generations of Irish-American women, beautifully wound through with euphonious Celtic folk tales and mermaid lore. Unfortunately, the mother and daughter at the center of the book have such large chips on their shoulders that it's a wonder they still walk upright; only the stoic Old Country grandmother kept this reviewer reading. Carey has a magical touch when it comes to descriptions of Irish country life—so despite my misgivings about this particular book, she's clearly a writer to keep an eye on. If relentlessly bad-tempered protagonists don't faze you, give this one a try. *Ghost Country* by Sara Paretsky (Delacorte) is an unusual book by the author of the popular V. I. Warshawski mysteries. Mystery fans were deeply disconcerted by the novel, but fantasy readers won't blink an eye—we're in familiar territory here. Paretsky has created an affecting tale about homeless women in the streets of Chicago and ancient myths in the modern world. *The Moor* by Laurie R. King (St. Martin's Press) is the latest in this author's Mary Russell series about "the wife of Sherlock Holmes." This one, which returns to the misty Dartmoor setting of *The Hound of the Baskervilles*, is a story seeded with the myths and legends of England's West Country. (King even uses a real-life folklorist, Reverend Sabine Baring-Gould, as a character.) It's a terrific book (but as a Dartmoor dweller, I admit to being biased here!). *Eucalyptus* by Murray Ball (Farrar, Straus & Giroux) is a realist story but follows a classic fairy tale theme: a man in western Australia has created a living museum of trees consisting of hundreds of different species of eucalyptus. When it comes time for his daughter to marry, her suitors must pass the test of correctly naming each tree on the property. It's an amiable, quirky little romance, embellished with nuggets of folklore, natural science and Australian history. *Faraday's Popcorn Factory* by Sandra Lee Gould (St. Martin's Press) is contemporary mythic fantasy set in a small Ohio town, blending African folk tales with a sensual, spiritual love story. This first novel has charming moments and lovely descriptive passages; it doesn't quite hang together as a whole, but is worth a look. *Holding Out* by Anne O. Faulk (Simon & Schuster) is an entertaining page-turner inspired by Aristophanes's *Lysistrata*. In this good-natured political satire, women across America are encouraged to go on sexual strike until certain social changes are made. . . . It's light, but a lot of fun. *Medea* by Christa Wolf (Doubleday) is a more ponderously feminist work based on the Medea legend (with an introduction by Margaret Atwood). After German unification, it was discovered that Wolf had been a Stasi informant for many years—which gives her exploration of the much-maligned Medea figure additional levels of meaning.

Fantasy in the Mainstream

Magical books on the mainstream shelves can be harder to spot than those grouped tidily under a fantasy label, so each year we try to point the way to books you might otherwise overlook. This year, the best of these are the Day, Doud, Erdrich, Hogan, Knox, and McCrumb books listed previously, but here are a handful of others which are also strongly recommended: *Oyster* by Janette Turner Hospital (W. W. Norton) is another stunning novel by the Australian author of *The Last Magician*. In her latest, Hospital paints a shattering portrait of a charismatic doomsday cult leader who takes over a remote town of opal miners in the Australian outback. It's a densely layered novel, shot through with elements of surrealism and aboriginal myth. The plot is compelling, even hypnotic, and leaves you stunned at the book's end. Another book I recommend highly is *Semaphore* by G. W. Hawkes (MacMurray & Beck), a coming-of-age tale about a boy who can foresee the future (his sister's death by drowning, his own marriage to the little girl next door . . .) and how he and his family live with this unsettling ability. It's a provocative premise, well executed. *Quarantine* by Jim Crace (Farrar, Straus & Giroux) is a beautifully penned novel imagining Jesus of Nazareth's forty days in the wilderness, set in a convincingly historical, non-miraculous context. This thoughtful, passionate book won the Whitbread Book of the Year Award and was short-listed for the Booker Prize. I recommend it highly even if, like me, you don't usually read Biblical fiction. *Ghost Children* by Sue Townsend (Soho Press) is darker than Townsend's usual work (the best-selling "Adrian Mole" series), concerning class issues, poverty, and child abuse in modern England. The plot involves the ghost of a teenage girl (among other unwanted children) who haunts a woman seventeen years after an abortion. It's a hard-hitting but compassionate book, complex in its moral outlook and brightened by flashes of the author's trademark humor. Don't be put off by the bleak topic—this is Townsend at her best. *The Notebooks of Don Rigoberto* by Mario Vargas Llosa, translated from the Spanish by Edith Grossman (Farrar, Straus & Giroux) is a sagacious, highly erotic new novel from this acclaimed Peruvian writer, a sequel of sorts to his comic novel *In Praise of the Stepmother*. Llosa is a magician with words, conjuring illusion and enchantment through a text layered with stories, notebook excerpts and anonymous letters, stitched together by the life and art of the painter Egon Schiele. *Ghost Town* by Robert Coover (Henry Holt) is another phantasmagorical novel consisting of stories embedded within stories, although in this case the effect is a postmodern one, comic but brutal. As in his gorgeous book *Briar Rose*, Coover is reworking mythic themes: this time, cowboy myths and outlaw tales of the American West.

Other mainstream novels of note: *The Passion Dream Book* by Whitney Otto (HarperCollins) is a novel that should have pushed all my buttons: a fantasia about women artists, starting in the Italian Renaissance and moving to Holly-wood, Harlem, and Paris in our own century. (The slight fantasy element here is the way in which the past entwines with the present.) Otto's book never quite engages, however, and the characters are oddly distant. The atmospheric Italian section is worth a look, but overall it's a disappointment. *Esperanza's Box of Saints* by Maia Amparo Escandon (Scribner), on the other hand, is fully engaging. The novel follows the journey of a beautiful widow searching for her missing daughter, guided by a box full of whispering santos. Ranging from a small village in Mexico to the streets of modern L.A., it's a beautifully redemptive novel, both comic and tragic. *The History of Our World Beyond the Wave* by R. E. Klein (Harcourt Brace) is a modern fable about a young man surfing the oceans in search of fellow survivors after a massive tidal wave engulfs the Earth. Full of big ideas and grand adventure, Klein's novel is quirky and better than it sounds. *Our Sometime Sister* by Norah Labiner (Coffee House Press) is the first novel by a young author mixing autobiographical material about a girl exiled to board-ing school with fragments of *Hamlet*. Some of the first novels coming out of Coffee House Press are a bit self-indulgent . . . but this one is an exception. It's a fat, ambitious book—not flawless, but unique and memorable.

Ximena at the Crossroads by Laura Riesco, translated from the Spanish by Mary G. Berg (White Pine Press) is about a young girl growing up in a wealthy Spanish family in 1940s Peru, slowly becoming aware of the gulf between her privileged life and the poverty of the native people, as well as of the world of politics impinging on her nation. The fantasy elements include the stories Xim-ena tells to connect to the adults in her life; it's a magically atmospheric book, but has little in the way of plot. *The Undiscovered Country* by Samantha Gillson (Grove Press) is the harrowing tale of a family of American researchers torn apart by their experiences in the rainforests of Papua New Guinea. This is another richly atmospheric book flavored with folk tales, myths and local color, yet it's flawed by irritating characters who seem almost to deserve their fate. (For a better book with a similar theme, try *The Poisonwood Bible* by Barbara Kingsolver instead.) *Flower in the Skull* by Kathleen Alcalá (Chronicle) is the sequel to last year's *Ordinary Spirits*. Unlike the previous volume, Alcalá strays away from magic realism here—but it's a beautiful story nonetheless, ranging from nineteenth-century Sonora, Mexico to modern-day Tucson, and readers who loved the previous volume will certainly enjoy this one as well. *The Sin Eater* by Alice Thomas Ellis (Moyer Bell) is another novel with little in the way of overt magic in it (although the theme and title of the book are based on an old Welsh folk tale), but fans of her last novel, *A Fairy Tale*, will want to give it a go. This one involves a Welsh family gathered around the death bed of its patriarch.

Persian Brides by Dorit Rabinyan, translated from the Hebrew by Yael Lotan (George Braziller) is a novel to steer clear of—don't be swayed by the laudatory reviews. This young author's book is woven through with folk tales and dark magic, but is ruined by characters who wail, whine, shriek, and giggle endlessly, then beat and sexually torment each other. It could have had the flavor of the Arabian nights; it's more like curdled milk. *The Long Sandy Hair of Neftoon Zamora* by Michael Nesmith (St. Martin's Press) is another one I'd give a miss—although, to be fair, my assistant loved it, as did mainstream reviewers. It's a first novel by a blues musician (and member of the Monkees—yes, *that* Mike Nesmith) involving a musician's quest through the New Mexico desert to track down a mysterious blues musician who may, or may not, turn out to be an Indian High Priestess . . . or a Martian. The book has the flavor of fantasy written by someone unfamiliar with similar books already published in the field; the mythic elements are earnestly utopian and didactic. Still, it has its moments.

Angels seem to be a popular theme in mainstream fiction these days. Some of these novels are dreadful and I won't attempt to list them here, but a few writers managed to avoid both sentimentality and cliché to create fine tales. The very best of them, hands down, is *The Vintner's Luck* by Elizabeth Knox (listed previously), but here are three more angel stories that I can recommend: *Falling to Earth* by Elisabeth Brownrigg (Firebrand Books), a comic novel about a closeted lesbian and her exasperating guardian angel; *River Angel* by A. Manette Ansay (Morrow), a lovely tale about the guardian angel of a river in Wisconsin; and *Rose's Garden* by Carrie Brown (Algonquin), an incandescent little novel about angels, grief, and gardening.

Reflections of Loko Miwa by Lilas Desquiron, translated from the French by Robin Orr Bodkin (University of Virginia Press) is an intense story about Haitian society, female sexuality, and the magical traditions of Haitian Vodoun. *Chocolat* by Joanne Harris (Viking) is an enigmatic tale about a mysterious woman in a French village who runs a chocolate shop and may, or may not, be a witch. *The Ruins* by Tracy Farrell (New York University Press) is a peculiar little book that won the N.Y.U. Press Prize for First Novel: a dark, mystical fable about a hapless shoeshine boy. *The Service of Clouds* by Delia Falconer (Farrar, Straus & Giroux) is a self-consciously magic realist novel set in the Blue Mountains of Australia. The turn-of-the-century period detail is very nice indeed, but the prose tends toward the overly-lyrical and sometimes floats away altogether. *Quite a Year for Plums* by Bailey White (Knopf) is a charming episodic book about small-town life in southern Georgia from a writer best known as a storyteller on National Public Radio. White's work is eccentric, whimsical and droll, with a quiet folksy appeal. *The Circus at the End of the World* by Rosalind Brackenbury (Fithian Press) is a curious magic realist tale about a young juggler who travels the world searching for love, and the mother who abandoned him as a child. *Hell* by Kathryn Davis (Ecco Press) is the latest from the author of the fine adult fairy tale novel *The Girl Who Trod on a Loaf*. Her new one is a darker book, braiding the stories of three households: the home of Edwina Moss (a 19th-century expert on domestic management), a suburban family of the 1950s, and a dollhouse family. The ideas here are interesting, even brilliant, but the author's style is challenging to the point of inaccessibility. *Gaff Topsails* by Patrick Kavanagh (Viking) is a dense, Joycean first novel set in a remote Newfoundland fishing village. This is another challenging read, but one that is worth the effort. Although Kavanagh sometimes goes over the top with self-consciously poetic prose, he tells a fascinating story of the conflict between the Christian religion and old pagan beliefs. *A Troubadour's Testament* by James Cowan (Shambhala) is a short, handsomely packaged book from the author of *A Mapmaker's Dream*. Hardcore medievalists may love this one, but for the rest of us it's a bit cerebral, based on the now-familiar conceit of an academic drawn into the past (in this case, 12th-century Provence) in the course of his research. Although billed as a novel, Cowan's book is really a slow meditation on spiritual love, more educational than moving. *D'Alembert's Principal: Memory, Reason, and Imagination* by Andrew Crumey (Picador) is another one that disappoints. Crumey calls this "a novel in three parts," set in the 18th century, exploring reality and mathematics. It's obscure rather than intriguing, and I'd give it a miss. *Empire of the Ants* by Bernard Werber (Bantam), a bestseller in its original French edition, was promoted by the publisher as "the *Watership Down* of ants." If that description attracts rather than repulses you, then give it a try. And if one bug book isn't enough, you can also look for *The Life of Insects* by Victor Pelevin, translated from the Russian by Andrew Bromfield (Farrar, Straus & Giroux), an allegory about modern Russian society told through anthropomorphic insects.

For good satiric fantasy, I recommend *The Smithsonian Institute* by Gore Vidal (Random House), a political saga set in Washington, D.C., in 1939. T., a teenage math prodigy with an uncanny ability to understand Einstein's formula, is sent to the Smithsonian to help work on the secrets of the bomb. After hours, the various Smithsonian dioramas come to life in a complex plot in which T. attempts to change history and to have a lot of sex. It's pure Vidal—an entertaining spoof enriched by his dazzling command of American history and politics. I also recommend *Second Coming Attractions* by David Prill (St. Martin's Press), a parody of the Christian film industry and religious fanaticism. Although perhaps not quite as tight as his previous novel, *Serial Killer Days*, it's pretty funny nonetheless, and pulls no punches. *Girlfriend in a Coma* by Douglas Coupland (HarperCollins) is a cynical, offbeat tale about a teenage girl who loses her virginity then lapses into a coma; she wakes up eighteen years later to find that the world and her friends have changed. *The House of Sleep* by Jonathan Coe (Knopf) is a thoughtful tale, both satiric and romantic, about sleeping, dreaming, and the shifting nature of reality. *Memories of My Father While Watching TV* by Curtis White (Dalkey Archive Press) is a sharply satiric fantasia about American family life and television culture.

Notable reprint editions: *Portrait of Jennie* by Robert Nathan (Tachyon Publications) is the reprint of a supernatural love story from the 1940s, with introductions by Peter S. Beagle and Sean Stewart. *Ashe of Rings and Other Writings* by Mary Butts (McPherson & Co.) revives the work of a British author who played a vibrant part in the expatriot literary community in Paris between the two wars. Her fiction, often autobiographical, is tinged with occult elements. The McPherson edition contains her first novel, *Ashe of Rings*, a novella, "Imaginary Letters," and three essays, including one on ghost fiction. *Doctor Faustus* by Thomas Mann (Knopf) has been newly translated by John E. Wood. If you haven't yet read this German classic about a musical genius who trades his soul in order to become a great composer, here's an opportunity to do so.

Oddities

The Best Peculiar Book distinction of 1998 goes to *An Unlikely Prophet* by Alvin Schwartz (MacMurray & Beck). Though billed as autobiography, this reads like fantasy to me—or else a Tom Robbins novel. Schwartz was a writer of the forties and fifties who hung out with the likes of Jackson Pollack and Saul Bellow, yet was best known as the author of *Superman* and *Batman* comic strips. Unlikely as it seems, writing *Superman* becomes the first step in a wild adventure involving a seven-foot-tall Tibetan tulpa, a time-traveling Hawaiian kahuna, and messages in Pollack's paintings. . . . What more can I say? The runner-up for this "award" is *Last Love in Constantinople: A Tarot Novel for Divination* by Milorad Pavic, translated from the Serbian by Christina Pribichevich-Zoric (Dufour Editions). Pavic's literary fantasy tale is set during the Napoleonic Wars; it comes complete with tarot cards designed by Pavic and instructions on how to use them in conjunction with the text. It's odd and ingenious, like so much of Pavic's work.

Raining Cats and Dogs

What is it with cat and dog books? Last year, so many were sent for review that we put them into a category of their own; this year, they are equally abundant. The best cat fantasy of the lot is *The Wild Road* by Gabriel King (Del Rey), the epic journey of a London house cat crossing the island to Cornwall. There are animal companions to aid the quest, an evil alchemist to be thwarted, and a world of enchantment conjured behind the backs of oblivious humans. This premise has the potential to end up being nauseatingly cute, but we're dealing with first-rate writers here (M. John Harrison and Jane Johnson, collaborating under the King pseudonym); as a result, the book is smart, clever, and sparkles with genuine magic. The best dog story is *A Dog's Head* by Jean Dutourd, translated from the French by Robin Chancellor (University of Chicago Press), a classic tale of French magic realism brought back to print after thirty-five years. It's a bittersweet, satiric novel—part Borges and part fairy tale—recounting the life story of a boy born with the head of a spaniel.

Others, briefly noted: *The Dogs* by Rebecca Brown (City Lights) is a bizarre novel written in the form of a "modern bestiary" about an American woman living in a small apartment with a pack of otherworldly Doberman pinschers, and her slow descent into madness. Very strange. *The Cat* by Pat Grey (Ecco Press) is an offbeat comic novel about the lives of Cat, Mouse, and Rat in a house whose owner has fallen down dead in front of the refrigerator. It's amusing, and very British. *Snow* by Betsy Howie (Harcourt Brace) is an indulgent semi-autobiographical "story of self-discovery" about a woman in an isolated winter cabin trying to stave off a nervous breakdown with the aid of two cats (one of whom talks) and Spam-loving bears. *Samurai Cat Goes to Hell* by Mark E. Rodgers (Tor) is the fifth and final book of this rather broad comedy series about the adventures of a feline samurai warrior and his nephew sidekick. *The Bridegroom Was a Dog* by Yoko Tawada, translated from the Japanese by Margaret Mitsutani (Kodansha) is a collection of three novellas by a young, award-winning Japanese writer. The title piece is a quirky erotic story about a teacher, her unconventional lover, and the fairy tale of a princess promised in marriage to a dog. It's . . . unusual. *Rover's Tales: A Canine Crusader and his Travels in the Dog World* by Michael Z. Lewin (St. Martin's Press) contains forty short stories, by a popular mystery writer, about a smart and lovable mutt. The tales range from funny to overly sentimental; the illustrations by Karen Wallis are delightful. *Cat on a Hyacinth Hunt* by Carole Nelson Douglas (Forge) is the latest in her "Midnight Louie" series about a feline detective. The book is light, but a page-turner and charming in an offbeat way. If you're interested in books *about* cats, try: *Icons of Power: Feline Symbolism in the Americas* edited by Nicholas J. Saunders (Routledge); or *The Mythology of Cats: Feline Legend and Lore Through the Ages* by Gerald and Loretta Hausman (St. Martin's Press). *99 Lives: Cats in History, Legend and Literature* by Howard Loxton (Chronicle) is lavishly illustrated with photographs and fine art, and would make a fine gift book. *Angel Cat* by Michael Garland (Boyd Mills Press) is a handsome picture book, and a lovely present for a child, or even an adult, whose cat has died.

Briefly Noted

The following fantasy novels hit the bestseller lists in 1998. Beloved by large numbers of readers across the country, they deserve mention: *A Knight of the Word* by Terry Brooks (Ballantine), *Running With the Demon* by Terry Brooks (Del Rey), *Queen of Demons* by David Drake (Tor), *Polgara the Sorceress* by Eddings & Eddings (Del Rey), *Krondor the Betrayal* by Raymond E. Feist (Avon Books), *Shards of a Broken Crown* by Raymond E. Feist (Avon), *Temple of the Winds* by Terry Goodkind (Tor), *Four and Twenty Blackbirds* by Mercedes Lackey (Baen), *Into the Fire* by Dennis L. McKiernan (Roc), *Sword-born* by Jennifer Roberson (DAW), and *The Demon Spirit* by R. A. Salvatore (Del Rey).

In the field of science fiction there are several books with magical elements that fantasy readers may also enjoy. The best of them is *Brown Girl in the Ring* by Nalo Hopkinson (Warner), a novel set in the economic ruins of 21st-century Toronto. Despite the SF premise, the book reads more like fantasy or magic realism, for it's a tale bursting with Afro-Caribbean myths, legends, folkways, voodoo, and spiritual beliefs. This book won the Warner Aspect First Novel Award, and Jamaican-born Hopkinson is clearly a writer to keep an eye on. I also recommend *Octoberland* by Adam Lee (Avon), a blend of science fiction, fantasy and postmodern phantasmagoria. Like all of A. A. Attanasio's fiction, including tales published under the Lee psuedonym, the book astonishes with its language, breadth, and sheer inventiveness. *Ark Baby* by Liz Jensen (Overlook Press) has both SF and fantasy elements. The book features two plot lines, one set in twenty-first-century Britain in which all women are mysteriously barren, the other set in the nineteenth century. Both plots are darkly humorous, unusual to the point of weird, and are tied together by Darwinian theories of evolution.

Time travel novels are usually properly classified as science fiction, but some of these tales can be of interest to fantasy readers as well. The best of these in 1998 is *To Say Nothing of the Dog* by Connie Willis (Bantam Spectra), a smart, hilarious romp ranging from the nineteenth to the twenty-first centuries, and stamping over every known genre boundary in the process. It's a unique homage to the fiction of Jerome K. Jerome, Dorothy Sayers, and P. G. Wodehouse. I also recommend *The Iron Bridge* by David E. Morse (Harcourt Brace) about a young woman from a dystopian future trying to prevent the building of the first iron bridge (and the Industrial Revolution). Morse's book is a first novel, and an impressive debut. *Making History* by Stephen Fry (Random House) is a new satiric novel by this well-known British actor/writer, about a history student who unwittingly falls into a time-travel plot to prevent Hitler's birth. Fry creates an extravagant story that stumbles a little along the way, but is enjoyable nonetheless. *Flesh Guitar* by Geoff Nicholson (Gollancz, U.K.; Overlook, U.S.) is about a woman who travels through time to jam with the greats of musical history (both real and invented). It's an unusual, moving tale—not flawless, but worth seeking out.

Children's Fantasy

The best children's fantasy novel of the year is the one on all the bestseller lists: *Harry Potter and the Sorcerer's Stone* by J. K. Rowling (Scholastic). This Scottish author's first novel is a fast-paced, sparkling dark comedy about a boy on scholarship at "Hogwarts School for Witchcraft and Wizardry." It won England's National Book Award, among other prizes, and is captivating audiences of all ages around the world. For fantasy readers, little in Rowling's tale will be startlingly original, but her narrative voice is wonderful and I recommend seeking the book out.

The best of the rest: *The Heavenward Path* by Kara Dalkey (Harcourt Brace) is a gorgeous, mythic, romantic novel set in twelfth-century Japan. This book is the sequel to Dalkey's *Little Sister*, and I recommend it highly. *Sirena* by Donna Jo Napoli (Scholastic) is another novel that shouldn't be missed—the lyrical story of a mermaid and a Greek warrior, by the author of *Zel*. *In a Dark Wood* by Michael Cadnum (Orchard) is a dark version of the Robin Hood myth, retold from the point of view of Lord Geoffrey, Sheriff of Nottingham. It's a taut, suspenseful portrayal of daily life in the Middle Ages. *Shadow Spinner* by Susan Fletcher (Atheneum) is an outstanding fantasy novel inspired by the stories of Scheherazade, poetically told from the point of view of a lame serving girl. *The Secret of Platform 13* by Eva Ibbotson (Dutton) is a clever, surprising story in which a London railway platform becomes the door to a magic island—a door which can only be opened, however, once every nine years. *Dark Lord of Derkholm* by Diana Wynne Jones (Greenwillow) is a tongue-in-cheek fantasy spoof about an inept wizard and tourists from another world—silly and fun. *Clockwork* by Philip Pullman (Scholastic) is a terrific new work from the award-winning author of *The Golden Compass*. This slim little volume contains the story of an apprentice clockmaker and the sinister stranger who comes to offer him his heart's desire. Reminiscent of old German folk tales but filled with unique Pullman twists and turns, the book is a treat, and beautifully illustrated by Leonid Gore. Pullman fans should also keep an eye out for *Count Karlstein* (Knopf), a deliciously Gothic tale in a small, illustrated edition.

I also recommend the following: *Circle of Magic: Sandry's Book, Tris's Book* and *Daja's Book* by Tamora Pierce (Scholastic), three books in the "Circle of Magic" quartet, involve young student mages in a landscape steeped in enchantment, vividly rendered. *The Long Patrol* by Brian Jacques (Philomel), the tenth book in the best-selling "Redwall" series, is the story of hedgehogs, hares, and shrews who band together to save Redwall Abbey from vicious vermin. *I Rode a Horse of Milk White Jade* by Diane Lee Wilson (Orchard) is a memorable tale with lovely period detail set in fourteenth-century China, about a lame girl, her grandmother (a Mongolian shaman), a talking horse, a tiger cat, and the court of Kublai Khan. *Dark Shade* by Jane Louise Curry (Atheneum) is a fine time-travel novel about two children in western Pennsylvania who walk through a dark forest into the French and Indian War of 1758. *The Boxes* by William Sleator (Dutton) is wonderful dark fantasy about two mysterious boxes . . . and what they contain. *The Islander* by Cynthia Rylant (DK Publishing) is a charming little edition by a Newbery Medal winner—a gentle story about the sea, a magic key, and a mermaid. Another good ocean story is *The Sea Man* by Jane Yolen (Philomel), a lyrical merman tale with illustrations by Christopher Denise (Philomel). *Twilight Boy* by Timothy Green (Rising Moon/Northland) is a mystical mystery novel set on the Navajo Indian reservation. Adult readers will prefer Tony Hillerman's books, which Green's story greatly resembles, but this is a good one to give to younger fantasy and mystery fans. *The Godmother's Web* by Elizabeth Ann Scarborough (Ace) is another Native-American tale, part of the "Godmother" series exploring the folklore of different cultures. I recommend the previous two volumes as well: *The Godmother* (European folklore) and *The Godmother's Apprentice* (Irish folklore). Other good books, noted briefly: *Switchers* by Kate Thompson (Hyperion), *Among the Hidden* by Margaret Peterson Haddix (Simon & Schuster), *Court Duel* by Sherwood Smith (Harcourt Brace), *The Darkling* by Charles Butler (McElderry), *Fire Arrow: The Second Song of Eirren* by Edith Pattou (Harcourt Brace), *Angels Turn Their Backs* by Margaret Buffie (Kids Can Press), and *Draugr* by Arthur G. Slade (Orca Books, Canada).

The best children's story collection of the year is *Even a Little is Something: Stories of Nong* by Tom Glass (Linnet), a volume of colorful tales set in a rural village in Thailand, illustrated by Elena Gerard. *Here There Be Ghosts* by Jane Yolen (Harcourt Brace) is also recommended: a volume of stories and poems on a ghostly theme, illustrated by David Wilgus. Also of note: *Enchanted Journeys: Fifty Years of Irish Writing for Children* edited by Robert Dunbar (The O'Brien Press, Ireland). This collection features eighteen Irish authors from the 1940s to the present, represented here with excerpts selected from previously published books. Although it is rarely satisfying to read snippets of larger works, Dunbar's anthology performs a valuable service in bringing fine writers like Marita Conlon-McKenna, Tom McCaughren, Elizabeth O'Hara (the pseudonym of Elis Ni Dhuibhne), Martin Waddell, Eilis Dillon, and others to our attention. *Maurice, or the Fisher's Cot* by Mary Shelley (Knopf) is a bittersweet "new" children's tale by the author of *Frankenstein*. Claire Tomalin's fascinating introduction recounts how Shelley's manuscript, lost for more than two hundred years, was recently rediscovered in a trunk in an old Italian palazzo. The book provides a good introduction to Mary Shelley's life and work—but it's likely to be more of interest to adults, and Shelley fans, than to children. There's been a lot of hoopla this year about a new story by J. R. R. Tolkien: *Roverandom*, edited and introduced by Christina Scull and Wayne G. Hammond (Houghton Mifflin). Tolkien first invented this shaggy dog, oops, I mean magical dog story on a family vacation. Eventually he wrote it down and submitted it to his British publisher, just after the success of *The Hobbit*. Wisely, his publisher declined it and requested another story instead: the story that eventually became Tolkien's masterpiece, *The Lord of the Rings*. Now, lo these many years later, the older piece has been revived. If you're a rabid Tolkien fan, check it out; otherwise give it a miss.

Notable reprint editions: Peter Glassman of "Books of Wonder" continues to produce gorgeous facsimile editions of classic Oz titles, complete with the old John R. Neill illustrations. Available this year are *The Lost Princess of Oz* by L. Frank Baum, *Rinkitink in Oz* by L. Frank Baum, and *The Royal Book of Oz* by Ruth Plumly Thompson (Morrow/Books of Wonder). Also for Oz fans (although not quite as handsome): *The Sea Fairies* by L. Frank Baum, illustrated by John R. Neill (Dover); and an original title: *Visitors from Oz* by Martin Gardner (St. Martin's Press), which brings Dorothy, the Scarecrow and the Tin Man to the streets of modern Manhattan (not a book meant for kids). The Antique Collector's Club has started a new line of books called "ACC Children's Classics," publishing venerable children's tales in new editions with contemporary illustrations. Their first publications are: *The Princess and the Goblin* by George MacDonald, *Peter Pan* by J. M. Barrie, *Mistress Masham's Repose* by T. H. White, and *Sailing Days: Stories and Poems about the Sea* compiled by Amy McKay. Another welcome reprint is *The Fisherman and His Soul and Other Fairy Tales* by Oscar Wilde (St. Martin's Press), a small hardcover edition published in the Bloomsbury Classic Series.

Single-author Story Collections

1998 has turned out to be a particularly strong year for collections, particularly within the fantasy genre. The top volume of the year, however, comes from a mainstream source: *Elementals: Stories of Ice and Fire* by A. S. Byatt (Chatto & Wyndus, U.K.). This edition features six extraordinary tales by this Booker Prize-winning author, including her French fantasia "A Lamia in the Cevennes" and her sensual fairy tale "Cold." It's the best one yet from Byatt—thoroughly magical, and presented in a handsome little volume with art by Edvard Munch. I also recommend *Moonlight and Vines* by Charles de Lint (Tor), the author's third collection of "Newford" stories (following *Dreams Underfoot* and *The Ivory and the Horn*). De Lint mixes the myths of Old World immigrants and New World native peoples, stirs them into a melting pot of contemporary urban fiction, and imbues them with music, magic, and an almost shamanic style of storytelling. *Smoke and Mirrors* by Neil Gaiman (Avon Books) is a flashy, versatile collection by a flashy, versatile writer who was named one of the "Ten Top Postmodern Writers in America" by *The Dictionary of Literary Biography*. In his new collection, Gaiman dazzles the reader with his storytelling powers—and with the sheer diversity of his work, ranging from pastiche to crystalline fairy tales to psychological horror. *The Night We Buried Road Dog* by Jack Cady (Dream-Haven) contains six ghostly tales, along with an introduction by Peter S. Beagle. Cady is one of the great writers of our day, with a distinctively American voice. The title novella is worth the price of the book alone. Karen Joy Fowler has been called "the American Angela Carter" and she shows how apt that label is in her fine new collection *Black Glass* (Henry Holt). It's another one that dazzles with diversity and literary panache. *Last Summer at Mars Hill* by Elizabeth Hand (HarperPrism) is yet another excellent volume, reprinting strong cross-genre tales like "The Erl-King," the title story, and a handful of other pieces that have, as Tappan King once described them, "heart and also sharp little teeth." *Going Home Again* by Howard Waldrop (St. Martin's Press) reprints nine classic Waldrop stories—witty, wacky, wonderful stuff from a World Fantasy Award-winning author. *The Cleft and Other Odd Tales* by Gahan Wilson (Tor) contains fine works of dark fantasy and horror: disturbing, often mesmorizing fiction accompanied by Wilson's art.

On the mainstream shelves, I recommend *Collected Fictions* by Jorge Luis Borges, translated by Andrew Hurley (Viking), an omnibus edition of this Argentinean master's distinctive short stories, dating from 1935 publications to never-before-translated tales. *The Knife Thrower and Other Stories* by Steven Millhauser (Crown) is a *tour de force* of Millhauserian phantasmagoria—demonstrating once again that this author is one of the finest fantasists of our day. *Flying Leap* by Judy Budnitz (Picador) is the debut collection of a talented young writer—primarily a realist work, but with several forays into fantasy. *The Woman with the Flying Head and Other Stories* by Kurahashi Yumiko, translated from the Japanese by Atsuko Sakaki (M. E. Sharpe), is the first English-language collection of stories by this award-winning writer. Yumiko's volume of eleven dreamlike stories, with erotic and surrealist elements, was published as part of M. E. Sharpe's "Japanese Women Writing" series.

Small press story collections this year include *Lost Pages* by Paul Di Filippo (Four Walls Eight Windows), a strong volume of tales reimagining the lives and adventures of such literary figures as Franz Kafka, Anne Frank, Henry Miller, Philip K. Dick, Joseph Campbell, Jack Kerouac, Theodore Sturgeon and others. *Weird Women, Wired Women* by Kit Reed (Wesleyan University Press) is a genre- and gender-bending collection by one of our most interesting writers. This volume draws tales from three decades of work, and contains three original pieces. *The Mirror of Lida Sal* by Miguel Angel Asturias, translated from the Spanish by Gilbert Alter-Gilbert (Latin American Literary Review), collects fabulous, very surreal little stories based on Guatemalan myths and legends. *Dance House* by Marshall Joseph III (Red Crane Books) is a collection of contemporary stories (and essays) by a member of the Sicunga Lakota Sioux nation. While most of these are realist tales, Joseph's poignant ghost story "Cozy by the Fire" is recommended to fantasy readers. *Sari of the Gods* by G. S. Sharat Chandra (Coffee House Press) is a collection of stories portraying the Indian-American immigrant experience. The middle section of the book, set in rural India in the 1950s and 1960s, is full of exotic, magical detail and thus recommended to fantasy readers. *The Music Behind the Wall: Selected Stories, Vol. 2* by Anna Maria Ortese, translated from the Italian by Henry Martin (McPherson), will be of interest to fans of surrealism and stylistic experimentation—as will *Hectic Ethics* by Francisco Hinojosa, translated from the Spanish by Kurt Hollander (City Lights Books), the first U.S. publication of this award-winning Mexican author's work.

Reprinted classics: *Farewell to Lankhmar* by Fritz Leiber (Borealis/White Wolf) is a new edition bringing Leiber's famous "Fafhrd and the Gray Mouser" stories back to print. Many fantasists today cut their teeth on Leiber's work, so if your own reading began with Jordan and Brooks, go get this volume at once.

The Avram Davidson Treasury by Avram Davidson, edited by Robert Silverberg and Grania Davis (Tor) is an elegant posthumous collection of the short fiction of this erudite writer, with afterwords by Ray Bradbury and Harlan Ellison, and story introductions contributed by a veritable who's who list of fantasy authors. The selections in the book span a period of thirty years (beginning in the 1950s), containing such classics as "Or All the Sea with Oysters" and "Manatee Gal, Won't You Come Out Tonight." *The Perfect Host: The Collected Short Stories of Theodore Sturgeon, Vol. 5*, by Theodore Sturgeon (North Atlantic) is the latest volume in a series collecting short fiction by yet another great writer who shaped the modern fantasy field. Going back a little further in time, there's a new collection of *Fairy Tales, Short Stories and Poems* by Johann Wolfgang von Goethe (Lang), an unattractive but useful edition of works by this great German Romantic, including his imagistic fairy tales, translated from the German by J. W. Thomas.

Anthologies

There are several fat anthologies devoted exclusively to fantasy fiction this year, but little that's new or innovative to get excited about. The best of them is probably *The Fantasy Hall of Fame* edited by Robert Silverberg (HarperPrism), a reprint volume containing stories chosen by the membership of the Science Fiction and Fantasy Writers of America organization. It's a worthy, solidly conservative book (despite a nod to Jorge Luis Borges), filled with the names you would expect and stories that have been anthologized before by Robert A. Heinlein, Poul Anderson, Fritz Leiber, Peter S. Beagle, Roger Zelazny, Gene Wolfe, Ursula K. Le Guin, etc. According to the book's promotional material, these are the authors and stories that have shaped and defined the modern fantasy field. Well now, this is true only if one ignores broad sections of the fantasy landscape of the 80s and 90s, which is more diverse (and contains far more women writers) than this book would lead you to believe. Yet within its limitations, this doorstop of a volume contains some fine, classic tales. I recommend it as a gift for young readers who have never ventured beyond commercial fantasy sagas. It's a good foundation volume, and better than your other choice: *A Magic Lover's Treasury of the Fantastic* edited by Margaret Weis (Warner), an uneven collection. Then there's *Legends* edited by Robert Silverberg (Tor), boasting brand new fiction by Robert Jordan, Stephen King, Terry Goodkind, Anne McCaffrey, Terry Pratchett and a host of others, each story set in a fantasy world the author has already made famous. Lavishly designed and illustrated by Darrell Sweet and Michael Whelan, if ever a book was designed specifically for the bestseller lists, this is it.

When we turn to anthologies mixing fantasy tales with science fiction and horror, things get a bit brighter. The best original anthology I read this year was *Starlight 2*, edited by Patrick Nielsen Hayden (Tor), the second installment in this astute editor's World Fantasy Award-winning series. Magical, highly literary tales by Susanna Clarke, Ellen Kushner, Ted Chiang, Angélica Gorodischer (translated from the Spanish by Ursula K. Le Guin), and others make this book of interest to fantasy readers, and I highly recommend it. Of the various reprint anthologies, I recommend three in particular. *Flying Cups and Saucers: Gender*

Explorations in Science Fiction and Fantasy edited by Debbie Notkin and "the Secret Feminist Cabal" (Edgewood Press) contains sharp, transgressive fiction by Lisa Tuttle, James Patrick Kelley, Ian McDonald, Delia Sherman, Kelley Eskridge, Ursula K. Le Guin and others—all tales that either won or were shortlisted for the James Tiptree, Jr. Award. *Dreaming Down-Under* edited by Jack Dann and Janeen Webb (Voyager, Australia) is a broad-ranging collection of fantasy, science fiction, horror, surrealism, and magical realism by Australian authors. There's some very fine work here by Lucy Sussex, Terry Dowling, and numerous others. *Great American Ghost Stories* edited by Frank D. McSherry, Jr., Charles G. Waugh, and Martin H. Greenberg (Rutledge Hill Press) is an unusually good reprint collection, ignoring genre boundaries to gather stories scattered across the fifty states by Ambrose Bierce, Seabury Quinn, Donald E. Westlake, Madeleine L'Engle, Manly Wade Wellman, Joyce Carol Oates, Jack Cady, Harlan Ellison, Dahlov Ipcar, and many more.

Other anthologies, mentioned briefly: *Lord of the Fantastic* edited by Martin H. Greenberg (Avon Books) is a lovely tribute volume honoring Roger Zelany (1937-1995), one of the finest writers to grace the SF and fantasy fields in the last half-century. The book features original fiction by Robert Silverberg, John Varley, Andre Norton, Steven Brust, and many more—mostly science fiction tales, but a small amount of fantasy, too. *The Best of Crank!* edited by Bryan Cholfin (Tor) collects weird and wonderful interstitial stories (first published in the *Crank!* small press journal) by the likes of Jonathan Lethem, Michael Bishop, and R. A. Lafferty. *In the Shadow of the Gargoyle* edited by Nancy Kilpatrick and Thomas R. Roche (Berkley) is a theme collection of stories about gargoyles—mostly horror fiction, but there's also some nice fantasy tucked within these pages. *Black Cats and Broken Mirrors* edited by Martin H. Greenberg and John Helfers (DAW) is the best of the many Greenberg theme anthologies this year, with nice original work from Nina Kiriki Hoffman, Charles de Lint, and Bruce Holland Rogers. *Imagination Fully Dilated* edited by Alan M. Clark and Elizabeth Engstrom (Cemetery Dance) is a small press edition of tales based on Alan M. Clark's macabre art. It's primarily of interest to horror and SF fans, but it contains a bit of fantasy too. *Things Invisible to See* edited by Lawrence Schimel (Circlet) is a small press collection of "gay and lesbian tales of magical realism," nicely packaged, with a particularly good contribution from Martha Soukup. *The Mammoth Book of Comic Fantasy* edited by Mike Ashley (Carroll & Graf) mixes old and new tales ranging from Lewis Carroll, Edward Lear, and James Thurber to Terry Pratchett, Tom Holt, and Douglas Adams.

For swords-and-sorcery fans: *Fantastic Worlds* edited by Paul Collins (HarperCollins) contains original tales from Australian writers; *Swords and Sorceresses* XV edited by Marion Zimmer Bradley (DAW) is the latest in a long-lived series which has given many young writers their start; and *Marion Zimmer Bradley's Fantasy Worlds* edited by Marion Zimmer Bradley and Rachel Holmen is a small press collection of original fiction (The MZB Literary Works Trust). For mystery fans: *Once Upon a Crime: Fairy Tales for Mystery Lovers* edited by Ed Gorman and Martin H. Greenberg (Prime Crime); and *Crossing the Line: Canadian Mysteries with a Fantastic Twist* edited by Robert J. Sawyer and David Skene-Melvin (Pottersfield Press, Nova Scotia). Also from Canada: *Arrowdreams* edited by Mark Shainblum and John Dupuis (Nuage Editions, Canada), stories exploring alternate versions of Canadian history. *Wandering Stars: An Anthology of Jewish Fantasy and Science Fiction* edited by Jack Dann (Jewish Lights) is a reprint edition of a book that has been out of print for twenty-five years.

Lovers of surrealist fiction should seek out *Leviathan 2: The Legacy of Boccaccio* edited by Jeff VanderMeer and Rose Secrest (Ministry of Whimsy Press), and *The Belgian School of the Bizarre* edited by Kim Connell (Fairleigh Dickinson University Press). *Prospero's Mirror: A Translator's Portfolio of Latin American Short Fiction* edited by Ilan Stavans (Curbstone) contains a range of stories from some of the best Latin American writers and translators working today, including magical realist works. *Cubana: Contemporary Fiction by Cuban Women* edited by Mirta Yanez, translated from the Spanish by Dick Cluster (Beacon Press), is another good collection ranging from realist to magic realist fiction. *Which Lilith* edited by Enid Dame, Lilly Rivlin, and Henry Wenkart (Jason Aronson) is an anthology collecting "women's responses to the Lilith myth in prose and poetry." It's a wildly uneven volume with some very good essays and poetry, but the fiction has an amateur feel. If you're interested in the subject check it out, but be forewarned.

I should also mention my own anthologies here, for the sake of the authors published in them: *The Essential Bordertown* co-edited with Delia Sherman (Tor) contains original urban fantasy stories on teenage coming-of-age themes by Ellen Kushner, Midori Snyder, Charles de Lint, Steven Brust, Patricia A. McKillip, and a host of others. *Sirens and Other Daemon Lovers* co-edited with Ellen Datlow (HarperPrism), contains original stories and poems on the theme of passion, obsession, and mytho-eroticism by Joyce Carol Oates, Tanith Lee, Ellen Kushner, Brian Stablefold, Neil Gaiman, Delia Sherman, Pat Murphy, and others.

Poetry

There is a great deal of magical and mythic poetry being published these days, but for the most part it's scattered across journals and magazines rather than collected into single volumes. I can recommend a few editions, however, that are well worth seeking out:

Autobiography of Red by Anne Carson (Knopf), billed as "a novel in verse," is a contemporary reworking of the myth of Geryon and Herakles—a passionate, extraordinary book which I recommend highly. *Proper Myth* by William F. Van Wert (Orchises Press) is a rich, thoughtful collection exploring Greek myths, along with the themes of race and gender. *Esperanza: Poems for Orpheus* by Holly Prado (Orchises Press) is a wonderful collection about ancient Greek myth, modern life, and the nature of inspiration. *Mrs. Dumpty* by Chana Bloch (University of Wisconsin Press) is a powerful, heart-breaking memoir-in-verse using themes from a classic nursery rhyme to portray the dissolution of a marriage. *Magic Words: Poems* by Edward Field (Gulliver Books) is a beautiful collection based on Inuit legends; although published for young readers, adults will enjoy these mythic poems too. My personal favorite of the year is *The Boy Changed into a Stag Cries Out at the Gate of Secrets* by Ferenc Juhasz. This lengthy mythic poem was first published in Hungary, then translated into English by Kenneth McRobbie and Ilona Duczynska as part of *The Plough and the Pen:*

Writings from Hungary (1963). Now Juhasz's powerful, disturbing work has been brought back to print in the June 1998 edition of *Agenda* magazine, edited by William Cookson, published in London.

The Magazines

The state of fantasy fiction in genre magazines was somewhat better this year than last. As you can see on our copyright and Honorable Mentions pages, a number of stories either reprinted or recommended this year came from the Big Three genre magazines: *The Magazine of Fantasy & Science Fiction* edited by Gordon Van Gelder; *Asimov's* edited by Gardner Dozois; and *Realms of Fantasy* edited by Shawna McCarthy. *F&SF*, in particular, has really picked up steam since editor Van Gelder came on board, and it is now a more reliable source for fine fantasy short stories. When it comes time to chose the stories for *The Year's Best Fantasy and Horror* annual, however, I truly notice the hole in the field left by the demise of *Omni* magazine (which gave up even its online edition in 1998). Under editor Ellen Datlow, *Omni* regularly published fiction of the highest literary quality—and had the money to attract some of the best writers working today. I greatly miss having that well to draw from when making selections for this annual volume. On a brighter note, Ellen Datlow's new venture, the online magazine *Event Horizon*, has begun to publish first-rate fiction (see the Kelly Link story reprinted here)—and I wish it every bit of success.

Unlike the horror field, which supports a wide variety of small press 'zines that are often sources for good horror fiction, I'm just not seeing memorable work in the semi-professional magazines that publish fantasy. The excellent *Century* magazine is dormant, and the rest of the 'zines that cross my desk seemed to be geared to adventure tales, not literature. If you're actually looking for adventure tales, however, *Marion Zimmer Bradley's Fantasy Magazine* edited by Rachel E. Holmen, is probably the most reliable of them (and Darrell Schweitzer's perceptive interview columns are always worth reading). The quality of the stories is uneven since Holmen and Bradley give a lot of their print space to new writers still earning their chops, but somebody has got to provide a forum for young writers, so bravo to them. Now if only someone would create an entry-level forum for young writers of literary fantasy and mythic fiction. . . . Three good web sites devoted to fantasy are good sources for reviews, news, and recommendations: *Legends* edited by Paula Katherine Marmor (http://www.legends.dm.net/); *Folk Tales* edited by Cat Eldridge (http://www.kinrowan.com/); and *Phantastes* edited by Staci Ann Dumoski (http://www.phantastes.com/). As for mainstream magazines and literary journals, fantasy continues to thrive out there, as long as it's labeled something else: magic realism, surrealism, or—my favorite—"post-realism." (No, I'm not making that up.) Stories and poems reprinted in this volume were culled from *The New Yorker, Ms., The New York Review of Books, The Tampa Tribune Fiction Quarterly, Pleiades, AGNI, The Sewanee Review, The Antioch Review, The Poetry Review* (U.K.), and *Southerly* (Australia). Many other journals provided tales for our Honorable Mentions list.

Art

The big art news of the year is the publication of Brian Froud's long-awaited sequel to *Faeries*, the ground-breaking, often-imitated art and folklore volume he created with Alan Lee twenty years ago. The new book, titled *Good Faeries/Bad Faeries* (Simon & Schuster), offers faerie mythology from around the world, viewed through Froud's unique art and vision. I was involved with the book (editing Froud's text), so I'm too close to the project to critique it, but any new work by this master faerie artist is an event, and worth checking out. You should also take a look at *Stardust*, another glimpse into the world of faerie: this time through the lovely Rackham-flavored art of Charles Vess, with text by Neil Gaiman. Originally published as four graphic novels, the story has been collected into a single beautiful edition (DC/Vertigo); both the text and the art have a wonderful turn-of-the-century feel, and create real magic. *Tibet: Through the Red Box* by Peter Sis (Farrar, Straus & Giroux) is an amazing, award-winning publication based on a true story. Sis's father, a filmmaker in Communist Czechoslovakia, was sent to film road contruction in China in the 1950s. Lost during a blizzard, separated from his crew, he ended up in Tibet, where he was nursed back to health by gentle monks (and even met the Dalai Lama). Sis grew up with tales of this dreamlike journey throughout his childhood, but only after his father's death did he read the diary of the journey (kept for decades in a red lacquer box), which in turn inspired the creation of this stunningly illustrated book. In the fine art field, I recommend *Paula Rego* (Thames & Hudson) highly, a 1997 book not seen until this year, published to coincide with a touring show organized by London's Tate Gallery. Born in Portugal, Rego is one of the finest figurative artists working in Britain today. Her work often incorporates Portuguese legends and disturbing fairy tale symbolism, and has some of the same dark, passionate feel as Angela Carter's fiction.

Here are other recommended art publications from 1998: *Wondrous Strange: the Wyeth Tradition* (Bulfinch Press) features the work of three generations of Wyeth painters, along with the art of Howard Pyle, in a book inspired by a show curated at the Delaware Art Museum. *The Life and Works of Sir Edward Burne-Jones* by Christopher Wood (Stewart, Tabori and Chang) is the best volume yet on a painter whose work was infused with myths and fairy tales. I also recommend an informative new biography: *Edward Burne-Jones* by Penelope Fitzgerald (Sutton Publishing). *Pre-Raphaelite Women Artists* by Jan Marsh and Pamela Gerish Nunn (Thames and Hudson) is a welcome look at the women associated with the Pre-Raphaelite and Arts-&-Crafts movements. *Juliet Margaret Cameron's Women* by Sylvia Wolfe (Yale University Press) is a book inspired by a recent exhibition of sixty-three works by this Victorian photographer associated with both the Pre-Raphaelite and Bloomsbury circles. *American Book Design and William Morris* by Susan Otis Thompson (Oak Knoll Books) looks at the pervasive, on-going influence of this brilliant, versatile designer. *Carl and Karin Larsson: Creators of the Swedish Style* edited by Michael Snodin and Elisabet Stavenow-Hidemark (Bulfinch Press) is a beautiful volume dedicated to the enchanted paintings and the colorful interior designs of this husband and wife team of artists from the turn of the century. For fans of surrealist art, there are four excellent volumes to chose from: *Mirror Images: Women, Surrealism, and Self-Representation* edited by Whitney Chadwick and Dawn Ades (MIT Press); *Leonora Carrington: A Retrospective Exhibition* (Americas Society); *Ernst* edited by Jose Maria Faerna, translated by Alberto Curotto (Abradale Press); and *The Fantastic Art of Beksinski*, Zdzislaw Beksinski (Morpheus International).

Also of note: *The Mole and the Owl*, written and illustrated by Charles Duffie (Hampton Roads Publishing), is a poignant, romantic fable set in the magical world of nature, packaged in an elegantly designed little edition. *Fairy Tales of Oscar Wilde: The Young King and The Remarkable Rocket* (NMB Publishing) is illustrated by P. Craig Russell in an attractive comic book format. *Minidoka (937th Earl of One Mile Series M)* by Edgar Rice Burroughs (Dark Horse) is the earliest surviving unpublished story by Burroughs, with a color cover painting and black-and-white interior art by Michael Wm. Kaluta. *Icon: A Retrospective by the Grand Master of Fantastic Art, Frank Frazetta* edited by Arnie and Cathy Fenner (Underwood): For those who like art of the muscular-barbarians-and-babes-in-chain-mail variety, Frazetta was indeed the Grand Master of this par-ticular genre. *Spectrum #5: The Best in Contemporary Fantastic Art* edited by Arnie and Cathy Fenner (Underwood): Much of the work in this annual edition is science fiction or swords-and-sorcery oriented, but for fans of a more romantic brand of magical art there are good contributions here from John J. Muth, James Christensen, and David Bowers. The Gold and Silver Awards in the Unpublished Category (by Phil Hale and Kirk Rienert respectively) are particularly fine. The judges for volume #5 were: Terry Lee, Joe Kubert, Donato Giancola, Joseph DeVito, John English, and Tom Dolphins.

Picture Books

Children's picture books are a wonderful showcase for magical storytelling and art. Here is a baker's dozen of the best to cross my desk this year (in alphabetical order):

The Crane Wife by Odds Bodkin, illustrated by Gennardy Spirin (Gulliver/ Harcourt Brace), a haunting Japanese tale with luminous paintings by a Russian master.

To Everything There is a Season by Leon and Diane Dillon (Blue Sky/Scho-lastic), a handsomely designed book with art based on visual imagery from all around the world.

Tales of Wonder and Magic by Berlie Doherty, illustrated by Juan Wijngaard (Candlewick Press), a collection of enchanted stories from cultures the world over, beautifully retold, gorgeously illustrated. Don't miss this one!

The Pied Piper of Hamlin by Robert Holden, illustrated by Drahos Zak (Houghton Mifflin), a poetic retelling of this German folk tale with unique, quirky illustration by an artist from the Czech Republic.

Old Mother Hubbard by David A. Johnson (McElderry), a lovely, gentle edition with a wonderful old-fashioned feel.

Pegasus by Marianna Mayer, illustrated by Kinuko Y. Craft (Morrow) is a fine retelling of this Greek myth adorned with Craft's distinctive, jewel-toned paint-ings. (Another good Pegasus retelling is *Pegasus the Flying Horse* by Jane Yolen, illustrated by Ming Li [Dutton].)

The Stone Fey by Robin McKinley, reprinting one of McKinley's finest stories in a romantic new edition illustrated by John Clapp (Harcourt Brace).

Beautiful Warrior: The Legend of the Nun's Kung Fu by Emily Arnold McCully (Levine/Scholastic), a rousing good tale about a beautiful Chinese Kung Fu master and a girl running away from marriage.

Animal Dreaming by Paul Morin (Harcourt Brace), a story of the Aboriginal Dreamtime, following a young aboriginal boy's rites of passage into adulthood.

King Stork by Howard Pyle, illustrated by Trina Schart Hyman (Morrow/Books of Wonder), a classic tale from Pyle's *The Wonder Clock*, with terrific new illustrations from this fine watercolorist.

Cendrillon: A Caribbean Cinderella by Robert San Souci, illustrated by J. Brian Pinkney (Simon & Schuster), a lively Cinderella variant set on the island of Martinique, with vibrant scratchboard art.

The Blind Fairy by Brigitte Schar, illustrated by Julia Gukova (North South), a memorable, unusual fairy tale by a Swiss writer (and expert on German folklore), brought to life by unusual work from this fabulous Russian artist.

Other titles I recommend seeking out, noted briefly: *Tales of Wisdom and Wonder* retold by Hugh Lupton, illustrated by Niamh Sharkey (Barefoot Books); *Joan of Arc*, a picture book biography by Diane Stanley (Morrow Junior); *A Dog's Tooth: A Tale from Tibet* by W. W. Rowe, illustrated by Chris Banigan (Snow Lion); *Baba Yaga and the Wise Doll*, a Russian story retold by Hiawyn Oram, illustrated by Ruth Brown (Dutton); *The Fox's Kettle*, a Japanese story by Laura Langston, illustrated by Victor Bosson (Orca); *The Legend of the Panda*, a Chinese tale retold by Linda Granfield and illustrated by Song Nan Zhang (Tundra Books); *The Chrystal Heart: A Vietnamese Legend* by Aaron Shepard, illustrated by Joseph Daniel Fielder (Atheneum); *Hanuman*, a retelling of India's Ramayana by Erik Jendresen and Joshua M. Greene (Tricycle Press); *A Gift for Abuelita: A Celebration of the Mexican Day of the Dead* (in both English and Spanish) by Nancy Leunn, illustrated by Robert Chapman (Rising Moon); *Grandmother's Song*, a Mexican tale by Barbara Soros illustrated by Jackie Morris (Barefoot Books); *The Tortilla Cat* by Nancy Willard, illustrated by Jeanette Winter (Harcourt Brace); *This Big Sky, Poems Inspired by the Land and Culture of the American Southwest* by Pat Mora, illustrated by Steve Jenkins (Scholastic); *The Legend of the White Buffalo Woman* by Paul Goble (National Geographic Society); *Touching the Distance: Native American Riddle-Poems* by Brian Swan, illustrated by Maria Rendon (Harcourt Brace); *The Legend of Sleeping Bear*, an Ojibwe tale about Lake Michigan retold by Kathy-Jo Wargin, illustrated by Gijsbert van Franenhuyzen (Sleeping Bear Press); and (particularly recommended) *The Barefoot Book of Princesses*, stories from around the world retold by Caitlin Matthews, illustrated by Olwyn Whelan (Barefoot Books).

Nonfiction

1998 has been another good year for works of nonfiction relevant to our field. The following four volumes are particularly recommended to readers and writers of fantasy: *No Go the Bogeyman* by Marina Warner (Chatto & Windus, U.K., 1998; Farrar, Straus & Giroux, U.S., 1999) is the latest work by the author of the study *From the Beast to the Blonde* (a dazzling examination of women and fairy tales in European history). Warner now turns her penetrating gaze to the darker images in myth, folklore, and popular culture: ogres, giants, bogeymen, and other figures of masculine terror. This is a fascinating, subversive, fiercely intelligent book; I can't recommend it too highly. *The Voice That Thunders* by Alan Garner (The Harvill Press, U.K.) is a stunning collection of autobiographical essays about myth, fantasy, and the creative process by this singular, brilliant writer, the author of *The Owl Service*, *Elidor*, and other classics. *Shaking a Leg: Collected Writings* by Angela Carter, edited by Jenny Upglow (Penguin) is a fine posthumous edition collecting Carter's journalism and essays, including musings on the subjects of fairy tales, folklore, magic realism, and feminism. *Mirror, Mirror on the Wall: Women Writers Explore Their Favorite Fairy Tales* edited by Kate Bernheimer (Doubleday), is a wonderful collection of essays and reflections by twenty-four contemporary authors including Margaret Atwood, A. S. Byatt, Fay Weldon, and a broad range of others from the well-known to the obscure. My only quibble with this excellent book (but it's a big one) is that no genre authors were included here, despite the fact that fine writers like Robin McKinley, Jane Yolen, Tanith Lee, Ursula K. Le Guin, Sheri S. Tepper, Patricia A. McKillip (I could go on and on here), have worked with fairy tales more extensively than most writers included in the volume. Pity.

Also recommended: *Wonders and the Order of Nature, 1150–1750* by Lorraine Daston and Katherine Park (MIT Press), an exploration of mankind's appetite for wonders, monsters, and the miraculous. This lengthy, broad-ranging volume examines the ways writers from the Middle Ages through the Enlightment used wonders to envision the natural world. Does this sound like the background to a John Crowley novel? As a matter of fact, Crowley reviewed this intriguing book for *The Washington Post*. *The Alphabet Versus the Goddess: The Conflict Between Word and Image* by Leonard Shlain (Viking) is a provocative investigation of the effect of written language on myth and gender issues—highly recommended. *Fantasy: the Liberation of Imagination* by Richard Mathews (Simon & Schuster/ Twayne) discusses fantasy as a literature of subversion and liberation, from ancient epics through William Morris to Tolkien and Le Guin. *Northern Dreamers* edited by Edo van Belkom (Quarry Press), contains interviews with twenty-two Canadian writers of speculative fiction including Charles de Lint, Dave Duncan, Elisabeth Vonarburg, and Tanya Huff. *Presenting Young Adult Fantasy Fiction* by Cathi Dunn MacRae (Simon & Schuster/Twayne) is a useful reference guide, including reading lists, comments from young readers, and writer biographies. *C. S. Lewis: Writer, Dreamer and Mentor* by Lionel Adey (Eerdmans) takes a fresh look at Lewis' work in all its many forms, as well as the biographical context in which the work was written. *Invisible Writer: A Biography of Joyce Carol Oates* by Greg Johnson (Dutton) is not a critical study but a proper life of this prolific, gifted author. *The Letters of Hildegard of Bingen, Vol. I*, translated from the Latin by Joseph L. Baird and Radd K. Ehrman (Oxford University Press), provides a tantalizing glimpse into the mind and magical life of this Christian mystic. For those interested in the writing process, I recommend the following two volumes: *Steering the Craft: Exercises and Discussions on Story Writing for the Lone Navigator or the Mutinous Crew* by Ursula K. Le Guin (Eight Mountain Press), a useful, supportive, thought-provoking volume that no would-be writer should be without. *Telling Stories: An Anthology for Writers* by Joyce Carol Oates

(W. W. Norton) is another excellent volume about the writer's craft, including an interesting section on retelling myths and fairy tales.

Mythology and Folklore

There were several excellent, highly useful reference volumes published this year. In particular, I recommend: *Encyclopedia of Folklore and Literature* by Mary Ellen Brown and Bruce Rosenberg (ABC-CLIO), an extensive volume documenting folklore and myth in the works of writers through the ages (as well as filmmakers, playrights, composers, and other creative artists); and *Folklore* edited by Thomas A. Green (ABC-CLIO), a two-volume encyclopedia of "beliefs, customs, tales, music and art," compiled by an international team of folklorists, designed to be of use to general readers as well as scholars. More tightly focused, but equally engrossing, is *The Encyclopedia of Native American Shamanism* by William S. Lyon (ABC-CLIO), a reference volume on Native-American myths, beliefs, and ceremonies. I also strongly urge you to seek out *The Book of Fabulous Beasts: A Treasury from Ancient Times to the Present* by Joseph Nigg (Oxford University Press). From Babylonian myth to Renaissance heraldry, from Herodotus to J. R. R. Tolkien, this dazzling book follows the tracks of magical beasts down through the ages. Two more helpful reference volumes from the Oxford University Press: *The Dictionary of Celtic Mythology* by James MacKillop; and *The Dictionary of Native American Mythology* by Sam D. Gill and Irene F. Sullivan.

Assorted Celtic and British works: *Animals in Celtic Life and Myth* by Miranda Green (Routledge) is a lucid, thorough reference volume. *Tales of the Celtic Otherworld* by John Matthews (Blandford) is an insightful text, with dramatic, rather startling illustrations by Ian Daniels. *Robin Hood: the Green Lord of the Wildwood* by John Matthews (Blandford) is a fresh, incisive look at this legendary figure. *Drinking from the Sacred Well: Personal Voyages of Discovery with the Celtic Saints* by John Matthews (HarperSanFrancisco) is an exploration of the lives and legends of twelve mystical Celtic saints, plus an overview of the history of Celtic spirituality. *The Grail Legend* by Emma Jung and Marie-Louise von Franz (Princeton University Press) is a strictly Jungian take on the grail mythos. *The Sacred Circle Tarot* by Anna Franklin, illustrated by Paul Mason (Llewellyn), offers a book and tarot deck combining standard tarot imagery with Celtic symbols (for instance, the Fool becomes the Green Man, the World becomes the World Tree, etc.). *Celtic Folklore Cooking* by Joanne Asala (Llewellyn) contains more than two hundred recipes discovered by the author (a folklorist) during travels through Europe and the British Isles, along with fairy tales, ballads, charms, riddles, etc. *Spirits, Fairies, Leprechauns and Goblins: An Encyclopedia* by Carol Rose (W. W. Norton) is a light but charming edition—and preferable to A *Field Guide to Irish Fairies* by Bob Curran (Chronicle Books). Not only is the art in the latter volume alarmingly derivative of *Faeries* (the classic volume by Alan Lee and Brian Froud), but the publisher then proclaims this "the first and only such guide available." Excuse me?

For myth, folk, and fairy tale material of particular interest to women, try: *Fearless Girls, Wise Women and Beloved Sisters: Heroines in Fairy Tales* edited by Kathleen Ragan (W. W. Norton), a terrific sourcebook of tales from all around the world, drawing upon older variants, highly recommended despite a steep cover price. *On the Edge of Dream: The Women of Celtic Myth and Legend* by Jennifer Heath (Plume) contains fifteen tales drawn from Celtic epics and the oral tradition. *The Women We Become* edited by Ann G. Thomas (Prima) is a light but pleasant edition of myths and folk tales about growing older. *Ventures into Childland: Victorians, Fairy Tales and Femininity* by U. C. Knoepflmacher (University of Chicago Press) is a fascinating study, published in a handsome package. *Scheherezade's Sisters: Trickster Heroines and Their Stories in World Literature* by Marilyn Jurich (Greenwood Publishing) is filled with useful reference information, but look for it at the library, because the price is astronomical. *The Gift of Life* by Bonnie Glass-Coffin (University of New Mexico Press) is a ground-breaking anthropological study of women, shamanism, and spirituality in northern Peru. *Lotus Seeds and Lucky Stars* by Shu Shu Costa (Simon & Schuster) is a gentle, mystical little book of Asian myths, folklore, and traditions surrounding pregnancy and birthing.

For myths and folklore in America, both native tales and transplanted ones, try: *Myths, Legends and Folktales of America* by David Leeming and Jake Page (Oxford University Press), an anthology encompassing everything from ancient indigenous stories to modern-day mythic figures like Superman, Elvis, and Billy the Kid. *The Mythology of Native America*, also by the team of Leeming and Page (University of Oklahoma Press) provides a good overview of the traditional lore of a variety of tribal peoples. *American Indian Trickster Tales* edited by Richard Erdoes and Alfonso Ortiz (Viking), is a superlative (and long-awaited) collection from this well-respected duo and highly recommended. *The Serpent's Tongue: Prose, Poetry and Art of the New Mexico Pueblos* (Dutton) is a gorgeous coffee table book full of wonderful tales, photographs, and art both old and modern. Good collections of tales from different tribes: *Living Stories of the Cherokee* edited by Barbara R. Duncan (University of North Carolina Press); *Grandmother, Grandfather and Old Wolfe* edited by Clifford E. Trafzer (Michigan State University Press), oral tales from the Northwestern tribal tradition; *Life With the Little People* by Robert Johnson Perry (The Greenfield Review Press), a look at creatures in Muskogea tales sometimes called "Indian Leprechauns"; *Hopi Animal Tales* edited by Michael and Lorena Lomatuway'Ma (University of Nebraska Press); *Nez Perce Coyote Tales: The Myth Cycle* by Deward E. Walker and Daniel N. Matthews (University of Oklahoma Press); and, my personal favorite, *Northern Tales: Stories from the Native People of the Arctic and Subarctic Regions* edited by Howard Norman (Pantheon Fairy Tale and Folklore Series).

Miscellaneous myths and folklore:

Aesop: the Complete Aesop's Fables, translated by Robert and Olivia Temple (Penquin): this uncensored translation has caused quite a stir, for it includes some rather ribald fables which have never seen print before in English. *Lilith's Cave* by Howard Schwartz (Oxford University Press) is a collection of Jewish supernatural tales. *The Monkey and the Mango Tree* by Harish Johari (Inner Traditions) contains twenty-five "teaching tales" drawn from the great Indian epics. *An Anthology of Russian Folk Epics*, translated by James Bailey and Tatyana Ivanova (M. E. Sharpe), offers epics and ballads drawn from the Russian oral tradition. Also available from the same publisher: *The Animal Tales: The Complete Russian Folktale, Vol. 2* edited by Jack V. Hanley. *Fairy Tales and*

Fables from Weimar Days edited by Jack Zipes (University of Wisconsin Press) is a good, slim collection of tales translated by a first-rate folklore scholar. *Kaua'i: Ancient Place Names and Their Stories* by Frederick B. Wichman (University of Hawaii Press) is a surprisingly fascinating little book of myths and legends behind the names on the island of Kauai, reminding us that we don't have to go to Middle Earth or Narnia to find lands of wonder. *At the Edge of the World: Magical Stories of Ireland* edited by John Lowings (Holt), is a striking edition of Irish fairy tales and ghost stories, illustrated with dramatic photographs of the Irish landscape. *Encompassing Nature: A Sourcebook* edited by Robert M. Torrance (Counterpoint Press) is an extensive guide (weighing in at a hefty 1,200 pages) to nature writing from around the world, including nature myths and legends. *Longing for Darkness: Kamante's Tales from Out of Africa* by Peter Beard (Chronicle) is a captivating edition (which Jacqueline Kennedy Onassis had a hand in before her death) featuring fables and autobiographical tales related by the hero of Isak Dinesen's *Out of Africa*, along with Kamante's watercolors and photographs by Dinesen and the adventurer/photographer Peter Beard. This one's a real treat.

A handful of good editions for children: *Favorite Medieval Tales* retold by Mary Pope Osborne, illustrated by Troy Howell (Scholastic); *Hearsay: Strange Tales from the Middle Kingdom*, magical tales of China by Barbara Ann Porte (Greenwillow); *Why Goats Smell Bad and Other Stories from Benin* edited by Raouf Mama (Shoe String Press); *American Indian Fairy Tales* by W. T. Larned (Derrydale); *The Deekatoo: Native American Stories about the Little People* edited by John Bierhorst (Morrow); and *American Fairy Tales: From Rip Van Winkle to Rootabaga Stories* edited by Neil Philips, with an introduction by Alison Lurie (Hyperion).

Music

Traditional music is of interest to many fantasy lovers because it draws on some of the same cultural roots as folk tales and other folk arts. Contemporary "world music" can be compared to certain kinds of fantasy fiction, for artists in both fields are updating ancient folkloric themes for a modern age. There is so much good traditional music these days that it's hard to keep recommendations down to a length that won't overwhelm this summary, but I've collaborated with writer/musician Charles de Lint and Ellen Kushner (host of the "Sound and Spirit" program for Public Radio International) to come up with a pared-down list of favorites that you shouldn't miss.

From Charles: "My top album of the year is Robbie Robertson's *Contact from the Underworld of Redboy* (Capitol), a stunning, evocative mix of traditional Native-American chants and drumming, contemporary music, and sampled sounds. Roots/narrative-based music had a couple of real highlights: first there was the debut release from transplanted Irish native Bap Kennedy, *Domestic Blues* (E Squared), featuring Peter Rowan, Jerry Douglas, Roy Husky Jr. (his last recording), Nanci Griffith, and Steve Earl (who also co-produced as part of the Twangtrust). Then later in the summer Earl's sister Stacey released her debut, *Simple Gearle* (Gearle Records), a collection of acoustic songs that hark back to the old high, lonesome sound of the hills while remaining very contemporary.

And do I even have to mention that Lucinda Williams finally has a new release? *Car Wheels on the Gravel Road* (Mercury) is everything her fans could have hoped for. In Celtic music, Solas released *The Words That Remain* (Shanachie), yet another matchless collection of instruments and songs. Donny Lunny finally got out from behind the producer's chair to release his second, long awaited album, *Coolfin* (Metro Blue)—a mix of Celtic, European and original material that is worth the wait. If there was a rave scene in Celtic music, Bongshang would be leading it. Their second release, *The Hurricane Jungle* (Bongshang) is an infectious blend of traditional and drum and bass. The Poozies lost the talented Sally Barker, but gained the equally talented Kate Rusby to replace her. She appears with them on *Infinite Blue*, and on a three-song EP of her own, *Cowsong* (both on Pure Records). Some of the most fascinating experiments with traditional music seem to be happening on the Latin music scene. My favorite this year was the self-titled *Los Super Seven* (RCA), featuring members of Los Lobos and the Texas Tornadoes; but the self-titled *Ozomatli* (Almo Sounds) runs a close second with their tougher, more rocking sound. *The Black Light* by the Tucson band Calexico (Quarterstick) offers an Anglo's take on the Tex-Mex border flavor, while traditionalists will delight in the nouveau flamenco of Robert Michael's *Utopia* (Melaby/WEA)."

From Ellen: "The most exciting musical moment for me of 1998 was getting to meet the African musician Stella Chiweshe of Zimbabwe in connection with the release of her collection *The Healing Tree: the Best of Stella Chiweshe* (Shanachie). Her music is not merely beautiful; in the Shona tradition music is essential for summoning spirits of the ancestor (and when you meet Chiweshe, you realize that this is a person who is magic, yet real) in the modern world, through an ancient tradition that has not died. 1998 also marked the 900th anniversary of the birth of the mystic, scientist, poet, and composer Abbess Hildegard von Bingen. Many brilliant recordings of her music have been released, including a superb historical recreation by the groups Sequentia and Anonymous 4 on *Tapestry's Celestial Light* (Telarc), which includes not only Hildegard's own music, but a stunning contemporary piece based on her words. Last but not least, the absolutely perfect 1998 release for fantasy readers is Ruth MacKenzie's *Kalevala: Dream of the Salmon Maid* (Omnium). This is the 'original cast recording' of McKenzie's performance piece based on an ancient Finnish epic. "Salmon Maiden" retells the story of Aino, whose mother tries to marry her against her will to the musician Vainamoinen; Aino escapes by transforming herself into a fish. The music is a thrilling combination of rock, traditional Finnish women's music, even pagan animal hollers . . . and if those names sound kinda familiar, yes, J. R. R. Tolkien drew on the Kalevala myth and language in *The Silmarillion*." For more information on these artists and extensive playlists of music, see the *Sound & Spirit* Web site: http://www.wgbh.org/wgbh/pages/pri/spirit/index.html

I second the previous recommendations, and have a few of my own to add. My favorites of the year were: *Red and Rice*, a dazzling two-CD set by the young English singer/musician Eliza Carthy, a very contemporary take on the folk music of the British Isles (Topic); and *Mahk Jchi* by Ulali (Corn, Beans & Squash), a trio of Native-American women singers (featured on Robbie Robertson's Red

Road Ensemble) who blend traditional songs with jazz, blues, and gospel influences in a unique and gorgeous way. I also highly recommend *Omaiyo*, a terrific CD from master percussionist Robin Adnan Anders of Boiled in Lead (Ryko). In this solo work, he has created gorgeous pieces of music which he calls "tone poems"—each one based on a brief story by, variously, Jane Yolen, Neil Gaiman, Ellen Kushner, Steven Brust, Will Shetterly, Emma Bull, and other writers from the fantasy field.

Other British/Celtic music recommendation: *Alloy* is the latest from the legendary Minneapolis rock-and-reel band Boiled in Lead (Omnium), combining a selection of tunes from previous CDs with live and alternative-mix tracks. A *Certain Smile* by Bachue is a lovely CD of Scottish music with jazz influences. *Crossing the Bridge* by Eileen Ivers (Sony) mixes Irish music performed by this world class fiddler combined with music from cultures around the globe. Deaf Shepherd is a hot young band out of Scotland; check out their infectious second release, *Synergy* (Greentrax). If you're looking for good Celtic vocals try: *On Air* by the peerless June Tabor (Strange Fruit), *Circle of the Sun* by Aine Minogue (RCA), *Women of Ireland* by Ceoltoiri (Maggie's Music), *Starry Gazy Pie* by Nancy Kerr and James Fagan (Fellside), *Lights in the Dark*, a CD of Sacred Irish songs produced by Hector Zazou (Detour), and *Celtic Voices*, an excellent compilation CD (Green Linnet). The best traditional instrumental CD I heard all year was *Spellbound: The Best of Sharon Shannon*, from a wizard on the accordion (Green Linnet). For music of the Loreena McKennitt type, try Kate Price's new release, *Deep Heart's Core* (Omtown). For a bardic CD of fine storytelling and Celtic harp music, try *The Language of Birds* from Scotland's Fiona Davidson (Watercolor Music). Another good harp release is Savourna Stevenson's *Calman the Dove* (Cooking Vinyl), inspired by the 1400th anniversary of the death of St. Columba on the mystic island of Iona. And for a real treat, try Abby Newton's Celtic music for the cello (yes, the cello), titled *Crossing to Scotland* (Culburnie).

On our own shores, there were a number of first-rate CDs this year mixing traditional Native American music with jazz, blues, and other contemporary rhythms: *Things We Do* by Indigenous (Pachyderm); *Spirit Nation* by Spirit Nation (V2 Records); *Orenda* by Joanne Shenandoah & Lawrence Laughing (Silver Wave); *Big Medicine* by the R. Carlos Naki Quartet (Canyon); and *Blood of the Land* by Burning Sky (Canyon). It was also an amazing year for magical music from the Celtic and Sami traditions of Scandinavia. I particularly loved two CDs of contemporary joik-songs from the Sami people of northern Finland: *The New Voice of the North* by Girls of Angeli (Warner Finlandia) and *ruossa eanan* by ulla pirttijarvi (Atrium). Other good Scandinavian CDs mixing ancient and contemporary rhythms, all released by Northside in Minneapolis: *Stolen Goods* by Chateau Neuf, *String Tease* by JPP, *Triakel* by Triakel, *Swap* by Swap, *Storsvartan* by Olov Johansson, and the *Northside 1998* compilation CD, which provides a good introduction to this kind of music. Also check out *Ranarop: Call of the Sea Witch*, a strong CD from the Finnish band Gjallarhorn (Warner Finlandia). From other parts of the world, give a listen to the nuevo flamenco music of La Esperenza (Higher Octave); folk music from the Andes performed by Inti-Illimani on *Lejania*, "next-wave Jewish roots music" by The Klezmatics on *The Well* (Xenophile); diverse styles from the Cuban tradition on *Rhythm &*

Smoke: the Cuba Sessions (Intersound); and great dance music on *Tarika: D* from Malgasy (Xenofile) and on the compilation CD *Salsa: the Rough Guide* (World Music Network).

Literary Conventions and Conferences

The World Fantasy Convention, an annual professional gathering of writers, illustrators, publishers, and readers of both fantasy and horror fiction, was held in Monterey, California this year, over Halloween weekend. The Guest of Honor was Gahan Wilson. The 1998 World Fantasy Awards (for works published in 1997) were presented at the convention. Winners were as follows: *The Physiognomy* by Jeffrey Ford for Best Novel; "Streetcar Dreams" by Richard Bowes for Best Novella; "Dust Motes" by P. D. Cacek for Best Short Fiction; *Bending the Landscape: Fantasy* edited by Nicola Griffith and Stephen Pagel for Best Anthology; *The Throne of Bones* by Brian McNaughton for Best Collection; Alan Lee for Best Artist; *The Encyclopedia of Fantasy* edited by John Clute and John Grant for Special Award/Professional, and Fedogan & Bremer (book publishers) for Special Award/Non-Professional. The judges were: Peter Crowther, Peter Schneider, David Truesdale, Janeen Webb, and L. E. Modesitt, Jr. For information on future World Fantasy Conventions, visit their Web site: http://world.std.com/~sbarsky/mcfi/wfc

Mythcon, a scholarly convention devoted to fantasy, sponsored by the Mythopoeic Society, was held in July in Wheaton, Illinois. The Guests of Honor were Paul F. Ford and Verlyn Flieger. Winners of the 1998 Mythopoeic Award were as follows: *The Djinn in the Nightingale's Eye* by A. S. Byatt (Adult Literature category), The "Young Merlin" trilogy by Jane Yolen (Children's Literature category); *The Encyclopedia of Fantasy* edited by John Clute and John Grant (Scholarship Award for Myth & Fantasy Studies); and *A Question of Time: Tolkien's Road to Faerie* by Verlyn Flieger (Scholarship Award for Inklings Studies). The award is judged by the membership of the Mythopoeic Society. For information on future Mythcons, visit their Web site: http://www.mythsoc.org

The WisCon Feminist Science Fiction and Fantasy Convention was held, as it has been for several years, at the end of May in Madison, Wisconsin. The Guests of Honor were Ellen Kushner, Delia Sherman, and Sheri S. Tepper. The 1998 James Tiptree, Jr. Award, for work addressing gender issues, went to Raphael Carter for the story "Congenital Agenesis of Gender Ideation," published in *Starlight* 2. Judges for the award were: Kate Schaefer (chair), Ray Davis, Candas Jane Dorsey, Sylvia Kelso, and Lisa Tuttle. For information of future WisCons, visit their Web site: http://www.sf3.org/wiscon

The International Conference on the Fantastic in the Arts, a scholarly conference devoted to all forms of fantasy, science fiction, horror, and magical realism, was held (as always) in Ft. Lauderdale, Florida in March. They present the Crawford Award every year; this year's honors went to *Children of Amarid* by David B. Coe. For information on future IAFA conferences, visit their Web site: http://ebbs.english.vt.edu/iafa/iafa.home.html

The British Fantasy Convention and the British Fantasy Awards are covered in Ellen Datlow's Summary.

That's an overview of the year in fantasy—now on to the stories themselves.

As usual, there are stories we were unable to include in this volume, but which are among the year's very best. I encourage you to seek out the following:

James P. Blaylock's "The Old Curiosity Shop" in the February issue of *F&SF*.

Richard Bowes's "Diana in the Spring" in the August issue of *F&SF*.

Angélica Gorodischer's "The End of a Dynasty," translated by Ursula K. Le Guin, in *Starlight 2*.

Tim Nickles's "Glisten and Beyond Herring" in *The Ex Files*.

And in particular: Ian R. MacLeod's alternative history novella "The Summer Isles" in the Oct./Nov. issue of *Asimov's*.

I hope you will enjoy the stories and poems that follow as much as I did. Many thanks to the authors, agents, and publishers who allowed us to reprint them here.

—T. W.
Devon, U.K. and Tucson, US
1998–1999

Summation 1998: Horror

Ellen Datlow

Book Publishing News

Two giant maws, Bertelsmann and Barnes & Noble, continued to devour and incorporate more of the publishing industry throughout 1998. The German media conglomerate Bertelsmann announced its intention to acquire the United States's largest consumer-group publisher, Random House and merge it with Bantam Doubleday Dell. The move created the largest trade-publishing company in the world, combining annual revenues of about $1.22 billion for Random House and $679 million for BDD. The Authors Guild and the Association of Authors' Representatives filed objections with the FTC to prevent the merger, claiming that the combined company would control more than 36 percent of the U.S. adult trade book market. Despite this, the merger was approved in early May. Bertelsmann also bought a majority stake in Springer Verlag, one of Germany's most admired literary publishers, and further surprised the industry by first announcing that it was starting an online bookselling division, then instead buying a 50 percent stake in barnesandnoble.com. In turn, Barnes & Noble stunned the publishing world with its announcement that it plans to buy the wholesaler the Ingram Book Group. These last two deals finally prompted the Federal Trade Commission to investigate, and were still up in the air at the end of 1998.

Meantime, the American Booksellers Association launched an antitrust suit in California against the Barnes & Noble and Borders chains, alleging that both use their clout with publishers to obtain preferential treatment and terms.

Doubleday cancelled several high-profile (and high-priced) contracts early in the year. First the company cancelled its contract for Steve Alten's *Fathom*, the follow-up to the heavily promoted but commercially disappointing novel *Meg*. Alten filed suit for breach of contract. Doubleday then cancelled contracts with country music star LeAnn Rimes after her first book sold fewer than projected, and with Paul Alexander, author of a biography of J. D. Salinger, stating that the biography was "not editorially acceptable."

Tor Books, a subsidiary of St. Martin's Press since its purchase in 1986, became an equal partner of the Holtzbrinck Publishing Holdings in early February. The changes simplify the chain of command for Tor, which will only report to John Sargent, chairman of Holtzbrinck Publishing Holdings Limited Partnership and Von Holtzbrinck Publisher Services. He is now vice-chairman of Tor, St. Martin's Press, Farrar, Straus & Giroux, and Henry Holt, and will report directly to Dieter von Holtzbrinck, who remains chairman.

Farrar, Straus & Giroux purchased a majority stake in Faber and Faber, Inc., the U.S. subsidiary of British literary publisher Faber and Faber, Ltd., which will remain a minority stockholder in the U.S. unit. Faber and Faber, Inc. will no longer originate its own titles but will publish and distribute in the U.S. titles acquired by the British side. The U.S. subsidiary closed down its offices outside of Boston, terminated its distribution agreement with Cornell University Press, and moved its operations to New York City by the end of the year. Faber & Faber, Inc. published about 100 titles a year.

Picador USA, an imprint of St. Martin's Press since 1995, is to become an independent publisher that will now reprint more hardcovers published by Farrar, Straus & Giroux in addition to publishing its own titles and reprinting titles from SMP and elsewhere. Editorial director George Witte was made publisher, reporting to a board consisting of various executives of Holtzbrinck, SMP, and FS&G. Picador will be increasing their titles from 50–55 to 75–100 a year. This gives FS&G a needed paperback-reprint arm.

Carroll & Graf was sold to Publishers Group West through its Avalon Publishing Group subsidiary. President Herman Graf and Publisher Kent Carroll will acquire equity in Publishers Group, Inc. and will continue to run the company. Susan Reich, COO of Avalon, will join the C&G board. C&G has published Michael Cadnum, Brian Stableford, Kim Newman, Thomas Ligotti, Brian Aldiss, and Stephen Jones's *Mammoth Book of Horror* (in the U.S. called *Best New Horror*). Avalon also acquired the assets of Blue Moon Books, rescuing Grove Press founder Barney Rosset from bankruptcy. Blue Moon was forced to file for Chapter 11 bankruptcy in late 1997, after the assets of its distributor, Barricade Books, were frozen by a court order following a $3 million libel judgment against Barricade publisher Lyle Stuart. Barricade was forced into bankruptcy, and Rosset was forced to follow.

Susan Allison was named associate director, editorial, Berkley and will continue as Berkley vice-president and editor-in-chief of Ace; Shelley Shapiro, previously executive editor of Del Rey Books, has been promoted to editorial director.

Leisure Books editor Don D'Auria has, with little fanfare, launched a horror line, becoming the only commercial publisher now doing so, and publishing such titles as Elizabeth Massie's Stoker Award–winning novel *Sineater* in mass market, and books by Ed Gorman, Douglas Clegg, Tom Picirilli, and others.

Magazine News

General Media International let go *Omni* Internet's staff of five as of April 1, 1998, ceasing publication. *Omni*, first published in October, 1978—brainchild of Kathy Keeton and Robert Guccione—was the only slick magazine combining science and science fiction. Ellen Datlow was with the magazine more than eighteen years, for most of that time as fiction editor, adding the titles of producer, and senior editor for the Internet edition. In mid-August, Datlow and her former *Omni* colleagues launched *Event Horizon: Science Fiction, Fantasy, and Horror*, a monthly Web zine devoted to those three genres. Datlow is editor and fiction editor while Robert K. J. Killheffer is nonfiction editor. The Web zine also features weekly online author chats.

In March, DNA Publications, Inc., publisher of *Absolute Magnitude* and *Dreams of Decadence*, announced the addition of *Weird Tales*, "the oldest genre magazine," to its publication list. The first quarterly issue was set to appear the summer of 1998. For the past couple of years the venerable magazine has been called *Worlds of Fantasy and Horror* because its publishers did not own rights to the *Weird Tales* name, but new publisher Warren Lapine renegotiated for the use of the *Weird Tales* name. George Scithers and Darrell Schweitzer continue as editors; *Amazing Stories*, the oldest science fiction magazine, was resurrected by Wizards of the Coast, the gaming company that bought TSR, former owner of *Amazing*. The new version includes media tie-in fiction and nonfiction, in addition to traditional SF, and intends to reach a younger audience than the other SF/F magazines. The first issue of the quarterly was launched at the Worldcon in Baltimore. Kim Mohan is the editor. *Cemetery Dance* went from a quarterly to a bi-monthly schedule and added John Pelan as a columnist.

Closings: Debbie Smith and J. F. Gonzalez folded *Phantasm* magazine, citing a dwindling subscription base and distribution avenues as their main reasons. But Smith's television work and Gonzalez's own writing were also making increasing demands on their time; *Plot*, edited by Christina C. Russell, folded after nine issues; *White Knuckles*, edited by John Platt, folded after eight issues; Pirate Writings Publishing went out of business and *Pirate Writings* magazine was sold to DNA Publications. Unfortunately, *Epitaph: Dark Tales of Fantasy & Horror*, edited by Tom Piccirili and published by *Pirate Writings*, was forced to cease publication; *Crank!*, the literary SF/F magazine edited by Bryan Cholfin, officially suspended publication; and Paula Guran's ambitious horror start-up *Wetbones* ceased publication for financial reasons after two issues.

U.K. News

After eight years with HarperCollins-U.K., Malcolm Edwards left to become managing director of Orion Books Ltd., where he assumes responsibility for the Orion and Millennium imprints as well as the children's, media, and business lists. The French company Hachette bought a majority stake in the Orion Publishing Group and agreed to back expansion of the group, increasing its presence in the U.S. and in other English-language markets. Hachette acquired about 70 percent of the company from three venture capital investors. The remaining 30 percent is owned by Orion founder and CEO, Anthony Cheetham, his wife and co-founder, Rosemary, and Peter Roche, now COO and managing director. Soon after, Orion bought Cassell, significant to science fiction, fantasy, and horror, because Cassell owns Victor Gollancz, publishers of the long-running horror anthology series *Dark Terrors*, edited by Stephen Jones and David Sutton. The SF books will be published as Gollancz hardcovers and Millennium paperbacks. Simon Spanton and Jo Fletcher will be the acquiring editors and Caroline Oakley, in charge of Orion paperbacks, will continue to edit some genre authors; British publisher Tanjen ceased publication.

Three prominent HarperCollins-U.K. authors threatened to quit the publishing house when Rupert Murdoch, its owner, forced executives there to drop plans to publish the memoirs of Chris Patten, the former governor of Hong Kong. Authors Doris Lessing, Penelope Fitzgerald, and Peter Hennessey (not to mention the publishing world) expressed outrage over the decision by HarperCollins to cancel the book, expected to be critical of China. Critics have said that Murdoch scrapped the book because he was nervous it might damage his business interests in the expanding Chinese market. The senior Harper executive who had defended the book, Stuart Proffitt, was ousted as a result and Murdoch made as close to a public apology for his handling of the situation as he's ever done. Macmillan-U.K. snapped up the book.

A plaque dedicated to M. R. James was unveiled at St. Peter's Church, Great Livermere (Suffolk, U.K.), September 26, 1998.

Australian News

In Australia, the Australian Horror Writers was officially dismantled the first week in January by its president, Bryce Stevens, after a long struggle with financial difficulties and a lackluster response to the annual dues notice, which drew five responses from eighty members. The organization published *Severed Head: The Journal of the Australian Horror Writers*, edited by Aaron Stern. Ticonderoga Publications editor Russell B. Farr announced that it would shut down by December 1999 after the publication of two more collections by Sean Williams and Stephen Dedman.

General News

In March, the Horror Writers Association announced revisions in the Stoker Award rules, adding the following new categories effective immediately: anthology; comic book, graphic novel or other illustrated narrative; screenplay; work for young readers; and other media. There are also new rules to cover no award and "to allow for the dropping of any category for which there are insufficient recommendations in a given year." Also effective immediately is the associate-member class amendment, establishing membership for "editors, illustrators, literary agents, booksellers, anthologists, and other nonwriting professionals able to show a professional interest in horror or dark fantasy." They are a nonvoting class.

At the Horror Writers Association banquet, the Bram Stoker Awards for superior achievement in horror for 1997 were given to: Novel: *Children of the Dusk*, by Janet Berliner and George Guthridge; First Novel: *Lives of the Monster Dogs*, by Kirsten Bakis; Novelette: "The Big Blow" by Joe R. Lansdale; Short Story: "Rat Food" by Edo van Belkom and David Nickle; Collection: *Exorcisms and Ecstasies* by Karl Edward Wagner; Nonfiction: *Dark Thoughts: On Writing* by

Stanley Wiater; Life Achievement: William Peter Blatty, Jack Williamson; Specialty Press Award: Richard Chizmar (Cemetery Dance); Hammer Award: Sheldon Jaffery.

The small press energetically continued to take up the slack in horror publishing. Subterranean Press inaugurated a short novel series with Norman Partridge's "Wildest Dreams" and Joe R. Lansdale's "The Boar." Silver Salamander published Jack Ketchum's short novel "Ladies Night," and Cemetery Dance inaugurated an original novella series with "Spree" by Lucy Taylor and "The Wilds" by Richard Layman. Interestingly, most of these novellas/short novels are deeply ingrained in reality and have minimal supernatural elements in them.

There were a few excellent pieces of fiction this year that I would very much like to have picked but just didn't have room for. I urge you to go out and find the following stories and read them: "The Space Between the Lines" by Peter Crowther from *Imagination Fully Dilated*, "As Above, So Below" by Brian Hodge from his collection *Fallen Idols*, "Amid the Walking Wounded" by Jack Ketchum from *The UFO Files*, "The Death of Heroes" by Bill Congreve from his collection *Epiphanies of Blood*, and two stories by Kurahashi Yumiko from *The Woman with the Flying Head*: "The Woman with the Flying Head" and "The Witch Mask."

Note: Addresses of various resources and small press publishers are at the back of this section.

Novels

Oyster by Janette Turner Hospital (Norton) is a riveting mystery taking place in and around a tiny outback town. Outer Maroo is caught up in millennial paranoia and opal fever, and these factors, combined with the arrival of a charismatic cult leader, make for an explosive situation. *Oyster* is told from several points of view and from several different points in time, so that the reader only sees the whole picture at the end. Hospital, author of *The Last Magician*, another excellent dark novel, weaves a richly textured portrait of a town overwhelmed by its intricate web of deception, suspicion, xenophobia, and greed. While being fiercely critical of the rape of mother nature she creates fascinating characters and an unusual world in which a reader can lose one's self.

Irrational Fears by William Browning Spencer (White Wolf) is a humorous horror novel with very serious undertones. Jack Lowry has been drinking steadily since his lover was murdered by her crazy husband. He goes into detox, becoming immersed in the politics of Alcoholics Anonymous and embroiled in very strange goings-on connected with jealousy, the Lovecraft mythos, immortality, and ghosts. As ever, an imaginative *tour de force* by this wonderful writer who regularly creates characters caught on the border between reality and fantasy.

The Ballad of Frankie Silver by Sharyn McCrumb (Dutton) is an entertaining dark mystery by an author who has made Appalachia her own territory. Sheriff Spencer Arrowood becomes fascinated by two murders committed almost 140 years apart. Nineteen-year-old Frankie Silver was charged, found guilty, and hanged for the murder of her husband in 1832. Fate Harkyder is now on death row for a slaying he committed twenty years ago. The murders have nothing in common but their brutality and the unease they cause in the sheriff. McCrumb immerses the reader in the rough life of mountain folk who have never expected and rarely received justice from those in town.

The Hunt Club by Brett Lott (Villard) also takes advantage of the divide between two cultures—the rich professional men of Charleston and their poorer neighbors who populate the Low country of South Carolina—to write a lively murder mystery. The story is told by Huger Dillard, the fifteen-year-old boy who helps his blind Uncle Leland get around. The discovery of the mutilated body of a prominent doctor on the grounds of the Hunt Club initiates a chain of events that reveal long kept secrets, not least of which is the circumstances behind Uncle Leland's blinding in a fire that killed his wife. The finely wrought characters, sense of place, and skillful pacing make for an engrossing read.

Blood Work by Michael Connelly (Little, Brown) is a suspense novel-police procedural about a former FBI agent sidelined by a heart transplant. His career hunting serial killers finally has taken its toll, and now all he wants to do is work on his boat. But when the sister of the woman whose heart he received asks him to track down her killer, he cannot turn her away. Although *Blood Work* refers to events that presumably took place in *The Poet* this does nothing to diminish the effectiveness for the first time reader.

Sunset Express by James Lee Burke (Doubleday) is a beautifully told convoluted tale of family secrets, past injustices, racism, cruelty, and revenge. In this new Dave Robicheaux novel, the children of a labor organizer who was crucified against a barn wall in the fifties, return to New Iberia. The orphaned siblings have grown up to be successful adults, but their veneer of success can't erase their childhood hurt or soothe the hate they feel for those they believe responsible for their father's unsolved murder. As in all Burke's novels the plot is filled with colorful characters who are rarely merely good or evil.

The Physiognomy by Jeffrey Ford (Avon Books) takes place in a world where the measurements of your face and body determine your role in life and your guilt or innocence. A dictator, who is very arbitrary in the reward and punishment of his subjects, runs the Well-Built City with an iron fist. The protagonist, a Physiognomist, has the power to inconvenience, disrupt, or destroy lives and at the beginning of this odd novel does so with all the arrogance of one raised to be at the top of the heap. But a *new* assignment leads him into unknown territory, challenging the bedrock of his beliefs. This winner of the World Fantasy Award is an original and potent mixture of science fiction, fantasy, and horror.

Bombay Ice by Leslie Forbes (Farrar, Straus & Giroux) is a flawed but atmospheric first novel set in contemporary India. A half-Indian-half-Briton journalist returns to India at the behest of her half sister, who is married to a famous filmmaker whose first wife died suspiciously. There is a wealth of information on a wide range of Indian lore: brilliant bits about the life cycle of the monsoon and its relationship to chaos theory; the lives of the hijra—eunuchs considered holy by some, accursed by others; and what to do when faced with a deadly cobra. And running throughout is the making of the "Bollywood" version of Shakespeare's *The Tempest* and several murders. The flaws can be distracting, but still the novel is worth a look.

Blindness by José Saramago (Harcourt, Brace) is a disturbing allegory by the Portuguese fabulist, who won the Nobel Award for literature in 1998. *Blindness* has a real plot, inspires real terror, and—although we never learn their names—is about believable, sympathetic characters. A man driving down the street is suddenly struck blind, setting off a highly contagious plague of "white sickness." The authorities take immediate but futile action by quarantining victims and potential victims in an ill-equipped, abandoned mental hospital. Things rapidly deteriorate as food is hoarded, factions develop, and anarchy reigns. The one true hero is the "doctor's wife," who willingly accompanies her blind husband, although she can still see, and acts as a liaison between the blind and the rest of the world.

Freezing by Penelope Evans (Soho Press) has an unlikely detective as its hero—a misfit with a frightening appearance who works as a morgue photographer. Stewart Park lives alone with his crazy, demanding father, finding solace playing computer games and in the company of his two young nephews. But the arrival at the morgue of the frozen corpse of a young woman fished out of the Thames changes his life, as he's galvanized into discovering her identity and finding out what happened to her.

The Ogre's Laboratory by Louis Buss (Jonathan Cape-U.K.), a beautifully told modern gothic, is surprising, moving, and quite satisfying. When a young Catholic priest is transferred to the country parish where his predecessor mysteriously committed suicide, his keen interest in history draws him into the murky past of the aristocrat family whose estate looks down over the village. Once upon a time there was a real ogre: the local noble, a giant suspected of atrocities worthy of Gilles de Rais. His deeds still haunt the children of the village in nightmares. Was he the ogre upon which that the fairy tale "Jack and the Beanstalk" was based, and is his evil influence still being felt in the village?

Night Train by Martin Amis (Harmony) is a short, sharp shock of a mystery about the apparent suicide of the brilliant and beautiful beloved daughter of the top cop in a major American city. A veteran detective who spent some weeks drying out in her boss's home several years earlier and thus, feels beholden to him, is asked to investigate. What transpires is a tour of the suicide victim's perfect universe that simultaneously takes the detective on her own inner journey. Amis has worked in the crime/mystery genre before with his early novel *Other People* and more recently with *London Fields*.

Noir by K. W. Jeter (Bantam Spectra) is an energetic and imaginative noir SF thriller by the author of the raw, proto-cyberpunk novel *Dr. Adder* and the brilliant *In the Land of the Dead*. McNihil is your classic antihero, a former government enforcer of the penalty for copyright violation—death. A Machiavellian corporate type traps him into investigating the murder of a young lower-level executive. One of several grotesque jokes is that the "trophies" (living brain tissue housing personality) taken from the copyright violators are transmuted into antique toasters, garbage disposals—whatever the victim of the copyright infringement wishes. This brave new world also resurrects the bodies and brains of debtors, forcing them to continue to pay off their outstanding credit charges. Jeter zings some nice surprises, keeping his readers on their toes in this hate letter to L.A.

One of Us by Michael Marshall Smith (HarperCollins-U.K./Bantam) has some superficial similarities to *Noir*: both are L.A. stories about illegalities, underground economies, and men who get entangled in conspiracies against their will.

Although there's a fair measure of violence in *One of Us*, the novel maintains the lighter tone evident in Smith's first novel *Only Forward*. In this future the appliances have personality—lots of it—and there are some laugh-out-loud encounters between Hap and his misguided alarm clock. People with money can hire others on whom to unload their bad dreams—or their bad memories. Hap, whose illegal but high-paying job it is to be the temporary receptacle of these dreams and memories, gets stuck with the memory of a murder. If he's caught with it *he* rather than the person whose memory it is can be convicted of the crime. As hapless as his name, this petty and pretty harmless criminal is (like McNihil) forced into investigating a murder with no apparent connection to him. But then Smith gets *really* wonky as the book launches itself into "Man Who was Thursday" territory. Does this work? I'm not sure but it is a lot of fun getting there.

As mentioned earlier, Subterranean Press launched its short novel series with two excellent books: *Wildest Dreams* by Norman Partridge, a fast-moving, hard-boiled supernatural novel about a hired gun who can see ghosts. Clay Saunders will kill whomever he's hired to kill—and anyone else who gets in his way. Despite his moral emptiness he's moved by the lonely ghost of a girl he encounters, and he promises to visit her again. But first he's got to deliver the severed head of a cult leader to the ambitious daughter who paid for his murder. Published in a 500 signed and numbered hardcover edition and 26-copy signed/lettered edition; the second novel is *The Boar* by Joe R. Lansdale, an excellent adventure-coming-of-age story brimming with authenticity and warmth towards its characters. The locale is east Texas, the period is the middle of the Depression and although times are hard, they aren't all *that* much harder than usual for the poor farmers who eke out their existence. The adult narrator recounts his fifteenth summer, a milestone year for two reasons: he decides to become a fiction writer, and a crazed wild boar with razor-sharp tusks brings mayhem to the area. After the seemingly invincible creature kills the family dogs and attacks the boy and his pregnant mother, the boy and his best friend swear to destroy it. Lansdale says that the father in *The Boar* is obliquely based on his own father. The love shows. Dust jacket art is by Mark A. Nelson, designed by Gail Cross, and interior art is by Keith Minnion. Available in two limited editions.

The Haunted Tea Cozy: A Dispirited and Distasteful Diversion for Christmas by Edward Gorey (Harcourt Brace) is cause for celebration. This story by the reclusive eccentric first appeared in *The New York Times Magazine* in 1997 and this is its first book publication.

Novels

Bag of Bones by Stephen King (Scribner); *In a Child's Eye* by Tim Wilson (St. Martin's Press); *Cold in Earth* by Melissa Jones (St. Martin's Press); *Now It's Time to Say Goodbye* by Dale Peck (Farrar, Straus & Giroux); *Head Injuries* by Conrad Williams (The Do-Not Press, U.K./ Dufour Editions); *Kissing the Beehive* by Jonathan Carroll (Nan A. Talese/Doubleday); *Burning Bright* by Jay S. Russell (St. Martin's Press); *Desmond: A Novel of Love and the Modern Vampire* by Ulysses G. Dietz (Alyson); *Sisters of the Night: The Angry Angel* by Chelsea Quinn Yarbro (Avon Books); *Galen* by Allan Gilbreath (Ronin Enterprises); *Voo-*

doo Child by Michael Reaves (Tor); Nothing Burns in Hell by Philip Jose Farmer (Forge); Malpertuis by Jean Ray, translated by Iain White (Atlas Press, U.K.)—originally published in France in 1943. This is its first English translation; The Crow: The Lazarus Heart by Poppy Z. Brite (HarperPrism); Night Prayers by P. D. Cacek (The Design Image Group); Journey of the Dead by Loren D. Estleman (St. Martin's Press); Carmilla: The Return by Kyle Marffin (Design Image Group); Terror by Graham Masterton (Severn House, U.K.); Where the Children Cry by Jenny Jones (Gollancz, U.K.); The Book of the Dark by William Meikle (Hafod Publishing—electronic); Retribution by Elizabeth Forrest (DAW); Burnt Offerings by Laurell K. Hamilton (Ace); When Shadows Fall by Brian Scott Smith (Leisure); House of Bones by Graham Masterton (Scholastic/Point, U.K.); The Violet Hour by Richard Montanari (Avon Books); The Highwayman by Jessica Berens (Hutchinson-U.K.); Silk by Caitlin R. Kiernan (Roc); The Dark Room by Julia Cameron (Carroll & Graf); Reaper by Ben Mezrich (HarperCollins); The Flesh Eaters by John Gordon (Walker Books, U.K.); The Shadowy Horses by Susanna Kearsley (Roundhouse Publishing); Dracula: The Definitive Edition (Barnes & Noble Books)—bound in black cloth without a dustjacket, with interior illustrations by Edward Gorey, taken from his Dracula: A Toy Theatre published in 1979, an introduction by Marvin Kaye, two appendices containing a sampler of contemporary opinions on the novel, a look at the author, and an annotated bibliography of Stoker's principal writings; The Vampire Armand by Anne Rice (Knopf); Control Freak by Christa Faust (Rhinoceros); Vampyrrhic by Simon Clark (Hodder & Stoughton, U.K.); The Hanging Tree by Paul Stewart (Point Horror, U.K.); Dust by Charles R. Pellegrino (Avon Books); The Stillest Day by Josephine Hart (The Overlook Press); Raven Stole the Moon by Garth Stein (Pocket Books); Faces Under Water by Tanith Lee (The Overlook Press); Violation by Darian North (Dutton); Shadowchild by Joseph A. Citro (Hardscrabble); Shadow on the Wall by Jonathan Aycliffe (HarperCollins, U.K.); Wine of Angels by Phil Rickman (Macmillan, U.K.); The Sleeper in the Sands by Tom Holland (Little, Brown, U.K.); Deliver Us from Evil by Tom Holland (Warner, U.K.); Shadow of the Beast by Margaret L. Carter (Design Image); Storytellers by Julie Anne Parks (Design Image); Ungrateful Dead by Gary L. Holleman (Leisure); Superstition by David Ambrose (Warner); The Halloween Man by Douglas Clegg (Leisure); Eyes by Joseph Glass (Villard); The Haunting by Joan Lowery Nixon (Delacorte); The Double by Don Webb (St. Martin's Press); Dracul: An Eternal Love Story by Nancy Kilpatrick (Lucard Ltd.); A Coming Evil by Vivian Vande Velde (Houghton Mifflin-YA); Ghost of a Hanged Man by Vivian Vande Velde (Cavendish-YA); Soho Black by Christopher Fowler (Warner, U.K.); Mannequin by J. Robert Janes (Soho); The Widow Killer by Pavel Kohout, translated by Neil Bermel (St. Martin's Press); A Song of Stone by Iain Banks (Simon & Schuster); A Perfect Crime by Peter Abrahams (Ballantine Books); The Chimney Sweeper's Boy by Barbara Vine (Harmony Books); Rampage by Susan Taylor Chechak (Doubleday); Trick of Light by David Hunt (Putnam); Riven Rock by T. Coraghessan Boyle (Viking); Ark Baby by Liz Jensen (The Overlook Press); Soft! by Rupert Thomson (Alfred A. Knopf); The World I Made for Her by Thomas Moran (Riverhead Books); Lampshades by Carole Morin (The Overlook Press); Eleven Days by Donald Harstad (Doubleday); The Sensualist by Barbara Hodgson (Chronicle Books); Shame by Alan Russell (Simon & Schuster); Double

Image by David Morrell (Warner Books); *The House of Sleep* by Jonathan Coe (Knopf); *Solibo Magnificent* by Patrick Chamoiseau (Pantheon); *Cows* by Matthew Stokoe (Creation, U.K.); *Santa Steps Out* by Robert Devereaux (Dark Highway Press); *Dawn Song* by Michael Marano (Tor); *Hearts and Bones* by Margaret Lawrence (Avon Books); *Father of Lies* by Brian Evenson (Four Walls Eight Windows); *The Face Changers* by Thomas Perry (Random House); *Vespers* by Jeff Rovin (St. Martin's Press); *The Last Voice They Hear* by Ramsey Campbell (Forge); *Defiance* by Carole Maso (Dutton); *The Martyring* by Thomas Sullivan (Forge); *Twitchy Eyes* by Joe Donnelly (Michael Joseph-U.K.); *An Instance of the Fingerpost* by Iain Pears (Riverhead); *Everybody Dies* by Lawrence Block (William Morrow & Co.); *Mendel's Dwarf* by Simon Mawer (Harmony Books); *Bloodstained Kings* by Tim Willocks (Random House); *The Extremes* by Christopher Priest (Simon & Schuster, U.K.); *The Uncanny* by Andrew Klavan (Crown); *Ingenious Pain* by Andrew Miller (Harcourt Brace); *The Angel of Darkness* by Caleb Carr (Random House); *The Tattoo Murder Case* by Akimitsu Takagi, translated by Deborah Boliver Boehm (Soho); *Enduring Love* by Ian McEwan (Nan A. Talese/Doubleday); *Someplace to Be Flying* by Charles de Lint (Tor); *Skull Session* by Daniel Hecht (Viking); *Hush* by Mark Nykanen (St. Martin's Press); *Bad Chemistry* by Gary Krist (Random House); *Delirium* by Douglas Cooper (Hyperion); *Mr. In-Between* by Neil Cross (Jonathan Cape-U.K.); *Second Coming Attractions* by David Prill (St. Martin's Press); *Homebody* by Orson Scott Card (HarperPaperbacks); *The Passion* by Donna Boyd (Avon Books); and *King Rat* by China Miéville (Pan).

Anthologies

Imagination Fully Dilated edited by Alan M. Clark and Elizabeth Engstrom (CD Publications) is a wonderfully varied anthology of twenty-eight stories (all but one original to the volume) inspired by twenty-eight pieces of art by the talented and versatile Alan Clark. The book has hand tipped-in art by Clark and was published in a small limited hardcover edition that's signed by all the authors, including F. Paul Wilson, Thomas F. Monteleone, Ramsey Campbell, Poppy Z. Brite, Lucy Taylor, and Jack Ketchum. Not all the stories are horror but they're all very good, and there's certainly enough disquieting material to please any connoisseur of the dark.

Dreaming Down-Under edited by Jack Dann and Janeen Webb (HarperCollins, Australia) is a hefty volume of original science fiction, fantasy, and horror by Australians. There is enough excellent horror in this trade paperback for readers to run out and order it.

Dark Terrors 4: The Gollancz Book of Horror edited by Stephen Jones and David Sutton (Victor Gollancz—U.K.) continues to be the only game in town when it comes to original, non-theme horror anthologies. More than two-thirds of the stories are excellent, with no real duds among the rest.

Brothers of the Night edited by Michael Rowe and Thomas S. Roche (Cleis Press) was published too late in 1997 for me to cover it. Its eleven gay vampire stories are for the most part readable without being especially noteworthy. Most of them go more for the groin than the throat.

The UFO Files edited by Martin H. Greenberg (with Ed Gorman credited on the title page but not on the cover) (DAW) is a surprisingly varied collection of SF/fantasy/horror stories about alien sightings, encounters, misunderstandings, and monsters by a distinguished group of writers. Although not horror, Robert Charles Wilson's story is excellent.

Noirotica 2: Pulp Friction edited by Thomas S. Roche (Rhinoceros) is the second installment of erotic crime stories. As with the first volume it's a mixed bag with some well-told stories and others that seem mere excuses to write dirty vignettes. The best are by authors known for their horror tales such as Brian Hodge, Lucy Taylor, Caitlín R. Kiernan, and a few others.

Demon Sex edited by Amarantha Knight (Rhinoceros) is yet another erotic horror anthology. Most of the demons are pretty ho-hum but there are very good stories by Gemma Files and Neil Gaiman.

More Monsters from Memphis edited by Beecher Smith (Zapizdat Publications) does a better job than the first volume at capturing the southern ambiance, but there isn't enough variety.

Dark Whispers edited by Ivan S. Graves (Hard Shell Word Factory) is an electronic anthology, available on CD-ROM, of seventeen horror stories, eleven of which are original. The reprints include stories by Douglas Clegg, Stephen Dedman, Brian Hodge, and Nancy Kilpatrick. The originals include two zombie stories reminiscent of those of Stephen King and Dan Simmons, a good story about guilt by Gary A. Braunbeck, and a lot of disappointments.

The Conspiracy Files by Martin H. Greenberg and Scott Urban (DAW) is a mediocre *X-Files* rip-off with a handful of stories that are better than average.

Hot Blood X edited by Jeff Gelb and Michael Garrett (Pocket Books)—the series chugs on with some chilling erotic horror. Perhaps not surprisingly, some of the best stories are not erotic at all. Original except for one Ramsey Campbell reprint.

In the Shadow of the Gargoyle edited by Nancy Kilpatrick and Thomas S. Roche (Ace) is based on a wonderful subject—those weird waterspouts that live eternally on medieval structures. There have been some fine stories about gargoyles, such as Greg Bear's "Petra" and Sara Douglass's "The Evil Within," so as far as I'm concerned *In the Shadow of the Gargoyle* has a lot to live up to— and I was on the whole disappointed. There were a few standouts, but for all the recognizable names featured, very few stories stuck once I closed the book.

Horrors! 365 Scary Stories edited by Stefan Dziemianowicz, Robert Weinberg, and Martin H. Greenberg (Barnes and Noble Books) was a trudge rather than fun. The majority of these tiny vignettes are clichés, with the setup in the first paragraph signaling the ending a mile off. So it came as a surprise to discover a few gems in which the authors actually conjure up a convincing, frightening world in only the 750 words.

The Crow: Shattered Lives & Broken Dreams edited by J. O'Barr and Ed Kramer (Del Rey) is primarily for Crow fans—for whom this will be a unique treat. However, only a few of these stories will appeal to those not interested in the graphic novel or movie series. Each story is illustrated, by an excellent crew of artists including Thomas Canty, Rick Berry, Phil Hale, Charles Vess, James O'Barr, creator of "the Crow," and others.

Fresh Blood 2 edited by Mike Ripley and Maxim Jakubowski (The Do-Not Press—U.K.) is a refreshing crime anthology with a variety of edgy stories.

Murder for Revenge edited by Otto Penzler (Delacorte) is a terrific collection of dark mystery stories by Joyce Carol Oates, David Morrell, Lawrence Block, and eight other writers—capped by the brilliant, cruel novella by Peter Straub called "Mr. Clubb and Mr. Cuff."

Other Anthologies

Black Cats and Broken Mirrors edited by Martin H. Greenberg and John Helfers (DAW) is an unmemorable original anthology about superstitions; *Going Postal* edited by Gerard Daniel Houarner (Space & Time) is unfortunately a case wherein the title is cleverer than most of the stories within; *The Darkest Thirst* (no editor named) is a vampire anthology published by the Design Image Group, a new small press horror publisher in Illinois. The book is printed in a made-to-last trade paperback format; *The Kiss of Death: An Anthology of Vampire Stories* (no editor) (The Design Image Group) is yet another undistinguished vampire anthology with one or two good stories; *A Terrifying Taste of Short & Shivery* by Robert D. San Souci (Delacorte—middle readers) adapts thirty scary stories from around the world for children; *Eros ex Machina* edited by M. Christian (Rhinoceros) is mostly about sex revolving around machines as per the title but it's got a few horror stories; *Gravity's Angels* edited by Gary Couzens, Trevor Denyer, Sarah Ellender, Trevor Mendham, and Martin Owton is a mixed genre anthology of fourteen original and reprinted stories published by the T Party Writers' Group in Beckenham, England; *The Ghost of Carmen Miranda and Other Spooky Gay and Lesbian Tales* edited by Julie K. Trevelyan and Scott Brassart (Alyson) is a mostly original anthology by nongenre writers; *Don't Read this! and Other Tales of the Unnatural* (no editor) (A Groundwood Book) is an anthology of children's stories of the supernatural with the proceeds benefitting the International Board of Books for Youth, an international organization "committed to giving children access to books with high literary and artistic standards;" *At the Edge of the World: Magical Stories of Ireland*, illustrated with contemporary photographs by John Lowings (Henry Holt); *Marion Zimmer Bradley's Fantasy Worlds* edited by Marion Zimmer Bradley and Rachel E. Holmen (The Marion Zimmer Bradley Literary Works Trust) was published in a 300 signed and numbered copy edition. There are a few darker stories but it's mostly fantasy; *The Annual Macabre 1998* assembled and introduced by Jack Adrian (Ash-Tree Press) focuses on six male authors not normally associated with the supernatural tale, including Ford Maddox Ford, Hilaire Belloc, and John Buchan, and others. All six stories had been out of print since their initial publication, some for as long as ninety years; *Aklo: A Volume of Enthusiasms* edited by Mark Valentine, Roger Dobson, and R. B. Russell (Tartarus Press/Caermaen Books) continues the tradition of the original magazine by publishing rare and previously unpublished material by Count Stenbock and Alain Fournier, new studies of writers and artists, and contemporary fiction; *Eternal Lovecraft: The Persistence of Lovecraft in Popular Culture* edited by Jim Turner (Golden Gryphon) is a selection of stories published over the past thirty-five years, demonstrating the lasting influence of H. P. Lovecraft on writers as diverse as Stephen King, William Browning Spencer, Gene Wolfe, Nancy A. Collins, Robert Charles Wilson, and Fred Chappell; *Great Ghost Stories* selected and illustrated by Barry Moser (Books of Wonder/Morrow) is a wonderful collectable for fans of artist Moser, best known for his illustrations of *Alice's Adventures in Wonderland, Frankenstein,* and *The Wizard of Oz.* Here he selects stories by Philippa Pearce, Madeleine L'Engle, Joyce Carol Oates, H. G. Wells, and nine other authors; *Cutting Edge: Best and Brightest Mystery Writers of the 90s* edited by Janet Hutchings (Carroll & Graf) includes stories from *Ellery Queen's Mystery Magazine* by Ray Bradbury, Lawrence Block, and Ruth Rendell, among others; *Twelve Tales of Murder* edited by Jack Adrian (Oxford University Press); *Twelve Mystery Stories* edited by Jack Adrian includes stories by Wilkie Collins and Arthur Conan Doyle (Oxford University Press); *Twelve Irish Ghost Stories* edited by Patricia Craig (Oxford University Press); *The Best of Cemetery Dance* edited by Richard Chizmar (CD Publications) is one of the most historically significant reprint anthologies of 1998 because it celebrates nine years of what has evolved into the only professional magazine in the horror field. There are at least two stories that were chosen for *The Year's Best Fantasy and Horror,* and a Stephen King story that would have been, could we have procured permission at the time. An interview with Chizmar by Bob Morrish explains the impetus for starting CD, and its change from a strictly horror magazine to one that encompasses dark suspense; *Tales of the Cthulhu Mythos* by H. P. Lovecraft and others (Del Rey) is the first trade edition of this anthology, first published by Arkham House and edited by Lovecraft; *Classic Ghost Stories II* edited by Glen Bledsoe and Karen Bledsoe (Lowell House) is a YA with eight stories by M. R. James, Mary Wilkens Freeman, and others; *Creepy Classics II* edited by Doris Stuart (Lowell House), another YA anthology with eight horror stories by Edgar Allan Poe, E. Nesbit, and others; *The Year's Best Australian Science Fiction and Fantasy: Volume Two* edited by Jonathan Strahan and Jeremy G. Byrne (HarperCollins, U.K.) provides an excellent overview of what's happening in Australian fantastic fiction with thirteen stories ranging from the award-winning SF collaboration by Janeen Webb and Jack Dann to the horror of Rick Kennett and Terry Dowling (both reprinted in this volume); *The Year's 25 Finest Crime and Mystery Stories: Seventh Annual Edition* edited by Ed Gorman and Martin H. Greenberg with an introduction by Jon L. Breen and an afterword by Edward D. Hoch, has stories by Lawrence Block, Joyce Carol Oates, and Simon Brett; *The Best American Mystery Stories,* 1998 selected by guest editor Sue Grafton (series editor, Otto Penzler) (Houghton Mifflin) reprints twenty stories. Three overlap with the aforementioned, "best of" anthology; *The Mammoth Book of 20th Century Ghost Stories* edited by Peter Haining (Carroll & Graf) reprints thirty stories by Jack London, P. G. Wodehouse, Muriel Spark, and Ruth Rendell, among others; *Great Irish Tales of Horror* edited by Peter Haining (Souvenir Press) has twenty-four stories by George Bernard Shaw, Jack Higgins, Bram Stoker, and other Irish authors. Cumberland House has inaugurated an attractive new trade paperback series of regional anthologies about vampires with *Blood Lines: Vampire Stories From New England* edited by Lawrence Schimel and Martin H. Greenberg, collecting nine reprints and one original by Schimel; *Streets of Blood: Vampire Stories from New York City* edited by Lawrence Schimel and Martin H. Greenberg, collects nine reprints and one original by Schimel; *Southern Blood: Vampire Stories of the American South* edited by Lawrence Schimel and Martin H. Greenberg collects nine reprints, including Dan Simmons's novelette "Carrion Comfort" and originals by Schimel and Billie Sue Mosiman; *Fields of Blood: Vampire Stories of the Heartland* edited by Lawrence Schimel and Martin H. Greenberg with thirteen stories, three of them originals; *The Young Oxford Book of Nasty Endings* edited by Dennis Pepper (Oxford University Press) contains a good mix of stories from everyone from E. Nesbit and T. H. White and John Collier to Ray Bradbury (the over-anthologized "The Veldt"), Richard Matheson, Ramsey Campbell, and Evan Hunter; *Ghosts in the Cloisters* edited by Mark Bryant (Hodder & Stoughton, U.K.) collects a variety of clerical tales of mystery and the supernatural; *The Unexplained: Stories of the Paranormal* edited by Ric Alexander (a pseudonym for Peter Haining) (Orion, U.K.) is a 430-plus page volume collecting stories about the paranormal with a wide variety of contributors including Robert A. Heinlein, Ursula K. Le Guin and Olaf Stapledon, Gerald Kersh, Richard Matheson, J. G. Ballard, Arthur Machen, and others. There is an original story by Richard Laymon; *The Mammoth Book of Best New Horror Volume 9* edited by Stephen Jones (Robinson, U.K./Carroll & Graf) overlaps with our own *The Year's Best Fantasy and Horror: Eleventh Collection* with only one story this year, and reprints two novellas that were highly recommended by myself—"The Zombies of Madison County" by Douglas E. Winter and "Coppola's Dracula" by Kim Newman. Includes an extensive introduction and short but cogent commentary on the horror's newest literary mutation—"extreme horror," a splinter from the splatterpunks, and a necrology; *The Best of Crank!* edited by Bryan Cholfin (Tor)—recently closed down by its editor, *Crank!* was a small-press magazine with a title that perfectly reflected its editor—and perhaps not coincidentally, published eclectic and sometimes excellent science fiction, science fantasy, fantasy, and just plain weird stories for several years; *The Reel Stuff* edited by Brian Thomsen and Martin H. Greenberg (DAW) reprints eleven popular SF stories that were made into movies or television episodes; *Mistresses of the Dark: 25 Macabre Tales by Master Storytellers* selected by Stefan Dziemianowicz, Denise Little, and Robert Weinberg (B&N Books) is a 500-plus page bug-crusher with stories by Margaret Atwood, Joyce Carol Oates, Shirley Jackson, Patricia Highsmith, and surprisingly, Ursula K. Le Guin; *100 Twisted Little Tales of Torment* selected by Stefan Dziemianowicz, Robert Weinberg, and Martin H. Greenberg (B&N Books); *The Ex Files* edited by Nicholas Royle (Quartet, U.K.) has stories about ex-spouses and ex-lovers by Pat Cadigan, Michael Marshall Smith, and Joel Lane, among others but is far more gentle than one would think; 11th Hour Productions produced a series of limited edition chapbooks of stories by authors who have participated in Chicago's Twilight Reading series: *Dangerous Dames* edited by Tina L. Jens presents stories and poems by ten women; *Tales of Forbidden Passion* edited by Tina L. Jens presents six reprints and originals signed by the authors; and *Strange Creatures* presents ten reprints and originals. *The Innsmouth Cycle: The Taint of the Deep Ones in 13 Tales* selected and introduced by Robert M. Price, series editor (Chaosium Books) contains one original story; *The Raven and the Monkey's Paw* (ed. anonymous) (Random House/Modern Library) has eight poems by Poe, and stories by him, Saki, Wharton, etc.; *Flying Cups & Saucers: Gender Explorations in Science Fiction & Fantasy* edited by Debbie Notkin and the Secret Feminist Cabal (Edgewood Press) is the first anthology honoring and explaining the James Tiptree, Jr. Award. There is an interesting mix of SF and fantasy, occasionally going over into horror territory; *Classic Ghost Stories* edited by John Grafton (Dover) has eleven stories by the usual suspects; *The Dedalus Book of French Horror: The Nineteenth Century* edited by Terry Hale (Dedalus) provides a representative selection of the century's horror by Charles Baudelaire, Guy de Maupassant, Alexandre Dumas, and others.

Collections

1998 was a very good year for collections, as some of the most respected names in horror had their work collected by either the mainstream or small press. The revival of older work by Ash-Tree Press, Sarob Press, and others continues, bringing a historical perspective to a new generation of readers (although the limited nature of the editions and relatively high prices of these hardcover collectibles might be prohibitive to younger readers).

Crypt Orchids (Subterranean Press) is David J. Schow's fourth collection and includes two original stories, a previously unpublished play adaptation of a Robert Bloch story, and nine reprints from various magazines and anthologies. Schow is a powerful storyteller and his fiction often has incisive commentary on Hollywood. This classy-looking hardcover limited edition was originally meant to be titled *Look Out He's Got a Knife!* and it has an introduction by Robert Bloch, who, according to Schow, influenced several of the stories. The effective and attractive jacket design is by David J. Schow, Bob Morrish, and Gail Cross. Interior illustrations are by Tim Caldwell.

Last Summer at Mars Hill by Elizabeth Hand (HarperPrism) collects all of the author's short work, including the marvelous World Fantasy Award–winning title novella—a passionate exploration of grief and hope; "The Erl King," a very dark, bleak contemporary rendition of the traditional tale; "Justice" and "The Bacchae," harsh, unforgiving reactions to violent men and patriarchy; "In the Month of Athyr" and "The Boy in the Tree," brilliant SF/horror stories about scientific research gone bad and other stories, equally provocative and well written. There *is* one humorous story. Hand writes vividly, creates interesting characters, and often puts the ancient religious "mysteries" to appropriate and chilling use. She is one of a handful of contemporary writers who glide effortlessly among the SF, fantasy, and horror genres to create gems in each.

The Barrens and Others by F. Paul Wilson (Tor) reprints twelve stories and novellas published by Wilson between 1987 and 1998. It includes a stage adaptation of his antifur story, "Pelts" (along with the original story) and "Glim," an original teleplay. Wilson is an excellent storyteller. Each story has an introduction that in itself is an enjoyable tale.

One Day Closer to Death by Bradley Denton (St. Martin's Press) is the first trade edition of the two-volume World Fantasy Award–winning limited edition of Denton's short fiction. Some of the eight stories in this collection are science fiction or fantasy but at least two are quite dark. "The Conflagration Artist" is about a journalist delving into the motives of a woman who has made an art of setting herself on fire and diving, burning into a small pool of water. Denton acknowledges his debt to Kafka's "The Hunger Artist" in his introduction, and as with some of the most affecting horror, the story is as moving as it is horrific. And as a treat for readers who loved *Blackburn*, his novel about a sympathetic serial killer, there is a brand-new "Blackburn" story, about the late Jimmy Blackburn's sister.

Smoke and Mirrors: Short Fictions and Illusions by Neil Gaiman (Avon Books). Although better known in the world-at-large as the creator of the *Sandman* series of graphic novels, Gaiman has, over the past ten years, also written many marvelous stories, tales, vignettes, and poems. This volume collects thirty of them—some published here for the first time and others never collected before.

The Cleft and Other Odd Tales by Gahan Wilson (Tor), is amazingly, the first collection of the beloved cartoonist's short stories, although he's been writing them for more than thirty-five years. Twenty-three of the stories were published between 1962 and 1998 in *Playboy, Omni*, and *The Magazine of Fantasy & Science Fiction*, and in all kinds of anthologies. The title story is original to the collection. Not every work is a horror story, but they're all twisted in some way—and they all have in common Wilson's dark wit. One of my very favorites is "The Sea Was Wet as Wet Can Be," even more mordant than Lewis Carroll's original "The Walrus and the Carpenter." Each story has a full-page black-and-white illustration by Wilson.

The Collector of Hearts: New Tales of the Grotesque by Joyce Carol Oates (Dutton) collects twenty-seven horror stories by this prolific and multitalented author who is one of the few mainstream writers to acknowledge her horror credits and awards. Two stories were first published in 1998. Of the others at least seven were published in genre anthologies and magazines and two were reprinted in earlier volumes of this series.

Extremities by Kathe Koja (Four Walls Eight Windows) is the first collection by a winner of the Bram Stoker Award for first novel, *The Cipher*. Her subsequent novels and some of her short fiction prove her a master stylist of dark fiction with the ability to pin down the areas where art and obsession intersect. While her characters may not always be likable, they are utterly believable. Of the sixteen stories here, two are published for the first time.

Personal Demons by Christopher Fowler (Serpent's Tail, U.K.) collects recent stories, seven original to the collection, of urban horror including the award-winning "Wageslaves."

The Night We Buried Road Dog by Jack Cady (DreamHaven Books) collects this multi-award-winning author's short fiction published between 1991 and 1996. Of these six stories and novellas, most are instilled with a ghostly quality. Peter Beagle has provided the foreword and Cady has written a preface. This is a beautiful package, with John Berkey jacket art, a title page photograph by Nancy Garcia, and beautiful forest-green frontpapers.

Flowers From the Moon and other Lunacies by Robert Bloch (Arkham House) is the first posthumous collection by this master of the macabre who died in 1994. It contains some of his early stories from *Weird Tales, Strange Stories*, and *Rogue* (some under pseudonyms), a number of which have never been anthologized before.

Are You Loathsome Tonight by Poppy Z. Brite (Gauntlet Press) is the author's second collection. There are four original pieces of fiction, including the title story: a short, utterly believable little ode to Elvis in his last days. Brite's short work is richly atmospheric, and her characters are always believable as they act out their obsessions. With a strange yet entirely appropriate introduction by Peter Straub and an afterword by Caitlín Kiernan. The cover art and interior illustrations are by J. K. Potter.

Black Butterflies: A Flock on the Dark Side by John Shirley (Mark V. Ziesing) collects sixteen dark, previously uncollected stories (including the creepy "The Rubber Smile") and two stories published here for the first time. Done as a trade paperback with excellent interior, and cover art and design by John Bergin.

Falling Idols by Brian Hodge (Silver Salamander Press) is the second collection by the author of *Nightlife*, *Prototype*, and *The Darker Saints*. It includes the World Fantasy Award–nominated novella "The Dripping of Sundered Wineskins" and two new stories, one a brilliant novella. Published in a limited edition of 860 copies of three states: leather-bound, cloth, and in perfectbound trade paperback.

Manitou Man: The Worlds of Graham Masterton is the British Fantasy Society's first serious foray into book publishing. It's a solid package, collecting ten of Masterton's horror stories, (including three originals) with a short biography, a bibliography, and intersticial critical material on the author's themes. Unfortunately, the book is badly designed—its typeface is too tiny and too light, and there are no running heads for each individual story (a design fault found in far too many collections). The interior illustrations are by Bob Covington, and the cover illustration is by Les Edwards. Trade paperback and limited slipcased editions available.

Epiphanies of Blood by Bill Congreve (MirrorDanse Books, Australia) is an excellent collection of six dark stories. The book is an attractive trade paperback with black-and-white interior illustrations by Marianne Plumridge and front cover art by Kyla Ward. Three of the stories are original to the book.

Cannibals of the Fine Light by Simon Brown (Ticonderoga Publications, Australia) collects twelve stories (one original) by this talented newcomer in an attractive, durable trade paperback edition.

The Exit at Toledo Blade Boulevard is Jack Ketchum's first collection (Obsidian) and ranges widely, from a moving zombie story intended for the last *Book of the Dead* and the timely gut-wrencher, "The Rifle," to an original dark fantasy story and a reminiscence about writer Henry Miller. Richard Laymon provides a gracious introduction to the volume and Ketchum supplies fascinating tidbits about each story. The excellent cover art and interior illustrations are by Alan M. Clark. The hardcover is limited to 500 copies signed by the contributors and numbered.

Ghosts and Grisly Things by Ramsey Campbell (Pumpkin Press, U.K.) is a nice retrospective of some of Campbell's short fiction over the past twenty-five years. It contains twenty stories, with one original novelette. Published in three editions: Limited, trade hardcover, and trade paperback with a wonderfully mysterious and creepy cover by Les Edwards.

Vengeful Ghosts by C. E. Ward (Sarob Press, U.K.) is an attractive hardcover limited edition with cover art and interior illustrations by Paul Lowe. The book collects eight excellent examples of the classic ghost story (two previously unpublished). *Skeletons in the Closet* by William I. I. Read is also a hardcover limited edition collecting nine stories, six of which are original. Cover art and all story illustrations are by Nick Maloret.

The Collected Strange Papers of Christopher Blayre by Edward Heron-Allen (Tartarus Press, U.K.). Heron-Allen was a British scientist and polymath who used the Blayre pseudonym to protect his identity until after his death. The "strange papers," deposited with the fictional Christopher Blayre, registrar of the University of Cosmopoli, are the weird and supernatural experiences of the professorial staff of the university. In the book is the rare story "The Cheetah-Girl," which Tartarus also published as a separate book in 1998 (which sold out, upon publication). In late December, the publisher brought out a new impression of Arthur Machen's classic *Tales of Horror and the Supernatural*. All the Tartarus titles are limited editions done up simply and attractively.

The Paladin Mandates by Mike Chinn (Alchemy Press, U.K.) is a good-looking paperback collecting six original and reprinted tales about Damian Paladin: adventurer, gallant, and dead. This is a lot of fun as Paladin teams up in the twenties and thirties with a daughter of the Romanovs to open a nightclub, fight ghosts and banshees, and gets into all kinds of trouble. Appropriately illustrated by Bob Covington.

A Coven of Vampires by Brian Lumley (Fedogan & Bremer) collects thirteen vampire stories written over twenty-five years by the author of the popular Necroscope series. The book, published in limited and trade editions, has a foreword by the author and a wraparound cover by Bob Eggleton.

The Dagger of Tsian and Other Tales of Adventure collects for the first time eleven of the best pulp adventures by Hugh B. Cave and *Escapades of the Eel* collects fifteen of Cave's tales about the Eel, a gentleman correspondent. Both are from Tattered Pages Press.

Candles for Elizabeth by Caitlín R. Kiernan (Meisha Merlin) is a chapbook with three stories by this up-and-coming writer. One of the stories is original. Kiernan introduces each story and Poppy Z. Brite wrote the introduction. Cover art by Ken Meyer, Jr.

The Curse of the Magazine Killers by Gary Jonas (Ozark Triangle Press) is a chapbook of four stories accepted by various magazines that bit the dirt before publishing the stories. Three of the stories are horror, one a dark heroic fantasy. Cover art by Brand Whitlock.

The Woman with the Flying Head and Other Stories by Kurahashi Yumiko, translated by Atsuko Sakaki (East Gate-M. E. Sharpe) is by an award-winning Japanese surrealist, fantasist, and teller of grotesque tales who has been compared to Franz Kafka and Kobo Abe. The eleven stories, taken from different stages in her career, are often erotic and sometimes shocking but always strongly flavored with Japanese culture.

Weird Family Tales III: Maledictio Redux by Ken Wisman (Dark Regions Press) continues the saga of a very strange bunch of people. In trade paperback with illustrations by Don Schank.

Death Drives a Semi by Edo Van Belkom (Quarry Press, Canada) collects twenty horror stories by this up-and-coming Canadian writer, including his Bram Stoker Award–winning collaboration with David Nickle, "Rat Food."

Penumbra by Stephen Studach (Galley Press, Australia) collects an interesting mixture of seven stories by an Australian newcomer in a sturdy and attractive trade paperback with cover photography and design by Ashley Temple.

The Canadian publisher, Ash-Tree Press published two volumes of stories by contemporary authors in 1998: John Whitbourn's marvelous collection of originals and reprints, *Binscombe Tales: Sinister Saxon Stories*, brings to life an old-fashioned sort of town peopled by a likable group of eccentrics. Many of the

stories are told from the point of view of Mr. Oakley, a relative newcomer to
the town, and many emanate from the Duke of Argyll, the local pub. This book
is a must for readers looking for new traditional ghost stories and weird fiction;
and Steve Duffy's *The Night Comes On*, which contains mostly unpublished
stories by another talented creator of traditional horror and ghost stories. Other
Ash-Tree titles: *Out of the Dark*, the first in a proposed two-volume set collecting
Robert W. Chambers's supernatural short fiction, edited and with an introduction by Hugh Lamb. *The Clock Turns Twelve* by H. R. Wakefield contains all
eighteen stories and the introduction from the 1946 Arkham House edition, as
well as three other Wakefield stories, two previously uncollected; *Twilight and
Other Supernatural Romances* by Marjorie Bowen, edited by Jessica Amanda Salmonson. This volume contains previously unpublished stories and an article by
Bowen. It also has an introduction by her son Hilary Long; *The Fellow Travellers
and Other Stories*, a collection of Sheila Hodgson's supernatural tales, many of
which feature M. R. James. In May, Ash-Tree Press inaugurated a series of occult
detective stories. Each book, edited by Jack Adrian, will feature a different set
of psychic detective tales from the 1910s, 1920s, and 1930s. The first volume
was *Aylmer Vance: Ghost-Seer* by Alice and Claude Askew. *The Black Reaper* by
Bernard Capes is an expanded edition of a hard-to-find collection originally published in the U.K. a decade ago as an Equation-Chiller edition. *Nightmare Jack
and other Stories* by John Metcalf collects the best of Metcalf's horror fiction
from *The Smoking Leg* and *Judas*, the complete short novel, *The Feasting Dead*,
and five additional stories, edited and with an introduction by Richard Dalby;
Lady Ferry and Other Uncanny People collects eleven stories by Sarah Orne Jew-
ett, and inaugurates the "Grim Maids" series, which intends to bring back into
print neglected supernatural tales by women. *Lady Ferry* is edited and has an
introduction by Jessica Amanda Salmonson; *The Death-Head's March & Others*
by Hugh B. Cave and Geoffrey Cave (Black Dog Books) is a collection of four
oriental detective tales that first appeared in *Oriental Stories* and *Magic Carpet*.
It has an introduction by Hugh Cave; *The Terror by Night* by E. F. Benson, edited
and introduced by Jack Adrian, is the first volume of a five-volume Spook Stories
series. The series will bring together all of E. F. Benson's known tales of the
strange and the supernatural, including all the recently discovered weird tales.
Adrian will rearrange them into their chronological order of composition and
publication; *Nights of the Round Table* by Margery Lawrence, edited and introduced by Richard Dalby, is the first volume of an extended series of Lawrence's
works which Ash-Tree will be producing over the next few years.

Other collections include *The Migration of Ghosts* by Pauline Melville
(Bloomsbury, U.K.) twelve original occult, fantasy, and mainstream stories (not
seen); *Thirty Strange Stories* by H. G. Wells (Carroll & Graf) with its introduction by Stephen Jones vividly illustrates Wells's talent for writing dark tales of
revenge, weird tales, and ghost tales; *The Umbrella Man and Other Stories* by
Roald Dahl (Viking Children's Books) takes thirteen stories from various Dahl
adult collections; *The Complete John Silence Stories* by Algernon Blackwood (Dover); *The Complete Pegana* by Lord Dunsany (Chaosium) is an omnibus of three
collections, edited and with an introduction by S. T. Joshi; *While the Light Lasts
and Other Stories* by Agatha Christie (HarperCollins, U.K.) includes seven previously uncollected stories by the author, some of them supernatural; *Ashe of*

Rings and Other Writings by Mary Butts (McPherson & Company) includes the title novel plus another and two essays; A Warning to the Curious and Other Stories by M. R. James (Phoenix) collects sixteen stories, selected and with an introduction by Philip Gooden; Here There Be Ghosts by Jane Yolen (Harcourt, Brace) combines reprinted and original stories and poems for children by the author called "America's Hans Christian Andersen." Moaning Bones: African-American Ghost Stories by Jim Haskins (Lothrop, Lee & Shepard Books-YA); Lovely Biscuits by Grant Morrison (Oneiros Press, U.K.) collects four stories and two plays by this writer best known for his graphic novels.

From the Dark Regions selected poetry series: Poking the Gun, twenty-eight poems by John Grey with an introduction by Michael Arnzen and cover and interior illustrations by Dale L. Sproule; and Anubis on Guard collects some excellent SF and dark-fantasy poetry by Don Webb and has wonderful illustrations by Linda Reynolds. If you have any interest in genre poetry, these simply yet attractively designed chapbooks are a bargain at $4.95 each. Shadows of Light and Dark by long-time U.K. book editor Jo Fletcher (Airgedla'mb Publications and The Alchemy Press, U.K.) combines poetry about the dark fantastic with dark non genre poems about love and loss. More of Bruce Boston's poetry appeared in Cold Tomorrows (Gothic Press). Anamnesis Press published several poetry chapbooks including Satan is a Mathematician: Poems of the Weird, Surreal and Fantastic by Keith Allen Daniels, with nice cover art by Rodger Gerberding; Imprinting by Terry McGarry (Anamnesis Press) with mostly reprints but a few original poems, mostly fantasy, some dark fantasy; and Steve Utley's This Impatient Ape collecting more than thirty tiny poems.

Mixed Genre Collections

Black Glass by Karen Joy Fowler (Henry Holt) is a mixed bag by a master of fantasy, dark fantasy, science fiction, and alternate history. An edginess that should appeal to readers of dark fiction pervades many of the stories, two of which are published for the first time; Going Home Again by Howard Waldrop (St. Martin's Press) is the first trade edition of this fourth collection by an important weird fantasy/SF writer. I published more than half of the material in Omni so obviously I'm biased, but Waldrop's a national treasure and should be read by everyone. It's got a gonzo introduction by Lucius Shepard and an afterword to each story by the author; Weird Women, Wired Women by Kit Reed (Wesleyan University Press) is another mixed bag of satire that often strays into horror by an author who writes psychological thrillers under the name Kit Craig. Connie Willis wrote the foreword; I Sing the Body Electric! and Other stories by Ray Bradbury (Avon Books) is an omnibus of I Sing the Body Electric! and Long After Midnight; Beaker's Dozen, in author Nancy Kress's consistently elegant prose, mixes some of her best science fiction (some dark) and fantasy (again, some of it very dark) written between 1991 and 1996; The Perfect Host: Volume V: The Complete Stories of Theodore Sturgeon continues to collect all the short fiction by the author of the classics Some of Your Blood and More Than Human. In this volume are two stories never before published; Time Pieces by Michael Bishop (Edgewood Press) collects the poetry by this writer best known for his SF and fantasy in an attractive trade paperback edition; Charity is Mark Rich-

lxxii ·· Ellen Datlow

ard's (Nan A. Talese/Doubleday) second collection marketed as mainstream but infused with the weird—a child sees ghosts, angels, and Death; a man seduces by telling real ghost stories; *The Knife Thrower and Other Stories* by Steven Millhauser (Crown), winner of the World Fantasy Award and no stranger to this anthology series, is the author's fourth collection; *The Explanation & Other Good Advice* by Don Webb (Wordcraft of Oregon) combines reprints and originals of Webb's very odd fictions, some of them occasionally detouring into dark territories; *Dark Tales and Light* by Bruce Boston (Dark Regions Press) reprints ten stories by this eclectic writer; Elmore Leonard, justly famous these days for his crime fiction, actually started out by writing westerns. *The Tonto Woman and other western stories* (Delacorte) collects nineteen of them; *The Avram Davidson Treasury* edited by Robert Silverberg and Grania Davis (Tor) is a tribute collection of twenty-six stories by this brilliant short story writer who died in 1993. Each story has an introduction and afterword by notables such as Ursula K. Le Guin, Ray Bradbury, William Gibson, Harlan Ellison, Thomas M. Disch, and others. One can hope that this important book, along with the recently published novella *The Boss in the Wall* will bring Davidson new readers to appreciate his accomplishments; *Flying Leap* by Judy Budnitz (Picador) introduces a new mainstream writer who veers into the surreal and weird with her exuberant and imaginative stories—including a cabal of cheerleaders dedicated to upholding the spirit of their high school . . . no matter what—a female T. Coraghessan Boyle; *Hit Man* by Lawrence Block (William Morrow) finally brings together all the terrific Keller (a hit man with a sense of fair play) stories that have been published over several years (although the publisher attempts to disguise the fact that they're stories: the titles are used as "chapter headings" and there is no table of contents).

Recommended Artists with Work in the Small Press

Rob Kiely, Donna Johansen, Barb Armata, Alan Hollingsworth, Larry Wessel, Poppy Alexander, Kenneth Scott, Martin Springett, Augie Wiedemann, Stephen E. Fabian, Jason Van Hollander, Dominic Harman, Darryl Sloan, Pete Queally, David Checkley, Gerald Gaubert, Kenneth B. Haas III, Cliff Nielsen, Adam Rex, Beryl Bush, Dallas Goffin, Douglas Walters, Rob Suggs, Shaun Tan, Keith Boulger, Paul Swenson, Wolf Read, Tom Simonton, Bob Hobbs, Eric Turnmire, Cathy Buburuz, Bob Crouch, Wendy Down, Liam Hemp, Jon C. Gernon, Lee Seed, Paul Lowe, Steven Denton, Harry O. Morris, Joseph Campbell, Rodger Gerberding, Jamie Oberschlake, Chris Pelletiere, Jeffrey Thomas, Lisa Fillingham, Leslie Miyuki Obata, Gordon Klock, Bruce Young, Robert Paes, Roddy Williams, Allen Koszowski, Dino Flatline, Stefan Valent, Alan Gilmore, and Iain Maynard.

Magazines and Newsletters

With the failure of *Horror*, the two best sources for regular horror news are found on the Internet: *DarkEcho* edited by Paula Guran and *Hellnotes* edited by David B. Silva. *DarkEcho* has the stamp of Guran's voice, making it more personal and quirky. Both weekly newsletters cover the news of the field equally well.

DarkEcho, bascially a one-woman operation, often has incisive commentary about the field. *Hellnotes* generally has a long interview with a horror notable, short horror reviews by various people, and a view from England by Peter Crowther. *DarkEcho* is free and supports itself with advertising. To subscribe, e-mail darkecho@aol.com with "subscribe" as your subject. *Hellnotes* is subscription based. E-mail subscriptions are available for $10 per year. Hardcopy subscriptions are available for $40 per year payable to David B. Silva, *Hellnotes*, 27780 Donkey Mine Road, Oak Run, CA 96069. E-mail address: dbsilva@hellnotes.com or mailto:pfolson@up.net.

On the other hand, horror *does* have a major critical magazine in the quarterly *Necrofile: The Review of Horror Fiction* edited by Stefan Dziemianowicz, S. T. Joshi, and Michael A. Morrison. *Necrofile* has a varied stable of writers who, among them, cover the full spectrum of horror fiction. With lengthy pieces, a regular column by Ramsey Campbell, shorter (but no less informative) reviews by the editors, and listings of horror books in the U.S. and the U.K., *Necrofile* is indispensable to the serious horror reader. A subscription is $12 payable to Necronomicon Press, P.O. Box 1304, West Warwick, RI 02893.

Heliocentric Writer's Network edited by Lisa Jean Bothell is an informative bimonthly newsletter with interviews, market reports, news, mini-reviews, and short articles on writing. It's $3 for a sample; $18 a year (six issues) payable to Heliocentric Writer's Network, 17650 1st Avenue S, Box 291, Seattle, WA 98148. E-mail: bastmedia@aol.com.

The Gila Queen's Guide to Markets edited by Kathryn Ptacek is published every six weeks and is one of the best guides, covering all kinds of fiction and nonfiction. $34 for a 12-issue subscription payable to Kathryn Ptacek, GQHQ, P.O. Box 97, Newton, NJ 07860-0097.

Bare Bones, offshoot of the late lamented *The Scream Factory*, is edited by Peter Enfantino and John Scoleri. It seems to be covering mysteries and thrillers more than horror, particularly in the spring issue. It's meant to be a quarterly but has not yet kept to its proposed schedule. Single issues are $5 and a four-issue subscription is $16 payable to Deadline Press, P.O. Box 2808, Apache Junction, AZ 85217. E-mail: (Scoleri) resrvrdog@earthlink.net and (Enfantino) DiePool@aol.com.

Niekas Science Fiction and Fantasy #45 edited by Ed Meskys and Joe Christopher doesn't usually cover dark fantasy and horror as extensively as issue #45—which is dedicated to those genres. The magazine tries to alternate a general issue with special single-subject issues. Issue #45 begins with a reprinted essay by Darrell Schweitzer explaining why people like horror fiction and the whole thick issue is jam-packed with essays about horror. Read about the Lovecraftian influence on Stephen King, and about the light horror of John Bellairs, about believability in Stoker's *Dracula*, the ecology of vampires, and about Tod Browning's classic movie *Freaks*. *Niekas*, c/o Ed Meskys, RR #2 Box 63, 322 Whitter Highway, Center Harbor, NH 03226-9708.

Video Watchdog edited by Tim and Donna Lucas continues to entertain and illuminate with its bimonthly coverage of fantastic video. This is a must for anyone interested in quirky reviews and columns. A one-year subscription is $24 payable to Video Watchdog, P.O. Box 5283, Cincinnati, OH 45205-0283. E-mail: Videowd@aol.com.

Psychotronic Video edited by Michael J. Weldon is the other indispensable magazine specializing in weird genre videos. It's very different from *Video Watchdog*, which is more of a guide. *Psychotronic* runs interviews or profiles of such characters as R. G. Armstrong, Conrad Brooks (a regular in Ed Wood movies), and Mary Woronov. It also has movie, video, and book reviews. If you're the type who used to read the TV listings for the descriptions of each movie (hey, I am), this is for you.

Most small press magazines are labors of love and come and go with amazing rapidity. It's difficult to recommend buying a subscription to those that haven't proven themselves but I urge readers to buy at least a single issue of something that sounds interesting. There isn't room to mention every small-press horror magazine being published at any given time so the following handful are those that I thought were the best in 1998:

Ghosts & Scholars edited by Rosemary Pardoe is an excellent biannual magazine devoted to continuing the M. R. James tradition of ghost stories. Its combination of original and reprinted stories, book reviews, and scholarly articles make it a must for any reader interested in the traditional ghost story. A four issue subscription (two years) is $25 (surface)/$29 (air) payable to R. A. Pardoe, Flat One, 36 Hamilton Street, Hoole, Chester CH2 3JQ, England. Single issues can be purchased from Richard Fawcett, 61 Teecomwas Drive, Uncasville, CT 06382. E-mail: pardos@globalnet.co.uk

Weird Tales is back with a mix of dark fiction and reviews by Douglas E. Winter and Darrell Schweitzer. Now published by DNA Publications, editors George H. Scithers and Darrell Schweitzer assert that they will now be able to keep to a quarterly schedule. Single copies are $4.95 with a one-year subscription (four issues) $16 payable to DNA Publications, P.O. Box 2988, Radford, VA 24143-2980.

Mythic Delirium is a new magazine edited by Mike Allen with original and reprinted dark poetry by Charlee Jacob, Bruce Boston, Ann K. Schwader, and others with illustrations by Margaret B. Simon, Cathy Buburuz, and Charles S. Fallis. Allen intends to publish irregularly but a two-issue subscription is $9 payable to Mike Allen, P.O. Box 13511, Roanoke, VA 24034-3511.

Lore edited by Rod Heather, published only one issue in 1998 but it was a good one, with excellent art, particularly by Jamie Oberschlake, who did the cover and some interior illustrations. $4 for a single copy in the U.S., $5.25 elsewhere (US funds only). $15 for four issues payable to Rod Heather, P.O. Box 381, Matawan, NJ 07747-0381. The magazine goes from officially being a quarterly to semi-annual as of its ninth issue.

Enigmatic Tales edited by Mick Sims and Len Maynard is a promising new horror quarterly, published in England. Each issue features a combination of original and classic reprints, the latter introduced by such luminaries as Hugh Lamb and Richard Dalby. It's perfect bound and nicely illustrated. Single issues are 2 pounds sterling or $6 (U.S.) and a four-issue subscription is 8 pounds sterling or $20 (U.S.) payable to M. Sims, 1 Gibbs Field, Bishops Stortford, Herts CM 23 4EY, England.

Nasty Piece of Work edited by David A. Green, now in its third year of publication, is very uneven in quality. Each time it looks to be leaving behind the titillating and offensive vignettes of mutilation and sexual violence, I experience a burst of optimism in my assessment of the magazine's contribution to horror. But then, inevitably, the next issue sinks back into the adolescent morass of disgust and special-effect gore without chills. Still, eight stories made my honorable mention list in 1998 so it's definitely worth a look. A single copy is $4 and a subscription to this quarterly is $15 payable to David A. Green, 20 Drum Mead, Petersfield, Hants Gu32 3AQ, England.

Dark Regions/The Year's Best Fantastic Fiction is a perfect bound, irregularly published (two–four times per year) combination of half original horror fiction and reprints from various small press magazines. Joe Morey and Mike Olson edit *Dark Regions*. They, plus John Rosenman and poetry editor Bobbi Sinha-Morey, edit the *Year's Best Fantastic Fiction*. The reprints are usually a good mix from some of the better small press mixed-genre magazines and the originals include some strong entries. *DR #* 10 was SF, a "virtual reality" issue. The other half was what is left of *Horror*, the ambitious horror news magazine modeled on *Locus* that never managed to take off. Unfortunately, it doesn't work as a separate section that comes out irregularly. Subscriptions are $9 a year payable to Dark Regions, P.O. Box 6301, Concord, CA 94524.

One of the best reasons to join the Ghost Story Society is that members get three issues of *All Hallows*, a perfect-bound journal filled with articles, news, and usually excellent original ghostly fiction. But another good reason is the support of an organization dedicated to providing admirers of the classic ghost story with an outlet for their interest. Membership is only $23 per year. For more information visit the Ash-Tree Press Web site or write to P.O. Box 1360 Ashcroft, BC VOK 1AO. http://www.ash-tree.bc.ca/GSS.html

Peeping Tom edited by David Bell continues to publish an interesting mix of horror fiction. A four-issue subscription is 8 pounds sterling payable to Peeping Tom, Yew Tree House, 15 Nottingham Road, Ashby de la Zouch, Leicestershire LE 65 1DJ, U.K.

Dark Horizons edited by Peter Coleborn, Mike Chinn, Phil Williams, and Joel Lane is one of the excellent magazines received by members of the British Fantasy Society. For more information see the useful organizations section.

Night Terrors edited by D. E. Davidson has good production values for the small press and consistently readable fiction. A subscription costs $18 (four issues), payable to D. E. Davidson, *Night Terrors*, 1202 West Market Street, Orrville, OH 44667-1710. Ohio residents add 5.75 percent tax. A single issue costs $6.

Flesh & Blood edited by Jack Fisher is quite good. Issue #3 had an interview with Ed Bryant and some very good fiction. $11 (three issues) or $4 single copy payable to Jack Fisher, 121 Joseph Street, Bayville, NJ 08723.

Some of the best horror and dark fantasy fiction can be found in mixed genre magazines such as the pros—*Asimov's Science Fiction* edited by Gardner Dozois and *The Magazine of Fantasy & Science Fiction* edited by Gordon Van Gelder, although the former deliberately tries to avoid the supernatural. *Realms of Fantasy* edited by Shawna McCarthy occasionally publishes some good dark material. *Interzone* edited by David Pringle, often publishes several excellent horror-tinged stories per year. *Interzone*: 217 Preston Drove, Brighton, BN1 6L, U.K. *Event Horizon: Science Fiction, Fantasy, and Horror* which I edit has published some horror since its debut on the Web mid-August. Also promised in the future are horror reviews and columns by Douglas E. Winter and David J. Schow.

A few of the best mixed-genre small press magazines are:

Eidolon edited by Jonathan Strahan and Jeremy G. Byrne is an important source of excellent fiction, some of it horror. It's published in Australia and runs science fiction, fantasy, and horror. The 25/26 issue, which officially came out in December 1997 but didn't show up in the U.S. till January, contained two knock-out horror stories. Although in the past, *most* of the fiction has been by Australians, the publication of issue 27 instituted a policy of accepting fiction *only* by Australian citizens or residents. This policy does not affect nonfiction— that's a good thing, because Howard Waldrop is now writing "Crimea River," a column about whatever he wants. Subscription rates are in Australian dollars only: $(A) 45 (international airmail) for four issues or $(A)35 (international sea-mail) payable to Eidolon Publications, P.O. Box 225, North Perth, WA 6906 Australia. http://www.eidolon.net.

The Third Alternative edited by Andy Cox, is, along with *Interzone*, the most consistently interesting and entertaining genre magazine regularly published in the U.K. The artwork is elegant and often stark, the fiction dark and disturbing SF/fantasy/cross-genre. Every issue has a column about a mainstream writer of interest to our genres (e.g., John Fowles, Kurt Vonnegut). It is published quarterly with subscriptions $22 payable to TTA Press, 5 Martins Lane, Witcham, Ely, Cambs CB6 2LB, U.K. If you're wondering where excellent cross-genre fiction is, this is where.

Talebones edited by Patrick and Honna Swenson, is a quarterly with consistently attractive full-color covers and a variety of fiction, reviews, and interviews. Subscriptions are $16 for one year payable to *Talebones*, 10531 SE 250th Place, #104, Kent, WA 98031; *Space and Time* edited by Gordon Linzner is one of the longest-running small press magazines and its move to a glossy full-sized format makes it look more professional. A biannual, with two-issue subscriptions $10 payable to *Space and Time*, 138 West 70th Street 4B, New York, NY 10023-4468; *The Urbanite* edited by Mark McLaughlin is always worth reading. Most issues have a broad theme and a three-issue subscription is $13.50 payable to Urban Legend Press, P.O. Box 4737, Davenport, IA 52808; *Transversions* edited by Dale L. Sproule hails from Canada. The big double issue 8/9 has an especially good cover by Wolf Read. *Transversions* is published three times a year and a four-issue subscription is $18 (U.S. or Canadian) payable to Paper Orchid Press, 216 Woodfield Road, Toronto, Ontario M4L 2W7 Canada; *Odyssey*, the new glossy SF/fantasy bimonthly from the U.K. published a few dark stories but concentrates on SF and fantasy. Edited by Liz Holliday; *Cyber-Psychos AOD* edited by Jasmine Sailing is a hefty annual specializing in culture on the fringe, and is filled with interviews, profiles, articles, reviews, and fiction. For the most part there's not much to do with horror but it's worth a look to see what's just over the edge.

Aurealis edited by Stephen Higgins and Dirk Strasser published some very good SF and fantasy (with a wee bit of dark material) in 1998. Issue #19 only reached me in 1998, although the copyright was 1997. A four-issue subscription is $35 Australian seamail (or $43 airmail) payable to Chimaera Publications. Credit card sales acceptable. P.O. Box 2164, Mt. Waverley, Victoria 3149, Australia. *Aurealis* online features interviews and market listings: http://www.aurealis.hl.net.

Kimota No. 8 edited by Graeme Hurry is a good-mixed genre magazine published biannually in association with the Preston Speculative Fiction Group. 9 pounds sterling payable to G. Hurry, Graeme Hurry, 52 Cadley Causeway, Preston, Lancs, PR2 3RX, U.K.

Nonfiction Books (Film)

James Whale: A New World of Gods and Monsters by James Curtis (Faber & Faber) is a biography of the director of *Frankenstein, The Bride of Frankenstein,* and *The Invisible Man; Hollywood Rat Race* by Ed Wood, Jr. (Four Walls Eight Windows) is the previously unpublished memoir/how-to by the infamous director of *Plan 9 From Outer Space* and other really bad movies. This is the book Ed Wood fans have been waiting for! *Dark City: the Lost World of Film Noir* by Eddie Muller (St. Martin's Griffin) takes the reader on a lively and knowing trip to the urban landscape of sexy women and burned out (or approaching burn-out) men of film noir. Lots of photographs and knowing tidbits about the actors and directors of the era make for entertaining browsing; *Buñuel* by John Baxter (Carroll & Graf); *Censored Screams: British Ban on Hollywood Horror in the Thirties* by Tom Johnson (McFarland & Co.); *The Ingrid Pitt Bedside Companion for Vampire Lovers* by Ingrid Pitt (Batsford, U.K.); *Horror and Science Fiction Films IV* by Donald C. Willis (Scarecrow); *Children of the Night* by Randy Loren Rasmussen (McFarland & Co.); *The Films of Lon Chaney* by Michael F. Blake (Vestal); *Screams and Nightmares: The Films of Wes Craven* by Brian J. Robb (The Overlook Press); *Drums of Terror: Voodoo in the Cinema* by Bryan Senn (Midnight Marquee) provides film-by-film reviews of voodoo films from the 1930s to the 1990s with black-and-white photos; *Son of Guilty Pleasures of the Horror Film* edited by Gary and Susan Svehla (Midnight Marquee) with black-and-white photos throughout; *Dracula: The Shade and the Shadow* edited by Elizabeth Miller (Desert Island) is a collection of critical papers presented at Dracula '97, a centenary celebration and conference; *Dracula Unearthed,* annotated and edited by Clive Leatherdale (Desert Island); *Poe Cinema: Critical Filmography of Theatrical Releases Based on the Works of Edgar Allan Poe* by Don G. Smith (McFarland & Co.); *The Essential Monster Movie Guide* by Stephen Jones (Titan); *"They're Here . . ."* edited by Kevin McCarthy and Ed Gorman (Boulevard) is a tribute to the original movie version of *Invasion of the Body Snatchers*; and a completely revised edition of *The Outer Limits Companion* by David J. Schow (Crescendo Records).

Other Nonfiction

St. James Guide to Horror, Ghost & Gothic Writers edited by David Pringle (Gale/St. James Press) is an important reference book with an impressive list of contributors and an even more impressive list of writers covered. Of course, the usual, like Stephen King and Anne Rice, are included but what is of more interest is the inclusion of writers usually not classified under the umbrella of horror fiction such as William S. Burroughs, Kingsley Amis, and Anne Rivers Siddons; *Out of the Loud Hound of Darkness: A Dictionarrative* by Karen Elizabeth Gordon (Pantheon) is the newest book on English language usage from a writer who uses the gothic to entertain while teaching. The author of *The Transitive Vampire* takes on difficult or often misused words and gently instructs in their proper usage; *Freakery: Cultural Spectacles of the Extraordinary* edited by Rosemarie Garland Thomson (NYU Press) is a fascinating book of essays on freaks, from the history of the freak show to a piece about the self-creation of freaks. The volume is not at all academic and although it overlaps somewhat with other books, it covers new ground in its analysis of the American perception of people from other cultures as exotic, and thereby "freaklike"; *Wonders and the Order of Nature 1150–1750* by Lorraine Daston and Katharine Park (Zone Books) is about the ways European naturalists used wonder and wonders to envision themselves and the natural world. Illustrated and academic but not too much so; *Flesh and Blood: A History of the Cannibal Complex* by Raey Tannahill (Little, Brown) is a witty and erudite update of a 1975 classic on the subject; *The Victorian Underworld* by Donald Thomas (NYU Press) is a colorful chronicle of the criminal element in Victorian England. Unlike most histories, this one brings the period vividly alive for the reader; *The Excruciating History of Dentistry: Toothsome Tales of Oral Oddities from Babylon to Braces* by James Wynbrandt (St. Martin's Press) is a lively history about the development of dentistry with lots of interesting tidbits such as that Pierre Fauchard, the father of dentistry, recommended rinsing out your mouth with your own urine to relieve dental pain; that so many teeth were harvested from corpses at the Battle of Waterloo that the teeth, used for implants and dentures were known as "Waterloo Teeth"; *Serial Killers: Death and Life in America's Wound Culture* by Mark Seltzer (Routledge) is a dry, academic cultural study that drains all the juice out of a premise that might be fascinating with a slightly looser approach; *Invisible Enemies: Stories of Infectious Diseases* by Jeanette Farrell (Farrar, Straus & Giroux) is a straightforward book for the young adult audience explaining the history of seven diseases, including smallpox, tuberculosis, and AIDS; *The Anatomy of Disgust* by William Ian Miller (Harvard University Press) is a fascinating study conceived of by the author in the tradition of Robert Burton's *The Anatomy of Melancholy*. He covers the notion of disgust from the most obvious—the rejection of food ("disgust" means unpleasant to the taste) to the more subtle (group stench and the class system); *The History of Torture* by Brian Innes (St. Martin's Press) is an overview, with photos and illustrations, of man's inhumanity to man and the use and abuse of power, both outside and within the legal system; *Murder Most Foul: The Killer and the Gothic Imagination* by Karen Halttunen (Harvard University Press) explores the changing view of murder from early New England sermons read at the public execution of murderers, through the nineteenth century when the secular and sensational replaced the religiously moral judgment of the crime, to today's true crime literature and tabloid reports. Halttunen skillfully uses the development of detective literature and the attitude toward evil in movies such as *Dead Man Walking* and *Seven* to make some of her points; *A Defense of Masochism* by Anita Phillips (St. Martin's Press) is a brief but passionate defense that opens with a working definition of masochism as "the agreement between two people to explore the roles of master and slave by acting them out for a specific time period." Phillips argues that it was early psychiatry that named masochism and moved it away from its more innocent meaning; *When We Die: What Becomes of the Body After Death* by Cedric Mims (Robinson, U.K.); *Ghosts in the Middle Ages: The Living and the Dead in Medieval Society* by Jean-Claude Schmitt (The University of Chicago Press); *The Encyclopedia of Hell* by Miriam Van Scott (St. Martin's Press); *The Book of Fabulous Beasts: A Collection of Writings from Ancient Times to the Present* by Joseph Nigg (Oxford University Press); *Taming the Beast: Charles Manson's Life Behind Bars* by Edward George with Dary Matera (St. Martin's Press); *Looking into the Eyes of a Killer: A Psychiatrist's Journey through the Murderer's World* by Drew Ross, M.D. (Plenum Trade); *Piercing the Darkness: Undercover with Vampires in America Today* by Katherine Ramsland (HarperPrism); *The Work of William F. Nolan: An Annotated Bibliography & Literary Guide, Second Edition* by Boden Clarke and James Hopkins (Borgo Press) is an extensively revised and updated version of the original 1988 edition; *Scaring Us to Death: The Impact of Stephen King on Popular Culture: Second Edition* by Michael R. Collings (Borgo Press) is a critical discussion of King's works, with chronology, selected bibliography, and index. It's an expanded and updated version of the 1987 Starmont House edition; *Reflections on Dracula: Ten Essays* by Elizabeth Miller (one essay co-written with Margaret Carter) (Transylvania Press); *The Shape of Fear: Horror and the Fin de Siècle Culture of Decadence* by Susan Jennifer Navarette (University Press of Kentucky) is a critical look at literary horror and decadence at the end of the nineteenth century. Notes, extensive bibliography, index. Illustrated by artists including James Ensor, Aubrey Beardsley, and Edvard Munch; *The Devil in the Shape of a Woman: Witchcraft in Colonial New England* by Carol D. Karlsen (Norton); *Charlotte Perkins Gilman's "The Yellow Wallpaper" and the History of Its Publication and Reception* edited by Julie Bates Dock (Pennsylvania State University Press); *The Encyclopedia Cthulhiana: A Guide to Lovecraftian Horror* by Daniel Harms (Chaosium) is an expanded and revised second edition; *The Necronomicon Files: the Truth Behind the Legend* by Daniel Harms and John Wisdom Gonce, III (Night Shade Books) is a collection of essays about Lovecraft's book, debunking claims of its existence; *Body Horror: Photojournalism, Catastrophe and War* by John Taylor (NYU Press) addresses the questions of why we are compelled to look at or not look at shocking photographs and how our "sense of politics, morality, and culture is affect when we are exposed to gruesome images of accidents and disasters, murder and execution, grief and death"; *The Big Book of Noir* edited by Ed Gorman, Lee Server, and Martin H. Greenberg (Carroll & Graf) features articles and interviews about noir in all its forms—movies, novels, television, radio, and graphic novels. Includes Stephen King writing about Jim Thompson; *Northern Dreamers: Interviews with Canadian Authors of Science Fiction, Fantasy and Horror* by Edo van Belkom (Quarry Press); *The Haunted Mind: The Supernatural in Victorian Literature* edited by Elton E. Smith and Robert Haas (Scarecrow Press); *Iconoclastic Departures: Mary Shelley After Frankenstein: Essays in Honor of the Bicentenary of Mary Shelley's Birth* edited by Syndy M. Conger, Frederick S. Frank, and Gregory O'Dea (Fairleigh Dickinson University Press); *Sisters of Gore: Seven Gothic Melodramas by British Women, 1790–1843* edited by John Franceschina (Garland Publishing); *Ghost Stories by Women: The British and American Tradition, an Annotated, Selected Bibliography* by Lynette Carpenter and Wendy K. Kolmar (Garland Publishing); *Fighting the Current: The Life and Works of Evelyn Scott* by Mary Wheeler White (Louisiana State University Press); *Mary Butts: Scenes from the Life* by Nathalie Blondel (McPherson & Company); *The Complete Book of Ghosts & Poltergeists* by Leonard R. N. Ashley (Barricade); *The Complete Book of Vampires* by Leonard R. N. Ashley (Barricade); *Invisible Writer: A Biography of Joyce Carol Oates* by Greg Johnson (Penguin/Dutton); *The Vampire Gallery: A Who's Who of the Undead* by J. Gordon Melton (Visible Ink) is a guide to vampires in books and film and includes an index, and sources for each entry; *Screams of Reason: Mad Science and Modern Culture* by David J. Skal (Norton) is a critical analysis of the role of the mad scientist in movies, books, and comics and how this view of science reflects cultural changes; *The Vampire: A Casebook* edited by Alan Dundes (University of Wisconsin Press) collects academic essays examining the roots of vampire legends; *Midnight Dreary: The Mysterious Death of Edgar Allan Poe* by John Evangelist Walsh (Rutgers University Press) is a biography that probes into the cause of Poe's death; *Manly Wade Wellman: The Gentleman from Chapel Hill: A Working Bibliography* by Phil Stephenson-Payne and Gordon Benson, Jr. (Galactic Central Publications); *Lovecraft Remembered* edited by Peter Cannon (Arkham House) collects early reminiscences by Lovecraft's friends and admirers in one volume for the first time; *A Guide to the Cthulhu Cult* by Fred L. Pelton (Armitage House); *Vampire Readings: An Annotated Bibliography* by Patricia Altner (Scarecrow Press); *Stephen King from A to Z: An Encyclopedia of His Life and Work* by George Beahm (Andrew McMeel); *Discovering Stephen King* edited by Tony Magistrale (Borgo Press) is revised and expanded from Starmont's *The Shining Reader* (1991); *Discovering Dean Koontz* edited by Bill Munster (Borgo Press) is revised from Starmont's *Sudden Fear* (1988); *Mary Shelley: Frankenstein's Creator: First Science Fiction Writer* by Joan Kane Nichols (Conart Press) is a young adult biography.

Limited Editions and Chapbooks

Tachyon Publications published "The Boss in the Wall: A Treatise on the House Devil," an original novella by the late Avram Davidson and his ex-wife Grania Davis. Vlad Smith and his family spend the night in a house they're about to buy. That night, after a mysterious attack, his uncle is dead and his young daughter sent into convulsions, and he is determined to find out what happened. This very creepy horror tale is told from several different points of view, including Vlad's and a group of academics secretly studying and following up on reports of a creature variously called "Paper-Man," "String-Fellow," "Clatterer," and "Boss in the Wall"—creatures—neither dead nor alive—that are said to haunt houses. Despite a few anachronisms that might have been eliminated, this is a fine legacy for a brilliant writer who died impoverished. This and *The Avram Davidson Treasury* ought to bring renewed attention to his work.

Durtro reissued a pricey but attractive edition of *The Book of Jade*, a book of decadent supernatural poems dedicated to Baudelaire originally published anonymously (by David Park Barnitz) in 1901. The book includes some writings not included in the original and has an introduction by Mark Valentine and an afterword by Thomas Ligotti on "The Joys of Collecting Decadent Poetry." Limited to 300 numbered copies.

Necro Publications brought out two short novels: Charlee Jacobs's first, A

Symbiotic Fascination is published in two limited editions, and Edward Lee and Elizabeth Steffen's *Portrait of the Psychopath as a Young Woman* is published in three limited editions.

Deadline Press published Richard Laymon's *A Writer's Tale*, an autobiographical tour through the author's life and work in two limited editions. The book contains a comprehensive overview of his novels, his early, uncollected short fiction, photos, and tips for writers.

Enigma Press inaugurated an inexpensive series of novellas beginning with "Moths," a supernatural story by L. H. Maynard and M. P. N. Sims about a legend of evil Japanese villagers come to life. Cover illustrations are by Gerald Gaubert.

Charon Press of South Carolina reprinted *The Stone Dragon*, a classic work of supernatural and decadent fiction by R. Murray Gilchrist in a 250-copy facsimile of the original edition in a slipcase and with an illustrated dust jacket.

The Hazelwood Press has issued a 300-copy numbered facsimile edition of the manuscript of W. W. Jacobs's "The Monkey's Paw," showing the revisions and corrections made by the author during the process of composition. Also included are: five commissioned essays on Jacobs examining the story's appeal and setting it in the context of his other work, a biographical introduction, a review of Jacobs's tales of terror, a look at the stage and screen adaptations of Jacobs's other works, and an essay by the owner of "The Monkey's Paw" manuscript.

Cemetery Dance Publications: *Fear Nothing* by Dean Koontz, beat out the trade hardcover by about two weeks and *Seize the Night*, its sequel. Both titles are offered in two deluxe editions, with full color illustrations by Phil Parks. The lettered edition of *Seize the Night* has a dust jacket different from the numbered edition, with the jacket of the numbered used as a frontispiece for the lettered edition. The limited edition of *Robert Bloch's Psychos*, the HWA anthology came out; *The Cellar* by Richard Laymon was published in a limited edition with an introduction by Bentley Little. Both *The Beast House* and *The Midnight Tour* by Laymon, were published as signed, limited editions. Richard Matheson's *The Twilight Zone Scripts*, collecting fourteen classics was published as two limited editions. Each screenplay is accompanied by new introductory comments by the author, there is a new interview with Matheson, photographs from the TV episodes, and an introduction by editor Stanley Wiater. Also the CD series of original hardcover novellas was launched with two crime stories: *The Wilds* by Richard Laymon with full-color dust jacket and interior illustration by Keith Minnion and *Spree* by Lucy Taylor with a full-color dust jacket and interior illustrations by Jill Bauman. Both these are available in two editions.

Talisman published an excellent poetry broadside by Bruce Boston, "Confessions of a Body Thief."

Meisha Merlin published a chapbook of three stories (one original) by Caitlín R. Kiernan. Each story comes with notes by the author about its inspiration and inception. Introduction by Poppy Z. Brite. The cover art is by Ken Mayer, Jr. and the cover design by Neil Seltzer.

Dark Raptor Press published chapbooks by John Pelan and Edward Lee, Edo van Belkom, P. D. Cacek, and Carol Anne Davis. Each is illustrated.

Hypatia Press continued to publish limited chapbooks by P. C. Hodgell, with an entertaining supernatural Sherlock Holmes story called "A Ballad of the White Plague." Collage work and preface by the author.

Robert Morgan founded Sarob Press of Wales as an imprint for quality limited, numbered editions of classic and modern supernatural novellas, novels, and short story collections; each book is hardcover with sewn signatures. First up is a limited edition of Sheridan Le Fanu's classic tale *Carmilla* and the aforementioned *Vengeful Ghosts*, the collection by C. E. Ward.

Subterranean Press published several chapbooks including a very good original noir story by Norman Partridge called "Red Right Hand," with cover art by Mark A. Nelson; and a terrific new Koko Tate story by Peter Crowther called "Fugue on a G-String," with illustration and cover art by Alan M. Clark. Each comes signed, in two limited editions; also, *Monsters and Other stories* by Richard T. Chizmar, is a limited edition chapbook with two original stories; *Testament: The Unpublished Prologues* interweaves two prologues of David Morrell's novel that he forgot he had written, with a long autobiographical piece; and original novelettes "The Night in Fog" by David Silva and "The Keys to D'Esperance" by Chaz Brenchley. All three chapbooks are published in two signed limited editions.

Gauntlet published a limited twentieth-anniversary edition of *What Dreams May Come*, the Richard Matheson novel released as a feature film in 1998. The book has a new preface by Matheson and an afterword by Douglas E. Winter; *Eyes of Prey* by publisher Barry Hoffman, is the sequel to his novel *Hungry Eyes*. It was published in two limited editions, with an afterword by Richard Christian Matheson and cover art by Harry O. Morris. The twenty-six-copy leather-bound, slipcased edition has a second afterword by Richard Chizmar, and two additional Morris illustrations.

Tartarus Press published a limited edition of Arthur Machen's 1907 novel *The Hill of Dreams*, containing all three of Sidney Simes's illustrations originally meant for the first edition (only one was used). Also included are the original introductions by Machen and Lord Dunsany and a new one by Mark Valentine; *Afterglow*, a series of sketches of decadent "Greek Egypt," peopled with courtesans and poets, philosophers, and pharaohs was first published by Mitchell S. Buck in America in 1924. Arthur Machen provided the introduction, "On Paganism." Also *The Secret Glory*, with all six chapters published together for the first time and with a new introduction by Godfrey Brangham.

RazorBlade Press, publisher of *Raw Nerve* magazine, published *Faith in the Flesh*, a book of two excellent original novellas by Tim Lebbon: "The First Law" about the survivors of a shipwreck who, reaching an island find their problems just beginning. It's a well-told suspenseful tale. "From Bad Flesh" is an excellent SF/horror story. The attractive trade paperback has an introduction by Peter Crowther. RazorBlade also published *The Dreaming Pool*, a new novel by Gary Greenwood. Both books have excellent covers, the latter by Chris Nurse.

Side Show published *Splatterspunk: The Micah Hays Stories*, by Edward Lee and John Pelan, in a limited trade paperback edition.

The U.K. publisher, Pumpkin Press, published all three volumes of Nancy Kilpatrick's "Power of the Blood" series in sturdy trade paperback editions plus hardcover and trade paperback editions of Dennis Etchison's Lizzy Borden novel, *Double Edge*, previously published only in a mass market edition in the U.S. They also published Campbell's collection, mentioned above.

Donald M. Grant, Publisher, re-released the first three books in Stephen King's "Dark Tower" series as a packaged set. *The Gunslinger* (originally published in 1982), is a third edition, and has been issued with a new dust jacket; *The Drawing of the Three* (1987), is a second edition, and was also issued with a new dust jacket, and with ten new prints by artist Phil Hale. The third book, *The Wastelands* (1991), will be from the first edition. The books are available only as a set in a single two-tone slipcase.

Fedogan & Bremer published Adam Niswander's Cthulhu novel, *The Sand Dwellers*, in a trade edition. The book has jacket art and interior illustrations by H. E. Fassl.

Silver Salamander published three limited editions of *Ladies' Night*, a short novel by Jack Ketchum. The British Fantasy Society published *Long Memories: Recollections of Frank Belknap Long* by Peter Cannon, with an afterword by Ramsey Campbell. This is a sixty-eight-page booklet detailing the final years of Frank and Lyda Long as seen through the eyes of Peter Cannon. Cannon was a close friend of the Longs, and this memoir is a moving biography.

Children's Books

Boshbloberbosh by J. Patrick Lewis and illustrated by Gary Kelley (Harcourt Brace Creative Editions) is a sprightly and informative biography of Edward Lear written and illustrated very much in the spirit of the Victorian gentleman's own nonsense verse. The reader follows Lear from his birth as the twentieth of twenty-one children, to his visits to the zoo, where he perfected his parrot drawings, to the drawing lessons that he gave to Queen Victoria, etc. Rich in material gleaned from a variety of sources, this is a wonderful entertainment for child and adult.

The Ink Drinker by Eric Sanvoisin; translated by George Moroz, illustrations by Martin Matje (Delacorte Press); is a twisted little story about a boy who hates reading and is stuck for summer break in his father's bookstore. One day he spies a strange man drinking from a book with a straw—a vampire who drinks ink! and follows him. This is a terrific gift book.

Alice's Adventures in Wonderland by Lewis Carroll, illustrated and with photographs by Abelardo Morell (Dutton) is an odd version of the classic. Abelardo has taken the Tenniel illustrations, cut them up and created collages overlapped with photographs of real objects—tables, tea sets, books—to give a three-dimensional effect. A cute gimmick, but it won't take the place of any other versions of the classic.

Baba Yaga and the Wish Doll retold by Hiawyn Oram and illustrated by Ruth Brown (Dutton Children's Books). In this version the old witch (pretty sexy, in fact) is surprisingly self-aware as her child-gobbling toads tell her "you are truly terrifying." The too-good little girl is thrown out of the house by her Horrid and Very Horrid sisters until she brings back one of the Baba Yaga's toads in a jewel-encrusted collar. The interior art is better than the cover would suggest.

The Crane Wife retold by Odds Bodkin and illustrated by Gennady Spirin

(Gulliver Books, Harcourt, Brace) is the story of a poor, lonely sailmaker who finds a beautiful but mysterious woman at his door one day. This simple rendition of a Japanese folk tale is heartbreaking. The illustrations are exquisite, making it a collectible for those who love Japanese art, as well as a lovely book for children.

The Little Buggers: Insect and Spider Poems by J. Patrick Lewis with pictures by Victoria Chess (Dial Books for Young Readers) contains charming odes to the rhinoceros beetle, doodlebugs, and a host of other insects and spiders, some of whom attend the wedding of the spider and the fly. Unfortunately, the groom disappears before the honeymoon is over. The poems are cute and the pictures wonderful. This is the perfect book to entrance young readers into the joys of studying (or at least, not grimacing with repugnance at) insects.

There's a Hair in My Dirt: A Worm's Story by Gary Larson (HarperCollins) is a charming, funny, and educational lesson in ecology and the lifestyles of some vertebrates and invertebrates as daddy earthworm tells the facts of life to his disgruntled son. By the imaginative author of *The Far Side*.

Squids Will Be Squids is a less successful collaboration than usual by the outstanding team of Jon Scieska and Lane Smith (Viking). Their two previous collaborations, *The True Story of the Three Little Pigs* and *The Stinky Cheese Man* have been clever, as well as silly and visually fun. While the illustrations by Smith in *Squids Will Be Squids* are as good as ever, the so-called fables themselves are simply silly, often missing their mark.

Douglas Florian uses splashes of watercolor to accompany his smart, instructive spider and insect poems in *Insectlopedia* (Harcourt Brace). He occasionally uses the type of the poetry to illustrate some of the creatures about which he writes, for example, the "Inchworm" poem is printed out to look like an inchworm. Another perfect example of how to introduce children to insects, spiders, and poetry—without terror.

My Town by William Wegman (Hyperion) finds Wegman transforming his weimaraners even more than ever into almost seamless dog-men and women as schoolboy Chip wanders around his town photographing the "townspeople" (all dogs) trying to think up an interesting topic for a school report.

It's Disgusting and We Ate it!: True Food Facts from Around the World and Throughout History by James Solheim and illustrated by Eric Brace (Simon & Schuster Books for Young Readers) is another educational and entertaining book for kids with straight facts and amusing illustrations about some of the stranger creatures eaten by humans.

Odds and Ends

A Morning's Work: Medical Photographs from the Burns Archive & Collection 1843–1939 (Twin Palms Publishers). Dr. Stanley Burns has been collecting and archiving early medical photographs for over twenty-five years, creating the most extensive (more than a half-million photographs) collection documenting the first century of medical photography. Dr. Burns annotates each of the 127 black-and-white and color plates, with details about the subjects and photographers plus some sociological commentary. Disturbing, shocking, thought provoking.

Special Cases: Natural Anomalies and Historical Monsters by Rosamond Purcell (Chronicle Books) is based on the exhibition curated by the author in 1994. Purcell is well known for her disturbing and beautiful photographs of medical subjects. This is the first book in which she adds her voice—erudite and enthralling—as she writes about the subjects of the historical images exhibited. Purcell has documented many of the rumors that surrounded "anomalous beings" throughout the centuries, creating a moving series of vignettes.

Police Pictures: The Photograph as Evidence (SF Moma/Chronicle Books) was published to accompany the eponymous exhibit at the San Francisco Museum of Modern Art. The text traces the history of crime photography and its use in support of the early pseudosciences physiognomy and phrenology. So the "evidence" is not only of crime scenes, but also the supposedly physical characteristics of the criminal mind as viewed by the camera. The photographs show prostitutes, one of the co-conspirators of the Lincoln assassination, Baby Face Nelson and Pretty Boy Floyd. Also shown are people made "criminal" by circumstance: Native Americans, Southern slaves, Algerian women photographed by French troops, and some of the thousands held by the Cambodian Khmer Rouge in their torture camp.

The Red Hourglass: Lives of the Predators by Gordon Grice (Delacorte) reads like a novel. The intrepid and obsessive Grice leads the reader on an exploration of the life and habits of the black widow spider, the preying mantis, the rattlesnake, the pig, and other predatory creatures. He's an expert observer of the minute. In his essay on the pig, he proposes that the Jewish and Muslim taboos on eating pigs might be derived less from the common wisdom that the meat might harbor parasites than the fact that the stony ground of Palestine made deep burial difficult and wild pigs would devour corpses.

Splendid Slippers: A Thousand Years of an Erotic Tradition by Beverly Jackson (Ten Speed Press) is a riveting, profusely illustrated history of the Chinese custom of footbinding. This book contends that the tradition was widespread in China by the 1890s and that nine-tenths of the women had bound feet. With gorgeous color photographs.

Paper Tiger, now an imprint of Collins & Brown-U.K. reissued the Peter Dickinson/Wayne Anderson collaboration *The Flight of Dragons*. In it, Dickinson semi-seriously speculates on the evolution, the life cycle, the means of locomotion, and the slaying of dragons using folk tales, legends, and historical evidence that they really did exist. Anderson's serious black-and-white sketches and usually whimsical color illustrations nicely complement the text.

Barlowe's Inferno by Wayne Barlowe (Morpheus International) combines the almost-repulsive with the beautiful. This talented artist imagines mutilated grotesques made of stone and other tortured figures worthy of a Clive Barker movie. The design of the book is utterly effective with the stark text by Barlowe juxtaposed with the denizens of hell. Tanith Lee contributes the introduction.

Peeping Tom by Leo Marks (Faber & Faber) contains the screenplay of the horror film directed by Michael Powell and a fascinating interview with Leo Marks, the screenwriter, whose job as head of Codes and Ciphers for SOE (Special Operations Executive) during World War II inspired the screenplay. *Peeping Tom* was so controversial at the time it was made that it destroyed Powell's career, but today it's considered a masterpiece of terror.

Prisoners by Arne Svenson (Blast Books)—Arne and his sister Kristina Svenson happened upon twelve stark, early twentieth-century glass-plate negatives of mugshots in an antique store. They tracked down a stash of 500. After more research, he discovered that the photographs were taken in Maryville, a town in the Sacramento Valley in California by a Mrs. Smith, who was contracted by the city for eight years to photograph all incoming prisoners. Svenson managed to piece together about 200 case histories to go with the portraits. What you get is a compelling book of early photography and a historical record of the crimes of that period.

Spectrum 5: The Best in Contemporary Fantasy Art edited by Cathy Fenner and Arnie Fenner proves without a doubt that fantasy and horror art is alive and flourishing. This year's volume is the most varied so far, showcasing breathtaking pieces of art in every medium from well-known artists and unknowns. Even the three-dimensional work (which in the past I've found pallid or just plain bad) is excellent. The editors also provide a useful overview of the field and define the various categories in which the art was judged. This belongs on every art lover's bookshelf.

A new book by Dave McKean is a must-have for anyone entranced by his artwork, as I am. *Option: Click* is a book of his photographs (Allen Spiegel Fine Arts/Hourglass) meant to accompany exhibitions of his art. Sepia tone images, single page mysteries, collage, superimposition, portraits, odd juxtapositions, the organic and inorganic, masks. With text provided by the artist and a brief introduction by Jon Hassell. Also, Kitchen Sink Press has collected McKean's *Cages* into one big beautiful hardcover edition.

Small Press Addresses

Ash-Tree Press, P.O. Box 1360, Ashcroft, BC V0K 1A0, Canada; E-mail: ash-tree@mail.netshop.net.

Alchemy Press: 46 Oxford Road, Acocks, Green Birmingham B27 6DT, England; E-mail: peter@alchemypress.demon.co.uk.

Borgo Press, P.O. Box 2845, San Bernadino, CA 92406-2845; fax: (909) 888-4942.

CD Publications: P.O. Box 943, Abingdon, MD 21009.

Dark Highway Press: 2519 South Shields #117, Fort Collins, CO 80526; E-mail: bovberg@frii.com.

Dark Raptor Press: P.O. Box 2242, Clay, NY 13041; E-mail: nightflier@mindspring.com.

Deadline Press: P.O. Box 2808, Apache Junction, AZ 85200; E-mail: diepool@aol.com.

Durtro: BM Wound, London WC1N 3XX, U.K.

Fedogan & Bremer: 3721 Minnehaha Avenue South, Minneapolis, MN 55406; E-mail: fedbrem@mail.visi.com.

Galley Press: 50 Arthur Street, Surrey Hills, NSW 2010 Australia.

Gauntlet Publications: 309 Powell Road, Springfield, PA 19064; E-mail: gauntlet66@aol.com.

Hard Shell Word Factory: P.O. Box 161, Amherst Jct., WI 54407; E-mail: books@hardshell.com.

The Hazelwood Press: 2633 Hazelwood Road, Lancaster, PA 17601.

Hobgoblin Press: P.O. Box 806, Bristol, RI 02809; E-mail: lordshazam@geocities.com.

Hypatia Press: c/o Escape Books, 225 W. 7th, Eugene, OR 97401; E-mail: hypatia@teleport.com.

Marion Zimmer Bradley Literary Trust, P.O. Box 249, Berkeley, CA 94701-0249.

MirrorDanse Books: P.O. Box 3542, Parramatta, NSW 2124 Australia.

Necro Publications: P.O. Box 540298, Orlando, FL 32854-0298; E-mail: necrodave@aol.com.

Obsidian: 37800 38th Avenue S., Auburn, WA 98001; E-mail: Mjobsidian @aol.com.

Pumpkin Books: P.O. Box 297, Nottingham NG2 4GW, U.K.; E-mail: pumpkinbooks@netcentral.co.uk.

Quarry Press: P.O. Box 1061, Kingston, Ontario K7L 4YS, Canada; E-mail: info@quarrypress.com.

RazerBlade Press: 186 Railway Street, Splott, Cardiff, CF2 2NH, Wales; E-mail: darren.floyd@virgin.net.

Sarob Press: Brynderwen, 41 Forest View, Mountain Ash, Mid Glamorgan, Wales CF45 3DU.

Sideshow Press: P.O. Box 945, Brewerton, NY 13029-0945 E-mail: sideshow@dreamscape.com

Silver Salamander Press: 4128 Woodland Park Ave. N., Seattle, WA 98103 E-mail: Jpelan@cnw.com

Subterranean Press: P.O. Box 190106, Burton, MI 48519, E-mail: wks@tir.com

Tachyon Publications: 1459 18th Street #139, San Francisco, CA 94107

Tartarus Press: 5 Birch Terrace, Hangingbirch Lane, Horam, East Sussex, TN21 0PA, England; E-mail: tartarus@pavilion.co.uk.

Tattered Pages Press, 13 Spring Lane, Barrington Hills, IL 60010.

Useful Organizations

The British Fantasy Society is open to anyone. For information write: The British Fantasy Society, the BFS Secretary, Peter Coleborn, 2 Harwood Street, Stockport, SK4 1JJ, U.K. Members receive the informative bimonthly Newsletter, *Prism*, in addition to *Dark Horizon* (mentioned above). The society organizes the annual FantasyCon, the British Fantasy Convention, and its membership votes on the British Fantasy Awards.

The Horror Writers Association is an organization of writers and publishing professionals dedicated to promoting the interest of writers of horror and dark fantasy. There is a bimonthly newsletter with market reports, useful columns, etc. The HWA also hosts an annual meeting and banquet at which the Bram Stoker Awards for Superior Achievement are given out in several categories. For information write to: P.O. Box 50577, Palo Alto, CA 94303 or check out the organization's Web pages at: http://www.horror.org/

Horror and Fantasy in the Media: 1998

Edward Bryant

It's the End of the World as We Know It . . .

As the western Christian millennium winds down, it is difficult for any one observer to keep track of such global phenomena as the screened entertainment business. 1998 was, for example, the year in which the massive Indian film industry, second in volume only to the U.S., complained mightily of cultural and fiscal imperialism. Filmmakers in Calcutta and Bengal and Madras pointed out that Hollywood was making significant inroads into their domestic box office grosses. Indian cinema, it should be pointed out, is a hotbed for potboilers chock-full of melodrama, fantasy, violence, and horrific elements.

If you're curious and have a local Indian video rental storefront placed right beside your Asian videotique, then you're in luck. Otherwise you'll have to start searching the Internet for obscure sources of the non-English grotesque. One of the best orientation manuals, defacto shopping guides, and invaluable information resources is *Mondo Macabro: Weird & Wonderful Cinema from Around the World* by Pete Tombs (St. Martin's Press, 1998). The book is exactly what the title suggests.

Here at home, 1998 was particularly notable for the number of mainstream films, both from independents and major studios, that incorporated elements of the fantastic. Generally this was done without fanfare or fuss.

To wit, the following. You'll find that my annotated list of examples is woefully incomplete. Adding your own discoveries is part of the fun.

The Coolest of the Cool

Gods and Monsters: This splendid film adaptation of Christopher Bram's speculative biographical novel of director James Whale, *Father of Frankenstein*, has done well for itself at the box office and in the awards ceremonies. Call *Gods and Monsters* something of a stealth meta-horror picture. It's written and directed by Bill Condon, director of *Candyman II: Farewell to the Flesh*. Clive Barker executive-produced. Ian McKellen, Lynn Redgrave, and Brendan Fraser all excelled in their roles. The movie has considerable to say about friendship, loyalty, and honesty, and does so with eloquence. It also incorporates into its structure—sometimes subtly, sometimes with unnerving gusto—a wide variety of horror film-based allusions and references. Ultimately it honestly and successfully wrenches at the viewer's emotions with an innocently ingenuous image in the rain-soaked night that should choke up all but the most jaded action-thriller-addicted viewers. Relationships and art—two universal concerns—are both splendidly treated. So far as I'm concerned, *Gods and Monsters* is the year's high point for the dark fantastic.

Beloved: Toni Morrison's novel of post-slavery (Ohio, 1873) black life. A woman (Oprah Winfrey in an earnest and solid role) deals with the unhappy ghost of the babe she murdered to save it from returning to slavery's chains. The ultimate healing (played more as a church-lady exorcism) is given a game try by a terrific cast and director Jonathan Demme. It bombed at the box office. Gorgeously shot, the earnest leaden pace attempts to capture the detail and texture of a literary novel. The poltergeist-haunted house/demonic child effects actually work against the author's original intention. But the power of intention still makes this one of the year's pictures to note and seek out if you didn't see it on the big screen.

Lawn Dogs: If you can believe it, this modest art-house indie starring Sam Rockwell and extraordinary newcomer Mischa Barton combines Russia's Baba Yaga legend with a surreal contemporary Kentucky landscape, something of a modern Southern Gothic. Written by Kentucky poet Naomi Wallace, it's directed by the very British John Duigan (*Sirens*). And yes, it is an unregenerate fantasy. Seek it out at your video store.

Pi: Filmed for virtually no budget at all in hyperkinetic grainy black and white for novice director Darren Aronofsky, this feature played the festivals and then was rapidly picked up for art house release. Sean Gullette's portrayal of Max, the hermetic mathematician who's built his own homegrown version of a supercomputer and believes he's found a way to order chaos, is suitably paranoid. And yes, it's an intellectual science/fantasy mystery/thriller about the enigmas of math. Oh, and Jewish mysticism, too. And massive oblique conspiracies on the part of maybe the government, perhaps Wall Street. The film's sheer chutzpah astonishes.

Dark City: I could quarrel just a bit with the story, but not with the visual look of this gorgeously realized noir vision of a grimy city that's Everywhere and No Place simultaneously, along with a beset hero (Rufus Sewell) and a whole gang of black-garbed alien revenants played by such actors as Richard O'Brien. This is director Alex Proyas's first film since the similarly dark visual feast, *The Crow*. Though Sewell, O'Brien, Kiefer Sutherland, William Hurt, Jennifer Connelly, and plenty of others in the cast are just fine, the city is the true visionary star of the piece—imagine Tim Burton's lovely Gotham, taken a quantum level higher. It's a banquet for the senses, and gives the film's equally dark mood a lovely park in which to play. If the unfolding plot's a bit too familiar for experienced fans of the written fantastic, that's a small quibble. *Dark City*'s aimed more for the eyeball than the brain.

The Butcher Boy: There's just enough outright fantasy in this adaptation by Neil Jordan of Patrick McCabe's darkly comedic novel. Young Eamonn Owens plays the increasingly disturbed Irish boy Francie Brady with dedicated relish. Stephen Rea plays Francie's drunken father convincingly as the boy spirals into a genuinely ghastly farrago of madness and violence. Oh yes, don't miss Sinead O'Connor as the Madonna. Yes, *that* Madonna. The Biblical original one....

The Truman Show: Peter Weir returns to direct Jim Carrey's most serious role since the underrated *Cable Guy.* The gimmick's not new to the hardened science-fiction audience, but the public was wowed. Poor Truman Burbank slowly discovers that his whole comfortable life has been continuously broadcast entertainment to the entire world and that his circumscribed environment is one huge set (in our reality, the disturbingly planned community of Seaside, Florida). Ed Harris plays the godlike director. This accumulation of talent keeps things moving. With his script for *The Truman Show,* Andrew Niccol offers some solid supporting evidence that he's becoming the most impressive exponent of SF in the mainstream cinema. Last year he wrote and directed the exemplary *Gattaca.*

Pleasantville: Also familiar but fun is Gary Ross's variation on a variety of vintage *Twilight Zone* scenarios. With an assist from a supernatural TV repairman (a scary Don Knotts), squabbling sibs Reese Witherspoon and Toby Maguire find themselves transplanted from the nineties into a literally black-and-white fifties family sitcom. And that is *really* scary. Catalyzed by the interlopers, a loss of innocence (characterized by the intrusion of color) begins to seep into the monochrome pocket-universe of the title. In his final role, the late J. T. Walsh enlivens the role of an unregenerate Chamber of Commerce head.

Striking the Offbeat Note

Apt Pupil: Have you noticed that many of the best Stephen King Hollywood adaptations are taken from his nonhorror works? I could cite *Stand By Me, Shawshank Redemption, Dolores Claiborne,* etc. *Apt Pupil* showcases Ian McKellen's other great role this year, playing the elderly Nazi war criminal who just wants to live out his life peacefully. But then he's uncovered by high school kid Brad Renfro who decides he'd rather soak up increasingly seductive stories of what the Third Reich was *really* like rather than turn the old guy in to the Nazi hunters. Bryan Singer *(The Usual Suspects)* tautly directs, cinematographer Newton Thomas Sigel gives the film a richly saturated look, and John Ottman's extraordinary score layers the mood expertly. Whether you've read King's novella or not, don't expect a Hollywood-ized upbeat version.

Smoke Signals: Adapted by Sherman Alexie from stories in his collection *The Lone Ranger and Tonto Fistfight in Heaven* and directed by first-timer Chris Eyre, this is a finely crafted film capturing the contemporary Native-American experience as no other movie has done. Quite aside from being a first-rate production, it affords the alert viewer and collector of cinematic and literary trivia the chance to spot one quick moment when one of the characters, commenting bemusedly on the interface of white literary culture with the American-Indian experience, lists *The Last of the Mohicans* and Connie Willis's "The Last of the Winnebagos."

Six-String Samurai: Apparently made for the cost of the average used car (or less), this is a highly odd but equally entertaining riff on the *Mad Max* approach to the future. Filmmaker Lance Mungia gives us a millennial vision of a devastated America in which the (musical) King is Dead and freelance musicians from all over the endless wasted landscape are converging on Las Vegas for the choosing of the new cultural icon. *Film Threat* gave it five stars. What can I say? The film includes music and an appearance early on by the Red Elvises.

Dangerous Beauty: The world of 16th-century Venice is so distant from most of us, this might as well be viewed as a lush fantasy. Directed by Marshall Herskovitz, Catherine McCormack stars as a courtesan simply attempting to survive and prosper in the court of the time. Based on the real life of Venetian beauty Veronica Franco, the film could be considered a genuinely literate bodice-ripper. Rufus Sewell also stars. Neat digital effects bring to life both the ancient city and its ship-filled harbor.

The Spanish Prisoner: David Mamet wrote and directed this paranoid suspense puzzle about the convolutions attending on the invention of a highly lucrative new scientific discovery. Campbell Scott's the out-classed inventor, Ben Gazzara's his calculating boss. Rebecca Pidgeon plays an all too innocent secretary. And Steve Martin carries off a wonderful turn as a charming mystery man who is all too full of engrossing stories. The film is every bit as complicated as the confidence game of the title.

Passion in the Desert: Writer/director/producer Lavinia Currier took on a major challenge when she decided to adapt an 18th-century story by Balzac about a young officer separated from Napoleon's Egyptian expeditionary force and lost in the desert. Played well by Ben Daniels, the officer totally detaches from civilization in order to survive, and ends up in an offbeat, sensual relationship with a leopard. The preternatural forces of the primeval desert are weird indeed. Gratifyingly, no cats or humans were seriously injured in the filming of this movie.

The Hanging Garden: The film starts with a perfectly normal-seeming marriage—until the bride's brother shows up after a ten year absence. When he left home, he was fat, unattractive, and fully in the closet. Now he's come out of his chrysalis (and closet). But he and the family are still working through enormous dysfunction. The resulting ghosts may or may not be literal, but they are the key to the twisted lives herein.

Déjà Vu: Henry Jaglom's a distinctive filmmaker, but never a predictable one. In this surreal mystery, Victoria Foyt, Vanessa Redgrave, Stephen Dillane, and Redgrave's mom all come together in a peculiar tale about love and loss, destiny and fate. Poor Foyt is a busy professional woman about to be married; then she meets an older woman with an affecting story about love and loss. The woman disappears, but leaves Foyt with a striking piece of jewelry—and that becomes the key to a convoluted journey through fractured but suspiciously familiar memories.

Bulworth: Warren Beatty plays the lead and is the creative brains behind this satire of American presidential politics. The title character is an incumbent liberal California senator who has a breakdown during the campaign primaries and takes (in the eyes of his staff) an alarming veer into candid speech and honest behavior. One might consider this a peculiar alternate world (pre-Clinton impeachment trial). Beatty's character empathizing with the black community and becoming a political rapper in the hip-hop world is worth the price of admission—or a rental.

Fallen: The year started out with this Denzel Washington thriller about a tough cop in a mano-à-mano with a demon who can possess humans and who passes from body to body by a simple touch. Dark and disturbing, the film works fine for most of its length, only falling a little short at the very end.

Henry Fool: Hal Hartley crafted this extremely Faustian tale in which a Queens garbageman abruptly transforms into a world-famous poet thanks to the good offices of the title character. James Urbaniak, Thomas Jay Ryan, and Parker Posey star.

Buffalo 66: Actor Vincent Gallo's first venture into direction is a doozy. Location filming in deepest winter in Buffalo, New York looks oddly parallel to the Antarctica of *The Thing.* No digitized shape-shifting monsters here. There are unholy creatures of a more realistic bent, however. Most of the cast portrays absolutely crazed individuals in eerily surreal terms. Christina Ricci adds sweet spice. Ben Gazzara and Anjelica Huston appear as parents hailing—maybe literally, perhaps metaphorically—from another space-time continuum.

A Touch of Evil: You want *real* horror? Orson Welles is still unforgettable in this restored, supplemented re-release of his 1958 masterpiece. In this tale of crime, betrayal, violence, and general chicanery in a tattered Mexican border town, Charlton Heston, Janet Leigh, Akim Tamiroff, and Marlene Dietrich all do very well indeed; but it's the masterful Welles, playing the corrupt, internally decaying local cop who rightfully steals the show.

The Medium and the Message

The X-Files: Fight the Future: Seeing Scully and Mulder deal with secret government/alien conspiracies on the very large screen is fun, but the feature doesn't come across as appreciably more ambitious than a two-part TV episode. The effects are nice, ranging from weird happenings in the corn-belt to an under-ice alien repository in the Antarctic. Producer/creator Chris Carter had said that the movie would be both intriguing for series fans and intelligible to the new viewer. He may have been half right.

Star Trek: Insurrection: I can never recall whether the conventional wisdom says it's the odd or the even *Star Trek* movies that are the good ones. . . . I think *ST: Insurrection* is number nine, for what that's worth. At any rate, this is a serviceable installment in which Captain Picard (the always dependable Patrick Stewart) and crew deal with aliens, interstellar politics, and beset indigenes living in a (what else?) virtual Eden. Anthony Zerbe's a Federation admiral in cahoots with fairly bland aliens led by F. Murray Abraham. The heroics are all suitably so. Donna Murphy lends considerable spark to the role of a, well, mature woman who takes a hankering to the Captain.

Lost in Space: The Robinson family returns from TV purgatory, this time with William Hurt and Mimi Rogers as the parents, accompanied by their three often obnoxious kids. Gary Oldman has some presence as the villainous Dr. Smith. Matt LeBlanc's the pilot. And yes, the robot's back. There are plenty of effects:

morphing space armor, literal cybernetic bugs, hyperspace travel. You know the drill. Really, the only thing missing is a coherent story.

Nothing's More Certain Than Death, Taxes, and Vampires

Meet Joe Black: Ah, there's nothing like attempting to show the human side of death. "Suggested by" 1934's *Death Takes a Holiday, Meet Joe Black* spent three hours accomplishing a much less magical job of depicting the personification of Death entering our world, checking out the human condition, and ultimately falling in love. As the avatar of the Grim Reaper, Brad Pitt did a pretty fair job of playing an alien attempting to adapt to a (to him) strange landscape. Unfortunately the four-authored script gave his character all manner of misleading signals. As the soon-to-be-terminal mortal who initially intrigues Mr. Death, Anthony Hopkins displayed his customary accomplished style. Is director Martin Brest's film a provocative and affecting meditation on mortality and its finality? Only for the very young. Is it flossy brain candy for all ages? Definitely. Don't miss the startlingly violent scene early on when Pitt's mortal avatar gives up the ghost so that Death can have a body.

What Dreams May Come: Rather more ambitious than *Meet Joe Black,* Richard Donner's *What Dreams May Come* adapts the thoughtful novel by Richard Matheson in an attempt to treat the nature of death and what comes after. Robin Williams plays the poor schnook who gets a pungent taste of Job by first losing his two kids, then dying himself as a good samaritan in a stupid car disaster, *then* has to cope post-life with his despondent wife's suicide. He's got to develop latent personal inner resources with a bit of divine guidance from Cuba Gooding, Jr. While the viewer's brain may tend to glaze over with the picture's leaden pace and slogging philosophical dialogues, the eye is entranced. Visually the film's splendid, whether the imagery captures heavenly landscapes depicted literally as inhabited painted canvases, or the dark inverted cathedral devised by the dead widow as her personal hell. The heaven-and-hell debates may remind you of being trapped in a gaggle of argumentative Unitarians after a box social.

Blade: On the vampire front, two films made a fair splash. For my jaded sensibility Wesley Snipes's *Blade* easily outdistanced *John Carpenter's Vampires.* Though Stephen Norrington directed *Blade,* Wesley Snipes is the motive force behind this adaptation of Marvel Comics' series about the half-human, half-vampire hybrid who carries quite a grudge about his unhuman heritage. As the eponymous character, Snipes lends a great deal of power and charisma to the role. He is never upstaged by an exceedingly grizzled-looking Kris Kristofferson as a helpful human scientist. Steven Dorff effectively evokes the head bad guy, an ambitiously ultra-contemporary vampire with serious upwardly mobile aspirations. *Blade's* solid entertainment value has been rewarded with word that a sequel is on the way.

John Carpenter's Vampires: This modest director achieves the dubious goal of capturing the very worst tone of Sam Peckinpah. Based loosely on John Steakley's *Vampire$,* the film sensibly cast James Woods as the obsessed Jack Crow, contemporary contract-slayer of vampires for the Vatican. Played out in the arid landscape of the Southwest, this film tries to demonstrate some macho bonding by tough-minded, action-oriented guys; even as the lone significant female character demonstrates a hard time speaking, acting, or even justifying taking up useful space. It's Peckinpah country, but not a *good* Peckinpah homage. *John Carpenter's Vampires* will never be mistaken for a *Wild Bunch* with stakes and garlic. If you want to see James Woods handle much more painful cinematic violence with crazed aplomb, check out Larry Clark's (*Kids*) impressive *Another Day in Paradise*.

Tripping the Dark Fantastic

Ever After: Drew Barrymore thoroughly enchants as a resourceful and self-sufficient young woman in this period piece taking as its conceit the notion that the Cinderella story really did have historical roots. Anjelica Huston breathes life into the role of the stepmother, not so much cruel as rationally pragmatic. As something of a bonus, Leonardo da Vinci shows up in sixteenth-century France.

Babe: Pig in the City: Director George Miller returns us to the genuinely entertaining world of *Babe*—excepting this time stranding the bright and resourceful pig in a fantabulous city with the wife (Magda Szubanski) of the bedridden farmer. After discovering a humane old hotel that accepts (and even encourages) beasts of the field and street, the out-of-towners find themselves scrambling to save their new colleagues from the obsessed clutches of the animal control bureau. The humor here is a tad more somber—and more forced—than in its predecessor. But the city, a deliberate visual mishmash of everything from Sydney to Hollywood, charms. And I'll always be a sucker for that supporting character staple, Ferdinand the duck.

The Mask of Zorro: With Anthony Hopkins playing the older, retired masked hero and Antonio Banderas recruited as the new generation Zorro-in-training, this latest version of the classic period pulpy adventure in Old Spanish California manages plenty of colorful action and screwy over-the-top wit without (at least most of the time) tipping over into complete camp. It does the job as a thoroughgoing entertainment. As the love interest, Catherine Zeta Jones plays her young woman as both gorgeous and independent.

The Mighty: Want a terrific modern fantasy blended skillfully with Arthurian legend? British actor/ director Peter Chelsom has done the trick expertly with *The Mighty*, adapted by Charles Leavitt from the Rodman Philbrick novel, *Freak the Mighty*. Set in bleakest Cincinnati, the unlikely friendship of the frail, birth defect-affected Freak (Kieran Culkin) and the enormous, traumatized, silent Max Kane (Elden Henson) is highly manipulative, but in thoroughly defensible ways. No mawkishness here as troubled kids learn about friendship and boldness of spirit. The grownups—Sharon Stone, Harry Dean Stanton, Gena Rowlands, Meatloaf, Gillian Anderson—are fine, but this is first and foremost a wonderfully affecting depiction of children's courage and soul.

A Pack of Splat with Mixed Results

Psycho: I've got to admit that I thought long and hard about whether I really wanted to go see Gus Van Sant's oddly faithful shot-by-shot remake of *Psycho*. Morbid curiosity won out. Anne Heche is quite an attractive update of Janet

Leigh's role, but she does end up in a most unflattering nude pose sprawled over the edge of the motel tub with her rear high in the air. Then there's Vincent Vaughan mugging Anthony Perkins in the Norman Bates part. Vaughan can be a fine villain—check out his psycho killer turn in the same year's thriller *Clay Pigeons*. In *Psycho* he cranks it up a touch too high on the old camp-o-stat. On the other hand, William H. Macy does just fine recapping Martin Balsam's detective role. Probably the worst problem the film can't overcome is that the original was designed for black and white—the visual look was shadowy Gothic. Ultimately, when the lights came up, I walked out of the theater shaking my head sadly. The new *Psycho*'s not really a bad movie. It is a heartbreakingly unnecessary one.

Halloween: H20: 1998 was the twentieth anniversary of John Carpenter's marvelous *Halloween*, with the younger Jamie Lee Curtis executing a wonderful performance as a young woman with brains, resourcefulness, and toughness battling the unstoppable psycho killer. So how did Miramax celebrate 20 years of masked Michael Myers running amuck with large knives? *Halloween: H20*. Jamie Lee Curtis returns as Laurie Strode two decades older, increasingly worn down by facing all the various issues of terrible memories and the knowledge that her bratty brother Michael is still out there. Now Laurie's got a teen son and is working as a college administrator, two horrific fates in themselves. Michael, of course, comes to visit with all the attendant mayhem. The devil is in the primary plot. It's business as usual in the abbatoir trade. The fun is in the details. There's a great set-piece scene when a mother traveling cross-country with her little daughter enjoys a most disquieting experience at a nearly deserted roadside rest area women's room. Janet Leigh has a cameo as her real-life daughter's secretary. But Laurie Strode's final auto-therapeutic act with a large ax somehow doesn't do justice to 20 years of suspense.

Urban Legend: Probably the best *Scream* clone of the year. Mostly shot in Canada by director Jamie Blanks from a script by Silvio Horta (a classic *Star Trek* fan perhaps?), the melodrama is set on a Northeastern college campus where a mysterious killer's (usually dressed modestly as an Eskimo in full winter garb) *modus operandi* is to orchestrate a series of murders based on all the best-known urban myths. You know the drill. It's all pretty standard stuff, but done with enthusiasm and some style. Robert Englund has a minor role as a collegiate urban folklore lecturer. If there's a pony in the cast, it's Loretta Devine playing a campus cop who devours old Pam Grier flicks and is better armed than any college officer this side of the hall monitors at Beirut Polytechnic.

I Still Know What You Did Last Summer: Yeah, yeah, the guy with hood and the hook is back. Director Danny Cannon doesn't add much to the tried-and-true teen psycho gore formula. Jennifer Love Hewitt, Brandy, Mekhi Phifer, Freddie Prinze, Jr., and most of the rest of the cast are all, well, *young*. Jeffrey Combs is a welcome token Old Guy.

Nightwatch: Ewan McGregor stars as a budget-conscious law student who takes a night shift job patrolling the creepy old medical examiner's building—with attendant morgue. Then there's the escalating matter of falling under suspicion as a serial killer who steals his victim's eyes. The film starts off creepy, but punks out. Josh Brolin plays an exceedingly suspicion-provoking best friend, Patricia Arquette is the loyal girlfriend, and Brad Dourif (what a surprise) plays a weird morgue doctor. But the real oddment is Nick Nolte, playing a troubled cop. One version of Nolte's ability to take a role over the top netted him an Oscar nomination for *Affliction*. *Nightwatch* is another version. I don't think it'll be seriously considered by the Academy.

Bride of Chucky: This sequel to three previous killer-doll movies comes awfully close to working very well indeed. Hong Kong director Ronny Yu's version contains a considerable amount of real wit for most of its length as white trash vamp Jennifer Tilly reveals an unusual old relationship with Brad Dourif before his soul was trapped in the midget body of a Chucky doll. The key phrase is "violently funny." As the film heads for its final half hour, the humor diminishes as the violence and gore crank up. Too bad. It's a near miss.

They're So *Animated*, He Said

Small Soldiers: If you liked the level of animation displayed in *Toy Story*, then this was your cup of tea. The old idea of kids' toys coming to life is more-or-less rationalized science fictionally, but the real appeal is, of course, the adventures of these high tech midgets as they attempt independent existence out in the world, but still obliged to cope with their toy manufacturer's programming. Tommy Lee Jones makes a great gung-ho leatherneck named Major Chip Hazard. The late Phil Hartman takes his final turn on the big screen as a terminally vague parent. The action's sufficient for the kid audience; the satiric commentary on merchandising, toys, and war will keep the adults awake.

Antz: Don't expect to learn a lot of real entymology from animated bug movies. *Antz* at least portrays its title characters as having six legs, but plays fast and loose with the ratio of male to female inhabitants in the ant colony. The script's funny enough, with a few very adult lines and Woody Allen supplying the protagonist's voice. It's a good cast, also including Sharon Stone, Christopher Walken, and Sylvester Stallone. All great fun, even if you find yourself itching as the closing credits roll.

A Bug's Life: This film's even less likely to get an award for popularizing real science. The ants in this one are all quadrupeds. At any rate, this is Pixar's entry into the world of insects, featuring the voices of such as Kevin Spacey, Julia Louis-Dreyfus, Phyllis Diller, and Dave Foley as Flik, the smartest ant in the story. The plot revolves around an ant colony freeing itself from bondage to an oppressive management by grasshoppers. The script appears to be more broadly aimed at an exceedingly wide audience, and doesn't have the cool in-jokes that *Antz* boasts.

Prince of Egypt: DreamWorks plays it utterly safe with this mainstream version of the story of Moses (the voice of Val Kilmer, who also gets to play God). Danny Glover does well as Moses' father-in-law, Jethro. Ralph Fiennes plays Rameses and Patrick Stewart expands upon his Capt. Picard role as Pharaoh Seti. Unsurprisingly, Old Testament savagery is toned down here. There's even a run at political correctness. As priests of Ra, Steve Martin and Martin Short do their best to get laughs. But there's certainly no joking about mass drownings in the Red Sea, the tossing of Hebrew infants to the crocodiles, or the arrival of the Angel of Death.

Mulan: Disney's entry into this year's animation sweepstakes is quite a good one. This is based on an old Chinese folk tale about the eponymous young woman, a loyal daughter who disguises herself as a man and fights in the Emperor's army in order to keep her parents alive and well. The fighting and action sequences are particularly effective. Eddie Murphy lending his voice to a wise-cracking pocket dragon seems a touch inappropriate. Actress Ming-Na Wen lends Mulan a good character voice. Forget the music by Matthew Wilder and David Zippel. Is the film an empowerment fantasy? Yep, and it works.

Killer B's

Tarzan and the Lost City: Novice director John Bruno filmed this harmless and amusing chapter whatever of the Tarzan saga on location in Africa. Casper Van Dien *(Starship Troopers)* plays the Lord of the Jungle with reasonable panache. As a bonus, the lost city of Opar shows up, though without La or many other trimmings. In this case, low budget means clean lines and a lack of flab.

Deep Rising: Once upon a time, apparently, this was going to be a big-budget major event sort of film. Something came a cropper in the pre-production process. The plot question: something big and hungry has taken over the world's largest cruise ship. Most of the crew and passengers have vanished—somewhere—when a gang of piratical hijackers comes on board. Dumb but fun, especially for such moments as a party of survivors venturing into a still-functional elevator. As they descend into the bowels of the ship, they hear a distant sinister sound of something big and probably ravenous. One asks with trepidation, "What *is* that?" Another adventurer, caught up in the still functioning Muzak, answers, "The Girl From Ipanema." Okay, I'm easily amused.

Phantoms: Dean Koontz's 1983 bestseller fared better in its translation to film than have most of his other books brought to screen. This is the one about the small Colorado mountain town in which a handful of bemused survivors try to figure out what suddenly caused most of the natives to disappear. Spotters of early appearances by young actors can rack up points for noticing such cast members as Ben Affleck and Rose McGowan. For older watchers, there's a comfortably worn Peter O'Toole.

Soldier: Kurt Russell had perhaps a dozen lines of dialogue in his role as a futuristic genetically modified super-soldier. The plot calls for him to be marooned on a distant junkyard planet so he can save the peaceful settlers by going up against his old masters. Directed by *Event Horizon*'s Paul Anderson, this is a nostalgically familiar plot. Worked for westerns. Works here on an unsophisticated basic level.

Sphere: With Samuel Jackson, Sharon Stone, Dustin Hoffman, and Peter Coyote in the cast, this adaptation of Michael Crichton's novel about a mysterious alien spacecraft found at the ocean's bottom should have had the cast and clout to be a major effort. But the script seems to have dictated otherwise. This is definitely a B-movie!

Between a Rock and a Hard Place

Deep Impact: Last year the cinematic Earth was ravaged by volcanos. This time, the summer doldrums were brightened by asteroid impacts. I hate to dignify escapist disaster fare with *too* much deep think, but *Deep Impact* probably out-pointed its rival for serious concerns. In other words, there was at least lip service paid to motivating character roles and attempting to point out some of the moral issues of surviving global devastation. Probably the most memorable scene for me was Tea Leoni's touching father-daughter reunion on the coast as a zillion-foot high blast wave rolls in from the sea. Come to think of it, it *did* remind one just a trifle of the novel *Lucifer's Hammer*.

Armageddon: Imagine John Wayne's portrayal of ace extinguisher-of-oil-well-infernos Red Adair in *The Hellfighters*, translated to sending Bruce Willis at the head of a crew of experienced roughnecks out into near-Earth space to blow up a chunk of space rock the size of Texas, and you can get your mind around *Armageddon*. Every time the plot action slows, the script directs a few more meteor fragments toward Paris or Beijing. Lots of sound and fury, but roughly as memorable as your last extra-large bag of movie popcorn. You might consider this Michael Bay's accompanying music video for Aerosmith's Oscar-nominated tune on the soundtrack.

Don't Play It Again, Sam. Please

Godzilla: Remakes aren't always a good idea. Take two: Remakes are *rarely* a good idea. Flush with clout and cash from *Independence Day*, director Roland Emmerich and producer Dean Devlin tackled that great, lovable, sushi-eating lizard, *Godzilla*. Looking at what turned out, one could wish that perhaps Gammera and Rodan should have been resuscitated too so that misery could be shared. This version of the big G is technologically superior—no short guy in a zippered rubber suit. These days Godzilla is much more a velociraptor sort of critter than the stately lumberer from decades past. But for all the effects budget, the monster's something of an enigma as he munches, crunches, and beds down in New York City. First, his relative size seems to fluctuate for no good reason. Second, when he smashes into a Manhattan office tower and uses it as his entrée to the Big Apple underworld for nefarious purposes of his (her?) own, nobody can figure out where that great reptile's disappeared. There don't seem to be a lot of contemporary mountain men present who can deduce that a monster-sized entrance wound with no corresponding exit hole in a major building just *might* be a clue. Matthew Broderick's on hand in a harmless counterpart to Raymond Burr's walk-on in the first *Godzilla*. French actor Jean Reno's a welcome relief later on, but he doesn't provide enough fresh air to sustain an entire stifling audience.

The Avengers: Oh, dear. Where's Patrick Macnee when you need him? Or Diana Rigg? Honor Blackman? Even Linda Thorson? What you get in this version of the characters recalled with great affection by many of us from the classic British TV show are Ralph Fiennes and Uma Thurman wearing a lot of really nifty clothes. The whole film is a beautifully designed compilation of sets and costumes. Hmm. Is it simply a two-hour fashion commercial? Very possibly. The script neglects to include significant plot or characterization. Even Sean Connery as the bad guy cannot inject vitality into this revenant. Knowledgeably nostalgic audiences stir and murmur at the moment when Patrick Macnee's disembodied voice briefly invigorates an invisible character, but the moment passes all too quickly. If only the balance of the film had done likewise. Sacrilege.

Rhymes (Loosely) With Niche

Practical Magic: Alice Hoffman supplied the magical book; Sandra Bullock and Nicole Kidman provide the good girl and confused girl characterizations respectively as the descendants of a long line of East Coast witchy women. A longstanding curse ensures that men don't last long in romances here. Things get worse when Kidman makes a classic bad choice and brings back a particularly obnoxious suitor from the grave. It's all reasonably amusing, but studiedly mainstream and very lightweight. It would seem director Griffin Dunne's not intending to delve far beneath the surfaces here.

Rough Magic: Director Clare Peploe's transmogrification of a 1944 James Hadley Chase novel called *Miss Shumway Waves a Wand* isn't *quite* a nineties equivalent of a classic screwball comedy, but it's close. Bridget Fonda plays a fifties L.A. magician's assistant who's on the lam for Mexico after her boss and mentor is shot, and she's none too keen on waiting around for her disastrous fiancé (D. W. Moffett) to make her life all better. Fonda takes her yellow Buick convertible and strikes out for the jungles of Mexico. She finds genuine shamanic magic, powerful hallucinogens, and a chance at genuine romance with a cynical journalist (Russell Crowe). Wit and intelligence keep things moving smartly.

One I Forgot Last Year

Kissed: Combine a Canadian first-time director named Lynne Stopkewich and a script based on a story by Barbara Gowdy, and—*voilà!*—you have an affectingly literate account of a young woman coming of age and her obsession with necrophilia. *Kissed* requires a deft and delicate hand, and director Stopkewich supplies it. Actress Molly Parker empathically brings to life girl-next-door Sandra—who, it happens, has from childhood entertained a sincere fascination with the secret life of the dead. Sensual and sincere, *Kissed* gives meaningful relationships with the deceased a true respect.

Bright Light, Small Screen

Babylon 5: Thanks to TNT, J. Michael Straczynski's enormously ambitious and complex five-year story arc for the universal crossroads of the giant Babylon 5 space station successfully completed its run, offering up two accompanying made-for-TV movies as a bonus. The final episode wrapped up most issues with Bruce Boxleitner's role as commander-in-chief coming to the end of his borrowed 20 years in the story framework. One neat added bonus was series creator Straczynski's cameo as the maintenance guy who actually turns out the lights and starts the self-destruct sequence when the obsolete B5 station is being decommissioned. If all goes well, *Crusade*, the follow-up series, will start airing in the summer of 1999. *Babylon 5* has been a magnum opus against which it will be difficult for even the original creator to match. But J. Michael Straczynski's talent is broad and deep enough to do it.

Buffy the Vampire Slayer: Joss Whedon's teen comedic drama of high school demon hunters attempting to keep their bucolic California town free of the denizens of the underlying Hell Mouth continued to skate along, thanks to a great cast and sharp writing. One semi-regular character got killed off; another was consigned to hell for his misdeeds. Other regulars learned to deal with becoming, variously, a witch, a shapeshifting werewolf, and a guy who'll apparently always have uncertain luck with girls. Besides solid, frequently inspired, writing, *Buffy*'s possessed of genuine warmth and charm. The creators are getting ready to pack a couple of the characters off to L.A. for an urban spinoff.

The X-Files: Indications are that 1998 is Chris Carter's hit series' penultimate season. As has become customary, the episodes bounced between the longtime major story arc of insidious alien invasion and massive conspiracy and coverups, and freestanding, wider ranging encounters with the paranormal. Two of the most notable episodes generated from outside the Carter shop: the enormously anticipated Stephen King episode about a cursed doll up there in Maine went through a variety of changes and apparently ended up as a child of compromise. The startling episode title was "Chinga." In interviews, King said that was just a random name, the appellation of the child's doll. On the other hand, many viewers familiar with idiomatic Spanish realized that the title was also the imperative form of the verb meaning to have sexual congress with, a phrase frequently linked with *"tu madre."* Whatever. The other notable "outsider" episode was "Kill Switch" by William Gibson and Tom Maddox, two writers well known for their cyberpunk expertise. The script concerned a rogue artificial intelligence and folded in a variety of intriguing characters both unfamiliar and regulars from the cast. The texture of plot and incident was more the complexity of the short story form rather than what most people associate with series television. In any case, agents Scully and Mulder continue subtly to evolve their image and their relationship, and the series still holds considerable value for entertainment and provocation.

Millennium: Thanks in large part, I suspect, to Chris Carter's *other* series, *Millennium*'s Frank Black (Lance Henriksen) continues to hang on to another season. Things change. Frank's now widowed, his little daughter orphaned, and he's parted company from the suspiciously paranoid and perhaps evilly subverted Millennium Group. So it's back to laboring for the FBI. The series is at its best with the freestanding episodes, particularly a holiday segment about psychic healing. The hour begins with three wiseguys taking a fourth colleague out into the snowy forest to shoot him. The killers are all singing Christmas carols. Now *that's* show business!

Brimstone: This Fox supernatural series died, coincidentally enough, after 13 episodes. One could wish it had stuck around a bit longer. Peter Horton played a cop sent to hell after killing the guy who raped his wife. The Devil cuts a deal with him: there's been a "jailbreak" in the Infernal Regions. More than a hundred of history's worst have fled back to Earth in the 1990s. Go back, catch them all (generally one a week . . .), and you'll earn a second chance at life. It's played semi-seriously with John Glover quite amusing and occasionally chilling as Old Scratch himself. The overall story arc contained some neat twists, such as when series regular, cop Terri Polo, turned out to be a deep-cover demon herself.

Cupid: This ABC series starring Jeremy Piven as Cupid himself, exiled by the gods to our contemporary world until he recruits 100 enduring love matches, was one of the genuine highlights of the television season. The writing, the conversational repartee, is sensational. Romance, wit—and first-rate characters.

Charmed: Aaron Spelling's new series is something of an attempt to be a *Buffy* for younger grown-ups. Problem is, *Buffy*'s adroit enough to fill that need for most age groups already. Shannen Doherty's back as the oldest of three sisters, all of whom have witchy powers and are trying to come to terms with being twenty-something young moderns in the city. The tongue-in-cheek moments are welcome; the chilling bits usually aren't cold enough. Ultimately the show just does not seem to be carving out its own personality with any great precision.

Xena and *Hercules:* Yep, they're still around and cranking right along. U.S. Secretary of State Madeleine Albright said, while visiting New Zealand, the home of Xena actress Lucy Lawless, "One of my role models, Xena, the warrior princess, comes from here." No word on whether, say, George Stephanopolous has said the equivalent thing about Herc.

Moby Dick: This cable miniseries might not appear on the surface to be science fiction. But Herman Melville was a sufficiently brilliant writer, he could have evolved, right? Adapted. Filmed in and around Australia, the saga of the doomed *Pequod* with its obsessed captain and unfortunate crew is slickly produced. But with Patrick Stewart cast as Capt. Ahab, it was hard not to view this production as an oddly faithful version of a *Star Trek* movie. Thinking of the wonderfully played Queequeg as being in the Klingon role helps. Never mind. It worked for *me.*

Live and in Person

Slava's Snowshow: This year I saw a considerable amount of live theater, but I'll constrain myself to mentioning only two productions of note. *Slava's Snowshow* is basically a one-man production that stopped in Denver on its way to Broadway. Slava Polunin's a gifted Russian student of classic clowning and the creator, author, and star of his *Snowshow.* He admits to taking inspiration from everyone from Stanislavski and Artaud to Meyerhold and Beckett. Typical of his sketches is a wonderful sequence in which he sails a boat/brass bed in the midst of a fog-shrouded stage; suddenly, without warning, another clown with a shark fin fixed to his back sails out from the side of the stage belly-down on a skateboard or some such, circles the bed, and then streaks back to safety. In another set-piece, Slava reacts in best mime-fashion to an approaching loud buzz, the sound of something huge but as yet invisible. At the propitious moment, a huge mutant insect drops onto the stage. It's all surreally funny. Slava possesses a strong sense of interaction with the audience. That's where the encore piece with huge inflated balls moving from the stage to the audience comes in. But to fully appreciate it, you'll have to participate, and I do unhesitatingly recommend that.

Theatre of the Vampires: Anne Rice biographer Katherine Ramsland and others have documented the proliferation of theater groups inspired by the Paris vampire performance group in *Interview With a Vampire.* One of the most accomplished and longest-tenured groups is based in Boulder, Colorado. It was my pleasure in 1998 to attend their single Halloween performance in a large and technically proficient theater. They're quite accomplished, combining eclectic music, dance, low trapeze art, sensual melodrama, and a touch of *Grand Guignol*. All in all, very impressive.

The Face of the Future

So what do the shifting features of the future hold for us in terms of mass entertainment? If I knew, I'd get the big bucks as a highly paid consultant. So I satisfy myself for the moment with trying to spot semiotic clues.

Instead of a crystal ball, I have before me a snow globe from PolyGram Video. This has to be the significant movie artifact of the year. Packaged with Poly-Gram's deluxe version of the videotape of the Coen brothers' terrific black comedy, *Fargo*, the globe elaborately encloses an outdoors scene with Sheriff Marge drawing down on a saintly-featured blonde dude cramming a shod and trousered human lower leg into the wood chipper. Do you all recall the scene? The "snow" that lazily drifts through the globe's fluid interior is a mix of white and crimson. You betcha, don't cha know!

There is a counterpart snow globe accompanying the reissue of *Halloween*, but the miniaturized drama isn't nearly so accomplished as it is in the *Fargo* scene. This coming year you might expect to see more elaborate globes with audio chips recapturing the dialog. Cool. It's all even more impressive than my electric roaring chomping *Godzilla* toilet paper dispenser.

Sometimes the film industry seems to possess an unexpected sense of profound irony. Whether deliberate or stochastic, good for them! See you at the movies.

Comics: 1998

Seth Johnson

The last decade has seen the explosion of the comic book and the graphic novel into a wider range of genres than has been seen since the earliest days of the medium. From fantasy and horror to science fiction, autobiography to satire, such a wealth of material awaits comics readers that a short column like this can only begin to cover it by offering up some of the best:

Jeff Smith's *Bone* (Cartoon Books), Dave Sim's and Gerhard's *Cerebus* (Aardvark-Vanaheim) and Mark Crilley's *Akiko* (Sirius) have all been mentioned in this column for the last three years, and they have again earned their place among the year's best comics. Fantastic art, epic storytelling, and tales that read well either in single-issue installments or trade paperback collections—these are comic storytelling at the top of its form.

Writer Caitlin R. Kiernan turned her talents to comics this year with *The Dreaming* (DC), weaving tales from the threads spun in Neil Gaiman's *The Sandman*. Gaiman himself has moved on to a number of projects since his World Fantasy Award-winning series came to a close. Among them was *Stardust*, Gaiman's prose fairy tale of a young man's quest for love and a fallen star. DC Comics, publisher of the original four installments of *Stardust*, released a limited-edition hardcover this year that included Charles Vess's beautiful illustrations. Those who have yet to read *Stardust* may have trouble locating that collector's item, but should be able to find either DC's trade paperback edition or Gaiman's stand-alone prose, released as the launch of Avon Books's Spike imprint in early 1999.

Prose released by comics publishers seemed to be a theme of 1998, as *Stardust* was followed by Dark Horse Comics's release of *Minidoka: 937th Earl of One Mile Series M*, a heretofore unreleased story by Edgar Rice Burroughs. Though it doesn't rank among Burroughs's best stories, it's worth reading for historical value, the fantastic illustrations by Michael Kaluta and the wonderful J. Allen St. John cover.

DC Comics's Vertigo imprint continues to maintain its reputation as one of the best places to find powerful, literate graphic storytelling. Not only does the imprint publish several of the titles already mentioned above, it's also the home of such varied ongoing series as Garth Ennis and Steve Dillon's twisted yet fascinating *Preacher*, Warren Ellis and Darrick Robertson's *Transmetropolitan*—the future as explored by rebel-with-a-laptop Spider Jerusalem, and Grant Morrison's labyrinthine conspiracy tale *The Invisibles*. But their shorter-term projects are just as worthy of attention, like Matt Howarth and Michael Avon Deming's one-shot update of 1940s DC detective *Doctor 13*, weaving the "skeptical rationalist" into a web of mystery, marital problems, madness, and electronic ghosts. To keep an eye on what Vertigo and its talented corps of creators are up to, pick up their annual *Winter's Edge* holiday special—this year's sampler featured not only ongoing Vertigo titles, but also Steve Gerber's *Nevada* and Ed Brubaker and Michael Lark's *Scene of the Crime*. Highly recommended.

An odd subset of horror comics currently on the shelves is the growing category of horror-humor. Check out Sergio Aragones' *Bogeyman* (Dark Horse Comics), Brian Augustyn's *Gross Point* (DC), William Morton's *Bar Crawl of the Damned* (MORTCO), and Steven Weissman's *Yikes!* (Alternative Press).

It's to be expected that fans of fantasy would eventually start creating comics about . . . well, fans of fantasy. Luckily, they're willing to admit how funny they can be. *Knights of the Dinner Table* (Kenzer & Company), by Jolly Blackburn, follows the misadventures of a fantasy role-playing group as they blitz and blunder through the best-laid plans of their gamemaster. *Dork Tower*'s John Kovalic (Corsair Publishing) also centers his stories around a gaming group, but leaves the kitchen table and follows its members as they stumble through their interactions with the rest of the world.

Speaking of fans—from *Mallrats* to *Chasing Amy*, director Kevin Smith has always featured comic books prominently in his movies. In 1998 he got the chance to write comics of his own, and he showed that his talents weren't limited to film. His popular Jay and Silent Bob characters (the latter played in his movies by Smith himself) starred in their own four-issue road trip from Oni Press, a hilarious story involving drugs, porno movies directed by Neil Patrick Harris (of *Doogie Howser, M.D.* fame), and a runaway orangutan. A pair of specials (also released by Oni) continued the story of his movie *Clerks*, chronicling the ongoing adventures of minimum-wage slaves. Finally, he signed on for a run of Marvel Comics's *Daredevil*, the beginning of which marked a major upswing in sales for the book as comics fans followed Smith's rising star.

One project that attracted an astounding array of talent from across the medium was Kitchen Sink Comix's *The Spirit: The New Adventures*, as writers and artists got the chance to pay homage to Spirit creator Will Eisner by telling new stories of Central City's masked-and-fedoraed crimefighter. Kitchen Sink also released three of four projected volumes bringing together Scott McCloud's acclaimed science fiction/superhero series *Zot!*, but sadly late in 1998 financial problems drove the venerable company to close its doors. Whether the last volume of the collected *Zot!* or any further new adventures of the Spirit will ever be released remains to be seen.

Crime comics continue to thrive in tune with the growing popularity of hard-boiled tales in movies and television. David Lapham's *Stray Bullets* (El Capitan) isn't coming out as regularly as it once did, but it's well worth the wait to catch the latest installment of his dark story of crime and cynicism. Brian Azzarello and Eduardo Risso told their own tale of hard luck on the tough streets with

Jonny Double (Vertigo), a Chandleresque saga of a tough gumshoe caught up in a scheme to steal seven million dollars from the mob.

Frank Miller took a vacation from his *Sin City* in 1998 to produce *300*, the story of three hundred Spartan soldiers's stand against the Persian army at Thermopylae. It's a powerful and groundbreaking story; we can only hope that the inevitable followers turning out historical comics (as Miller's *Sin City* pioneered the current wave of crime comics and his *The Dark Knight Returns* helped redefine the way superhero comics were written in the late 1980s) manage to imitate even a degree of his storytelling ability.

Miller made an appearance—in the form of one of his addresses on the First Amendment—in *Free Speeches* (Oni Press), a benefit comic supporting the Comic Book Legal Defense Fund. Neil Gaiman, Dave Sim, and a multitude of comics talents also contributed, along with Nadine Strossen, president of the ACLU. *Free Speeches*, and the CBLDF, are a reminder that comics which break the boundaries—like many of those mentioned in this column—come at a price beyond that printed on the cover, one of constant vigilance against would-be censors. (Those who don't understand why censors might want to attack a "kids' medium" like comics are directed to the organization's highly informative Web site at *www.cbldf.org*.)

Pushing the boundaries of comics with subtlety and a surreal sense of humor in 1998 were two very strange comics: *Sky Ape (les aventures)* (Slave Labor Graphics), by Phil Amara, Tim McCarney, and Richard Jenkins was on the surface an homage to the pulp magazines of yesteryear as it followed the adventures of a jetpack-wearing gorilla on a quest. But below that was a very strange story involving sodium pentothal-laced 'truth burgers,' references to the Smothers Brothers, and the long-lost Suspense Jacket. Just as hard to follow—but just as much fun—was Tony Millionaire's *Sock Monkey* (Dark Horse Comics), where the cloth animal of the title engaged in strange misadventures that usually involved strong drink and invariably ended in disaster. Very strange, but also very funny.

Alan Moore, the reclusive comics guru, turned out a few stories here and there but spent much of the year either on projects outside the medium or preparing for the launch of his "America's Best Comics" line by Wildstorm in 1999. For those who needed their fix in the meantime there was *Alan Moore's Songbook* (Caliber Comics), a collection of Moore's lyrics and poetry originally printed in Caliber's respected anthology titled *Negative Burn*. It's powerful and playful material (a mournful lament by Godzilla: "I'm so tired of trampling Tokyo. No interest remains/in eating cars or tearing down the elevated trains...."), beautifully illustrated by a host of terrific artists ranging from Dave Gibbons and James A. Owen to Colleen Doran and Phillip Hester.

Every time it's lamented that superhero comics have finally gone narratively bankrupt, someone picks up the torch and proves them all wrong. On this leg of the run the torch has been carried by Kurt Busiek, who continued to astound and amaze in 1998 with his deft storytelling. In *Thunderbolts* (Marvel) he tells the story of a group of villains masquerading as heroes who slowly and surprisingly find themselves adapting to their new roles. It's a story fraught with emotion, complexity, and resonance as Busiek reveals the inner cores of characters who were once nothing more than bank-robbing cannon fodder clashing with unitard-clad do-gooders. But Busiek saves his big guns for *Kurt Busiek's Astro City* (Wildstorm), where he shows that it's not just those in costumes who are comics's complex characters, that everyone from the starry-eyed kid just off the bus to the wife and children of a vigilante has a fascinating story to tell. Darn close to perfection.

Though they've slimmed down their line, DC Comics' Paradox Press imprint continued to expand its *Big Books* series in 1998 with *The Big Book of Vice* and *The Big Book of the Weird Wild West*. Both were chock full of factoids, anecdotes, and wit, and illustrated by artists recruited both from within and well outside the comics mainstream.

The comics and graphic novels in this essay should be available at your local comic shop, along with many other titles there wasn't room to mention. If you don't frequent a comic shop, you can find one by calling the Comic Shop Locator Service toll-free at 1–888–COMIC–BOOK.

Thanks to the folks at Pic-a-Book in Madison, Wisconsin and the fellows at FM International Distribution for their help in finding materials for this year's column.

Obituaries: 1998

Each year as inevitable as the passing of each season into the next, so the seasons of creative lives pass. Fertile, creative minds grow old, cease to bear fruit, inevitably give way to fresh, young developing talents that were unformed or even unborn not many seasons previous. And other talented creators meet with untimely death, through accident or illness, to leave a gap that none would have expected, which all mourn. So this past year we were lessened by the exit of many talented people. If any of these are unfamiliar to you, do yourself a kindness and discover the joys of the fruits of their talents.

Bob Kane, 83, created the Batman comic and a number of other characters. He was a trailblazer in the comic book industry, innovating with a "superhero" who didn't have super powers. Batman remains an enduring icon in modern comics, and has even survived translation to both big and little screen. **Akira Kurosawa,** 83, was a major film director, many of whose films employed elements of fantasy or the supernatural. He developed a style both powerful and distinctive, and was a major influence on film around the world. **Alan D. Williams,** 72, was a major editor of thrillers and literary fiction. He edited Stephen King at The Viking Press in the 1980s, and worked with a number of other fine authors. He was extremely well respected for his judgment and editorial skills. **Jerome Bixby,** 73, was a fine writer and screenwriter. His published fiction was almost entirely short stories; he also wrote a number of screenplays and teleplays. The most memorable image from his *oeuvre* is probably from an original *Twilight Zone* episode he wrote, based on his own short story, "It's a *Good* Life," which helped establish the young Billy Mumy as a frighteningly intense child actor. **Jo Clayton,** 58, was a science fiction and fantasy writer who wrote more than thirty novels, including the "Wild Magic," "Dancer," and "Duel of Sorcery" fantasy series. Her work was exciting and challenging, infused with the verve of her skillful storytelling, and tackling feminist themes in unusual ways. **Paul Lehr,** 67, was a realistic and surrealistic artist who made an indelible imprint on book covers of science fiction and fantasy. Though the majority of his work was in science fiction, his work had a wonderfully evocative sense of the fantastic that transcended genre. He worked in other areas as well, especially in childrens' literature. Whatever the subject, Lehr's art was uncannily intriguing, suggestive. One might say it was possessed by a sense of wonder in all things. **Naomi Mitchison,** 101, was a prolific science fiction and fantasy writer best known for her historical fantasies, in particular *The Corn King and the Spring Queen,* but with broad range and interests. She was involved in socialist politics in England when she was young, and was a freethinker. Her entire life she flouted convention and defied narrow-minded critics, asserting her individuality and intelligence in many directions. **Robert A. "Doc" Lowndes,** 81, was a science fiction fan, writer, editor, agent, collaborator . . . in the 1930s and 1940s he did it all, editing magazines, writing, being an active member of the Futurians club that spawned so many well known professionals in the field. He edited fantasy and horror as well as science fiction, and remained active in the field well into the 1980s. **Michael D. Weaver,** 36, wasn't very prolific, but he was a rare talent in both science fiction and fantasy. His "Bloodfang" trilogy was an intriguing, different kind of fantasy and his novel *Mercedes Nights* was an exciting science fiction novel with a fresh, strange, and unique sensibility, and a sheer sense of gonzo fun. **Octavio Paz,** 84, was Mexico's premier poet and essayist and a towering man of letters. He won the Nobel Prize in Literature in 1990 and produced more than 40 volumes of poetry and essays. **Ralph Arnote,** 71, was a salesman, sales and marketing director, and quintessentially in charge of ID (wholesale) distribution of mass-market paperbacks. He worked for Pocket Books when they distributed Ballantine Books (including *Lord of the Rings* by J. R. R. Tolkien). He ended his career with Tor Books as their ID sales manager and was instrumental in gaining acceptance and distribution for their SF, Fantasy, and Horror lists. He also wrote contemporary thrillers.

Joe Orlando, 71, got his start doing horror comics for E.C. Comics before moving on to *Mad* Magazine and finally to DC comics where he was responsible for the revival of DC's horror comics line. His most popular creation (with Len Wein and Bernie Wrightson) was *Swamp Thing.* **Archie Goodwin,** 60, was a comics writer and editor for Warren Publications, then Marvel Comics, and finally DC comics. **Antonio Prohias,** 77, was a Cuban exile who became famous for his "Spy vs. Spy" comic strip in *Mad* magazine and now on *Mad TV.* **Jean-Claude Forest,** 68, was most famous for creating the comic book character *Barbarella,* which was the basis for the film starring the young Jane Fonda.

Sean Moore, 33, was a young fantasy writer and game designer who had written several quite good *Conan* novels and was working on his first independent horror novel. His interests extended beyond the genre, and he had several projects in the works when he died in a car crash. **T. A. (Thomas) Waters,** 60, was a science fiction writer of a different color. His most intriguing work was *The Probability Pad,* one of a very loosely connected trilogy which he crafted along with Michael Kurland and Chester A. Anderson. Possessed of a feel for and knowledge of magic and an offbeat sense of humor, his work struck a chord with readers for whom science fiction and fantasy are a continuum. **Alain Doremieux,** 64, was one of the most influential figures in the French SF/Fantasy publishing community. He was a writer, but his far greater contribution was as editor, introducing French readers to many major British and American writers, editing both magazines and lines of books that dared to do the new and different. **Frank**

D. McSherry, Jr., 69, co-edited many ghost story anthologies, mostly with Martin H. Greenberg and Charles G. Waugh. He was also a writer and illustrator of considerable accomplishment. **Lawrence Sanders,** 78, was a brilliant thriller writer several of whose novels were translated with varying success to film. He wrote a single fantasy novel, *Dark Summer*, under the name Mark Upton. **Rachel Cosgrove Payes,** 75, was the author of more than forty-five books, including science fiction and fantasy. Her first love was Oz, and her first published novel was an Oz book, *The Hidden Valley of Oz*. **Dominique Aury,** 90, wrote the erotic bestseller *The Story of "O"*. **Hermann Lenz,** 85, was one of Germany's most significant and prolific authors. He wrote the *Swabian Chronicle*.

Lloyd Bridges, 85, was an actor of film and television for many years, known best for his continuing role in the series *Sea Hunt* and the film *Airplane*. He appeared in many other films and television programs, including the film adaptation of Jules Verne's *Twenty Thousand Leagues Under the Sea* and *The Outer Limits*. **Richard Denning,** 85, was a popular star of many "B" films in the forties and fifties, including a number of fantasy and horror vehicles. **Peter Lind Hayes,** 82, was a popular radio, television, and film actor who was best known for his work with his partner and then wife, Mary Healy. He had a prominent role in the film *The 5,000 Fingers of Doctor T.* **Shari Lewis,** 65, was beloved by several generations of children of all ages for her work as a puppeteer featuring her most famous hand puppet, Lamb Chop, on television. She wrote more than sixty children's books, and conducted symphony orchestras as well. **E. G. Marshall,** 84, was a veteran actor of stage, screen, and television. He starred or played supporting roles in many television productions with fantasy motifs. **Roddy McDowell,** 70, was a well-known actor in films and television productions for decades. His work ranged across many genres, but many will remember him for his work in ape-face in the "Planet of the Apes" films and television series. **Derek Newark,** 65, was a British actor in many horror films and on television. **Leo Penn,** 77, was a television director with numerous credits including *Ghost Story*, among other projects with fantasy elements. He also was the father of actor-director Sean Penn. **Leslie Stevens,** 74, was a producer, mainly for television, whose credits included the 1950s series *The Outer Limits*.

Julian Green, 97, was an expatriot American literary novelist. Some of his works, most notably *If I Were You* and *Shall the Dust Return*, contained fantasy elements. **Wolf Mankowitz,** 73, was a talented novelist and screenwriter. Some of his work was fantasy, notably his novel *A Kid for Two Farthings*. He also wrote a biography of Edgar Allan Poe, *The Extraordinary Mr. Poe*. **Dame Catherine Cookson,** 91, was a prolific and talented romance novelist. She also wrote the children's fantasy *Mrs. Flannagan's Trumpet*. **Hammond Innes,** 84, was a very popular thriller writer, many of whose works were popular with fantasy and science fiction readers because of their powerful conflicts between good and evil. Epic, in their own way. **Mary Elizabeth Grenander,** 79, was a professor of English and an authority on Ambrose Bierce. **Edward H. (Ted) Irving, Jr.,** 75, was an Old English scholar with a particular interest in *Beowulf* and Anglo-Saxon poetry. He was married to SF writer Judith Moffett. **José Paulo Paes**, 72, was a Brazilian critic, poet, editor, and translator who wrote a number of perceptive essays about such seminal works as Mary Shelley's *Frankenstein*, among others. **Robert Marasco,** 62, was the successful playwright who wrote *Child's Play*. His first novel,

Burnt Offerings, was horror, and became a film. His writing was eclectic and effective. **A[lfred] L[eslie] Rowse**, 93, wrote several collections of short stories based on the folklore of Cornwall and the antiquity of Oxford. **George Hay**, 75, was a SF and horror writer and edited the Spearman edition of *The Necronomicon*. **Daniel Farson**, 70, was a journalist and horror writer. He was also a grandnephew of Bram Stoker. **Joshua Charles Armitage**, 84, known as "Ionicus," was a great cartoonist for the British magazine *Punch*. **Francelia Butler**, 85, was a champion of children's literature. **Marshall Barer**, 75, wrote the music for *Once Upon a Mattress*. **Eric Ambler**, 89, was a thriller writer who elevated the genre to literature. **Hilda Morley**, 81, wrote poetry shaped by abstract expressionism. **Jack Biblo**, 91, ran a reprint house, Canaveral Press, that issued previously unpublished works by Edgar Rice Burroughs, and sold used books.

Philip Sterling, 76, was an actor of stage and television. **Theresa Merritt**, 75, was a television and film actress. **Philip Abbott**, 72, was a television and film actor. **James Nelson Algar**, 85, was a director and animator. **John Ashley**, 62, was an actor and producer. **Ramsay Ames**, 78, was an actress. **Michael Balfour**, 79, was a British character actor. **Eva Bartok**, 72, was a Hungarian-born actress. **Hal Baylor**, 79, was a character actor. **Norman Fell**, 74, was a film and television actor. **Jack T. Collis**, 75, was a production designer and art director. **Beverley Cross**, 66, was a British playwright who also wrote screenplays. **Frederic Downs**, 81, was a character actor. **Gene Evans**, 75, was a veteran character actor. **Bernard Girard**, 79, was a director of both films and television productions. **Richard C. Glouner**, 66, was a cinematographer. **Patricia Hayes**, 88, was a British actress. **Jonathan Hole**, 93, was a veteran character actor. **David King**, 67, was an actor. **Andrew Keir**, 71, was a film actor. **Ben Bagley**, 64, was a producer of off Broadway hits. **James Villiers**, 64, was a genre actor. **Ferdy Mayne**, 81, was a genre actor. **Charles Bryant Lang**, 96, was a cinematographer and director whose work included *The Uninvited* and *The Magnificent Seven*. **Mark Williams**, 38, was a film effects expert. **William Griffis**, 81, was a stage and televison actor.

Junior Wells, 63, was a blues singer and harmonica player who was one of the major players of Chicago's dynamic, funky, electric blues sound in the late 1950s and 1960s. **Patrick Clancy**, 76, helped start the Irish folk revival of the 50s and 60s. **Michel Petrucciani**, 36, was a French jazz pianist and composer. **Marie-Louise von Franz**, 83, was a doctor of Jungian psychology and interpreted more than 65,000 dreams throughout her career. **Daniel Crowley**, 76, was an anthropologist who took part in and chronicled the world's carnivals, festivals and other folk celebrations. **Ross Wetzsteon**, 65, helped create the Obie Awards for off Broadway and off off Broadway theater. **J. Gordon Lippincott**, 89, was a design consultant who helped design the "Tucker" automobile, as well as the interior for the "Nautilus," the Navy's first nuclear submarine. **Eldridge Cleaver**, 62, was a Black Panther who later became a G.O.P. conservative, whose memoir *Soul on Ice* made him a symbol of black rebellion. **Loren MacIver**, 90, was a painter of dreamlike, half-abstract landscapes, close-ups of natural forms, and city views. **Buster Cleveland**, 55, was a Dadaist known for his zany collages and mail art.

—James Frenkel

KELLY LINK

Travels with the Snow Queen

Kelly Link is a new writer who is quickly making a name for herself. This year, she has placed two stories in this volume—a horror story published elsewhere in these pages, and the following adult fairy tale based on Hans Christian Andersen's "The Snow Queen." Link hails from North Carolina, and currently lives in Boston, Massachusetts. She has published short fiction in various venues including Century *and* Asimov's Science Fiction *magazine.*

This story, published in the small zine Lady Churchill's Rosebud Wristlet, *fell between the cracks of the 1997 and 1998 publishing years. We're reprinting it now because we don't want readers to miss this highly original tale—which tied with Candas Jane Dorsey's "Black Wine" for the James Tiptree, Jr. Award.*

—T. W.

Part of you is always traveling faster, always traveling ahead. Even when you are moving, it is never fast enough to satisfy that part of you. You enter the walls of the city early in the evening, when the cobblestones are a mottled pink with reflected light, and cold beneath the slap of your bare, bloody feet. You ask the man who is guarding the gate to recommend a place to stay the night, and even as you are falling into the bed at the inn, the bed which is piled high with quilts and scented with lavender, perhaps alone, perhaps with another traveler, perhaps with the guardsman who had such brown eyes, and a mustache that curled up on either side of his nose like two waxed black laces, even as this guardsman, whose name you didn't ask calls out a name in his sleep which is not your name, you are dreaming about the road again. When you sleep, you dream about the long white distances that still lie before you. When you wake up, the guardsman is back at his post, and the place between your legs aches pleasantly, your legs sore as if you had continued walking all night in your sleep. While you were sleeping, your feet have healed again.

You were careful not to kiss the guardsman on the lips, so it doesn't really count, does it.

Your destination is North. The map that you are using is a mirror. You are always pulling the bits out of your bare feet, the pieces of the map that broke off and fell on the ground as the Snow Queen flew overhead in her sleigh. Where you are, where you are coming from, it is impossible to read a map made of paper. If it was that easy then everyone would be a traveler. You have heard of other travelers whose maps are breadcrumbs, whose maps are stones, whose maps are the four winds, whose maps are yellow bricks laid one after the other. You read your map with your foot, and behind you somewhere there must be another traveler whose map is the bloody footprints that you are leaving behind you.

There is a map of fine white scars on the soles of your feet that tells you where you have been. When you are pulling the shards of the Snow Queen's looking-glass out of your feet, you remind yourself, you tell yourself to imagine how it felt when Kay's eyes, Kay's heart were pierced by shards of the same mirror. Sometimes it is safer to read maps with your feet.

Ladies. Has it ever occurred to you that fairy tales aren't easy on the feet?

So this is the story so far. You grew up, you fell in love with the boy next door, Kay, the one with blue eyes who brought you bird feathers and roses, the one who was so good at puzzles. You thought he loved you—maybe he thought he did too. His mouth tasted so sweet, it tasted like love, and his fingers were so kind, they pricked like love on your skin, but three years and exactly two days after you moved in with him, you were having drinks out on the patio. You weren't exactly fighting, and you can't remember what he had done that had made you so angry, but you threw your glass at him. There was a noise like the sky shattering.

The cuff of his trousers got splashed. There were little fragments of glass everywhere. "Don't move," you said. You weren't wearing shoes.

He raised his hand up to his face. "I think there's something in my eye," he said.

His eye was fine, of course, there wasn't a thing in it, but later that night when he was undressing for bed, there were little bits of glass like grains of sugar, dusting his clothes. When you brushed your hand against his chest, something pricked your finger and left a smear of blood against his heart.

The next day it was snowing and he went out for a pack of cigarettes and never came back. You sat on the patio drinking something warm and alcoholic, with nutmeg in it, and the snow fell on your shoulders. You were wearing a short-sleeved T-shirt; you were pretending that you weren't cold, and that your lover would be back soon. You put your finger on the ground and then stuck it in your mouth. The snow looked like sugar, but it tasted like nothing at all.

The man at the corner store said that he saw your lover get into a long white sleigh. There was a beautiful woman in it, and it was pulled by thirty white geese. "Oh, her," you said, as if you weren't surprised. You went home and looked in the wardrobe for that cloak that belonged to your great-grandmother. You were thinking about going after him. You remembered that the cloak was woolen and warm, and a beautiful red—a traveler's cloak. But when you pulled it out, it smelled like wet dog and the lining was ragged, as if something had chewed on it. It smelled like bad luck: it made you sneeze, and so you put it back. You waited for a while longer.

Two months went by, and Kay didn't come back, and finally you left and locked the door of your house behind you. You were going to travel for love, without shoes, or cloak, or common sense. This is one of the things a woman can do when her lover leaves her. It's hard on the feet perhaps, but staying at home is hard on the heart, and you weren't quite ready to give him up yet. You told yourself that the woman in the sleigh must have put a spell on him, and he was probably already missing you. Besides, there are some questions you want to ask him, some true things you want to tell him. This is what you told yourself.

The snow was soft and cool on your feet, and then you found the trail of glass, the map. After three weeks of hard traveling, you came to the city.

No, really, think about it. Think about the little mermaid, who traded in her tail for love, got two legs and two feet, and every step was like walking on knives. And where did it get her? That's a rhetorical question, of course. Then there's the girl who put on the beautiful red dancing shoes. The woodsman had to chop her feet off with an axe.

There's Cinderella's two stepsisters, who cut off their own toes, and Snow White's stepmother, who danced to death in red-hot iron slippers. The Goose Girl's maid got rolled down a hill in a barrel studded with nails. Travel is hard on the single woman. There was this one woman who walked east of the sun and then west of the moon, looking for her lover, who had left her because she spilled tallow on his nightshirt. She wore out at least one pair of perfectly good iron shoes before she found him. Take our word for it, he wasn't worth it. What do you think happened when she forgot to put the fabric softener in the dryer? Laundry is hard, travel is harder. You deserve a vacation, but of course you're a little wary. You've read the fairy tales. We've been there, we know.

That's why we here at Snow Queen Tours have put together a luxurious but affordable package for you, guaranteed to be easy on the feet and on the budget. See the world by goose-drawn sleigh, experience the archetypal forest, the winter wonderland; chat with real live talking animals (please don't feed them). Our accommodations are three star: sleep on comfortable, guaranteed pea-free box spring mattresses; eat meals prepared by world-class chefs. Our tour guides are friendly, knowledgeable, well-traveled, trained by the Snow Queen herself. They know first aid, how to live off the land; they speak three languages fluently.

Special discount for older sisters, stepsisters, stepmothers, wicked witches, crones, hags, princesses who have kissed frogs without realizing what they were getting into, etc.

You leave the city and you walk all day beside a stream that is as soft and silky as blue fur. You wish that your map was water, and not broken glass. At midday you stop, and bathe your feet in a shallow place, and the ribbons of red blood curl into the blue water.

Eventually you come to a wall of briars, so wide and high that you can't see any way around it. You reach out to touch a rose, and prick your finger. You suppose that you could walk around, but your feet tell you that the map leads

directly through the briar wall, and you can't stray from the path which has been
laid out for you. Remember what happened to the little girl, your great-
grandmother, in her red woolen cape. Maps protect their travelers, but only if
the travelers obey the dictates of their maps. This is what you have been told.

Perched in the briars above your head is a raven, black and sleek as the cur-
licued moustache of the guardsman. The raven looks at you and you look back
at it. "I'm looking for someone," you say. "A boy named Kay."

The raven opens its shiny beak and says, "He doesn't love you, you know."

You shrug. You've never liked talking animals. Once your lover gave you a
talking cat, but it ran away and secretly you were glad. "I have a few things I
want to say to him, that's all." You have, in fact, been keeping a list of all the
things you are going to say to him. "Besides, I wanted to see the world, be a
tourist for a while."

"That's fine for some," the raven says. Then he relents. "If you'd like to come
in, then come in. The princess just married the boy with the boots that squeaked
on the marble floor."

"That's fine for some," you say. Kay's boots squeak; you wonder how he met
the princess, if he is the one that she just married, how the raven knows that
he doesn't love you, what this princess has that you don't have, besides a white
sleigh pulled by thirty geese, an impenetrable wall of briars, and maybe a castle.
She's probably just some bimbo.

"The Princess Briar Rose is a very wise princess," the raven says, "but she's
the laziest girl in the world. Once she went to sleep for a hundred days and no
one could wake her up, although they put one hundred peas under her mattress,
one each morning."

This, of course, is the proper and respectful way of waking up princesses.
Sometimes Kay used to wake you up by dribbling cold water on your feet. Sometimes he woke you up by whistling.

"On the one hundredth day," the raven says, "she woke up all by herself and
told her council of twelve fairy godmothers that she supposed it was time she
got married. So they stuck up posters, and princes and youngest sons came from
all over the kingdom."

When the talking cat ran away, Kay put up flyers all around the neighborhood.
You wonder if you should have put up flyers for Kay.

"Briar Rose wanted a clever husband, but it tired her dreadfully to sit and
listen to the young men give speeches and talk about how rich and sexy and
smart they were. She fell asleep and stayed asleep until the young man with the
squeaky boots came in. It was his boots that woke her up.

"It was love at first sight. Instead of trying to impress her with everything he
knew and everything he had seen, he declared that he had come all this way to
hear Briar Rose talk about her dreams. He'd had been studying in Vienna with
a famous Doctor, and was deeply interested in dreams."

Kay used to tell you his dreams every morning. They were long and complicated and if he thought you weren't listening to him, he'd sulk. You never
remember your dreams. "Other people's dreams are never very interesting," you
tell the raven.

The raven cocks its head. It flies down and lands on the grass at your feet.

"Wanna bet?" it says. Behind the raven you notice a little green door recessed in the briar wall. You could have sworn that it wasn't there a minute ago.

The raven leads you through the green door, and across a long green lawn towards a two-story castle that is the same pink as the briar roses. You think this is kind of tacky, but exactly what you would expect from someone named after a flower. "I had this dream once," the raven says, "that my teeth were falling out. They just crumbled into pieces in my mouth. And then I woke up, and realized that ravens don't have teeth."

You follow the raven inside the palace, and up a long, twisty staircase. The stairs are stone, worn, and smoothed away, like old thick silk. Slivers of glass sparkle on the pink stone, catching the light of the candles on the wall. As you go up, you see that you are part of a great, grey rushing crowd. Fantastic creatures, flat and thin as smoke, race up the stairs, men and women and snakey things with bright eyes. They nod to you as they slip past. "Who are they?" you ask the raven.

"Dreams," the raven says, hopping awkwardly from step to step. "The Princess's dreams, come to pay their respects to her new husband. Of course they're too fine to speak to the likes of us."

But you think that some of them look familiar. They have a familiar smell, like a pillow that your lover's head has rested upon.

At the top of the staircase is a wooden door with a silver keyhole. The dreams pour steadily through the keyhole, and under the bottom of the door and when you open it, the sweet stink and cloud of dreams are so thick in the Princess's bedroom that you can barely breathe. Some people might mistake the scent of the Princess's dreams for the scent of sex; then again, some people mistake sex for love.

You see a bed big enough for a giant, with four tall oak trees with red and gold leaves for bedposts. You climb up the ladder that rests against the side of the bed to see the Princess's sleeping husband. As you lean over, a goose feather flies up and tickles your nose. You brush it away, and dislodge several seedy looking dreams. Briar Rose rolls over and laughs in her sleep, but the man beside her wakes up. "Who is it?" he says. "What do you want?"

He isn't Kay. He doesn't look a thing like Kay. "You're not Kay," you tell the man in the Princess's bed.

"Who the fuck is Kay?" he says, so you explain it all to him, feeling horribly embarrassed. The raven is looking pleased with itself, the way your talking cat used to look, before it ran away. You glare at the raven. You glare at the man who is not Kay.

After you've finished, you say that something is wrong, because your map clearly indicates that Kay has been here, in this bed. Your feet are leaving bloody marks on the sheets, and you pick a sliver of glass off the foot of the bed, so everyone can see that you're not lying. Princess Briar Rose sits up in bed, her long pinkish-brown hair tumbled down over her shoulders. "He's not in love with you," she says, yawning.

"So he was here, in this bed, you're the icy slut in the sleigh at the corner store, you're not even bothering to deny it," you say.

She shrugs her pink-white shoulders. "Four, five months ago, he came through, I woke up," she says. "He was a nice guy, okay in bed. She was a real bitch, though."

"Who was?" you ask.

Briar Rose finally notices that her new husband is glaring at her. "What can I say?" she says, and shrugs. "I have a thing for guys in squeaky boots."

"Who was a bitch?" you ask again.

"The Snow Queen," she says, "the slut in the sleigh."

This is the list you carry in your pocket, of the things you plan to say to Kay, when you find him, if you find him:

1. I'm sorry that I forgot to water your ferns while you were away that time.

2. When you said that I reminded you of your mother, was that a good thing?

3. I never really liked your friends all that much.

4. None of my friends ever really liked you.

5. Do you remember when the cat ran away, and I cried and cried and made you put up posters, and she never came back? I wasn't crying because she didn't come back. I was crying because I'd taken her to the woods, and I was scared she'd come back and tell you what I'd done, but I guess a wolf got her, or something. She never liked me anyway.

6. I never liked your mother.

7. After you left, I didn't water your plants on purpose. They're all dead.

8. Goodbye.

9. Were you ever really in love with me?

10. Was I good in bed, or just average?

11. What exactly did you mean, when you said that *it was fine that I had put on a little weight, that you thought I was even more beautiful, that I should go ahead and eat as much as I wanted*, but when I weighed myself on the bathroom scale, I was exactly the same weight as before, I hadn't gained a single pound?

12. So all those times, I'm being honest here, every single time, and anyway I don't care if you don't believe me, I faked every orgasm you ever thought I had. Women can do that, you know. You never made me come, not even once.

13. So maybe I'm an idiot, but I used to be in love with you.

14. I slept with some guy, I didn't mean to, it just kind of happened. Is that how it was with you? Not that I'm making any apologies, or that I'd accept yours, I just want to know.

15. My feet hurt, and it's all your fault.

16. I mean it this time, goodbye.

The Princess Briar Rose isn't a bimbo after all, even if she does have a silly name and a pink castle. You admire her dedication to the art and practice of sleep. By now you are growing sick and tired of traveling, and would like nothing better than to curl up in a big featherbed for one hundred days, or maybe even one hundred years, but she offers to loan you her carriage, and when you explain that you have to walk, she sends you off with a troop of armed guards. They will escort you through the forest, which is full of thieves and wolves and princes on quests, lurking about. The guards politely pretend that they don't notice the trail of blood that you are leaving behind. They probably think it's some sort of female thing.

It is after sunset, and you aren't even half a mile into the forest, which is dark and scary and full of strange noises, when bandits ambush your escort, and slaughter them all. The robber queen, who is grizzled and grey, with a nose like an old pickle, yells delightedly at the sight of you. "You're a nice plump one for my supper!" she says, and draws her long knife out of the stomach of one of the dead guards. She is just about to slit your throat, as you stand there, politely pretending not to notice the blood that is pooling around the bodies of the dead guards, that is now obliterating the bloody tracks of your feet, the knife that is at your throat, when a girl about your own age jumps onto the robber queen's back, pulling at the robber queen's braided hair as if it were reins.

There is a certain family resemblance between the robber queen and the girl who right now has her knees locked around the robber queen's throat. "I don't want you to kill her," the girl says, and you realize that she means you, that you were about to die a minute ago, that travel is much more dangerous than you had ever imagined. You add an item of complaint to the list of things that you plan to tell Kay, if you find him.

The girl has half-throttled the robber queen, who is now on her knees, gasping for breath. "She can be my sister," the girl says insistently. "You promised I could have a sister, and I want her. Besides, her feet are bleeding."

The robber queen drops her knife, and the girl drops back onto the ground, kissing her mother's hairy grey cheek. "Very well, very well," the robber queen grumbles, and the girl grabs your hand, pulling you farther and faster into the woods, until you are running and stumbling, her hand hot around yours.

You have lost all sense of direction; your feet are no longer set upon your map. You should be afraid, but instead you are strangely exhilarated. Your feet don't hurt anymore, and although you don't know where you are going, for the very first time you are moving fast enough, you are almost flying, your feet are skimming over the night-black forest floor as if it were the smooth, flat surface of a lake, and your feet were two white birds. "Where are we going?" you ask the robber girl.

"We're here," she says, and stops so suddenly that you almost fall over. You are in a clearing, with the full moon hanging directly overhead. You can see the robber girl better now, under the light of the moon. She looks like one of the bad girls who loiter under the street lamp by the corner shop, the ones who used to whistle at Kay. She wears black leatherette boots laced up to her thighs, and a black, ribbed T-shirt and grape-colored plastic shorts with matching suspenders. Her nails are painted black, and bitten down to the quick. She leads you to a tumbledown stone keep, which is as black inside as her fingernails, and smells strongly of dirty straw and animals.

"Are you a princess?" she asks you. "What are you doing in my mother's forest? Don't be afraid. I won't let my mother eat you."

You explain to her that you are not a princess, what you are doing, about the map, who you are looking for, what he did to you, or maybe it was what he didn't do. When you finish, the robber girl puts her arms around you and squeezes you roughly. "You poor thing! But what a silly way to travel!" she says. She shakes her head and makes you sit down on the stone floor of the keep, and show her your feet. You explain that they always heal, that really your feet are quite tough, but she takes off her leatherette boots and gives them to you.

The floor of the keep is dotted with indistinct, motionless forms. One snarls in its sleep, and you realize that they are dogs. The robber girl is sitting between four slender columns, and when the dog snarls, the thing shifts restlessly, lowering its branchy head. It is a hobbled reindeer. "Well go on, see if they fit," the robber girl says, pulling out her knife. She drags it along the stone floor to make sparks. "What are you going to do when you find him?"

"Sometimes I'd like to cut off his head," you say. The robber girl grins, and thumps the hilt of her knife against the reindeer's chest.

The robber girl's feet are just a little bigger, but the boots are still warm from her feet. You explain that you can't wear the boots, or else you won't know where you are going. "Nonsense!" the robber girl says rudely.

You ask if she knows a better way to find Kay, and she says that if you are still determined to go looking for him, even though he obviously doesn't love you, and he isn't worth a bit of trouble, then the thing to do is to find the Snow Queen. "This is Bae. Bae, you mangy old, useless old thing," she says. "Do you know where the Snow Queen lives?"

The reindeer replies in a low, hopeless voice that he doesn't know, but he is sure that his old mother does. The robber girl slaps his flank. "Then you'll take her to your mother," she says. "And mind that you don't dawdle on the way."

She turns to you and gives you a smacking wet kiss on the lips and says, "Keep the shoes, they look much nicer on you than they did on me. And don't let me hear that you've been walking on glass again." She gives the reindeer a speculative look. "You know, Bae, I almost think I'm going to miss you."

You step into the cradle of her hands, and she swings you over the reindeer's bony back. Then she saws through the hobble with her knife, and yells "Ho!" waking up the dogs.

You knot your fingers into Bae's mane, and bounce up as he stumbles into a fast trot. The dogs follow for a distance, snapping at his hooves, but soon you have outdistanced them, moving so fast that the wind peels your lips back in an involuntary grimace. You almost miss the feel of glass beneath your feet. By morning, you are out of the forest again, and Bae's hooves are churning up white clouds of snow.

———

Sometimes you think there must be an easier way to do this. Sometimes it seems to be getting easier all on its own. Now you have boots and a reindeer, but you still aren't happy. Sometimes you wish that you'd stayed at home. You're sick and tired of traveling towards the happily ever after, whenever the fuck that is—you'd like the happily right now. Thank you very much.

When you breathe out, you can see the fine mist of your breath and the breath of the reindeer floating before you, until the wind tears it away. Bae runs on.

The snow flies up, and the air seems to grow thicker and thicker. As Bae runs, you feel that the white air is being rent by your passage, like heavy cloth. When you turn around and look behind you, you can see the path shaped to your joined form, woman and reindeer, like a hall stretching back to infinity. You see that there is more than one sort of map, that some forms of travel are indeed easier. "Give me a kiss," Bae says. The wind whips his words back to you. You can almost see the shape of them hanging in the heavy air.

"I'm not really a reindeer," he says. "I'm an enchanted prince."

You politely decline, pointing out that you haven't known him that long, and besides, for traveling purposes, a reindeer is better than a prince.

"He doesn't love you," Bae says. "And you could stand to lose a few pounds. My back is killing me."

You are sick and tired of talking animals, as well as travel. They never say anything that you didn't already know. You think of the talking cat that Kay gave you, the one that would always come to you, secretly, and looking very pleased with itself, to inform you when Kay's fingers smelled of some other woman. You couldn't stand to see him pet it, his fingers stroking its white fur, the cat lying on its side and purring wildly, "There, darling, that's perfect, don't stop," his fingers on its belly, its tail wreathing and lashing, its little pink pointed tongue sticking out at you. "Shut up," you say to Bae.

He subsides into an offended silence. His long brown fur is rimmed with frost, and you can feel the tears that the wind pulls from your eyes turning to ice on your cheeks. The only part of you that is warm are your feet, snug in the robber girl's boots. "It's just a little farther," Bae says, when you have been traveling for what feels like hours. "And then we're home."

You cross another corridor in the white air, and he swerves to follow it, crying out gladly, "We are near the old woman of Lapmark's house, my mother's house."

"How do you know?" you ask.

"I recognize the shape that she leaves behind her," Bae says. "Look!"

You look and see that the corridor of air you are following is formed like a short, stout, petticoated woman. It swings out at the waist like a bell.

"How long does it last?"

"As long as the air is heavy and dense," he says, "we burrow tunnels through the air like worms, but then the wind will come along and erase where we have been."

The woman-tunnel ends at a low red door. Bae lowers his head and knocks his antlers against it, scraping off the paint. The old woman of Lapmark opens the door, and you clamber stiffly off Bae's back. There is much rejoicing as mother recognizes son, although he is much changed from how he had been.

The old woman of Lapmark is stooped and fat as a grub. She fixes you a cup of tea, while Bae explains that you are looking for the Snow Queen's palace.

"You've not far to go now," his mother tells you. "Only a few hundred miles and past the house of the woman of Finmany. She'll tell you how to go—let me write a letter explaining everything to her. And don't forget to mention to her that I'll be coming for tea tomorrow: she'll change you back then, Bae, if you ask her nicely."

The woman of Lapmark has no paper, so she writes the letter on a piece of dried cod, flat as a dinner plate. Then you are off again. Sometimes you sleep as Bae runs on, and sometimes you aren't sure if you are asleep or waking. Great balls of greenish light roll cracking across the sky above you: at times it seems as if Bae is flying alongside the lights, chatting to them like old friends. At last you come to the house of the woman of Finmany, and you knock on her chimney, because she has no door.

Why, you may wonder, are there so many old women living out here? Is this a retirement community? One might not be remarkable, two is certainly more than enough, but as you look around, you can see little heaps of snow, lines of smoke rising from them. You have to be careful where you put your foot, or you might come through someone's roof. Maybe they came here for the quiet, or because they like ice fishing, or maybe they just like snow.

It is steamy and damp in the house, and you have to climb down the chimney, past the roaring fire, to get inside. Bae leaps down the chimney, hooves first, scattering coals everywhere. The Finmany woman is smaller and rounder than the woman of Lapmark. She looks to you like a lump of pudding with black currant eyes: she wears only a greasy old slip, and an apron that has written on it, "If you can't stand the heat, stay out of my kitchen."

She recognizes Bae even faster than his mother had, because, as it turns out, she was the one who turned him into a reindeer, for teasing her about her weight. Bae apologizes, insincerely, you think, but the Finmany woman says she will see what she can do about turning him back again. She isn't entirely hopeful. It seems that a kiss is the preferred method of transformation. You don't offer to kiss him, because you know what that kind of thing leads to.

The Finmany woman reads the piece of dried cod by the light of her cooking fire, and then she throws the fish into her cooking pot. Bae tells her about Kay and the Snow Queen, and about your feet, because your lips have frozen together on the last leg of the journey, and you can't speak a word.

"You're so clever and strong," the reindeer says to the Finmany woman. You can almost hear him add, *and fat*, under his breath. "You can tie up all the winds in the world with a bit of thread. I've seen you hurling the lightning bolts down from the hills as if they were feathers. Can't you give her the strength of ten men, so that she can fight the Snow Queen and win Kay back?"

"The strength of ten men?" the Finmany woman says. "A lot of good that would do! And besides, he doesn't love her."

Bae smirks at you, as if to say, I told you so. If your lips weren't frozen, you'd tell him that she isn't saying anything that you don't already know. "Now!" the Finmany woman says, "take her up on your back one last time, and put her down again by the bush with the red berries. That marks the edge of the Snow Queen's garden; don't stay there gossiping, but come straight back. You were a handsome boy—I'll make you twice as good-looking as you were before. We'll put up flyers, see if we can get someone to come and kiss you."

"As for you, missy," she says. "Tell the Snow Queen now that we have Bae back, that we'll be over at the Palace next Tuesday for a couple rubbers of bridge. Just as soon as he has hands and not hooves."

She puts you on Bae's back again, giving you such a warm kiss that your lips unfreeze, and you can speak again. "The woman of Lapmark is coming for tea tomorrow," you tell her.

The Finmany woman lifts Bae, and you upon his back, in her strong, fat arms, giving you a gentle push up the chimney.

Good morning, ladies, it's nice to have you on the premiere Snow Queen Tour. I hope that you all had a good night's sleep, because today we're going to be traveling quite some distance. I hope that everyone brought a comfortable pair of walking shoes. Let's have a head count, make sure that everyone on the list is here, and then we'll have introductions. My name is Gerda, and I'm looking forward to getting to know all of you.

Here you are, at last, standing before the Snow Queen's palace, the palace of the woman who enchanted your lover, and then stole him away in her long, white sleigh. You aren't quite sure what you are going to say to her, or to him. When you check your pocket, you discover that your list has disappeared. You have most of it memorized, but you think maybe you will wait and see, before you say anything. Part of you would like to turn around and leave, before the Snow Queen finds you, before Kay sees you. You are afraid that you will burst out crying, or even worse, that he will know that you walked barefoot on broken glass across half the continent, just to find out why he left you.

The front door is open, so you don't bother knocking, you just walk right in. It isn't that large a palace, really. It is about the size of your own house, except that the furniture, which is Danish modern, is carved out of blue-green ice as are the walls and everything else. It's a slippery place, and you're glad that you are wearing the robber girl's boots. You have to admit that the Snow Queen is a meticulous housekeeper, much tidier than you ever were. You can't find the Snow Queen and you can't find Kay, but in every room there are white geese, who, you are in equal parts relieved and surprised to find, don't utter a single word.

"Gerda!" Kay is sitting at a table, fitting the pieces of a puzzle together. When he stands up, he knocks several pieces of the puzzle off the table, and they fall to the floor and shatter into even smaller fragments. You both kneel down, picking them up. The table is blue, the puzzle pieces are blue, Kay is blue, which is why you didn't see him when you first came into the room. The geese brush up against you, soft and white as cats.

"What took you so long?" Kay says. "Where in the world did you get those ridiculous boots?" You stare at him in disbelief.

"I walked barefoot on broken glass across half a continent to get here," you say. But at least you don't burst into tears. "A robber girl gave them to me."

Kay snorts. His blue nostrils flare. "Sweetie, they're hideous."

"Why are you blue?" you ask.

"I'm under an enchantment," he says. "The Snow Queen kissed me. Besides, I thought blue was your favorite color."

Your favorite color has always been yellow. You wonder if the Snow Queen kissed him all over, if he is blue all over. All the visible portions of his body are blue. "If you kiss me," he says, "you break the spell and I can come home with you. If you break the spell, I'll be in love with you again."

You refrain from asking if he was in love with you when he kissed the Snow Queen. Pardon me, you think, when *she* kissed *him*. "What is that puzzle you're working on?" you ask.

"Oh, that," he says. "That's the other way to break the spell. If I can put it together, but the other way is easier. Not to mention more fun. Don't you want to kiss me?"

You look at his blue lips, at his blue face. You try to remember if you liked his kisses. "Do you remember the white cat?" you say. "It didn't exactly run away. I took it to the woods and left it there."

"We can get another one," he says.

"I took it to the woods because it was telling me things."

"We don't have to get a talking cat," Kay says. "Besides, why did you walk barefoot across half a continent of broken glass, if you aren't going to kiss me and break the spell?" His blue face is sulky.

"Maybe I just wanted to see the world," you tell him. "Meet interesting people."

The geese are brushing up against your ankles. You stroke their white feathers and the geese snap, but gently, at your fingers. "You had better hurry up and decide if you want to kiss me or not," Kay says. "Because she's home."

When you turn around, there she is, smiling at you, like you are exactly the person that she was hoping to see.

The Snow Queen isn't how or what you'd expected. She's not as tall as you— you thought she would be taller. Sure, she's beautiful, you can see why Kay kissed her (although you are beginning to wonder why she kissed him), but her eyes are black and kind, which you didn't expect at all. She stands next to you, not looking at Kay at all, but looking at you. "I wouldn't do it if I were you," she says.

"Oh come on," Kays says. "Give me a break, lady. Sure it was nice, but you don't want me hanging around this icebox forever, any more than I want to be here. Let Gerda kiss me, we'll go home and live happily ever after. There's supposed to be a happy ending."

"I like your boots," the Snow Queen says.

"You're beautiful," you tell her.

"I don't believe this," Kay says. He thumps his blue fist on the blue table, sending blue puzzle pieces flying through the air. Pieces lie like nuggets of sky-colored glass on the white backs of the geese. A piece of the table has splintered off, and you wonder if he is going to have to put the table back together, as well.

"Do you love him?"

You look at the Snow Queen when she says this, and then you look at Kay. "Sorry," you tell him. You hold out your hand, in case he's willing to shake it.

"Good grief!" he says. "You're sorry! What good does that do me?"

"So what happens now?" you ask the Snow Queen.

"Up to you," she says. "Maybe you're sick of traveling. Are you?"

"I don't know," you say. "I think I'm finally beginning to get the hang of it."

"In that case," says the Snow Queen, "I may have a business proposal for you."

"Hey!" Kay says. "What about me? Isn't someone going to kiss me?"

You help him collect a few puzzle pieces. "Will you at least do this much for me?" he asks. "For old time's sake. Will you spread the word, tell a few single princesses that I'm stuck up here? I'd like to get out of here sometime in the next century. Thanks. I'd really appreciate it. You know, we had a really nice time, I think I remember that."

The robber girl's boots cover the scars on your feet. When you look at these scars, you can see the outline of the journey you made. Sometimes mirrors are maps, and sometimes maps are mirrors. Sometimes scars tell a story, and maybe someday you will tell this story to a lover. The soles of your feet are stories—hidden in the black boots, they shine like mirrors. If you were to take your boots off, you would see reflected in one foot-mirror the Princess Briar Rose as she sets off on her honeymoon, in her enormous four-poster bed, which now has wheels and is pulled by twenty white horses.

It's nice to see women exploring alternative means of travel.

In the other foot-mirror, almost close enough to touch, you could see the robber girl whose boots you are wearing. She is setting off to find Bae, to give him a kiss and bring him home again. You wouldn't presume to give her any advice, but you do hope that she has found another pair of good sturdy boots.

Someday, someone will probably make their way to the Snow Queen's palace, and kiss Kay's cold blue lips. She might even manage a happily ever after for a while.

You are standing in your black laced boots, and the Snow Queen's white geese mutter and stream and sidle up against you. You are beginning to understand some of what they are saying. They grumble about the weight of the sleigh, the weather, your hesitant jerks at their reins. But they are good natured grumbles. You tell the geese that your feet are maps *and* your feet are mirrors. But you tell them that you have to keep in mind that they are also useful for walking around on. They are perfectly good feet.

STEVE DUFFY

Running Dogs

Steve Duffy was born in 1963. He has lived in Norfolk and London, and currently makes his home on the North Wales coast. He is an information technology professional but has been writing in a variety of genres, more for the pleasure of it than the money. He specializes in the ghost story, having been inspired by the works of Robert Aickman and M. R. James. His stories have been published in Ghosts & Scholars, *and in the anthology* Midnight Never Comes.

According to Duffy, "Running Dogs" was written in 1996 and the title suggested the story. It borrows most of its setting from a discarded (and untitled) fragment and was inspired by Dorothy L. Sayers's tale, "The Cyprian Cat," which the author had recently reread. "Running Dogs" was originally published in The Night Comes On, *Duffy's first collection.*

—E. D.

In those days,' (began the gentleman in the first-class carriage, as the train pulled out of Liverpool Street) 'I travelled extensively on the local lines, my status as a gentleman of leisure and my inquisitive nature providing me with adequate means and motive to explore the more unfrequented corners of the countryside. Different times, and pleasant enough times they were, to be sure: rural inns and hostelries, cathedral closes, halls and abbeys, minsters and manses and dilapidated piles the length and breadth of England. Hard to imagine nowadays, I suppose, now that so much seems to have changed.'

'Most pleasant,' I assented, 'and yes, rather hard to imagine in the present age. I envy you the experience.' His account of such an agreeable way of life, according as it did so well with my own tastes, heightened the curiosity with which I observed this elderly, punctilious gentleman, my sole companion in the dimly-lit carriage, and I sought to draw him out further than perhaps was warranted by our briefest of acquaintances. 'Of course, the exploration of our rich national heritage can prove most stimulating—I myself have often wished that my own meagre finances would run to such adventures.'

'Adventures, you call them,' said the elderly gentleman with a slight smile, 'you overstate the case, I fear. Of all my various experiences, I should be hard put to apply the term "adventure" to more than one or two.'

'One or two,' I interjected; 'then perhaps on these occasions there transpired events of—how shall I put it—more than usual interest?' My fellow-traveller (to whom I shall henceforth refer as Mr Smith, because that was the name above the station bookstall at which I first met him, as we jostled politely for a copy of the latest *Blackwood's*) sighed a little, and I was on the verge of apologising for my regrettable tendency towards prying when he spoke again, as one who makes his mind up to an inevitable, and possibly an uncomfortable, disclosure.

'It is true,' said Mr Smith, 'that on one occasion in particular my travels led me to an altogether unexpected occurrence. For reasons which still seem to me defensible and valid, I am not in the practice of relating the details of this event, least of all to strangers'—my heart sank at this perceived rebuff—'however, these are perhaps extraordinary circumstances.'

'How so?' said I, wondering at his choice of words.

'Well, to begin with, I must confess to having perpetrated a trivial subterfuge,' rejoined Mr Smith, to my bemusement. 'At the bookstall, my intervention in your purchase of this periodical'—he indicated the magazine which lay unopened on the seat at my side—'was, I am ashamed to say, little more than a ruse—a stratagem by which to strike up your acquaintance. For reasons which will perhaps become clear, I harbour these days an extreme unwillingness to engage in railway travel unaccompanied, and as a result I am occasionally forced to employ a degree of artifice to the end of securing a travelling companion of however brief an acquaintance. On this occasion, you were my victim, to use a somewhat melodramatic expression, and as such it may be no more than your due to learn something of the circumstances behind such outlandish behaviour.'

'My curiosity is now fully aroused,' I said, leaning forward in my seat and taking out my pipe. 'We have some hours to pass before arriving at our destination: please take a fill from this excellent tobacco and relate in your own time and fashion such particulars as you think suitable.'

Mr Smith accepted my invitation, and proceeded to tell the following tale, here reproduced as nearly as I can manage the thing. As you will appreciate, it is not an anecdote likely to be forgotten by its hearers: indeed, the words seem to rush to my pen as I write, and I am once again in that smoky rattling carriage, the Essex countryside rushing by invisible in the dark, listening to the careful, somewhat pedantic tones of Mr Smith as he set out the details of his story, thus.

This particular visit was some forty years ago, to Ashburgh on the north Norfolk coast. Do you know the place at all? You would not know it now: I believe the Army took over that portion of the coast some years before the War, and used it as an artillery range, and the village is long since gone. No great loss, architecturally speaking: a poky little church with nothing in particular to commend it, a village inn with a view of the harbour and the estuary, a rough shale beach too hard to walk, and the countryside around dull enough to try the patience of a saint. Not one of my more rewarding visits—I could wish now that I had never set foot in the place.

Be that as it may, I could at least leave at my convenience: accordingly, I presented myself at the railway station, Ashburgh Halt, about a mile out of town, early on the second evening of my visit, with the intention of catching the eight-thirty train for London. I might say that nothing became Ashburgh like the leaving of it, for the evening was magnificent—you know those wonderful summer evenings, when the air is so utterly languid and unmoving, charged still with all the heat of the day, and the last of the light seems to linger an eternity in the west? Well, picture the station on just such an evening, deserted save for the passengers and the porter, who was now and again to be spied as he wandered desultorily in and out of the ticket office.

I say passengers: there was just one other besides myself, a little further down the platform. He was a rather florid, burly man, and I placed him without too much difficulty as one of the commercial travellers who, along with myself, had constituted the entire clientele of the inn at Ashburgh. Indeed, on the platform before him there was a large samples case, upon which his feet rested as he reamed out his pipe. He looked round gratefully at my approach, sprang to his feet, and extended a hand, calling out in a rather familiar manner, 'At last! I thought it was a Sunday or something for all the life there is in the place! Another human being at last—come and sit down, sir, won't you?'

Needless to say, I should not have chosen him for a travelling companion; however, he seemed so pleased to see me that it would have appeared churlish to refuse. We exchanged formalities, then, and sat down on the bench; his name, he said, was Joseph Babcock ('Joe Babcock, sir, at your service'), and he travelled in alcoholic beverages for a large London firm.

'But these yokels, sir, they have their own little thruppenny-ha'penny breweries, and will they touch a drop of the real right stuff? They won't, and I don't know why, for I'd rather be shot than poisoned, myself, any day of the week.'

He was lively enough at any rate, and if he was a little coarse in his way of speaking, that was only to be expected. One must take as one finds, on public transport—present company excepted, of course. He was voluble in his dislike of Ashburgh: 'A poisonous little hole, I call it, sir: sort of place where the only fun of a Saturday night's to sit and watch the trains go by—and don't I feel sorry for them as stops here! Drab little inn, with its miserable old cuss of a landlord and his rotten great brute of a dog—I hate 'em, sir, dogs, I'm more of a cat man, myself, and they think more of their dogs in Ashburgh than they do of the human beings, if you want my opinion. All got 'em—big ugly things, that'd have the throat out of you soon as look at you. Give 'em a kick as I go past, I do, when their owners aren't looking—so long as they're tied up, ha-ha!'

Myself I do not particularly mind dogs—or at least, I did not at that time—and I cannot say I had been unduly bothered by the landlord's specimen, a large beast with an appearance of the wolf-hound or Alsatian about it, which I daresay made an excellent guard-dog. But I could see that Babcock might have excited the animosity of the locals if he had expressed his prejudices in the matter, and I took that to be the reason for any little difficulty he might have experienced.

The time passed quickly enough; the evening continued pleasant, and the train was due within ten minutes or so when Babcock's eye was caught by a movement at the further end of the platform. 'Look!—d'you see—down there—

it's a woman, to be sure. Lord! so they have women nowadays, round these parts!'

A woman, dressed modestly in grey and wearing a neat straw hat, with no luggage that I could see, was sitting on a bench by herself, her head inclined away from us. We had not noticed her before; perhaps we had been too intent on our own little chat. At any rate, Babcock suddenly seemed eager to take his side of the conversation elsewhere.

'I—ahem! I'll just wander down and see whether the signal's gone up yet, shall I?' And under his breath I heard him mutter, 'Nice—very . . .' as he rose to his feet.

He strolled elaborately down the platform in the direction of the lady on her bench, whistling a little air through his fashionably drooping moustache. My sense of propriety being somewhat more acute, I remained seated, observing from a distance. Babcock drew level with the woman, stopped, and apparently made some remark by way of greeting; she started visibly, shrank back on the bench, and ducked her head. For a moment I thought Babcock had said something off-colour, and I got to my feet in case there should be any unpleasantness. However, Babcock saw me rise, and beckoned me over, calling, 'Mr Smith! Won't you come and meet our new companion?'

For all I had little wish to be thus compromised, I had no choice: I went over to where he stood, and was introduced by him to the lady on the bench, whose name, I learned, was Miss Holt. 'Mr Smith,' she said, almost in a whisper, her accent suggestive of local origin; she peeped up from beneath the brim of her hat, and for the first time I was able to see her face. Her eyes were round, and wonderfully brown, with large dark pupils and deep irises, her features were sharp and a little pointed, and when she smiled as we shook hands, I noticed that her teeth were a shade too prominent for conventional standards of beauty, and her fingernails as long as a Chinaman's—as the saying goes; I have never met a Chinaman, myself.

'Miss Holt is for our train,' explained Babcock, with an air almost of possessiveness in his voice, eyeing her with obvious admiration.

'How fortunate,' I rejoined, thinking that if Babcock intended to 'expand,' as the saying goes, any further, then two might be company and three a most unwelcome crowd. 'If you will excuse me: I have some papers to look over before the train arrives. Miss Holt: a pleasure.'

She acknowledged me with a nod, looking all the while at Babcock: he, for his part, said, 'Ah, yes; of course,' casting a look of mixed gratitude and complicity in my direction, and favouring me—I regret to say—with a surreptitious and rather vulgar wink. Looking over my shoulder as I retraced my steps along the platform, I saw Babcock engage Miss Holt in conversation, he standing, she remaining seated; politeness restrained me from attempting to eavesdrop.

Back on my own bench, reading over my scanty notes from the visit to Ashburgh, I glanced over from time to time at my fellow-passengers. The distance between them never varied: he stood on the platform, bending slightly from the waist, thumbs hooked into the watch-pockets of his waistcoat, while she sat on her bench in prim rigidity, gazing up at him with her head cocked a fraction to one side. The image of Squire So-and-so and his faithful hound came to mind, in one of those rather commercial paintings you may see in the better class of hotel, price eleven guineas or thereabouts, title *Master of the Hunt.*

Presently Babcock came over and sat down alongside me, and signalled in a confiding way. I bent to hear him, and he whispered, 'I say, that's a very rum sort of girl, you know. Pretty enough, and well-brought up in a parson's-daughter sort of way, but absolutely no conversation—none whatsoever. She nods, and smiles, and looks at you, and that's all she'll do: I've tried to bring her out a bit, but I can't get the first thing out of her. Funny, isn't it? Lot of inbreeding goes on in these little villages, I daresay: not exactly lacking, you know, just a little slow on the uptake. Or perhaps it's just my city ways: the girls you'd take to the Alhambra or the Holborn Empire are a bit more sparky, you know, and they'll chaff a fellow and banter, that's what I like about 'em.'

If Miss Holt did not wish to exchange chaff, or banter, or anything else, with Babcock, that was her prerogative, as far as I could see, and I expressed this opinion as delicately as I could. 'Oh, absolutely,' he said, looking a trifle wounded: 'just passing the time of day, you know—no harm in it, no harm whatsoever,' and he got up and wandered back down the platform to Miss Holt's side once more. I resumed the scrutiny of my notes; the train was due in five minutes.

A whistle heralded its arrival, far off in the heavy evening air; I saw Miss Holt look up abruptly, then begin to rise, and Babcock put out a hand as if to assist her. She turned quickly to him, and again I thought for an instant that he had overstepped the mark, so swiftly did she respond; and then she merely let her hand rest upon his arm till she was quite on her feet. Babcock began to walk back down to where I sat, and Miss Holt followed close behind, making little darting steps alongside and past him, first this side, then the other, trying to see where the train might come into view.

The engine rounded the bend and drew up with much hissing and exhalation of steam at the platform; we were closest to the door of the rearmost carriage, which Babcock opened up with a flourish: the porter was nowhere in sight, curiously enough. He handed Miss Holt up into the carriage, and held the door ajar for me: I stepped forward, reaching for the bags at my side—and found, much to my perplexity, that the bags had gone, both my large suitcase and the smaller valise.

Babcock appraised the situation at a glance. 'What's up—bags? Bags gone? I say, that's pretty rum. Call the porter chappie: see if he's put them in the guard's van or whatever.' Good advice, and I sought to put it into effect: but the booking window of the porter's office was empty, and I could see no trace of him any-where on the station. I even went so far as to look inside the office: a deep growl came from below the counter, and I shut the door hurriedly on seeing a large brindled mastiff rise from its basket and eye me balefully, baring all its teeth in a dangerous lip-curling snarl.

I heard a whistle and a chuff of steam, and Babcock's voice, shouting some-thing unintelligible: alarmed, I retreated to the platform, where fresh calamity awaited. The signal had apparently been given to pull away—by whom, I have no idea—and the train had already almost cleared the platform as I hurried after it, flagging with both arms in frantic semaphore and shouting for it to wait. Babcock hung from the open carriage door, waving his hand at me, or at the driver, I know not which, and he called out, 'They've gone off, the fools,' (this much I could see for myself). 'I shouted to wait, but they can't have heard me.'

The train pulled clear of the station, and I slowed my pursuit as I reached the edge of the platform, dividing my muttered imprecations between the precipitate driver, the absent porter, and poor Babcock, who had done me no more harm than to continue to wave as he was borne off into the far distance. And then arose a circumstance which for a moment gave me fresh hope; the train began once more to slow down, as it approached a curve in the line which would take it between two low cuttings in the undulating sandy terrain, and so out of sight from the station. This, I later found out, was regular practice on the part of the drivers on that stretch; but I did not know that then, and assumed the train was slowing down in order that I might catch up and explain the situation. As far as I knew, it was the last train out of Ashburgh Halt that night, and if it would wait for me, till my luggage had been located and brought aboard, then so much the better.

I began to trot along the side of the track towards the train, now almost stationary; the way was difficult, with loose gravel shifting treacherously underfoot, but I managed to keep my footing. One or two village dogs, I noticed from the corner of my eye, were also pursuing the train in amongst the sand dunes; as I ran, I remembered Babcock's earlier assertion, that the only entertainment in Ashburgh consisted of watching the trains, and thought how he might smile to see the dogs bear him out in it. But indeed he must have seen it, for he was still hanging by an arm from the carriage and exhorting me onwards, though I could not hear him above the racket of the engine and my own exertions.

Then one of the dogs veered across the line, into my way; I tripped, I stumbled, and I was precipitated with some force onto the hard sharp edges of the gravel, skinning most painfully the palms of my hands and entirely ruining the knees of my trousers. You may imagine with what ardour I cursed the brute, and I flung a handful of the gravel after it as it raced ahead; some of the stones pattered onto its back, and it faced round quickly and snapped out a vicious bark in my direction before turning once more to the chase.

The train now began to pick up speed again, and by the time I had regained my feet it had almost vanished round the bend. Babcock was still waving and yelling at me from the last carriage with redoubled vehemence, swinging from an arm and a leg like some great ape, though I was still unable to make out what it was he shouted. He suddenly lurched outwards, and I thought for a moment that he must surely fall; perhaps it was the train's jerking movement as it began to accelerate away. At any rate, he did not fall: the arm of Miss Holt shot out as if to restrain a small boy, and seized him by the collar. For a long moment they were balanced thus, Babcock wriggling as if trying to regain his equilibrium, groping for the arm of Miss Holt behind his back; and then by some prodigious effort she jerked him clean backwards into the carriage, seeming to overbalance them both in the act, and I could see them no more in the open doorway. I heard Babcock cry out one last time, but the train whistle sounded and the sense of it was lost to me; and then the last of the carriage rounded the bend, and was lost from view behind the sandy cuttings. The dogs raced round the corner after it, some three or four of them by now; for my part, I was left to limp back down the line to the station, in my foulest temper yet.

Had the porter by now reappeared, he should have taken the brunt of my wrath; but the station was deserted still, and I found none but inanimate objects on which to vent my spleen. After a little while, the village dogs that had chased the train reappeared, trotting down the line to take up a sitting position opposite the platform on which I stood, consulting the station timetable in the gathering twilight.

The situation was not as hopeless as I had at first feared: there was another train that evening, due to leave in half-an-hour. What cannot be cured must be endured, and I resolved to sit and wait, bottling up my rancour against the reappearance of the porter. I walked over to the bench, and encountered still another surprise, or at least a variant on the first: there were my bags, as if they had been there all the time, placed carefully beside the bench just as I had left them on first sitting down. You may imagine the frame of mind in which I now awaited the return of the porter; and it was some ten minutes later, after I had puffed my way through a pipe full of tobacco like a small Vesuvius, that I became fully aware of the dogs across the track.

I have said that there were at first three or four of these dogs, village animals or perhaps strays; now there must have been between twelve and fifteen of the brutes, sitting on their haunches in a rough semi-circle facing me, tongues lolling from their jaws as they panted and grinned. As I said, I had no special dislike of the canine species, having been reasonably successful in facing down a variety of animals ranging from the foolish and yapping to the plain vindictive; still, there were many of them, and only one of me, and I observed them with a caution not unmixed with perturbation. They made no move, and were perfectly quiet; I sat slowly and carefully on my bench, and they continued to stare at me, and I at them. From time to time, one of them yawned noiselessly, or raised a long muzzle to sniff at the air; for my part, I refilled my pipe and lit it again, letting the blown-out match fall lightly from my fingers rather than casting it away as was my usual habit.

Before long, more of the animals came ambling in ones and twos; some from the direction of the sand dunes and the village beyond, others from down the line where the train had gone, all pattering up to join the others and taking their place in the formation. By the end, I should say there were some twenty-five dogs facing me and staring me down. They were all largish, heavy, more or less of a breed save one or two, with a look of that Alsatian owned by the landlord of the village inn, and if they had taken it into their heads to turn on me, I daresay I might have been in for a tight time of it, being armed with nothing more than a walking-stick; but as I say they did nothing more than watch me, and I them. I should have been glad to see even the porter, by the time half-an-hour of that had elapsed, but the station remained silent and empty throughout, save for myself—and, I now recalled, mentally recalculating the odds canine-versus-human once again, that guard dog in the porter's office.

It was the queerest thing I had ever experienced, in its way: the distinct impression was that I was being watched, much as a prisoner may be watched from the peephole in his cell-door, though you may smile at the comparison. If I had whistled, or thrown a stick for them to fetch, I do not think I should have met with much response; if I had approached them, or attempted to leave the platform, I have no way of knowing what might have become of it. Gradually, I realised that this was no ordinary experience; there was something more to it than just a pack of strays that ranged around the dunes of an evening and chased after the trains. There was a sensation abroad in the air, difficult to define yet growing by the minute in intensity and queerness; and it emanated from the dogs.

If I likened the sensation to hypnosis, that might give you an idea of it; hypnosis in which direction, at whose instigation, and to whose will, I would find it hard to say. There was something of the hypnotist's trance in my utter absorption, certainly, for to keep close watch on beasts which may turn vicious is one thing, but there was more of lassitude than alertness in my bearing as I sat and watched—I never once felt like sleeping, you understand, but there was no power in me, no vigour, no adrenalin. For the life of me, all I could do was stare. As I stared, I wool-gathered; strange notions came into my head, half-formed and instinctive, thoughts such as I had never entertained before, though now it was if I had known them all my life. I thought how dogs had been the first beasts Man bent to his purpose, when he came down from the trees and walked and stood upright. Was that the power of human will at work upon a lesser beast, I asked myself; or was it not instead something more of a covenant, a tacit, unacknowledged recognition of some dim and distant kinship? How distant indeed might that remove be; or how near? These and other equally curious speculations moved through my mind, as the shadows lengthened among the sand-dunes and were swallowed at last in the soft thick blur of dusk. I wondered whether our ancestors might not have looked out from their caves on such a night, and seen dark eyes, such as I saw now, stare back at them; and I wondered what commerce might have passed between the two, in those days before Fate led them in such very opposite directions.

At length the absolute stillness of that weird and unsettling scene was interrupted by the whistle of an oncoming train; at its shrill report, all the dogs rose as if controlled by wires and bolted for the dunes, and were gone in an instant. Now, at last, the porter reappeared, but by this time I was too confused to give him the upbraiding he so richly deserved, merely asking him where he had been for the last half-hour, and whether he had taken my bags earlier.

'I don't know what you mean, sir,' he said in a curious sleepy kind of voice, running a hand over his thick unshaven jowls; 'I was in the office, all along; you'd have seen me, if you was but to step inside.'

I dismissed him for an idiot, and busied myself in loading my bags into the train—I did not trust him not to vanish with them again, if I left the job to him. Thus established in the carriage, I swung the door to, and as the train drew away from the platform I saw the last of Ashburgh Halt recede in the now almost perfect darkness, the porter standing where I had stood at the end of the platform, watching the train out of sight round the bend in the track.

And yet I could not settle. The affair with the dogs had played queerly on my mind, and even though I had slept rather poorly the night before, I found myself unable, or unwilling, to succumb to the drowsiness I now felt. Time and again I was on the verge of sleep, and would jerk awake with some inconsequential remembrance or other; Miss Holt and the angle of her head as she sat and listened to Babcock; the porter's voice as he spun his fabrication of having been in his office all the time; the way Babcock had swung from the carriage and shouted to me, and how Miss Holt had hauled him back when he seemed to pitch forwards; and mixed in with all these, the dogs, that sat and watched me like a jury of my peers for fully half-an-hour in the dusk. I remembered one in particular, a greyhound that had come late to join the pack; how it sat on its slim haunches across the track, trembling a little in that coiled-spring way particular to the breed, licking now and again at its lips and muzzle.

Perhaps at the end I did sleep, or come close to it; I seemed to remember Babcock at the carriage-door, both hands free of the frame, toppling outwards and Miss Holt's arm pistoning out to hold him: like a fish on a gaff, I thought abstractedly; like a dog on a leash. At that moment Babcock must have been a hundred yards away in reality, and yet in my dream, or my fancy, I thought I could see magnified the expression on his face, and hear—if not what he shouted, at least the tone of his voice above the train whistle. Much at odds they were with the comfortable rumbling vulgarity of Babcock on the platform; far from the cheerful Cockney caricature he presented so guilelessly, to Ashburgh and to the world at large. I seemed to see his features distorted, as if in terror, and his voice was shrill and harsh, more of a scream than a holloa; it woke me up, or recalled me to my senses, and Babcock's scream merged with the whistle of my own train, now pulling into the next station on the line.

Very likely Babcock had screamed, I reflected; and why should he not appear alarmed? He had, after all, been on the verge of a reasonably serious accident, a fall from a moving train, and only Miss Holt's prompt actions had saved him. Still, I wondered a little at her strength, now I came to consider it: Babcock was a grown man, and must have weighed in excess of sixteen stone, and that slip of a girl had hauled him in like—like a fish on a gaff, as I had thought before, or like a dog hauled back on its leash.

The matter was dispelled from my mind for the time being by a rapping on the carriage window. I opened the door, thinking it to be some passenger awaiting entrance, and discovered instead two officials of the Railway, one tall and thin, one stout and rather shorter—as is often the case with two such men. 'Excuse me, sir,' said the taller, licking his lips as if his mouth were dry; 'did you board the train at Ashburgh Halt, by any chance?'

'Yes; here is my ticket,' I said, proffering the pasteboard slip for inspection.

'It isn't that, sir,' said the shorter of the two, and I noticed that both their faces were white as sheets in the gloom. 'I'm afraid it's something a bit more unpleasant, like. The fact is___' And he broke off, leaving the other to finish.

'There's been an accident, sir, a rather nasty accident, on the train before yours. We wired up to Ashburgh, and they say a gentleman answering your description was delayed from catching that train by a matter of luggage, or some such: it seems you were talking to another gentleman on the platform . . .' He trailed off, and again his companion stepped into the breach.

'And we was wondering, sir, whether you could undertake to identify that gentleman?'

'Babcock? Of course,' said I, and got down from the train in some perturbation. 'But what, is he wounded—seriously—gravely? Has there been a crash of some description? An explosion of the boiler? And there was a woman in his carriage—a Miss Holt—is she hurt too?'

'You'd better follow us, sir,' was all the men would say, and I suffered myself to be led across to a siding, in which the train I had missed, and Babcock caught, stood with its engine damped and cooling, the other passengers cleared from the carriages, while a little knot of railway folk stood outside the rear most bearing lanterns. Among them was a policeman; he detached himself from their midst and came to my side, and I saw that he, like my twin Cicerones, was pale in the extreme, and very much ill at ease.

'Officer? Please tell me what has happened.'

'Excuse me, sir—you're the passenger from Ashburgh? Well, sir, I'm afraid I have some rather upsetting news for you: the gentleman you were talking to on the platform there—the fact of it is, he's dead, sir,' he said simply, and in that instant I felt a great sadness such as I would not have credited on an acquaintance of at the most fifteen minutes, and a fondness for poor boastful Babcock and all his ridiculous ways. But I was still in the dark as to the manner of his death, and I pressed the policeman for information.

'As to that, sir—it's not pretty, I'm afraid,' he said earnestly. 'I'm afraid I shall have to ask you to make an identification if you can, sir, and I warn you now, you'll need a strong stomach, for it's all I can do to look in the door, let alone close up.' He turned half-away in what I fancied was shame, and while still somewhat anaesthetised by the very suddenness of it all I took from his hand the lantern, and mounted to the carriage door.

What I saw inside that carriage will never leave me, I suppose: I still see it at night, sometimes, when my nerves are bad. The hot brassy reek of blood comes through, the reek that permeated the whole compartment; my flesh crawls now as it crawled then, when I think of what was left of Babcock. Whatever had killed him had all but torn him apart; I have never been in India, but I imagine a tiger might leave such a carcass behind, for the scavengers of carrion to finish off and pick clean down to the bone. The clothing, what shreds remained, was Babcock's; as to the body, it might have been anyone's, and I told the policeman so afterwards, once I had regained my mettle. That was afterwards; in that first shock of taking it all in, I swayed and almost fell, and they had to grab at me and catch me lest I injure myself, and the first thing that imprinted itself on my mind amidst the horror was this—*Babcock had not stumbled.* I knew it in that instant of falling myself. He had not fallen: what I had seen was Babcock trying to jump clear of the carriage, having turned from the open door and looked back inside, and seen—what? That which had caught him; that which had pulled him back, to a death worse than that of any animal, for a man is sensible of his doom, even as the claws sink in, and the teeth rend and tear. As soon as I was able, I asked what had become of Miss Holt.

'Excuse me, sir,' the policeman said, his brow creased in perplexity, 'but there wasn't any other passenger mentioned by the folks up at Ashburgh. Just the gentleman there and yourself, he said, sir; no one else. And there was no one else in the carriage, when we came to find him: he was quite alone.'

'Quite alone' was the verdict of the inquest, too, when it came around: the porter was called to give evidence before me, and he told the court that he had seen no other passengers save Babcock and myself on the platform that evening, nor had he sold a ticket to any young woman such as I described. The name of Holt was said to be unknown in those parts, and police investigations failed to trace anybody of that description in connection with the affair. My own statement of the facts was taken into evidence and weighed against the porter's; I did not mention my intuition concerning Babcock's near-fall from the train; nor did I mention the dogs, for I knew how it would sound, and in those days I was a vainer man than I am now. I did, however, say that I thought the porter had prevented me from boarding the train by concealing my luggage, but this he denied, and was believed in his denial. In his laughably provincial summing-up, the coroner suggested that anyone might have jumped out of the train once it had passed out of my sight, and equally, anybody might have got on board. Anybody; or call it anything; for the injuries poor Babcock had sustained were found to be of a violence and ferocity consistent more with the animal kingdom than with the run of normal homicide. Murder by person or persons unknown, was the verdict; and against that I had nothing to say, particularly. But I thought of the dogs, that had followed the train out of sight while it was still travelling slowly enough to be caught up with; I thought of Miss Holt, and of the grey-hound that had stared me down across the railway track; and I thought of Bab-cock, in life and in death, and I think of him still to this day. And I thank you for letting me share this carriage with you; for while I am able to avoid dogs for the most part—unless I am on a shooting-holiday, or on a crowded street where it is a little easier—I still have to use the railway if I am to go about my business in the world, and that is difficult if the carriage is empty, you see.

Such was the singular and paradoxical story told to me by the old gentleman I have called Mr Smith; he got out at Cambridge, thanking me again for my company, and for my indulgence in hearing him out. For my part, I stayed on till King's Lynn, and travelled as far as Sheringham the next morning, on business of my own. Upon the conclusion of that business, I found I had a day to spare before travelling back to London, and from London to my college; you will perhaps not be surprised if I tell you that I took a rented motor-car as far along the coast towards Ashburgh as proved feasible.

The road ran out against a wire fence, some few miles from the town; I instructed the driver to wait for me, essayed the wire, and walked on along the sand-blown, weed-cracked roadway. There was little left of the town, when I reached it: the artillery practice of the Army had been thorough, and not a house was undamaged, with many destroyed completely. I turned further east, and located with no great difficulty the station; the line was of course completely overgrown, and the station-house much dilapidated. Impressed with that sense of melancholy attendant upon all such marks of Time's firm impartial hand, I poked around the booking-office, and inside the porter's room; posters and time-tables from twenty years before lay higgledy-piggledy, hither and yon, and the station sign creaked plaintively in a thin North sea breeze.

Outside, I turned my steps once more towards the west, where waited the car, and it struck me to wonder what became of the villagers, when the Army took over the land. As I walked on, pondering the matter, and revolving in my mind all those details of Mr Smith's outlandish story, I noticed away up on a sand-dune to my right a dog, which might have been a greyhound; I am not very good in these things, but I thought it very feminine and graceful, and yet powerful, too, and watchful, even in silhouette. It sat atop the dune and looked at me for a second; and then it leapt up and was gone, whither I cared not follow it.

MARISA DE LOS SANTOS

Wiglaf

Marisa de los Santos holds an MFA from Sarah Lawrence College and a Ph.D. in literature and creative writing from the University of Houston. Her recent publications include poems in Southwest Review, Prairie Schooner, and Chelsea.

In the following poem, de los Santos takes a fresh look at the Beowulf story, beautifully weaving its ancient themes into modern life. It is reprinted from The Antioch Review, published in Yellow Springs, Ohio and edited by Robert S. Fogarty.

—T. W.

"Wiglaf the foot-warrior sat near the shoulder of his King, wearily sprinkling water on his face to wake him. He succeeded not at all."

—*Beowulf*

It is the saddest part of a sad story:
a young man in an old man's heavy shirt,
his helmet, arm-rings, all the gold gone dull

and gummed with blood. The gutted dragon lies
there twitching, and cowards—seasoned fighters—
are dragging themselves, shamefaced, from the woods.

Wiglaf's own eyes saw his master's body
caught up by waves of flame, saw long teeth tear
the great one's throat. Through clots of smoke, he

found the weak spot, struck, and found out later
what is worse than dragons. Kings die slowly,
gasping words. Young Wiglaf loved his king

and carried water to him, in his hands.
This story is and isn't old. My half-brother's
sixth-month-born, three-pound daughter was alive

an hour last December, and, in spring, he's
saying this, "You haven't seen her room, yet"
although he knows I have, the crib and stack

of folded blankets, silver brush and comb
his wife lifts up to dust beneath and then
puts back. Fat bears and grinning tigers dance

across the wall. Foot-warrior Wiglaf knew
the king was dead, and still he bathed his face
to wake him, sprinkling water, while the others

watched. We are standing in my brother's yard,
where a single mimosa, bloom-decked, leans
in careful arabesque. He's choking, weary,

on his loss, and I see how love, once started,
can become a thing apart from us,
a being all its own, unstoppable,

just watching as we waste our human gestures
on the air, and who can say if it's
the monster or the hero of our lives?

SUSANNA CLARKE

Mrs Mabb

Susanna Clarke is a British writer who specializes in works of historical fantasy fiction. Her exquisite adult fairy stories (reminiscent of the works of Sylvia Townsend Warner) have been published in Starlight 1; The Sandman: Book of Dreams; *and* Black Swan, White Raven. *She shares a home in Cambridge, England with writer Colin Greenland, and is at work on her first novel.*

"Mrs Mabb" is reprinted from Starlight 2, *edited by Patrick Nielsen Hayden.*

—*T. W.*

In the late spring of 18_____ a lady in the village of Kissingland in D____shire suffered a bitter disappointment.

Mrs Fanny Hawkins to Mrs Clara Johnson

"... and I know, my dear Clara, that you will share my vexation when I tell you what has happened. Some months ago my sister, Miss Moore, had the good fortune to captivate an officer in the Regulars. Captain Fox shewed a decided preference for Venetia from the start and I was in great hopes of seeing her respectably settled when, by a stroke of ill fortune, she received a letter from an acquaintance, a lady in Manchester who had fallen sick and was in need of someone to nurse her. You may imagine how little I liked that she should leave Kissingland at such a time, but I found that, in spite of all I could say, she was determined to undertake the expense and inconvenience of the journey and go. But now I fear she is too well punished for her obstinacy, for in her absence the wretched Captain Fox has forgot her entirely and has begun to pay his respects to another lady, a neighbour of ours, Mrs Mabb. You may well believe that when she comes back I will always be quarrelling with her about it ..."

Fanny Hawkins' amiable intention of quarrelling with her sister proceeded, not merely from a general wish to correct faulty behaviour, but also from the realization that if Venetia did *not* marry Captain Fox then she must look to Fanny for a home. Fanny's husband was the curate of Kissingland, a person of no particular importance in the society of the place, who baptised, married, and buried all its inhabitants, who visited them in their sick-beds, comforted them in their griefs, and read their letters to them if they could not do it for themselves—for all of which he received the magnificent sum of £40 a year. Consequently any moments which Fanny could spare from domestic cares were spent in pondering the difficult question of how an income which had never been sufficient for *two* might now be made to support *three*.

Fanny waited for her sister's return and, with great steadiness of purpose, told Mr Hawkins several times a day how she intended to quarrel with her for letting Captain Fox slip his bonds. "To go off like that with the business entirely unsettled between them. What an odd creature she is! I cannot understand her."

But Fanny had a few oddities of her own, one of which was to delight in fancying herself disagreeable and cold-hearted, when in truth she was only ill-used and anxious. When at last Miss Moore returned to Kissingland and when Fanny saw how white and stricken the poor girl was to hear of her lover's defection, all of Fanny's much-vaunted quarrelsomeness dwindled into a shake of her head and, "Now you see, Venetia, what comes of being so obstinate and liking your own way above what other people advise"; and even this she immediately followed with, "There, my dear, I hope you will not distress yourself. Any man who can play you such a shabby trick as this is not worth thinking of. How is your friend in Manchester?"

"Dead." (This in a tearful whisper.)

"Oh! . . . Well, my dear, I am very sorry to hear it. And Mr Hawkins will say the same when I tell him of it. Poor girl!—you have a sad homecoming."

That evening at supper (a very small amount of fried beef to a great deal of boiled turnip) Fanny told Mr Hawkins, "She has gone to bed—she says she has a shocking headache. I dare say she was a great deal more attached to him than we believed. It was never very likely that she should have escaped whole-hearted from the attentions of such a man as Captain Fox. You may recall I said so at the time."

Mr Hawkins said nothing; the Hawkins' domestic affairs were arranged upon the principle that Fanny supplied the talk and he the silence.

"Well!" continued Fanny, "We must all live as cheaply as we can. I dare say there are more savings I can make." Fanny looked around the shabby parlour in search of any luxuries that had hitherto gone undiscovered. Not finding any, she merely remarked that things lasted a great deal longer than those people supposed who always like to have every thing new; indeed it had been a very long time since Fanny had had any thing new; the worn stone flags of her parlour floor were bare, the chairs were hard and inconvenient, and the wallpaper was so ancient and faded that it appeared to shew withered garlands of dead flowers tied up with dry brown ribbons.

The next morning Fanny's thoughts ran upon the subject of her grievances against Captain Fox and her anger against him was such that she found herself obliged to speak of it almost incessantly—while at the same time continually advising Venetia to think of Captain Fox no more. After half an hour Venetia said with a sigh that she thought she would walk in the fresh air for a while.

"Oh!" said Fanny, "Which way do you go?"

"I do not know."

"Well, if you were to go towards the village then there are several things I need."

So Venetia went along Church-lane to Kissingland and, though it would benefit the dignity of the Female Sex in general to report that she now despised and hated Captain Fox, Venetia was not so unnatural. Instead she indulged in many vain sighs and regrets, and tried to derive such consolation as she could from the reflection that it was better to be poor and forgotten in Kissingland, where there were green trees and sweet flowery meadows, than in Manchester where her friend, Mrs Whitsun, had died in a cold grey room at the top of a dismal lodging house.

Captain Fox was a tall Irishman of thirty-six or seven who bore the reputation of having red hair. Indeed in some weathers and lights it did appear to have a little red in it, but it was more his name, his long ironical grin and a certain Irish wildness that made people believe they saw red hair. He also had a reputation for quite unheard-of bravery, for he had once contradicted the Duke of Wellington when all around were most energetically agreeing with that illustrious person.

It had been a question of boots. The boots (ten thousand pairs of them) had been proceeding east from Portugal upon the backs of seventy mules to where the British army, with boots entirely worn out, anxiously awaited them. Without the new boots the army was entirely unable to begin its long march north to retake Spain from the French. The Duke of Wellington had been in a great passion about it, had talked a great deal about the nuisance of delay and what the British might lose by it, but in the end he had admitted that the soldiers could do nothing without new boots. Upon the contrary, Captain Fox had cried; it would be better by far for the boots to travel along a more northerly path to the city of S____ where they could meet the army on its way north—which would mean that for the first part of the march the men would be coming ever closer to their new boots—a cheerful thought that would doubtless encourage them to go faster. The Duke of Wellington had thought for a while; "I believe," he had said at last, "that Captain Fox is right."

Upon turning the corner at Blewitt's yard Venetia came in sight of a substantial stone house. This was the residence of Mr Grout, a well-to-do lawyer. So vigorous were the roses in Mr Grout's garden that one of the walls of his house seemed to be nothing but a trembling cliff of pale pink; but this delightful sight only served to remind Venetia that Captain Fox had been excessively fond of pale pink roses, and had twice told her with significant glances that, when he married and had a garden of his own, he did not think he would have any other sort.

She determined upon thinking of something else for a while but was immediately thwarted in that resolve when the first person she saw in the High-street was Captain Fox's servant, Lucas Barley.

"Lucas!" she cried, "What! Is the Captain here?" She looked about her hastily, and only when quite certain that the Captain was not in sight did she attend properly to Lucas. She saw with some surprize that he had undergone a strange transformation. Gone was his smart brown coat, gone his shining top boots, gone his swaggering air—the air of someone with a proper consciousness of the fact that his master had once given the Duke of Wellington a flat contradiction. In place of these he wore a dirty green apron several sizes too big for him and wooden patterns on his feet. He was carrying two enormous pewter tankards that slopped beer into the mud. "What are you doing with those jugs, Lucas? Have you left the Captain's service?"

"I do not know, Miss."

"You do not know! What do you mean?"

"I mean, Miss, that should I ever lay eyes on Captain Fox again I shall certainly ask him for his opinion on that point; and if he should ask me for my opinion on that point I shall certainly say to him that I do not care about it one way or the other. You may well look surprized, Miss—I myself am in a state of perpetual astonishment. But I am not alone in that—the Captain is parting with all his old friends."

And, having no hands disengaged to point with, Lucas indicated by a sort of straining expression of his face that Venetia should look behind her, to where a most beautiful brown-black mare was being led into Mr Grout's mews.

"Good Lord!" cried Venetia, "Belle-dame!"

"A message has come from Mrs Mabb's house that she is to be sold to Mr Grout, Miss."

"But is the Captain quitting the regiment?"

"I do not know, Miss. But what will such a little, round man as Mr Grout do with such a horse as that? He had better take care that she does not mistake him for a turnip and eat him."

Indeed the mare seemed to have some thoughts of her own in that direction; the disdainful light in her wild brown eye shewed that she was aware of having come down in the world, and thought someone ought to suffer for it, and was at this moment turning over in her mind exactly whom that someone ought to be.

"It happened like this, Miss," said Lucas, "The morning after you left, Mrs Mabb sent a message to the Captain to ask him if he would make a fourth at cards; and I went with him—for someone once told me that Mrs Mabb has a great number of aunts and nieces and female relations living with her, every one of them more beautiful than the last—and I hoped to make myself acquainted with any as was not too proud to speak to me. But when we got to the house I was made to wait in a little stone antechamber as cold as a tomb and furnished with nothing but a few bones in the hearth. I waited and I waited and I waited and then I waited some more; and I could hear the sound of the Captain talking and the sound of female laughter, high and loud. And after a while, Miss, I saw that my fingernails were getting longer and I felt that my chin was all bristles— which gave me quite a fright as you may suppose. So, the front door being open, I shot through it and ran all the way back to Kissingland, where I discovered that I had been standing in Mrs Mabb's little stone room for three days and three nights."

"Good Lord!" cried Venetia. She pondered this a moment. "Well," she said at last with a sigh, "If people discover they were mistaken in their affections or find that they like another person better . . . I suppose she is very beautiful?"

Lucas made a scornful sound as though he would like to say something very cutting about the beauty of Mrs Mabb and was only prevented by the fact of his never having seen her.

"I do not think that Mrs Mabb ought to be named with you in the same day, Miss. The Captain told me several times, Miss, that you and he would marry soon and that we would all go off to Exeter to live in a little white house with a garden and a trellis of pink roses; and I had made myself a solemn vow, one morning in church, to serve you very faithfully and honourably—for you were always very kind to me."

"Thank you, Lucas . . ." said Venetia, but she found she could get no further. This picture of what would never come to pass affected her to strongly and her eyes filled with tears.

She would have liked to have given Lucas a little money but there was nothing in her purse but what would pay for the bread that she had come out to buy for Fanny.

"It is of no consequence, Miss," said Lucas, "We are all of us a great deal worse off on account of Mrs Mabb." He paused. "I am sorry I made you cry, Miss."

Which remark, said with a great deal of kindness, was enough to make her glad to hurry away to the bakery where melancholy fancies of Captain Fox gaily abandoning his career for the sake of Mrs Mabb, and Mrs Mabb laughing loudly to see him do it, so took off her attention from what she was doing that when she got home and opened up the packages she found to her surprize that she had bought three dozen French milk-rolls and an apricot-jam tart—none of which were the things that Fanny had wanted.

"What in the world were you thinking of?" cried Fanny in great perplexity when she saw what Venetia had done. Fanny was quite appalled by the waste of money and under the baneful influence of the milk-rolls and the jam tart became snappish and cross, a mood that threatened to last all day until Venetia remembered that, just before she died, her friend Mrs Whitsun had given her some curtains as a wedding-present. Now that there was to be no wedding it seemed both proper and kind for Venetia to fetch the curtains down from her bedroom and make a present of them to Fanny. The material was very pretty—primrose-yellow with a fine white stripe. Fanny's good humour was restored upon the instant and with Venetia's help she set about altering the curtains for the parlour window and when they were settled at their work, "Fanny," asked Venetia, "Who is Mrs Mabb?"

"A very wicked person, my dear," said Fanny, happily brandishing her large black scissors.

"In what way is she wicked?"

But Fanny had no precise information to offer upon this point and all that Venetia could learn was that Mrs Mabb's wickedness chiefly consisted in being very rich and never doing any thing if she did not like it.

"What does she look like?" asked Venetia.

"Oh, Lord! I do not know. I never saw her."

"Then she is quite recently come into the neighbourhood?"

"Oh, yes! Quite recently. . . . But then again, I am not quite sure. Now that I come to think of it I believe she has been here a great long while. She was certainly here when Mr Hawkins came here fifteen years ago."

"Where does she live?"

"A great way off! Beyond Knightswood."

"Near to Dunchurch, then?"

"No, my dear, not near Dunchurch. Nearer to Piper than anywhere, but not particularly near there either . . ." (These were all towns and villages in the neighbourhood of Kissingland.) ". . . If you leave the turnpike road just before Piper and go by an overgrown lane that descends very suddenly, you come to a lonely stretch of water full of reeds called Greypool, and above that—atop a little hill— there is a circle of ancient stones. Beyond the hill there is a little green valley and then an ancient wood. Mrs Mabb's house stands betwixt the stones and the wood, but nearer to the wood than the stones."

"Oh!" said Venetia.

The next day Fanny declined Venetia's offer to walk to the village again to buy bread and instead sent her off with a basket of vegetables and some soup to pay a charity visit to a destitute family in Piper. For, as Fanny said, mistakes in purchases came expensive, but if Venetia were so inattentive as to give the soup to the wrong paupers it would not much signify.

Venetia delivered the basket to the destitute family in Piper, but on the way back she passed an opening in a hedge where a narrow, twisting lane descended steeply from the turnpike road. Massive ancient trees grew upon each side and their branches overarched the path and made of it a confusing, shadowy place where the broken sunlight illuminated a clump of violets here, three stalks of grass there.

Now all of English landscape contained nothing that could hold Venetia's gaze quite as rapt as that green lane, for it was the very lane that Fanny had spoken of as leading to the house of Mrs Mabb, and all of Venetia's thoughts ran upon that house and its inhabitants. "Perhaps," she thought, "I will just walk a little way along the lane. And perhaps, if it is not too far, I will just go and take a peep at the house. I should like to know that *he* is happy."

How she proposed to discover whether or not the Captain was happy by looking at the outside of a strange house, she did not consider too exactly, but down the lane she went and she passed the lonely pool and climbed up to the ancient stones and on and on, until she came to a place where round green hills shut out the world.

It was a quiet and empty place. The grass which covered the hills and the valley was as unbroken as any sheet of water—and, almost as if it were water, the sunshiny breeze made little waves in it. On the opposite hill stood an ancient-looking house of grey stone. It was a very tall house, something indeed between a house and a tower, and it was surrounded by a high stone wall in which no opening or gate could be discerned, nor did any path go up to the house.

Yet despite its great height the house was overtopped by the bright sunlit forest wall behind it, and she could not rid herself of the idea that she was actually looking at a very small house—a house for a field mouse or a bee or a butterfly—a house which stood among tall grasses.

"It will not do to linger," she thought. "Suppose I should chance to meet the Captain and Mrs Mabb? Horrible thought!" She turned and walked away quickly, but had not gone far when she heard the drumming of hooves upon the turf behind her. "I shall not look behind me," she thought, "for, if it is Captain Fox, then I am sure that he will be kind and let me go away undisturbed."

But the sound of hooves came on and was joined by many more, till it seemed that a whole army must have risen up out of the silent hills. Greatly amazed, she turned to see what in the world it could be.

Venetia wore a queer old-fashioned gown of fine blue wool. The bodice was embroidered with buttercups and daisies and the waist was low. It was none too long in the skirt but this was amply compensated for by a great number of linen petticoats. She mused upon this for a moment or two. "It appears to be," she thought, "a costume for a milkmaid or a shepherdess or some such other rustic person. How odd! I cannot recall ever having been a milkmaid or a shepherdess. I suppose I must be going to act in some play or other—well, I fear that I shall do it very ill for I do not remember my speeches or any thing about it."

"She has got a little more colour," said Fanny's anxious voice, "Do not you think so, Mr Hawkins?"

Venetia found that she was in Fanny's parlour and Mr Hawkins was kneeling on the flagstones before her chair. There was a basin of steaming water on the floor with a pair of ancient green silk dancing slippers beside it. Mr Hawkins was washing her feet and ankles with a cloth. This was odd too—she had never known him do such a thing before. When he had finished he began to bathe her face with an air of great concentration.

"Be careful, Mr Hawkins!" cried his wife, "you will get the soap in her eyes! Oh, my dear! I was never so frightened in my life as when they brought you home! I thought I should faint from the shock and Mr Hawkins says the same."

That Fanny had been seriously alarmed was apparent from her face; she was commonly hollow-eyed and hollow-cheeked—fifteen years' worrying about money had done that—but now fright had deepened all the hollows, made her eyes grow round and haunted-looking, and sharpened up her nose until it resembled the tip of a scissor blade.

Venetia gazed at Fanny a while and wondered what could have so distressed her. Then she looked down at her own hands and was surprized to find that they were all scratched to pieces. She put her hand up to her face and discovered tender places there.

She jumped up. There was a little scrap of a looking-glass hung upon the opposite wall and there she saw herself, face all bruises and hair pulled this way and that. The shock was so great that she cried out loud.

As she remembered nothing of what had happened to her it was left to Fanny to tell her—with many digressions and exclamations—that she had been found earlier in the day wandering in a lane two or three miles from Piper by a young man, a farmer called Purvis. She had been in a state of the utmost confusion and had answered Mr Purvis's concerned enquiries with queer rambling monologues about silver harness bells and green banners shutting out the sky. For some time Mr Purvis had been unable to discover even so much as her name. Her clothes were torn and dirty and she was barefoot. Mr Purvis had put her on his horse and taken her to his house where his mother had given her tea to drink and the queer old-fashioned gown and the dancing slippers to wear.

"Oh! but, my dear," said Fanny, "do not you remember any thing at all of what happened?"

"No, nothing," said Venetia, "I took the soup to the Peasons—just as you told me—and then what did I do? I believe I went somewhere. But where? Oh! Why can I not remember?"

Mr Hawkins, still on his knees before her, put his finger to his lips as a sign that she should not be agitated and began gently to stroke her forehead.

"You tumbled into a ditch, my dear," said Fanny, "That is all. Which is a nasty, disagreeable thing to happen and so naturally you don't wish to dwell upon it." She started to cry. "You always were a forgetful girl, Venetia."

Mr Hawkins put his finger to his lips as a sign that Fanny should not be agitated and somehow contrived to continue stroking Venetia's forehead while patting Fanny's hand.

"Fanny," said Venetia, "Was there a procession today?"

"A procession?" said Fanny. She pushed Mr Hawkins' hand away and blew her nose loudly. "Whatever do you mean?"

"*That* is what I did today. I remember now. I watched the soldiers ride by."

"There was no procession today," said Fanny, "The soldiers are all in their lodgings, I suppose."

"Oh! Then what was it that I saw today? Hundreds of riders with the sunlight winking on their harness and the sound of silver bells as they rode by. . . ."

"Oh! Venetia," cried Fanny in great irritation of spirits, "do not talk so wildly or Mr Hawkins and I will be obliged to send for the physician—and then there will be his guinea fee and all sorts of medicines to buy no doubt. . . ." Fanny launched upon a long monologue upon the expensiveness of doctors and little by little talked herself up into such paroxysms of worry that she seemed in grave danger of making herself more ill than Venetia had ever been. Venetia hastened to assure her that a physician was quite unnecessary and promised not to talk of processions again. Then she went up to her room and made a more detailed examination of her own person. She found no injuries other than scrapes and bruises. "I suppose," she thought, "I must have fainted but it is very odd for I never did so before." And when the household sat down to supper, which was rather late that evening, Venetia's strange adventure was not mentioned again, other than a few complaints from Fanny to the effect that the Purvises had still got Venetia's gown.

The next morning Venetia was stiff and aching from head to toe. "I feel," she thought, "as if I had tumbled two or three times off a horse." It was a familiar sensation. Captain Fox had taught her to ride in the previous November. They had gone up to a high field that overlooked Kissingland and Captain Fox had lifted her up onto Belle-dame's back. Beneath them the village had been all a-glow with the ember colours of autumn trees and the candlelight in people's windows. Wisps of vivid blue smoke had drifted up from bonfires in Mr Grout's gardens.

"Oh! how happy we were! Except that Pen Harrington would always contrive to discover where we were going and insist on coming with us and she would always want the Captain to pay attention to her, which he—being all nobility—was obliged to do. She is a very tiresome girl. Oh! but now I am no better off than she is—or any of those other girls who liked the Captain and were scorned by him for the sake of Mrs Mabb. It would be far more natural in me to hate the Captain and to feel sisterly affection towards poor Pen . . ."

She sat a while trying to arrange her feelings upon this model, but at the end of five minutes found she liked Pen no better and loved the Captain no less. "I suppose the truth is that one cannot feel much pity for a girl who wears a buttercup-yellow gown with lavender trimmings—buttercup-yellow and lavender look so extremely horrid together. But as for what happened yesterday the most likely explanation is that I fainted in the lane and Mr Purvis found me, picked me up and put me on his horse, but subsequently dropped me—which would account for the bruises and the holes in my clothes. And I suppose that he now is too embarrassed to tell anyone—which I can well understand. The Captain," she thought with a sigh, "would not have dropped me."

That morning as the sisters worked together in the kitchen (Venetia shelling peas, Fanny making pastry), they heard the unexpected sounds of a horse and carriage.

Fanny looked out of the window. "It is the Purvises," she said.

Mrs Purvis proved to be a fat, cheerful woman who, the moment she set eyes upon Venetia, gave a delighted cry and embraced her very heartily. She smelt of sweet milk, new bread and freshly turned earth, as if she had spent the morning in the dairy, the kitchen and the vegetable-garden—as indeed she had.

"I dare say, ma'am," said Mrs Purvis to Fanny, "you are surprized at my warmth but if you had seen Miss Moore when John first brought her in, all white and shaking, then I think you would excuse me. And I know that Miss Moore will excuse me for she and I got to be great friends when she was in my kitchen."

"Did we, though?" thought Venetia.

"And you see, my dear," continued Mrs Purvis, delving in a great canvas bag, "I have brought you my little china shepherdess that you liked so much. Oh! Do not thank me. I have half a dozen other such that I scarcely look at. And here, ma'am . . ." She addressed Fanny respectfully, ". . . are asparagus and strawberries and six beautiful goose eggs. I dare say you will agree with me that it is scarcely any wonder that our young ladies faint dead away when they let themselves get so thin."

Fanny always liked visitors and Mrs Purvis was precisely the sort to please her—full of harmless gossip, and deferring to Fanny as a farmer's widow should defer to a curate's wife. Indeed so pleased was Fanny that she was moved to give each of the Purvises a small biscuit. "I did have a bottle of very good madeira-wine," she told them, "but I fear it is all drunk." Which was true—Mr Hawkins had finished it at Christmas eight years before.

Of the queer, old-fashioned gown Mrs Purvis had this to say: "It was my sister's, Miss Moore. She died when she was about your age and she was almost as pretty as you are. You are welcome to keep it, but I expect you like to have everything of the new fashion like other young ladies."

The visit ended with Mrs Purvis nodding and making signs to her son that he should say something. He stammered out his great pleasure in seeing Miss Moore looking so much better and hoped that she and Mrs Hawkins would not object to his calling upon them again in a day or two. Poor man, his blushing countenance seemed to shew that Venetia had not been alone in sustaining some hurt from the previous day's adventures; her rescuer also appeared to have received a blow—in his case to the heart.

When they were gone Fanny said, "She seems a very worthy sort of woman. It is however extremely provoking that she has not brought back your clothes. I was several times upon the point of asking her about it, but each time I opened my mouth she began to talk of something else. I cannot understand what she means by keeping them so long. Perhaps she thinks of selling them. We have only her word for it that the clothes are spoiled."

Fanny had a great deal of useless speculation of this sort to get through but she had scarcely begun when she discovered that she had left her huswife in her bedroom and sent Venetia upstairs to fetch it.

In the lane beneath Fanny's bedroom window Mrs Purvis and her son were making ready to drive away. As Venetia watched John Purvis took a big wooden pail out of the back of the ancient gig and placed it upside-down on the ground as an extra step for his mother to mount up to the driver's seat.

Venetia heard Mrs Purvis say, "Well, my mind is much eased to see her looking so much better. It is a great blessing that she remembers nothing about it."

Here Purvis said something, but his face was still turned away and Venetia could not hear what it was.

"It was soldiers, John, I am sure of it. Those great slashes in her gown were made by swords and sabres. It would have frightened them both into fits—as much as it frightened me, I am sure—to see how cut about her clothes were when you found her. It is my belief that this Captain Fox—the same I told you of, John—must have set on some of his men to frighten her off. For all that he has treated her so cruel she may still love him. With such a sweet nature as she has got it is the likeliest thing in the world. . . ."

"Good God!" whispered Venetia in great astonishment.

At first the horror which she ought to have felt was quite overtaken by her indignation on the Captain's behalf; "I dare say she was very kind to take me in, but she is a very stupid woman to invent such lies about Captain Fox, who is every thing that is honourable and would never do harm to any one—always excepting, of course, in pursuit of his military duties." But then, as images of her poor, ill-treated gown rose up before her fancy, the disagreeable impression which Mrs Purvis's words had created grew until Venetia was thoroughly frightened. "What in the world can have happened to me?" she wondered.

But she had no satisfactory answer.

On the following day after dinner, Venetia felt in need of fresh air and told Fanny that she thought she would walk out for a while. She went down Church-lane and turned the corner at Blewitt's yard; looking up she saw something behind the walls of Mr Grout's kitchen garden—Oh! the most terrible thing in all the world!—and the fright of it was so great that her legs gave way beneath her and she fell to the ground.

"Young lady! Young lady! What is the matter?" cried a voice. Mr Grout appeared with his housekeeper, Mrs Baines. They were very shocked to find Venetia crawling on the ground and she was scarcely less shocked to be found. "Young lady!" cried Mr Grout, "What in the world has happened to you?"

"I thought I saw a strange procession coming towards me," said Venetia, "but now I see that what I took for pale green banners fluttering in the breeze are only the tops of some birch trees."

Mr Grout looked as if he did not very well understand this.

Mrs Baines said, "Well, my dear, whatever it was, a glass of marsala-wine is sure to put it right."—and, though Venetia assured them that she was quite well and was certain to stop shaking in a moment, they helped her into the house where they made her sit down by the fire and gave her marsala-wine to drink.

Mr Grout was an attorney who had been settled many years in Kissingland, where he had lived quietly and inexpensively. He had always appeared friendly and was generally well thought of, until he had suddenly got very rich and bought two farms in Knightswood parish. This was all quite recent, yet long enough for Mr Grout to have acquired a reputation as a most unreasonable landlord who bullied the farmers who worked his land and who increased their rents just as it suited him.

"You will eat something, perhaps?" said Mr Grout to Venetia, "My excellent Mrs Baines has been baking this morning if I am not mistaken. I smell apple tarts!"

"I want nothing, sir. Thank you," said Venetia and then, because she could not think of any thing else to say, she added, "I do not think I was in your house, sir, since I was a little girl."

"Indeed?" said Mr Grout, "Then you will see a great many improvements! It is a curious thing, young lady, but wealth don't suit everybody. The mere notion of great quantities of money is enough to make some people uneasy. Happily I can bear the thought of any amount with equanimity. Money, my dear, does more than provide mere material comforts; it lifts the burden of cares from one's shoulders, it imparts vigour and decisiveness to all one's actions and a delicate clearness to the complexion. It puts one in good humour with oneself and all the world. When I was poor I was not fit to be seen."

Money did indeed seem to have worked some curious changes in Mr Grout: his lawyer's stoop had vanished overnight, taking with it all his wrinkles; his silver hair shone so much that, in certain lights, he appeared to be sanctified; and his eyes and skin had a queer sparkle to them, not entirely pleasant to behold. He was known to be more than a little vain of all these new graces and he smiled at Venetia as though inviting her to fall in love with him on the spot.

"Well, sir," she said "I am sure that no one could deserve good fortune more. You made some cunning investments no doubt?"

"No, indeed. All my good fortune has sprung from the same noble source, a great lady who has employed me as her man of business—for which I may say I have been very handsomely rewarded. *Mrs Mabb* is the lady's name."

"Oh!" said Venetia, "She is someone I have a great curiosity to see."

"I do not doubt it, young lady," said Mr Grout, laughing pleasantly, "For she has got your sweetheart, the bold Captain Fox, has she not? Oh! there is no need to pretend that it is not so, for, as you see, I know all about it. There is no shame in being seen from the field by such a rival as Mrs Mabb. Mrs Mabb is a pearl beyond price and praise. The soul delights in the smallest motion of her hand. Her smile is like the sunshine—No! it is better than sunshine! One would gladly live in darkness all the days of one's life for the sake of Mrs Mabb's smile. Oh, young lady! The curve of Mrs Mabb's neck! Her eyebrow! Her smallest finger-nail! Perfection every one!"

Venetia sighed. "Well," she said and then, not knowing very well how to continue, she sighed again.

"In her youth, I believe," continued Mr Grout, "she was most industrious in managing her estates and ordering the affairs of her relations and dependents—who are very numerous and who all live with her—but at length the follies of the world began to disgust her and for many years she has lived a very retired life. She stays at home where she is very busy with her needle. I myself have been privileged to examine yard upon yard of the most exquisite embroidery, all of Mrs Mabb's production. And all her spinster cousins and maiden aunts and other such inferior females as she condescends to keep about her embroider a great deal too, for Mrs Mabb will not tolerate idleness."

"She lives near Piper, does she not?" said Venetia.

"Piper!" cried Mr Grout. "Oh no! Whatever gave you that idea? Mrs Mabb's house is not half so far and in quite another direction. It is reached by the little path that crosses the church-yard and goes out by the ivy-covered arch. The path, which is somewhat overgrown with cow parsley and foxgloves, passes a little pool full of reeds and then climbs a smooth green hill. At the top of the hill the visitor must climb through a gap in a ruined wall of ancient stones—whereupon he finds himself in Mrs Mabb's garden."

"Oh!" said Venetia. "How strange! For I am sure that someone told me that she lived near Piper. But, sir, I promised my sister that I would not be gone long and she is sure to grow anxious if I do not return soon."

"Oh!" said Mr Grout, "But we are just beginning to get acquainted! My dear, I hope you are not one of those prim young misses who are afraid to be alone with an old friend. An old friend, after all, is what I am, for all I look so young."

In Church-lane Venetia climbed up and looked over the churchyard-wall. "So that is the path that leads to Mrs Mabb's house, and there is the ivy-covered arch!"

She could not remember ever having observed either of them before. "Well! I do not think it can do any harm to go up very quietly and privately to look at her house."

And so, quite forgetting that she had told Mr Grout that Fanny would worry if she did not return home soon, she slipped into the churchyard and beneath the ivy-covered arch, and climbed the hill and passed the pool and came at last to the broken wall.

"I wonder that such a great lady should have no better entrance to her house than this inconvenient gap in an ancient wall!"

She passed through.

Majestic trees of great age and height stood about a great expanse of velvety green lawn. The trees had all been clipped into smooth rounded shapes, each one taller than Kissingland church tower, each one a separate mystery, and each one provided by the evening sun with a long shadow as mysterious as itself. Far, far above a tiny moon hung in the blue sky like its own insubstantial ghost.

"Oh! How quiet and empty it is! Now I am quite certain that I ought not to have come, for I was never in so private a place in my life. Any moment now I shall hear silver bells and hooves upon the turf, I know I shall! And as for the house I do not see one."

Yet there was something; at the one end of the lawn stood a round tower built of ancient-looking, grey stones, with battlements at the top and three dark slits for windows very high up. It was quite a tall tower, but in spite of its height it was overtopped by a monstrous hedge of pale roses that stood behind it and she could not rid herself of the idea that the tower was actually very tiny—a tower for an ant or a bee or a bird.

"I suppose it is that monstrous hedge that confuses one. It must be a summerhouse. I wonder how you get inside—I do not see a door. Oh! someone is playing a pipe! Yet there is no one here. And now a drum! How odd it is that I cannot see who is playing! I wonder if . . . Two steps forward, curtsey and turn. . . ."

The words came from nowhere into her head and the steps came from nowhere into her feet. She began to dance and was not at all surprised to find that, at the appropriate moment, someone took her outstretched hand.

Someone was crying very quietly and, just as before, Mr Hawkins knelt by Venetia's chair and washed her feet.

"And yet," she thought, "they will never be clean if he washes them in blood."

The water in the basin was bright red.

"Fanny," said Venetia.

The crying stopped and a small sound—something between a squeak and a sniff—seemed to shew that Fanny was nearby.

"Fanny, is it evening?"

"It is dawn," said Fanny.

"Oh!"

The curtains in Fanny's parlour were drawn back, but in the grey light of early dawn they had lost all their primrose colour. And everything outside the window—Fanny's vegetable-garden, Robin Tolliday's barn, John Harker's field, God's sky, England's clouds—all could be seen with perfect clarity but all had lost their colour as if all were made of grey water. Fanny began to cry again. "Perhaps she is in pain," thought Venetia, "For there is certainly a pain somewhere."

"Fanny?" she said.

"Yes, my love?"

"I am very tired, Fanny."

Then Fanny said something which Venetia did not hear and Venetia turned her head and when she opened her eyes she was in bed and Fanny was sitting in the wicker-chair, mending a hole in Mr Hawkins's shirt, and the curtains were drawn against the bright sunshine.

"Oh, Venetia!" said Fanny with a sigh and a despairing shake of her head, "Where in the world have you been? And what in the world have you been doing?"

It was not the sort of question that expected an answer but Venetia attempted one anyway; "I remember that I drank a glass of wine at Mr Grout's house, but I told him very plainly that I must come home, for I knew you were waiting for me. Did I not come home, Fanny?"

"No, Venetia," said Fanny, "you did not." And Fanny told Venetia how she and Mr Hawkins and their neighbours had searched through the night, and how, just before dawn, John Harker and George Buttery had looked into the churchyard and seen the pale shape of Venetia's gown billowing out in the darkness.

She had been under the big yew tree, turning and turning and turning, with her arms spread wide. It had taken both of them holding tight on to her to make her stop.

"Two pairs of shoes," sighed Fanny, "One entirely gone and the other in tatters. Oh, Venetia! Whatever were you thinking of?"

Venetia must have fallen asleep again for when she woke it seemed to be late evening. She could hear the clatter of plates as Fanny got the supper ready downstairs; and as Fanny went back and forth between parlour and kitchen she talked to Mr Hawkins: ". . . and if it should come to that, she shall not be sent to the madhouse—I could not bear that she should go to one of those horrid places and be ill-treated. No, indeed! Take warning, Mr Hawkins, that I expressly forbid it. . . ."

"As if he would suggest such a thing!" thought Venetia, "So good as he is to me."

". . . I dare say that mad people are no more expensive to keep than sane ones—except perhaps in the articles of medicines and restraining chairs."

Early next morning Fanny, Venetia and Mr Hawkins were at breakfast in the parlour when there was a loud knocking at the door. Fanny went to the door and returned in a moment with Mr Grout, who wasted no time upon apologies or explanations but immediately addressed Venetia in accents of great displeasure.

"Young lady! I am expressly sent to you by Mrs Mabb who has bid me tell you that she will not have you creeping around and around her house!"

"Ha!" cried Venetia, so loudly that Fanny started.

"Mrs Mabb's relations and dependents," continued Mr Grout with a severe look at Venetia's exulting expression, "have all been frightened out of their wits by your odd behaviour. You have given her aged uncles bad dreams, made the children afraid to go asleep at night and caused the maids to drop the china upon the floor. Mrs Mabb says that there is not one complete dinner service left in the house! She says that the butter will not come in the churns because you have given her cows malicious looks—Miss Moore, will you stop tormenting this lady?"

"Let her give up Captain Fox to me," said Venetia, "and she shall never hear of me again."

"Oh, Venetia!" cried Fanny.

"But young lady!" cried Mr Grout, "It is Mrs Mabb that the Captain loves. As I think I have explained to you before, Mrs Mabb is as fair as the apple-blossom that hangs upon the bough. One glance of Mrs Mabb's eyes . . ."

"Yes, yes! I know!" cried Venetia impatiently, "You told me all that before! But it is just so much nonsense! It is *me* the Captain loves. Had it been otherwise he would have told me so himself—or at least sent me a letter—but I have neither seen nor heard any thing of him since I returned from Manchester. Oh! Do not tell me that Mrs Mabb forbade him to come or some such other foolishness—Captain Fox is not the man to be dissuaded from doing his duty by any body. No, depend upon it, this is another trick of Mrs Mabb's."

"Young lady!" cried Mr Grout, very much appalled, "It ill becomes a young person of no consequence, such as yourself, to go about slandering great people in all the dignity of their property!"

"Mr Grout!" cried Fanny, unable to keep silent a moment longer, "Do not speak to her so! Use milder language to her, sir, I beg you! Can you not see that she is ill? I am, of course, extremely sorry that Mrs Mabb should have been put to any inconvenience by Venetia's going to the house—though I must say you make a great piece of work of it—and merely remark, in justice to Venetia, that all these cows and uncles must be extraordinarily nervous creatures to have been put in such a pickle by a poor, sick girl looking at them! But I tell you what I shall do. To keep her from wandering abroad and causing further nuisance to our neighbours I shall hide the green slippers the Purvises gave her—which are the only shoes she has—where she cannot find them and then, you know," Fanny concluded triumphantly, "she must remain at home!"

Mr Grout looked at Venetia as though hopeful that she would admit defeat.

But Venetia only said sweetly, "You have my answer, sir, and I advise you to go and deliver it. I dare say Mrs Mabb does not tolerate procrastination."

For the next two days Venetia waited for an opportunity to go in search of Mrs Mabb but in all this time Fanny neither left her alone nor answered any of her inquiries about Mrs Mabb. But on the third day Fanny was called away after dinner to take some elderflower tea and peppermint cordial and other remedies to John Harker's maid who had a bad cold. As Fanny went up Church-lane to Harker's farm it seemed probable that among the things her basket contained were the green silk dancing slippers, for when Venetia came to look for them she could not find them anywhere.

So she wrapped her feet up in rags and went anyway.

In a golden light, by what the inhabitants of Kissingland were pleased to call a river and which other, less partial people would probably have called a stream, in a fresh green meadow, beneath blossoming May-trees, some children were playing. One boy with a tin whistle was the Duke of Wellington, another boy with a drum was the entire British army and four little girls in grass-stained gowns of blossom-coloured muslin gave a lively portrayal of the ferocity and indomitable spirit of Napoleon and his French generals.

By the time Venetia passed by in the lane in search of Mrs Mabb her feet were very sore. She thought she would stop and bathe them; but as she went down to the river the two boys began to play a melancholy air upon the whistle and the drum.

Upon the instant Venetia was seized by a terror so blind that she scarcely knew what she did. When she recovered herself she found that she was holding fast to the hand of a most surprized little girl of eight or nine years of age.

"Oh! I beg your pardon. It was only the music that frightened me," she said; and then, as the girl continued to stare at her in astonishment, she added, "I used to be so fond of music you see, but now I do not care for it at all. Whenever I hear a pipe and drum I am certain that I shall be compelled to dance forever and ever without stopping. Does not it strike you that way sometimes?"

The little girls looked very much amazed but did not answer her. Their names were Hebe, Marjory, Joan and Nan, but as to which was which Venetia had not the least idea in the world. She bathed her feet and lay down to rest—for she was still very weak—in the sweet green grass. She heard Hebe, Marjory, Joan or Nan observe to the others that Miss Moore had, as was well known, run mad for the love of handsome Captain Fox.

The little girls had got some daisies to pull apart and as they did so they made wishes. One wished for a sky-blue carriage spotted with silver, another to see a dolphin in Kissingland river, one to marry the Archbishop of Canterbury and wear a diamond-spangled mitre (which she insisted she would be entitled to do as an Archbishop's wife, though the others were more doubtful), and one that there would be bread and beef dripping for her supper.

"I wish to know where I may find Mrs Mabb's house," said Venetia.

There was a silence for a moment and then either Hebe, Marjory, Joan or Nan remarked contemptuously that every one knew that.

"Everyone, it seems, but me," said Venetia to the blue sky and the sailing clouds.

"Mrs Mabb lives at the bottom of Billy Little's garden," said another child.

"Behind a great heap of cabbage leaves," said a third.

"Then I doubt that we can mean the same person," said Venetia, "Mrs Mabb is a very fine lady as I understand."

"Indeed, she is," agreed the first, "The finest lady that ever there was. She has a coachman . . ."

". . . a footman . . ."

". . . a dancing master . . ."

". . . and a hundred ladies-in-waiting . . ."

". . . and one of the ladies-in-waiting has to eat the dull parts of Mrs Mabb's dinner so that Mrs Mabb only ever has to eat roast pork, plum-cake and strawberry jam . . ."

"I see," said Venetia.

". . . and they all live together at the bottom of Billy Little's garden."

"Do not they find that rather inconvenient?" asked Venetia, sitting up.

But Hebe, Marjory, Joan and Nan could not suppose that there would be any particular inconvenience attached to a residence at the bottom of Billy Little's garden. However, they were able to provide Venetia with the further information that Mrs Mabb drank her breakfast coffee out of an acorn-cup, that her chamberlain was a thrush and her coachman a blackbird, and that she herself was "about the size of a pepper-pot."

"Well," said Venetia, "what you tell me is very strange, but no stranger than many of the things that have happened to me recently. Indeed it seems to me to be all of a piece with them—and so perhaps you will have the goodness to shew me where I may find this curious house."

"Oh!" said one child, clapping her hand to her mouth in alarm.

"You had much better not," said another kindly.

"She could turn you into butter," said a third.

"Which might melt," observed the fourth.

"Or a pudding."

"Which might get eaten."

"Or a drawing of yourself on white paper."

"Which someone might set fire to, you know, without meaning to."

But Venetia insisted upon their taking her to Mrs Mabb's house straight away, which at length they agreed to do.

Billy Little was an ancient farm labourer of uncertain temper who lived in a tumbledown cottage in Shilling-lane. He was at war with all the children of

Kissingland and all the children of Kissingland were at war with him. His garden was at the back of the cottage and Venetia and Hebe, Marjory, Joan and Nan were obliged to bend low to creep past his uncurtained window.

Someone was standing on the window-sill. She wore a brightly coloured gown, and had a cross expression upon her face.

"There you are, at last!" said Venetia. She straightened herself and addressed this lady in the following words: "Now, madam! If I might trouble you to answer one or two questions. . . ."

"What are you doing?" hissed Hebe, Marjory, Joan or Nan and took hold of Venetia by her gown and pulled her down again.

"Oh! Do you not see?" said Venetia. "Mrs Mabb is just above us, on the windowsill."

"*That* is not Mrs Mabb!" whispered Hebe, Marjory, Joan or Nan. "*That* is only Billy Little's Betsy-jug, with his Toby-jug beside it."

Venetia popped her head back up, and this time she observed the china lady's china husband. The couple were indeed jugs for they had large handles sticking out of their backs.

"Oh! very well," said Venetia, crossly.

"But," she thought to herself, "I have half a mind to push her off the window-sill anyway—for it is my opinion that, where Mrs Mabb is concerned, you never can tell."

Beyond the heap of cabbage leaves and other dark, decaying matter, the path led past a sad-looking pond and up a steep bank. At the top of the bank was a smooth expanse of bright green grass, at one end of which a dozen or so tall stones and slates were piled together. It was possible they were intended for a bee-hive, but it was equally possible that they were simply left over from some ancient wall. Tall flowers grew behind them—meadowsweet, cow parsley and buttercups—so that it was the easiest thing in the world to fancy one was looking at a tower or castle-keep on the edge of an ancient wood.

"Now this is odd," said Venetia, "for I have seen this place before. I know I have."

"There she is!" cried one of the children.

Venetia looked round and thought she saw a quivering in the air. "A moth," she thought. She approached and the shadow of her gown fell across the stones. A dark, damp chill hung about them, which the sunlight had no power to dissipate. She stretched out her hands to break apart Mrs Mabb's house, but upon the instant a pale-green something—or a pale-green someone—flew out of a gap in the stones and sprang up into the sunlight—and then another, and another—and more, and more, until the air seemed crowded with people, and there was a strange glitter all around, which Venetia associated with the sight of sunlight glinting on a thousand swords. So rapid was the manner in which they darted about that it was entirely impossible to hold any of them in one's gaze for more than a moment, but it seemed to Venetia that they rushed upon her like soldiers who had planned an ambush.

"Oh!" she cried, "Oh! You wicked creatures! You wicked, wicked creatures!"; and she snatched them out of the sparkling air and crushed them in her hands. Then it seemed to Venetia that they were dancing, and that the steps of their dance were the most complicated ever invented and had been devised on purpose to make her mad; so she took great pleasure in knocking them to the ground and treading upon their pale green clothes. But, though she was certain that some were killed and dozens of others were sent away injured, there never appeared to be any diminution in their number. Gradually the strength of her own passion began to exhaust her; she was sure she must sink to the ground. At that moment she looked up and saw, just beyond the battle's fray, the pale, heart-shaped face of a little girl and Venetia heard her say in a puzzled tone, " 'Tis only butterflies, Miss Moore."

Butterflies? she thought.

"It was only butterflies, my love," said Fanny, smoothing Venetia's cheek.

She was in her own room, laid upon her own bed.

"A cloud of pale-green butterflies," said Fanny. "Hebe, Marjory, Joan and Nan said that you were crying out at them and beating them down with your fists and tearing them apart with your fingers until you fell down in a faint." Fanny sighed. "But I dare say you remember nothing about it."

"Oh! But I remember perfectly well!" said Venetia, "Hebe, Marjory, Joan and Nan took me to Mrs Mabb's house, which as you may know is at the bottom of Billy Little's garden, and Captain Fox was inside it—or at least so I suppose—and had Mrs Mabb not sent the butterflies to prevent me, I would have fetched him out, and—"

"Oh, Venetia!" cried Fanny in exasperation.

Venetia opened her hand and found several fragments of a pale-green colour, like torn paper yet not half the thickness of paper and of no weight whatsoever: the broken remains of two or three butterflies.

"Now I have you, Mrs Mabb," she whispered.

She took a scrap of paper and folded the broken butterflies up inside it. Upon the outside she wrote, 'For Mrs Mabb'.

It was not difficult for Venetia to prevail upon Mr Hawkins (who loved her dearly and who was particularly anxious about her at this period) to deliver the folded paper to Mr Grout.

Next morning Venetia waited hopefully for the return of Captain Fox. When he did not appear she determined to go in search of him again—which both Fanny and Mr Hawkins seemed to have expected, for Fanny had hidden Venetia's dancing slippers in an empty rabbit-hutch in the garden and Mr Hawkins had fetched them out again half an hour later. Mr Hawkins had placed them upon Venetia's bed, where Venetia found them at three o'clock, together with a page torn from Mr Hawkins's memorandum book upon which was drawn a map of Kissingland and the surrounding woods—and deep within those woods, the house of Mrs Mabb.

Downstairs in the kitchen Mr Hawkins was blacking Fanny's boots and—what was very strange—doing it very ill, so that Fanny was obliged to stand over him and scold him about it. She never heard Venetia slip out of the front door and run down the lane.

The map shewed Mrs Mabb's house to be much deeper in the woods than Venetia had ever gone before. She had walked for an hour or so—and was still some way off from Mrs Mabb's house—when she came to a wide glade surrounded by great oaks, beeches, elders and other sweet English trees. At the furthest end of this glade a cloud of insects rose up suddenly against the sunlit wood and a man appeared. But whether he had stepped out of the wood or out of the cloud of insects would have been impossible to say. His hair had the appearance of being a sort of reddish-brown, and he wore the blue coat and white britches of General ____'s regiment.

"Venetia!" he cried the moment he saw her, "But I thought you had gone to Manchester!"

"And so I did, my dear, dear Captain Fox," said she, running towards him in great delight, "and am now returned."

"That is impossible," said Captain Fox, "for we parted only yesterday and I gave you my watch-chain to wear as keepsake."

They argued about this for some time and Venetia said several times how almost four months had passed since last they met and Captain Fox said how it was nothing of the sort. "It is very odd," thought Venetia, "His virtues are all exactly as I remember them, but I had entirely forgot how very exasperating he is!"

"Well, my love," she said, "I dare say you are right—you always are—but perhaps you will explain to me how the trees in this wood got so heavy with leaves and blossoms and buds? I know they were bare when I went away. And where did all these roses come from? And all this sweet fresh grass?"

At which Captain Fox crossed his arms and looked about him and frowned very hard at the trees. "I cannot explain it," he said at last. "But, Venetia," he said more cheerfully, *"you will never* guess where I have been all this time—with Mrs Mabb! She sent me a message asking me to make a fourth at Casino but when I arrived I found that all she wanted was to talk love and all sorts of nonsense to me. I bore with it as long as I could, but I confess that she began to try my patience. I tell you, Venetia, she is a very odd woman. There was scarcely a stick of furniture in the place—just one chair for her to sit on and then everybody else must prop himself up against the wall. And the house is very queer. One goes through a door—thinking perhaps to fetch a cup from the kitchen or a book from the library—and suddenly one finds oneself in a little wood, or upon some blasted heath, or being drenched by the waves of some melancholy ocean. Oh! And someone—I have not the least idea who—came several times to the house. Which put all the family and servants in a great uproar, for it was a person whom Mrs Mabb most emphatically did not wish to see. So they were at great pains to get rid of this unwelcome visitor. And what a piece of work they made of it! The third time several of them were killed outright. Two bloody corpses were brought home not more than an hour ago— wrapped in paper—which was a little odd, I thought—with 'For Mrs Mabb' written on the top. I observed that Mrs Mabb grew pale at the sight of them and declared that the game was not worth the candle and that, much as she detested yielding to any body, she could not allow any more noble spirits to be destroyed in this cause. I was glad to hear her say so, for I fancy she can be obstinate at times. A little while afterwards she asked me if I should like to go home."

"And what did you do, my love, while Mrs Mabb's servants were removing this troublesome person?" asked Venetia sweetly.

"Oh! I dozed quietly in the back-parlour and let them all rampage about me if that was what they wished. A soldier—as I think I have told you before, Venetia—must be able to sleep any where. But you see how it is: if the head of a household is governed by passion instead of by reason—as is the case here— then confusion and lack of discipline are quickly communicated to the lower orders. It is the sort of thing one sees very often in the army. . . ." And as Captain Fox expounded upon the different generals he had known and their various merits and defects, Venetia took his arm and led him back to Kissingland.

They walked for some time and had a great deal to say to each other and when twilight fell it brought with it a sweet-smelling rain; and birds sang on every side. There were two lights ahead—at the sight of which Venetia was at first inclined to feel some alarm—but they were immediately discovered to be lanterns—only lanterns, the most commonplace articles in the world; and almost as quickly one of the lanterns swung up to reveal Fanny's thin face and; "Oh, Mr Hawkins!" came her glad cry, "Here she is! I have found her!"

RICK KENNETT

Due West

Rick Kennett is an Australian writer who has published one space opera, A
Warrior's Star, *but is now recognized more as a writer of dark fantasy in the
tradition of M. R. James and William Hope Hodgson—an interest that led
directly to his collaboration on a booklet of "Carnacki" pastiches with English
writer Chico Kidd.*

*Kennett's best-known stories feature motorbike-riding reluctant ghost-
hunter, Ernie Pine. Some of these stories were collected in the booklet* The
Reluctant Ghost-Hunter *by Rosemary Pardoe's Haunted Library. A novel
featuring Pine,* Abracadabra, *was recently published. Kennett does still write
the occasional space opera, most notably in the Cy Chauvin series of stories.
He has a web page (although he's not online): http://www.freeyellow.com/
members6/csfuqua/*

*"Due West" is, like many of Kennett's ghost stories, based upon an actual
event. It was originally published in* Eidolon *25/26.*

—E. D.

One afternoon, Arthur Lewisham peered through the keyhole of an empty
room in his own home and regretted it for ever after.

Lewisham had lived in the house nearly two years: a neat and recently
built cottage on Murphy Road in the town of Graxton, a hundred miles
due west of Brisbane in the vast back country of Queensland. While others had
flocked to the cities for what little work there was in the middle of the Great
Depression, Lewisham, a retired history teacher, had retreated to this quiet country town to write his book on the causes and consequences of the Gallipoli
campaign of 1915. It had taken his son Michael, and he was determined to make
what sense he could of it.

The cottage, one of a scattering along Murphy Road, had two bedrooms. Mr
Lewisham slept in the smaller of them, using the master bedroom at the back
to store his excess of books, journals and papers. As a result, the master bedroom
was rarely entered.

On one of these occasions, late on a busy writing day, Lewisham deposited a
pile of papers and books on the floor of the back bedroom, beside another pile

of books and in front of another pile of papers. He straightened up, feeling the bones click down his spine. He knew he'd been hunched over his typewriter too long, that he should get out for some exercise, even if it was just a short bicycle ride along Murphy Road. But his writing had reached the Battle of Lone Pine, a point of particular and personal interest. Besides, it was late in the day; the afternoon sun slanted faint red through the window.

He hurried out and closed the door. It had never latched properly, so long ago he had contrived to keep it shut by looping a rubber band over the doorknob and knotting the other end around a nail hammered into the jamb. However, as soon as he'd stretched the band over the doorknob it occurred to him he couldn't recall if he had switched off the room's light. Electricity had only reached Graxton the year before, and the house had been wired just a few weeks previous. Two years away from cities had made Lewisham unused to light switches.

He muttered to himself. His writing called and it was all too much trouble to unhook the band from around the doorknob again, open the door and see. He peeped through the keyhole.

All was dark within, which satisfied him—though only for an instant. As he lifted his eye away it occurred to him that it was *too* dark. Where was the light from the side window?

He peered through again. Was there something there, obstructing his view? Had he left a coat hanging on the inside doorknob?

Feeling a martyr to curiosity he took the few seconds to stretch the rubber band off and open the door.

Afternoon light shone weakly through the side window, giving the room a sense of twilight. Diffuse shadows stretched from piles of books and papers, and pooled beneath and behind an old armchair, broken and unstuffed. He craned his head around the door and made sure there was nothing hanging from the inside knob. He stepped into the room and put his eye to the keyhole. He saw part of the room's wall and part of the door frame.

Again he went to the other side and, holding the door ajar, looked through from there. His view took in part of a wall, the piles of books, the broken chair, all plainly visible.

Closing the door and holding it shut with his hand, he pressed an eye yet again to the keyhole.

Darkness.

"Bloody queer." He swept the door open, as if to surprise the mystery. But the room stood as it should.

By now he had forgotten his eagerness to return to the typewriter. Determined not to be defeated by this puzzle, he tried various experiments. He fetched the key of the room and locked and unlocked the door as it stood open, then looked again, seeing nothing more or less than what he should. He shone a lantern though either side and saw its light each time without obstruction. He took a stepladder into the room and sat the lantern on its top step so that it shone directly at the keyhole. He then went out, shut the door and peered through into the room. He saw only darkness.

"Damnation!"

He made to push the door open again, but stopped when he saw the darkness was *not* complete. As if his eye were becoming accustomed to a night scene, it seemed he could now make out stars in a night sky.

They were dim and needed time to be perceived clearly, but it soon grew on Lewisham that he was seeing the incredible through the keyhole of his back bedroom door. And not only stars: the features of a landscape, silhouettes of trees, a grassy paddock hedged by an old-fashioned fence of ironbark poles, all bathed in a full moonlight that grew stronger as he looked. Arthur Lewisham pulled his eye from the keyhole. It scared him, it bewildered him, but above all it filled him with a sense of wonder unfelt since childhood.

> Lone Pine was a knowing sacrifice of the youth of Australia. It was supposed to be a feint to distract the Turks from a British landing at Suvla Bay. Instead it turned into a massacre for both sides in mostly hand-to-hand fighting, the ferocity of which has been unmatched in—

Arthur Lewisham stared at the unfinished sentence in his typewriter; stared without really seeing. The sun had since set and the swiftness of a bush night had settled over Graxton, Murphy Road and Arthur Lewisham. For the first time in a long while he was not thinking of the useless waste of his son's life in the World War. He was not thinking of anything. Electric light blazed all through the house. Every so often he raised his eyes and turned his head to look through the kitchen to the back bedroom door. It hadn't so much as trembled in the three hours since he'd backed away from it in awe. He wanted to look again, but dared not. What if something looked back?

Maybe something is looking back, right now, watching me through the keyhole sitting here like a frightened child, too scared to act, to think, to do anything but sit in the light.

At length he bestirred himself, going over his notes and the finished portion of his manuscript. But it all seemed a jumble of meaningless words and he soon found his attention drifting back, his head turning again to that door, knowing that sooner or later he would be once more pressing his eye to its keyhole.

As it was, Nature rather than the Bizarre called first. The earth closet was in the back yard, so he put off his body's urgings for as long as he could with any spurious excuse his mind could find. He checked his notes again. He stacked wood and kindling beside the kitchen stove. He even thought of going out the front and into the empty paddock opposite. But in the end he stood up and strode out the back, passing the back bedroom door as if it didn't really matter.

The stars were sharp and clear in the night sky. He was no astronomer or bushman and was unable to say whether they were the same constellations seen through the keyhole. The trees, on the other hand . . .

He held up his lantern and looked hard at the trees in the paddock behind his property. Were they the same as those in the keyhole?

He tended his urgent business, after which he again studied the trees. He moved out amongst them. With some imagination they might be made to stand in the same positions as those in the vision now etched into his memory. Only these seemed taller.

He lowered his lantern and looked at the sky, so black and brilliant with stars.

It was a sight alien to city nights with their garish lights, as was the intense silence all around: unknown in the noisy city. The silence felt as if it had power to weigh down on him, to squeeze from all sides and crush him.

Feeling oppressed, almost stifled, Lewisham chanced to glance down and saw narrow wheel tracks close by his boots in the dirt.

He crouched to look more closely. Wagon tracks. Farmers roundabout still used horse-drawn vehicles, and he'd often seen such tracks on Graxton's dirt roads. These were recently made if he judged aright the crispness of the imprint. One of the tracks, he saw, wove in and out slightly as if the wheel that made it wobbled. He looked back along the track and saw his own lighted back door. He looked the other way and saw only the darkness of the bush and the vague shapes of trees.

"Imposs____" he began, then held his tongue. It was a word that had that day lost all meaning for Arthur Lewisham. He stood and followed the tracks into the trees. They kept straight on for four or five hundred yards, then varied slightly to left and right. Lewisham followed for about a quarter of a mile and was about to give up and return to his house when the tracks suddenly swerved hard to the right and, after another couple of hundred yards, ran across the top of a spur and dropped out of sight.

Lewisham hesitated. Anything could happen here. It was a lonely place, and dark but for his lantern. He held it up, the squeak of its handle so loud in the utter silence. He swept its light into the hollow, tracing the tracks down the slope. At its utmost limit he thought he could discern shapes: big shadows by the trees, prone oblongs in the grass.

The place smelt of blood, reeked of dread and fear beating up out of the dark with a strength and intensity that totally overwhelmed him. It entered seeping, pushing, leaping, bellowing into his mind until suddenly, aimlessly, irrationally he turned and fled from the hollow darkness.

Back along the tracks he went, back through the trees, running like a boy, frightened as a child, not looking behind, not daring, never stopping until he reached, panting and blowing, falling, stumbling, feeling all his years, the wooden back wall of his earth closet.

Alice Flynn opened her provisions store at eight o'clock on a bright blue morning, just as she had every day except Sundays and Christmas for the past thirty-seven years. Passing farm wagons and motor trucks kicked up dust along Graxton's main street. Other doors on other stores opened here and there, and another day began. What made this one different from the usual run of workdays for Alice Flynn was the sight of Arthur Lewisham propped up beside her door, fast asleep with his bicycle leaning against the wall beside him.

She bent down, looking closely into his face. Mr Lewisham was a regular customer, never failing to drop by whenever he dragged himself away from his work and came into town. She knew him to be of sober manner and appearance. At least he had been until now. There was no drink on his breath, but his clothes were rumpled as if he'd slept in them all night, and they were grass stained, too, and dirty as if he'd spent the night in a paddock.

Alice dashed back into the shop and roused her husband, Len, from his break-fast. By the time they returned, Mr Lewisham was already bestirring himself.

Mumbling apologies but no explanations, he climbed to his feet and brushed himself down as best he could.

"What—" began Flynn, but stopped at a sharp glance from his wife.

"Come and have a cup of tea in the back, Arthur," said Alice, and guided him into the shop.

Flynn sat Lewisham down in his own chair and joined Alice at the kitchen stove as she stoked up the embers to warm the kettle. "Looks like he's had a nasty turn," he said in a low voice.

Alice nodded. "Something's shook him up. Maybe something's wrong out at his house."

"I'll go take a look. You be all right here?"

"I'll manage. Do you think you should go by way of the police station?"

"Let's see what's what first, Alice, before we go bothering the coppers."

Unnoticed by Lewisham who was staring at the jar of raspberry jam on the table, Len Flynn grabbed his hat and left the room. He mounted Lewisham's bicycle and trundled down Graxton's main street in the direction of Murphy Road.

Alice poured hot water into the teapot and set it down on the table. "Let's give it a few minutes to brew," she said to Lewisham. She drew out the seat opposite him and waited for him to speak.

His eyes wandered about the kitchen, coming back to the jam jar with something like a flinch. He said, "I . . . I just need to be with people a bit, sit calm and tell you, and you're the only people I really know in Graxton, and . . ." He gave it all out then in a rambling, repeating, hesitating way: the keyhole, the tracks, and what they led to.

"You probably think I'm mad," he said finally. "I would in your place. I don't know what it means. All I know is that I saw it, and no one will convince me otherwise."

"Wagon tracks," said Alice with an odd expression on her face—an expression that'd been growing as Lewisham had told his story. "A moonlit night. Arthur, have you been talking to any of the old residents of the town?"

Lewisham shook his head. "The only person I talk to during the day, apart from myself, is Mary who comes and does the housework three times a week. How old do you mean?"

"People our own age: fifties, sixties. Mary's only twenty and probably wouldn't know."

"Know what?"

"I was thinking perhaps you had heard some talk and had dreamed, but I don't think you're the type." Alice leaned forward. "Arthur, if it wasn't for that keyhole business I might say someone is trying to give you a fright. Wheel tracks can be faked, but that keyhole business is too uncanny to get round. You're sure what you saw?"

"Did I not say so? I hope my writing's not so boring as to cause me to fall asleep and dream! On the other hand, if you're implying someone is playing the fool, to frighten me for whatever reason . . ." He hesitated and spread his hands. "Who would possibly do such a thing?"

" 'Who would possibly do such a thing?' Arthur, they were the very words they used thirty-seven years ago."

"There is something here you're not telling me."

"Would it put you out if you moved away from Murphy Road?"

"You mean run away from a haunted house?"

"You did last night. You ran from your yard and slept in the paddock opposite, so you tell me."

"I hardly *slept*, Alice."

"Perhaps all the more reason to go elsewhere. Perhaps—and I say this as a friend—away from Graxton."

"Why? What's here in Graxton I should avoid?"

"A piece of this town's history we don't much like to discuss, such a time ago that it was." She leaned through the kitchen door as the first customers of the morning entered. "At any rate, I think it's a story a man should tell you. You'll understand when Len comes back." She stood and strode into the shop, saying over her shoulder, "I'll wager he finds nothing."

Len Flynn did find nothing. He told his wife as much when he returned twenty minutes later. "See, I said there was no need to involve the coppers. Nothing wrong at his house, anyway." He glanced through into the kitchen where Lewisham was sitting over his cold tea. "Did you find out what's up?"

"Did you check the yard?"

"Naturally."

"I mean for tracks."

"What sort of tracks?"

"Wagon tracks. With one wobbly wheel."

Flynn blanched. "What did he say he saw? For god's sake, Alice, what's he been at?"

"Poor bloke's either got the DTs or there's ghosts in his house."

As she repeated Lewisham's story to him, Flynn felt as if a chill wind had crept into the shop.

"He doesn't seem to know the story," said Alice, "yet he knows about the wheel marks, the full moon the night it happened, and the place where it happened. Whatever his shakes are about I think he deserves to know what happened once out on Murphy Road."

Len Flynn nodded and stepped into the kitchen, closing the door behind him.

"You can always tell them, Arthur. They always stop in the same place along Murphy Road. Tourists mostly. Doesn't happen much nowadays, so long after the event and what with money so tight and people less able to travel. But we used to see it a lot before the war and through the Twenties. Usually they'd lean on the fence and stare out at the paddock right where your house is now. It's easy—and maybe a bit ugly—to guess what they're thinking, looking out at the field and the trees beyond. There were no houses along Murphy Road back in 1898. Back then it was wooded right up to the road. Thirty-seven years ago it happened, in that paddock, among the trees, and under the light of a brilliant full moon.

"It had to do with the Henleys, who were a large family working a grazing farm about five miles up from Graxton on Murphy Road. They were a well-liked and respected part of Graxton's farming community; not particularly wealthy, but comfortable for all that. There were eight Henley children in all, but what happened involved the three middle children: the oldest boy Douglas, twenty-seven, and the two girls; Celeste who was twenty-four and Myra, who had just turned nineteen. I have only vague recollections of them because Alice and I had been in Graxton just six months, and custom was slow to build in those early days. We arrived in June, 1898, and this . . . this thing happened towards the end of the Christmas season of that year—the night of Boxing Day, the 26th of December.

"Douglas and the girls left their parents' farm that evening in their sulky to go to a dance at the Divisional Board's Hall, just where Murphy Road runs into the main street here. Turned out the dance was cancelled because of low attendance, and at nine o'clock they closed the hall. A witness saw the three Henleys drive by in their sulky at ten minutes past nine. When they saw the hall closed they turned about and started up Murphy Road again, towards their home. They never arrived.

"In the morning, when their parents woke and found they had not returned, they sent their son-in-law, Kevin O'Donnell who was visiting . . . they sent him on horseback along Murphy Road to look for them. The sulky had a loose wheel, and they were worried there'd been an accident. At least it was easy to follow the crooked track it made in the dirt.

"Kevin followed the sulky's tracks towards Graxton, but it wasn't until he got to the sliprails at the entrance of a place called Quinn's Paddock that he saw any tracks coming back. It seemed that the sulky hadn't stopped at the entrance, but had swept right through the sliprails and on into the trees. Kevin took the sliprails down—they had the marks of the sulky's wheels upon them—and followed the tracks in.

"They bore due west for a distance, then wandered between west and south-west as if the driver wasn't sure of his direction. After something like a quarter of a mile, the tracks suddenly swerved to the south and kept a straight line for two or three hundred yards. Kevin O'Donnell followed them over a spur and looked down into a hallow.

"The first thing he thought when he saw them was that they were having a picnic. Celeste and Myra were lying on a rug together under a spotted gum tree whose trunk looked from a distance splattered with something red and lumpy; Douglas lay a little distance away, beside the sulky. All three were lying in the same direction, heads to the west, feet to the east. Their horse was slumped in the sulky's shafts. Kevin didn't go any closer. He turned about and galloped straight to the police barracks. His first words there were, 'The Henleys are lying dead in Quinn's Paddock, and such a mess you've never seen in your life!'

"A medical examination showed that Douglas had been shot in the head at close range. The girls had both been raped, and then bludgeoned with terrible violence. Their skirts were in disarray, their corsets undone and their petticoats splattered in blood and semen. There were scratches and other injuries about their . . . um, lower persons, if you follow my meaning. A thick, knotty stick was found nearby covered in blood and brain. Yet apart from the bodies themselves, there was no sign of a struggle: neither the rug they were on—all smooth and tidy—nor the ground round about, which should've been torn up something fierce, but wasn't. And of course the three of them, all arranged perfectly east-west."

In the sanity of the morning sunshine, Arthur Lewisham returned to Murphy Road. There were no tracks in his backyard, and nothing to show they had ever been there. Nothing within the cottage had been disturbed and the same unfinished sentence remained poking out of the typewriter.

Determined to fight this down, he went out into the woods behind his house, and after some searching found what he thought was his hollow of the night before. But he couldn't be sure. No shapes, no fears or dreads. On the far side was a spotted gum, like the one Flynn had mentioned found besplattered with 'something red and lumpy'. If this was the same tree, it had been cleaned by years of rain and insects. He didn't inspect it. He returned home.

"They never found out who did it," Flynn had said. "Lots got questioned—newcomers to the district, swagmen and the like. They even looked at me pretty hard at one time, seeing as we'd only been here six months. People going up and down Murphy Road that night said they'd seen a man standing by the sliprails, like he was waiting for someone. No one ever did identify him and no one ever did get charged."

Lewisham thought this over as he reached his backyard again and gazed back into the woods. For a long time he debated with himself about looking through the back room keyhole again. In the end he did, and the moon and stars, fence and trees were still there. He drew away, revolted, knowing now what it all meant.

Later that day Len Flynn came up to the house and, at Lewisham's solemn invitation, put his eye to the back bedroom keyhole.

"Do you see it?" asked Lewisham. "Do you see it?"

"Yes," said Flynn in an odd sort of voice.

"I'm glad."

They talked the matter over in the front room.

"Perhaps," said Lewisham, "a constant observation of the vision might eventually reveal the instigator of the outrage. Perhaps it's like a cinema film on an endless loop, going round and round."

"Do you have the nerve to keep your eye on it?" said Flynn.

Lewisham made no answer to that. Though he had as yet seen no movement in the starry scene, just the expectation, just the thought that he *might* see something if he looked too long frightened him. After Flynn had left he sat far from the door and pondered.

East and West. Was it just coincidence the way the three bodies had fallen, or was there meaning in their alignment? The thought was repugnant: it smacked of cabalistic practices. Black magic, here in the bush; here among level-headed farming folk. It was ridiculous.

Yet, leaving aside the unlikeliness of the setting, wasn't "direction" the theme of an occult book he had once read? *Compass Obeisance*. Much emphasis, he recalled, had been placed on compass points, particularly the West, in the various occult acts the book examined. No corpses had been involved, of course, but those of the Graxton Mystery could have been an independent refinement or addition. The head, so these things said, was the temple of the soul, and the bodies of Douglas, Celeste and Myra had all been laid head-first due West.

Human sacrifices were supposed to be a common thing in black magic, though Lewisham doubted it occurred a tenth as frequently as people thought. However, he had heard rumoured that sex magic was often practised at black masses by those who fancied themselves witches and sorcerers. That man Crowley in England, for instance; a sordid poet of no great distinction, he had found a greater fame or infamy in his promotion of sex magic, earning him the title of The Great Beast, England's Worst Man and The Wickedest Man in the World.

Lewisham had always considered such hyperbole as examples of yellow journalism and Crowley himself as a mere charlatan. But now, as he sat musing over last night and all that Len Flynn had told him, he was not so sure. Thirty-seven years ago, when Crowley was beginning his career in magic—actual, fake or self-delusional—had someone else in Graxton reached a peak in their own?

It was not just the westward alignment of the bodies—any madman could do that. It was the other details Flynn had touched on in their discussion which had brought Lewisham to thinking this way: the lack of signs of a struggle at the murder scene, though the ground was soft; the lack of tracks save those of the sulky going in, with none going away; the absence of anything heard or seen by others passing along Murphy Road on that bright, moonlight night; the two sets of four claw marks found side-by-side some distance from the scene which an aboriginal had identified as crocodile claws; the scrap of parchment found in the paddock some days later scribbled over in no known writing; the empty meat tin with the hole punched through its bottom, found in the sulky; the reason the Henleys went into Quinn's Paddock to begin with . . .

Such was Arthur Lewisham's train of thought, which he soon left off because of the lack of answers to any of these mysteries. Yet during the day, in which he sat at his work desk and wrote nothing, his mind returned again and again to the idea of the Graxton Mystery as Occult Act.

> "In Memory of Douglas aged twenty-seven, Celeste aged twenty-four, Myra aged nineteen. The dearly beloved children of James and Amelia Henley, who were the victims of a horrible tragedy perpetrated near Graxton on December 26th, 1898. Requiescant In Pace. This Monument has been erected by public subscription to the memory of the above innocent victims."

It was a warm afternoon, as most afternoons were in the Queensland countryside. The sky was blue and the grass a crisp yellow. Lewisham waved flies away with his hat and stepped back to get the grey stone obelisk into perspective; in Graxton's little cemetery of simple crosses and modest stones it was a monster. He had never in his life visited a graveyard outside of a funeral, the last time being sixteen years ago when his wife had died in the flu epidemic following the Great War. He wasn't sure why he was here now; perhaps to prove to himself that Douglas, Celeste and Myra had really existed; perhaps to see that nothing cabalistic had been scrawled on their stone. As he walked around its rusting iron railing he reflected with a grim smile that this was not the best place for a man with a newly acquired belief in ghosts. It could be just asking for trouble.

He stopped and thought that over. Perhaps he *was* asking for trouble. Unconsciously, perhaps, he was daring them—whoever, whatever they may be. *Here I am*, he thought. *Do your worst.* Feeling defiant, he scanned the graveyard, the road, the bush and fields beyond.

Crows made lazy calls in the surrounding wattles and gums, and flapped between branches. Something rustled through the grass. Flies darted and droned about Lewisham's head, getting in his ears, buzzing.

Something stirred on the other side of the obelisk. He leaned around it, expecting to surprise a lizard or rabbit. Instead he beheld a figure all in black, stooping before the Henley grave. His heart raced, as did his brain, filling with fear, regretted bravado and visions of death's-head spectres. He cried out. The figure stood, revealing itself to be a man in dark tweed, a string tie and wide-brimmed hat.

Lewisham let out a deep sigh and felt rather foolish, especially when he saw the wreath the man had just placed against the stone.

Smiling, the stranger said, "I'm sorry. Did I startle you?"

"I suppose you did. I turned myself around not half a minute ago, yet never saw you coming."

"Perhaps I approached in such a line as to be hidden by the monument."

"That must be it," said Lewisham with a little desperation. He glanced down at the wreath—Turk's Cap lilies—then up at the stranger's face. He guessed his age as forty, and thought he looked something like Michael, had he been alive now: the same nose, something of the same eyes. "Are you a relative?"

"No," said the stranger. "Are you?"

"No. But I have an interest."

"I trust not a morbid one. You know the history?"

"I was told it this morning, although I've lived in the town almost two years now. Which is odd, come to think of it, as I would've thought the story to be well known hereabouts."

"Only the older folk of the district remember. Graxton's population has shifted in the last few years, and a good many who lived through the event have long since moved away or died. The young might think they know, and others who weren't here, but only at second and third hand. Time and retelling breaks truth into rubble. I fancy you have heard some garbled version involving frozen expressions of horror on the faces of the victims, mutilation of the horse, unexplained parchments and animal prints found nearby. It is one of history's passing sensations, best forgotten."

"And yet you lay flowers on their grave."

"I knew the two girls."

"Then you must be older than you look and know the facts of the matter."

The stranger smiled. "You flatter me. Questions without answers are only torments to yourself and a burden to others. There are no answers here."

"You mean in the cemetery?"

"I mean in Graxton. There are no truths to be found out; none within human reach at least. Don't believe all you hear. Let mysteries lie. Good day, sir."

The stranger touched the brim of his hat and stalked off among the stones. Lewisham watched him disappear into the scrub, then turned and made his way back to his bicycle leaning by the cemetery gates. All the way he swatted flies from his face, and it was only then he realized he hadn't seen the stranger bothered by a single insect.

When he arrived home Lewisham checked the scene in the keyhole. It was exactly as it had been the time before and the time before that. He didn't think of it now as an endless loop of film but rather as an overture awaiting the raising of a curtain. He felt he was tempting fate by peeking, even for a second. Who was to say when the curtain may fly up and he be witness to the whole hideous business.

His sleep that night was fitful, shot through with slices of incoherent dream; formless but triggering a jumble of emotions: fear, anger, dread, awe. At one o'clock he jerked awake and stared into the darkness. Had a door just slammed in his silent house?

He held his breath and listened. But all he heard was the all-encompassing bush silence, and the footsteps come creeping he feared never eventuated. He breathed again. Just a dream noise sounded in the mental ear. Doors were preying on his mind. This sort of thing had happened before, he recalled. Other places, other times. One morning in his Melbourne flat he'd woke to the sound of clawed feet scuttling across kitchen linoleum, fading into infinite distance. On another morning years later he distinctly heard someone yell "Beee-eeeeeee" right outside his room. There was no sequel or explanation for either event.

Tricks of the mind, he told himself, lying there in the dark. But then his Melbourne flat hadn't had a bizarre history; its keyholes weren't haunted.

Keyholes. Realization startled him. He sat up. Keyholes. Why just the back bedroom keyhole? Why not the back door? The front door? His own bedroom door? What might they not show?

Half eager, half afraid, he swung out of bed and groped for the matches and candle on the night stand. In rural areas electricity was often deemed unnecessary in the wee hours, and suppliers acted accordingly. With the candle lit and left burning on the stand, he left his room, closed the door and peered through the keyhole.

For some moments he saw nothing. Not blackness, not a night scene slowly resolving on the eye, but a grey murk. Then it seemed that there *was* something after all: something very small, very far away emerging, swaying from the grey. A figure, tiny and indistinct, walking slowly and deliberately towards him. Was it imagination, or did it wear dark clothes and a black, wide-brimmed hat? Surely it was too far away to see such detail. Yet at one moment he was sure, while in the next it was again but an undefined stick figure.

The back door was next. With intense foreboding, for the door faced west, he peered into its keyhole.

A naked figure stood erect against a sky aflame in dying sunset, its body all scrawny and wasted, thin arms crooked and outstretched. Eyes—small, black and hard—stared from a head too long, too narrow for its grinning mouth. Wishbone legs hooped an arch on bare feet resting on the ridged backs of two crocodiles gripping the ground with crocodile claws.

Lewisham backed away, reeling from the macabre vision. He retrieved the candle from his room with shaking hands and made his way to the front door. He stooped and looked through the keyhole.

"Michael!"

Len Flynn was taking the morning air outside his shop when he spotted Arthur Lewisham shuffling up the middle of the main street. Looking neither left nor right he performed miracles of chance in not being struck down by passing wagons and motors. Flynn dashed into the road and guided Lewisham safely to his verandah. He sat him down on a wooden chair, then glanced through the window, but for the moment was unable to catch his wife's eye as she busied herself serving a customer.

"You've seen something," Flynn said.

Lewisham nodded, and in a shaken, broken way, almost a repeat of the previous morning, he told Flynn what he'd seen, holding back only the keyhole apparition of his west-facing back door.

"But what has your son to do with it?" asked Flynn.

"Good god, man!" Lewisham burst out of his lassitude. "Don't you think I've asked myself that same question all these hours? I've sat in my room and babbled to myself all morning. I'm going mad, Len. Those damned ghosts are driving me out of my mind." He went on to describe the man he'd met in the graveyard, but neither Len Flynn nor Alice, when she came out from the shop, was able to put a name to him.

"I thought not," said Lewisham in a tone of self-satisfaction.

In the Flynns' kitchen he was given a splash of brandy in a glass to steady his nerves. He drank it readily, despite the fact he was an almost total abstainer.

"Those clothes you say this bloke was wearing," said Flynn as Lewisham coughed down his liquor. "Reminds me of the way a swagman around here used to dress. Always wore dark tweed and a hat like the one you described. Round about thirty-odd and beardless, which was unusual for the time, particularly for a swaggie. Drifted in and out of town, wouldn't be seen for months, then he'd turn up again and work a while at a farm or at the butchers, sling his swag and disappear. Not that I'm saying he's the fellow you asked about. He hasn't been seen hereabouts for donkey's years. Come to think of it . . . Alice, wasn't he found dead in Sydney round about 1903 or 4?"

She squinted, remembering. "Seems I did hear something like that. Maybe secondhand and long afterwards; maybe someone from hereabouts was in Sydney when they read about him being found dead in the gutter. Face down in his own vomit, he was."

"*He* got questioned by the coppers, just like me. They really looked at him hard at one stage, so I heard," said Flynn.

"And his name was . . . Knight," said Alice, face brightening with remembrance. "Yes. I remember him now. Used to come in here sometimes. He'd be the last one you'd pick for a swagman. He used words that went right over my poor head. 'Necro-pol-is' was one I recall. In fact I recall it well because it was the day of the Henley burials. He had his work clothes right enough, did Knight, but he always travelled dressed to the nines. Some used to think he was a gentleman who'd come down in the world."

"Years on the track would knock the polish off a man like that," Flynn said. "Or kill him. It's catch as catch can on the road; only the selfish and the ruthless survive a life like that. And you know," he said, rubbing his chin, "there *was* something of that about Knight; something about him that made you think you never saw all round him."

"Yes, well, swaggie or not," said Lewisham, "this fellow I met in your cemetery certainly wasn't a seventy-year-old. In fact, though he looked hardly old enough, he said he knew the Henley girls."

"Lots of people round here knew the Henleys," said Alice. "They were a well respected family. You'll have read on their stone how it was paid for by public subscription."

"It's a shame," said Lewisham with the air of someone thinking out loud, "that there are no photographs of this man Knight."

"Who says not?" said Flynn.

"Are there?" said Lewisham.

"When this happened the town came alive with newspaper men and their photographers, and that's to say nothing of police photographers and everyone else who could work a Kodak. Graxton's photographer of the time, old Frank Benson, bequeathed most of his to the people of the district. They're kept at the town hall."

As they made their way to Graxton Town Hall through the bright morning sunshine, Flynn said, "When you saw your boy through the front door keyhole, what was he doing?"

"How do you mean?"

"You said the other figure was walking towards you; was Michael walking towards you too?"

For a long moment Lewisham didn't answer, then glanced at Flynn, surprised. "I don't know. Queer, that. I have no memory of *what* I saw, yet I know I saw him."

"And you remember what you saw at the others?"

Lewisham nodded, pensive.

"What about the back door keyhole? You never mentioned that."

"No, I haven't. And I'd rather not, at least for the time."

At the town hall they were directed down an echoy passage, cool and dim to the library. After a lengthy wait, several boxes labelled F....E. BENSON BEQUEST were brought out.

"Old Benson had set his shop up here long before my time," Flynn whispered as they spread yellowing photographs over the library table, "and he didn't pass away until just a few years ago, so his collected works are quite substantial."

The bulk of the several hundred photographs were portraits done in Benson's studio. All but a few of the later prints were strangers to Lewisham, posed stiffly solo or grouped around items of furniture before various backdrops. Flynn with his thirty-seven years residence now and then made noises of recognition as some forgotten face was unearthed. Some of the prints of places were more familiar, however: the Station Hotel; the Brian Boru Hotel; various of the outlying farmhouses, particularly those along Murphy Road ("That's the Henley place," Flynn said, tapping one of these with a finger); the streets, emptier then but still dirt and dust; the stores and shops along the main drag, often housing a different merchant or tradesman than they did today.

"Ah," said Flynn. "Here's a picture of the Henleys." He passed it across: a middle-aged man and woman sitting on chairs in an outdoor setting, behind them a row of eight boys and girls ranging from child to late twenties. "The young fellow standing behind the old gent, the one wearing the moustache, that's Douglas. The two girls on the right are Myra and Celeste."

Lewisham bent over the picture for a time, studying it in silence, looking into each set of eyes in turn, trying not to imagine this upright young man and those two lovely girls lying broken and violated in Quinn's Paddock.

"The surviving children have long since moved away," said Flynn. "Though James Henley and his wife Amelia never left the district, despite all, and both passed away in the twenties only months apart. They're out in the cemetery not far from their children's monument. The old lady used to visit it every Sunday and cry and wail something piteous."

"I read a book on folklore once," said Lewisham, his eyes on Amelia Henley sitting with her husband and children in happier times. "It said too much grief and sorrow could bring a ghost back because it stopped it from resting. I wonder . . . It said dogs could see ghosts, and if you looked between a dog's ears you would see the same ghost the dog saw. And if you gazed steadily through the eye of a needle . . . I wonder if all small apertures . . ." He trailed off vaguely as somewhere above them the town hall clock struck the hour.

"Arthur, I really should be getting back to the store. Will you be all right here?" Lewisham nodded and Flynn left, promising to return later to help pack up.

Lewisham carried on sifting through the photos, looking for the man in dark tweed, beardless, thirtyish. Before long, however, he felt the missing hours of sleep creeping upon him, the unnatural stress of the last couple of days, and the monotony of passing tired eyes over more posed strangers, more half-familiar landscapes. He leaned back in his chair, closed his eyes a moment, then with an effort resumed his work.

Here was one of a bush scene, lightly wooded, a horseless sulky to one side tilted down on its shafts. In the foreground an Aborigine crouched. Lewisham turned it over and read in pencil: "Quinn's Paddock 28 Dec. '98. Henley sulky and black tracker Paddy Perkins."

"I doubt you found tracks that led anywhere in this world, eh, Paddy," said Lewisham. He put it down and picked up another at random. This was an oddity among the rest: a night view of an empty road, lit by a full moon. The next photo was a copy of the last . . . or was it? Lewisham examined it closely: same road, trees, ironbark post and rail fence picked out in the same garish moonlight. Same deep shadows gathered beside the road in the foreground . . . No! Where the shadow in the first was unbroken, something had pushed out from it in the second. The third photo he picked up was much the same, save that the thing pushing out of the shadows had moved out a little further and there was now something coming along the road: a one-horse sulky carrying three people.

Without looking, without questioning, Lewisham picked up another photograph. The sliprails into Quinn's Paddock were down and wheel tracks, one side wobbly, traced their way through.

By now his heart was pounding and his hands were far from steady as they picked up another picture. He didn't want to see. But his hand came up just the same and practically pushed the ghastly thing into his face.

Here was his picture of Knight. Here was the man in dark tweed and string tie, half turned into the moonlight showing ugly emotion on that beardless, thirtyish face, *doing it*; the educated, well spoken swaggie with his trousers open, *doing it*, with a thick branch in his upswung hands, *doing it*; three more for the necro-pol-is lying terrified there half in moon shadow on the grass, all heads pointing West where distant but distinct the grinning thing stood on crocodile backs stretching out its thin gathering arms.

Lewisham looked up, horribly shaken. Douglas, Myra and Celeste sat with him at the table. They were smiling. He thought, *Why are you smiling? Don't you know? Don't you care?* Still smiling, the girls' heads sloughed off at the sides. Bone and brain and brain-fluid gushed forth, splattered on the table, on the photos. Blood squirted from a neat round hole in Douglas's forehead, spraying over Lewisham, salty and warm.

Horror tightened in his chest. He fell face-forward into the photographs and gore, dimly aware he was having a heart attack.

At the Ipswich Hospital, halfway east to Brisbane, the doctors diagnosed a heart flutter, though tests showed his heart was strong and they puzzled over the cause. Lewisham knew better than to tell them. He spent his time fearing the moment a nurse would smile and say, "You're going home tomorrow." He did not look forward to leaving hospital. He did not relish the thought of sleeping again in his neat little Murphy Road cottage.

But three days later, feeling like a recaptured fugitive, he was given a bottle of tablets and returned all those miles west to Graxton.

"And how are we today, Mr Lewisham?"

"Why is it," he said, staring up at the ceiling of his room, "that the moment someone is incapacitated otherwise normal people begin referring to him in the collective first person?"

"Beg yours?" said the young woman at the door of his room.

"Never mind. You're late today, Mary. You might like to give the typewriter an extra dusting."

Mary dropped her bag at the bedroom door and put her hands into her apron pockets. "I saw the amount of dust that was on it when I was here on Wednesday, Mr L. That same page is still sticking out of it that was sticking out of it two weeks ago."

"I've only been out of hospital a few days. Your local G.P., Machen, told me to take it slowly."

"I heard what Doctor Machen said . . . As if you do get yourself excited, couped up here most days like a prize barnyard fowl. But there are limits to taking it slow. You'll rust away just lying there."

"Ah, Mary. You're getting more and more like the daughter I never had." Lewisham popped a tablet into his mouth and washed it down with a glass of water. "Writing's not all pounding out words on a typewriter. There's a lot of researching to be done. Which reminds me, have those books come in from the State Library yet?"

Mary hefted her bag and brought out two large tomes. "That's why I was late. I was waiting at the station. They were on the eleven o'clock train that didn't come in till twenty past."

"Aha!" He took the two books and began thumbing through them with almost childish eagerness.

"Mr L, coming from the Smoke as you do, you probably don't reckon I'm too sharp on such matters, but I have eyes in me head and I read the papers sometimes. Them books there that you ordered special from Brisbane got nothing to do with the War. I know who Crowley is and I looked 'thaum-at-urgy' up in father's dictionary on the way here. That's blasphemy those books are."

"Nonsense, m'dear." He was turning pages slower now, stopping to read headings and study sketch drawings. "They *are* about the War. Crowley started it. He was pulling rabbits out of a hat and by mistake pulled the Kaiser out by his whiskers. Isn't being pulled out of a hat by your whiskers excuse enough to send a hundred million young men to kill each other?"

"You're not talking sense, Mr L."

Lewisham peered at her over the top of the book and frowned. "No. I'm not. But that's because there was scarce sense to begin with. Tell me, Mary, have you ever heard of the Henleys?"

The change of subject threw her for a second, but she quickly regained her balance. "Henleys. Yeah . . . I know the story," she said, sounding like she knew less than she was saying. "They's the ones that got murdered a long time ago somewhere around here."

"Yes. Somewhere around here."

"A man and his two sisters went into a paddock one night because . . . well, you know."

"Know what?"

"They were at it." She tittered nervously.

"Eh? What do you mean 'at it'?"

"You know . . . at it." She darted her eyes sideways a couple of times, and gave an embarrassed laugh. "But their father caught them and bashed their brains in with a stick and then shot the horse and cut off its thing and then he went and hung himself."

Lewisham regarded her first with astonishment then with a tolerant smile. "Dust, Mary, dust!"

Time and retelling breaks truth into rubble, the cemetery stranger had said. When Len Flynn had come visiting in Ipswich Hospital, he'd told Lewisham he'd visited the Henley monument. But where Lewisham had seen a wreath of lilies laid, Flynn had found only a scattering of dead flies.

Lewisham plunged into the books, but had read only a couple of minutes when he called to Mary sweeping the front room carpet.

She poked her head around the door again. "Yes?"

"Mary, do you know what a poltergeist is?"

"Yes," she said. "I do know what a poltergeist is. It's a ghost that chucks things about. And well I should know, too."

She made to go again, but he called out, "Wait! What do you mean well you should know? Have you had one in your house?"

"No, not in my house—in gran's house . . . father's parents had one throwing things about when he was just a boy. Smashed anything that could be smashed it did, and turned the whole place inside out, so they tell me."

"When was this?"

"Well, like I said, when me dad was a boy."

"Yes, yes, Mary, but what year? What year?"

"Mr L, don't get excited. Remember your heart. Well, I reckon it must've been round the turn of the century."

"1898?"

"Suppose."

"Have you ever heard other stories of poltergeist activity in Graxton round about that time?"

She leaned on her broom. "You hear stories, Mr L. Towns like this are rife with stories about this and that. Who's to say what's true and what's been made up to be better than the neighbours? But they say there were other houses and other farms here and there about Graxton with poltergeists in them round the same time. Copycats, I reckon. Wanted to go one better."

"Thank you, Mary." He returned to his thaumaturgy book where his finger still rested on the heading "Residue Phenomena: Poltergeists, Apparitions, etc."

> Immediately after such ceremonies and experiments, random poltergeist activity is often experienced at distances of up to a mile or more. These dissipate after a few days. However, more substantial phenomena occur at the focus, and can continue in discrete form for many years. This can include what is popularly known as ghosts, and is not always connected with the original Magic.

Later, when Lewisham was giving Mary her shillings for the week, he asked, " 'Poltergeist' is not a word many people know, town or country. How did you come to hear it?"

"Well, it was Gran's word when she told the story."

"And where did she learn it?"

"From a man who worked some of the farms round about. A swaggie he was, but he knew some odd things for all that, so Gran said."

Lewisham sat up sharply. "Was he called Knight?"

"Yeah. Ridley Knight; that was his name."

After Mary left, Lewisham swung himself gingerly out of bed and pressed his eye to his bedroom keyhole. Something dark and blurred and shot through with oscillating light occupied the whole view. He caught glimpses of a skull face in too-close-up and imagined he heard the clack of bone against bone. He crept across the kitchen's stone floor, still wet from Mary's mop, glanced briefly through the back door keyhole, then turned away again with a shudder, unable to face what grinned there. He returned to the front door. Michael was there in its keyhole, glancing left and right in a sick anxiety. The stars and bush and fence were still visible in the back bedroom keyhole. What's more, he was sure something was now moving there in the moonlight.

All that afternoon and into the night he pored over the book on magic and the book on Crowley and how he worked that magic. At half past ten power was cut off. He lit two candles and continued reading.

> Bradley and Montpelier completed the incantations at sunset and killed one of the two injured cats. They then raised a gold ring each to an eye and gazed through it, seeing the expected Devil astride its reptiles miles to the West, although the basement wall was but a few yards away. Obeisances were enacted. Promises of power were made by the Devil. Whether these promises were kept is difficult to ascertain. Bradley died in an unexplained accident two years later in that very same basement, the house then standing vacant. At the time of his

death he had not visibly gained in material wealth or spiritual power. Montpelier, however (and here it must be remembered that it was he who drew the original Parchment) did gain some notoriety within arcane circles, but died in penniless obscurity in his sixtieth year. His last words were reputed to have been: "Has it all come to nothing?"

The failure of the Bradley-Montpelier Experiment is often blamed on a lack of will to carry it through properly. Something of far more personal value than a stray cat should have been given for proper returns. There were rumours which persisted for years afterwards that a re-enactment of the Ceremony could be seen through the keyhole of the basement door. Figures usually described as being something like Bradley and Montpelier were often reported in the house during their lifetimes and long after their deaths. The cries of cats were said to drift through its corridors. Unexplained figures were met with during the one formal investigation of the house subsequent to the Ceremony; these have been variously theorized as unconnected memories and ghosts of later tenants, or entities which slipped through a gap opened unintentionally by Bradley and Montpelier. An example of this is a young man of a liquid appearance often seen leaning out of an upstairs window crying, "Fire!" though there had never been a fire at this house. The apparition of an ugly woman was sometimes seen chasing an amorphous mist which some perceived to be a child. Those who saw the woman never saw the child and those who saw the child never saw the woman, save as a formless darkness. It is sometimes thought the reappearance of Bradley and Montpelier were attempts by the essence of the men, both during life and afterwards, to re-establish a level from which they could regain power through the use of captured 'spirits' which were attached to and brought in by subsequent dwellers in the house.

At one o'clock, with his head swirling, Lewisham put out his candles and fell into a deep sleep in which he dreamt that Michael was standing guard over him. In the morning he awoke from the best night's rest he'd had since this thing had begun.

Later that morning he dropped himself down on the back doorstep with his bottle of heart tablets, a pencil and notebook, and began work on his Gallipoli book again. But writing came hard that morning, and he found himself coming back to ponder his earlier words about the Battle of Lone Pine having been a "knowing sacrifice of the youth of Australia". Sometimes he'd cast a glance towards the woods beyond his yard. At one point he made a tube of his hands, like a telescope, but did not dare bring it to his eye. There was no door, no barrier here; just the backyard stretching off into the woods and the horrible hollow beyond. Eventually he put everything aside, went in and fetched out the two library books.

Len Flynn visited around lunch time and brought a thermos of tea and some bread and jam. For a while they spoke of nothing in particular, and at times lapsed into long awkward silences.

This got to Lewisham after a while and he suddenly interrupted Flynn's small talk, saying, "Did you take another look through the Benson photos?"

"Well . . . yes," Flynn said, happy at last to drop pretense. He took an oblong of cardboard out of his shirt pocket and gave it face down to Lewisham. "Are you sure?" He looked up at the wide blue Queensland sky. "It was broad daylight in the library too."

Lewisham said nothing but, hesitating only briefly, flipped over the old photograph.

Knight. Not waiting in the shadows of Murphy Road, not committing the unspeakable in a moonlit paddock, not the unreal photos. Knight in his dark tweeds and hat and string tie. Knight standing beardless in the backyard of the Graxton police station in 1898. Though the clothes were the same as those of the stranger he met in the cemetery, the face was dissimilar, and Lewisham recalled how he'd imagined he'd looked like Michael, had his son lived to age forty. The thing that had left a wreath of flies at the Henley monument had deliberately mocked him.

I knew the two girls, it had said with a smile.

"Do you think that's wise, Arthur?" said Flynn, indicating the two books of arcane knowledge sitting on the step beside him.

"Yes," said Lewisham in as steady a voice as he could muster, though he felt sick. He briefly outlined to Flynn what he'd read of the Bradley-Montpelier Experiment. "Do you see, Len? Bradley tried to stop it by going back and facing it, but he hadn't the necessary power behind him. He hadn't made much of a sacrifice." He handed the photo back, face up. "I have, in Michael. That's what Knight is after."

"Come away, Arthur," said Flynn suddenly. "Come away."

Lewisham pulled away from his friend's hand plucking at his sleeve. "Leave me be."

"Sell this place. Sell it, burn it down."

"And go where? Back to Melbourne? Back where I came from? Or somewhere with no ghosts? There are ghosts everywhere, Len. I might as well try to run from my own thoughts, and I'm getting too old for that. You have to face them down—ghosts of all sorts—or they'll beat you mind and body. Leave me be. Tell Alice I'll come visit as soon as the doctor allows."

So Flynn left and Lewisham returned to his work with renewed vigor.

In the late afternoon a cloud—or so he thought at first—crossed the sun. He looked up. There was no cloud. The sun shone brightly behind the tall apparition standing swaying above him.

"The Henleys are lying dead in Quinn's Paddock, and such a mess you've never seen in your life."

Lewisham nodded quietly to it and the figure turned and stalked across the yard, losing thickness and detail until it was a thin shadow lost amongst the trees.

He stood. Knight would be there in the hollow. He had to be, for his skull face was no longer stumbling in and out of view in the keyhole. Dead these many years. Dead like Bradley and Montpelier had died; like he expected Crowley, already on a slide, to die—in poverty, powerless and alone. He who made the greater sacrifice would prevail. Knight's wasn't a sacrifice; Knight had lost *nothing*.

Lewisham moved off on faltering steps, past the earth closet, gently through the trees due west, following the wheel tracks, one side wobbly.

CATHARINE SAVAGE BROSMAN

Kokopelli

Catharine Savage Brosman was born in Colorado and educated in Texas and France; she currently lives in New Orleans. She is the author of four collections of poetry: Watering, Abiding Winter, Journeying from Canyon de Chelly, *and* Passages, *as well as a memoir,* The Shimmering Maya and Other Essays. *She has edited numerous books on modern French literature, culture, and literary biography, and has published poems in a wide variety of literary journals.*

Kokopelli is a well-known figure among the indigenous people of the American Southwest. Many are the tales in which this magical spirit (symbolically pictured as a hump-backed flute player) seduces young women and brides. The hump on his back is often described as a sack containing enticing gifts. Brosman's evocative poem comes from The Sewanee Review *(published in Sewanee, Tennessee, edited by George Core), and will be included in her forthcoming poetry collection* Places in Mind.

—T. W.

Kokopelli, humpbacked dancer from a past
with neither wheel nor beasts of burden,
but with music—brought across the strait
among the snows and down the continental
spine, or carried like an amulet by those
who sang over the vast and variable sea

and drank from skins below unshaded blue,
until they heard the shore birds answer—
Kokopelli, dancer, piper to the Anasazi,
we, the desert dwellers of these latter
days, are listening for you, as you make
your sweet and silent music on the stone,

inscribed forever with the sacred corn,
melodious still beside the sun and clouds,
the hunters who pursued the bighorn sheep
and slew the deer. Like all enchanters,
you were feared—by husbands and old men—
but brides and virgins secretly rejoiced

at Kokopelli's flute, and followed him—
perhaps too far, along the canyon streams
through hoary cottonwoods, or to the edge
of mesas, where they swooned in ecstasy,
and good and evil mingled in their blood
till time was born again. It is beyond

us, all—the spirit winds that hiss around
the arches, sculpting stone to emptiness;
the indwelling visions which imagined gods
with flesh, then vanished with the autumn
grass; the willow music of desire sounding
in the wilderness, as if it would not end.

BRUCE GLASSCO

Taking Loup

Bruce Glassco is a new writer to keep your eye on. His first story, a brilliant retelling of the ballad of "True Thomas," was published in the adult fairy tale anthology Black Swan, White Raven. *"Taking Loup" is his second published story. It comes from the "erotic fantasy" anthology* Sirens and Other Daemon Lovers.*

"Taking Loup" is a dark fantasy looking at gender issues from an unusual perspective. For such a brief tale, it packs quite a punch.

Glassco lives in Virginia, where he teaches English at Eastern Shore Community College.

—T. W., E. D.

You study your date's fingers intently when you give her the flowers, because you read in a magazine once that women on loup have unusually wide knuckles. You don't know the exact dimensions of a normal woman's knuckle, though, so you don't learn much. Her fingers are long and slim, and you've heard that's a good sign, but the nails look awfully strong, and they curve downwards a bit at the ends.

You remember when it all started, how men were warned to watch out for hair growing in unusual places. But women had been shaving their bodies for years, so that wasn't much help. Men might not even have known what an unusual place was, back then; they might have thought an armpit was unusual. Linda's hair is as black as the night, and if she changed and it covered her she would blend into the night and you would never see her coming.

The fact is, there aren't any signs. The fact is, if a woman is taking loup you won't know it until it's too late, until she's already ripping your chest open and swallowing your heart. The fact is, as Linda takes your flowers and admires them and goes to the kitchen for a vase, her freezer might be filled with parts from a dozen dates, ready to be thawed out for a late-night snack. The fact is, you thought you were sure about the last woman, and you were wrong.

You try not to think about that as she comes back with her handbag and leads the way to the parking lot. She's small, a lot smaller than you, but mass doesn't count for much anymore. Pete Wilhelm at your new job weighs twice as much as his wife, but all summer he came into work wearing long-sleeved shirts. Sometimes there are bandages on his face, and he claims that he cut himself shaving or fell through a window. Sometimes he doesn't come to work at all.

You were fifteen when you first heard about loup. It started with athletes, you think: some kind of steroid that worked a bit too well. They've studied it for years, but they still don't know exactly how it works or where it comes from. All they know for sure is that it doesn't work on men. Something about chromosomes and estrogen and the phases of the moon.

There is a brief quarrel over whether you're going in her car or in yours, but you give in after some token resistance. She opens the passenger door of a silver Porsche. As you sit down you check the velour seat covers for fur or blood.

Tom Schneider was a kid from your hometown—your age, but from a different school. You'd never met him. He hitchhiked home from an away game one night, and no one ever saw him again. You joined the hunt, moving as straight as you could across a meadow, peering in clumps of grass and bushes, bored and scared at the same time. They found a shinbone with tooth marks on it, and that was all they ever found.

You made sure to tell your roommate exactly where you would be, exactly when you expected to get in, who to call if you were late. You wish you could say that you took no chances, but if that was true you would have stayed at home.

At the restaurant there is an awkward pause. You were brought up to offer to take a woman's coat. That's not the custom anymore, and for a moment it looks like she's going to try to take yours. Finally you each awkwardly shrug off your own, and then you take them both to the coatroom while she sees about her reservations.

New customs are hard. New customs—an oxymoron. On the freeway she was listening to the Cleveland Howlers against the Green Bay Pack. Sheila Breen, Cleveland's best runner, had carried the bag to midfield when the Pack caught up with her, and between them they tore the bag to ribbons. It was the fifth new bag of the game. Sometimes you miss football.

"So tell me about yourself," you say when you sit down, and she happily goes into her story. She's on the fast track at an ad agency—a campaign for those new quadrupedal workout areas. Your roommate Karl didn't tell you much about her when he set the two of you up. He just said you'd been moping around too much, you needed to get out more. Only a few women do the stuff, he said, and most of the ones who do aren't dangerous. Most of them are nice. And of course you know that, except for deep down in your gut where you remember heavy paws on your chest, where you remember hot hot breath and saliva and pointed teeth grinning inches away from your face.

Still, you let him make the date for you, because you hate it when it gets cold at night and the only warm place in the bed is the place where you are. She seems nice enough, stopping to ask you a few questions and sounding as if she's interested in your answers. On the other hand, she orders the steak. She's carving it up and popping chunks into her mouth and chewing heartily, and suddenly you feel your supper shifting inside you. She catches your look and asks you what's wrong.

The first time you left your wife, you called a friend to come pick you up in the middle of the night. She changed back to her trueform then, standing on the lawn apologizing and begging as you drove off. She was so beautiful that you almost told him to turn around, but you could see your blood on her fingernails in the moonlight as you held your bandaged arm.

She must have rubbed some of the blood on one of the tires in the confusion. You can't think how else she could have traced you to the hotel, later that night. She had to pay for eight hundred dollars in damages to that room, and you went to the hospital with a broken rib.

The next time, you planned your exit more carefully. You left work early, went to the bus station, and never looked back. No, that's not true. Sometimes you miss her so much it burns; sometimes you would go back and serve her your liver on a platter, if only she would eat it and smile and tell you it was good.

Linda is very kind, she's holding your hand as you tell her the story, and she's telling you how sorry she is you've been hurt. She asks if you still want to go to the movie, and you say not really, you'd rather go home.

She parks in the street behind your car, outside her apartment. Then she leans on your hood for twenty-five minutes and tries to persuade you to come inside. I won't pressure you once you're in, she says. Truly I won't. I just want somebody to talk to. I want to hear your story.

There's something about her that still makes you uneasy: the way the moon looks over her shoulder, the way her hair moves when there wasn't any wind, the way her nostrils flare when there is. Finally, though, you give in. She's stroking your arm, and her voice is gentle, and the bed in your own apartment is cold.

When you get inside she offers you a glass of wine and puts on some soft music. There's a dull ache inside you like a lump of congealed blood, and you aren't sure whether it's lust or loneliness or fear. You hope it's not just fear. You want her the way you want air, the way you want your nightmares to leave you alone. A part of you is screaming no, no, we've done this before, but when she reaches up and strokes your cheek the lump in your gut dissolves, and there's nothing you can do anymore. You need to touch her, need to touch someone, there's an empty feeling in your fingertips like parts of them are missing. You stroke her arm and she kisses you. Her mouth is as hot as blood.

She pulls you toward the bedroom and you don't resist. She pulls off your clothes and lays you out on the bed, then climbs on top of you and engulfs you. Her hands clutch your shoulders and she cries out as she forces you inside her. For this one moment you're important to someone else; for this moment you're her world. As she rides you and cries out into the night, you are a part of something larger than yourself, for you are hers. Even as her arms stiffen and grow hair, even as the fingers on your shoulders grow heavy and sharp, still you are hers and she is yours, and as you see her teeth shine in the moonlight you climax in ecstasy and fear.

Some women never turn all the way. Sometimes it's just an ear pointing, a claw sharpening, a muscle that tenses suddenly with the strength of wind. "That was wonderful," she says, and you see the loup passing from her face like a shadow; the newly grown hair fades and turns wispy and falls like snow. Her nose is still wide, though, and she sniffs the air above you. "You're afraid, darling," she says. "I'm sorry, I should have warned you. Were you scared that I would hurt you like your wife did?"

Mutely, you nod. She climbs off and lies down beside you, resting her head on your shoulder. "Not all of us do that," she says. "That's not really what loup is about." She strokes your chest for awhile with a thick finger, and then she says softly, "I'll protect you, darling. I'll keep you safe."

"What *is* it about?" you ask, and you turn to look into her deep gray eyes. You think you see the answer inside them: It's something that's strong, and young, and very, very old.

"The night is where we belong," she says finally. "Out where the moon burns white-hot at midnight. The stars go on forever, and the only thing for us to be afraid of now is the sound that the moon makes in our blood. Do you know what that's like?"

I remember, you tell her. I remember.

Later you fall asleep. You dream that you are lying in the moonlight, and dark shapes are gathered around you. They are ripping you open and feasting on your warm insides, but you feel no pain. If anything, you are glad to be a part of them, for it is good to feel needed. Then one of them moves up and kisses you with bloody lips, and you see that the eyes on her dark face are your own.

You wake up and check to make sure you are still in one piece, and you think back to the time when a woman's heart would grow cold at the sound of a man's footstep in a lonely place at midnight. How long, you wonder, how long until both of the moon's twin children will be able to walk beneath her without fear? And without fear, would love still taste as sweet?

She is sleeping behind you, her breasts pressed against your back, her arms around your chest. The backs of her hands are covered with short black down, and her fingernails are as thick as dimes. Her breath on the back of your neck is hotter than blood.

Feeling her hot breath on your skin, staring into the darkness, you lie awake until dawn.

SARA DOUGLASS

The Evil Within

Sara Douglass was born in Penola, South Australia and raised in Adelaide. She worked as a nurse until she "escaped . . . into the preferable world of writing." Since the publication of BattleAxe, Book One *of the Aurealis Award– winning* Axis Trilogy *in 1995, Douglass has become Australia's premier best- selling fantasy novelist. In addition to the other two novels of the trilogy, she is the author of* Sinner *and* Pilgrim, *the first two books of the* Wayfarer Redemption Trilogy; Threshold; *and a young adult novel,* Beyond the Hanging Wall. *She is also author of such nonfiction titles as* Images of an Educational Traveler in Early Modern England. *She currently lives in Bendigo, Victoria.*

"The Evil Within" is one of Douglass's rare short stories. She asserts that she has always wanted to write a story based on the world as medieval people perceived and literally saw it. The fourteenth-century heretics of the village of Montaillou inspired the setting and some of the characters. Douglass has succeeded brilliantly in bringing alive a world that we've seen only in the art of Hieronymus Bosch. The story was originally published in Dreaming Down- Under, *edited by Jack Dann and Janeen Webb.*

—E. D.

This world, this wasteland, lies heavy with evil. Here writhe serpents, here sting pests, here rot grub worms, here raven wolves, here sin issues in glistening rivulets from the mouths of the dead. Here evil roams on the breath of wind and the dance of dust motes, here evil shrouds itself in the shadows of earth clods and the cavities of human bodies. Here live men and women, the sinful fruit of Adam's weak loins and Eve's vile womb. For her sin, they are condemned to this wasteland, to their toil in the dust, to their scratch- ings at the boil of plague and the bite of pest. Here, amid all this wretchedness, lies the seed of their salvation and the terror of their damnation: battle the evil without and conquer the sin within; succumb to the evil without, and suffer the worms of Hell for all eternity.

Here, this world, this wasteland.

It was an age of gloom and despondency. The population of Europe lay decimated by the creeping pestilence, forests encroached upon untended fields, wolves ranged into villages, and the darkness crept down from the mountain slopes even at the crest of the noonday sun.

Night was an abomination, the haunt of demons and devils, incubi and sharp-toothed fairies, and black ravening dogs that no place on God's earth. Screeches and howls wailed through the most tightly shuttered window, and the most carefully tended infant was vulnerable to forces unnameable.

Hell incarnate roamed abroad, and no pathway was safe, no barred home a haven.

Especially not from the evil within.

His hands stiff with cold, Friar Arnaud Courtete wrapped his cloak a little more tightly about him and slowly raised his eyes into the wind. Before him a narrow trail wound upwards about the grey mountainside before disappearing into the uncertainty of low rain clouds.

Should he continue? The day was half gone already, and the village of Gebetz an afternoon's walk away. But Arques was already a day behind him, and Courtete had no wish to spend another night in the open.

Besides, he could not turn back. Bishop Fournier would not be pleased.

"Holy Virgin, guide my steps," Courtete mumbled, one hand fumbling at the cross about his neck, and then hefted his staff and stepped forward.

Although Fournier had no jurisdiction over Courtete's mendicant order, he was a powerful and influential bishop, and when he had asked Courtete to visit Gebetz, the friar had little option of refusal.

But Gebetz!

Courtete had been there several times in the past, but that had been years ago, and he'd been a young man, both his body and spirit strong. Now his age made his footsteps falter, and a lifetime of priestly asceticism battling frail human need had left his spirit vulnerable.

Courtete hoped he had the faith to endure whatever he might find in Gebetz.

"The priest there is young," Fournier had told Courtete. "Inexperienced and idealistic. A fatal combination in these malignant days. I have heard Gebetz is troubled."

"And if it is 'troubled'?" Courtete had asked the bishop.

"Then send down the mountain to me for Guillaume Maury. I will send him. And his pack."

Gebetz might only be a small and poor village, but it was strategically positioned, straddling the high trails of the northern Pyrenees. If Gebetz succumbed to godless forces, then the trails would be closed, no man would be able to drive his sheep into the rich summer pastures, nor any pilgrim wend his way to Santiago. The mountain passes would be lost to Christendom forevermore.

It was the only reason Fournier was willing to even entertain the idea of letting Maury and his pack move so far from the cathedral.

Courtete shuddered, and hoped that Gebetz wasn't so besieged that it needed Maury and his creatures. Courtete wasn't sure what he feared more—evil in whatever form it took, or Maury and his fiendish spawn.

But was there any difference?

"Holy Virgin, Mother of God," he whispered, "light my way, guide my feet, cradle my soul, save me, save me, save me. . . ."

As Courtete climbed further into the mountains, strange shapes danced in and out of the shadows of his wake. Some took the form of fish with the jointed legs of locusts, others were formed like creatures of the earth, but with perverted, elongated or scaled forms and the slavering jaws of nightmares. Still more creatures were vaguely man-like, save for odd horns, or extra limbs, or the half-lumped flesh of the graveyard.

All faded into the mist whenever Courtete spun about, his eyes wild.

The dusk had gathered and Courtete's limbs were shaking with exhaustion and fear by the time he rounded the final bend into Gebetz. He stopped, his breath tight in his chest, and looked down from the trail to where the village nestled in the hollow formed by the convergence of three mountains.

It was still, silent.

Had darkness won, then?

Courtete gripped his staff tighter and fought the urge to run.

Run where? Night was falling, and he was in the mountains!

Above him a bell pealed, and Courtete cried out. He spun around, frantically looking about him, his staff falling from nerveless hands.

An icy wind whistled between the mountains, lifting his robe and cloak so that the coarse material wrapped itself about his head, obscuring his vision and stifling his breathing.

Courtete's hands scrabbled desperately until he freed his face, his eyes darting about to spot the demon that had attacked him.

Nothing. No one.

Gebetz lay still and silent.

Even the chimneys were smokeless.

Courtete's hand groped for his cross, and he steadied his breathing.

The bell pealed again, and this time Courtete heard a foreboding mumble follow it.

"Where are you?" he screamed, his hand now so tightly gripped about his cross its edges cut into his flesh. *"Come forth and face me!"*

Again the peal, much closer now, and a rumble of voices sounded with it.

"Who are you?" Courtete whispered this time, sure that demons slid down the mountain sides towards him, hidden by the gloom and mist.

A light flared some fifteen paces above him, and Courtete's eyes jerked towards it.

The bell pealed again, frantic itself now, as if whoever—whatever—held it had succumbed to the jerking madness, and a rabble of voices rose in the mist.

"Lord God, Redeemer!"

"Bloodied Jesus!"

"Holy Virgin—"

"Save us! Save us! Save us!"

Courtete slowly let his breath out in relief. It was the villagers who were above him, and no doubt the young priest Bernard Planissole who wielded the bell.

"Holy Redeemer—"

"Crucified God—"

"Drive evil from our homes—"

"And from our fields—"

"And from the paths of the shepherds!"

The bell tolled again, far closer, and Courtete jumped yet again. Holy Mother, he thought, they are engaged in a Perambulation Against Evil!

Was it *this* bad?

Without warning a black figure jumped down from the mist onto the road before Courtete. It was a young, wild-eyed man, black-robed in the service of Christ. In one hand he carried a bell, in the other a spluttering, smoking torch.

He thrust both in Courtete's face, the bell shrieking and bellowing.

"Get you gone!" the priest screamed. "In the name of God, and of the Son . . . and . . . and . . ."

"And by the Virgin, Planissole!" Courtete said, recovering his own clerical composure and the authority of his age in the presence of the young priest's panic. "Can you not see that *I* walk in Christ's footsteps, too?"

And he held forth the small cross from his neck.

Planissole abruptly stopped yelling, although he still tolled the bell. He stared at Courtete, wet black hair plastered across his forehead, green eyes startling in a white face, the flesh of his cheeks trembling, a sodden robe clinging to a thin body.

"I am Friar Arnaud Courtete," Courtete said, extending his hand. "Here to aid you and strengthen God's word in this sorrowful place."

Other figures now stepped out of the undergrowth and mist to stand behind Planissole. Without exception they were stark-eyed and gaunt-cheeked, their faces contorted with the trails of sleepless nights, their clothes clinging damply to bodies shaking with fear, the pale skin of their faces and hands smudged with grime and fatigue, their mouths still moving with invocation and prayer, although no sound issued forth.

Save us, save us, save us!

"Planissole," Courtete said as evenly as he could manage, "will you tell me what is wrong?"

Planissole stared, then dropped the bell, put his hands to his face, and began to keen, a thin wail of fear that echoed about the mountains.

The bell rolled over the edge of the trail and bounced down the side of the hill, jangling and clamouring, until it landed in a small gutter that ran beside a row of houses.

There it lay half submerged in grey-streaked sewage, its tongue finally silenced.

Planissole led Courtete through the village, the villagers trailing behind them in a muttering, jittery crowd. Planissole's eyes never ceased to move right and left as they walked, and Courtete found his heart thudding violently every time the breeze billowed the mist about them. Yet he maintained an outward composure, for surely Planissole and his flock were close to a fateful panic. Finally they drew close to the great stone church that stood at the far end of the village. There was nothing beyond the church, save a trail that led yet further into the uncertainty of the mist and mountains.

Planissole saw Courtete study the trail. "No one has come down that trail for the past week," he said. "And yet there must still be shepherds and pilgrims trapped in the mountains. Dead. Or worse."

Courtete turned from the trail to Father Planissole, but thought it wisest to say nothing, and after a moment the priest led him inside the church.

It was a large, substantial and well-appointed church, catering for the transient population of shepherds and pilgrims as well as villagers. A beautifully carved rood screen separated altar from nave, and carvings of the saints, apostles and of the vices and virtues adorned the sixteen pillars supporting the roof. The windows were small, but beautifully blocked with stained glass, and the walls and roof had been plastered and then painted with stories of the bible.

The smell of roasting pig was entirely out of character.

Planissole's thin face assumed an expression of fretful guilt as he saw Courtete stare at the pig spitted above a fire towards the rear of the nave.

"Forgive our insult to our Lord and the Saints," Planissole said, "but for the past eight days and nights the entire population of the village has lived in this church. It is better protected against the foes of the night. Of necessity we must cook in here as well."

Courtete graced the man with a smile, and waved a vague absolution for the sacrilege.

The villagers had crowded in behind the two priests, and Planissole and Courtete stepped to one side to give them room. Some sank down to rest on piles of bedding heaped amid scattered baskets behind the pillars, several women moved to the fire, setting prepared pots of food among the coals, and the rest grouped about the two priests.

"It is too dangerous to live beyond these sanctified walls?" Courtete asked.

Planissole nodded. "Will you sit?" He waved to the warmth of the fire and they settled down, the villagers spread in a respectful circle about them. "Let me tell you our story."

Even as he took breath to speak, grating noises came from the roof, and an unearthly wailing from beyond the walls.

"Night has fallen," said a woman some paces away, and she hurriedly crossed herself.

"*Evil* has fallen," Planissole said softly, and then he began his tale.

It was far worse than Courtete had feared. The corruption had struck four weeks previously, growing progressively stronger with each night and feeding off the fear and helplessness of the villagers.

The village dogs had been the first to sense the demonic onslaught.

"They fled one night," Planissole said to Courtete. The priest had calmed now the church doors were safely bolted, and Courtete realised that he spoke very well for a simple parish priest. Too well, perhaps. Almost bespeaking an education beyond that of most mountain clerics.

"After the Sabbath sunset the dogs began howling," Planissole continued, not realising Courtete's interest in him, "then they ran into the streets, growling and screaming and speaking in strange—"

"*Speaking?*" Courtete said.

"Speaking," Planissole repeated softly. "They spoke in a language I have never heard before, but which I now believe to be the tongue of Lucifer's minions. After the passage of the first part of the night they massed and fled into the night . . . into the mountains."

"Up the trail that extends beyond this church?" Courtete asked, and Planissole nodded.

"From that night on we have been visited by terror. Great winds that have lifted the roofs of houses and torn the babes from their mother's arms. Food has rotted within an hour of being cooked, and worms have wriggled from bread freshly baked and broken. Great . . ." Planissole took a deep breath, and forced himself to continue. "Two days ago great cracks appeared in the fields, and from them periodically has issued the sulphurous stench of Hell."

"Mother Mary of Jesus!" Courtete cried, "say it is not so!"

"The rents in the earth have deepened, and now they snake close to the village. Out of them crawl abominations."

"Father," one of the village women said, "our priest relates only the truth, and only a part of what we have had to endure. Look at us!" She swept an arm about the assembled gathering. "We fear to venture out at night—'twould be madness to even think of it!—and during the day we walk the streets and field with our elbows tucked tight against our bodies lest we bump the ghosts who throng about!"

A middle-aged man, his clothes hanging about his thin frame all patched and worn, his face weather-beaten, his eyes dull, now stepped forth and spoke. "And yet what this village endures is paradise compared to the inferno that burns within the mountain passes."

"And you are?" Courtete asked.

"My name is Jaques. I am a shepherd. I wander the mountain trails with my sheep, searching for sweet pasture and a dry place to lay down at night. But . . . forgive me, Father . . . I cannot speak of it."

"Jaques, and several other shepherds struggled out of the mountains nine nights ago," Planissole said. "They were wild with fear. They said that a great dark shape that shrieked and wailed ate their sheep, and while it was so occupied, they fled. They'd run for three days and two nights, not stopping, not daring to."

"And no one else has come down from the mountains?" Courtete said, thinking that the dogs had fled *into* the mountains. Was that where the evil was concentrated? *What had they gone to meet?*

"Only one man," Planissole said, and indicated a curly black-haired young man wrapped in a dark cloak sitting against one of the pillars. "A pilgrim. Winding his way home from Saint James of Santiago de Compostella. He arrived five nights ago. Maybe the Saint protected him through the mountains, for none have followed him out."

Courtete stared at the man, who nodded politely. He was reasonably well-dressed, but not ostentatiously. A staff and pilgrim's scrip lay on the floor next to him, and Courtete noticed that there were several badges on the shoulders of the man's cloak. He'd been travelling a while to have collected so many pilgrim badges, and Courtete thought he was probably the son of a merchant or minor nobleman, on pilgrimage to atone for some youthful escapade.

Courtete looked about at the fear-worn faces of the villagers, and listened to the howlings and rappings outside.

"Wait here," he said, laying a hand on Planissole's shoulder, and he rose and walked with heavy heart to a small window in the back wall of the nave that

normally framed the deformed faces of lepers too contagious to be allowed inside
for mass.

Now the glass revealed something more horrible even than the contagion of
leprosy.

A creature, half donkey, half man, was careering in and out of the thickening
mist. Part of one malformed limb had been eaten away.

As frightful as that creature was, to one side something else caught Courtete's
attention, and he pressed his face closer to the glass.

A black imp with thin shoulders, grotesque pot belly, and overly-large hands
and feet squatted on the ground, chewing on the stolen flesh.

It looked up from its meal and saw Courtete staring. Its mouth opened in a
silent laugh, its shoulders and belly wobbling, and it held out a long-fingered
hand in invitation.

Come join me, priest. We could have fun, you and I.

And then it dropped its hand to its swollen genitals and rubbed energetically,
its face glazing over in lust.

Courtete tried to drag his eyes away, but found it impossible.

The imp's movements grew more vigorous, as did the whispered words of
invitation in Courtete's mind, and it was only when the imp succumbed so
entirely to its lust that its eyes rolled up and it collapsed in a quivering heap on
the ground that Courtete could break free from the window.

The friar took a moment to steady his mind and his own physical trembling
before he rejoined Planissole and the villagers.

"Bishop Fournier sent me here to help you," Courtete whispered, then cleared
his throat and managed to speak more strongly. "He will spare no effort to
contain this evil, and then to drive it back."

"I *have* tried everything!" Planissole said. "Every prayer that has ever been—"

"Hush, my son," Courtete said. "There is yet one more thing we can do—"

"No!" Planissole cried, and the villagers shifted and mumbled. "No!"

"My son, I am sorry, but I must. I have *seen* what . . . what scurries outside.
At first light I will send a man with a letter for Bishop Fournier. He will send
Maury . . . and his pack."

"No," Planissole said yet again, but his voice was very quiet now and his eyes
resigned. "Is there no other way?"

"Evil is rampant," Courtete said, "and it must be driven back by the strongest
of means."

The church was spacious, and there was bedding room for all the villagers, but
bedding itself was at a premium, and Courtete shared Planissole's blankets behind the altar. Although both blankets and Planissole were warm, and Courtete's
limbs and eyes weary from the journey to Gebetz, the scrapings on the roof and
the scratchings at the windows and doors kept the friar awake with black memories of the imp's energetic hand.

Neither could Planissole sleep. "I have heard of Maury," he whispered, feeling
Courtete fidget under the blanket.

"You have not seen him, or them?"

"No. I was educated much farther north, and took my orders at the great
cathedral of Notre Dame."

"Ah, you are of the Parisian Planissole family, then?" No wonder the priest spoke so well! Courtete wondered what one of the aristocratic Planissoles was doing in this God-forsaken parish.

"Yes. I . . ."

Courtete's mouth thinned. A sin, then. No doubt the anonymity of the night would prompt Planissole to confess to whatever had condemned him to Gebetz, and Courtete did not know that he was in a mood to listen to a sinner's babbling.

"I became affectionate towards another novice, Father."

Courtete took a horrified breath, for the lust of one man for another was among the most appalling of sins. How was it that one man could lay the hands of lust upon another man? And force himself into another man's body? Unasked, repulsive images filled Courtete's mind, and he drew himself as far away from Planissole's body as he could. "No doubt the bishop found you rutting beneath the kitchen stairs."

"May God forgive my lusting," Planissole whispered.

Courtete wished he had chosen to spend the dark hours on his knees before the altar, and not behind it, twisted in a blanket with Planissole. "In forty-five temptation-ridden years I have befouled neither my body nor my vows of chastity, Planissole," he said. "God will exact penance as he chooses, you may be sure of that."

Courtete hesitated, then spoke again, his hatred of sodomites forcing the words from his mouth. "Considering your own sin, Planissole, I find it hard to believe you regard Maury with such abhorrence."

Planissole rolled away and stood up. "I have loved my fellow man," he said quietly, "not coupled with one of the hound-bitches of Hell."

And he walked away into the darkness.

The next day Courtete sent the fittest of the village men down the mountain with a message for Bishop Fournier.

It took five days for Maury to arrive. In those five days the situation at Gebetz slid from the desperate to the abysmal. No one now dared leave the precincts of sanctified ground; the entire population of the village, as well as those transients who had sought shelter with them, was confined to the church, churchyard and adjoining graveyard. Beyond these boundaries blackened and blistered imps scurried, even during daylight hours. The legions of the dead blocked the streets, choking the gutters with their rotting effusions. The tumults of Hell wailed up through the great rents in the earth which now reached almost to the church itself, and at night immense gouts of fire speared into the night.

Evil reigned.

It would take the infernal to combat this depth of wickedness, thought Courtete as he stood in the churchyard looking down into the village. Prayers to God were useless in the face of this onslaught.

Planissole joined Courtete silently, and the friar glanced at him. Had Planissole's sin attracted this evil? But surely not even the most lascivious of sodomies could attract *this* much horror . . . could it?

Courtete returned his gaze to the streets, watching as a horned and turtle-backed demon seized a skeletal wraith and forced it to the ground for a momentary and brutal rape. Both creatures scuttled into the shadows as soon as it was done, but the vision had spread a stain across Courtete's mind and soul, and he wondered if even Maury could remove it.

Or if, perchance, he would add to it.

How *could* a man couple with a creature as foul as that imp had been?

There was a commotion in the street, and Courtete's gaze sharpened. The horned demon, so recently the aggressor, was now jumping from shadow to shadow, screaming as if God himself was after him.

"Oh Lord save us!" Planissole cried, and grabbed Courtete's sleeve. "Look!"

A creature the size of a large calf was bounding down the street. It was horned and bearded, and great yellow fangs hung from its gaping jaws. It had the paws of a dog, the tail of a lion, and the ears of a donkey, but its twisted and grotesque naked body was horrifyingly human-like.

It was female, for thin breasts swung almost to the ground.

With a shriek the she-thing pounced on the demon, pinning it to the ground, and tearing its head off with a single snap of her jaws.

Then she raised her head and stared at the two priests. She half snarled, half laughed, and bounded back into the village, looking to feed once again.

Another appeared momentarily in the doorway of the village tavern, a male-thing this time, his snake-like head buried in the belly of a yellow-scaled sprite, his talons scrabbling at the wooden doorposts, his body—as horribly human-like as the last—writhing in an agony of satisfaction.

The sprite whimpered, and dissolved, and its killer tipped back his head and howled.

Abruptly Planissole turned to one side, doubled over, and vomited. He coughed, and then straightened, wiping his mouth with the back of one hand.

"Maury's get," he said tonelessly.

"Aye," Courtete said. "The gargoyles."

As his gargoyles chased demons in and out of the houses and snapped at the heads of imps peering over the edges of chasms, Maury himself scampered down the street towards the church, apparently unconcerned about the hellish battles surrounding him. He was a twisted, wizened old man who leaned heavily on a staff, but he had merry brown eyes and a mouth almost permanently gaping in a scraggle-toothed grin.

Maury found much in life to amuse him.

He stopped before the two priests, and peered at them. "Fournier said you had a plague of evil," he said. "But I had not thought you would lay such a good table for my pets."

"Is it done?" Planissole asked.

Maury howled with laughter. "Done? *Done?* Good Father? It will take a week at least to "do" this village. But what have *you* done to attract such wretchedness? Eh? Depravity this dark does not congregate for no reason."

Again Courtete's mind filled with the memory of the imp tugging gleefully at its genitals, and to his horror the friar realised that it roused in him more than just disgust. Appalled, Courtete lost his equilibrium.

"And of depravity you would know much, wouldn't you, Maury?" he said.

Dismayed and frightened by Courtete's attack—had not the friar invited Maury himself?—Planissole laid a restraining hand on Courtete's arm, but the friar paid it no heed. "For have you not an *intimate* acquaintance with depravity?"

Maury's grin faded, and he snapped his fingers. From the window of the nearest house a gargoyle leaped to the ground and scurried over, fawning at his feet. Maury scratched the man-thing's head, but did not take his eyes from Courtete, and he understood many things.

"They are my beloveds, priest, and they will save you and yours! Do not think to condemn what you yourself—"

"Your sons and daughters do you proud," Planissole interrupted, stumbling over his words in his haste to soothe, "and for their service we may forgive the sin of their mother."

Maury's grin slowly stretched out across his face again as he looked at Planissole. "The sin of their mother, priest? She was no sin to me. She kept me warm at night, and she did not overburden me with useless chatter. And," he switched his eyes back to Courtete, "she were more willing than any *woman*, more accommodating than any *wife*, and the litters she has dropped have proved more useful to true believers of God than any *priest!*

"Besides," Maury's voice dropped to a conspiratorial level, holding Courtete's eyes, "*someone* had to couple with her, and I volunteered to save good priests the embarrassment!"

He ran an over-plump and moist tongue slowly around his lips, as if remembering his nights of abandon, and one hand scratched absently at his crotch.

Courtete's face flamed.

Maury chuckled. "Keep the villagers within the church, priests. I can keep my pets from disturbing them there."

"But—" Courtete began.

"They'll hunt down *any* evil, friar. Including the evil that these good souls harbour within them. Can you claim that any here are free of sin, free of evil? Are they not all sons of Adam and daughters of Eve?"

Maury paused, then whispered, "Are *you* not a son of Eve, friar?"

Courtete dropped his eyes and did not reply.

"And while you huddle within the church, good priests, think about what attracted this evil to Gebetz. See how these chasms reach for the church. Something here is as a beacon to it. Find it. Destroy it."

And with that he was gone.

Back to his misbegotten children.

For two days and nights Maury led them in an ecstatic hunt through the village and its enveloping clouds of sulphurous gases, hunting out the demons, imps and sprites that continually spilled out from the rents in the earth. During that time Planissole kept his flock within the church, only allowing people out four by four to use the hastily dug communal privy pit under the alder by the graveyard. During the day the villagers huddled as close to the altar as they could get, speaking in whispers, their round, fearful eyes drifting to the bolted doors every so often.

At night they were silent, and slept in protective heaps that made Courtete shake his head and mutter prayers over them lest individuals' lusts overcame their need for salvation.

Who knew what wanton communion took place among those twisted bodies?

The five or six shepherds sat by themselves several paces to the west of the altar, and the lone pilgrim, the bravest of all of them, spent his days wandering the church, studying the fine carvings and inscriptions that littered the walls.

Courtete found himself curious about the man, and yet in that curiosity, somewhat unnerved by the man's lack of perceptible fear.

At dusk of the third day after Maury's arrival, Courtete wandered over to the pilgrim as he stood by a narrow window in the eastern transept. The window was of rose glass held in lead, but even so Courtete could see the occasional dark shapes cavort outside—whether demons, imps or gargoyles, or even possibly Maury, Courtete did not know.

"Are you not afraid?" he asked the pilgrim.

The pilgrim slowly turned his eyes towards Courtete.

They were the most vivid blue Courtete had ever seen in a man.

"Afraid? In God's house? No, good friar. We are all safe within these walls."

There was a faint thump and then a scrabbling on the roof, but both men ignored it.

"Your faith is strong and lively," Courtete said, and watched the man smile cynically. "May I ask your name, and your origin?"

"My name is Malak. I come from the east, and I travel west."

Courtete opened his mouth to ask for more specifics, but was halted by the expression in Malak's eyes. The man had no desire to be further interrogated, and Courtete wondered what he had to hide.

And what an unusual name! It jarred at something in Courtete's mind, but he could not place it.

"Have you seen the gargoyles before?" he asked. There were several cathedral packs in the east and north of France, and some in the German princedoms and northern Italian states, but if Malak had come from yet further east, this might be the first time he'd encountered them.

"Not this close," Malak said, and he tightened his cloak about him.

Courtete raised his eyebrows. He *was* afraid, then! "They are unsettling creatures," he prompted.

"I find it strange," Malak said softly, "that men of God fight evil with creatures that are birthed of evil and abomination."

The rooftop scrabbling came again, but more distant now.

"Good sometimes fails to—"

"Which Pope was it," Malak said, now facing Courtete again, "that decided that a mating between a man and a hound-bitch of Hell would produce a creature capable of fighting back the vilest of infamies, the darkest of Lucifer's creatures?"

"I don't know who—"

"And what kind of man *willingly* consents to plant his seed in a creature so hideous I find it difficult to imagine he could even contemplate the act of generation, let alone perform it."

There was a horribly uncomfortable quiet as each man stared at the other, each knowing the other's mind was consumed by visions of the loathsome coupling.

"Some men have a taste for such things," Courtete said and, despite himself, glanced out the rose-coloured glass as if he might again spot the imp engaged in its infernal fondling.

Malak laughed softly, as if he could read Courtete's innermost fears. "And where," he said, so softly Courtete had to lean closer to hear him, "does the Church find the hound-bitches of Hell for men to couple with in the first instance?"

Courtete was silent a long time before he finally, reluctantly, replied. "In some places on God's earth the borderlands between this world and the Hellish regions under Lucifer's sway are narrow indeed. Sometimes it is possible to capture one of the Prince of Darkness's hounds."

"Aye," Malak said, "in some places the borders between this world and Hell *are* almost indefinable, indeed." He paused. "*Have* you taken a good look down those chasms outside, my friend? Do you *want* to? Might you see something down there you might *desire?*"

And with that he was gone.

Appalled that Malak could so accuse him, Courtete would have gone after the pilgrim, but just as he took his first step a horrible wailing rose from outside.

"Oh! Oh! Oh, my pretty! Oh my lovely! What do you there! Come down! Come down!"

Courtete opened the door, Planissole at his shoulder, to see Maury standing several yards away, staring at the roof. The pack of gargoyles sat yet further distant, under the low hanging eaves of a nearby house.

They were ignoring the imps that peeked at them from a nearby window, looking instead between Maury and the church roof.

"Something is wrong," Courtete murmured, and eased out the door. Planissole checked that the villagers were safely grouped about the altar, then followed, closing the door behind him.

The two priests moved to Maury, then followed his gaze upwards.

There was a gargoyle precariously balanced on the spine of the steep roof, the remains of a long-snouted imp under its claws.

It didn't look happy.

It whined, and twisted about slightly, scrabbling with its feet as it almost overbalanced. From where it sat, there was at least a twenty-pace drop.

Maury wailed.

"What is the gargoyle doing up there?" Courtete asked.

Maury twisted his hands to and fro. "She chased the imp up there . . . up *that!*"

He pointed to a rough ladder that leaned against the wall of the nave, near where it angled out into the eastern transept.

"*Who put that there?*" he shouted, and turned to Planissole, his face twisting in fury.

Planissole backed away a step. "Several weeks ago one of the villagers was engaged in relaying the slate of the roof. When the evil gathered, and everyone fled inside the church, he must have left the ladder there. But I don't understand why—"

"They *loathe* heights!" Maury said, now looking back to his gargoyle. She was still now, tense. "What if she falls?"

Planissole looked at Courtete, but the friar's face was working with what was probably disgust as he stared at the she-creature on the roof, and so the young priest gathered his courage and addressed the gargoyle keeper. "Maury, surely you can tempt her down? Speak to her soft words of reassurance? If she climbed the ladder in the first place, then—"

"What if she falls?" Maury wailed again. "How could I bear to lose her?"

And without further ado he hurried over to the ladder and began to climb it himself. "My lovely," he called, his voice soothing. "My beautiful . . . come here to me . . . come . . . yes, my pet, yes . . . come . . ."

Maury reached the top of the ladder and held out his hands to the gargoyle. "Come, my pretty, come!"

The gargoyle, reassured by the closeness of her father, slowly inched her way down the roof.

"Maury!" Planissole called. "Be careful! That ladder is—"

The gargoyle's paws slipped in the slimy residual muck of the imp. She screamed, twisted, fell on her flank, and began to slide down the roof.

Straight towards Maury.

He leaned yet further forward, thinking to break her fall with his arms, but the gargoyle was large, as heavy as a mastiff, and when she crashed into him the ladder tipped back and both Maury and the gargoyle sailed into space.

The ladder teetered, then slapped back to rest against the high guttering.

Courtete and Planissole stared, appalled. It seemed to them that the twisted forms of the gargoyle and Maury hung in space for several heartbeats, then both crashed the fifteen paces to the ground.

They landed in thick mud. There was a momentary stillness, then movement as the gargoyle struggled to her feet and limped away a few feet.

Planissole took one step forward, but Courtete grabbed his arm and hauled him back.

"Maury's dead!" he hissed. "See how still his form lies?"

"But—"

"We've got to get back inside. But move slowly, Planissole. Slowly."

"But we've got to see if—"

"By the Holy Virgin, Planissole! Maury's *dead!* Don't you understand? He was the *only* one who could control those gargoyles!"

Planissole's eyes slid towards the pack of gargoyles by the house. They were shifting anxiously, their eyes moving between the body of Maury and the two priests.

One of them lifted its head towards the priests, and snarled.

Planissole took a step back, then one more, then turned and ran. Courtete cursed, and bolted after him. Behind him he heard the pack of gargoyles raise their voices in a shrieking clamour.

"*Lord save me!*" he screamed and, now only a breath behind Planissole, ducked inside the church, slamming the door behind him.

Planissole threw down the heavy bolt. "We're safe!"

"We're *trapped!*" Courtete said. "What is to prevent those gargoyles attacking us now?"

"But we are not the evil."

Suddenly there was a scream outside, and something heavy thundered against the door.

Planissole leapt back, his hand fumbling at his cross.

A murmuring rose among the villagers, still grouped about the altar, then one cried out as a shadow flashed across one of the windows.

There was a howling outside, and numerous claws scratching at the door.

"Why us," one of the village women cried, "when the village still swarms with fiends?"

Malak, the pilgrim, strode forth from the group. His face was taut with anger, and his eyes shone very, very bright.

He stopped just before the two priests. "Do something!" he said. "You are responsible for all our safety! Was it not enough to be surrounded by the minions of Hell? Why now are we attacked by those meant to save us?"

"You would do better," Courtete said, "to go back to the villagers and employ whatever spiritual insight you have acquired as a pilgrim to lead them in a prayer of salvation. Planissole and I will join you shortly."

Malak stared at him, then wheeled about and rejoined the villagers. He shot Courtete and Planissole a dark look, then laid his hand on the shoulder of a man and lowered his head in prayer.

The growlings and scratchings outside grew worse, more frantic. A dreadful musty odour penetrated the door; it reminded Courtete of the smell of desiccated corpses in cathedral tombs.

"Why hunt *us*?" Planissole cried.

Courtete stepped close to Planissole, and spoke quietly. "Listen to me. We are all sinners, all born of Eve. We all harbour evil within. Even you, Planissole, have freely confessed to . . . sordidness."

Planissole flinched, but spoke with angry voice. "Do you say there is no hope? Should we open the door and let the gargoyles feed at will?"

"*Listen* to me! Maury said that something acted as a beacon to attract this evil to Gebetz. *What*, Planissole? What is there in this village that would attract this much evil?"

Planissole was silent.

"If we can find this evil, and turn the gargoyles' minds to it, then we may yet be saved. What, Planissole? What?"

The young man shook his head. "What village sin could attract this much retribution? There has been no great sin committed here. No murders. No invocations to the Prince of Darkness. Nothing but the daily sins of ordinary men and women."

"No incest? How can you know what goes on in the crowded beds of the village houses? I know peasants." Courtete's voice thickened with disgust. "Entire families share the one precious bed. Fathers huddle with daughters, mothers with sons. Flesh is weak, Planissole, and temptation strong. Who knows what happens when a man stretches out his hand in the night and encounters the breast of his daughter, a woman the manhood of her son. No doubt—"

"Your mind is consumed with the temptations of the flesh, is it not, Courtete?" Planissole said flatly. "You accuse all around you of impurity, yet of what do *you* dream at night? The saints? Or of the humping blankets of peasant beds? Do you yearn to lift the corners of those blankets to watch, Courtete? *Do you?*"

Planissole turned away momentarily, taking a deep breath to calm his anger. What is the greater sin, he thought. The sin of the flesh committed yet confessed, or the sins of the mind not admitted? "My parishioners sin no more than those in Arques, Courtete, no more than those in Toulouse or Orleans or Paris itself. I have no reason to put forward for this all-consuming evil that has attacked *us*."

"What? Are you sure that *you* have not sullied the innocence of a shepherd boy, Planissole? Are you *certain* you have not engaged in an 'affection' with one of those young dark-eyed boys? Or were the sheep more compliant, perhaps?"

Planissole grabbed the front of Courtete's robe. "I do not think it *me* lusting for the sheep, Brother Courtete!"

Courtete blanched, and trembled. "Lucifer himself must be guiding our tongues, Planissole. Fighting between ourselves will not aid us, nor the villagers. My son, I suggest we lead these poor souls in prayer, and hope that the Lord hears our entreaties."

Planissole jerked his head in assent—and some residual disgust—and let go Courtete's robe. "You speak sense, Brother. 'Tis the Lord God only who can forgive sin."

He walked over to the villagers, and gathered them for prayer. Courtete joined him, and together they led the assembly in a prayer for salvation even as the gargoyles renewed their attack on the church doors.

"From those that reareth wars, from those that maketh tempests, from those that maketh debate between neighbours and manslaughter therewith, from those that stoketh fires, and those that bloweth down houses, steeples and trees—"

"Free and defend us, O Lord!"

"From the stratagems and snares of the devil—"

"Free and defend us, O Lord!"

"From the onslaught of malignant fiends—"

"Free and defend us, O Lord!"

"From ourselves—"

"Free and defend us, O Lord!"

As the response faded, Courtete opened his mouth to begin a litany against hopelessness, when Malak laughed loudly.

His eyes were still angry.

"Do you think to drive back such as assaults this church with such pitiful words, priest?"

"It is all we have, my son."

Malak's mouth twisted. "It is the evil within that makes the gargoyles attack, Courtete. Perhaps *your* evil. How many of these women have you lusted after, Courtete? And how many of the boys, Planissole?"

He turned and addressed the villagers. "Perhaps we should just throw the *priests* to the gargoyles! Prayer will not save us! Well, what say you? Shall we throw those tainted creatures outside the tainted minds of these priests?"

"Be still, Malak!" Courtete roared, and at the name he spoke Planissole went white with shock. "Can you claim to be free of sin yourself?"

But Malak did not answer him. He was staring at Planissole, and his teeth bared in a cold smile.

"You know my name, do you not, priest?"

Planissole slowly sunk to his knees, his face now rigid with dread. He opened his mouth, but no sound came forth.

Courtete stared at Malak, then at Planissole. "My friend," he said gently, "what is it?"

"Malak," Planissole whispered harshly, "is an ancient word for angel."

He threw himself to the stone flagging, prostrating himself before the angel. "Save us! Save us!"

Malak the angel stepped back and laughed. "Nay, not I!"

Courtete fought down the cold terror within—had the angel seen the visions of the imp that filled his mind?—and addressed the angel as calmly as he could. "What do you here? Why do your immortal feet tread this earth?"

"I come bearing word from God, to all sinners on earth."

"And that word is . . . ?"

"The word is being acted out about you, Courtete. Sin inundates this wasteland, and grows worse each day. The evil within, within you," the angel pointed at Courtete, "and within you," his finger stabbed towards Planissole still face down on the flagging, "and within all of you," the accusing finger swept over the huddled, frightened villagers, "has grown so great that Lucifer's legions have surged out of Hell to greet it! God's wrath increases with each imp that scampers into the light of day, and He has grown of the mind that He should abandon you to your fate."

"No!" Courtete cried, and also fell to his knees. "Say it is not so! What must we do? How can we save ourselves?"

The angel stepped forward and grabbed Courtete's hair, twisting his face up. "Are you prepared to throw yourself to the gargoyles, Courtete? Will you sacrifice yourself for these villagers as Christ sacrificed himself for mankind? And you, Planissole? Will you also let the gargoyles tear you apart as Christ endured the spear and nails for your sakes?"

Both Courtete and Planissole were silent. Then, "If it will save these good folk, then, yes, I will so offer myself," Planissole said, rising to his knees.

His voice was almost joyous.

After a momentary hesitation, Courtete also spoke. "And I."

"Then spend the night in prayer," the angel said, "in the hope that God will accept your souls. At dawn I will open those doors and you will step forth to assuage the anger of the gargoyles."

The interior of the church was shadowed, the only light cast by the flickering candles on the altar.

No one slept.

The villagers and shepherds were now at the rear of the nave, seated stiff and frightened against the back wall, as far from the angel as they could get.

He, for his part, sat cross-legged in the very centre of the nave, staring towards where the folded rood screen revealed the altar.

There knelt the two priests, their backs to the angel, deep in prayer.

Or so it seemed.

"Something is not as it should be," Courtete murmured.

"Be joyful, brother. We will save the villagers with our deaths."

"No, no. It is not a lack of acceptance that makes me so uneasy. There is *something* not right."

Planissole decided not to reply, and the silence deepened between them.

Eventually Courtete whispered again. "If he is God's messenger, then why does he linger *here?*"

Planissole was silent.

"Should the angel not be out, spreading God's message? Is that not his mission?"

Planissole began murmuring the Pater Noster, but Courtete knew he was listening.

"Planissole, the angel is as afraid of those gargoyles as we are. He has stayed within this church because he is terrified of them!"

Planissole continued murmuring, but the words of the prayer were broken now. Faltering.

"No angel should fear a gargoyle," Courtete continued. "Not unless he . . . unless he . . ."

Planissole breathed in sharply. "Unless he is a *fallen* angel!"

"Angels can sin as much—greater!—than man! Is not Lucifer himself a fallen angel? And does not Lucifer gather to him all angels who have fallen from grace?"

"*He* is the beacon which has attracted the evil to Gebetz! Our plight worsened significantly after he arrived." Planissole paused. "Perhaps . . . perhaps Lucifer has thought to open Hell about us here so that the angel may join him. Thus the rents in the earth, the sulphurous odours!"

"Aye. Perhaps the angel thinks to escape to the nearest chasm while the gargoyles are occupied with us."

Planissole grinned in the dark. "I have an idea. One to rid us of angel, gargoyles *and* evil."

Outside the gargoyles paced back and forth, occasionally scratching at the wooden doors, occasionally howling and screaming their frustration.

They wanted the evil within.

At dawn the angel rose and walked over to the two priests still bowed in prayer. He laid a hand each on their shoulders.

"It is time."

The two men rose stiffly to their feet. Planissole looked ashen and sweaty, his eyes frightened.

"I . . . I . . ." he stumbled. "My bowels . . . I am sorry."

And he rushed towards some stairs that wound up to a store room built among the roof beams. Beneath the staircase was a small closet with a pot set up for the effluent of mortals; few now wished to venture out to the open privy under the alder.

The angel hissed in frustration.

"He is young," Courtete said, "and scared. It is to be expected."

The angel looked at Courtete. The man's face was calm and relaxed.

"You should, perhaps, exhibit more fear yourself, friar. Too soon you will be torn—" The angel stopped, then cried out in anger. "See! He thinks to escape!"

Instead of stepping inside the small closet, Planissole had leaped onto the stairs and was now climbing rapidly.

"Fool!" Courtete cried enthusiastically. "Accept your fate!"

And he sprinted towards the stairs.

The angel screamed in fury, the unearthly sound echoing about the church, and then he, too, ran for the stairs that now both priests were climbing as fast as they could.

The stairs twisted in a tight, narrow circular fashion, and when the angel reached their base all he could see was the climbing feet of Courtete high above.

Planissole was nowhere to be seen.

The angel's hands tightened into talons as he grabbed hold of the railings, and he bounded up the stairs three at a time, howling as he climbed.

His face twisted and contorted into that of a bearded demon, his back humped into grotesque lumps, and his clothes burst from him.

Courtete turned as he heard the angel step onto the platform behind him, and almost screamed.

All semblance of the man had gone. The angel had now assumed the form of a multi-armed, pot-bellied, toad-skinned creature.

It snarled, flecks of yellow foam splattering about.

Courtete swallowed, and flung his hand towards the open window. "He's climbed out onto the roof!"

The angel-demon scurried over to the window and looked out, twisting to view the slope of the roof above. "Where?" it growled.

"He . . . he . . ." Courtete found it almost impossible to force the words out. "He has climbed over the spine of the roof. Perhaps he hopes to escape down the ladder on the other side."

The angel-demon hissed, then, its claws scrabbling furiously for purchase, lifted itself out of the window and onto the roof.

Courtete heard its feet thudding as it climbed.

"Lord save us!" he screamed, and slammed the shutters of the window shut.

In an instant Planissole leapt out of his hiding place behind a set of hessian-wrapped bells and helped his fellow priest bolt the window closed.

"Are you sure there is no other way he can get down from the roof?" Courtete gasped.

"No! No . . . *listen!*"

Something horrible was jabbering on the roof above them. It whispered and shrieked and scampered, and the priests could hear the promise of Hell in its voice.

"Quick!" Courtete said. "We have no time to waste!"

And as fast as they had climbed the stairs, they hurried down.

Once back to the church floor they did not waste a glance at the villagers still huddled in a silent mass, but ran to the door. Courtete put his ear to the wood and listened intently.

"Nothing," he whispered. "Silence."

Then something screamed high above them, and one of the village women wailed.

Courtete and Planissole shared a look, then unbolted the door, hurriedly crossed themselves, and stepped outside.

The space before the church was empty.

There were no gargoyles to be seen.

As one, both men turned towards the ladder.

It was swarming with gargoyles. Already the first was clambering onto the roof, another at its tail. As the men watched, the final gargoyle on the ground climbed onto the first rungs of the ladder.

"Sweet Jesu," Planissole whispered. "Climb! Climb!"

Above, the angel-demon shrieked and gibbered. The men could hear it scrambling about agilely enough, but now four or five gargoyles were creeping their careful way towards it. Not long, and they would have it trapped.

Courtete made as if to move forward, but Planissole held him back with a cautionary hand. "Wait . . . wait . . . *now!*"

They darted forward as the final gargoyle made its way onto the roof, seized the ladder in shaking hands, and pulled it backwards until it toppled to the ground.

"Done!" Courtete yelled. *"Done!"*

The gargoyles took no notice, but the angel-demon—now clinging to the cross that rose from the centre of the roof above the nave—began to rain curses down upon them.

"May demons eviscerate you for this! May imps violate your mothers! May you be cursed to the pits of Hell for . . . *ah!*"

A gargoyle bit down on one of its arms, and then another sank its teeth deep into its belly, and another its neck.

The angel-demon screamed and tried to tear itself free, but the gargoyles tore deeper.

An arm came free, black blood spraying across the roof.

What was left of the angel-demon tried to curl into a ball to protect its belly— but it was too late, green-grey entrails already spilled about its knees, and the creature slipped in its own mess and was instantly covered by the pack of gargoyles.

The priests watched silently as the gargoyles tore the evil thing apart.

And then . . . silence.

Nothing. The gargoyles crouched to the slate, as if suddenly realising where they were. The wind dropped. No howls. No shrieks.

Planissole looked back into the village.

Houses still leaned helter skelter into great cracks in the earth, but now no sulphurous fumes rose skyward. No blackened imps' heads poked above the edges of the fissures.

Lucifer had closed the gates of Hell, his disciple destroyed.

"Praise the Lord the evil was strong enough to tempt those gargoyles to the roof," Courtete said.

One of the creatures glanced down . . . and growled.

"Praise God the evil *above* was the greater temptation," Planissole said.

Six months later Courtete returned to the village of Gebetz. The sky was lightly clouded, but sun fell on the village, and at the top of the mountain track Courtete stopped and leaned on his staff, astonished.

It seemed that this place did not know the meaning of evil, let alone be a site that had nurtured such horror only a half year earlier. Carefully tended fields spread up the mountains, and where the slope grew too steep for cropping, there flourished sweet pastures.

Within the village itself the houses had been repaired; all stood straight and even. The streets were paved, and flowers grew in window boxes.

People wandered the streets, gossiping or bargaining at the produce stalls, their eyes free of anything save laughter and good cheer.

Courtete looked to the church, and his wonder grew.

It lay swathed in sunshine amid emerald lawns. The doors were flung wide open so that God's goodness and mercy might spill down upon the village.

Crouched about the roof were the immobile shapes of the gargoyles.

Courtete slowly descended into the village, passing a few words here and there with villagers who remembered him.

When he approached the church, Planissole stepped forth and hurried down the slope to meet him.

"My friend! It is good to see you again!" he cried.

Then Planissole's face grew serious. "What did Bishop Fournier say? Was he angry?"

"Nay, Planissole. Do not fret. Fournier was naturally somewhat upset at the loss of the pack, but they were useless without Maury to control them. Tell me, do they give you any trouble?"

"None. At night we sometimes hear them move about, but mostly they crouch at the extremities of the roof, as they are now. In fact, no one has seen or heard them move for several weeks."

"And the evil?"

"None. No evil dares approach Gebetz now the gargoyles stand sentinel upon the church roof. Even the mountain trails are clear."

Courtete raised his eyes to the roof again, thinking about what he would say to Fournier when he returned to Arques. What a God-given answer to dealing with the problem of evil *and* the perennial problem of coping with the fractious packs of gargoyles! Fournier had ordered another pack from the gargoyle breeding groves of the Black Forest—but why not simply station them on the roof of the cathedral and send their keeper packing?

After all, what God-fearing man could trust someone who *enjoyed* fornicating with a hound-bitch from Hell? Courtete shuddered, and tried unsuccessfully to force the visions of unnatural intercourse from his mind.

"One day," he said quietly to Planissole, "every church roof in Christendom shall bristle with such as these."

"And that," the younger priest replied, "should leave us to devour our sheep in complete freedom, should it not, Courtete?"

LARRY FONTENOT

Wile E. Coyote's Lament

Larry Fontenot was born in Louisiana and now lives in Houston, Texas, where he is a member of the Twitching Limes Ensemble, a local troupe of poets active in the Gulf Coast area. He has had poetry published in Arrowsmith, Bayousphere, Chachalaca, Poetry Review, i.e. Magazine, and many other journals. He was the Featured Poet at the Houston Poetry Fest in 1996 and a Juried Poet in 1998. His collection Choices & Consequences won the Maverick Press Southwest Poet Series chapbook competition.

Fontenot's delightful poem "Wile E. Coyote's Lament" is reprinted from Conspire, an internet poetry magazine. You can find it on the Web at: http://www.conspire.org

—T. W.

A drop of a thousand feet
and the canyon becomes
a coffin.
Nature's ability to swallow
everything whole
gives it power.
Poised at the top.
I have exhausted memory
searching for a charitable way out.
All I feel
are the best of times,
a simple loss
of a thousand
dreams
floating past
on the back of
Colorado breezes.

I have hiked and died
a thousand times

in this country.
All the things
I thought missing
I found in simple flowers
braced against the wind.
bushes
lodged in the lip of a cliff,
streams
rubbing up against muddy banks.
But even here,
among a solitude so forgiving,
something desperate calls.
and sometimes a drop
of a thousand feet seems like
only the next step forward.

MARY ROSENBLUM

The Rainmaker

I have long considered Mary Rosenblum to be one of the best of the new generation of writers, but since the bulk of her work is science fiction, we've been unable to include her in The Year's Best Fantasy and Horror *volumes—until now. Rosenblum's novels include:* Chimera, The Drylands, *and* The Stone Maiden. *She's published a collection of short stories,* Synthesis and Other Virtual Realities, *and writes mysteries under the name Mary Freeman.*

The following coming-of-age story is set in American farm country, and works with a classic American myth. It is reprinted from the October/November issue of The Magazine of Fantasy & Science Fiction, *edited by Gordon Van Gelder.*

—T. W.

So he's a fraud?" Dad said.

"Well, have *you* ever heard of a genuine rainmaker?" Uncle Kenny cut a neat triangle out of his stack of pancakes. "Sandy, I swear these could be Mom's hotcakes. I never could get 'em right."

"You'd say anything for a free breakfast, little brother." Mom ruffled his hair the way she does mine, and she flipped three more of the browned cakes onto a plate. "Better eat these, Donny, before your uncle talks me out of 'em. So how come you don't arrest this man, if he's a fraud? You're the Sheriff." She planted her hands on her hips. "It's a crime, cheating folks around here. Who has any money to waste, with the cattle market so bad?"

"We sure as hell don't." Dad pushed his chair back. "Got to check those heifers." He reached for his hat. "We're gonna run out of pasture in about two weeks," he said in a tired voice. "Guess I'll have to ship a bunch out, in spite of the beef prices. Once they start losing weight, I won't get squat for 'em anyhow."

"Hey, you could hire this rainmaker." Uncle Kenny speared the last sticky forkful of pancake and wiped the syrup from his plate with it.

"I kind of wish I could." Dad wasn't smiling. For a moment he held Uncle Kenny's narrow stare, then he turned away. My uncle shook his head.

"John sounds like he wants to get religion." He laughed.

"Don't, Kenny." Mom was collecting dishes. "It's tough right now."

"It's always tough for him, isn't it? This rainmaker dude is slick." He changed the subject abruptly. "He doesn't promise anything. Not in writing, anyway. If folks want to be stupid and give him money, it's not a crime."

"He's trading on faith." Mom's face had gotten tight. "That's a sin, even if it's not a crime."

"I sure agree with you." Uncle Kenny sighed, and kissed her as he got to his feet. "Wish you made the laws, Sis. So, Donny-boy." He grinned down at me. "You ready to ride?"

Mom was looking at me, and I had to say yes. I'd been just about willing to kill to ride with Uncle Kenny, sitting shotgun beside him as he tooled the green and white Sheriff's Department Jeep through the sage that was mostly what makes up Harney County. Everybody liked Uncle Kenny. It used to make me feel real important, seeing how respectful everyone treated him. I licked my lips, trying to think of an excuse not to go. "Sure," I finally said, and pretended not to notice Mom's eyes get narrow.

"You'll make a good deputy, kid." He slapped me on the shoulder—hard enough to hurt. "Let's go."

Uncle Kenny put his sunglasses on when he got into the car. I didn't say much as we drove back into town. It was hot, and I had the window down all the way, but the July heat washed over me, making me hotter. There isn't much to Burns. The high school. A few streets on either side of Highway 20. A lot of sage beyond that, in gray-green clumps. You got rocks, too, and dust the color of a buckskin mustang's hide. I saw a ghost in the distance, just walking through the sage. He was carrying a bucket.

I see them a lot—the ghosts. Sometimes I think the desert preserves them, like it does the old homesteaders' cabins that are scattered all through the sage. Or maybe the ghosts are everywhere, but it's just easier to see them out here. I told my mom about them when I was six. She went in the bedroom and cried, after. I heard her through the door. I never talked about 'em after that. They don't pay us any attention anyway. I wonder if they even know we're here?

"You're sure talkative," Uncle Kenny spoke up. "Can't shut you up for a second. Something eating at you, Donny-boy?"

"No sir." I could feel his eyes on me, but I couldn't stop looking at the ghost.

"Maybe we need to talk," he said in a real quiet voice.

I sneaked a quick look at him then, and yeah he was looking at me. I stared at my twin faces in the mirrored surface of his glasses, and my stomach kind of folded in on itself, so I could feel the lump of the pancakes I'd eaten. Then his head jerked a little and he turned sharp without warning, so that I had to grab the door. We were pulling into the parking lot of the motel across the street from the high school, tires squealing. No siren.

This was Wednesday in late July. The lot should have been empty—too early in the day for the truckers to be stopping, or the folks passing through on their way to somewhere else. But it was full—so full that Uncle Kenny pulled up behind two big Ford rigs slantwise, not even bothering to look for a parking space. A green and orange patio umbrella stuck up over the crowd at the back of the lot, out where the asphalt left off and the sage began. Everybody was back there, crowding around like it was a booth at the county fair.

"Let's go, Donny." Uncle Kenny threw off his seatbelt like he was mad. "Time to further your education."

Relieved, I scrambled out after, wondering if I could find someone I knew and get myself invited over for the afternoon. Uncle Kenny would buy that.

The crowd around the umbrella parted to let my uncle through, and I followed, looking hard for a face . . . any face. I saw a bunch of people I knew—Mr. Franke, who managed the Thriftway, and the lady who always worked the cash register at the Payless. No kids, though. Then I saw Mrs. Kramer, my English teacher. I stopped short, like I was skipping school, even though it was summer. It made me feel funny, seeing her there in blue jeans like anybody, with my uncle pushing past her.

"We see the world clearly, when we're children." A man's rich voice rose over the murmur of the crowd. It sounded like velvet feels and it sent shivers down my back. "When we're very young, we believe what we see. It's only as we grow up that we learn to doubt—to disbelieve the things that we once knew were real. When we were children, we knew we could summon the rain—or wish it away."

"I don't remember making it rain." Mrs. Kramer spoke up in her late-homework tone and I craned my neck trying to see, because I bet that guy was cringing.

"Our yesterdays change to suit today's belief." The man sounded like he was smiling. "Haven't you ever listened to the arguments at a family reunion? You don't really need me, but if you can't remember how to bring the rain yourselves, you can pay me to do it."

I forgot about Uncle Kenny and pushed forward, not even noticing who I was shouldering past. The man's words made me shiver again—inside this time, like taking too deep a breath of frosty winter air. I was waiting for Mrs. Kramer to cut him off at the knees, like she does when you tell her how the goat ate your homework, but she didn't say anything.

"You got a vendor permit, mister?" Uncle Kenny spoke quietly, but everybody stopped talking right away. He was like that. He could walk into a noisy bar and talk in a normal voice and everybody would shut up to hear him. "You got to have a permit to peddle stuff in this town." He stepped forward, and I could see the man now, squinting from the umbrella's shade. He didn't look like he sounded. He was small, kind of soft and pudgy, with a round sweating face and black hair that Mom would have wanted to neaten up. I was disappointed, I guess.

"I'm sorry, Sheriff." He spread his hands. "I didn't know I needed a permit to talk."

"Folks work hard for their money around here." My uncle hooked his thumbs in his gun belt. "The government takes a big bite and maybe, if beef prices are high enough, we can pay the mortgage and feed our kids on what's left." He paused, looking around at the faces that surrounded him. Everybody had moved back a little, making a ring, like you do when there's a fight out behind the gym. "What you do should be against the law." He turned his attention back to the little man. "It isn't, but we don't have to put up with your slimy kind." He let his fingers curl loosely over the top of his holstered .44. The little man nodded at the gun, his lips pursed.

"Are you threatening to beat me up or shoot me?" he asked mildly.

The silence around us got real tight and I looked away, thinking of the winter night when I had watched through the steamed-up windshield as Uncle Kenny beat up this ranch hand who'd been starting a lot of ugly bar fights in town. "Sometimes you got to know the right language," he had said when he returned to the car. He had wiped the blood from his hands carefully on a towel he pulled from under his seat. "Jail doesn't scare his kind much. But now—he'll mind his manners. I'm just tryin' to save him from knifing somebody one night, and getting himself a prison sentence for it."

I'd believed him. I watched my uncle's lips tighten.

"Tell you what," he said in a hard voice. "You're so sure you're God's messenger, Mister Rainmaker, let's make a little wager. You make it rain on my place, I'll pay triple your fee." He tilted his head slowly back to stare at the hot, hard sky. Not a cloud anywhere—not even a wisp of cirrus. "It don't rain, then you move on and don't ever set foot in Harney County again." He lowered his head, his eyes as hard as the sky. "You willing to put it on the line, Rainmaker?"

"Whatever you want." The man shrugged. "But I don't make rain. I just call it."

"How 'bout you call it right now?"

"I can start right now." The Rainmaker pursed his lips into a little frown. "It takes time for weather to happen. I don't do Hollywood special effects. We're talking a shift in the jet stream, cold fronts and warm fronts. Big masses of air and moisture. Takes time to move that much around."

"Yeah, got you." Uncle Kenny turned around slow, talking to the crowd now. "So if it rains sometime next Christmas, you did it?" He winked. "That's how it works?" People laughed, but the clear space got bigger around the umbrella and the little man. Only Mrs. Kramer didn't move.

"I don't think my cows can wait till Christmas," someone said.

"It won't take that long." The man answered solemnly, as if Uncle Kenny had asked a real question. "Couple of days—maybe four." He shrugged. "When it gets close, I'll let you know."

"And it'll rain right on my land, huh? Just there?"

"Why not our south pasture?" I spoke up. "Grass'd sprout in a couple of days back there if it rained. Dad could put the heifers in instead of sellin' 'em." I looked at my uncle. "You don't have any cattle. You don't need the rain."

"Good idea." Hiram Belker, our neighbor to the east, spoke up from the crowd. "Maybe some of that there water'll land on my back forty." He guffawed—was answered by more laughter.

"Why not?" Uncle Kenny slid his sunglasses into place and turned his shiny mirrored gaze on me. "Hell, do my poor brother-in-law a favor. We'll make it a public event. I'll put up a notice on the bulletin board in the Courthouse lobby when our wizard here decides the rain's comin'. We can party." He grinned around at the crowd. "Don't forget your umbrellas, folks."

He turned away and people turned with him, like he'd given an order. I looked to see if the Rainmaker was mad about that, but he just looked tired. He noticed me looking and gave me a small smile. I smiled back, wondering how he meant to do it, then flinched as my uncle's hand landed hard on my shoulder.

"How 'bout we go get a burger, Donny-boy? We can watch for the clouds to show up."

"It's kind of early for lunch." My voice sounded squeaky.

He opened his mouth to reply, but just then one of my uncle's deputies tapped him on the shoulder. "Kenny? Ronny Carter just called in." He shook a Marlboro out of the squashed pack in his uniform pocket. "You'll never guess what he found out in the sage on his summer range—over by White Horse Creek? The Rojas kid's old beater Chevy."

"Is he sure it's Rojas's?" Uncle Kenny pushed his hat back on his head. "I thought he took off to Mexico to visit his mother, way back in November. Did he find a body?"

"Nope." The deputy dragged on his cigarette and blew out a blue lungful of smoke. "Found the registration. Coyotes had all winter."

Uncle Kenny turned to me. "Let's go, Donny-boy."

"Excuse me." The Rainmaker had finished folding his umbrella. "I don't know my way around here." He brushed dust carefully from gray slacks that looked prissy alongside the jeans everybody else pretty much wore. "Perhaps your nephew could show me where you expect this rain to fall? Or are you free to escort me?"

"Sure," I said, before Uncle Kenny could say anything. "I'll show you."

Uncle Kenny just looked at me, long and hard, and then shrugged and spat. "Whatever you want, kid." He turned his back on us, and walked off with his deputy.

The motel lot was almost empty now. The crowd had left a scatter of crumpled burger wrappers, pop cups, and cigarette butts to mark where it had been. I remembered our one trip to the beach, when I was eight—how the tide had left the same litter of dead seaweed, trash, and broken shells on the clean white sand. I'd found a dead seal, all bloated, with empty eye sockets and grinning yellow teeth. There were ghosts there, too—harder to see, like shadows, but they were there.

"What's your name?" The Rainmaker was looking at me with this thoughtful sort of expression.

"Donald," I said.

"Dimitri." He offered me a pudgy hand and I shook it solemnly. Dimitri sounded foreign. Russian or something. "Saturday hours are precious ones," he went on. "Thank you for giving up a few of them for me. Here." He handed me the folded umbrella, nodded at a dusty blue Dodge Caravan parked on the far side of the lot.

It wasn't a good car for the desert. But when he opened the back, I saw camping gear, some canned stuff in a box, and a couple of five-gallon water jugs. Full. Okay, he wasn't stupid anyway. I got into the front seat beside him, wondering how he'd explain it when the rain didn't come. "What?" I said, when he just sat there staring at me.

"Your seatbelt."

I buckled it. Only Mom ever nagged me about the seatbelt. "Left on Highway Twenty," I said. "Take the first right after the gas station."

He turned the key, frowned as the engine sputtered. When it finally caught, he gunned it and pulled out of the motel lot. Clogged fuel injectors, I wanted to tell him. Pour some cleaner in the gas tank before you have to pay to get 'em fixed. "Turn here," I said, when we got to the track that led back to our spring pasture. "I'll get the gate." A ghost was walking along the fence line as if he was checking the wire. He had a weathered face and wore tattered work pants held up by suspenders. I waited until he passed by before I unhooked the wire gate and pulled it aside.

When I climbed back into the front seat, the Rainmaker was staring at the place where the ghost had vanished. He looked at me, nodded, but didn't say anything more as we bounced slowly along the track. Something metal was rattling in the back. Pots and pans, sounded like.

"Do you really call the weather?" I licked my dry lips, wishing he'd go faster so we'd get a breeze. "Or are you a phony?"

"That's a refreshingly direct question." He chuckled. "Your uncle thinks I'm a phony." We topped a rise and the Rainmaker halted the car. Turned off the engine and opened the door. "This feels like a good place," he said.

He walked away from me and stopped right on the edge of the slope. A pronghorn lifted her head from the sage, eyed us for a second, then trotted slowly away, her white sides flashing in the scorching sun. I wiped my face on my sleeve. I swear the Rainmaker wasn't even sweating. He stood there, looking like he was standing on a city street, just staring out at the sage and rock and dust that stretched to the horizon. This time of year, dry as it was, there wasn't any grass left to speak of. Just sage, and greasewood, and rabbit brush.

I got out, too, thinking that this was stupid, that this guy was a scam, and he'd wave his hands around, and then sneak off when nobody was looking. And I realized I was thinking all this in my uncle's voice. So I quit. And just listened to the desert. It talks, you know. Real quiet—the sound of dust sifting against rock, and wind whispering through sage stems, sand shifting under a mule deer's hoof or a jackrabbit's paws. It doesn't notice us much. I told Mom about that, too. Once. She didn't cry, but it bothered her. I could tell.

The Rainmaker stood there in the blazing sun, arms at his sides, just staring into space with this kind of distant look on his face. And for a moment . . . just a few seconds, I guess . . . I felt something. It was like the air got solid. I don't mean I couldn't breathe or anything. But it was like I could *feel* it—the air, could feel the clouds in it, hung up and leaking on the Cascade Mountains, could feel the cool dampness beyond them where all that water evaporating from the summer ocean was pushing inward. And I could feel . . . a weak spot. Where that nice damp air could push our way.

A ground squirrel scuttled over my toes. I jumped back, startled, and lost the feeling. Figured I'd just imagined it. I kicked a shower of dust after the vanished critter. Looked up to see the Rainmaker smiling at me.

"Tomorrow evening," he said, like he was agreeing with me. "We were lucky—finding that weakening in the high pressure ridge."

I nodded and swallowed. Because his eyes were older even than old Mr. Long's, and he was a hundred and two. The Rainmaker looked out over Dad's pasture again, and now he just looked sad. "It's tough to believe in what you see," he said softly. "When everyone knows it can't be true. Come on. I'll take you home."

I shivered, and didn't answer him as I got back into the car. He drove me back down the track, and then up the main driveway to our house. And it wasn't until I had gotten out at the front door and he was driving away that I realized I'd never told him where I lived.

The sky was clear that night, with just a sliver of a moon, and the Milky Way swept a white path across the sky, so clear that you could believe that it was a road, like in the old Indian tales, where you could ride a horse up it, right up into that sky.

"Hey, it's gonna rain tomorrow." Uncle Kenny had dropped by for dinner, like he did just about every night. "Can't you tell?"

"I'd sure take it, if it came." Dad popped another beer. "Hell, I'd pay the man." He helped himself to a slice of meat loaf with a grunt. "Pass me the potatoes, will you, Sandy?"

"Did I tell you we found the Rojas kid's car?" Uncle Kenny said. "Back along White Horse Creek." He reached for the meat loaf. "I guess the coyotes cleaned things up."

"Julio?" Mom paused, the steaming bowl of potatoes in her hand. "He went back to Oaxaca. To visit his mother."

"Guess not." Uncle Kenny forked meatloaf onto his plate. "Drug deal gone bad, is my guess."

"No!"

"Don't kid yourself, Sandy." My uncle chewed, reached for his beer. "He was selling. Everybody knew it."

"Hard to believe." Dad tilted his beer can to his lips. "He was a hard worker, that kid. Worth his pay—and that's rare enough these days. Kids don't know how to work anymore. They grow up and figure that an hour with a shovel'll kill 'em." He looked at Mom. "You gonna hold onto those all night?"

Mom looked down at the bowl in her hands. With a jerky movement, she set it in front of Dad. Then she carried her untouched plate into the kitchen. Uncle Kenny finished his dinner and went over to click through the TV channels. Dad opened another beer. I slipped out of the house and walked up the rise behind the barn. You could see over toward the spring range from up here. Julio used to sit on a rock that stuck out over the dry wash behind the barn and play his guitar. He taught me chords. He told me how it was, growing up in Mexico. I told him about the ghosts once. He told me that his family had a party for the dead every year—that they're around. Same as us. I was about to go back to the house when I spotted a ghost walking along the lip of the wash. It disappeared near the rock where Julio used to sit. Early in the spring, I found some withered flowers on that rock. I went back to the house where Mom shoved a too-big piece of apple pie at me and didn't ask me where I'd been.

"Sky cloudin' up yet? Smellin' rain in the air?" Uncle Kenny laughed and forked pie into his mouth, but the look he gave me stung like the flick of a quirt.

I told Mom I was tired, and went on up to bed.

"He's in love," I heard Uncle Kenny say as I climbed the stairs. "He's got all the signs."

I got onto the bed, but it was still hot up here, even with the fan on. I turned the light off and just lay on top of my sheets in my T-shirt and shorts. When I heard Mom's footsteps on the stairs, I realized I'd been waiting for her to come up. I pulled the sheet over me and sat up in the dark.

She didn't turn on the light, and she didn't say anything, but I felt the edge of the bed sink. For a while we both just sat there. The air was thick with heat up here, and for a moment, I felt it again—clouds, rain, wind—like a giant quilt that was constantly changing, shifting, moving above us. "Uncle Kenny's a good Sheriff, right?" The words sort of came out on their own. I didn't mean to say anything, hoped she'd let it pass.

"Yes, he is." She brushed the hair off my forehead, like she did when I was sick. "Julio didn't do it, you know? Sell drugs. He was so lonely." Her voice faltered. "He was in love with a girl in Oaxaca. He made up songs for her on his guitar. What's wrong, Donny?" She had her hand under my chin now, so that I couldn't look away from her. "What happened between you and Kenny?"

I swallowed, but the words had balled up in my throat. I could only shake my head, glad it was dark.

"This is a hard place to live." She stood up. "He's a good man, Donny, even if he has to be hard, at times. Justice means everything to him. That's why he's good for the county."

I didn't have anything to say to that. She took her hand away after a while, and stood up without saying anything more. I lay on my back, staring up at the ceiling for a long time after she went downstairs. I heard my uncle drive away in his county Jeep, I heard my parents come upstairs to bed. Dad stumbled on the stairs and it sounded like he fell. Mom said something in the tone she uses when a cow is having trouble calving. I waited until their door closed, then I got up and went to the window. It was cool outside now, and the stars still glittered. But as I leaned over the sill into the night, I could feel the distant rain pressing against the air, pushing at it. It was on its way.

I waked before the sun was up and left the house just as it got light. The eastern sky had gone pink and soft gray as I followed the wash down across the east pasture. When it rained, the steep-sided little canyon filled up with water. Fast. My dad and I had had to ride out in a freak storm one spring, to move cattle out from where they'd holed up in the bottom, before it flooded. I remember that afternoon real well—lightning breaking across the sky in blue forks, rain falling in stinging sheets, the horses snorting and trying to bolt. The cattle milled in the shelter of the willow brush in the bottom, not wanting to move. Uncle Kenny had showed up on his rangy black mustang to help, still in uniform because he was on duty. The three of us had finally gotten the twenty or so cows and calves started up the bank—just as a wave of brown water had come foaming down the bed. It had caught my pony, and he had reared, belly-deep in an instant. I knew we were goners. But then Uncle Kenny had grabbed the reins and hauled us both out of the flood. "Too cold for swimmin'," he'd said, and laughed.

I left the wash and climbed the slope, squinting at the first blaze of sun above the distant horizon. I stopped to get my breath on the ridge. Down below, near the highway fence, a dusty blue Dodge Caravan was parked by a crooked juniper. The Rainmaker was sitting on a little folding stool beside the car, a steaming mug in his hand. He smiled and nodded as I reached him, and stood up as if he'd been waiting for me to show. "You can tell me the good place for breakfast," he said.

The good place, he'd said. I thought about that. "The Spur," I said.

The parking lot was crowded. The Rainmaker didn't say anything as he parked at the edge of the lot. He turned off the engine and started to open the door.

"Can I do it?" I said. My voice sounded too loud, or too soft, I wasn't sure which.

"Do what?" He didn't turn around to look at me.

"Call the rain." I swallowed. "I can feel it coming. It's gonna get here soon."

"Tonight." He still didn't look at me. I thought he'd be glad, but his shoulders drooped, the way Mom's did when Dad had to take out the loan to pay the feed bills. "Yes." He went quiet again for a minute. "You can do it. But once you do—you don't live in the same world with everybody else anymore. Think about that." He opened the door suddenly, letting in a gust of hot dusty wind. Got out.

I wanted to ask him more—lots more—but he wasn't going to answer me, so I didn't say anything as we went inside. It was crowded. The booths and formica-topped tables were mostly full and cigarette smoke drifted beneath the wagon-wheel lights with their yellow globes. It felt like evening instead of bright morning. And it got quiet while the waitress hustled us over to a table. I recognized a couple of faces from the motel parking lot yesterday. And Uncle Kenny was there—drinking coffee in his regular booth by the door where he could see the whole room. He was sitting with one of his deputies, and I could feel him looking at me as I walked past like I hadn't seen him.

I sat down with my back to him and stared at the typed menu in its plastic sleeve. The words didn't make any sense, but I wasn't hungry anyway. "Can I have coffee, please?" I asked the impatient waitress. "And a cinnamon roll."

The Rainmaker ordered the breakfast special—steak and eggs with hash browns and toast. He looked up as the waitress bustled away and Uncle Kenny took her place. "Good morning, Sheriff." He smiled a bland, kind of tired smile.

"It ain't raining." Uncle Kenny pulled a chair out with a scrape that sounded way too loud in the utter silence that now filled the room. "So you chose up sides, huh, kid?"

From the corner of my eye, I caught a glimpse of movement. A gray-haired old man was making his way down the aisle with a check in his hand. As he reached the cash register, he vanished.

"I'm talkin' to you, kid." My uncle's tone pulled my head back around like he'd tied a string to my jaw. "Your mom know you're here?"

I nodded, wondering who the old man had been, why he walked here, and made myself meet my uncle's eyes. She loves you. The words started swelling inside me like bread dough. Do you know that? That she loves you? More than me. More than Dad, even. *Little brother.*

"Easy," the Rainmaker murmured. Like I'd spoken out loud.

Uncle Kenny looked away—at the wall, with its pictures of bronc and bull riders, Warm Springs Indians on rough-coated Paints riding beside cowgirls with satin shirts, spangles, and silver-mounted tack in rodeo parades. "So when's the show?" He pushed his chair back, talking to the Rainmaker like he'd forgotten

I was there. "When do we get our rain?" He was talking loud and everybody in the place was listening to him. "Hey, we're spending the money. We want to be there when the curtain goes up."

"It'll probably rain tonight." The Rainmaker leaned back a little as the waitress plunked the big oval platter with his steak and eggs down in front of him, set down the smaller plate piled with toast, and whipped the coffee pot over his cup. She didn't fill mine, gave me a dirty look like I was drinking whiskey and not coffee as she paraded away.

"You don't sound too sure." Uncle winked around the restaurant, got chuckles and skeptical grunts on cue.

"No." The Rainmaker cut a precise rectangle of steak. "Nothing is certain in real life." He placed the meat neatly in his mouth.

Uncle Kenny snorted and turned his back. "I'll come wait with you tonight." He didn't look back as he strode across the restaurant. "You all are invited, too." He gave the room one last grin that seemed to focus on every person there. Got a couple of hoots in reply. "It's my party. Take the gate just west of the Highway Motel . . . north side of the highway. Look for my rig on the road. And bring your umbrellas." Chuckling, he pushed through the door. I heard his car start up outside.

The Rainmaker didn't seem to notice the stares as he ate his breakfast. They made me want to crawl under the table, but I sat up straight and turned my empty cup around and around, wishing the waitress would give me more coffee. Finally he was done and we got up to go. When the cashier told us he was $1.50 short, he looked up at her so sharp she flinched. "He never got his cinnamon roll," he said, with a nod in my direction.

He had noticed, and not said anything.

I wasn't sure if I was pissed or not.

We drove back out to the dry wash where we sat in the shade of a twisted juniper, watching its shadow creep across the ground. Waiting for the rain, I guess. The flowers on the rock had blown away a long time ago. "You were going to tell me," I said. "How to do it."

"I never said that." The Rainmaker gave me a severe look. "It's not something you can teach. So you have decided to stop being a part of the human race?"

"You're human." I tossed a pebble at a fence lizard basking under a clump of bittergrass, watched it scuttle indignantly away. I tossed another when he didn't say anything. I kept remembering the way people had looked at him in the restaurant. "It's just because you're a stranger in town." The words didn't sound very convincing.

"You better tell your mother where you are." He crossed his arms on his knees. "She's worrying."

I got up, dusting off my jeans. Because she was. Movement flickered across the draw. The ghost again. You can't see them very well in the bright sun. I don't think it really shines on them, or even through them. The light sort of covers them up instead. This one sat on the shelf of rock where the flowers had been. The Rainmaker noticed him, too. He looked at me and raised one eyebrow, but I turned my back on him and ran up the side of the wash, and all the way home, so that I came into the kitchen soaked with sweat.

Mom met me with her fists on her hips, face stiff with anger, as if I'd skipped my chores. "Kenny told me where you were." Her voice trembled. "You go straight to your room, young man."

"Why?" I blurted out the word, angry myself, now. "What's wrong with having breakfast with . . ." I couldn't remember his name. "With the Rainmaker," I finished lamely.

"He's a fraud." She got angrier. "Where are your brains?"

"He's not a fraud."

"He's a crook. Cheating people."

"Who has he cheated, huh? You tell me who."

"Kenny said . . ."

"You always believe Uncle Kenny." I was yelling now. "Uncle Kenny is so damn perfect. You won't believe me, but anything he says . . ."

She slapped me.

For a moment I stared at her, face burning where her palm had struck, the sudden silence ringing in my ears. Then I turned and ran out of the kitchen, pounding up the stairs to my room. I slammed the door, and threw myself down on the bed. Mad at her. Mad at myself. Because a part of me had wanted her to tell me for sure that he was a fraud.

I lay on the bed, waiting for her to come upstairs, watching the sun move across the cloudless sky and sweating in the still heat of the upstairs. What if it didn't rain? I wasn't sure how I'd feel about that—or maybe I just didn't want to know. But she didn't come upstairs, and that hurt, too. And I guess I fell asleep after a while, because it was dark when I woke up, and Mom was setting a tray on my desk.

"I brought your dinner up." She turned on the light and straightened, pushing wisps of hair back from her forehead. "It must be ninety up here. Why didn't you turn on the fan?" She snapped on the old box fan, her fingers brisk and impatient on the switch. The sudden gust of air felt cool on my face, and I imagined for a second that I could smell rain, the way the animals can.

"Your uncle went down to where that . . . man is camped." Mom sounded uneasy. "He's worried that a lot of people might show up. That they might get . . . rowdy."

"They'll come because he told 'em to." I didn't look at her. "They'll beat up the Rainmaker. Because he wants them to."

"No."

"Don't you get it, Mom?" I leaned forward, but she wouldn't look at me. "People always do what he wants 'em to do."

"Don't talk about your uncle like that." But she said it mechanically, in a dull tone without anger. "We couldn't make it without him. I couldn't make it." She got to her feet and walked out of the room.

I went over to the window, a fist squeezing my stomach until I thought I'd be sick. To the west—in the direction of the distant ocean—the stars ended in a band of pure darkness above the horizon. I felt the fist in my stomach loosen a hair, fixed my eyes on a small pair of dim stars. They vanished. A twinkling yellow star above them vanished a moment later. "Mom," I called out. "Clouds."

She came back to stand silently beside me at the window. I heard her swallow.

"Let's go down there," she said softly. "Your dad was going to haul the heifers to auction tomorrow."

We went downstairs together, tiptoeing through the living room, where my dad snored on the sofa, one hand loosely curled around a can of beer. I had never heard him snore before. His face looked soft and flushed. "Dad?" I stopped.

"He's all right." Mom's face was as still as a winter pond before a flight of geese lands. "He's just drunk." Her voice was without inflection.

I had never seen my father drunk. But I remembered his uncertain tread on the stairs every night, and her tone as she coaxed him to bed.

I thought Mom would take the truck, but she walked into the sage, as sure in the faint moonlight as if she came this way every day. I stumbled after her, tripping over sage stems and clumps of grass. I didn't catch up with her until she had reached the lip of the wash. The Rainmaker's camp was visible in the light from a single propane lantern. At least a dozen men milled in a loose circle around him. I recognized Uncle Kenny. He wasn't in his uniform. Suddenly he stepped forward, one hand closing on the front of the Rainmaker's shirt, lifting him onto his toes.

"You think we're a bunch of dumb cowboys, don't you?" His voice came to me on the wind, edged with violence. "We'll just grin and shuffle our feet and hand over our money to you, 'cause you're so smart, and we're just dumb hicks."

The men around them growled and shuffled forward, as if they were puppets, and he'd yanked all their strings at once. I took a step forward, caught my toe in a sage stem, and fell flat on my face. Eyes full of grit, I struggled to my knees, spitting dust. I knew what was going to happen—could see it, like on a movie screen. My face was wet and I wiped it on my sleeve. Crying, I thought, as I staggered to my feet. I'm not crying.

"Kenny!" Mom's voice was shrill and strange, and down below, my uncle paused, his fist drawn back, his other hand clutching the Rainmaker's shirt front. He looked up at her.

More water hit my face. Cold water. I looked up and laughed.

It was raining.

The stars had vanished, and the rain came down all at once, like someone had upended a cosmic bucket. It pounded on the dry ground and made the sage shiver. Below, the bunched, angry men were milling like nervous cattle. Uncle Kenny still held the Rainmaker by the shirt, but he had lowered his hand. My mom was running down to him, her wet hair plastered to her head. She looked like a kid and I realized suddenly how old my dad was. One of the men whooped, and somebody pounded on the Rainmaker's back.

By the time I got down to the Rainmaker's camp, I was soaked to the skin and muddy. People were still hanging around. I knew who they were. All of them. They were watching the first streams of brown water run down the bottom of the wash. I looked up at the rock shelf where I found the flowers, and yeah, the ghost was there, standing on the very edge. And it was really dark, but I could see him better than I ever had before—like there was a spotlight shining on him.

Julio Rojas.

He looked sad. I looked at my mom, and she was staring at that rock, too, but she didn't see him. She had her hands pressed tight against her chest, like she hurt inside. And Uncle Kenny was looking at her, too. Water was starting to fill the wash, brown and foamy as chocolate, pouring down into the low land across the highway. When I looked again, Julio had gone from his rock, and I thought about the flowers, and my mom running down through the sage like she knew the way.

And I could feel the water, like I'd felt the rain. I guess it *was* rain—only on the ground now, and not in the sky. And if it ran down the east side of the draw, it would cut away a lot of the dirt beneath the rock shelf. I took a step away from everyone, staring at that chocolate flood, feeling it like it was a wet rope sliding through my hands, and I didn't really think about it, I just started to pull.

A thin stream welled over a low berm of silt and stones from last winter's floods, pushed a small rock out of the way. I was sweating. The rock tumbled down the slope and more water welled after it, pushing more stones out of the way, dissolving the dirt. Then, suddenly, the berm gave way and was gone as if it had never been. The flood divided, sweeping now along the steep east wall of the wash, eating away the dirt below the shelf.

Uncle Kenny stepped up beside me, not noticing me, his eyes on that dissolving bank. His shoulders were hunched and his hands clenched into fists. The rock shelf tilted and wavered, and I heard him take a fast, short breath.

It tilted some more, slid very slowly into the churning water, smashing flat the sparse willow stems that lined the sides. Something showed in the hole left in the bank. Something not dirt colored. "Look!" I pointed. "Over there, along the bank."

I guess a couple of people looked, because someone broke away from the crowd and walked along the lip of the wash, hat pulled down against the still-steady rain, water soaking his shirt and jeans. Mr. Walker. Owner of the Bar Double D. He stopped above the light-colored object and stepped quickly back. "It's a body," he yelled to us. "My God. Someone was buried here."

Everybody went running over, boots splashing through the water, a half dozen tall shapes in wet clothes and pulled down hats. My uncle didn't go. Neither did my mom. They were both looking at me. "It's Julio," I said. My mom's face didn't change, but she made a small sound, like a hurt animal.

"I was sleeping over the night he disappeared." My uncle spoke up in that slow, lazy drawl he uses when he breaks up a fight. "Remember, Sandy?" He turned to her, smiling a little, his hand on her shoulder. "Dave and I got to drinking, and I slept on the sofa. After we put Dave to bed."

I could feel his words turning solid in the air, reaching back over the weeks to change yesterday. I could feel my mom's relief as she started to nod. "No," I said. "You left. Dad watched TV after you were gone." And I had sneaked out, because the moon was full, and I couldn't sleep.

"Donny . . ." Mom whispered. "Don't."

Uncle Kenny had saved me when the flood caught my pony. He helped us a lot. When Dad was drunk. *We couldn't make it without him. I couldn't make it.* I heard my Mother's voice. Words took shape in my throat, stuck there like fish bones: *Oh yeah, I remember now. You slept over. Sorry, Uncle Kenny.*

The Rainmaker was looking at me, and he looked sad. Julio had taught me how to chord on his old, battered guitar. He had laughed, and missed the girl he had loved. Up on the bank, two of the ranchers were bending over Julio Rojas's body. I couldn't look at Mom. "I saw you," I said to my uncle. "I was up in the sage."

For a moment, my uncle stared at me, his face all edges, as if the flesh had eroded away, leaving nothing but bone. "You're dreaming, kid. I was in the house, asleep, when he took off. Ask your mom." His laugh sounded like something breaking. "You're the crazy kid who sees ghosts and talks to the damn desert. Who's gonna believe you?"

She had told him. I couldn't look at her, wondering who else he had told, chuckling about it over a beer maybe, in the Spur at night. The rain was running into my eyes, but I didn't try to wipe my face, just stood there waiting for her to agree with him. Because I was only a crazy kid who saw ghosts, and back home, Dad had passed out, and there were the cattle to deal with. The ranch.

"He's not crazy, Ken." Mom spoke softly. "And he's right." Her voice sounded empty and cold. "You left. I remember because . . . I had a hard time getting Dave up the stairs by myself that night."

For a long moment, my uncle and my mom stared at each other. Then my uncle turned away and slogged back toward the road. Only the Rainmaker saw him go. He was looking at me, standing hatless in the rain, his face as round and calm as the moon.

"Donny?" My mother's voice trembled. "Julio used to play his guitar for me." She closed her eyes briefly as we heard Uncle Kenny's car start. "He was so young and full of hope. He was a poet—he made those songs up himself. That's all that happened between us. I swear it."

I nodded, but I couldn't speak. There wasn't anything inside of me. Just night and rain. After a moment Mom turned away. I watched her trudge toward the road after Uncle Kenny. You couldn't cross the wash anymore. She would have to take the long way home—back to the empty house where my dad snored on the sofa. I flinched as the Rainmaker put a hand on my shoulder.

"I have to," I said. "Don't I?"

He squeezed my shoulder. "I'll make you some tea," he said, and his voice sounded as old as the desert. Sad. Two of the ranchers went running back to their parked cars. To find the Sheriff? I wondered. "No, thank you," I said politely. "Mom's waiting for me."

And she was—up on the road—hugging herself in the pouring rain. She straightened as I got close. "Are you going to go with him?" she asked softly.

I shook my head. "I used to listen to Julio play, too," I said. "He was really good. We'll have to tell someone."

She nodded once, eyes closed, then opened them and smiled at me. "We will." Then she reached for my hand, and as we walked along the road to our driveway together, the rain began to diminish to a slow, steady shower.

MICHAEL MARSHALL SMITH

A Place to Stay

Michael Marshall Smith was born in England in 1965, grew up in the United States, South Africa, and Australia, then returned to the U.K. He now lives in North London, with his wife Paula, two cats, and "enough computers to launch a space shuttle."

His short fiction has been published in Omni, *the* Mammoth books, Peeping Tom, Chills, Touch Wood: Narrow Houses 2, Dark Voices, Shadows Over Innsmouth, The Anthology of Fantasy and the Supernatural, *both* Darkland *anthologies,* Dark Terrors, Lethal Kisses, Best New Horror, *and* The Year's Best Fantasy and Horror. *He has won the British Fantasy Award for short fiction three times and the August Derleth Award for his critically acclaimed first novel* Only Forward. *His second novel,* Spares, *was optioned by Steven Spielberg's company, DreamWorks SKG. His third novel,* One of Us *was published in 1998 and has been optioned by Warner Brothers and Di Novi Pictures. He is currently working on a number of feature screenplays and his fourth novel. A collection of short stories was published by HarperCollins-U.K. in May 1999.*

Smith perfectly captures the ambiance and allure of the French quarter of New Orleans in "A Place to Stay," originally published in Dark Terrors 4.

—E. D.

John, do you believe in vampires?"

I took a moment to light a cigarette. This wasn't to avoid the issue, but rather to prepare myself for the length and vitriol of the answer I intended to give—and to tone it down a little. I hardly knew the woman who'd asked the question, and had no idea of her tolerance for short, blunt words. I wanted to be gentle with her, but if there's one star in the pantheon of possible nightmares which I certainly *don't* believe in, then it has to be bloody vampires. I mean, really.

I was in New Orleans, and it was nearly Hallowe'en. Children of the Night have a tendency to crop up in such circumstances, like talk of rain in London. Now that I was here, I could see why. The French Quarter, with its narrow streets and looming balconies frozen in time, almost made the idea of vampires credible, especially in the lingering moist heat of the fall. It felt like a playground for suave monsters, a perpetual reinventing past, and if vampires lived anywhere, I supposed, then these dark streets and alleyways with their foetid, flamboyant cemeteries would be as good a place as any.

But they *didn't* live anywhere, and after another punishing swallow of my salty Margarita, I started to put Rita-May right on this fact. She shifted herself comfortably against my chest, and listened to me rant.

We were in Jimmy Buffet's bar on Decatur, and the evening was developing nicely. At nine o'clock I'd been alone, sitting at the bar and trying to work out how many Margaritas I'd drunk. The fact that I was counting shows what a sad individual I am. The further fact that I couldn't seem to count properly demonstrates that on that particular evening I was an extremely *drunk* sad individual too. And I mean, yes, Margaritaville is kind of a tourist trap, and I could have been sitting somewhere altogether heavier and more authentic across the street. But I'd done that the previous two nights, and besides, I liked Buffet's bar. I was, after all, a tourist. You didn't feel in any danger of being killed in his place, which I regard as a plus. They only played Jimmy Buffet on the juke box, not surprisingly, so I didn't have to worry that my evening was suddenly going to be shattered by something horrible from the post-melodic school of popular music. Say what you like about Jimmy Buffet, he's seldom hard to listen to. Finally, the barman had this gloopy eye thing, which felt pleasingly disgusting and stuck to the wall when you threw it, so that was kind of neat.

I was having a perfectly good time, in other words. A group of people from the software convention I was attending were due to be meeting somewhere on Bourbon at ten, but I was beginning to think I might skip it. After only two days my tolerance for jokes about Bill Gates was hovering around the zero mark. As an Apple Macintosh developer, they weren't actually that funny anyway.

So. There I was, fairly confident that I'd had around eight Margaritas and beginning to get heartburn from all the salt, when a woman walked in. She was in her mid-thirties, I guessed, the age where things are just beginning to fade around the edges but don't look too bad for all that. I hope they don't, anyway: I'm approaching that age myself and my things are already fading fast. She sat on a stool at the corner of the bar and signalled to the barman with a regular's upward nod of the head. A minute later a Margarita was set down in front of her, and I judged from the colour that it was the same variety I was drinking. It was called a Golden something or other, and had the effect of gradually replacing your brain with a sour-tasting sand which shifted sluggishly when you moved your head.

No big deal. I noticed her, then got back to desultory conversation with the other barman. He'd visited London at some point, or wanted to—I never really understood which. He was either asking me what London was like, or telling me; I was either listening, or telling him. I can't remember, and probably didn't know at the time. At that stage in the evening my responses would have been about the same either way. I eventually noticed that the band had stopped playing, apparently for the night. That meant I could leave the bar and go sit at one of the tables. The band had been okay, but very loud, and without wishing them any personal enmity I was glad they had gone. Now that I'd noticed, I realized they must have been gone for a while. An entire Jimmy Buffet CD had played in the interval.

I lurched sedately over to a table, humming "The Great Filling Station Hold-up" quietly and inaccurately, and reminding myself that it was only about twenty after nine. If I wanted to meet up with the others without being the evening's comedy drunk, I needed to slow down. I needed to have not had about the last four drinks, in fact, but that would have involved tangling with the space-time continuum to a degree I felt unequal to. Slowing down would have to suffice.

It was as I was just starting the next drink that the evening took an interesting turn. Someone said something to me at fairly close range, and when I looked up to have another stab at comprehending it, I saw it was the woman from the bar.

"Wuh?" I said, in the debonair way that I have. She was standing behind the table's other chair, and looked diffident but not very. The main thing she looked was good-natured, in a wary and toughened way. Her hair was fairly blonde and she was dressed in a pale blue dress and a dark blue denim jacket.

"I said—is that chair free?"

I considered my standard response, when I'm trying to be amusing, of asking in a soulful voice if *any* of us are truly free. I didn't feel up to it. I wasn't quite drunk enough, and I knew in my heart of hearts that it simply wasn't funny. Also, I was nervous. Women don't come up to me in bars and request the pleasure of sitting at my table. It's not something I'd had much practice with. In the end I settled for straightforwardness.

"Yes," I said. "And you may feel absolutely free to use it."

The woman smiled, sat down, and started talking. Her name, I discovered rapidly, was Rita-May. She'd lived in New Orleans for fifteen years, after moving there from some God-forsaken hole called Houma, out in the Louisiana sticks. She worked in one of the stores further down Decatur near the Square, selling Cajun spice sets and cookbooks to tourists, which was a reasonable job and paid okay but wasn't very exciting. She had been married once and it had ended four years ago, amidst general apathy. She had no children, and considered it no great loss.

This information was laid out with remarkable economy and a satisfying lack of topic drift or extraneous detail. I then sat affably drinking my drink while she efficiently elicited a smaller quantity of similar information from me. I was thirty-two, she discovered, and unmarried. I owned a very small software company in London, England, and lived with a dozy cat named Spike. I was enjoying New Orleans' fine cuisine but had as yet no strong views on particular venues—with the exception of the muffelettas in the French Bar, which I liked inordinately, and the po-boys at Mama Sam's, which I thought were overrated.

After an hour and three more Margaritas our knees were resting companion-ably against each other, and by eleven-thirty my arm was laid across the back of her chair and she was settled comfortably against it. Maybe the fact that all the dull crap had been got out of the way so quickly was what made her easy to spend time with. Either way. I was having fun.

Rita-May seemed unperturbed by the vehemence of my feelings about vam-pires, and pleasingly willing to consider the possibility that it was all a load of toss. I was about to raise my hand to get more drinks when I noticed that the bar staff had all gone home, leaving a hand-written sign on the bar which said LOOK, WILL YOU TWO JUST FUCK OFF.

They hadn't really, but the well had obviously run dry. For a few moments I bent my not inconsiderable intelligence towards solving this problem, but all that came back was a row of question marks. Then suddenly I found myself out on the street, with no recollection of having even stood up. Rita-May's arm was wrapped around my back, and she was dragging me down Decatur towards the Square.

"It's this way," she said, giggling, and I asked her what the hell I had agreed to. It transpired that we were going to precisely the bar on Bourbon where I'd been due to meet people an hour and a half ago. I mused excitedly on this coincidence for a while—until Rita-May got me to understand that we were going there because I'd suggested it.

"Want to buy some drugs?" someone asked, and I turned to peer at Rita-May.

"I don't know," she said. "What have you got?" This confused me until I realized that a third party had asked the original question, and was indeed still standing in front of us. A thin black guy with elsewhere eyes.

"Dope, grass, coke, horse . . ." the man reeled off, in a bored monotone. As Rita-May negotiated for a bag of spliffs I tried to see where he was hiding the horse, until I realized I was being a moron. I turned away and opened my mouth and eyes wide to stretch my face. I sensed I was in a bit of a state, and that the night was as yet young.

It was only as we were lighting one of the joints five minutes later that it occurred to me to be nervous about meeting a gentleman who was a heroin dealer. Luckily he'd gone by then, and my attention span was insufficient to let me worry about it for long. Rita-May seemed very relaxed about the whole deal, and as she was a local, presumably it was okay.

We hung a right at Jackson Square and walked across towards Bourbon, sucking on the joint and slowly caroming from one side of the sidewalk to the other. Rita-May's arm was still around my back, and one of mine was over her shoulders. It occurred to me that sooner or later I was going to have to ask myself what the hell I thought I was doing, but I didn't feel up to it just yet.

I wasn't really prepared for the idea that people from the convention would still be at the bar when we eventually arrived. By then it felt as if we had been walking for at least ten days, though not in any bad way. The joint had hit us both pretty hard, and my head felt as if it had been lovingly crafted out of warm brown smoke. Bourbon Street was still at full pitch, and we slowly made our way down it, weaving between half-dressed male couples, lean local blacks and pastel-clad pear-shaped tourists from Des Moines. A stringy blonde popped up from nowhere at one point, waggling a rose in my face and asking "Is she ready?" in a keening, nobody's-home kind of voice. I was still juggling responses to this when I noticed that Rita-May had bought the rose herself. She broke off all but the first four inches of stem in a business-like way, and stuck the flower behind her ear.

Fair enough, I thought, admiring this behavior in a way I found difficult to define.

I couldn't actually remember, now we were in the area, whether it was the Absinthe Bar we were looking for, the *Old* Absinthe Bar, or the *Original Old* Absinthe Bar. I hope you can understand my confusion. In the end we made the decision on the basis of the bar from which the most acceptable music was pounding, and lurched into the sweaty gloom. Most of the crowd inside applauded immediately, but I suspect this was for the blues band rather than us. I was very thirsty by then, partly because someone appeared to have put enough blotting paper in my mouth to leech all the moisture out of it, and I felt incapable of doing or saying anything until I was less arid. Luckily Rita-May sensed this, and immediately cut through the crowd to the bar.

I stood and waited patiently for her return, inclining slightly and variably from the vertical plane like some advanced form of children's top. "Ah ha," I was saying to myself. "Ah ha." I have no idea why.

When someone shouted my name, I experienced little more than a vague feeling of well-being. "They know me here," I muttered, nodding proudly to myself. Then I saw that Dave Trindle was standing on the other side of the room and waving his arm at me, a grin of outstanding stupidity on his face. My first thought was that he should sit down before someone in the band shot him. My second was a hope that he would continue standing, for the same reason. He was part, I saw, of a motley collection of second-rate shareware authors ranged around a table in the corner, a veritable rogues' gallery of dweebs and losers. My heart sank, with all hands, two cats and a mint copy of the Gutenburg Bible on deck.

"Are they the people?"

On hearing Rita-May's voice I turned thankfully, immediately feeling much better. She was standing close behind, a large drink in each hand and an affectionate half-smile on her face. I realized suddenly that I found her very attractive, and that she was nice, too. I looked at her for a moment longer, and then leant forward to kiss her softly on the cheek, just to the side of the mouth.

She smiled, pleased, and we came together for another kiss, again not quite on the mouth. I experienced a moment of peace, and then suddenly I was very drunk again.

"Yes and no," I said. "They're from the convention. But they're not the people I wanted to see."

"They're still waving at you."

"Christ."

"Come on. It'll be fun."

I found it hard to share her optimism, but followed Rita-May through the throng.

It turned out that the people I'd arranged to meet up with *had* been there, but I was told that they had left in the face of my continued failure to arrive. I judged it more likely that they'd gone because of the extraordinary collection of berks they had accidentally acquired on the way to the bar, but refrained from saying so.

The conventioneers were drunk, in a we've-had-two-beers-and-hey-aren't-we-Bohemian sort of way, which I personally find offensive. Quite early on I realized that the only way of escaping the encounter with my sanity intact was pretending that they weren't there and talking to Rita-May instead. This wasn't allowed, apparently. I kept being asked my opinion on things so toe-curlingly dull that I can't bring myself to even remember them, and endured fifteen minutes of Davey Wank-face telling me about some GUI junk he was developing. Luckily Rita-May entered the spirit of the event, and we managed to keep passing each other messages on how dreadful a time we were having. With that and a regular supply of drinks, we coped.

After about an hour we hit upon a new form of diversion, and while apparently listening avidly to the row of life-ectomy survivors in front of us, started—tentatively at first, then more deliciously—to stroke each others' hands under the table. The conventioneers were now all well over the limit, some of them having had as many as four beers, and were chattering nineteen to the dozen. So engrossed were they that after a while I felt able to turn my head towards Rita-May, look in her eyes, and say something.

"I like you."

I hadn't planned it that way. I'd intended something much more grown-up and crass. But as it came out I realized that it was true and that it communicated what I wanted to say with remarkable economy.

She smiled, skin dimpling at the corners of her mouth and wisps of her hair backlit into golden. "I like you too," she said, and squeezed my hand.

Wow, I thought foggily. How weird. You think you've got the measure of life, and then it throws a curve-ball. It just went to show. "It just goes to show," I said, aloud. She probably didn't understand, but smiled again anyway.

The next thing that I noticed was that I was standing with my back against a wall, and that there wasn't any ground beneath my feet. Then that it was cold. Then that it was quiet.

"Yo, he's alive," someone said, and the world started to organize itself. I was lying on the floor of the bar, and my face was wet.

I tried to sit upright, but couldn't. The owner of the voice, a cheery black man who had served me earlier, grabbed my shoulder and helped. It was him, I discovered, who'd thrown water over me. About a gallon. It hadn't worked, so he'd checked my pulse to make sure I wasn't dead, and then just cleaned up around me. Apart from him and a depressed-looking guy with a mop, the bar was completely empty.

"Where's Rita?" I asked, eventually. I had to repeat the question in order to make it audible.

The man grinned down at me. "Now I wouldn't know *that* would I?" he said. "Most particularly 'cos I don't know who Rita *is*."

"What about the others?" I managed. The barman gestured eloquently around the empty bar. As my eyes followed his hand, I saw the clock. It was a little after five a.m.

I stood up, shakily thanked him for his good offices on my behalf, and walked very slowly out into the street.

I don't remember getting back to the hotel, but I guess I must have done. That, at any rate, is where I found myself at ten the next morning, after a few hours of molten sleep. As I stood pasty-faced and stricken under the harsh light of the bathroom, I waited in horror while wave after wave of The Fear washed over me. I'd passed out. Obviously. Though uncommon with me, it's not unknown.

The conventioneers, rat-finks that they were, had pissed off and left me there, doubtless sniggering into their beards. Fair enough. I'd have done the same for them.

But what had happened to Rita-May?

While I endured an appalling ten minutes on the toilet, a soothing fifteen minutes under the shower, and a despairing, tearful battle with my trousers, I tried to work this out. On the one hand, I couldn't blame her for abandoning an unconscious tourist. But when I thought back to before the point where blackness and The Fear took over, I thought we'd been getting on very well. She didn't seem the type to abandon anyone.

When I was more or less dressed I hauled myself onto the bed and sat on the edge. I needed coffee, and needed it very urgently. I also had to smoke about seventy cigarettes, but seemed to have lost my packet. The way forward was clear. I had to leave the hotel room and sort these things out. But for that I needed shoes.

So where were they?

They weren't on the floor, or in the bathroom. They weren't out on the balcony, where the light hurt my eyes so badly I retreated back into the gloom with a yelp. I shuffled around the room again, even getting down onto my hands and knees to look under the bed. They weren't there. They weren't even *in* the bed.

They were entirely absent, which was a disaster. I hate shoes, because they're boring, and consequently I own very few pairs. Apart from some elderly flip-flops which were left in the suitcase from a previous trip, the ones I'd been wearing were the only pair I had with me. I made another exhausting search, conducting as much of it as possible without leaving the bed, with no success. Instead of just getting to a café and sorting out my immediate needs, I was going to have to put on the flip-flops and go find a sodding shoe store. Once there I would have to spend money which I'd rather commit to American-priced CDs and good food than on a pair of fucking *shoes*. As a punishment from God for drunkenness this felt a bit harsh, and for a few minutes the walls of the hotel room rang with rasped profanities.

Eventually I hauled myself over to the suitcase and bad-temperedly dug through the archaeological layers of socks and shirts until I found something shoe-shaped. The flip-flop was, of course, right at the bottom of the case. I tugged irritably at it, unmindful of the damage I was doing to my carefully stacked shorts and ties. Up came two pairs of trousers I hadn't worn yet—one of which I'd forgotten I'd brought—along with a shirt, and then finally I had the flip-flop in my hand.

Except it wasn't a flip-flop. It was one of my shoes.

Luckily I was standing near the end of the bed, because my legs gave way. I sat down suddenly, staring at the shoe in my hand. It wasn't hard to recognize. It was a black lace-up, in reasonably good condition but wearing on the outside of the heel. As I turned it slowly over in my hands like some holy relic, I realized it even smelled slightly of Margaritas. Salt had dried on the toe, where I'd spilt a mouthful laughing at something Rita-May had said in Jimmy Buffet's.

Still holding it in one hand, I reached tentatively into the bowels of my suitcase, rootling through the lower layers until I found the other one. It was underneath the towel I'd packed right at the bottom, on the reasoning that I was unlikely to need it because all hotels had towels. I pulled the shoe out, and stared at it.

Without a doubt, it was the other shoe. There was something inside. I carefully pulled it out, aware of little more than a rushing sound in my ears.

It was a red rose, attached to about four inches of stem.

The first thing that strikes you about the Café du Monde is that it isn't quite what you're expecting. It isn't nestled right in the heart of the old town, on Royal or Dauphin, but squats on Decatur opposite the Square. And it isn't some dinky little café, but a large awning-covered space where rows of tables are intermittently served by waiters of spectacular moroseness. On subsequent visits, however, you come to realize that the *café au lait* really is good and that the beignets are the best in New Orleans; that the café is about as bijou as it can be given that it's open twenty-four hours a day, every day of the year; and that anyone wandering through New Orleans is going to pass the Decatur corner of Jackson Square at some point, so it is actually pretty central.

Midday found me sitting at one of the tables at the edge, so I wasn't surrounded by other people and had a good view of the street. I was on my second coffee and third orange juice. My ashtray had been emptied twice already, and I had an order of beignets inside me. The only reason I hadn't had more was that I was saving myself for a muffeletta. I'd tell you what they are but this isn't a travel guide. Go and find out for yourself.

And, of course, I was wearing my shoes. I'd sat in the hotel for another ten minutes, until I'd completely stopped shaking. Then I'd shuffled straight to Café du Monde. I had a book with me, but I wasn't reading it. I was watching people as they passed, and trying to get my head in order. I couldn't remember what had happened, so the best I could do was try to find an explanation that worked, and stick with it.

Unfortunately, that explanation was eluding me. I simply couldn't come up with a good reason for my shoes being in my suitcase, under stuff which I hadn't disturbed since leaving London.

About nine months before, at a convention in England, I rather over-indulged in the dissolute company of an old college friend. I woke the next morning to find myself in my hotel bed, but dressed in different clothes to those I'd been wearing the night before. Patient reconstruction led me to believe that I could *just about* recall getting up in the small hours, showering, getting dressed—and then climbing back into bed. Odd behaviour, to be sure, but there were enough hints and shadows of memory for me to convince myself that's what I had done.

Not this time. I couldn't remember a thing between leaving the Old Original Authentic Genuine Absinthe Bar and waking up. But strangely, I didn't have The Fear about it.

And then, of course, there was the rose.

The Fear, for those unacquainted with it, is something you may get after very excessive intake of drugs or alcohol. It is, amongst other things, the panicky conviction that you have done something embarrassing or ill-advised that you can't quite remember. It can also be more generic than that, a simple belief that at some point in the previous evening, something happened which was in some way far from ideal. It usually passes off when your hangover does, or when an acquaintance reveals that yes, you did lightly stroke one of her breasts in public, without being requested to do so.

Then you can just get down to being hideously embarrassed, which is a much more containable emotion.

I had mild Fear about the period in Jimmy Buffet's, but probably only born of nervousness about talking to a woman I didn't really know. I had a slightly greater Fear concerning the Absinthe bar, where I suspected I might have referred to the new CEO of a company who was a client of mine as a "talentless fuckwit."

I felt fine about the journey back to the hotel, however, despite the fact I couldn't remember it. I'd been alone, after all. Everyone, including Rita-May, had disappeared. The only person I could have offended was myself. But how had my shoes got into the suitcase? Why would I have done that? And at what point had I acquired Rita-May's rose? The last time I could remember seeing it was when I'd told her that I liked her. Then it had still been behind her ear.

The coffee was beginning to turn on me, mingling with the hangover to make it feel as if points of light were slowly popping on and off in my head. A black guy with a trumpet was just settling down to play at one of the other sides of the café, and I knew this guy from previous experience. His key talent, which he demonstrated about every ten minutes, was that of playing a loud, high note for a very long time. Like most tourists, I'd applauded the first time I'd heard this. The second demonstration had been less appealing. By the third time I'd considered offering him my Visa card if he'd go away.

And if he did it now, I was likely to simply shatter and fall in shards upon the floor.

I needed to do something. I needed to move. I left the café and stood outside on Decatur.

After about two minutes I felt hot and under threat, buffeted by the passing throng. No one had yet filled the seat I'd vacated, and I was very tempted to just slink right back to it. I'd be quiet, no trouble to anyone: just sit there and drink more fluids. I'd be a valuable addition, I felt, a show tourist provided by the town's Management to demonstrate to everyone else how wonderful a time there was to be had.

But then the guy with the trumpet started a rendition of "Smells Like Teen Spirit" and I really had to go.

I walked slowly up Decatur towards the market, trying to decide if I was really going to do what I had in mind. Rita-May worked at one of the stores along that stretch. I couldn't remember the name, but knew it had something to do with cooking. It wouldn't be that difficult to find. But should I be trying to find it? Perhaps I should just turn around, leave the Quarter and go to the Clarion, where the convention was happening. I could find the people I liked and hang for a while, listen to jokes about Steve Jobs. Forget about Rita-May, take things carefully for the remaining few days, and then go back home to London.

I didn't want to. The previous evening had left me with emotional tattoos, snapshots of desire which weren't fading in the morning sun. The creases round her eyes when she smiled; her tongue, as it lolled round the rim of her glass, licking off the salt; the easy Southern rhythm of her speech, the glissando changes in pitch. When I closed my eyes, in addition to a slightly alarming feeling of vertigo, I could feel the skin of her hand as if it was still there against my own. So what if I was an idiot tourist. I was an idiot tourist who was genuinely attracted to her. Maybe that would be enough.

The first couple of stores were easy to dismiss. One sold quilts made by American craftspeople; the next wooden children's toys for parents who didn't realize how much their kids wanted video games. The third had a few spice collections in the window, but was mainly full of other souvenirs. It didn't look like the place Rita-May had described, but I plucked up my courage and asked. No one of that name worked there. The next store was a bakery, and then there was a fifty-yard open stretch which provided table space for the restaurant which followed it.

The store after the restaurant was called The N'awlins Pantry, and tag-lined "The One Stop Shop for all your Cajun Cooking Needs." It looked, I had to admit, like it was the place.

I wanted to see Rita-May, but I was scared shitless at the thought of just walking in. I retreated to the other side of the street, hoping to see her through the window first. I'm not sure how that would have helped, but it seemed like a good idea at the time. I smoked a cigarette and watched for a while, but the constant procession of cars and pedestrians made it impossible to see anything. Then I spent a few minutes wondering why I wasn't just attending the convention, listening to dull, safe panels like everybody else. It didn't work. When I was down to the butt I stubbed my cigarette out and crossed back over the road. I couldn't see much through the window even from there, because of the size and extravagance of the window display. So I grabbed the handle, opened the door and walked in.

It was fantastically noisy inside, and crowded with sweating people. The blues band seemed to have turned on a second bank of amplifiers, and virtually everyone sitting at the tables in front of them was clapping their hands and hooting. The air was smeared with red faces and meaty arms, and for a moment I considered just turning around and going back into the toilet. It had been quiet in there, and cool. I'd spent ten minutes splashing my face with cold water, trying to mitigate the effect of the joint we'd smoked. While I stood trying to remember where the table was, the idea of another few moments of water-splashing began to take on a nearly obsessive appeal.

But then I saw Rita-May, and realized I had to go on. Partly because she was marooned with the conventioneers, which wouldn't have been fair on anyone, but mainly because going back to her was even more appealing than the idea of water.

I carefully navigated my way through the crowd, pausing halfway to flag down a waitress and get some more drinks on the way. Because obviously we needed them. Obviously. No way were we drunk enough. Rita-May looked up gratefully when she saw me. I plonked myself down next to her, glared accidentally at Dave Trindle, and lit another cigarette. Then, in a clumsy but necessary attempt to rekindle the atmosphere which had been developing, I repeated the last thing I had said before setting off on my marathon journey to the gents. "It just goes to show," I said.

Rita-May smiled again, probably in recognition at the feat of memory I had pulled off. "Show what?" she asked, leaning towards me and shutting out the rest of the group. I winked, and then pulled off the most ambitious monologue of my life.

I said that it went to show that life took odd turns, and that you could suddenly meet someone you felt very at home with, who seemed to change all the rules. Someone who made stale, damaged parts of you fade away in an instant, who let you feel strange magic once again: the magic of being in the presence of a person you didn't know, and realizing that you wanted them more than anything else you could think of.

I spoke for about five minutes, and then stopped. It went down very well, not least because I was patently telling the truth. I meant it. For once my tongue got the words right, didn't trip up, and I said what I meant to say. In spite of the drink, the drugs, the hour, I said it.

At the same time I was realizing that something was terribly wrong.

This wasn't, for example, a cookery store.

A quick glance towards the door showed it also wasn't early afternoon. The sky was dark and Bourbon Street was packed with night-time strollers. We were sitting with the conventioneers in the Absinthe Bar, I was wearing last night's clothes, and Rita-May's rose was still behind her ear.

It was last night, in other words.

As I continued to tell Rita-May that I was really very keen on her, she slipped her hand into mine. This time they weren't covered by the table, but I found I didn't care about that. I did, however, care about the fact that I could clearly remember standing outside the Café du Monde and wanting her to touch my hand again.

In the daylight of tomorrow.

The waitress appeared with our drinks. Trindle and his cohorts decided that they might as well be hung for a lamb as for an embryo, and ordered another round themselves. While this transaction was being laboriously conducted I stole a glance at the bar. In a gap between carousing fun-lovers I saw what I was looking for. The barman who'd woken me up.

He was making four Margaritas at once, his smooth face a picture of concentration. He would have made a good photograph, and I recognized him instantly. But he hadn't served me yet. I'd been to the bar once, and been served by a woman. The other drinks I'd bought from passing waitresses. Yet when I'd woken up, I'd recognized the barman *because he'd served me*. That meant I must have bought another drink before passing out and waking up in the bar by myself.

But I couldn't have woken up at all. The reality of what was going on around me was unquestionable, from the smell of fresh sweat drifting from the middle-aged men at the table next to us to the way Rita-May's skin was cool and smooth despite the heat. One of the conventioneers had engaged Rita-May in conversation, and it didn't look as if she was having too bad a time, so I took the chance to try to sort my head out. I wasn't panicking, exactly, but I was very concerned indeed.

Okay, I *was* panicking. Either I'd spent my time in the toilet hallucinating about tomorrow, or something *really* strange was happening. Did the fact that I hadn't been served by the barman yet prove which was right? I didn't know. I couldn't work it out.

"What do you think of Dale Georgio, John? Looks like he's really gonna turn WriteRight around."

I didn't really internalize the question Trindle asked me until I'd answered it, and my reply had more to do with my state of mind than any desire to cause offence.

"He's a talentless fuckwit," I said.

Back outside on the pavement I hesitated for a moment, not really knowing what to do. The N'awlins Pantry was indeed where Rita-May worked, but she was out at lunch. This I had discovered by talking to a very helpful woman, who I assume also worked there. Either that, or she was an unusually well-informed tourist.

I could either hang around and accost Rita-May on the street, or go and get some lunch. Talking to her outside the store would be preferable, but I couldn't stand hopping from foot to foot for what could be as long as an hour.

At that moment my stomach passed up an incomprehensible message of some kind, a strange liquid buzzing that I felt sure most people in the street could hear. It meant one of two things. Either I was hungry, or my mid-section was about to explode taking the surrounding two blocks along with it. I elected to assume I was hungry and turned to walk back towards the Square, in search of a muffeletta.

At Café du Monde I noticed that the dreadful trumpet player was in residence, actually in the middle of one of his trademark long notes. As I passed him, willing my head not to implode, the penny dropped.

I shouldn't be noticing that he was there. I knew he was there. I'd just been at Café du Monde. He was one of the reasons I'd left.

I got far enough away that the trumpet wasn't hurting me any more, and then ground to a halt. For the first time I was actually scared. It should have been reassuring to be back in the right time again. Tomorrow I could understand. I could retrace my steps here. Most of them, anyway. But I couldn't remember a thing of what had happened in the cookery store. I'd come out believing I'd had a conversation with someone and established that Rita-May worked there. But as to what the interior of the store had been like, I didn't have a clue. I couldn't remember. What I could actually *remember* was being in the Absinthe Bar.

I looked anxiously around at tourists dappled by bright sunshine, and felt the early-afternoon heat seeping in through my clothes. A hippy face-painter looked hopefully in my direction, judged correctly that I wasn't the type, and went back to juggling with his paints.

On impulse I lifted my right hand and sniffed my fingers. Cigarette smoke and icing sugar, from the beignets I'd eaten half an hour ago. This had to be real.

Maybe there had been something weird in the joint last night. That could explain the blackout on the trip back to the hotel, and the Technicolor flashback I'd just had. It couldn't have been acid, but some opium-based thing, possibly. But why would the man have sold us it? Presumably that kind of thing was more expensive. Dealers tended to want to rip you off, not give you little presents. Unless Rita-May had known, and had asked and paid for it—but it didn't seem very likely either.

More than that, I simply didn't believe it was a drug hangover. It didn't feel like one. I felt exactly as if I'd just had far too much to drink the night before, plus one strong joint—except for the fact that I couldn't work out where in time I actually was.

If you close one of your eyes you lose the ability to judge space. The view flattens out, like a painting. You know, or think you know, which objects are closer to you—but only because you've seen them before when both of your eyes have been open. Without that memory, you wouldn't have a clue. The same appeared to be happening with time. I couldn't seem to tell what order things should be in. The question almost felt inappropriate.

Suddenly thirsty, and hearing rather than feeling another anguished appeal from my stomach, I crossed the road to a place that sold po-boys and orange juice from a hatch in the wall. It was too far to the French Bar. I needed food immediately. I'd been okay all the time I was at Café du Monde—maybe food helped tether me in some way.

The ordering process went off okay, and I stood and munched my way through French bread and sauce piquante on the street, watching the door to the N'awlins Pantry. As much as anything else, the tang of lemon juice on the fried oysters convinced me that what I was experiencing was real. When I'd finished I took a sip of my drink, and winced. It was much sweeter than I'd been expecting. Then I realized that was because it was orange juice, rather than a Margarita. The taste left me unfulfilled, like those times when you know you've only eaten half a biscuit, but can't find the other piece. I knew I'd bought orange juice, but also that less than a minute ago I had taken a mouthful of Margarita.

Trembling, I slugged the rest of the juice back. Maybe this was something to do with blood sugar levels.

Or maybe I was slowly going off my head.

As I drank I stared fixedly at the other side of the street, watching out for Rita-May. I was beginning to feel that until I saw her again, until something happened which conclusively locked me into today, I wasn't going to be able to stabilize. Once I'd seen her the day after the night before, it had to be that next day. It really had to, or how could it be tomorrow?

Unless, of course, I was back in the toilet of the Absinthe Bar, projecting in eerie detail what might happen the next day. About the only thing I was sure of was that I wanted to see Rita-May. I realized that she probably wouldn't be wearing what I'd seen her in last night, but I knew I'd recognize her in an instant. Even with my eyes open, I could almost see her face. Eyes slightly hooded with drink, mouth parted, wisps of clean hair curling over her ears. And on her lips, as always, that beautiful half-smile.

"We're going," Trindle shouted, and I turned from Rita-May to look blearily at him. They hadn't abandoned me after all: they were leaving, and I was still conscious. My habitual irritation towards Trindle and his colleagues faded somewhat on seeing their faces. They'd clearly all had a lovely time. In a rare moment of maturity, I realized that they were rather sweet, really. I didn't want to piss on their fireworks.

I nodded and smiled and shook hands, and they trooped drunkenly off into the milling crowd. It had to be well after two o'clock by now, but the evening was still romping on. I turned back to Rita-May and realized that it hadn't been such a bad stroke of luck, running into the Trindle contingent. We'd been kept apart for a couple of hours, and passions had quietly simmered to a rolling boil. Rita-May was looking at me in a way I can only describe as frank, and I leaned forward and kissed her liquidly on the mouth. My tongue felt like some glorious sea creature, lightly oiled, rolling for the first time with another of its species.

After a while we stopped, and disengaged far enough to look in each others' eyes. "It just goes to show," she whispered, and we rested our foreheads together and giggled. I remembered thinking much earlier in the evening that I needed to ask myself what I thought I was doing. I asked myself. The answer was "having an exceptionally nice evening" which was good enough for me.

"Another drink?" It didn't feel time to leave yet. We needed some more of being there, and feeling the way we did.

"Yeah," she said, grinning with her head on one side, looking up at me as I stood. "And then come back and do that some more."

I couldn't see a waitress so I went to the bar. I'd realized by now that the time switch had happened again, and I wasn't surprised to find myself being served by the smooth-faced barman. He didn't look too surprised to see me either.

"Still going?" he asked, as he fixed the drinks I'd asked for. I knew I hadn't talked to him before, so I guessed he was just being friendly.

"Yeah," I said. "Do I look like I'm going to make it?"

"You look fine," he grinned. "Got another hour or so in you yet."

Only when I was walking unsteadily back towards our table did this strike me as a strange thing to have said. Almost as if he knew that in a little while I was going to pass out. I stopped, turned, and looked back at the bar. The barman was still looking at me. He winked, and then turned away.

He knew.

I frowned. That didn't make sense. That didn't work. Unless this was all some flashback, and I was putting words into his mouth. Which meant that it was really tomorrow. Didn't it? Then why couldn't I remember what was going to happen?

I turned back towards Rita-May, and it finally occurred to me to ask her about what was going on. If she didn't know what I was talking about, I could pass it off as a joke. If the same thing was happening to her, then we might have had a spiked joint. Either way I would have learned something. Galvanized by this plan, I tried to hurry back through the crowd. Unfortunately I didn't see a large drunken guy in a check shirt lurching into my path.

"Hey! Watch it," he said, but fairly good-humouredly. I grinned to show I was harmless and then stepped back away from the curb. The woman I'd thought was Rita-May hadn't been. Just some tourist walking quickly in the sunshine. I looked at my watch and saw I'd been waiting opposite the store for only twenty minutes. It felt like I'd been there for ever. She had to come back soon. She had to.

Then:

Christ, back here again, I thought. The switches seemed to be coming on quicker as time wore on, assuming that's what it was doing. Eating the food hadn't worked.

By the time I reached the hotel I'd started to forget, but I'd had enough sense left in me to take Rita-May's rose from my pocket and slip it into one of my shoes. Then I buried the shoes as deeply in the suitcase as I could. "That'll fuck you up," I muttered to myself. "That'll make you remember." I seemed to know what I meant. It was six in the morning by then, and I took a random selection of my clothes off and fell onto the bed. My head was a mess, and my neck hurt. Neither stopped me from falling asleep instantly, to find myself on Decatur, still waiting opposite the N'awlins Pantry.

That one took me by surprise, I have to admit. I was beginning to get the hang of the back and forth thing, even if it was making me increasingly terrified. I couldn't stop it, or understand it, but at least it was following a pattern. But to flick back to being at the hotel earlier that morning, and find that I'd hidden the shoes myself, was unexpected.

It was all getting jumbled up, as if the order didn't really matter, only the sense.

The people on the po-boy counter were beginning to look at me strangely, so I crossed back over to stand outside N'awlins Pantry itself. It felt like I had been going back and forth over the road for most of my life. There was a lamppost directly outside the store and I grabbed hold of it with both hands, as if I believed that holding something solid and physical would keep me where I was. All I wanted in the whole wide world was for Rita-May to get back.

When she did, she walked right up to the table, straddled my knees and sat down. She did this calmly, without flamboyance, and no one on the nearby tables seemed to feel it was in any way worthy of note. I did, though. As I reached out to pull her closer to me, I felt like I was experiencing sexual attraction for the very first time. Every cell in my body shifted nervously against each other, as if aware that something rather unusual and profound was afoot. The band was still pumping out twelve-bar at stadium concert volume, which normally blasts all physical sensation out of me: I can't, to put it bluntly, usually do it to music. That didn't appear to be the case on this occasion. I nuzzled into Rita-May's face and kissed her ear. She wriggled a little closer to me, her hand around the back of my head, gently twisting in the roots of my hair. My entire skin felt as if it had been upgraded to some much more sensitive organ, and had I stood up too quickly, in those jeans, I suspect something in my trousers would have just snapped.

"Let's go," she said suddenly. I stood up, and we went.

It was about three a.m. by then, and Bourbon Street was much quieter. We went up it a little way, and then took a turn to head back down towards Jackson Square. We walked slowly, wrapped up in each other, watching with interest the things our hands seemed to want to do. I don't know what Rita-May was thinking, but I was hoping with all of my heart that we could stay this way for a while. I was also still girding myself up to asking her if she was having any problems keeping track of time.

We got to the corner of the Square, and she stopped. It looked very welcoming in the darkness, empty of people and noise. I found myself thinking that leaving New Orleans was going to be more difficult than I'd expected. I'd spent a lot of my life leaving places, taking a quick look and then moving on. Wasn't going to be so easy this time.

Rita-May turned to me, and took my hands. Then she nodded down Decatur, at a row of stores. "That's where I work," she said. I drew her closer. "Pay attention," she smiled. "It's going to be important."

I shook my head slightly, to clear it. It was going to be, I knew. I was going to need to know where she worked. I stared at the N'awlins Pantry for a moment, memorizing its location. I would always forget, as it turned out, but perhaps that is part of the deal.

Rita-May seemed satisfied that I'd done my best, and reached up with her hand to pull my face towards hers.

"It's not going to be easy," she said, when we'd kissed. "For you, I mean. But please stick with it. I want you to catch up with me some day."

"I will," I said, and I meant it. Slowly, I was beginning to understand. I let go of the lamppost with my left hand, and looked at my watch. Only another minute had passed. There was still no sign of Rita-May, just the slowly swarming mass of tourists, their bright colours warm in the sun. From a little way down the road I could hear the peal of one long trumpet note, and it didn't sound so bad to me. I glanced down Decatur towards the sound, wondering how far away she was, how many times I would have to wait. I decided to ask.

"As long as it takes," she said. "Are you sure this is what you want?"

In a minute Rita-May would give me the rose, and I'd go back to the bar to pass out as I had so many times before. But for now I was still here in the silent square where the only sign of life was a couple of tired people sipping *café au tait* in darkness at the Café du Monde. The air was cool, and soft somehow, like the skin of the woman I held in my arms. I thought of my house, and London. I would remember them with affection, but not miss them very much. My sister would look after the cat. One day I would catch up with Rita-May, and when I did, I would hold on tight.

In the meantime the coffee was good, the beignets were excellent, and there would always be a muffeletta just around the corner. Sometimes it would be night, sometimes day, but I would be travelling in the right direction. I would be at home, one of the regulars, in the corner of all the photographs which showed what a fine place it was to stay. And always there would be Rita-May, and me inching ever closer every day.

"I'm sure," I said. She looked very happy, and that sealed my decision for ever. She kissed me once on the forehead, once on the lips, and then angled her head.

"I'll be waiting," she said, and then she bit me softly on the neck.

LISA GOLDSTEIN

The Fantasma of Q___

Lisa Goldstein is one of the finest of the post-Tolkien generation of fantasists. She won the American Book Award with her first novel, The Red Magician, *inspired by Jewish folk tales and the stories her mother told her of growing up in Hungary. Since then, she has experimented with different forms of the fantastic: magical realism in* Tourists, *surrealism in* The Dream Years, *science fiction in* A Mask for the General, *historical fantasia in* Strange Devices of the Sun and Moon, *among other memorable works. Her short fiction has been collected in* Daily Voices *and* Travellers in Magic. *Goldstein lives in the Bay Area of Northern California.*

"The Fantasma of Q_____," one of Goldstein's most engaging stories to date, comes from the March/April issue of Ms. *magazine.*

—T.W.

I think I've seen her again.

It was on one of my rare forays into London, rare, perforce, because my old bones cannot stand the continuous jarring motion of the train into town and the even worse jostling of the people packed into the underground. It is galling to me that I, who have ventured into nearly every continent and seen sights most men can only dream of, should be confined to a little village, that I should have to plan for a trip to the capital with all the care and precision of a voyage to the interior of Africa. However, it cannot be helped.

I went to London to deliver to my publishers the latest installment of my memoirs—and to be treated to a rich dinner at my editor's club, one of my few indulgences nowadays. Over a glass of very good port I hinted at the marvels I would reveal in later episodes—the hippogriff, the centaur, the phoenix I had tracked down in Arabia.

My editor listened, as engrossed as a child, and when I had finished he remarked that the first volume of my memoirs had done very well. "People love to read about these journeys to exotic places," he said. "Especially now that civilization is making inroads nearly everywhere. In another ten years, I wager, most of these wonderful creatures will be extinct, or will have hidden themselves so well they'll never be found."

"Ten years, is it?" I said. "Fortunately I'll probably be dead by then."

He laughed, uncertain whether I had made a joke or not.

After dinner I left him and walked, a little unsteadily, to the nearest underground station. The train I wanted was just closing its doors, and I knew that I would not be able to run for it. *She* ran, however, flying past me, and slipped into the car just before the train pulled out.

It was she, I was almost certain of it. She looked exactly the same. Forty years had not changed her in the slightest. Well, they wouldn't, would they?

Now the question is, do I tell Wallis? He has less reason to love her than I do.

I have just telephoned Wallis. I had no idea whether or not he still lived in London; for all I knew he had returned to the States. And yet the operator I spoke to found him after a wait of only a few minutes, which seemed nearly as marvelous as anything I have encountered on my travels. Perhaps the wonder has not died out of the world after all.

He sounded, like myself, years older and years more tired. "Hello," I said. "Is this Samuel Wallis?"

"Yes," he said. "Who is this?"

"James Arbuthnot," I said.

There was a long silence. "Arbuthnot," he said finally. "What brings you to phone me?"

"I think I've seen her. She's in London, Wallis."

There was another silence. I thought he was going to ask me who "she" was, but he of course remembered her as vividly as I did. "Is she?" he said.

"Yes. I saw her on the underground."

"And what do you expect me to do about it? Scour London for her? I don't want to see her again—you of all people should know that. And you know why."

"I thought you might keep your eyes peeled. I don't live in London—"

"Yes, I know. I've read the first volume of your memoirs. Are you going to mention her, mention that episode, in the next volume?"

"I don't know. I hadn't thought to—"

"Good. Leave it alone, Arbuthnot. It won't do either of us any good."

"—but perhaps I will now," I said, moved by an impulse I didn't entirely understand. "Perhaps I'll find her, and ask her—"

"Leave it alone," Wallis said again, and put the phone down.

Over the next few days I couldn't settle down to continue my memoirs. Was I going to mention her? I hadn't planned to, but now I found that I could think of nothing else.

There was no help for it. I would have to get that incident out of the way, get it clear in my mind, before I could go on.

It started as so many of my journeys did, with the chance word spoken at the Royal Explorers Club. The club itself unfortunately no longer exists, though the building still stands, a massive pillared structure once filled with animals and plants, statuary and stelae, jewels and mummies, urns and reliquaries, all our marvels collected from all over the world.

I went there in the autumn of 1885, to give a talk about my unsuccessful voyage to Crete to seek out the Minotaur. Afterward a few of the members, some known to me and some not, settled back in the club's plush leather chairs to reminisce. "Do you know," one of the fellows said, "a friend of mine claims to have sighted a fantasma in the north," and he named a forest near the village of Q_____.

I was interested, of course. More than a little interested, if the truth be known, because a friend of mine, a man named Witherspoon, had told me a few months earlier that he had invented a device that made it possible to identify a fantasma. (Witherspoon, you may remember from the first volume of my memoirs, is the man who invented the oneiroscope, a device for capturing dreams.) They look like us, like ordinary people, though the consensus among explorers is that there are more females than males among them. The ancient Greeks called them Muses, and had distinguished nine of them, all women. Sightings by members of the Explorers Club seem to suggest that there are more than nine, though perhaps not many more; they are very elusive. A man who had captured one, or who was even in the presence of one, would be filled with ideas that would seem to burst from him; he would never lack for inspiration and creative force. I paid a visit to Witherspoon and arranged to borrow the device he had invented, which he called a musopticon.

The musopticon proved to be a bulky, boxlike structure about two feet on each side. Witherspoon had constructed it of mahogany, and the levers, dials, and gears of brass; it was also bound with decorations of brass along the sides, so that the whole thing was extraordinarily heavy. I brought it to a craftsman who had done work for me before and had him make me a knapsack of canvas so that I could carry it on my back; he also made pockets in the knapsack for my other instruments.

I took a train to Q_____ and a cab to my lodgings. I would be staying with Mrs. Jones, a woman who rented out rooms in her house. It was late afternoon by the time I finished unpacking, and I went downstairs to see if Mrs. Jones had made tea. I was very displeased to discover that she had other guests, a young man and woman. More people than I had heard the rumors about the fantasma, and I hoped that these other guests were not here for the purpose of finding her. Surely, I thought, an explorer would not bring his wife along on an expedition. And yet what other reason was there to travel to this remote village?

We made our introductions. The man was Samuel Wallis and his wife was Adele; from their accents I judged they were Americans. Wallis was lean and fit, with long glossy hair parted in the middle. Mrs. Wallis was as young as he and rather beautiful, with hair the same mahogany as my musopticon and wide slate-gray eyes. We settled down to our tea.

"Are you Arbuthnot the explorer?" Wallis asked me.

I admitted that I was.

"And does that fantastical instrument I saw being carried upstairs belong to you?" he asked. I hesitated, and he went on. "You don't have to admit anything if you don't want to. I should warn you, though, that we may both be after the same thing. Have you heard there may be a fantasma in the area?"

I confess that my heart sank at his words. "Yes," I said. "That's why I'm here."

"Good man," he said. "It's best to get these things out in the open, don't you think?" He held up his teacup, and I saw that he intended to propose a toast, as though we were drinking spirits. "May the best man win."

I could not argue with that. We clicked our cups together and drank. Mrs. Jones bustled out from the kitchen. "Can I get you more tea?" she asked. "Or sandwiches?"

Wallis' eyes were shining eagerly. And I, too, felt a sudden strong urge to be off, to implement some ideas I was beginning to have, to start combing the woods for the fantasma. "Have you made any discoveries I might be familiar with?" I asked him.

"This is my first expedition," he said. Mrs. Jones began to clear away the tea things. "But one has to start somewhere, don't you think? And I believe I have some rather original ideas about where to look."

"And what does your wife intend to do while you are away?"

"Oh, I'm going with him," Mrs. Wallis said. I said nothing. It is commonplace knowledge that women lack the stamina and initiative needed for the long, arduous journeys of exploration. I was starting to feel more optimistic; Wallis was a rank beginner and clearly posed no threat to me.

We left early the next day. We ate the hearty breakfast Mrs. Jones prepared for us, and then I bade farewell to Wallis and his wife in the chill dawn light and set off toward the forest, carrying the musopticon and my other instruments on my back.

The forest was ancient, perhaps a remnant of the huge wood that had once covered much of England. I had taken only a few steps in when the light around me grew dim; the trees began to arch toward each other, their leaves and branches plaiting overhead to form a living canopy. Oak and ash, alder and thorn, they grew thickly around me and their leaves underfoot muted my steps. I stopped, took the compass from my pack and got my bearings, then headed north.

The forest was terribly silent; I heard no birds, no small animals scurrying in the undergrowth. When it came time for me to take my bearings again, the gloom was so intense that I could not see the face of the compass or the brass dials of the musopticon, and had to light a lucifer match to be able to read them.

I shouldered the musopticon and continued on. As I tramped through the woods I wondered how Wallis and his wife were faring in this strange place, whether Mrs. Wallis, or even her husband, had grown oppressed by the gloom and turned back. We were all amateurs in the literal sense, all of us adventuring for love and not for money, but a sort of professional ethic had arisen among the members of the Explorers Club, and Wallis did not seem one of our sort.

Around midday I felt the first stirrings of hunger. I took out my pocket watch and lit another match to check the time, then ate the bread and cheese Mrs. Jones had prepared. Shortly after that I deemed it best to start back. I took another reading with the musopticon, recorded no activity once again, and began to head south, toward the village of Q_____.

The forest seemed even darker as I walked back; oppressively so. I began to go faster, as fast as my various instruments would allow; they made a wild chiming noise together in my pack as I ran. I was eager to see people again, eager even to see Mr. and Mrs. Wallis. I reached the end of the forest at four in the afternoon and came to Q_____ and Mrs. Jones's homely house shortly thereafter.

To my chagrin I found that the Wallises were still out. Mrs. Jones fluttered around me (if so stout a woman can be said to flutter), helping me off with my pack, bringing me tea and sandwiches. "Are you certain they haven't returned?" I asked as I settled down with a chipped plate of sandwiches on my knee.

"I've been here all day," Mrs. Jones said. "I'd have seen them if they'd come back."

The stresses of the day were beginning to take their toll. I settled back in an overstuffed chair and watched as Mrs. Jones turned up the gas lights and lit the fire. Her tea towel, I noticed, was a souvenir from the Great Exhibition at the Crystal Palace, over thirty years ago—probably the last time the poor dear had been away from home. I must have been in hundreds of parlors just like this one, I reflected, and the familiarity of my surroundings worked a strange kind of magic on me. I grew certain that I would find the fantasma, if not tomorrow, then sometime during my stay at Q_____; in my tired state I even thought I knew which paths within the forest to pursue. At that moment Mr. and Mrs. Wallis came into the parlor, talking to one another and laughing, Mrs. Jones hurried into the kitchen for more sandwiches.

"Arbuthnot, good afternoon," Wallis said. He caught sight of the bulky pack near my chair and laughed louder. "Good Lord, Adele, look at all this equipment. Come, sir, who are you really—the White Knight in Carroll's *Through the Looking Glass?*"

"And where's Alice?" Mrs. Wallis asked.

"Why, you must be Alice, my dear," Wallis said. "But then who am I?"

Their banter annoyed me. "How was your day in the forest?" I asked, as politely as I could.

"Oh, very good, very good," Wallis said. "Well, we haven't discovered anything yet, but we have some ideas where to look. And you?"

"The same," I said shortly. My annoyance with them grew. To me, and to my fellows at the club, exploration was almost a sacred task; certainly we felt that it should not be approached in such a lighthearted, frivolous spirit. And what were these ideas they claimed to have had?

"Dark in there, though, isn't it?" Wallis said.

"A bit."

"A bit! Listen to him, Adele! I suppose you have gas lamps in that pack of yours? Along with a full set of Dickens?"

"I have matches, certainly. Don't you?"

"Matches!" he said, smiting his forehead in what was intended to be a comical manner. "I knew we forgot something."

Mrs. Jones returned with more sandwiches. I stood and shouldered my pack. "I'm afraid I'll have to leave you," I said. "I must write my journal entry for today." And in truth I was anxious to return to my room; I wanted to record the insights I had had while relaxing and taking tea.

"Good afternoon," Wallis said. His manner seemed to soften. "I hope we haven't offended you—we were only joking."

"Oh, no," I said, abstracted. I nodded to the couple and began to climb the stairs.

I set off eagerly the next morning, so early that I did not encounter the Wallises. The night before I had started a map of the forest, sketching in the areas I had already explored. It seemed to me I had found a spot the fantasma might frequent, a lonely place about a mile away that was halfway between Q_____ and the nearest village. Some of the writers I had consulted before I set out thought that these creatures preferred places of solitude and quiet.

Now I skirted the forest, holding the compass in one hand and my rough map in the other. The sun rose higher in the sky. As I walked, though, I began to wonder what had made me so certain I would find the fantasma in this area. It looked the same as any other part of the forest, as deserted and as far from civilization as anything I had already seen. If you could count the Wallis couple as civilization, I thought, and laughed bitterly to myself.

My thoughts turned to the encounter I had had with them the evening before. What had they discovered? What were the ideas they said they had? How galling it would be, I thought, if these utter beginners were to find the fantasma before I did.

When I had judged that I had walked a mile from Q_____, I entered the forest. The great trees clustered around me, dark and silent, as I passed. I performed all the same actions as before, lighting matches, getting my bearings from the compass, checking the various dials and gauges on the musopticon. By the time I was ready for my midday meal I had grown tired and irritated, certain I was wasting my time.

My evil mood grew worse as I turned back, and continued to plague me as I walked toward my lodgings. I opened the door to Mrs. Jones's house and heard Wallis laughing. His wife said something I couldn't hear and Wallis laughed harder.

It is strange to relate, I know, but I felt happy and carefree just at hearing their voices. Gone were the fears that they would find the fantasma before I did, the annoyance I had felt the day before at their lighthearted banter. I was eager to see people, I suppose, and I hurried forward as though they were old friends.

Mr. and Mrs. Wallis were sitting in the parlor, Mrs. Jones setting out the tea things. "Look, it's the White Knight!" Mr. Wallis called out cheerfully. "How goes it, old chap?"

I slung my knapsack from my shoulders and settled into one of the overstuffed chairs. For some reason, perhaps to check on my equipment, I thought to open my pack and look inside. Every one of the musopticon's dials was vibrating madly.

I excused myself as soon as I could and went up to my room to think. The fantasma was here, in this very house. It was Adele Wallis, I was almost certain of it. Or could it be Samuel? No—the creatures were mostly women, and my intuitive feeling, the one that every good explorer learns to trust, was urging me toward the wife.

This revelation created almost more problems than it solved, however. Did her husband know? If he did, why had he come all this way, and why did he claim to be searching for a fantasma? And if he didn't, why hadn't she told him?

But so many other things seemed to make sense now. The clarity I had felt in her presence, the way I had seemed to generate one fresh idea after another about where to explore next. Even the happiness that surrounded the couple, that they seemed to bring with them wherever they went: surely the act of creation is accompanied by exactly that sort of joy.

What should I do now? There were rooms and rooms upstairs at the Explorers Club containing the strange things that I and other members had found, the salamanders and rocs and mermaids. If I could bring Adele Wallis to London, the club would never lack for ideas; we would explore forever; we would move from triumph to triumph. And I would get the credit; all of this would be due to me.

I vowed to talk to Adele Wallis, to get her away from her husband somehow.

I had my opportunity a few days later. The wait was irksome, as I had to pretend to be searching for the fantasma lest her husband become suspicious. I would leave the house and trek toward the forest, then turn back and spend the day in the village, drinking tea and talking to the inhabitants. It seemed to me that even these rude villagers had more than their share of creativity, that, for example, their speech was full of unexpected poetic conceits. Could this blossoming be the result of Adele Wallis' visit?

Then Mrs. Wallis fell ill. I feigned illness myself and spent the day in Mrs. Jones's parlor, covered in a shawl and drinking tea. Mrs. Jones moved around me, wearing her everlasting apron, dusting her fusty knickknacks and sweeping.

As the hours passed I began to grow impatient, and wildly excited; it became more and more difficult to sustain my pretense of illness. I saw myself traveling the world, Mrs. Wallis at my side, making the kinds of discoveries most explorers only dream of. I would return to England, speak at conferences and meetings around the country. Perhaps there would even be a knighthood.

At last, around teatime, Adele Wallis made her way down the stairs. I had set the musopticon down near my chair, and as she came into the room I opened the pack and took a look at it. As I had hoped, all the pointers in all the dials were vibrating as one. Mrs. Wallis accepted a cup of tea and settled in her chair.

"Oh, dear, are you ill too?" she asked me.

"I wanted to talk to you, Mrs. Wallis," I said.

She looked up quickly at that. I saw plain fear in her eyes, and she glanced at Mrs. Jones to make sure we wouldn't be left alone together. "What about, Mr. Arbuthnot?"

"I know what you are," I said.

Now she looked puzzled. "Do you, Mr. Arbuthnot?" she said. "And what am I?"

"You're the fantasma. You're what I've come all this way to find, I and your husband as well."

She threw back her head and laughed. "I am, am I?" she said. "And what brings you to this extraordinary conclusion?"

"Look here." I showed her the musopticon, the rapid agitation of the dials. "This device says that that is what you are."

"Does it? Well, then, one of us is mistaken, either me or that device. I am not the fantasma, Mr. Arbuthnot. I'm not what you think I am."

"Come back with me to London," I said urgently. "Let me present you to the Explorers Club, show them what you are."

"And then what? My husband's told me all about your club. Will you lock me in a cage, along with all the other unfortunates you've picked up on your travels? No, thank you."

"No, of course not," I said, though in truth I hadn't worked out all the logistics of the thing. How would I keep her at the club during those times when we weren't traveling? Well, I would solve that problem when we got there. "Just come with me. Travel with me back to London."

It was at this point, unfortunately, that Mr. Wallis came into the parlor.

What followed was like something from a bad French farce. Mr. Wallis accused me of trying to steal his wife, I tried to explain that I wanted his wife for a higher, more scientific, purpose, and Mrs. Wallis, for some reason, kept referring to me as "that horrible man." Finally, after I had repeated the word "fantasma" at least a dozen times, the anger appeared to drain out of him.

"You're saying that Adele is—Adele is the fantasma?" he said.

"Yes," I said.

He looked at his wife. "No, of course I'm not, Sam," Mrs. Wallis said with some asperity. "Don't you think you would know it if I was?"

"I don't know," Wallis said, bemused. "How would I know? You might be."

"Don't be ridiculous," Mrs. Wallis said.

"Look at this," I said. "It's a musopticon, made by the inventor Witherspoon. Look at these dials. They're recording the presence of a fantasma right here, right in this room."

"I have had plenty of ideas lately," Wallis said. "It seems as if I've been full of ideas, more than one man can possibly follow up in one lifetime. My dear, if you are—"

"I'm not. I'm Adele Ambrose Wallis, of Boston. You've known my family for years, for God's sake."

"Don't swear, dear," Wallis said.

"And if I were the fantasma, what did you plan to do with me? This horrible man here wants to bring me to London, to put me in a cage along with the dragons and werewolves and God knows what else. And you? What would you do?"

"Why, nothing, dear. You'd still be my wife, my beloved wife. I'd keep you close to me—"

"So you could take advantage of all the ideas you'd have?"

"You would of course be a help with my explorations. My muse and inspiration, as well as my wife. I would make the most amazing discoveries—there would be no stopping me. Why, I might even be eligible for membership in the Explorers Club."

"And here I thought I was your companion!"

"You are that as well, of course—"

"But you wouldn't mind using me for your own ends—"

"For our ends, dear. Your talent would benefit both of us."

"For the very last time, I'm not the fantasma."

"Then how do you explain those dials?" Wallis said.

"I don't know," Mrs. Wallis said angrily. "Ask Mr. Arbuthnot—it's his machine."

With that she left the room. A moment later we heard the front door slam.

"Adele!" Wallis said, following her. "Adele, dearest—"

I sat where I was, too astonished by this recent turn of events to do anything else. I happened to glance down at that moment; the dials of the musopticon were, if anything, more violent in their action than before.

The only other person in the room was Mrs. Jones. I looked up at her, too startled to speak.

"Yes," she said.

"Would you—would you come back with me to London?"

"No, of course not. Not after what Mrs. Wallis said. Is it true you put your discoveries in cages?"

"Some—some of them." I felt paralyzed before her. Her face was ancient calm, wise. She seemed to have wings—or were those just the ties on her apron?

"I'll have to leave you now, Mr. Arbuthnot," the fantasma said.

She spoke a few words. The room and everything in it vanished; I stood out in the open, with the village of Q_____all around me. The sun was setting. Far away, on the high street, I could see laborers walking home. Adele Wallis was marching toward the train station; her husband ran at her side, gesturing frantically.

I have thought about that incident nearly every day in the forty years since then. I heard through the Explorers Club that Samuel Wallis and his wife got a divorce; Adele Wallis went back to her family in Boston. Samuel made a few discoveries, nothing of importance, and then seemed to give up exploring, or at least his name was never mentioned again at the club.

What I wondered about most of all, though, was why I had failed to recognize the fantasma. I had prided myself on having the intuition of a true explorer, an intuition that had stood me in good stead on many of my voyages of discovery. Seldom have I been so terribly wrong.

It is only now, writing this, that I think I begin to understand. I am—I was—an explorer; I thought I could solve the mysteries that beset our lives by chasing after the exotic, the unique, the rare. But Mrs. Jones showed me another aspect of our condition, what I could only call the mystery of the commonplace. The mystery that exists in aprons, and tea towels, and knickknacks, the inspiration that can come from all these things. I am sorry now that I never settled down long enough to know any of this.

I am preparing to undertake my last expedition. I will go to London, to the underground stations, and search for her there. And if I find her I will not attempt to capture her, but will tell her—tell her what?—tell her that at long last I understand.

RALPH SALISBURY

Hoopa, the White Deer Dance

Native American writer Ralph Salisbury is Professor Emeritus of English at the University of Oregon, and the award-winning author of many works of fiction, nonfiction, and poetry including One Indian and Two Chiefs, Spirit Beast Chant, Going to the Water, *and* Between Thunder and Lightning. *The following story comes from his most recent collection,* The Last Rattlesnake Throw, *a hard-hitting work inspired by his Cherokee heritage and his experiences in Vietnam.*

The subtle magic in "Hoopa, the White Deer Dance" is the healing power of an ancient ritual as it works its potent "medicine" on contemporary lives. It is a beautiful story of modern mythic fiction—a category of fiction that straddles the fantasy genre/mainstream divide.

—T. W.

C alifornia sun, hot between collar and hair, the sun of Kentucky or Vietnam, odor of oak leaves, shriveling in heat, unfamiliar, Havel answered, "Only sure thing's I'm here, I guess," though he knew Ann's concern was, Did it hurt being back in Hoopa, where he'd been a small child abandoned by his mother?

Havel had lived twenty-four years of questions. Was he Indian or was he white? Was he gay, because he did not join troops in raping Vietnamese women? Was there a purpose to Life on Earth, which most Native American Studies students seemed to find peace in labeling "Our Sacred Mother," the earth in which Havel's Hupa-Hispanic mother had been buried twenty-two years, his Cherokee-English father since the Korean War?

From farming the hill to which forebears had fled when white mobs took the family plantation, Havel's dad had been drafted, trained in Japanese, and awarded a battlefield commission during "The War Against Totalitarianism," then recalled to active duty and killed in "The Crusade Against Communism." Havel's father's father having "made the supreme sacrifice" in "The War to End

All Wars," half of Havel's ancestors having dispossessed and subjugated the other half, Havel wondered did the new U.S. slogan, "Make Love, Not War," only mean make soldiers for future invasions?

University had taught Havel that matter may neither enter nor leave the universe, but that it changes, geniuses and fools to end as fertilizer—the U.S. to end as a Miss America swimsuit named "bikini" after a nuclear test site—as a rocket switch fossilized at "Launch"—those artifacts to join family bones and arrowheads, which some of Havel's Native American Studies classmates were intent on liberating from museums.

Havel didn't give a damn about liberating bones or artifacts. He needed museums, just as he needed books, to liberate him from ignorance—about the people who'd created him, Indian and White—about who he was, or might become. He needed to be himself, not just a faulty job of welding in the U.S. reproduction line—what the classmate he tried to laugh off as "The Official Indian" had termed a "cultural schizophrenic."

For Ann, while driving to Hoopa, The Official Indian had summed his and Havel's "Identity Crises" as, "Two races got together in bed, and we have to get them together in our heads," but, for some Hupa whom Ann had interviewed, then left, he'd introduced Havel as "My Cherokee brother," ignoring their white ancestors and not knowing about Havel's mother.

"Cherokee? Like them big vee-hickles?" an old man with more smile than teeth had responded, leaning down from his seat atop a pickup truck cab to shake hands. "Maybe Tonka Toys will manufacture a Hupa."

"Seriously, my people are Tsalagi—Cherokee who survived the Trail of Tears," The Official Indian had insisted, grin a toothpaste advertisement in his tanned-to-the-utmost, joylessly mature young face.

The Official Indian read histories and offered a "Native American Perspective" on world affairs. Havel's own perspective had been that of any reluctant soldier, drinking beer, inhaling joyful smoke, pontificating about baseball, reading, or, in precarious solitude, seeking solace from a girl's magazine photo—eternalized Temple of the Soul, till forced to kill—then, falling himself, bullet-shattered ankle bones grating, onto the Sacred Earth of Asia—from which Indians had probably migrated. Blinded by blood spraying from slashed throat, he'd shot at every sound until his buddy sneaked up barefoot, wrenched away the weapon, and—still barefoot, risking poisoned punjee stakes—carried Havel to a medical helicopter. Even though Havel's buddy had been black and only twenty, he had been the capable, stalwart father Havel had known from two to five, then only known as his grandmother's memories. "Wasted" was all Havel learned of his buddy's death.

"In Vietnam," The Official Indian had told the old man atop the pickup truck cab, "my unit forced thousands onto reservations—into concentration camps, really, same as Nazis did to German Jews—same as the U.S. did to Japanese Americans—and to our American Indian forebears.

"Democracy? Hypocrisy. Autocracy."

"You saying our boys was wrong in defending our country over there?"

"I was one of the ones over there, and Havel was, too, but, in the Old Time, his people weren't on The Trail of Tears. Havel is Tsaragi," The Official Indian had explained, turning and, as usual, staring for a befuddled moment at Havel's

Z-scarred throat before remembering that Havel was six inches taller, though hangdog, guilt-ridden and slouched. "Tsaragi," The Official Indian had lectured, "are the so-called 'Hard Rock Cherokee' who hid out in the mountains, to remain on our Sacred Ground back east."

Arthritis-twisted right hand pulling The Official Indian's thin, new hair-braid taut, left strumming, the old man had laughed. "I thought Hard Rock was this loud music young folks seem to think so much of." Then, braid flopping like a snake which had missed, old fingers had clamped hard onto Havel's short-haired head, as if it were a bowling ball, fingers digging into one temple, thumb into the other. "While tape-recording us elders' wisdom, your walkie-talkie woman, she asked about your momma, and I recall your granddaddy as a singer. Can you sing?"

"No," Havel had mumbled, worried that Ann might have turned this class research trip into a dull, meaningless family reunion with strangers, strangers who'd pressure him to feel a bond he couldn't feel, and try to persuade him not to feel angry, cheated, and betrayed. "My father was a singer, a real singer," he'd hastened to say. "A real Cherokee, my grandmother called him, meaning I was too educated, too modern and too young to be one. My dad knew stuff from Grandmother's brother, but the two of them died before I learned much of anything."

"Your mother's brother was a dancer, a real Hupa dancer, and he moved as if he was walking on the plumes of eagles. Can you dance?"

"I can't dance. I'm too—hung up."

"Hung up?"

The TV formula phrase questioned, Havel had felt as he'd felt in school, mispronouncing words which his grandmother, who'd only had four years of schooling, had learned from newspapers, without ever having heard them said. "My father could dance very gracefully," Havel had heard himself mumbling awkwardly. "Stomp dancing. Green corn dance"—words learned from his grandmother—"waltz, foxtrot, jitterbugging"—words learned from his stepmother, before she'd remarried and left.

"I keep hearing about your father, my young, blue-eyed man." Against blue sky above his pickup truck cab, the old man's eyes had been the dark brown of acorns he'd strung into a necklace for a little girl, maybe his granddaughter, before she'd slid down windshield glittering like ice in hot sun. Black wiper blade a twanging tuning fork, she'd rolled off hood and fender, acorn necklace breaking and scattering. Then, dodging between cars backing out of parking places and cars parking, she'd run to splash with other children in the cool river, the old fashioner of the necklace she'd so quickly broken murmuring, just loud enough to be heard above the children's clamoring, "I never met that Cherokee father of yours, but your being here proves he could fuck. What about you?"

Havel had only been able to bashfully mumble, "My walkie-talkie woman seems to think we're doing more than talking."

The Official Indian had inched away from Havel, but the old man had laughed and had let go of Havel's head, Havel's own relieved laughter throbbing in dents hard fingers had left.

"White girls turn into fancy laundry-ger-ie and purrri-fumes and powder," the old man had observed, crooked thumb pointing toward some pale, bare-shouldered, middle-aged tourist women hastening through parking-lot dust seeking air-conditioned cars. "You come back home, and you'll learn what it is to fuck. You don't need none of those hard drugs and that Hard Rock music. All you need is a hard cock, and women with loving feelings tender as acorn mush they mashes between stones for soup."

"Speaking of women, we have to find our brainy walkie-talkie classmate, who's helping with the mashing," the Official Indian had worried, his tone the tone that had made Havel jealous on the drive here.

Ann had been as easy to find as a white blaze-mark cut to indicate a trail among brown tree trunks, and while she went on mashing acorns, and waiting to eat with the women, Havel and The Official Indian had offered bread bought with money from the Student Research Fund, and had been invited to share bland acorn soup and oakwood barbecue smoke—flavored salmon, as they sat at one of several oak picnic tables spaced among oaks, whose centuries of shade reached from roots to the three stones of a White Deer ceremonial ground.

The Official Indian gone to ask when the next dance might start, Havel sprawled on the warm earth his mother's people held sacred, fast, cold river soothing his ankle swelled around sharded bullet, California September sun hot between collar and hair, a reminder of returning to Kentucky in July, after his year of war, to visit his father's and his grandmother's graves.

"Only sure thing's I'm here, I guess," he'd said, although knowing he was again failing to share his deepest feelings, knowing he was in danger of losing Ann and in danger of losing some sense of himself, which was always ahead of him, always just ahead, or lost somewhere in his past.

"Young as your mother was—worrying about a husband she'd known only briefly before he went to war—it's no wonder that she couldn't care for you," Ann told Havel. The river's reflections and the wading children's shadows were moving across her lips, tongue, and teeth as she went on talking. "You should forgive her. During the White Deer Ceremonies, the Hupa forgive every insult, real or imagined, every hurt, intended or accidental, Horseman says." Horseman what The Official Indian insisted was his Cherokee totem name. "People become one again. Centuries of wrong are forgiven. I can come, to observe and study and learn. Any white can come—even those whites I overheard threatening to sue a tourist agent for sending them where there are no war dances, no war bonnets, and nothing to buy.

"After what Horseman told me, I noticed people talking intensely, then hugging, and I hugged the woman I was working with," Ann murmured. "My hands were covered with the acorn mush we had ground for soup, but I held her with my forearms, and she held me and left the memory of her old twisted hands in acorn mush crusted on my shoulders. 'I'm sorry,' I told her, maybe meaning that I'm white, or that she is old and I'm young, it just came out, 'I'm sorry,' I didn't know for what, but she said, just as if she did know, had always known, and would always know, 'It's all right, daughter, it's all right.'

"It takes a lot of acorns to make a bowl of soup, but in my impulsive joy or grief I'd spilled a handful I'd finally ground successfully. This beautiful old woman's twisted hands wiped the mush off the picnic bench and scattered it, giving it back to the earth, under the planks of the picnic table sawed from oaks, and we went on working under the shade of the leaves of the oaks whose acorns we were preparing for food.

"One acorn hulled and ground, and the next and the next," Ann murmured, "moments, days, years, lives, like the hundreds of little red woodpecker scalps the Hupa stitched into ceremonial garments generations ago, and have reverently preserved to wear in their dances today—like particles of acorn meal eaten, and human cells growing, and children's children forming.

"I forgive my mother. For the years of slaps and fear. For her insane urge to browbeat me into being forever a child so she wouldn't feel old. I forgive my mother for becoming what a sick, affluent, brainwashed society trained her to be."

Ann's "forgive" made Havel uneasy, because fall semester had added the question of abortion to all the questions he could not answer, and Ann, in his arms, in bed, had had to make the decision alone. "Your mother's brother was a dancer, a real Hupa dancer," the old gent perched atop his pickup truck had said, and Havel wondered if all the people here had forgiven his mother. She'd left Hoopa to go to college, she'd got pregnant, she'd married a Cherokee-white soldier she'd met from a World War Two Japanese Language class, and, while her husband was fighting in the Solomon Islands, she had, according to Havel's father's mother, taken to drink, taken lovers, and, just weeks before she'd died in a car crash, she'd left her mixed-blood two-year-old son with her parents, from whom Havel's father had reclaimed him, after the war.

"I forgive my father for being so weak he let everything happen," Ann said, as they joined men, women, and children assembling in front of three ceremonial stones, "and I forgive myself, but I'm not alive to go on making mistakes."

"Hate, Hate! Hate! Hate!" it seemed men, wearing animal skins on heads and bodies, were chanting, while standing in a line, pivoting and swaying, the pelts of white deer, held on staffs, turning and rising and falling and rising and falling.

"Hate, Hate! Hate, Hate!" but it wasn't, though it was followed by what sounded like war cries. "Hate, Hate! Hate, Hate!" But it wasn't, and the war cries weren't necessarily war cries. Though Havel had heard a lecture and had read a text book, he didn't understand the dance, and he knew that he would never understand. But he was feeling, feeling the heat of the early afternoon sun and feeling the drumbeats. He was swaying in rhythm with the line of white deer come alive—in rhythm with two elderly Hook Dancers, their mostly bare, fur-clad bodies moving toward each other, eagle-bone whistles shrilling between set lips, green plant bundles cradled, black stone knives outthrust. Brows sweat-silvered under fur caps edged with the hook-shaped tusks of walrus hunted centuries back, the dancers were gliding past each other, gliding past the albino deer skins hundreds of years old. The corpulent, elderly men were moving, "as if dancing on eagle plumes," the way the textbook had said it should be, the way it had been with Havel's mother's Hupa people for centuries.

They hadn't had to endure a death march like The Trail of Tears. They had suffered, but they had not been forced from the sacred home of their ancestors. They were the people they had always been, and they had not lost the religion of which the White Deer Dance was a part.

As Horseman had told Ann, quoting the textbook he and Havel shared, the Hupa forgave and sought forgiveness. Its transports bringing home—from the supposed "Native American migration debarkation point," Asia—no booty, only bodies to bury, the U.S. had not acknowledged wrong, as other defeated aggressors had been forced to do. Instead of confessing to war crimes committed against a small population and against its own people, the U.S. had inscribed stone with the names of citizen soldiers killed, and had continued piracy as a basis for wasteful prosperity, though nuclear destruction might be the judgment that would fit the crime.

"Hate, Hate! Hate, Hate!" But it wasn't. It was a ceremonial chant, followed by what sounded like war cries, the cries of Americans in an assault on enemy bunkers, the cries of defending Vietnamese. "Hate, Hate! Hate, Hate!" But it wasn't, and the war cries weren't necessarily war cries. Havel didn't understand, but, in his deepest mind, deepest spirit awareness, he asked forgiveness of the men, women and children whose lives he had unwillingly taken, asked forgiveness for being alive while a better, a more courageous, kind, generous person, his buddy, had been killed.

Having heard his heavy footsteps as he limped over twigs and stones, Ann was standing, her hair bright as a ceremonial eagle plume above the dark heads of Hupa women moving past her, and Havel knew that, before his mind lost its sense of who she was and of who he was, he must ask her the question his father had asked of two women—ask, or he would lose her, lose her to Horseman or to someone else.

"Will you marry me?"

"No."

"I don't mean just because of the abortion, I mean—everything. Will you think about it and answer later?"

"I have thought about it," she told him, eyes, blue intensified by sun, like river blazing between leaves, "before my abortion and after. When I finally got courage enough to confront my dad, he said he didn't want to put me at odds with my mother by keeping her from beating me. It was a gender thing, mother and daughter, he said. He thought he was some kind of pop psychologist by way of being a personnel manager, I guess. I guess you think I spill my guts too much while you are being the noble, afflicted, silent Native American."

Havel tried to answer, couldn't.

"Silence, silent suffering, that's all I got from my dad, and I need more than that from a lover. Friends kid me that I'm hung up on being your Great White Mother, and maybe they're right. I won't be a wannabe Indian. I won't be a wannabe wife. And I already know what a don't-want-to-be mother is like. I'm going to stop trying for a symbolic rewrite of my girlhood. I'm going to live what Horseman calls my own Medicine Path, my own destiny, with my best sense of myself, whatever that means."

She walked rapidly away, leaving Havel confused, not sure of what he could have said, might still say. Just as he caught up to Ann again, the line of Hupa women she was following stopped, and then began veering, as far as brambles would allow, on one side of the road to the parking lot. It seemed the women were avoiding a huge, pink-shirted man who was staggering drunkenly and waving several new bills as green as ceremonial plant-bundle blades, trying to buy a white deerskin from a puzzled old Hook Dancer. Finally giving up and stuffing his money back into a Thunderbird-embossed billfold, the pink-shirted man said, "If you don't know how to make money, it's no skin off my ass. You've got one hell of a tourist attraction here, yelling that 'Hate, Hate, Hate!' at folks whose taxes feed you—half dressed men older than I am blowing those toy whistles while slinking back and forth, over and over—the same damned thing, and, if it was just going to be rehearsal, over and over, why the hell not let the tourist bureau know not to send folks to drive here all the way from L.A.?"

Horseman came alongside and warned Ann that the Hupa women had veered because women were supposed to keep a respectful distance from the sacred skins. "Not a gender-egalitarian religion," he whispered, "but there's at least one Medicine Woman." Horseman had learned that Navajos did not point, for fear of being thought witches, and, though his professors had not named any Hupa taboos, he was playing it safe, tactfully inclining his smoothly tanned, blunt nose toward an elderly lady. Having stood, as everyone, old and young, had, through-out the dance just ended, she was now settling onto an aluminum-framed chair gleaming in the shade of an oak, her black eyes staring, over Ann's blond hair, at Havel's brown face. Then, as if The Official Indian's pointing nose had worked the witchcraft he'd sought to avoid, shriveled forearms still at rest on rose-printed lap, she began slowly sinking.

Everyone nearby was moving fast, but Ann and the old man who'd called her a walkie-talkie woman, nearest and fastest, each seized a spindly arm and raised the Medicine Woman, to totter between them, a tiny, frail figure, whose eyes, huge in shrunken brown face, concentrated sun into intense black light. Behind her, the folding chair lay crumpled, a lopsided Z like the bayonet scar on Havel's throat which he learned again, with his fingers, every day when he shaved.

While Ann and the old man continued their support, Havel took a piece of the wood still piled beside coals of the salmon-grilling fire, and hammered until the chair was again connected to its braces and strong enough for the Medicine Woman to resume sitting in dignified silence.

Pointing at the oak chunk, splintered from striking chair braces, the old man remarked, "That's a quite a tool you got, young man, but a tool is only as good as the job it does." Merry old eyes looked at Ann's slender, white-bloused, tan-skirted body and looked, then, at children tumbling out of newly arrived autos.

A woman screamed, glass shattered, and, like a delayed and amplified echo of Havel's pounding, metal banged against metal. Through billowing, sunlit dust, Havel saw a little brown body roll over a glittering blue car's rear fender, tumble upright, and run to join kids already splashing in the cool river.

The big, pink-shirted drunk who'd tried to buy the deerskin got out of his car, and, leaning menacingly over a skinny Hupa man, yelled, "So, you nigger-skinned so-called Native American, to miss somebody's damned kid I backed into your rattletrap truck! No parking attendant. The god-damned tribe can pay for your headlight!"

"Hate, Hate! Hate, Hate!" Havel was recalling the chant as what it was not. He was hearing what he was feeling, and, when the big man pushed the skinny Hupa and sent him reeling backward, Havel moved. Horseman was moving ahead of him, but, amid a confusing swirling of bodies, it was Ann who hit the big man, in the solar plexus, doubling his huge chest down over his big, pink-clad paunch.

"Get out of here," she whispered, half to herself, half to the drunk. "Get out of here and back where you belong. You are destroying more than a truck head-light. Get out!"

Instead, the big guy threw a roundhouse punch, but Horseman defected the fist past Ann's face, caught the thumb, and compressed it back against its joint.

The big man screaming "I'll pay!" Horseman let him fumble the price of a headlight from his machine-stamped, Thunderbird-embossed billfold, and, as the big car drove off, Horseman muttered, "He never even noticed when he sent us 'nigger-skinned' soldiers to Nam, but now he knows that some of us got back."

Slender shoulder twisting out from under Havel's arm, Ann said, "You two can catch the college bus. I'm going to drive alone and do some thinking."

Brown faces were silvered by sun reflected off ripples which gleaming bodies of children splashed. The river's ceaseless mumbling over rocks, the cries of play, the rise and fall of people talking together, the rumble of a huge truck from the road above the ceremonial grounds, and the shrieks of military planes on ma-neuvers persisted as Havel walked between rows of bright autos, too tall, too light-skinned, not belonging here, not belonging anywhere, not with his Native American people, not with his European American people, not with university people, who'd no memory of sixteen-hour workdays on a grandparent's farm, not with other veterans, who seemed to feel no guilt about killing, not with Ann, not with any woman who was ready for marriage and children, and not with days body and mind were living.

He had no idea for any kind of research paper he might write. He hadn't learned anything. He still didn't feel that he'd ever had a mother. He didn't even know what he'd hoped to feel about her, about anything.

The Medicine Woman was standing, watching Ann's hair moving like a bright bird wing over the crests of bushes. Beside the old woman, the chair Havel had repaired was no longer in the shade. The metal frame felt hot as Havel tested it, his weight bearing down on his hands. It held. He picked up the chair, and set it beside the Medicine woman, in the shade.

She didn't say, "Thank you." She didn't say anything, but the old gent with more grin than teeth told Havel, "Just like I said. You need you some girls tender as the acorn mush they mashes. That walkie-talkie woman's all fancy laundry-ger-ie, purrrfume, and powerder," and he limped off to join some other old men.

"Don't listen to your poor, dead momma's old fool friend," the Medicine Woman said, so softly Havel only heard with his mind's shaping of what his ears could scarcely separate from the river's murmuring. "It's not all so easy. Your momma she was young, no older than you are now. She lived like what some men wanted her to be, and she wasn't herself any more. Then, she was gone into the ground. You were a soldier, that pretty-haired woman told me. You lived too much men things in war. Time now to live so your children can some-day stand at your grave. That woman with the hard little fist—you've lived you some life together, you know each other, and she might be the one for you and you the one for her. Don't stand around like some gawking tourist not knowing what to do, not knowing how to live one breath of his life let alone live some years of grandkids from now. You go after that young woman. You take that chance." Her wrinkles shadowed deep as scars, her taut mouth shaping pity and strength, the old woman looked like pictures of Havel's mother's mother.

"I'm all hung up—crazy," Havel said. "I don't belong with anyone, I don't belong anywhere."

"You belong anywhere you draw breath," the Medicine Woman said, and sat down on the flimsy chair in the shade of an oak grove, in the place where she'd been born, where she'd die, reflections of the river quivering and flickering like a school of little trout over the ripples of her skin. "You didn't just fix a chair," she said. "I watched you. You done you some living with wood. You felt you were that oak chunk you knew to use as a tool. You felt you were this metal that's holding up my old body, and you felt your own body, old, and needing this chair, and sitting in this chair. You don't have to say anything, and you don't have to do anything. You are one of us, and you always will be. Don't be like my pitiful niece, your momma, too timid to take the big risks and ending with less than nothing. You get going after your woman, and you keep going," Havel's old kinswoman told him. "Keep going, as long as it takes."

He got going, ignoring the pain in his ankle, walking fast, Ann's hair, bright above dusty bushes, all he could see of her, glimpsed and vanished, and glimpsed and vanished again.

When he reached the line of vehicles parked along the road above the ceremonial grounds, and saw that Ann's car was already dust between bordering oaks in the distance, he felt relieved. Ann had told the truth. She had been a mother to him. Maybe she'd been mothering her father all the years he'd been abused by his tyrannical wife. Havel knew he should respect Ann's refusing to marry him—knew she'd maybe done the right thing for him, as well as for herself. He'd be lonely, as he'd been for two years, till he'd met Ann, but he knew he had to live with his own problems, had to forgive his mother, his country, and himself.

The goodbye note he expected was not in the mailbox, and not taped to the door. Sun hot between collar and hair, he fumbled out his key, and, as he entered the apartment he had shared with Ann for a year, he saw hair bright against shadows and heard Ann's voice, imitating his, throwing his own words back at him; "Only sure thing's I'm here, I guess."

Nothing's sure, he thought, but he was moving, and he kept on moving—moving, trying, despite his limp, to move as his mother's Hook Dancer brother would have moved, "as if on the plumes of eagles," toward Ann's arms, meeting her eyes' question, beginning to live the answer, whatever it was.

STEPHEN KING

That Feeling, You Can Only Say What It Is in French

Stephen King needs little introduction, being one of the most widely read and beloved writers of our day, acclaimed for his highly effective novels of supernatural and psychological horror. His most recent novels are Bag of Bones *and* The Girl Who Loved Tom Gordon. *His stories have been published in such diverse venues as* Omni, Redbook, Shock Rock, Cemetery Dance, *and* Prize Stories: The O. Henry Awards.

"That Feeling, You Can Only Say What It Is in French" comes from the pages of The New Yorker *magazine and is something of a departure for King, being a tale of contemporary fantasy rather than horror—although it certainly has a disturbing edge. It is a beautifully crafted work of fiction exploring the fragile intimacies of memory, time, and relationships.*

—T. W.

Floyd, what's that over there? Oh shit. The man's voice speaking these words was vaguely familiar, but the words themselves were just a disconnected snip of dialogue, the kind of thing you heard when you were channel-surfing with the remote. There was no one named Floyd in her life. Still, that was the start. Even before she saw the little girl in the red pinafore, there were those disconnected words.

But it was the little girl who brought it on strong. "Oh-oh, I'm getting that feeling," Carol said.

The girl in the pinafore was in front of a country market called Carson's— "Beer, Wine, Groc, Fresh Bait, Lottery"—crouched down with her butt between her ankles and the bright-red apron-dress tucked between her thighs, playing with a doll. The doll was yellow-haired and dirty, the kind that's round and stuffed and boneless in the body.

"What feeling?" Bill asked.

"You know. The one you can only say what it is in French. Help me here."

"Déjà vu," he said.

"That's it," she said, and turned to look at the little girl one more time. *She'll have the doll by one leg,* Carol thought. *Holding it upside down by one leg with its grimy yellow hair hanging down.*

But the little girl had abandoned the doll on the store's splintery gray steps and had gone over to look at a dog caged up in the back of a station wagon. Then Bill and Carol Shelton went around a curve in the road and the store was out of sight.

"How much farther?" Carol asked.

Bill looked at her with one eyebrow raised and his mouth dimpled at one corner—left eyebrow, right dimple, always the same. The look that said, *You think I'm amused, but I'm really irritated. For the ninety-trillionth or so time in the marriage, I'm really irritated. You don't know that, though, because you can only see about two inches into me and then your vision fails.*

But she had better vision than he realized; it was one of the secrets of the marriage. Probably he had a few secrets of his own. And there were, of course, the ones they kept together.

"I don't know," he said. "I've never been here."

"But you're sure we're on the right road."

"Once you get over the causeway and onto Sanibel Island, there's only one," he said. "It goes across to Captiva, and there it ends. But before it does we'll come to Palm House. That I promise you."

The arch in his eyebrow began to flatten. The dimple began to fill in. He was returning to what she thought of as the Great Level. She had come to dislike the Great Level, too, but not as much as the eyebrow and the dimple, or his sarcastic way of saying "Excuse me?" when you said something he considered stupid, or his habit of pooching out his lower lip when he wanted to appear thoughtful and deliberative.

"Bill?"

"Mmm?"

"Do you know anyone named Floyd?"

"There was Floyd Denning. He and I ran the downstairs snack bar at Christ the Redeemer in our senior year. I told you about him, didn't I? He stole the Coke money one Friday and spent the weekend in New York with his girlfriend. They suspended him and expelled her. What made you think of him?"

"I don't know," she said. Easier than telling him that the Floyd with whom Bill had gone to high school wasn't the Floyd the voice in her head was speaking to. At least, she didn't think it was.

Second honeymoon, that's what you call this, she thought, looking at the palms that lined Highway 867, a white bird that stalked along the shoulder like an angry preacher, and a sign that read "Seminole Wildlife Park, Bring a Carful for $10." *Florida the Sunshine State. Florida the Hospitality State. Not to mention Florida the Second-Honeymoon State. Florida, where Bill Shelton and Carol Shelton, the former Carol O'Neill, of Lynn, Massachusetts, came on their first honeymoon twenty-five years before. Only that was on the other side, the Atlantic side, at a little cabin colony, and there were cockroaches in the bureau drawers. He couldn't stop touching me. That was all right, though, in those days I wanted to*

*be touched. Hell, I wanted to be torched like Atlanta in "Gone with the Wind,"
and he torched me, rebuilt me, torched me again. Now it's silver. Twenty-five is
silver. And sometimes I get that feeling.*

They were approaching a curve, and she thought, *Three crosses on the right
side of the road. Two small ones flanking a bigger one. The small ones are clapped-
together wood. The one in the middle is white birch with a picture on it, a tiny
photograph of the seventeen-year-old boy who lost control of his car on this curve,
one drunk night that was his last drunk night, and this is where his girlfriend and
her girlfriends marked the spot—*

Bill drove around the curve. A pair of black crows, plump and shiny, lifted off
from something pasted to the macadam in a splat of blood. They had eaten so
well that Carol wasn't sure they were going to get out of the way until they did.
There were no crosses, not on the left, not on the right. Just roadkill in the
middle, a woodchuck or something, now passing beneath a luxury car that had
never been north of the Mason-Dixon Line.

Floyd, what's that over there?

"What's wrong?"

"Huh?" She looked at him, bewildered, feeling a little wild.

"You're sitting bolt upright. Got a cramp in your back?"

"Just a slight one." She settled back by degrees. "I had that feeling again. The
déjà vu."

"Is it gone?"

"Yes," she said, but she was lying. It had retreated a little, but that was all.
She'd had this before, but never so *continuously.* It came up and went down,
but it didn't go away. She'd been aware of it ever since that thing about Floyd
started knocking around in her head—and then the little girl in the red pinafore.

But, really, hadn't she felt something before either of those things? Hadn't
it actually started when they came down the steps of the Lear 35 into the
hammering heat of the Fort Myers sunshine? Or even before? En route from
Boston?

They were coming to an intersection. Overhead was a flashing yellow light, and
she thought, *To the right is a used-car lot and a sign for the Sanibel Community
Theatre.*

Then she thought, *No, it'll be like the crosses that weren't there. It's a strong
feeling but it's a false feeling.*

Here was the intersection. On the right there *was* a used-car lot—Palmdale
Motors. Carol felt a real jump at that, a stab of something sharper than disquiet.
She told herself to quit being stupid. There had to be car lots all over Florida
and if you predicted one at every intersection sooner or later the law of averages
made you a prophet. It was a trick mediums had been using for hundreds of
years.

Besides, there's no theatre sign.

But there was another sign. It was Mary the Mother of God, the ghost of all
her childhood days, holding out her hands the way she did on the medallion
Carol's grandmother had given her for her tenth birthday. Her grandmother had
pressed it into her hand and looped the chain around her fingers, saying, "Wear
her always as you grow, because all the hard days are coming." She had worn it,

all right. At Our Lady of Angels grammar and middle school she had worn it, then at St. Vincent de Paul high. She wore the medal until breasts grew around it like ordinary miracles, and then someplace, probably on the class trip to Hampton Beach, she had lost it. Coming home on the bus she had tongue-kissed for the first time. Butch Soucy had been the boy, and she had been able to taste the cotton candy he'd eaten.

Mary on that long-gone medallion and Mary on this billboard had exactly the same look, the one that made you feel guilty of thinking impure thoughts even when all you were thinking about was a peanut-butter sandwich. Beneath Mary, the sign said "Mother of Mercy Charities Help the Florida Homeless—Won't *You* Help *Us?*"

Hey there, Mary, what's the story—

More than one voice this time; many voices, girls' voices, chanting ghost voices. There were ordinary miracles; there were also ordinary ghosts. You found these things out as you got older.

"What's wrong with you?" She knew that voice as well as she did the eyebrow-and-dimple look. Bill's I'm-only-pretending-to-be-pissed tone of voice, the one that meant he really *was* pissed, at least a little.

"Nothing." She gave him the best smile she could manage.

"You really don't seem like yourself. Maybe you shouldn't have slept on the plane."

"You're probably right," she said, and not just to be agreeable, either. After all, how many women got a second honeymoon on Captiva Island for their twenty-fifth anniversary? Round trip on a chartered Learjet? Ten days at one of those places where your money was no good (at least until MasterCard coughed up the bill at the end of the month) and if you wanted a massage a big Swedish babe would come and pummel you in your six-room beach house?

Things had been different at the start. Bill, whom she'd first met at a crosstown high-school dance and then met again at college three years later (another ordinary miracle), had begun their married life working as a janitor, because there were no openings in the computer industry. It was 1973, and computers were essentially going nowhere and they were living in a grotty place in Revere, not on the beach but close to it, and all night people kept going up the stairs to buy drugs from the two sallow creatures who lived in the apartment above them and listened endlessly to dopey records from the sixties. Carol used to lie awake waiting for the shouting to start, thinking, *We won't ever get out of here, we'll grow old and die within earshot of Cream and Blue Cheer and the fucking Dodgem cars down on the beach.*

Bill, exhausted at the end of his shift, would sleep through the noise, lying on his side, sometimes with one hand on her hip. And when it wasn't there she often put it there, especially if the creatures upstairs were arguing with their customers. Bill was all she had. Her parents had practically disowned her when she married him. He was a Catholic, but the wrong sort of Catholic. Gram had asked why she wanted to go with that boy when anyone could tell he was shanty, how could she fall for all his foolish talk, why did she want to break her father's heart. And what could she say?

It was a long distance from that place in Revere to a private jet soaring at forty-one thousand feet; a long way to this rental car, which was a Crown Victoria—what the goodfellas in the gangster movies invariably called a Crown Vic—heading for ten days in a place where the tab would probably be . . . well, she didn't even want to think about it.

Floyd? . . . Oh shit.

"Carol? What is it now?"

"Nothing," she said. Up ahead by the road was a little pink bungalow, the porch flanked by palms—seeing those trees with their fringy heads lifted against the blue sky made her think of Japanese Zeros coming in low, their underwing machine guns firing, such an association clearly the result of a youth misspent in front of the TV—and as they passed a black woman would come out. She would be drying her hands on a piece of pink towelling and would watch them expressionlessly as they passed, rich folks in a Crown Vic headed for Captiva, and she'd have no idea that Carol Shelton once lay awake in a ninety-dollar-a-month apartment, listening to the records and the drug deals upstairs, feeling something alive inside her, something that made her think of a cigarette that had fallen down behind the drapes at a party, small and unseen but smoldering away next to the fabric.

"Hon?"

"Nothing, I said." They passed the house. There was no woman. An old man—white, not black—sat in a rocking chair, watching them pass. There were rimless glasses on his nose and a piece of ragged pink towelling, the same shade as the house, across his lap. "I'm fine now. Just anxious to get there and change into some shorts."

His hand touched her hip—where he had so often touched her during those first days—and then crept a little farther inland. She thought about stopping him (Roman hands and Russian fingers, they used to say) and didn't. They were, after all, on their second honeymoon. Also, it would make that expression go away.

"Maybe," he said, "we could take a pause. You know, after the dress comes off and before the shorts go on."

"I think that's a lovely idea," she said, and put her hand over his, pressed both more tightly against her. Ahead was a sign that would read "Palm House 3 Mi. on Left" when they got close enough to see it.

The sign actually read "Palm House 2 Mi. on Left." Beyond it was another sign, Mother Mary again, with her hands outstretched and that little electric shimmy that wasn't quite a halo around her head. This version read "Mother of Mercy Charities Help the Florida Sick—Won't *You* Help Us?"

Bill said, "The next one ought to say 'Burma Shave.' "

She didn't understand what he meant, but it was clearly a joke and so she smiled. The next one would say "Mother of Mercy Charities Help the Florida Hungry," but she couldn't tell him that. Dear Bill. Dear in spite of his sometimes stupid expressions and his sometimes unclear allusions. *He'll most likely leave you, and you know something? If you go through with it that's probably the best luck you can expect.* This according to her father. Dear Bill, who had proved that just once, just that one crucial time, her judgment had been far better than her father's. She was still married to the man her Gram had called "the big boaster." At a price, true, but everyone paid a price.

Her head itched. She scratched at it absently, watching for the next Mother of Mercy billboard.

Horrible as it was to say, things had started turning around when she lost the baby. That was just before Bill got a job with Beach Computers, out on Route 128; that was when the first winds of change in the industry began to blow.

Lost the baby, had a miscarriage—they all believed that except maybe Bill. Certainly her family had believed it: Dad, Mom, Gram. "Miscarriage" was the story they told, miscarriage was a Catholic's story if ever there was one. *Hey, Mary, what's the story,* they had sometimes sung when they skipped rope, feeling daring, feeling sinful, the skirts of their uniforms flipping up and down over their scabby knees. That was at Our Lady of Angels, where Sister Annunciata would spank your knuckles with her ruler if she caught you gazing out the window during Sentence Time, where Sister Dormatilla would tell you that a million years was but the first tick of eternity's endless clock (and you could spend eternity in Hell, most people did, it was easy). In Hell you would live forever with your skin on fire and your bones roasting. Now she was in Florida, now she was in a Crown Vic sitting next to her husband, whose hand was still in her crotch; the dress would be wrinkled but who cared if it got that look off his face, and why wouldn't the feeling *stop?*

She thought of a mailbox with "Raglan" painted on the side and an American-flag decal on the front, and although the name turned out to be "Reagan" and the flag a Grateful Dead sticker, the box was there. She thought of a small black dog trotting briskly along the other side of the road, its head down, sniffling, and the small black dog was there. She thought again of the billboard and, yes, there it was: "Mother of Mercy Charities Help the Florida Hungry—Won't *You* Help Us?"

Bill was pointing. "There—see? I think that's Palm House. No, not where the billboard is, the other side. Why do they let people put those things up out here, anyway?"

"I don't know." Her head itched. She scratched, and black dandruff began falling past her eyes. She looked at her fingers and was horrified to see dark smutches on the tips; it was as if someone had just taken her fingerprints.

"Bill?" She raked her hand through her blond hair and this time the flakes were bigger. She saw they were not flakes of skin but flakes of paper. There was a face on one, peering out of the char like a face peering out of a botched negative.

"Bill?"

"What? Wh—" Then a total change in his voice, and that frightened her more than the way the car swerved. "Christ, honey, what's in your hair?"

The face appeared to be Mother Teresa's. Or was that just because she'd been thinking about Our Lady of Angels? Carol plucked it from her dress, meaning to show it to Bill, and it crumbled between her fingers before she could. She turned to him and saw that his glasses were melted to his cheeks. One of his eyes had popped from its socket and then split like a grape pumped full of blood.

And I knew it, she thought. *Even before I turned, I knew it. Because I had that feeling.*

A bird was crying in the trees. On the billboard, Mary held out her hands. Carol tried to scream. Tried to scream.

"Carol?"

It was Bill's voice, coming from a thousand miles away. Then his hand—not pressing the folds of her dress into her crotch, but on her shoulder.

"You O.K., babe?"

She opened her eyes to brilliant sunlight and her ears to the steady hum of the Learjet's engines. And something else—pressure against her eardrums. She looked from Bill's mildly concerned face to the dial below the temperature gauge in the cabin and saw that it had wound down to 28,000.

"Landing?" she said, sounding muzzy to herself. "Already?"

"It's fast, huh?" Sounding pleased, as if he had flown it himself instead of only paying for it. "Pilot says we'll be on the ground in Fort Myers in twenty minutes. You took a hell of a jump, girl."

"I had a nightmare."

He laughed—the plummy ain't-you-the-silly-billy laugh she had come really to detest. "No nightmares allowed on your second honeymoon, babe. What was it?"

"I don't remember," she said, and it was the truth. There were only fragments: Bill with his glasses melted all over his face, and one of the three or four forbidden skip rhymes they had sometimes chanted back in fifth and sixth grade. This one had gone *Hey there, Mary, what's the story* . . . and then something-something-something. She couldn't come up with the rest. She could remember *Jangle-tangle jingle-bingle, I saw your daddy's great big dingle*, but she couldn't remember the one about Mary.

Mary helps the Florida sick, she thought, with no idea of what the thought meant, and just then there was a beep as the pilot turned the seat-belt light on. They had started their final descent. *Let the wild rumpus start*, she thought, and tightened her belt.

"You really don't remember?" he asked, tightening his own. The little jet ran through a cloud filled with bumps, one of the pilots in the cockpit made a minor adjustment, and the ride smoothed out again. "Because usually, just after you wake up, you can still remember. Even the bad ones."

"I remember Sister Annunciata, from Our Lady of Angels. Sentence Time."

"Now, *that's* a nightmare."

Ten minutes later the landing gear came down with a whine and a thump. Five minutes after that they landed.

"They were supposed to bring the car right out to the plane," Bill said, already starting up the Type A shit. This she didn't like, but at least she didn't detest it the way she detested the plummy laugh and his repertoire of patronizing looks. "I hope there hasn't been a hitch."

There hasn't been, she thought, and the feeling swept over her full force. *I'm going to see it out the window on my side in just a second or two. It's your total Florida vacation car, a great big white goddam Cadillac, or maybe it's a Lincoln—*

And, yes, here it came, proving what? Well, she supposed, it proved that sometimes when you had déjà vu what you thought was going to happen next really, did happen next. It wasn't a Caddy or a Lincoln after all, but a Crown Victoria—what the gangsters in a Martin Scorsese film would no doubt call a Crown Vic.

"Whoo," she said as he helped her down the steps and off the plane. The hot sun made her feel dizzy.

"What's wrong?"

"Nothing, really. I've got déjà vu. Left over from my dream, I guess. We've been here before, that kind of thing."

"It's being in a strange place, that's all," he said, and kissed her cheek. "Come on, let the wild rumpus start."

They went to the car. Bill showed his driver's license to the young woman who had driven it out. Carol saw him check out the hem of her skirt, then sign the paper on her clipboard.

She's going to drop it, Carol thought. The feeling was now so strong it was like being on a an amusement-park ride that goes just a little too fast; all at once you realize you're edging out of the Land of Fun and into the Kingdom of Nausea. *She'll drop it, and Bill will say "Whoopsy-daisy" and pick it up for her, get an even closer look at her legs.*

But the Hertz woman didn't drop her clipboard. A white courtesy van had appeared, to take her back to the Butler Aviation terminal. She gave Bill a final smile—Carol she had ignored completely—and opened the front passenger door. She stepped up, then slipped. "Whoopsy-daisy, don't be crazy," Bill said, and took her elbow, steadying her. She gave him a smile, he gave her well-turned legs a goodbye look, and Carol stood by the growing pile of their luggage and thought, *Hey there, Mary . . .*

"Mrs. Shelton?" It was the co-pilot. He had the last bag, the case with Bill's laptop inside it, and he looked concerned. "Are you all right? You're very pale."

Bill heard and turned away from the departing white van, his face worried. If her strongest feelings about Bill were her only feelings about Bill, now that they were twenty-five years on, she would have left him when she found out about the secretary, a Clairol blonde too young to remember the Clairol slogan that went "If I have only one life to live," etc., etc. But there were other feelings. There was love, for instance. Still love. A kind that girls in Catholic-school uniforms didn't suspect, a weedy species too tough to die.

Besides, it wasn't just love that held people together. Secrets held them, and common history, and the price you paid.

"Carol?" he asked her. "Babe? All right?"

She thought about telling him no, she wasn't all right, she was drowning, but then she managed to smile and said, "It's the heat, that's all. I feel a little groggy. Get me in the car and crank up the air-conditioning. I'll be fine."

Bill took her by the elbow (*Bet you're not checking out my legs, though*, Carol thought. *You know where they go, don't you?*) and led her toward the Crown Vic as if she were a very old lady. By the time the door was closed and cool air was pumping over her face, she actually had started to feel a little better.

If the feeling comes back, I'll tell him, Carol thought. *I'll have to. It's just too strong. Not normal.*

Well, déjà vu was never normal she supposed—it was something that was part dream, part chemistry, and (she was sure she'd read this, maybe in a doctor's office somewhere while waiting for her gynecologist to go prospecting up her fifty-two-year-old twat) part the result of an electrical misfire in the brain, causing new experience to be identified as old data. A temporary hole in the pipes, hot water and cold water mingling. She closed her eyes and prayed for it to go away.

Oh, Mary, conceived without sin, pray for us who have recourse to thee.

Please ("Oh puh-lease," they used to say), not back to parochial school. This was supposed to be a vacation, not—

Floyd, what's that over there? Oh shit! Oh SHIT!

Who was Floyd? The only Floyd Bill knew was Floyd Dorning (or maybe it was Darling), the kid he'd run the snack bar with, the one who'd run off to New York with his girlfriend. Carol couldn't remember when Bill had told her about that kid, but she knew he had.

Just quit it, girl. There's nothing here for you. Slam the door on the whole train, of thought.

And that worked. There was a final whisper—*what's the story*—and then she was just Carol Shelton, on her way to Captiva Island, on her way to Palm House with her husband the renowned software designer, on their way to the beaches and those rum drinks with the little paper umbrellas sticking out of them.

They passed a Publix market. They passed an old black man minding a roadside fruit stand—he made her think of actors from the thirties and movies you saw on the American Movie Channel, an old yassuh-boss type of guy wearing bib overalls and a straw hat with a round crown. Bill made small talk, and she made it right back at him. She was faintly amazed that the little girl who had worn a Mary medallion every day from ten to sixteen had become this woman in the Donna Karan dress—that the desperate couple in that Revere apartment were these middle-aged rich folks rolling down a lush aisle of palms—but she was and they were. Once in those Revere days he had come home drunk and she had hit him and drawn blood from below his eye. Once she had been in fear of Hell, had lain half-drugged in steel stirrups, thinking, *I'm damned, I've come to damnation. A million years, and that's only the first tick of the clock.*

They stopped at the causeway toll-booth and Carol thought, *The toll-taker has a strawberry birthmark on the left side of his forehead, all mixed in with his eyebrow.*

There was no mark—the toll-taker was just an ordinary guy in his late forties or early fifties, iron-gray hair in a buzz cut, horn-rimmed specs, the kind of guy who says, "Y'all have a nahce tahm, okai?"—but the feeling began to come back, and Carol realized that now the things she thought she knew were things she really did know, at first not all of them, but then, by the time they neared the little market on the right side of Route 41, it was almost everything.

The market's called Corson's and there's a little girl out front, Carol thought. *She's wearing a red pinafore. She's got a doll, a dirty old yellow-haired thing, that she's left on the store steps so she can look at a dog in the back of a station wagon.*

The name of the market turned out to be Carson's, not Corson's, but everything else was the same. As the white Crown Vic passed, the little girl in the red dress turned her solemn face in Carol's direction, a country girl's face, although what a girl from the toolies could be doing here in rich folks' tourist country, her and her dirty yellow-headed doll, Carol didn't know.

Here's where I ask Bill how much farther, only I won't do it. Because I have to break out of this cycle, this groove. I have to.

"How much farther?" she asked him. *He says there's only one road, we can't get lost. He says he promises me we'll get to the Palm House with no problem. And, by the way, who's Floyd?*

Bill's eyebrow went up. The dimple beside his mouth appeared. "Once you get over the causeway and onto Sanibel Island, there's only one road," he said. Carol barely heard him. He was still talking about the road, her husband who had spent a dirty weekend in bed with his secretary two years ago, risking all they had done and all they had made, Bill doing that with his other face on, being the Bill Carol's mother had warned would break her heart. And later Bill trying to tell her he hadn't been able to help himself, her wanting to scream, *I once murdered a child for you, the potential of a child, anyway. How high is that price? And is this what I get in return? To reach my fifties and find out that my husband had to get into some Clairol girl's pants?*

Tell him! she shrieked. *Make him pull over and stop, make him do anything that will break you free—change one thing, change everything! You can do it—if you could put your feet up in those stirrups, you can do anything!*

But she could do nothing, and it all began to tick by faster. The two overfed crows lifted off from their splatter of lunch. Her husband asked why she was sitting that way, was it a cramp, her saying, Yes, yes, a cramp in her back but it was easing. Her mouth quacked on about déjà vu just as if she weren't drowning in it, and the Crown Vic moved forward like one of those sadistic Dodgem cars at Revere Beach. Here came Palmdale Motors on the right. And on the left? Some kind of sign for the local community theatre, a production of "Naughty Marietta."

No, it's Mary, not Marietta. Mary, mother of Jesus, Mary, mother of God, she's got her hands out . . .

Carol bent all her will toward telling her husband what was happening, because the right Bill was behind the wheel, the right Bill could still hear her. Being heard was what married love was all about.

Nothing came out. In her mind Gram said, "All the hard days are coming." In her mind a voice asked Floyd what was over there, then said, "Oh shit," then *screamed* "Oh shit!"

She looked at the speedometer and saw it was calibrated not in miles an hour but thousands of feet: they were at twenty-eight thousand. Bill was telling her that she shouldn't have slept on the plane and she was agreeing.

There was a pink house coming up, little more than a bungalow, fringed with palm trees that looked like the ones you saw in the Second World War movies, fronds framing incoming Learjets with their machine guns blazing—

Blazing. Burning hot. All at once the magazine he's holding turns into a torch. Holy Mary, mother of God, hey there, Mary, what's the story—

They passed the house. The old man sat on the porch and watched them go by. The lenses of his rimless glasses glinted in the sun. Bill's hand established a beachhead on her hip. He said something about how they might pause to refresh themselves between the doffing of her dress and the donning of her shorts and she agreed, although they were never going to get to Palm House. They were going to go down this road and down this road, they were for the white Crown Vic and the white Crown Vic was for them, forever and ever amen.

The next billboard would say "Palm House 2 Mi." Beyond it was the one saying that Mother of Mercy Charities helped the Florida sick. Would they help her?

Now that it was too late she was beginning to understand. Beginning to see the light the way she could see the subtropical sun sparkling off the water on their left. Wondering how many wrongs she had done in her life, how many sins if you liked that word, God knew her parents and her Gram certainly had, sin this and sin that and wear the medallion between those growing things the boys look at. And years later she had lain in bed with her new husband on hot summer nights, knowing a decision had to be made, knowing the clock was ticking, the cigarette butt was smoldering, and she remembered making the decision, not telling him out loud because about some things you could be silent.

Her head itched. She scratched it. Black flecks came swirling down past her face. On the Crown Vic's instrument panel the speedometer froze at sixteen thousand feet and then blew out, but Bill appeared not to notice.

Here came a mailbox with a Grateful Dead sticker pasted on the front; here came a little black dog with its head down, trotting busily, and God how her head itched, black flakes drifting in the air like fallout and Mother Teresa's face looking out of one of them.

"Mother of Mary Charities Help the Florida Hungry—Won't *You* Help *Us?*"
Floyd. What's that over there? Oh shit.
She has time to see something big. And to read the word "Delta."
"Bill? *Bill?*"
His reply, clear enough but nevertheless coming from around the rim of the universe: "Christ, honey, what's in your *hair?*"

She plucked the charred remnant of Mother Teresa's face from her lap and held it out to him, the older version of the man she had married, the secretary-fucking man she had married, the man who had nonetheless rescued her from people who thought that you could live forever in paradise if you only lit enough candles and wore the blue blazer and stuck to the approved skipping rhymes. Lying there with this man one hot summer night while the drug deals went on upstairs and Iron Butterfly sang "In-A-Gadda-Da-Vida" for the nine-billionth time, she had asked what he thought you got, you know, after. When your part in the show is over. He had taken her in his arms and held her, down the beach she had heard the jangle-jingle of the midway and the bang of the Dodgem cars and Bill—

Bill's glasses were melted to his face. One eye bulged out of its socket. His mouth was a bloodhole. In the trees a bird was crying, a bird was *screaming*, and Carol began to scream with it, holding out the charred fragment of paper with Mother Teresa's picture on it, screaming, watching as his cheeks turned black and his forehead swarmed and his neck split open like a poisoned goiter, screaming, she was screaming, somewhere Iron Butterfly was singing "In-A-Gadda-Da-Vida" and she was screaming.

"Carol?"
It was Bill's voice, from a thousand miles away. His hand was on her, but it was concern in his touch rather than lust.

She opened her eyes and looked around the sun-brilliant cabin of the Lear 35, and for a moment she understood everything—in the way one understands the tremendous import of a dream upon the first moment of waking. She remembered asking him what he believed you got, you know, *after*, and he had said you probably got what you'd always thought you *would* get, that if Jerry Lee Lewis thought he was going to Hell for playing boogie-woogie, that's exactly where he'd go. Heaven, Hell, or Grand Rapids, it was your choice—or the choice of those who had taught you what to believe. It was the human mind's final great service: the perception of eternity in the place where you'd always expected to spend it.

"Carol? You O.K., babe?" In one hand was the magazine he'd been reading, a *Newsweek* with Mother Teresa on the cover. "SAINTHOOD NOW?" it said in white.

Looking around wildly at the cabin, she was thinking, *It happens at sixteen thousand feet, I have to tell them. I have to warn them.*

But it was fading, all of it, the way those feelings always did. They went like dreams, or cotton candy turning into a sweet mist just above your tongue.

"Landing? Already?" She felt wide awake, but her voice sounded thick and muzzy.

"It's fast, huh?" he said, sounding pleased, as if he'd flown it himself instead of paying for it. "Floyd says we'll be on the ground in—"

"Who?" she asked. The cabin of the little plane was warm but her fingers were cold. "Who?"

"Floyd. You know, the *pilot*." He pointed his thumb toward the cockpit's left-hand seat. They were descending into a scrim of clouds. The plane began to shake. "He says we'll be on the ground in Fort Myers in twenty minutes. You took a hell of a jump, girl. And before that you were moaning."

Carol opened her mouth to say it was that feeling, the one you could only say what it was in French, something *vu* or *vous*, but it was fading and all she said was "I had a nightmare."

There was a beep as Floyd the pilot switched the seat-belt light on. Carol turned her head. Somewhere below, waiting for them now and forever, was a white car from Hertz, a gangster car, the kind the characters in a Martin Scorsese movie would probably call a Crown Vic. She looked at the cover of the news magazine, at the face of Mother Teresa, and all at once she remembered skipping rope behind Our Lady of Angels, skipping to one of the forbidden rhymes, skipping to the one that went *Hey there, Mary, what's the story, save my ass from Purgatory.*

All the hard days are coming, her Gram had said. She had pressed the medal into Carol's palm, wrapped the chain around her fingers. *The hard days are coming.*

KAREN JOY FOWLER

The Travails

Karen Joy Fowler lives in Davis, California, and is the author of two novels,
Sarah Canary *and* The Sweetheart Season—*both of which received the New
York Times Notable Books distinction. Her short fiction has been published
in various anthologies and magazines, and collected in* Artificial Things *and*
Black Glass. *"The Travails" is reprinted from the latter.*

In last year's volume of The Year's Best Fantasy and Horror, *we published
a story called "Gulliver at Home" by John Kessel, inspired by Jonathan Swift's
satire,* Gulliver's Travels. *Fowler says that "The Travails" was written in
response to Kessel's story.*

—T. W.

I hope I may with Justice pronounce myself an Author perfectly blameless, against whom Tribes
of Answerers, Considerers, Observers, Reflectors, Detecters, Remarkers, will never be able to
find Matter for exercising their Talents.   —LEMUEL GULLIVER

September 28, 1699

Dear Lemuel,

When you think of us, think of us missing you. As Betty cleared the Table
from Breakfast this morning, she burst into Tears. "There is Papa," she said,
pointing to a Crumb of Bread. And I perfectly comprehended her. I saw you in
my Mind, your Speck of a Boat, no bigger than a Crumb on the whole of the
Kitchen Table. God speed you back to us.

And then we sat no longer, because of all the daily Work to be done. Now
it is Evening and I take Time to write. I hope you received my Letter of July
3rd. Our Betty is Ten Years today and, though only Months have passed since
your Departure, I believe she is much altered and not the little Girl you left. I
feel the Passage of Years more acutely in the Children's Lives than in my own.
With a ten year Daughter, I cannot be accounted young. Already she is more
than half as old as I when you came courting. I imagine therefore that she is
already half done with being mine. A melancholy Thought.

But the Days grow ever more beautiful, so I shall look outside rather than in.

How do you endure a Day at Sea with no Trees about you? The Elm at our Window is all turned, its Leaves as golden as Egg Yolks. The Moon tonight is as big as a Tea Tray, but of course you have that too, wherever you are.

Johnny is growing out of all his Clothes, and Betty and I are kept forever sewing. I never pass Mrs. Nardac in the Shops but that she informs me that the Islands where you are sailing are filled with Women who wear no Stitch of Clothing. If they cover their Bodies at all, she says, they do it with their Hair, which is longer and thicker and more lustrous than anything any Woman in London can do with Wigs. Mermaids then, I say, teasing. No, no, they are quite real, she assures me. She thinks you will not come Home this time and she wishes me to know she thinks this.

But I know otherwise! And such an Adventure we had when the Weather first chilled. Suddenly we were overrun with Ants. What you now picture, double. Ants poured into the House from every Crack in every Wall. Not just the Kitchen, they assaulted us in the Parlour and even the Bed Chambers. Oh, it was War and went on for three whole Days. I plotted and laid Traps. You would imagine we had every Advantage, from Size to Cunning, and yet we could not win through. In truth, they seemed uncannily clever at times. Johnny even made use of a Weapon I must leave you to imagine. His Face when I came upon him! "I washed away great Hordes of them," he insisted, but I took him to Bed by his Ear and it has taken me many Days of scrubbing to see the Humour in it. And then, with no more Warning than we had at the Beginning, they vanished and we are at Peace again.

Mrs. Nardac thinks that Johnny should be sent away to School, but of course he is far too young still. I know I anticipate your Wishes in the Matter by keeping him at Home for now. When you return, you will find us all,

Your loving Family and,
Your Mary

Yuletide, 1701

Dearest, dearest,

I have received Word today from a dear Mrs. Biddle that you are recovered from the fast Grip of the Sea and safe aboard her Husband's Ship. What joyous Tidings! What Joy to write a Letter I know you will receive! I ran all the way Home and shouted the News without pausing to every Soul I passed. Then Betty and I wore ourselves out with the Weeping and Relief. You are on your way Home to us and we are anxious to see you healthy and unchanged in your Regard. In truth, something in Mrs. Biddle's Letter betrayed Concern regarding your State of Mind, although I remind myself that she has also written here, *twice* in one Letter, that you are well. Eat and rest now, my Darling. Take care of your Dear Self.

We are all healthy here. Carolers came to the Window last Night. They sang of good King Wenceslas and Bethlehem. Snow fell, but gently, on their Scarves and Caps, while their Voices rose into the Air. Tonight all is Snow-Silent and I cannot choose which it is I like best, the Silence or the Noise of the World. Greedily, I would have them both. The Whole of it is the only thing that will suit me tonight. Mrs. Biddle said that you have such Stories to tell us. And we, you!

Such a Merry Christmas God has given us!
Your Mary

August 8, 1702

Dear Lemuel,

I have been melancholy since you left. I so wanted you Home, and then nothing matched my Hopes. I am sorry for the Quarrels and sorry, too, that you made your Department while we were still quarrelling.

You have made fine Provision for us and left me no Fear that we shall ever fall upon the Parish. The little Flock of Sheep you left has already increased its Number by Five. For this I am grateful. The new House is Tight and Warm, in spite of being so Large. Since you spent so little Time in it, it often feels entirely mine. I cannot picture you at the Table or in the Bed. I never see you, sleeping under a Book in the Parlour, as I did in our old, damp Cottage. And since you chose, much against my Wishes, to send Johnny to School—really, he is not nearly so grown as you think him—it is a quiet House with me sometimes in one End of it, and Betty far away in the other. I find myself missing even Mrs. Nardac.

But I do confess I often enjoy the Size of it. Not when I am dusting, perhaps! But I like a Room up the Stairs. As I write this, from my Desk I look down on the Fields and Lanes and Gardens as if I had the Eyes of the Trees. I look down on all the other tiny Nests of the tiny People. They love, they fight, they dispute, they cheat, they betray, but I am far above it and absolutely untouched. And then Betty comes, with a Scrape or a Slight to suffer over. A Letter arrives from Johnny, and between those Words the Headmaster has allowed him to send, I can read his Misery. I am part of the World again, with all its Hurts and Affections. And I cannot remember why I ever thought it best to be otherwise.

Yesterday Betty found a Fledgling blown from its Nest. She has brought it inside and made the softest Box, but its Wing is damaged and I fear we can never release it. She is kept up constantly, even at night, with feeding. No one is more tender with Small Creatures than a Young Girl, and yet my Heart rebels against a Wild Thing kept forever in a Box.

We complete our Menagerie with Rats! Large as Dogs they sound as they pound over the Roof, but I have engaged a Man to deal with them. Money can buy Men for many but perhaps not all Purposes.

Mary

October 5, 1706

Dear Lemuel,

Where does this find you? This is a Letter I shall have to send in a Bottle with a Cork, by a strong Arm. It will wash ashore some months hence in Paradise and the Natives will read it, wondering if such a Place as green as England can really exist.

I fear my last Letter was uncharitable. I meant to be generous, but forgot. You know my Temper, little as you have seen it over the Years. I wished the Letter back as soon as I had sent it. Likely you did not receive it and are reading this in Wonder of what I might have written.

So I will only repeat that I was disappointed by your hasty Departure, but this time I was not surprised. We no longer seem to fit together, you and I.

When you are Meditative, I wish to be Doing: when I am larkish, you choose that Moment to be sober. You are so credulous, I must learn again each time not to teaze. We are two Magnets, with an attractive but also a repulsive Power over one another. I fear the closer we stand, the more the Latter is evident.

"You married a Dreamer," Mrs. Balnibarb said to me in the Lanes but yesterday, "and no Woman can live in the Clouds." Yet I think I am one Woman who could, and wait only the Invitation. Time would teach us to mesh again, but Time is the one thing I never have from you.

Betty has a Beau in Mrs. Balnibarb's middle boy, William. Are you pleased? He calls each Thursday and is as clean and polite as you could ask. He is a Farmer's Son and I count his Prospects tolerable. Her Feelings are more difficult to discern. She colours if his Name is spoken but makes no effort in his Presence to delight him. She is still so young and I will counsel Delays if my Counsel is sought. I am sure this is as you would wish.

We shall at least want him a more sensible Man than his Father. Mr. Balnibarb often walks the Lanes so lost in Thought, I have seen William forced to cuff him soundly on the Ear, lest he walk into a Tree! And he has now given up that Farming proved over the Centuries, in favour of new Methods of Planting and Irrigation designed by a Scientist in London and circulated in our little County by Pamphlet. This Pamphlet argues the Water will have more Vitality if it is Pumped uphill before being spread downhill. Its Author has surely never seen a Field in his Life. As a result, all the Farms but Balnibarb's enjoyed a most bountiful Harvest.

Our own Walnut Tree was so loaded with Fruits this year, it was dangerous to walk beneath. Nuts, like missiles, rained down at the slightest Breeze. We sit in front of the Fire and have our Pleasure, picking out the Meats and dreaming away the Evenings.

I do request that you discourage Johnny from going to Sea. I fear your Stories have had the opposite Effect. This is most unfair to me.

Rats on the Roofs, again, but I know just the Man to engage for it.

Mary

February 7, 1708

Dear Lemuel,

A short Letter today, and sad, to inform you of the Death of your Father. Betty and I were able to wait on him in his final Days. I know it is Customary to assure the Bereaved that the Sufferings were slight and not of long Duration. I wish I could, in Honesty, tell you this. Betty wept and wished him back, but I do not. He had already outlived his Health and Happiness, and if ever Death came as a Release, it came so to him. He missed you deeply and spoke of you often.

The Night after his Death he came to me in a Dream. He told me with great Clarity of his Willingness to be shed of a World he had always seen as Wicked. I was greatly impressed by the Vividness of this Dream, but as I have spoken of it, I have learnt that such Dreams are common on the Night of a Death. Whimsical Mr. Lugg believes the Dead have the one Night to return and tell us what needs to be said. I wish I had known to expect him. What Questions you could ask the Dead with a little Forewarning!

There were many at his Funeral, and all so respectful and sorry for your Loss. Johnny stood for you.

Our own Health, mine and our Children's, continues good. Betty and William have reached an Understanding. They will be married when the Year's Mourning is over and Johnny, young as he is, will give her to William.

Your own,
Mary

January 23, 1710

Dear Lemuel,

Your last Visit has finally borne its Fruit. I send this Letter to let you know your new Son, Samuel, has arrived. He came somewhat earlier than we antici- pated. More than a Month has passed since his Birth, and I am only now able to take up Pen to tell you so. The Passage was perilous this time, but we are in Safe Harbour. Betty insists he favours me, but perhaps your Face is not so familiar to her. For my Part, his Face is exactly that of our dearest Johnny at the same age.

Betty, too, expects her second Child, so Son and Grandchildren will all grow up cozy together. Her little Anne grows daily. I will write again in the New Year when I hope to be stronger and more at Leisure.

Your loving,
Mary

July 5, 1712

Dear Lemuel,

I cannot know if my last Letter arrived, scrawled as it was in my Haste and Panic. But I send this one quickly after to let you know that Samuel's Fever has ended and his Recovery seems assured. I could not bear to think of a Day without him or to imagine that he might pass from this World to the Next without you once setting Eyes upon his Face. How could you risk it?

I am too Joyous to scold, but I wonder at your Willingness to be so much away. There is something unnatural and inhuman about such Detachment, as if you cared no more for us than for the Sheep or the Horses.

Here we live in the Dailiness of each other, that Dailiness that you have fled. Enough. Betty is preparing a Feast, as Johnny arrives today from London. He set out at once on hearing of our Distress, but we were able to reach him by Post with our Joy. When he is finally here, my Joy will be Complete.

Your loving wife,
Mary

November 13, 1715

Dear Lemuel,

So much Time has passed since I had any Word of you, I fear the Worst. I console myself that you have never come to me in such a Dream as I had of your dear, departed Father. Perhaps this Letter will find you yet.

All is not as well as I could wish. I am sorely troubled for our darling Daughter's sake. She comes to the House with her Children much against William's Desires. Much against my Desires she returns to him. I have seen Marks upon her Wrists and Neck and wish, before I consented to the Marriage, that I had heeded the way he whips his Horses. They are the noblest of Animals and so mild little Anne, herself, can ride. Yet all have long, deep Scars along their Flanks.

I long to undress Anne and examine her own Legs but have not yet had a Moment to do so. Dearest Annie, who once bubbled like a Brook, has fallen silent and sucks on her Fingers. She hides in the Stables, preferring Beasts to People.

William was able to govern his Temper well enough when Johnny was at Home. He is, of course, within his Rights and so thinks us defenseless against him. He will find otherwise. A Man can be engaged for almost any Purpose, as I have had every Occasion to learn.

It is a wicked World. Your Father told me so when he was most in a Position to know. The more I see of it, the more I wonder at your Desire to see so much of it. We are a wicked Race, we People, and it is better to be acquainted with as few of us as possible.

Do I sound here like your own Mary? I feel quite altered. Johnny has gone to Sea at last and all is Desolation. He sailed for the Indies in September.

I once saw something in William's Face that surprised me. That something was your Face. And I thought, then, of your Father and wondered if he had ever told you of the World's Wickedness, had ever made you feel a Part of it. It has always been too easy to persuade you, my Love. All these years, all these Voyages—were you protecting us from yourself?

If you will be persuaded by someone, let it be me. First, I would have you believe that every Man and every Woman has a Kingdom of Evil somewhere in their Hearts. Yours is no bigger than some, and smaller than most. You are a Good Man and we are not afraid of you.

Second, you love us. Confess it, you are haunted by us. You can never go far enough to escape. We fill your Thoughts in spite of yourself. You mold your Memories about us, as if you had been here all along.

And now I will turn my Persuasions on myself; I will reason myself out of this Morbid Humour. My Life has not been a hard one. Perhaps I might have asked to be sheltered more. Perhaps I might have asked to live an Arm away from the Wicked World.

But I did not ask this. I asked to see the World, just as you did, so I will make no Complaint at seeing it. There are far worse things to be endured than an absent Husband, as Betty brings me constant Proof. And I am finished forever with blaming you for your Absence. I am hard at work to not blame you for Johnny's.

Indeed, I pray for your Return. Come Home to us now, surprise us just when everyone has said that this Time you are surely lost. Let us embrace again. We will find a way to live together, you and I, your Children and Grandchildren. Stay with us as long as you will, a valued Guest.

And then go. We have no Wish to hold you. We have become the People you would have us be, and you need never fear hurting us again. We will rejoice at your Coming; your Going will cause us no Moment of Suffering. More than this, I think, no Man can ask of his Family.

As always,
Mary

TERRY LAMSLEY

Suburban Blight

Terry Lamsley spent most of his childhood in the south of England. He has been living for seventeen years in Buxton, in Derbyshire, where many of his stories are set. For some time he's been employed by social services, working with disturbed adolescents and their families. His stories have been published in All Hallows, Cemetery Dance, Ghosts & Scholars, Midnight Never Comes, Dark Terrors: The Gollancz Book of Horror, *and* Lethal Kisses *and have been reprinted in* Best New Horror *and* The Year's Best Fantasy and Horror. *His self-published collection* Under the Crust *was nominated for the World Fantasy Award and the title novella won the award in 1994. Ash-Tree Press reprinted* Under the Crust *and also published his second collection,* Conference With the Dead. *Ash-Tree Press will publish a third collection in 1999.*

Lamsley considers "Suburban Blight" his first science fantasy story. That may be true, but it also is a quite horrific, wonderfully creepy tale. It was originally published in Dark Terrors 4.

—E. D.

W ell, they've started," Ann Hollins said. "I just drove past. They've knocked the front wall down and they're driving huge machines all over the place."

Her husband folded the newspaper he'd been reading and began to tap it on his knee. "They're digging them out then?"

"Not that I could see," Ann said. "Just tearing everything up, irrespective. Most of the trees are down already. They've simply uprooted them and set about them with chainsaws. The noise is terrible."

"But surely they're exhuming the bodies first?"

Ann shook her head. "As far as I can see, if they *are* digging the corpses out, and not just ploughing them in, they must be doing it with a JCB. It's all so undignified. There are men everywhere, smashing the headstones with iron bars and tossing the bits into skips."

"I suppose they want to get the job over as soon as they can," Hal Hollins said. "To cause as little inconvenience as possible to Copeland Comprehensive next door."

"That school should have been shut down while they did the work. It's a terrible thing for the children to go through, all that *desecration*. The kids can see everything that's going on."

"I expect the teachers will keep them away," Hal said, without much conviction.

"There were at least twenty pupils sitting on what was left of the wall watching the workmen when I went by. Hoping for the sight of a body, I expect."

Ann went into the kitchen to fill the kettle. "What bothers me," she shouted, "is that it was the last place around here where you could see trees. Real big old trees, like you get in the countryside. It's hard to remember what this area was like ten or fifteen years ago, before they built the estates. It was almost rural then. We used to say we lived in a village."

"Until now, there were still all sorts of animals living in that churchyard," Hal said. "Birds and rabbits and things. I've even seen foxes some evenings."

"Mr Singer says he thinks there were badgers," Ann said, returning to the room holding a tray. "He's noticed scratch marks like badgers make around one of the older family vaults. He thinks they might have been converting it into a set. They're protected creatures now, aren't they? It's illegal to dig them out, or disturb them in any way."

"Unless you work for the Council," Hal growled sourly.

"I wonder where the poor creatures will go now. There's nowhere left round here for them to build homes, is there?"

"That bloody factory started it all off," Hal observed. "When they knocked down Camber Woods to build that, and the car park to go with it, it was the beginning of the end. The whole location has changed now—lost its individuality."

Ann nodded. "It's become just another part of the city sprawl."

"I wish they'd knock the swimming baths down. The building is a disgrace, and dangerous too."

"The Council never answered the letter you sent them about it, did they?" Ann asked, pouring tea.

"I wrote again last week. Still no reply."

"Bastards," hissed Mrs Hollins, as she passed her husband a tin of biscuits. "You'll have to go to the Town Hall and talk to someone. I might come with you."

The Hollins' mournful dog, Chaplin, watched his master and mistress consume their afternoon refreshments with impatience. He moaned and fretted, and went and laid down close to the front door, giving the broadest possible hint to Hal of his requirements. Not that that was necessary: the Hollins household ran to a tight routine. At two-thirty exactly Mr Hollins took Chaplin's lead off its hook and the two of them set out on their afternoon excursion. It was something they both looked forward to. Hal Hollins, facing long-term, if not permanent unemployment, was glad of any chance he had of making himself useful, even if only to his pet.

Taking his time, because Chaplin was an old dog, he walked halfway around the high wire wall protecting the perimeter of Camber Polytechnic, nipped cautiously through the relentless traffic across City Road, and ventured through the edge of the menacing, deceptively uninhabited-looking New Ways Estate to take a short cut to the car park at the back of the baths. He felt it his duty, almost, to visit the building at least once a week, to monitor its decline. And it gave him some satisfaction to see the hated edifice slowly fall apart. A cheap thrill, he knew, but one he was addicted to.

The building's construction had been part of an ill-advised attempt by the Council of the nearby metropolis, in competition with a number of more prosperous rival cities in more attractive and temperate parts of the world, to be given the chance to host the Olympic Games. The venture had failed, and a number of arenas and sports grounds, specially built to tempt the world's top athletes to this unglamorous part of the North of England, remained scattered round the edges of the city: monuments to overweening civic ambition. The huge, unwanted swimming baths was one of them.

Someone had tried to set fire to the place since his last visit, Hal noticed. Bags of dumped rubbish had been piled up along the side wall and ignited. Sooty burn marks reached ten feet up the metal frames that contained the windows, and the glass in some of them had been shattered by the heat. The affected windows had been hastily blocked in with boards. The boarded area looked like an eye-patch on a vast flat face. Some yards away, at the same level, the sun was reflected in the remaining glass like a single glaring eye. A heavily padlocked door between was a grim, forbidding, tight-shut mouth.

The attempt at fire-raising had been unsuccessful because the building was mostly made of bricks and metal and glass, unlike the chemical plant that had once occupied the site and the much larger area of desolation that still lay beyond. That had gone up like a rocket one night, when protesters had destroyed the factory for fear of what it was rumoured was being created there. Hal had himself been active in the forefront of the campaign against the owners of the plant, who, it was suspected, were depositing unwanted byproducts from their manufactury in the underground river that ran beneath the site. Hal and many of his neighbours had been determined to get the place closed. He had not expected such a violent and drastic solution to the problem, but, when it had come, he had secretly welcomed it. Later, when the baths had been constructed on the vacant ground, he had taken it as a personal insult, but he soon discovered few others shared his strength of feeling, as there were many other more outrageous civic scandals in the offing at the time. Nevertheless, his resentment at what he considered to be cynically opportunistic and inappropriate exploitation of the site by the Council lingered on, and festered within him.

It was something of a miracle, Hal thought, as he circled the building, that so few of the dozens of big windows that formed at least seventy percent of the sides of the building had been smashed by the hordes of young vandals that roamed the area. Many of these lived in New Ways Estate, not two hundred yards away, but, apart from occasional sorties like the one that had produced the failed arson attempt, they kept away from the immediate vicinity of the baths. But then, the building always had, right from the start, a bad reputation.

An octogenarian hero of the Second World War had drowned in the shallow end, unnoticed by the baths' attendants, during a special over-sixties session in the first week of opening, and another bather had somehow managed to electrocute herself in the changing rooms less than a month later. These two incidents would probably have been forgotten eventually, and put down to bad luck, had it not been for the collapse of part of the viewers' balcony during the local schools' first Charity Swimming Gala, tipping tons of masonry and two rows of parents onto the children in the water below. This accident had resulted in five further deaths and more than twenty serious injuries. The general opinion after that was that the place was jerry-built. Others said the building was doomed, or even cursed.

The architect responsible for the design of the baths committed suicide before he could be summoned to the subsequent investigation, but this merely confirmed local people's feeling that the place was dangerous, somewhere to avoid. Perhaps it went back to the earlier use of the site by the biochemical company, who, it was believed, had permanently polluted the area. Even the students from the Polytechnic, whose subsidized custom had been relied upon to keep the baths out of the red, became reluctant to use the facility. The multiple rape of two nurses among the automatic fast-food and drinks dispensers in the otherwise unattended refreshments area one afternoon, by a gang of inner-city youths, put the lid on it, and the building was closed down.

The Councillors who, under a lot of local opposition, had pushed ahead with the construction of the baths and other stadiums intended for the Olympic Games, were keen to get their hands on the valuable site so they could sell it to regain some of the ratepayers' squandered money, but they were not in too much of a hurry to do this. A local election was not far off, and their political opponents would go for their throats over the conspicuous waste of money if the building was demolished after so short a life. They held on, and let the structure decay at its own speed, only patching it up as cheaply as possible when necessary, in the hope that its existence would be forgotten, temporarily. That was why they failed to respond to Hal's unwelcome letters of complaint about how dangerous the place was and what an eyesore it had become. They didn't want to know.

Hal stooped down to let Chaplin off the lead and left the old dog to hobble off on his own tour of inspection. The site was splattered with dozens of small heaps of dog turds, many of them Chaplin's own work, which provided him with inexhaustible interest. With nothing half as fascinating to occupy his mind, Hal went and stood close to the baths and peered through one of the dusty, greenish windows.

Inside, the building was beginning to look like an untended greenhouse. Strong winds had removed sections of the roof and the glass panels at one side soon after it had gone out of business. This damage had not been repaired until weeks later, by which time a great deal of dust and dirt had blown into the baths. The following spring's rains had leaked in through numerous cracks and brought to life thousands of seeds hidden in the dust, producing a variety of plants that had flourished for a while until a long dry spell had shrivelled most of them up. Then, two years later, the season had been milder and moister, creating within the building an atmosphere something like tropical, and the seeds and weeds that had survived in there had gone wild with gratitude and sprung into monstrous growth.

At first they'd formed a pleasant, multi-shaded green lawn in the bottom of the swimming pool, that had then stretched eagerly up towards the sun until it filled and overflowed the sides at the deep end. At about that time countless other plants, whose development had been hidden in the remains of the balcony, began to show their heads over the tops of the rows of seats and now, weeks later, Hal found he was staring into a dense, tangled jungle taller than himself.

An imprisoned jungle, that seemed desperate to get out. Branches of compressed shrubbery and small trees pushed hard against the glass in front of Hal's nose, like the arms of concentration camp victims pressing helplessly against the wire fences of their enclosures. The rapidity of the forced growth of the plants inside had been violent and unnatural, producing vegetation that looked virulent and somehow aggressive. There appeared to be a tremendous pressure building up in there that Hal, in a moment of vision, thought might soon demolish the building in some great explosion of concerted upwards and outwards thrust. Thickening tendrils of creepers that had already managed to force their way through unrepaired gaps in the wall clung like desperate fingers to the outer surface of the building, and were tugging at that against which they gripped, as though trying to haul their lower parts out into the car park and freedom.

One of them, tipped with angry pink buds, seemed to be reaching for Hal's throat. He hadn't noticed it when he had approached the building, and stepped back at once when he spotted it, grimacing somewhat shamefacedly. The peculiar plant looked particularly disgusting—obscene, even—but Hal wondered at the strength of his reaction to it. He had never before had the experience of being discountenanced by a mere vegetable.

The plant, whatever it was, belonged to a species unfamiliar to Hal, who fancied himself as something of an amateur horticulturist. His first thought was that it was from somewhere *else*, meaning he was certain it wasn't indigenous to the region or even the country: nothing like it, he was sure, grew naturally in an English garden. His hobbyist's curiosity overcame his revulsion after some moments, and he reached out and snapped off a section of the tip of the tendril to give it a closer inspection.

As he studied the cutting, one of three pink buds attached to it began to pulsate slightly, like a tiny heart, to Hal's astonishment. He held it closer to his face and saw that something inside the bud seemed to be struggling to get out. What appeared to be a miniature face emerged finally from between the tightly enfolded petals—a face with tiny, black, swerving eyes and a snapping mouth. Hal searched frantically in his pockets with his free hand for his reading glasses, to get a better look at the thing.

In his momentary preoccupation he missed most of what happened next, because he was swapping one pair of spectacles for the other when the creature broke free and flew up into the air close to his forehead. He did get a brief impression of its appearance as it hung for a moment in front of his eyes—it looked like a tiny bat with almost human features, but he was sure that was a false impression probably caused by its over-close proximity to his eyes.

Some kind of insect, then, he supposed—a moth, perhaps?

In his confusion, as he tried to get a better look at the thing that was now circling around his head, emitting a barely audible piping sound, he dropped the tendril bearing the bud from which the creature had emerged, and automatically bent down to retrieve it. When he stood up again, and got his glasses on his nose, the thing had vanished, though he fancied he could still hear the sound it had been making, somewhere above him.

At last, baffled, he shook his head and stowed away the sample twig he had snapped off in his jacket pocket. He intended to try to identify it later because it looked intriguingly ugly and *unhealthy*, and was also the breeding place of possibly pestiferous insects, assuming the creature he had seen was indeed some kind of insect. He had his doubts about that, but what else could it have been? Anyway, if, as he suspected, the plant itself was both rare and poisonous, it could be another stick he could beat the Council with, in his efforts to get the baths demolished.

Out in the middle of the car park, next to a burnt-out Datsun dumped by joyriders, Chaplin wuffed at him grumpily, bored already, and eager to continue on. Hal patted his thigh and held out the lead invitingly, but the mutt stood its ground, insisting his master went to *him*. A number of times in the past Hal had noticed Chaplin's reluctance to venture too near the walls of the derelict baths; a behavioural peculiarity that seemed to affect other visiting dogs, as there was a turd-free zone about ten feet wide all around the building. Since his pet was not normally stubborn, Hal gave way to the creature and went and connected the two of them together with the nylon umbilical. Chaplin lurched stiffly onto all four legs, staggered a little, and walked uncomfortably on ahead. It was a bad day for his bones and joints. The old dog was half-blind too, with a tendency to trip and bump over and into ever bigger things. Hal wondered how long their walks together could continue.

A couple of times, as they made their way towards one of the many gaps in the sagging fence that provided unofficial exits from the car park, Hal glanced at the sky above him, thinking he could hear the bleeping noise the insect that had escaped from the bud had made, but the air was empty up there, as far as he could see. Nevertheless, the sound continued even when all other noise was drowned in the din of heavy traffic grinding in and out of the industrial estate through which he made his way homeward by an oblique and bleakly over-familiar route.

"I agree," Ann said into the phone, "it's a bloody scandal, but what can we do?"

She flashed Hal a brief, humourless smile of welcome as he entered the room, and squirmed in her chair. She was obviously in a heated condition.

"God, don't I know it," she continued, "but people round here are *like* that! They'll moan and complain to each other, but, when it comes down to it, they'll do nothing to help themselves. If you try to give a lead, and go out on a limb for them, they'll drop you in the shit at the first sign of opposition."

She switched into a listening mode. Her eyes turned up and went out of focus, and her mouth dropped slightly open. Occasionally she grunted in emphatic agreement.

Hal unleashed Chaplin, removed his shoes and socks, sat down, and scratched his hot, damp feet.

At last Ann said, "He's here now, if you want a word with him. He's just got back." She thrust the phone towards her husband, with her palm clamped over the mouthpiece. "It's Mr Singer," she hissed conspiratorially. "He's been down to St Chad's."

Hal pulled a face and accepted the receiver reluctantly. After a moment he said, "No, I couldn't bring myself to go near the place today. I knew the sight of it would upset me."

"I couldn't believe what I was seeing," Mr Singer squawked. Outrage came easily to him, and he was wound up tight as a whelk with indignation now. "The Council is out of control. The lunatics have taken over." He sounded almost scared as well as angry, as though he had witnessed or been involved in some dangerous accident. Hal listened to his neighbour's ranting protestations and made a few mild, calming responses when given the opportunity. Ann watched him, and winked satirically from time to time.

"Well, he certainly feels strongly about the churchyard," Hal said when he was finally able to replace the receiver.

"Doesn't he just," Ann agreed. "It's not the usual sort of thing he gets worked up about though, is it? He's more a 'ban porn in the shops, violence on the telly, and castrate the gays' man. It's not often he gets involved in local, practical affairs." The Hollins were themselves active campaigners for and against a variety of issues of the day, and saw themselves as rather isolated, embattled figures as a result, though they enjoyed the notoriety generated by their rogue politicking.

"I never managed to get him to support me about the baths," Hal complained, slightly peevishly. "He seemed to think things like that don't matter."

"Anyway, we should encourage him now," Ann said. "He's a wild card, but he could be a useful ally. He could bore the opposition into submission. Can you imagine him marching through the Town Hall demanding justice at the top of his voice for hours on end?"

"That'd stir them up."

"I wonder *why* he's so concerned, all of a sudden. Could it be the badgers, do you think?"

"What does Singer know about badgers? Less than sod all, I should think," Hal said. "If there were badgers in that churchyard, I'll eat the dog's dinner. They're timid creatures, and it's too near the main roads. If they had been daft enough to take up residence there, some of them would have been run over, and we'd have seen their bodies. They travel about a lot at night, and they're hopeless at crossing roads. Those scratches old Singer spotted were probably made by kids trying to dig into the family tombs to look for rings on the corpses' fingers. It's the sort of thing they get up to nowadays. Nothing's sacred."

"It's not surprising, is it, with the example the Council's setting?" Ann observed. "I dread to think what effect the destruction of the graveyard will have on all those children in the school next door."

"Hardly any, probably. They see far worse things in the horror videos they watch that Singer gets so het up about. I don't suppose the sight of a few old stones and bones will give them nightmares, or lead them into depravity."

"Even so," Ann said, "I think that's the line we should take if we're going to protest to the Council. The corruption of innocent young minds is a hot issue at the moment. It's a good angle."

"*Are* we going to protest?" Hal said. "Is it worth it now the graveyard is in ruins?"

"Why not? We might make those bastards in the Town Hall sweat a little. I told Singer I'd help him have a go at them. Didn't you?"

"I said I'd take a look at the place this evening," Hal admitted, "to see what I think."

"There you go," Ann said. "United we stand. You'll have to help him stir the shit now, or he'll never stop bothering us. He thinks you're a shrewd operator, you know."

"You're joking," Hal interjected.

"His very words," Ann insisted. "So, if we support him now, he'll have to back you up about the baths. You know he's always going on about his sense of honour."

Hal took the point and groaned in submission.

Ann had never quite understood why her husband took the continued existence of the stricken public baths so personally, since it would obviously fall down in its own good time anyway, but she humoured his odd aversion.

Hal was sitting in his tiny study a couple of hours later when he heard the piping noise again. It seemed slightly louder now, perhaps because there was no ambient sound in the room to mask it. The double-glazed window was shut, as was the door, creating perfect silence within. After carefully closing the botanical book he had been perusing, using the section of the plant from the baths he had been trying to identify as a temporary bookmark, Hal removed his reading glasses and stood up.

The low ceiling, white-painted, was little more than a foot above his head. The room was full of light from the now setting sun. Hal tipped back his head, turned slowly around, and surveyed the inverted horizon above him. No sign at all of any small creature—not even a fly. The globular plastic light shade fitted almost flush with the ceiling. Hal reached up, unscrewed it and peered inside.

Empty.

He replaced it and stared all around him anxiously, aware that the tiny sound was continuing as he did so, somewhere close to his ears. It seemed to move about as he did.

Then the solution to its whereabouts dawned on him at last. He reached gingerly up with his right hand above the crown of his head, lowered his fingers, and touched something dry and quivering in his hair.

He snatched his hand sharply away in revulsion. He was not normally disturbed by the presence, however close, of insects, but this one felt different. It was hot, for one thing, and soft, like a ball of feathers. It yielded to his touch. And, if it was the thing he had seen on his recent visit to the baths, it had grown bigger. Quite a lot bigger. It must now be at least three times its original size.

He realized the thing had fallen silent, and wondered if it was still there. He hadn't felt it go away, but then, he hadn't felt it land in the first place. It couldn't, therefore, weigh much, he deduced.

So—what the hell was it?

Moving stiffly and slowly, and holding himself very erect as though he had a pile of books balanced on his head, Hal stepped out of his study and into the bathroom. He wiped the mirror on the cabinet above the wash basin, still misty from Ann's afternoon bath, with his shirtsleeve, and surveyed the uppermost section of his reflection. He could just see part of the thing's head and—well, yes, face; you had to call it a face—sticking up out of a swirl of his ginger hair. The rest of its form was hidden, as it had taken up position on top of the backward curve of his skull. He reached up as though to touch it again, but, as he did so, the thing began to bleep urgently, and Hal whipped his hand away before it made contact.

I need another mirror, he thought, to hold up behind me, to get a proper look.

There was a small one in among his wife's bottles of soaps and unguents on a table nearby. He fetched it, returned to the cabinet mirror, and manoeuvred the second glass into position, slanting it over the back of his head.

And couldn't see much that was new because the creature had wrapped itself in his hair. Worse—it seemed to have made a nest there, and looked very securely entwined. It must have dug and burrowed industriously to get itself so set. But how could it have done, without him feeling a thing?

Very *cautiously*, Hal supposed.

He moved up close to the mirror to get a look at the thing's grey face. He was convinced it was peering forward at his, Hal's, reflection with sharp little eyes, and it seemed to be taking an interest in what it saw. It's not stupid, Hal realized: it had a clever look.

It blinked a couple of times, almost lazily.

It didn't seem to have anything like a nose in the small gap under its eyes, but some of a wide mouth was partly visible. It was chewing something slowly—Hal could see the tiny muscles in its cheek stretch and contract—and it licked its lips from side to side continuously with a spike of black tongue.

What's it got in its mouth? Hal thought. What's the little bastard *eating*?

As if to show him, the thing yawned, and Hal got a glimpse of something—a pink bolus streaked with red, glistening between its jaws.

He jumped back from the mirror, yelped, and slapped at the back of his head with the flat of his hand without thinking. He felt a squidgy, sickening sensation as something sticky spread out under his palm.

"Got you," he shouted, in a burst of excitement, but he was wrong. After a few moments he felt the thing stir, then it started spinning and scratching wildly about in amongst his hair. Feet or claws dug into his scalp. The bleeping grew loud and angry. Hal slapped it again, to no effect. His hand was damp when he brought it down and he saw it was red with blood. His, or the creature's? Christ, was it trying to bore down into his skull?

Hal thumped the top of his head with his fist again and again, as hard as he could. He ran round the bathroom with his head down, like a crazed bull charging. At one point he attempted to get his head under the tap in the bath to try to wash the thing away. He even tried scrubbing it off with a nail brush but nothing, as far as he could tell, did anything to dislodge the creature. In the end he found some scissors and began blindly snipping away at his hair. That did have some effect, inasmuch as it seemed to enrage the thing a lot. The piping sound sharpened into a saw-like buzz that became a shriek.

It left Hal then, with some effort, as he could feel it jerking at what remained of his hair at the back of his scalp, and started flapping around him in an unsteady way that suggested it was injured or disorientated. Hal twirled around trying to keep it in sight, afraid it might try to get back into his hair. It was watching him as it encircled him, turning its face towards him constantly to glare at him over its thin, bat-like left wing. Hal made a couple of attempts to swat the thing with a towel, which seemed to upset it, because it started moving in closer to him with each turn it made. It was spinning in near to his ears.

Then it disappeared. It vanished over his left shoulder, and failed to reappear from behind his right. Hal had become dizzy, twisting to keep up with it, so he stood still to try to regain his equilibrium. He jerked around to look behind him, feeling, as he did so, a very peculiar sensation at the top of his head, as though a cold wind were blowing through his brain.

A freezing wind, full of flecks of snow.

The inside of his head became a vast, hollow space: an arctic waste, a desert of ice. At first it seemed like an empty, uninhabited place, but then Hal heard the sound of the insect, hugely amplified, but emanating from the far distance, or so it seemed. The sound echoed slightly, which was strange, because the inside of Hal's head was such a flat, featureless place, smooth and shining like a dance floor.

He looked all around for the creature, but there was no sign of it anywhere.

But he could hear it. Damn it—where *was* the bloody thing? There was no-where it could be hiding.

Hal searched in all directions inside his head to find it . . .

Ann said, "Hallam, what's wrong? You've hurt yourself."

Hal found he was sitting on the floor with his back to the bath. Ann was stooping over him, inspecting the back of his head.

"You've got a nasty cut," she said. "What on earth have you been doing? Trying to cut your own hair?"

Hal made an effort to get up. "Something got caught up in it," he said. His own voice sounded strange to him, and he had a terrible headache. "An insect. I was trying to cut it free. I think I must have fainted."

Ann smiled. "People don't faint," she said, "except in books. If you passed out, you must be ill. You'd better see the doctor."

"That won't be necessary," Hal said. The idea of a doctor inspecting his head, peering into his ears, and seeing—what? Glaciers? Shifting ice? An arctic waste?—was alarming. It still felt cold and bleak and *painful* in there. And he could still hear the bloody thing pinging softly, back in the deepest recesses of his mind.

Christ, what was happening to him? What had *got into him?*

"We'd better do something about that cut," Ann suggested.

"How does it look?"

Ann put both hands on his head on either side of the wound and gently parted his remaining hair. "Not good," she said. "Deep."

"It can't be," Hal protested, "because of the bone. There's no flesh above the skull."

Ann gave him a doubtful look and the wound a closer inspection. "What did you do, then? Stab yourself?"

"I can't remember," Hal replied, but he knew very well he had done nothing of the kind. Whatever damage had been done to his scalp had been done by the—insect—he still thought of it as an insect. No other classification offered itself.

"I probably fell and hit my head." He lied, because he couldn't bring himself to attempt to explain what had happened. His wife would think he was going crazy, and tell him so. He could do without that.

"Hold still," Ann said, as she swabbed his head with a wad of damp tissue. "This will sting. It's Dettol."

"You're sure you're up to it?"

"No problem, Ann. I feel fine now."

"You don't look it."

Hal had been aware that his wife had been covertly observing him anxiously from time to time since she had discovered him on the bathroom floor. He guessed he must look pretty awful, but had avoided confronting his own reflection in a mirror. If he looked as bad as he felt . . .

"I can take the bloody dog for a walk, you know," Ann insisted, "it's no big deal. Chaplin won't mind, just for once."

Not true, Hal thought: Chaplin was his pet, and knew it. And Ann walked too fast for the old dog's stiff legs.

"A walk will do me good!" Hal said, hustling Chaplin into a corner of the room so he could grab him to fix his lead. For some reason, and for the first time as far as Hal could remember, the mutt didn't seem to want his exercise. "And Singer needs sorting out, or he'll be calling us every ten minutes." Their garrulous neighbour had phoned again about the destruction of the graveyard, in an even greater state of indignation, and Hal had promised to meet him to plan some kind of retaliatory action.

"What's the matter with Chaplin?" Ann asked, as the dog whined in protest at being dragged into the open. "He's off his food, too. Didn't go near his dish tonight."

"He'll be okay," Hal said as the dog fled in an undignified fashion into the garden in front of him, dragging his master behind.

"It's a long time since I've seen him move so fast," Ann observed, as her husband was towed towards the front gate.

As Hal strode along towards St Chad's, with Chaplin stumbling swiftly and stiffly ahead, he slapped his head vigorously from time to time with his palm as though he were trying to eject something through his ears. Indeed, that was exactly what he was trying to do.

Singer, sitting on a bus stop bench close to the site of the now demolished church, watched his approach with mystification.

"G'd evening, Hallam," he said, when Hal took a place on the bench beside him. "Gnats biting, are they?"

"What gnats?"

"Saw you waving your hand about around your head."

"Oh! I see. No, I've got a strange sensation in my skull, to tell the truth. Rather unpleasant."

"Flu can do that. Had something like it myself a few weeks ago," Singer recalled. "Soon got over it," he added complacently, dismissing the subject. "Well, what d'you think, Hallam?" He jerked a thumb over his shoulder towards the churchyard behind them. "Have you ever seen anything so downright bloody disgraceful?"

Hal stood up, turned, and regarded the scene of desolation. The old church had vanished and its ancient graveyard was unrecognizable. The site looked as though giant worms had dug and tunnelled there, and voided huge casts of digested soil. It was a place of mounds and pits, and heaps of broken stone. Shattered monuments and gravestones lay about pell-mell, and the hulk-like trunks of debranched trees, some sliced in sections, sprawled among them. The tracks of earth-moving machines, now parked in what had been the nave of the flattened church, crisscrossed torn ground that had once supported grassy slopes rich with wild flowers. The air was sweet with the scent of wood smoke. The glowing remains of two big fires that had been built to burn the church's fitments smouldered in the background and were occasionally whipped into flame by the evening breeze.

"Amazing," Hal said, "to think they did all that in one day."

"They had to work fast, before we could put a block on them. I phoned the Town Hall a couple of days ago and mentioned the badgers. Perhaps I shouldn't have done, because I tipped them off about what I was planning. Anyway, they sounded quite worried when I told them I was going to get the RSPCA involved because the development of the site would disturb an established set. As it turned out, they didn't give me a chance."

"Are you sure about that?" Hal asked, resisting the temptation to push a finger into his left ear to try to dislodge something that seemed to be fluttering around in there. "About the badgers? I should think it's most unlikely."

"Can't be *sure*," Mr Singer said grudgingly, aware that Hal had briefly been involved in an organization to protect the creatures from gangs of would-be baiters, "but there appeared to be evidence of occupation to me."

"Where, exactly?"

Mr Singer rose from the bench with the assistance of his walking stick, then used it to point ahead of him.

"Over there," he said, indicating an area at the edge of the graveyard where least damage seemed to have been done. "Let's go and have a look, to see what you think. There might still be signs."

Once across the road Hal released Chaplin who, in spite of his infirmities, tottered eagerly away into the ruins. In contrast, both men stepped warily, like thieves or trespassers, as they entered the remains of the ancient churchyard, though no attempt had been made to discourage entry or keep them out. A cage-like structure had been erected around the more valuable and saleable stone and wood rescued from the ruins, but otherwise the area was open from all sides now the four surrounding walls had been breached.

A mob of kids were wandering noisily about, kicking and throwing things at each other. They jeered at the two men when they approached. At one point Singer seemed about to challenge them, but Hal was able to convince him that the gesture was unnecessary, and might cause trouble.

"Looks as though the workmen were just making a start here when it was time to go home," Singer said when they reached the spot he had designated. "Maybe we're not too late after all. There: look: do you see? What are those if they're not badger scrapings? You can see the claw marks."

He pointed his stick towards the base of a large family tomb that had had the lid pushed to one side, but had otherwise escaped further damage. The grass around it had been dug into quite deeply in places, but Hal saw at once the work had not been done by badgers. The individual marks were too wide and wayward. They did look as though they had been made by an animal, rather than with a tool, however, though it would have to have been a bloody big animal, Hal reflected, and powerful too, to have made such impressions. He bent to read some words carved into the side of the stone sarcophagus, and reached out towards them with his fingers.

"What d'you make of it?" Singer asked, when, after some time, Hal had volunteered no opinion as to the authors of the indentations.

Hal shook his head in a way that could have indicated bafflement, but said nothing.

Singer gave an impatient grunt at this lack of response and strode away around to the other side of the tomb to make his own investigations.

When his companion was out of sight, Hal fell on his knees, clutched his head, and groaned.

The reason he had not answered Singer's enquiry was that he had hardly been able to hear what his companion had said over the bleeping noise in his head, which had grown much louder as he had drawn closer to the tomb. As he had touched its crumbling side briefly, to clear some moss away from the inscription, the sounds inside his skull had almost deafened him. It was as though something was running around in there, screaming and shouting, and desperate to get out. Hal had an image of a huge moth-like thing hurtling from one part of the frozen, empty spaces of his brain to another, searching for an exit.

He forced himself back, almost rolling over as he did so, and stumbled a few paces away from the tomb. At once the sounds decreased, and the thing inside him became quieter and less restless. Nevertheless, Hal was somehow aware that the thing had not approved of his retreat from the tomb. He could sense its displeasure. It almost seemed to be speaking to him: the bleeping sounds, he realized, were a language he couldn't understand.

Or had not been able to until now, that was. Now it was becoming clear to him that the creature was trying to give him instructions and, after a few moments, he knew what it wanted him to do.

It wanted him to climb into the tomb, down through the space provided by the partly removed lid.

When Hal realized this, he didn't hesitate, but reached up to grasp the upper edge of the tomb and tried to haul himself on top.

Pain wracked his arms when they took the weight of his dumpy body, and his feet kicked wildly as he attempted to get a toehold in the indented inscription. He was pitifully unfit after two sedentary years of unemployment, but at last he got his bulk high enough to reach one arm down into the tomb and, in a burst of frantic effort, was able pull himself up and sit astride the top edge.

The bleeping moderated, and became something like a purr of satisfaction once he had established himself in this position. The thing in his head was pleased with him, and he was glad of that.

He understood that something was waiting down below in the earth: a meeting was about to take place. His mission was to climb inside, then he'd be free again.

Free of the thing inside his skull. That was what he wanted most of all at that moment. It was the *only* thing he wanted.

He was about to lower himself into the stone sarcophagus when he felt hands grasping his leg—the leg on the *outside* of the tomb.

"What the hell are you doing?" Singer shouted. "Bloody fool: you'll break your neck."

Singer was holding him fast with both hands just below the knee. Hal struggled and attempted to kick free, but was exhausted by his climb and felt himself slipping sideways.

The damned thing that had driven him where he was went wild again, and shrieked throughout the length and breadth of his mind, ordering him away, in the opposite direction to that in which he was being pulled.

Knowing he had no alternative, Hal flung himself forward into the tomb. Singer held on, but Hal was hardly aware of the pain in his contorted leg. He hung almost upside down and peered anxiously down into the darkness inside the vault, searching for he knew not what. But he was certain something was there, somewhere, waiting. He could feel its presence.

So could the creature—the parasite inside him.

From its movements, Hal realized it was preparing to leave him, if he could just give it time to get out.

Singer, meanwhile, was hanging all his weight on Hal's leg. The pain in Hal's thigh and crotch was so great now it made him yell out. He shouted to Singer to let him go, but the determined old fool redoubled his efforts to restrain him, and Hal felt himself being pulled in two directions, in and out of the tomb, as something like a muscular, rubbery blanket reached up from inside, engulfed his head and shoulders, and tried to pull him down, inch by inch.

He began to be drawn deeper into the tomb.

When Hal thought he was about to be split in half, his head exploded, or seemed to (something did) with a sound like a gunshot. Within the tomb whatever had held him let go abruptly, and he lurched into the air like a tailor's dummy tossed in a blanket. He cartwheeled out over the edge of the sarcophagus, arms and legs flying, and landed on top of Singer, who collapsed, with a succession of indignant grunts, underneath him.

Something wet, hairy, and foul-smelling flopped about over Hal's face.

He realized at once it was Chaplin's muzzle. He recognized the old dog's bad breath and tugged the hound away from him by his collar. He struggled to his feet, then helped Singer up and handed him his stick.

When he was able to hold himself erect and master his indignation enough to speak, Singer growled, "What in God's name did you think you were doing, Hollins?" He jabbed his stick towards the tomb. "You could have fallen down inside that thing and broken your neck."

"I'm sorry. Thanks for your help. Are you hurt?"

Singer looked as though he wasn't too sure, but he shook his head.

Hal saw the teenagers had drawn closer, attracted by the commotion, and were watching the two men and the dog with amusement. Their faces were predatory, contemptuous. One of them, catching Hal's eye, rolled his shoulders and took a step towards him in a meaningful way, as though setting an example to the others. A couple of them glanced at each other, but none of them seemed keen to take up the dare.

Perhaps it was something about Hal's demeanour that kept the group at bay long enough for him to lead Mr Singer and Chaplin swiftly out of the graveyard to the relative safety of the road. Hal was a small man, but with a determined jaw, and recent events had marked his face with a grim and possibly dangerous expression.

Singer insisted on walking him home, though Hal could have done without his company. He could think of nothing to say to justify his actions or explain his behaviour, in response to the prickly pensioner's blunt questioning.

"Are you crazy?" Ann asked her husband later, when Singer had told her what Hal had done in the churchyard. "Perhaps that bang on the head in the bathroom has something to do with it."

Singer insisted on being told about Hal's earlier misadventure, and at once became more conciliatory and sympathetic. He offered to drive Hal to the Accident Unit at the local hospital. Hal was tempted, but he still didn't want anyone looking too closely into his head, for fear of what they might find. He wasn't sure, yet, that it had been totally vacated.

He left Ann and Singer to discuss his problems and made his way up to his study to take another look at the section of branch, or whatever it was he had brought home from the swimming baths. If only he could identify it, what had happened to him since he had discovered it might be explained.

Chaplin, who seemed in an unusually nervous mood, followed awkwardly at his master's heels as he laboriously climbed the stairs to his study, then sat at his feet as Hal searched again through the colourful pages of his botanical books. After ten minutes Hal was quite sure there was nothing like his specimen in any of them. He slammed the last one shut and threw the now withering stick away from him across the room, towards the waste basket.

Chaplin, who had been observing every move Hal made, struggled to his feet and chased after the stick.

Hal jumped up and shouted, "No, boy: *leave* it," but was too late, because Chaplin got the fragment of branch firmly between his dribbling jaws and twisted around to return it triumphantly.

When Hal bent down to grasp the protruding end of the stick, Chaplin decided to make a game of it, and shook his head furiously as Hal's fingers were about to take hold. In imitation of the antics of his puppyhood that had earned him his clown's name, he ran off a little way and commenced spinning round on his hind legs, or trying to. Hal chased after him, calling his pet a fool, and snatching at the stick, but the old dog eluded him. Chaplin backed off again, as far as the top of the stairs before his legs, unused to this kind of violent exercise, let him down, causing him to stumble and tumble, tail over ears, to the ground floor.

Ann and Mr Singer, alarmed by the sound of Chaplin's indecorous descent, got to the dog seconds before Hal. While they inspected Chaplin for injuries, Hal looked about for the stick. There was no sign of it.

"He must have swallowed it," he said, "buds and all."

Ann looked up from patting the dog, who seemed mortified but unharmed, and said, "Swallowed what?"

"Oh, *nothing*," Hal said crossly, and returned to his study to think.

Over the next couple of days Ann grew more worried about Hal, and Hal became very concerned about Chaplin.

The dog had taken to hiding behind the television table, where no one could get to him, and he'd stopped eating. Also, when Hal stooped to switch on the set, he'd detected an unpleasant smell that he was sure was getting stronger. Ann had noticed it too, and had suggested taking Chaplin to the vet. Hal had shown no enthusiasm for this idea, and Ann had not pressed him on the point because she was sure her husband was himself ill, but was concealing the fact, or unsuccessfully trying to.

He looked extremely unwell. He too had lost his appetite and energy and, she noticed, the wound on the back of his head had swollen into a congealed lump of blood that rose more than an inch out of his hair, which he had taken to combing back over it in a way that made him look absurd.

Also, he'd started sleeping alone on the couch for some reason.

Mr Singer had phoned to enquire about him, but Hal had refused to speak to him, with the excuse of a severe migraine. In other ways, Hal seemed oblivious to his own condition, but, Ann was aware, he was constantly trying to establish contact with his pet, and attempting to lure him into the open with morsels of the dog's favourite food.

"He's not dead, is he?" she said at last, more than forty-eight hours after Chaplin's fall, when she caught Hal holding his nose with one hand and thrusting a cold pork sausage behind the TV with the other.

"Certainly not," Hal snapped, jerking guiltily upright.

"One way or the other, he's going to have to come out from there, Hal," Ann insisted. "He's a hygiene hazard. He needs help."

She went to the television and bent over to look behind it. Hal had pulled down the window blinds, so it was dark in the room. She couldn't see much except the black bulk of the dog down in the shadows at the back of the set. Chaplin, crouching back as far as he could, was peering up at her. She thought she saw his oily old eyes flicker. The stink of him made her step quickly back.

"Come on boy," she whispered encouragingly, when she heard the dog shift his ground slightly, "let's have a look at you."

She made a sudden grab at the TV table, lifted the nearest edge, and spun the thing out into the room. Hal groaned in protest, moved swiftly into the space she had opened up, and hunkered down over his pet before Ann could get a look at him. Chaplin, for his part, resented this intrusion, and ran out between his master's legs.

When Ann saw what had happened to the dog, she screamed briefly, and clasped her hand to her open mouth.

Chaplin ran about flapping the stubby wings that had sprouted from the back of his neck as though he was trying to get airborne. There was no hope he could lift his weight with such tiny appendages, however, and all he succeeded in doing was to stun himself on a chair leg he shortsightedly ran into almost at once. He fell on his side then, and lay flicking his wings fitfully and gasping noisily, in pain or for breath.

"Hallam, what is this?" Ann whispered, when she could speak at all. "What the hell has happened to the bloody dog?"

Hal shook his head. "I think it was something he ate, he said, "but that's *all* I know."

The pair of them stared incredulously down at Chaplin, who was beginning to show some signs of recovery. At last he was able to lift his belly off the ground and scuttle sideways towards the TV table. After a number of failed attempts to turn the corner, he managed to conceal himself in his old hiding place.

"You still want to take him to the vet?" Hal asked, sounding, Ann thought, unreasonably bitter—sarcastic, even.

"He can't stay in the house."

"Then someone will have to get him out of there again, and pick him up and *take* him away. You want to do it?"

Before Ann could answer, the doorbell rang. Ann, glad of the excuse to get away, ran to answer it. As soon as Hal heard Mr Singer's voice in the hall he pushed the TV table back in place, murmured a few words of reassurance to Chaplin, then stepped out of the room and closed the door firmly behind him.

"Hallam!" Singer bawled, "*There* you are. Good news about St Chad's. Have you heard? They had to stop work there. *My God*, what's the matter with you? You look half-dead."

"Migraine," Hal said, and put his hand to his brow as though the half-light in the hall was too strong for him to bear. "Didn't Ann explain?"

"She did, yes—but I had no idea you were as bad as that."

"It'll pass," Hal said. "What's that about St Chad's?"

"I don't know if it's because I phoned them up at the Town Hall after our visit, and gave them a bloody good bollocking, but it seems work there has come to a standstill. I went next morning and they were still at it like slaves, then I had to go that way again today, at lunchtime, and the place was deserted. Not a workman in sight, not even a caretaker. And the whole place shut off by this damn fence, as though it was some kind of military establishment—you know, 'Top Secret, Keep Out,' that sort of thing."

"You mean those signs were actually up?"

"No, of course not; but it looked like that sort of place—know what I mean?"

Hal nodded. "So what's happened? What's gone wrong?"

"Don't care. Work's stopped, that's the main thing. Those pen-pushers on the Council have been made to see sense at last. I got my message across. The power of protest, you know?"

Hal looked puzzled. "But there wasn't much protest, was there? I mean, just you and maybe a few others . . ."

"Perhaps they were impressed by the quality, not the quantity. After all, they've come up against *me* before, so they know what to expect."

"Hum."

"They've sent the kids home from the school as well," Singer continued. "I was talking to someone who said there was trouble at the graveyard this morning, and she thought some of the workmen on the site had been taken away. The Council will be in deep trouble if there's been an accident."

"Let's take a look," Hal suggested. "Are you free at the moment?"

Singer nodded enthusiastically. Ann objected that Hal was in no condition to go anywhere.

"I can't stay in here for ever," he said. "It's two days since I've been out. Fresh air might do me good." He put a flat cap firmly but carefully on his head, to hide the bloody lump, and led the way to the door, ushering Mr Singer ahead of him.

"Not bringing the dog," Singer observed, surprised.

"He's a bit off colour," Hal explained.

At the last minute, as they were leaving the house, Ann rushed out to join them. "I'm coming too," she said, as though she expected some opposition to the suggestion.

"Good," Hal said.

Ann leant towards him as they walked side by side, and put her mouth close to his ear. "I didn't want to be left alone with Chaplin," she whispered.

"This is a long way round," Singer objected, as Hal led them across City Road.

"I'd like to take a look at the baths first," Hal said.

"You're obsessed with that place," Singer said. "You've got a bee in your bonnet, if you ask me."

Hal grimaced painfully. "Maybe," he said. The inside of his head felt very peculiar indeed, in a way he could not have described to Singer or Ann. Bees weren't the problem, he was sure of that. It was something to do with the lump that had grown on the back of his skull over the last two days, which hurt too much to touch, and was too horrible to look at. The sight of it had made him physically sick when he'd lifted his hair off it in front of the mirror. He felt sick all over, in fact, and was uneasily aware he was getting worse.

When Hal saw the baths, he knew at once his earlier vision of the place exploding under the pressure of the forces pent-up inside had been erroneous. The plants growing in there no longer looked vigorous and healthy. They had slumped down: their branches now drooped and their leaves had withered and begun to lose their colour. They looked as bad as Hal felt. He'd had nightmares about their poisonous power during the last two days, on the few occasions he'd been able to get any sleep, and evidence of their vincibility cheered him a little.

Singer, with no knowledge of botany, was unmoved by the sight of the bizarre, outlandish growths, but Ann appreciated their unique ugliness at once, and would have stepped nearer to inspect them if Hal had not held her back.

"*Don't*—don't get too close," he said, grabbing her arm. She gave him a quizzical look. "They bite," he explained.

Singer made a show of laughing at what he took to be an example of Hal's, to him, incomprehensible humour. Then, when he saw the expressions on the couple's faces, he grunted abruptly, and looked puzzled and slightly embarrassed.

"What are they?" Ann asked, staring hard through the glass walls into the interior of the baths. Her voice conveyed her revulsion. "I've never seen anything remotely like them."

Hal shrugged, and the sudden movement made his head spin. He held tight to his wife, to stop himself reeling. "I think they are something quite new," he said. "Remember those rumours about what was being developed in the factory that used to stand on this site?"

"The one we campaigned against, that was shut down?"

"That was *burned* down."

"Well, the story was they were mutating extinct forms of life reconstructed from DNA samples, or something like that. Trying to create combination creatures from animal and vegetable sources."

Ann made a gesture towards the baths and its contents. "Well, those things, whatever they are, are dying, by the look of them."

"They're drying out. It's not rained for some time, so no water has got in through the roof and, luckily, their roots can't get through the floor. There's plenty of moisture down there, in the underground river, if they could reach it."

"If you're suggesting those things grew from substances released when the factory was destroyed, they could be growing anywhere, surely?" She looked anxiously around as though she expected to be surrounded by the things.

"Maybe, but I don't think so. There were very special and unusual conditions in there for a while, inside the baths. It must have been like a huge super-heated and very damp greenhouse. My guess is whatever got blown in by the wind was provided with the perfect environment to germinate and grow in, just by chance. But only for a short while."

Ann said, "You seem to have been giving the situation here a lot of thought. All this hasn't suddenly occurred to you."

"You're right, Ann. There's a few things I should have told you, but I haven't been able to bring myself to do it."

"Then tell me now," Ann insisted, alarmed by the extreme strain in her husband's voice. "Is it about your—accident—the other day?"

"Yes: that, and what came later."

"What *do* you mean?"

Hal, feeling suddenly very weak and unsteady, as though he was going to drop to the ground, was about to start to tell her, when Mr Singer interrupted.

"Look, this is all very well, and no doubt interesting, if unusual plants are your sort of thing, but we were supposed to be on our way to St Chad's to look at the graveyard." He sounded offended, perhaps because the recent conversation had excluded and not made any sense to him. He'd had no part in the campaign to close the factory and had even supported the project because of the jobs it had brought to the area.

Ann was all for letting Singer go on without them. Hal had his own reasons for wanting to visit the desecrated churchyard, but he wasn't quite sure what they were. He wasn't sure about anything any more: his understanding of everything was blurred, but he felt that if he went home and stopped moving, he might never start up again.

Mr Singer had exaggerated the extent of the fencing around the site. It wasn't very high and had obviously been put up in a hurry as a makeshift until a stronger and more elaborate one could be erected. Work on this had begun, but only a stretch of thirty yards or so was in place. A number of men erecting the more formidable structure, sinking steel support poles, were wearing protective clothing, and looked uncomfortable in the heat of the afternoon sun. Singer tried to get into conversation with two of them working closest to the road, but they were obviously under instructions not to talk.

"They told me to piss off and mind my own business," he said when he returned to where Hal and his wife were standing. He shook his stick in the air. "Damned impertinence. I'd have given them some of this if I could have got to them."

Hal said, "I see someone has taken the lid right off that tomb I was—inspecting. Looks as though they made a start on demolishing it."

"They didn't get far though," Singer observed, following Hal's gaze. "Something must have stopped them in their tracks."

A woman passing by overheard this remark. She stopped and said, "There's going to be big trouble over this, mark my words."

When Singer gave her his most interrogative stare, she continued, "Haven't you heard? About the missing children? Three of them vanished last night. They'd been playing in the graveyard. Lots of people saw them. None of them have been home since. Then, this morning, the workers found something bad in there, but nobody knows what, they won't say, but, putting two and two together . . ."

"Something bad . . . ? Ann queried.

"Something, or *things*. They took them away," the woman said.

"In an ambulance?"

"No. A big van. I wasn't here myself, but I was told it was like soldiers use. Painted all over with splotches."

"Camouflage," Singer pronounced pedantically. "Sounds damned odd, calling the army in. What's up, I wonder? I'm going to call the Town Hall. I've got contacts. I'll sort this out." He strode away towards a distant telephone booth, swinging his stick and looking quite jaunty now.

"He's got the bit between his teeth," Hal croaked.

The woman, previously distracted by the scandal of the lost children, had hardly glanced at Hal when she had been speaking. She looked at him now, and gasped. She stretched out an arm towards him in an involuntary gesture, as though to support him, and said, "My God, what's wrong with you?"

Hal felt like hiding his face in his hands, but he said nothing.

"You look—*rotten*." The woman emphasized the last word as though its meaning was insufficient to express her feelings, but her vocabulary was too small to provide a more suitable alternative. "You shouldn't be out," she snapped, maternally, and turned accusingly to Ann. "I'd get him home as quick as I can, dear," she advised. "He looks on his last legs."

"I'm not as bad as I seem," Hal protested, hearing, at the same time, how strange his voice had become. He sounded like someone talking on a radio with flat batteries. He spoke louder, to compensate, and his words took on a barking note that alarmed the woman, who took a few steps away from him.

A policeman, one of a number patrolling the area, attracted, perhaps, by Hal's shouts, appeared from somewhere, and sauntered towards the trio. He was a young man with a sparse moustache and pale, scared rabbit's eyes. "I'm *afraid* I must ask you to move on," he said. He sounded afraid. When he saw he was getting no response he added, "It's dangerous to hang about here. I advise you to go away."

"In what way dangerous?" Ann asked.

"There's been a leak of some kind."

"Of what?"

"I'm not sure. Chemicals, I think. The army are going to spray the area."

"Then why are you here, without protection—a mask or something—if it's not safe?"

The policeman looked confused, as though this hadn't occurred to him. "I'm not going to argue about it," he said after a moment. "I've got to keep people from hanging about round here. There's nothing to see. Please go home." The more he pleaded, the more boyish he became. Ann took pity on him. She linked arms with Hal, in anticipation that he might try to elude her, and drew him firmly away. "Come on," she said, "you *do* look terrible. Let's go."

"I'm not going home," Hal insisted. "Not just yet."

Ann hugged his arm tighter and said, "I was thinking of the hospital."

"I look that bad?"

"Worse by the moment."

"I am tired," Hal admitted. "There's a bench over there. Let's sit down for a moment." Ann had to agree, because her husband's legs were drooping and she could not have supported his weight much longer.

The bench was outside the school next to the graveyard. Normally, mothers sat there at three-fifteen in the afternoon, waiting to take their children home. Now, the bench was empty because the school had been closed.

Hal slumped down on the seat and stared at his knees. He realized they were shaking, then discovered his whole body was. He was quivering non-stop, as though his nervous system was short-circuiting. Inside his head it was cold and vast and bleak again, like the roof of the world. He thought something was flapping about, just beyond the rim of his inner vision, where his brain must be, but he couldn't get a proper sight of it, and tried to ignore it. In the distance, he thought he heard the bleeping sound again. He must have groaned aloud, because Ann put her arm around his shoulders and asked him what was wrong. She sounded almost in tears.

"Can't tell you," Hal said. "Don't know."

"What am I going to do with you?"

"Too late, I think, to do anything. Best just to leave me here."

"*Hal*," Ann said, outraged and hurt, "have some sense. You need—attention. What the hell has happened to you?"

"Something like what happened to the dog, I guess," Hal said. "It's out of control. So am I. So is Chaplin. It's got us, and we can't do anything about it."

"What has 'got' you?"

Hal made an ugly sound that could have been a snigger. "Blight," he said. "The ultimate suburban blight."

"For Christ's sake, Hal, talk sense," Ann insisted. "I don't understand you at all."

Hal seemed to be trying hard to explain himself, but his next words only confused Ann all the more, they seemed so irrelevant.

"The river, the *underground* river, that flows under the area around the swimming baths, also goes under the graveyard, he said, putting his words together with obvious difficulty. "The graveyard is downstream," he added, almost triumphantly, as though that fact explained everything. "The river is not far below the surface. Some of the graves must have fallen into it. Some of the *contents* of the graves. And stuff from the burned-out industrial complex would have washed down into the river and mixed with the human remains. I think something burrowed its way upward from the river . . ."

Hal's voice died away, but he continued to whisper to himself urgently, as though desperate to solve some problem.

Ann, assuming her husband was delirious, encouraged him to talk on, hoping he would reveal something of the cause of his condition. Hal's thoughts must have reached some conclusion then, because he suddenly started up halfway out of the seat and said, "The tomb—*of course*—it hid in there, where it could wait for the right moment. I was forgetting, the things will have intelligence, they could be very smart. They'd have to be. And there are probably a lot of them, biding their time!" Perplexed that Ann wasn't responding to what he had been saying, he gave her an imploring look, begging her to understand. She shrugged helplessly, and hugged him tight around the shoulders.

Mr Singer returned, obviously disgruntled. "Buggers," he snapped. "Tried to fob me off with some gas leak nonsense. Bloody jumped-up Town Hall desk monkeys. They don't think they're accountable for anything." He hit the back of the bench hard with his stick. "I'm going round there to get to the bottom of this. Want to come?"

Ann shook her head vigorously, and gestured towards her husband. Singer gave Hal a quick appraisal, then nodded conspiratorially. "See what you mean," he said.

Hal caught this last comment, and misunderstood it. He was snatching at straws. "Do you, Singer? Do you really? You see, I think it must be the freak weather we've had that gave them the chance of life. Something has been down there, in the soil, since the factory was destroyed, waiting for the right conditions. Probably it can adapt, to some extent, and maybe even be able to adapt and develop its environment to its own advantage, once it gets going. It's as though there's a male and female element. The plant thing is the male . . ."

"Sorry, Hallam, I'm not with you," Singer said impatiently. "Now if you want some help to get home, I've ordered a taxi to get me to the Town Hall. I can get the driver to drop you off where you like."

Ann started hauling Hal to his feet. As he allowed himself to be lifted from the seat, there was a loud, ominous rumbling sound from out in the graveyard. Hal turned in his wife's arms and stared towards the source of the sound, and gave a sharp yelp of satisfaction. "There," he said, glancing at Ann and Singer. "You see? I was right."

The vandalized tomb had vanished, as had the ground for many yards around it. Everything in the area, including part of the surrounding fence, had subsided into a huge crater that had opened below. Broiling dust billowed up. As the three of them watched, one of the big yellow earth-moving vehicles that had been used to flatten the graves jerked, dipped, and sank quickly into the ground as more of the graveyard fell away, including part of a wood fire that was still smouldering from the previous day's demolition work. When the red hot ashes reached a certain depth and came in contact with the underground river, clouds of steam hissed into the air, mingling with the dust and obscuring what happened next.

"Whatever it was that was in the tomb must have undermined the area collecting material to—consolidate—itself," Hal continued excitably, his voice becoming ever more strangulated and hard to understand. "The tunnels it made are collapsing under the weight of all those machines."

His energy left him then: his legs sagged and he drooped away from Ann's grasp like a child's cheap doll. Singer stepped up quickly and grabbed Hal's right arm, and he and Ann managed to stop him from falling.

At that moment Singer's taxi appeared. At first, the driver was reluctant to let them on board, because she assumed Hal was totally drunk. Mr Singer, however, with his vaguely military air of authority, was able to convince the woman of the truth of the situation enough for her to reluctantly allow them into the back of her vehicle, after Ann promised to pay for cleaning if Hal was sick.

On Singer's instructions, they headed for the Hollins' house. Ann had declared her intention to get her husband to bed as quickly as possible and call a doctor.

Hal, after a few moments, roused himself sufficiently to continue his fragmentary discourse. He seemed more troubled in mind than ever, and clutched at his head with both hands, as though in an effort to suppress his thoughts.

"Christ! *Pollination.* That's *it*," he croaked, at one point, "that's how they breed. In a few more days, the air would have been full of the small ones, the ones that can fly. But the heat was *too much for them*. They must have died, most of them, there in the baths. Only the few that were outside, nesting in the parts of the plants that had thrust out through the cracks in the wall, could have survived."

Hal's face became very grim then; at some further dark thought that had occurred to him, presumably. A thought that he did not try to share with Ann and Singer. He suddenly looked deeply depressed, and his face became tragically sad. He shut up completely, became speechless, and ignored Ann when she spoke to tell him they were home.

The taxi driver watched stone-faced as Ann and Singer manoeuvred Hal out onto the pavement, along the path to the front door, and into the house. His quaking body dangled between them like a bag of bones and he had become utterly helpless. He kept his hands clamped to his head, and his arms stuck out like handles on a jar. This made it even more difficult to move him.

Singer insisted on helping Ann haul her husband all the way into the house, upstairs, and onto the bed. They left him spreadeagled on his back, fully dressed, because Ann wanted to get a doctor round as quickly as possible. Before phoning, she slipped out to the taxi to contribute to the fare, and to thank Mr Singer for his help.

Singer accepted the money and the gratitude with equal ease. "You look after him, my dear. I've not seen a fellow looking as bad as that since I was out East. Be a great loss to the community if anything happened to him."

As he withdrew into the taxi he suddenly started flapping his hand around in front of his face in a slightly panicky way.

Ann said, "Is something wrong?"

"Some damned insect got in here with me," Singer said nervously. "I can't stand the buggers." He was slapping at the air in a panic.

Ann stuck her head down lower and peered into the back of the vehicle. "I can't see anything," she said.

"Nor can I now!" said Singer, still swerving about uneasily, "But I can hear it."

"It's probably a wasp," Ann said.

"Doesn't sound like a wasp," Singer objected. "Can't you hear it?"

Ann shook her head. "I must get back."

"Of course, of course," Singer said, his eyes darting all around him as he shut himself into the rear of the vehicle. "You'll let me know what the medico thinks, won't you?"

Ann ran back into the house.

The fact that the door to the front room was shut surprised Ann slightly, because it almost never was, but her mind was too full of worry to give the matter any thought. She burst into the room, grabbed the phone and the phone book, and began searching through the latter for the doctor's number. In her confused state, this was not easy, and at one point she slammed the book shut in frustration. This made quite a loud noise, which made her jump.

It also disturbed the other occupant of the room.

In his lair behind the TV, that which had once been Chaplin also moved suddenly, jerking the table he was under out into the room a few inches, and dislodging the TV. The precariously balanced set toppled back and forth, making a rattling noise that disturbed Chaplin further. He had been lying in the dark for a long time, becoming hungrier and hungrier, and more and more bad-tempered and afraid. The food that Hal had tossed him earlier, that he had once enjoyed so much, no longer seemed edible, and its presence even revolted him.

He wanted something else to eat, but he didn't know what.

He wanted something he had never seen or tasted or smelled before. He knew it was out there somewhere, but where and what it was, he did not know. He had an appetite, a huge appetite, that he could not satisfy. He had bitten everything around him, including the table legs, the carpet, the electric cable connected to the television (that had shocked him, but left him unharmed) and even taken bites out of his own front legs, but nothing had tasted anything like right, and had not assuaged his hunger.

He was in a foul, vicious, frightened state, and he was vaguely aware that things were happening to his body over which he had no control. He was getting a lot bigger back there, but was unable to turn his head to take a look at himself because his neck had gone rigid.

When the telephone book banged shut and Chaplin moved, Ann's blood seemed to turn to milk. All the troubles of the day returned to her, and crowded round like so many snapping dogs. She glanced across at the TV and saw it was edging forward across the table. At the same time the table rose slowly at an angle.

Then she remembered what had become of her husband's pet.

Behind the table, Chaplin was on the move again. He'd had enough of being cooped up and wanted to vent his furious anger. Rage and the terrible hunger overwhelmed him.

Keeping one eye on the corner of the room, Ann tore open the directory again. This time she found the number she needed at once, and started to dial. Her floundering, anxious fingers stamped out a wrong number and she heard an old lady she did not know talking in her ear. She swore at the woman, cancelled the call, and proceeded to dial again more carefully.

But, before she could finish, Chaplin rose swiftly upwards on his numerous legs, and felt a new strength and power as the table flew into the air, sending the TV up and away in an arc towards Ann.

The TV would have hit her had it not been for the aerial cable, which jerked the set away from her when it pulled tight. Nevertheless, she had to dive forward out of her seat onto the floor to avoid a vase of flowers that had rested on top of it, which smashed on the wall behind her head. Unimpeded, Chaplin came scuttling into view. He was foaming at the mouth like a bubble machine, and his cold yellow eyes glared at her with un-canine malevolence. Most of his fur had gone, replaced by a shiny, hard, emerald skin that resembled the surface of a succulent plant, and he unfurled the membranes of his now much larger wings experimentally as he drew closer.

Ann saw that he was producing a glistening grey cord from his rear end, like a single thread of a spider's web, as he advanced, and that a jumble of this substance formed a half-completed cocoon in the corner of the room. Something moved restlessly in this mess—something that was not part of Chaplin.

Perhaps because he had difficulty coordinating his new limbs and parts, that which Chaplin had become seemed to lack an accurate sense of direction. Although he continued to stare at Ann, and his intention to get to and *at* her was obvious, he kept swerving away, then had obvious difficulty trying to readjust himself. Though the layout of the room was well known to the old dog, it was a strange and unfamiliar place to the thing he had become.

Ann, on her knees, found herself powerless to do anything but watch the creature for some seconds. Then she became aware of the danger she was in.

She had dropped the telephone somewhere, but she still had the heavy directory in her hands. In a gesture that expressed disgust and revulsion as much as anger or fear, she flung the book at Chaplin's head. The spine of the volume hit him across the nose, where he must have been particularly sensitive, because he gave a high-pitched, twittering yowl, and reared up on his hind parts. He spread his wings wide, so their tips touched the walls on either side of him, stretched them forward, towards, but above, her, then fanned them back and forth. To Ann's absolute horror, he rose a couple of feet in the air. Once in this position, Chaplin suddenly looked less clumsy: at ease, in fact, as though he was in his element. He continued, rather gracefully, to ascend, all the time watching Ann with his unfathomable, alien eyes.

Ann left him there, hovering in the middle of the room. She crawled out, slammed the door behind her, and stood stock still for a moment, sobbing into her hands.

Behind her, Chaplin crashed against the far side of the door. She ran up the stairs. Chaplin renewed his attack. Ann thought she heard wood splintering.

She ran into the bedroom, shouting for Hal.

He was sprawling on the bed, just as she had left him. She tried to rouse him, but he was in a coma-like sleep. His hands still held his head, and his arms were so stiff, she wondered for a moment if he was dead. But, no; his heartbeat was surprisingly, even alarmingly, strong, as though he had recently been involved in some strenuous physical activity. This peculiar fact gave Ann new cause for concern. Nothing about Hal seemed right. She wanted to do something for him, but had no idea what.

There was a confusion of violent sounds from the ground floor, and Ann realized she had left the bedroom door wide open. She went to shut it, and glanced down the stairs.

Chaplin was staring up at her from ground level, snarling like the dog he had once been. Ann saw at once that he would not be able to fly up to the first floor because the stairwell was much to narrow for him to stretch his wings, and it was obvious from his stumbling and totally unsuccessful efforts to mount the first step that he would never reach the top. His new body wouldn't bend in the required places to enable him to redistribute his weight, and he kept over-balancing and falling back. He continued, single-mindedly, to make the attempt, however, and gave no impression that he was ever going to give up. His movements were mindless and mechanical, like an insect's.

Ann watched him lunging upwards and toppling back for some moments, and a slight feeling of relief glowed briefly somewhere inside her. This pleasant sensation was almost instantly replaced by a stunning tiredness that came to hang about her like heavy chains, pulling her down. She dragged herself back to where her husband was sprawled, and lay down beside him on the bed.

Her last thoughts before she slept were that it was unfortunate she and Hal had never had an extension to the phone installed in their bedroom, as they had long intended to do. It was dark when Ann woke up. The only illumination in the room was an ethereal, marigold light that penetrated as far as the foot of the bed, and cast foggy, damp-looking shadows.

For a moment Ann's mind was agreeably blank, and she remembered nothing of the day's events until she rolled over and felt the form of her husband beside her. Then, everything came back to her. She leaned harder against Hal, to get some reaction, but he didn't move. Ann lay still again then, listening to a slow, rhythmic thumping sound from somewhere in the house below. It was, she guessed, the thing she had once called Chaplin, still obsessively trying and failing to mount the first stair. She wondered how long he had been at it, and lifted her watch in front of her face. The time was just readable. It was 7.15 p.m. From the lack of light in the room, she'd assumed she'd been asleep much longer than that.

She lay back again, still exhausted, and closed her eyes. It was only gradually that she became aware that something, or very many *things*—tiny things—positively minute—were crawling across her face and hands.

And arms.

And legs.

They must have been light as dust, because, individually, they were hard to detect. They felt like a dry breeze blowing against her bare skin, but she knew there could be no breeze.

So what *was* there, moving softly and swiftly all over her body?

She sat up and started brushing her face and arms, but the sensation that she was infested remained.

Infested!

She screamed Hal's name, but he gave no answer.

Now Ann was fully awake, all her fears returned. She reached out blindly, grabbed Hal's arm and shook it. It was limp now. She realized he was no longer gripping hold of his head. She stretched over him, switched on the lamp on the table next to Hal's side of the bed, and turned slowly and deliberately back to look at him.

She realized why he had been clasping his head. He had been holding his cap over the back of his scalp. The cap lay on the pillow beside what was left of his head.

Hal must have turned over while she slept, because he was face down now. The back portion of the top of his skull was missing. A circular section more than six inches in diameter had somehow been removed.

Ann raised the lamp to cast a more direct light.

There was blood on the pillow, but not a lot. There was none at all inside Hal's head. Its contents had been devoured. The brain cavity was empty, except for the last few hundred of the countless tiny things, far smaller than the tip of a ballpoint pen, that hopped and darted out of their bony womb, and trickled and tumbled over the bed.

And all over Hal and Ann and the floor and the walls and even, Ann saw, in vast numbers, the windows—hence the darkness.

The young had almost all hatched out. The abandoned project had been, belatedly, a success.

The Blight had achieved the first of its endless series of rebirthings.

DENNIS ETCHISON

Inside the Cackle Factory

Dennis Etchison has been selling stories since the early 1960s and is one of the horror genre's most respected and distinguished practitioners. He has won three British Fantasy Awards and two World Fantasy Awards. His short fiction has been collected in The Dark Country, Red Dreams *(about to be reprinted by Alexander Publishing), and* Blood Kiss. *A new collection is scheduled for 1999. Etchison has published four novels—* Darkside, Shadowman, California Gothic, *and* Double Edge, *and has two new novels forthcoming. He is the editor of several acclaimed anthologies, including* Cutting Edge, *three volumes of* Masters of Darkness, Lord John Ten, *and* MetaHorror. *He also has written extensively for film and television.*

Etchison, a longtime resident of Los Angeles, has found the city rich territory to mine, with its paranoia and its obsessions with celebrity and "new product." Two earlier stories set in this milieu, "The Dog Park" and "The Dead Cop," were reprinted in previous volumes of our series. "Inside the Cackle Factory," another L.A. story, was originally published in Dark Terrors 4.

—E. D.

Uncle Miltie did not look very happy. Someone had left a half-smoked cigar on his head, and now the wrapper began to come unglued in the rain. A few seconds more and dark stains dripped over his slick hair, ran down his cheeks and collected in his open mouth, the bits of chewed tobacco clinging like wet sawdust to a beaver's front teeth.

"Time," announced Marty, clicking his stopwatch.

Lisa Anne tried to get his attention from across the room, but it was too late. She saw him note the hour and minute on his clipboard.

"Please pass your papers to the right," he said, "and one of our monitors will pick them up. . . ."

On the other side of the glass doors, Sid Caesar was even less amused by the logjam of cigarette butts on his crushed top hat. As the water rose they began to float, one disintegrating filter sloshing over the brim and catching in the knot of his limp string tie.

She forced herself to look away and crossed in front of the chairs to get to

Marty, scanning the rows again. There, in the first section: an empty seat with a pair of Ray-Bans balanced on the armrest.

"Sixteen," she whispered into his ear.

"Morning, Lisa." He was about to make his introductory spiel before opening the viewing theater, while the monitors retrieved and sorted the questionnaires. "Thought you took the day off."

"Number Sixteen is missing."

He nodded at the hallway. "Check the men's room."

"I think he's outside," she said, "smoking."

"Then he's late. Send him home."

As she hurried toward the doors, the woman on the end of row four added her own questionnaire to the pile and held them out to Lisa Anne.

"Excuse me," the woman said, "but can I get a drink of water?"

Lisa Anne accepted the stack of stapled pages from her.

"If you'll wait just a moment—"

"But I have to take a pill."

"Down the hall, next to the restrooms."

"Where?"

She handed the forms to one of the other monitors.

"Angie, would you show this lady to the drinking fountain?"

Then she went on to the doors. The hinges squeaked and a stream of water poured down the glass and over the open toes of her new shoes.

Oh great, she thought.

She took the shoes off and stood under the awning while she peered through the blowing rain. The walkway along the front of the AmiDex building was empty.

"Hello?"

Bob Hope ignored her, gazing wryly across the courtyard in the direction of the adjacent apartment complex, while Dick Van Dyke and Mary Tyler Moore leaned so close to each other that their heads almost touched, about to topple off the bronze pedestals. They had not been used for ashtrays yet today, though their nameplates were etched with the faint white tracks of bird droppings. She hoped the rain would wash them clean.

"Are you out here? Mister . . . ?"

She had let Angie check them in this morning, so she did not even know Number Sixteen's name. She glanced around the courtyard, saw no movement and was about to go back inside, when she noticed someone in the parking lot.

It was a man wearing a wet trenchcoat.

So Number Sixteen had lost patience and decided to split. He did not seem to be looking for his car, however, but walked rapidly between the rows on his way to—what? The apartments beyond, apparently. Yet there was no gate in this side of the wrought-iron fence.

As she watched, another man appeared as if from nowhere. He had on a yellow raincoat and a plastic-covered hat, the kind worn by policeman or security guards. As far as she knew the parking lot was unattended. She could not imagine where he had come from, unless there was an opening in the fence, after all, and the guard had come through from the other side. He stepped out to block the way. She tried to hear what they were saying but it was impossible from this distance. There was a brief confrontation, with both men gesturing broadly, until the one in the trenchcoat gave up and walked away.

Lisa Anne shook the water out of her shoes, put them on and turned back to the glass doors.

Marty was already into his speech. She had not worked here long enough to have it memorized, but she knew he was about to mention the cash they would receive after the screening and discussion. Some of them may have been lured here by the glamor, the chance to attend a sneak preview of next season's programs, but without the promise of money there was no way to be sure anyone would show up.

The door opened a few inches and Angie stuck her head out.

"Will you get *in* here, girl?"

"Coming," said Lisa Anne.

She looked around one more time.

Now she saw a puff of smoke a few yards down, at the entrance to Public Relations.

"Is anybody there?" she called.

An eyeball showed itself at the side of the building.

Maybe this is the real Number Sixteen, she thought. Trying to get in that last nicotine fix.

"I'm sorry, but you'll have to come in now . . ."

She waited to see where his cigarette butt would fall. The statues were waiting, too. As he came toward her his hands were empty. What did he do, she wondered, eat it?

She recognized him. He had been inside, drinking coffee with the others. He was a few years older than Lisa Anne, late twenties or early thirties, good-looking in a rugged, unkempt way, with his hair tied back in a ponytail and a drooping moustache, flannel shirt, tight jeans and steel-toed boots. A construction worker, she thought, a carpenter, some sort of manual labor. Why bother to test him? He probably watched football games and not much else, if he watched TV at all.

As he got closer she smelled something sweet and pungent. The unmistakable odor of marijuana lingered in his clothes. So that's what he was up to, she thought. A little attitude adjustment. I could use some of that myself right about now.

She held out her hand to invite him in from the rain, and felt her hair collapse into wet strings over her ears. She pushed it back self-consciously.

"You don't want to miss the screening," she said, forcing a smile, "do you?"

"What's it about?" he asked.

"I don't know. Honest. They don't tell me anything."

The door swung open again and Angie rolled her eyes.

"Okay, okay," said Lisa Anne.

"He can sign up for the two o'clock, if he wants."

Number Sixteen shook his head. "No way. I gotta be at work."

"It's all right, Angie."

"But he missed the audience prep . . ."

Lisa Anne looked past her. Marty was about finished. The test subjects were already shifting impatiently, bored housewives and tourists and retirees with nothing better to do, recruited from sidewalks and shopping malls and the lines in front of movie theaters, all of them here to view the pilot for a new series that would either make it to the network schedule or be sent back for retooling, based on their responses. There was a full house for this session.

Number Sixteen had not heard the instructions, so she had no choice. She was supposed to send him home.

But if the research was to mean anything, wasn't it important that every demographic be represented? The fate of the producers and writers who had labored for months or even years to get their shows this far hung in the balance, to be decided by a theoretical cross-section of the viewing public. Not everyone liked sitcoms about young urban professionals and their wacky misadventures at the office. They can't, she thought. I don't. But who ever asked me?

"Look," said Number Sixteen, "I drove a long ways to get here. You gotta at least pay me."

"He's late," said Angie. She ignored him, speaking as though he were not there. "He hasn't even filled out his questionnaire."

"Yes, he has," said Lisa Anne and ushered him inside.

The subjects were on their feet now, shuffling into the screening room. Lisa Anne went to the check-in table.

"Did you get Number Sixteen's?" she asked.

The monitors had the forms laid out according to rows and were about to insert the piles into manila envelopes before taking them down the hall.

Marty came up behind her. "Which row, Miss Rayme?" he said officiously.

"Four, I think."

"You think?" Marty looked at the man in the plaid shirt and wrinkled his nose, as if someone in the room had just broken wind. "If his form's not here—"

"I know where it is," Lisa Anne told him and slipped behind the table.

She flipped through the pile for row four, allowing several of the questionnaires to slide onto the floor. When she knelt to pick them up, she pulled a blank one from the carton.

"Here." She stood, took a pencil and jotted 16 in the upper right-hand corner. "He forgot to put his number on it."

"We're running late, Lees . . ." Marty whispered.

She slid the forms into an envelope. "Then I'd better get these to the War Room."

On the way down the hall, she opened the envelope and withdrew the blank form, checking off random answers to the multiple-choice quiz on the first page. It was pointless, anyway, most of it a meaningless query into personal habits and lifestyle, only a smokescreen for the important questions about income and product preferences that came later. She dropped off her envelope along with the other monitors, and a humorless assistant in a short-sleeved white shirt and rimless glasses carried the envelopes from the counter to an inner room, where each form would be tallied and matched to the numbered seats in the viewing theater. On her way back, Marty intercepted her.

"Break time," he said.

"No, thanks." She drew him to one side, next to the drinking fountain. "I got one for you. S.H.A.M."

"M.A.S.H.," he said immediately.

"Okay, try this. *Finders*."

He pondered for a second. *"Friends?"*

"You're good," she said.

"No, I'm not. You're easy. Well, time to do my thing."

At the other end of the hall, the reception room was empty and the doors to the viewing theater were already closed.

"Which thing is that?" she said playfully.

"That thing I do, before they fall asleep."

"Ooh, can I watch?"

She propped her back against the wall and waited for him to move in, to pin her there until she could not get away unless she dropped to her knees and crawled between his legs.

"Not today, Lisa."

"How come?"

"This one sucks. Big time."

"What's the title?"

"I don't know."

"Then how do you know it sucks?"

"Hey, it's not my fault, okay?"

For some reason he had become evasive, defensive. His face was now a smooth mask, the skin pulled back tautly, the only prominent features his teeth and nervous, shining eyes. Like a shark's face, she thought. A residue of deodorant soap rose to the surface of his skin and vaporized, expanding outward on waves of body heat. She drew a breath and knew that she needed to be somewhere else, away from him.

"Sorry," she said.

He avoided her eyes and ducked into the men's room.

What did I say? she wondered, and went on to the reception area.

A list of subjects for the next session was already laid out on the table, ninety minutes early. The other monitors were killing time in the chairs, chatting over coffee and snacks from the machines.

Lisa Anne barely knew them. This was only her second week and she was not yet a part of their circle. One had been an editorial assistant at the *L.A. Weekly*, two were junior college students, and the others had answered the same classified ad she had seen in the trades. She considered crashing the conversation. It would be a chance to rest her feet and dry out. The soggy new shoes still pinched her toes and the suit she'd had to buy for the job was damp and steamy and scratched her skin like a hair shirt. She felt ridiculous in this uniform, but it was necessary to show people like Marty that she could play by their rules, at least until she got what she needed. At home she would probably be working on yet another sculpture this morning, trying to get the face right, with a gob of clay in one hand and a joint in the other and the stereo cranked up to the max. But living that way hadn't gotten her any closer to the truth. She couldn't put it off any longer. There were some things she had to find out or she would go mad.

She smiled at the monitors.

Except for Angie they barely acknowledged her, continuing their conversation as though she were not there.

They know, she thought. They must.

How much longer till Marty saw through her game? She had him on her side, but the tease would play out soon enough unless she let it go further, and she couldn't bear the thought of that. She only needed him long enough to find the answer, and then she would walk away.

She went to the glass doors.

The rain had stopped and soon the next group would begin gathering outside. The busts of the television stars in the courtyard were ready, Red Buttons and George Gobel and Steve Allen and Lucille Ball with her eyebrows arched in perpetual wonderment, waiting to meet their fans. It was all that was left for them now.

Angie came up next to her.

"Hey, girl."

"Hey yourself."

"The lumberjack. He a friend of yours?"

"Number Sixteen?"

"The one with the buns."

"I never saw him before."

"Oh." Angie took a bite of an oatmeal cookie and brushed the crumbs daintily from her mouth. "Nice."

"I suppose. If you like that sort of thing."

"Here." She offered Lisa Anne the napkin. "You look like you're melting."

She took it and wiped the back of her neck, then squeezed out the ends of her hair, as a burst of laughter came from the theater. That meant Marty had already gone in through the side entrance to warm them up.

"Excuse me," she said. "It's showtime."

Angie followed her to the hall. "You never miss one, do you?"

"Not yet."

"Aren't they boring? I mean, it's not like they're hits or anything."

"Most of them are pretty lame," Lisa Anne admitted.

"So why watch?"

"I have to find out."

"Don't tell me. What Marty's really like?"

"Please."

"Then why?"

"I've got to know why some shows make it," she said, "and some don't."

"Oh, you want to get into the biz?"

"No. But I used to know someone who was. See you."

I shouldn't have said that, she thought as she opened the unmarked door in the hall.

The observation booth was dark and narrow with a half-dozen padded chairs facing a two-way mirror. On the other side of the mirror, the test subjects sat in rows of theater seats under several 36-inch television sets suspended from the ceiling.

She took the second chair from the end.

In the viewing theater, Marty was explaining how to use the dials wired into the armrests. They were calibrated from zero to ten with a plastic knob in the center. During the screening the subjects were to rotate the knobs, indicating how much they liked what they saw. Their responses would be recorded and the results then analyzed to help the networks decide whether the show was ready for broadcast.

Lisa Anne watched Marty as he paced, doing his schtick. He had told her that he once worked at a comedy traffic school, and she could see why. He had them in the palm of his hand. Their eyes followed his every move, like hypnotized chickens waiting to be fed. His routine was corny but with just the right touch of hipness to make them feel like insiders. He concluded by reminding them of the fifty dollars cash they would receive after the screening and the discussion. Then, when the lights went down and the tape began to roll, Marty stepped to the back and slipped into the hall. As he entered the observation booth, the audience was applauding.

"Good group this time," he said, dropping into the chair next to hers.

"You always know just what to say."

"I do, don't I?" he said, leaning forward to turn on a tiny 12-inch set below the mirror.

She saw their faces flicker in the blue glow of the cathode ray tubes while the opening titles came up.

The show was something called *Dario, You So Crazy!* She sighed and sat back, studying their expressions while keeping one eye on the TV screen. It wouldn't be long before she felt his hand on her forearm as he moved in, telling her what he really thought of the audience, how stupid they were, every last one, down to the little old ladies and the kindly grandfathers and the working men and women who were no more or less ordinary than he was under his Perry Ellis suit and silk tie. Then his breath in her hair and his fingers scraping her pantyhose as if tapping out a message on her knee and perhaps today, this time, he would attempt to deliver that message, while she offered breathless quips to let him know how clever he was and how lucky she felt to be here. She shuddered and turned her cheek to him in the dark.

"Who's that actor?" she said.

"Some Italian guy. I saw him in a movie. He's not so bad, if he could learn to talk English."

She recognized the co-star. It was Rowan Atkinson, the slight, bumbling everyman from that British TV series on PBS.

"Mr. Bean!" she said.

"Roberto Benigni," Marty corrected, reading from the credits.

"I mean the other one. This is going to be good . . ."

"I thought you were on your break," said Marty.

"This is more important."

He stared at her transparent reflection in the two-way mirror.

"You were going to take the day off."

"No, I wasn't."

The pilot was a comedy about an eccentric Italian film director who had come to America in search of fame and fortune. Mr. Bean played his shy, inept manager. They shared an expensive rented villa in the Hollywood Hills. Just now they were desperate to locate an actress to pose as Dario's wife, so that he could obtain a green card and find work before they both ran out of money.

She immediately grasped the premise and its potential.

It was inspired. Benigni's abuse of the language would generate countless hilarious misunderstandings; coupled with his manager's charming incompetence, the result might be a television classic, thanks in no small measure to the brilliant casting. How could it miss? All they needed was a good script. She realized that her mind had drifted long enough to miss the screenwriter's name. The only credit left was the show's creator/producer, one Barry E. Tormé. Probably the son of that old singer, she thought. What was his name? Mel. Apparently he had fathered a show-business dynasty. The other son, Tracy, was a successful TV writer; he had even created a science-fiction series at Fox that lasted for a couple of seasons. Why had she never heard of brother Barry? He was obviously a pro.

She sat forward, fascinated to see the first episode.

"Me, Dario!" Benigni crowed into a gold-trimmed telephone, the third time it had rung in less than a minute. It was going to be his signature bit.

"O, I Dream!" she said.

"Huh?"

"The line, Marty. Got you."

The letters rearranged themselves automatically in her mind. It was child's play. She had almost expected him to come up with it first. They had kept the game going since her first day at AmiDex, when she pointed out that his full name was an anagram for *Marty licks on me.* It got his attention.

"You can stop with the word shit," he said.

He sounded irritated, which surprised her. "I thought you liked it."

"What's up with that, anyway?"

"It's a reflex," she said. "I can't help it. My father taught me when I was little."

"Well, it's getting old."

She turned to his profile in the semidarkness, his pale, cleanshaven face and short, neat hair as two-dimensional as a cartoon cutout from the back of a cereal box.

"You know, Marty, I was thinking. Could you show me the War Room sometime?" She moved her leg closer to his. "Just you and me, when everybody's gone. So I could see how it works."

"How what works?"

She let her hand brush his knee. "Everything. The really big secrets."

"Such as?"

"I don't know." Had she said too much? "But if I'm going to work here, I should know more about the company. What makes a hit, for example. Maybe you could tell me. You explain things so well."

"Why *did* you come here?"

The question caught her off-guard. "I needed a job."

"Plenty of jobs out there," he snapped. "What is it, you got a script to sell?"

The room was cold and her feet were numb. Now she wanted to be out of here. The other chairs were dim, bulky shapes, like half-reclining corpses, as if she and Marty were not alone in the room.

"Sorry," she said.

"I told you to stay home today."

No, he hadn't. "You *want* me to take the day off?"

He did not answer.

"Do you think I need it? Or is there something special about today?"

The door in the back of the room opened. It connected to the hall that led to the other sections of the building and the War Room itself, where even now the audience response was being recorded and analyzed by a team of market researchers. A hulking figure stood there in silhouette. She could not see his features. He hesitated for a moment, then came all the way in, plunging the room into darkness again, and then there were only the test subjects and their flickering faces opposite her through the smoked glass. The man took a seat at the other end of the row.

"That you, Mickleson?"

At the sound of his voice Marty sat up straight.

"Yes, sir."

"I thought so. Who's she?"

"One of the girls—Annalise. She was just leaving."

Then Marty leaned close to her and whispered:

"Will you get out?"

She was not supposed to be here. The shape at the end of the row must have been the big boss. Marty had known he was coming; that was why he wanted her gone. This was the first time anyone had joined them in the booth. It meant the show was important. The executives listened up when a hit came along.

"Excuse me," she said, and left the observation booth.

She wanted very much to see the rest of the show. Now she would have to wait till it hit the airwaves. Was there a way for her to eavesdrop on the discussion later, after the screening?

In the hall, she listened for the audience reaction. Just now there must have been a lull in the action, with blank tape inserted to represent a commercial break, because there was dead silence from the theater.

She was all the way to the reception area before she realized what he had called her.

Annalise.

It was an anagram for Lisa Anne, the name she had put on her application—and, incredibly, it was the right one. Somehow he had hit it. Had he done so naturally, without thinking, as in their word games? Or did he know?

Busted, she thought.

She crossed to the glass doors, ready to make her break.

Then she thought, So he knows my first name. So what? It's not like it would mean anything to him, even if he were to figure out the rest of it.

She decided that she had been paranoid to use a pseudonym in the first place. If she had told the truth, would anybody care? Technically AmiDex could disqualify her, but the family connection was so many years ago that the name had probably been forgotten by now. In fact she was sure it had. That was the point. That was why she was here.

Outside, the rain had let up. A few of the next hour's subjects were already wandering this way across the courtyard. Only one, a woman with a shopping bag and a multi-colored scarf over her hair, bothered to raise her head to look at the statues.

It was disturbing to see the greats treated with such disrespect.

All day long volunteers gathered outside at the appointed hour, smoking and drinking sodas and eating food they had brought with them, and when they went in they left the remains scattered among the statues, as if the history of the medium and its stars meant nothing to them. Dinah Shore and Carol Burnett and Red Skelton with his clown nose, all nothing more than a part of the landscape now, like the lampposts, like the trash cans that no one used. The sun fell on them, and the winds and the rains and the graffiti and the discarded wads of chewing gum and the pissing of dogs on the place where their feet should have been, and there was nothing for any of them to do but suffer these things with quiet dignity, like the fallen dead in a veterans' cemetery. One day the burdens of their immortality, the birdshit and the cigarette butts and the McDonald's wrappers, might become too much for them to bear and the ground would shake as giants walked the earth again, but for now they could only wait, because that day was not yet here.

"How was it?" said Angie.

"The show? Oh, it was great. Really."

"Then why aren't you in there?"

"It's too cold." She hugged her sides. "When does the grounds crew get here?"

"Uh, you lost me."

"Maintenance. The gardeners. How often do they come?"

"You're putting me on, right?"

She felt her face flush. "Then I'll do it."

"Do—?"

"Clean up. It's a disgrace. Don't you think so?"

"Sure, Lisa. Anything you say . . ."

She started outside, and got only a few paces when the sirens began. She counted four squad cars with the name of a private security company stenciled on the doors. They screeched to a halt in the parking lot and several officers jumped out. Did one of them really have his gun drawn?

"Oh, God," said Angie.

"What's going on?"

"It's the complex. They don't like people taking pictures."

Now she saw that the man in the dark trenchcoat had returned. This time he had brought a van with a remote broadcasting dish on top. The guards held him against the side, under the call letters for a local TV station and the words EYEBALL NEWS. When a cameraman climbed down from the back to object they handcuffed him.

"Who doesn't like it?"

"AmiDex," Angie said solemnly. "They own it all." She waved her hand to include the building, the courtyard, the parking lot and the fenced-in apartments. "Somebody from *Hard Copy* tried to shoot here last month. They confiscated the film. It's off-limits."

"But why?"

"All I know is, there must be some very important people in those condos."

"In *this* neighborhood?"

She couldn't imagine why any VIP's would want to live here. The complex was a lower-middle-class housing development, walled in and protected from the deteriorating streets nearby. It had probably been on this corner since the fifties. She could understand AmiDex buying real estate in the San Fernando Valley instead of the overpriced Westside, but why the aging apartments? The only reason might be so that they could expand their testing facility one day. Meanwhile, why not tear them down? With its spiked iron fences the complex looked like a fortress sealed off against the outside world. There was even barbed wire on top of the walls.

Before she could ask any more questions, the doors to the theater opened. She glanced back and saw Marty leading the audience down the hall for the post-screening discussion.

She followed, eager to hear the verdict.

The boys in the white shirts were no longer at the counter. They were in the War Room, marking up long rolls of paper like doctors charting the vital signs in an intensive care ward. Lights blinked across a bank of electronic equipment, as many rack-mounted modules as there were seats in the theater, with dials and connecting cables that fed into the central computer. She heard circuits humming and the ratcheting whir of a wide-mouthed machine as it disgorged graphs that resembled polygraph tests printed in blood-red ink.

She came to the next section of the hall, as the last head vanished through a doorway around the first turn.

The discussion room was small and bright with rows of desks and acoustic tiles in the ceiling. It reminded her of the classrooms at UCLA, where she had taken a course in Media Studies, before discovering that they didn't have any answers, either. She merged with the group and slumped down in the back row, behind the tallest person she could find.

Marty remained on his feet, pacing.

"Now," he said, "it's your turn. Hollywood is listening! How many of you would rate—" He consulted his clipboard. "—Dario, You So Crazy! as one of the best programs you've ever seen?"

She waited for the hands to go up. She could not see any from here. The tall man blocked her view and if she moved her head Marty might spot her.

"Okay. How many would say 'very good'?"

There must not have been many because he went right on to the next question.

" 'Fair'?"

She closed her eyes and listened to the rustle of coat sleeves and wondered if she had heard the question correctly.

"And how many 'poor'?"

That had to be everyone else. Even the tall man in front of her raised his arm. She recognized his plaid shirt. It was Number Sixteen.

Marty made a notation.

"Okay, great. What was your favorite scene?"

The silence was deafening.

"You won't be graded on this! There's no right or wrong answer. I remember once, when my junior-high English teacher . . ."

He launched into a story to loosen them up. It was about a divorced woman, an escaped sex maniac and a telephone call to the police. She recognized it as a very old dirty joke. Astonishingly he left off the punchline. The audience responded anyway. He had his timing down pat. Or was it that they laughed *because* they knew what was coming? Did that make it even funnier?

The less original the material, she thought, the more they like it. It makes them feel comfortable.

And if that's true, so is the reverse.

She noticed that there was a two-way mirror in this room, too, along the far wall. Was anyone following the discussion from the other side? If so, there wasn't much to hear. Nobody except Marty had anything to say. They were bored stiff, waiting for their money. It would take something more than the show they had just seen to hold them, maybe *Wrestling's Biggest Bleeps, Bloopers and Bodyslams* or *America's Zaniest Surveillance Tapes*. Now she heard a door slam in the hall. The executives had probably given up and left the observation room.

"What is the matter with you people?"

The woman with the multi-colored scarf hunched around to look at her, as Marty tried to see who had spoken.

"In the back row. Number . . ."

"You're right," she said too loudly. "It's not poor, or fair, or excellent. It's a *great* show! Better than anything I've seen in years. Since—"

"Yes?" Marty changed his position, zeroing in on her voice. "Would you mind speaking up? This is your chance to be heard . . ."

"Since *The Fuzzy Family*. Or *The Funnyboner*." She couldn't help mentioning the titles. Her mouth was open now and the truth was coming out and there was no way to stop it.

Marty said, "What network were they on?"

"CBS. They were canceled in the first season."

"But you remember them?"

"They were brilliant."

"Can you tell us why?"

"Because of my father. He created them both."

Marty came to the end of the aisle and finally saw her. His face fell. In the silence she heard other voices, arguing in the hall. She hoped it was not the people who had made *Dario, You So Crazy!* If so, they had to be hurting right now. She felt for them, bitterness and despair and rage welling up in her own throat.

"May I see you outside?" he said.

"No, you may not."

The hell with Marty, AmiDex and her job here. There was no secret as to why some shows made it and other, better ones did not. Darwin was wrong. He hadn't figured on the networks. They had continued to lower their sights until the audience devolved right along with them, so that any ray of hope was snuffed out, overshadowed by the crap around it. And market research and the ratings system held onto their positions by telling them what they wanted to hear, that the low-rent talent they had under contract was good enough, by testing the wrong people for the wrong reasons, people who were too numb to care about a pearl among the pebbles. It was a perfect closed loop.

"*Now*, Miss Rayme."

"That isn't my name." Didn't he get it yet? "My father was Robert Mayer. The man who wrote and produced *Wagons, Ho!*"

It was TV's first western comedy and it made television history. After that he struggled to come up with another hit, but every new show was either canceled or rejected outright. His name meant nothing to the bean-counters. All they could see was the bottom line. As far as they were concerned he owed them a fortune for the failures they had bankrolled. If he had been an entertainer who ran up a debt in Vegas, he would have had to stay there, working it off at the rate of two shows a night, forever. The only thing that gave her satisfaction was the knowledge that they would never collect. One day when she was ten he had a massive heart attack on the set and was whisked away in a blue ambulance and he never came home again.

"Folks, thanks for your time," Marty said. "If you'll return to the lobby . . ."

She had studied his notes and scripts, trying to understand why he failed. She loved them all. They were genuinely funny, the very essence of her father, with his quirky sense of humor and extravagant sight gags—as original and inventive as *Dario, You So Crazy!* Which was a failure, too. Of course. She lowered her head onto the desktop and began to weep.

"Hold up," said Number Sixteen.

"Your pay's ready. Fifty dollars cash." Marty held the door wide. "There's another group coming in . . ."

The lumberjack refused to stand. "Let her talk. I remember *Wagons, Ho!* It was all right."

He turned around in his seat and gave her a wink as she raised her head.

"Thank you," she said softly. "It doesn't matter, now."

She got to her feet with the others and pushed her way out.

Farther down the hall, another door clicked shut. It was marked Green Room. She guessed that the executives from the other side of the mirror had decided to finish their argument in private.

Marty grabbed her elbow.

"I told you to stay home."

"You're hurting me," she said.

"But you just wouldn't take the hint, would you?"

"About what?"

"You can pick up your check in Payroll."

"Get your hands off me."

Number Sixteen came up next to her. "You got a problem here?"

"Not anymore," she said.

"Your pay's up front, cowboy," Marty told him.

"You sure you're okay?" asked Number Sixteen.

"I am now."

Marty shook his head sadly.

"I'll tell them to make it for the full two weeks. I liked you, you know? I really did."

Then he turned and walked the audience back to the lobby.

Farther down the hall, she saw Human Resources, where she had gone the first day for her interview, and beyond that Public Relations and Payroll. She didn't care about her check but there was a security door at the end. It would let her out directly into the courtyard.

Number Sixteen followed her.

"I was thinking. If you want some lunch, I've got my car."

"So do I," she said, walking faster.

Then she thought, Why not? Me, with a lumberjack. I'll be watching Martha Stewart while he hammers his wood and lays his pipe or whatever he does all day, and he'll come home and watch hockey games and I'll stay loaded and sit up every night to see *Wagons Ho!* on the Nostalgia Channel and we'll go on that way, like a sitcom. He'll take care of me. And in time I'll forget everything. All I have to do is say yes.

He was about to turn back.

"Okay," she said.

"What?"

"This way. There's an exit to the parking lot, down here."

Before they could get to it the steel door at the end swung open.

The rain had stopped and a burst of clear light from outside reflected off the polished floor, distorting the silhouette of the figure standing there. A tall woman in a designer suit entered from the grounds. Behind her, the last of the private security cars drove off. The Eyeball News truck was gone.

"All set," the woman said into a flip-phone, and went briskly to the door marked Green Room.

Voices came from within, rising to an emotional pitch. Then the voices receded as the door clicked shut.

There was something in the tone of the argument that got to her. She couldn't make out the words but one of the voices was close to pleading. It was painful to hear. She thought of her father and the desperate meetings he must have had, years ago. When the door whispered open again, two men in gray suits stepped out into the hall, holding a third man between them.

It had to be the producer of the pilot.

She wanted to go to him and take his hands and look into his eyes and tell him that they were wrong. He was too talented to listen to them. What did they know? There were other networks, cable, foreign markets, features, if only he could break free of them and move on. He had to. She would be waiting and so would millions of others, an invisible audience whose opinions were never counted, as if they did not exist, but who were out there, she was sure. The ones who remembered *Wagons, Ho!* and *The Funnyboner* and *The Fuzzy Family* and would faithfully tune in other programs with the same quirky sensibility, if they had the choice.

He looked exhausted. The suits had him in their grip, supporting his weight between them, as if carrying a drunk to a waiting cab. What was his name? Terry Something. Or Barry. That was it. She saw him go limp. He had the body of a middle-aged man.

"Please," he said in a cracking voice, "this is the one, you'll see. *Please . . .*"

"Mr. Tormé?" she called out, remembering his name.

The letters shuffled like a deck of cards in her mind and settled into a new pattern. It was a reflex she could not control, ever since she had learned the game from her father so many years ago, before the day they took him away and told his family that he was dead.

Barry E. Tormé, she thought.

You could spell a lot of words with those letters.

Even . . .

Robert Mayer.

He turned slightly, and she saw the familiar nose and chin she had tried so many times to reproduce, working from fading photographs and the shadow pictures in her mind. The two men continued to drag him forward. His shoes left long black skidmarks on the polished floor. Then they lifted him off his feet and he was lost in the light.

Outside the door, a blue van was waiting.

They dumped him in and locked the tailgate. Beyond the parking lot lay the walled compound, where the razor wire gleamed like hungry teeth atop the barricades and forgotten people lived out lives as bleak as unsold pilots and there was no way out for any of them until the cameras rolled again on another hit.

Milton Berle and Johnny Carson and Jackie Gleason watched mutely, stars who had become famous by speaking the words put into their mouths by others, by men who had no monuments to honor them, not here or anywhere else.

Now she knew the real reason she had come to this place. There was something missing. When she finished her sculpture there would be a new face for the courtyard, one who deserved a statue of his own. And this time she would get it right.

The steel door began to close.

Sorry, Daddy! she thought as the rain started again outside. I'm sorry, sorry. . . .

"Wait." Number Sixteen put on his Ray-Bans. "I gotta get my pay first. You want to come with me?"

Yes, we could do that. Simple. All we do is turn and run the other way, like Lucy and Desi, like Dario and Mr. Bean, bumbling along to a private hell of our own. What's the difference?

"No," she said.

"I thought—"

"I'm sorry. I can't."

"Why not?"

"I just . . . can't."

She ran instead toward the light at the end, hoping to see the face in the van clearly one last time as it drove away, before the men in the suits could stop her.

KURAHASHI YUMIKO

The House of the Black Cat

Kurahashi Yumiko is an acclaimed short story writer in her native Japan, active in Japanese experimental fiction since the 1960s. The range of her stories runs from mainstream to erotica, including works of surrealism, fantasy, and science fiction. Her books include The Adventures of Sumiyakist O *and* The Woman with the Flying Head; *and she has won the Tamura Toshiko, Izumi Kyoka, and Women's Literary prizes.*

"The House of the Black Cat," a peculiar little tale from the English edition of The Woman with the Flying Head, *gives a good taste of the disturbing, dreamlike world typically conjured by Yumiko. It is a variation on the "cat bride" tales to be found in both Japanese and Western folklore.*

—T. W.

I've rented a video from Kamiya. It looks interesting." When her husband told her this, Keiko replied, "Another homemade pornographic movie by Mr. Kamiya?" Kamiya, who had graduated from the same university as her husband, though a few years later, now worked for a TV station, as a producer. He also composed poems under a pseudonym. His award-winning anthology was—Keiko tried to recollect—entitled *The Black Cat*, if she's not mistaken. All the poems in it featured a black cat and dealt with a mysterious, apparently romantic relationship between a young man who appeared to be Kamiya himself and the black cat, "as noble as a prostitute, as coquettish as a dark goddess."

"I don't know if it's pornographic or not, but the video seems to be about the cat."

Keiko could hardly imagine Kamiya's work could be a straightforward portrayal of a cat's behaviors—it must be a visual version of the poems in *The Black Cat*. Keiko had made it a rule to watch such movies with her husband late at night, after her children had gone to sleep. For some reason, she felt awkward watching a provocative video all by herself, blushing and being aroused by it. It was a relief to have her husband beside her, for then it was just like watching movies or previews in the cinema with the rest of the audience.

The video *Black Cat* began with a shot of a house with white walls. The camera focused on a wall sunk in the pale, dim light of dusk or dawn. Then something like a charcoal line-drawing began to surface. Closer examination revealed that it was cat-shaped, and squirming slightly. It seemed as if a cat were in agony, confined in paint within the wall. This instantly reminded Keiko of Poe's "The Black Cat." She didn't much like that story, which featured the cruel killing of a cat.

"It's taken from Poe," said her husband, making the same connection.

One could never have become bored watching that picture of a cat moving and molding itself in the wall. Shortly thereafter, as the interior of the catlike outline was filled in with black, a pitch-black creature was revealed—and suddenly a pair of golden eyes was set aflame. No sooner had this occurred than a real black cat crawled out of the wall and came forward. The cat arched its supple back, drawing the Greek character omega—Ω—and then stretched itself.

Keiko gave a sigh of admiration. If it were a drawing, what an intoxicating curve that would seem!

"It looks more coquettish than the silhouette of a woman."

"Isn't it a woman in a cat's shape?"

"Its motions are exactly like those of a woman who just got out of bed."

This was true. There was something about the cat and its movements reminiscent of a woman languidly pacing around a room with the remnants of sleep in her disheveled hair. There were a skylight diagonally opposite the window, and a bed, a vanity table with three mirrors, and a chest, which the cat used as if they were its own furniture . . . and here, Keiko realized that miraculously, the cat was big enough to use the furniture the way a human being would—whether the furniture had shrunk or the cat had grown. Keiko took it for granted that the cat had become the same size as a human being. "This should be a woman in a cat figure after all," agreed her husband.

The black cat woman sat at the vanity table, with her glossy, hairy back to the screen. She raised her forepaws—or hands—forming a graceful diamond behind her neck, as if to comb her hair. Then she lined up cosmetics on the table and began to make up her face. How was she going to make up a feline face? Keiko took a strange interest. Did cats have lips to put lipstick on? As Keiko was wondering about this, the black cat took a light purple robe out of the chest, put it on, and walked out of the room on two legs.

In the next scene, the cat woman was sitting at table, having breakfast. It would no longer surprise Keiko to see her eat an omelet with a knife and fork and drink café au lait—in fact before Keiko had realized it, the cat-woman was doing just that. It would be even more natural for her husband or lover to be having breakfast opposite her—though Keiko was surprised, or rather, ill at ease, to find that he was human.

The man's back was to the camera, so the audience couldn't see how old he was or what he looked like. The cat-woman sat facing him. "What a beauty!" Keiko exclaimed again in admiration. It's a simple fact that some cats are prettier than others. A lover of cats since she was a child, Keiko had established standards for a cat's appearance. The face of this cat was so perfect it seemed as if it had accurately copied the ideal of cats in its profile and facial features. Especially its golden eyes, which had a slight green cast, were more beautiful than those of any woman. Keiko's husband sighed too. Keiko quivered unconsciously when the cat smiled at the man. The mysterious smile filled the viewer with the desire to be devoured by the cat.

Then the man disappeared—perhaps he had gone to work. What followed was a portrayal of the cat's everyday life. She now walked on four paws, jumped onto the windowsill, climbed the magnolia tree in the garden, and curled up to take a nap. The black cat had somehow shrunk to her normal size again.

When night fell, the cat grew as big as a human being again, and if Keiko had looked forward to watching the following scene, it was beyond even her expectations: an act of sexual intercourse of unearthly grace. It was not that the black cat was transformed into a human being, but with her cat's face and body, she embraced the man and made love to him exactly as any female human would. Keiko would never have imagined that a cat's limbs could so flexibly caress a person's body. Its rough tongue seemed very effective in this regard as well. The man's hand moved to stroke the cat's fur. Like any cat, she seemed to enjoy having her throat stroked. The cat's purring mingled with a song sung in a strange woman's voice, like background music. It sounded like a work by some contemporary composer, one that featured a soprano voice as a musical instrument, which would drive the listener crazy. The sound accompanied the physical movements of the exchange of pleasure. It seemed as if the cat woman were actually speaking erotically, while rippling the black curved line of her body.

The man's face always remained turned away from the camera. The pair began by making love in a standard position and then continued to move through one position after another. Eventually they assumed the beast's position. A part of the man's body seemed to be swallowed into the pitch darkness of the cat, rather than penetrating it. A long-lasting and high-pitched scream of pain or pleasure came as dawn's light broke abruptly through the screen.

"I wonder what technique he could possibly have used to shoot this?" Keiko's husband said in a voice dry with excitement. Her imagination too was so inflamed and swollen she was almost insensate. As was only natural in such a state, the couple couldn't do anything but reenact what they had just seen. Keiko tried to embody feline seductiveness, thinking of herself as a white cat when the strange music of a soprano voice began jumping in scat. Afterward, her husband said, "The white cat isn't bad, either."

For some strange reason, neither Keiko nor her husband was inclined to watch *Black Cat* again. They meant to return the video to Kamiya the next time he got in touch with them, but they never heard from him. Keiko's husband phoned the TV station and was told that Kamiya had taken a leave to travel abroad and had vanished without a trace.

"Is his wife at home?"

"He is married and has four children—female twins and male twins, I've heard."

"I'm rather worried. Why don't we go visit them someday?" Keiko said. She didn't like the idea of going by herself—something told her that something terrible might have happened.

It was on a Sunday afternoon, in the lingering chill before the cherry blossoms were in full bloom, that the two visited Kamiya's residence. The house they were looking for was built in the Spanish style, with elegant white walls. Dark red Japanese quinces were in flower, and a huge magnolia tree was swarming with blossoms in the garden.

"It's the same magnolia as in the video."

"It looks like that house with white walls at the beginning of it."

"Apparently no one's at home."

They were pushing open the wooden garden gate when they heard cats meowing above their heads. The black fruitlike things in the boughs of the magnolia turned out to be five black cats. As if to welcome the guests, the cats hung themselves headlong from the tree and climbed down to sit in a line on the white bench in the garden. The face of the biggest black cat looked familiar— this was undoubtedly the cat who had had sex with the man, the black cat-woman. Keiko was convinced that the cat's partner had been Kamiya—that this picturesque black cat must be his wife, and the other four his children.

"Where's your husband?" Without answering Keiko's question, the mother cat turned around and jumped to the windowsill, the others following her, and they disappeared into the house. From what Keiko and her husband could see of the inside, the house appeared inhabited. It didn't look like a deserted house whose master had taken flight. There was something unusual about the house though. Was it just Keiko's imagination that there was a slightly fishy, bloody smell hovering in the air? Was this smell from something the cats had eaten?

Her husband climbed in through the window and confirmed that no one was at home. The two decided it was time to leave. As they walked out of the garden and were taking another look back, Keiko thought she heard a woman speaking in the house.

"I was so scared. They came out of the blue."

"Did you hear something, Keiko?"

"No, not really," said Keiko.

JOHN KESSEL

Every Angel Is Terrifying

John Kessel was born in Buffalo, New York in 1950 and is currently a professor of American literature and fiction writing at North Carolina State University in Raleigh. Kessel's stories have been published in Cottonwood Review, Galileo, The Magazine of Fantasy & Science Fiction, Asimov's Science Fiction magazine, Omni, and other publications. He won an NEA Literature Fellowship in 1980. He won a Nebula Award for his novella "Another Orphan" and the Theodore Sturgeon Award for his story "Buffalo." His play Faustfeathers won the 1994 Paul Green Playwrights' Competition.

His first novel, Freedom Beach (with James Patrick Kelly) was published in 1985 and his second novel, Good News from Outer Space, was published in 1989. His most recent novel is Corrupting Dr. Nice. His short fiction is collected in Meeting in Infinity and The Pure Product.

Kessel's criticism has appeared in numerous venues, and he used to write a regular column for The Magazine of Fantasy & Science Fiction. Since 1985, with Mark L. Van Name, he has run the Sycamore Hill Writers' Conference. Kessel lives in Raleigh with his wife, graphic designer Sue Hall, their daughter Emma, and two cats.

Kessel is best known as a writer of "literary" science fiction and fantasy. So "Every Angel Is Terrifying," horror with a literary antecedent, is both like and unlike his usual fiction. The story was originally published in The Magazine of Fantasy & Science Fiction's October/November issue.

—E. D.

Railroad watched Bobby Lee grab the grandmother's body under the armpits and drag her up the other side of the ditch. "Whyn't you help him, Hiram," he said.

Hiram took off his coat, skidded down into the ditch after Bobby Lee, and got hold of the old lady's legs. Together he and Bobby Lee lugged her across the field toward the woods. Her broken blue hat was still pinned to her head, which lolled against Bobby Lee's shoulder. The woman's face grinned lopsidedly all the way into the shadow of the trees.

Railroad carried the cat over to the Studebaker. It occurred to him that he didn't know the cat's name, and now that the entire family was dead he never would. It was a calico, gray striped with a broad white face and an orange nose. "What's your name, puss-puss?" he whispered, scratching it behind the ears. The cat purred. One by one Railroad went round and rolled up the windows of the car. A fracture zigzagged across the windshield, and the front passenger's vent window was shattered. He stuffed Hiram's coat into the vent window hole. Then he put the cat inside the car and shut the door. The cat put its front paws up on the dashboard and, watching him, gave a pantomime meow.

Railroad pushed up his glasses and stared off toward the woodline where Bobby Lee and Hiram had taken the bodies. The place was hot and still, silence broken only by birdsong from somewhere up the embankment behind him. He squinted up into the cloudless sky. Only a couple of hours of sun left. He rubbed the spot on his shoulder where the grandmother had touched him. Somehow he had wrenched it when he jerked away from her.

The last thing the grandmother had said picked at him: "You're one of my own children." The old lady had looked familiar, but she didn't look anything like his mother. But maybe his father had sown some wild oats in the old days—Railroad knew he had—could the old lady have been his mother, for real? It would explain why the woman who had raised him, the sweetest of women, could have been saddled with a son as bad as he was.

The idea caught in his head. He wished he'd had the sense to ask the grandmother a few questions. The old woman might have been sent to tell him the truth.

When Hiram and Bobby Lee came back, they found Railroad leaning under the hood of the car.

"What we do now, boss?" Bobby Lee asked.

"Police could be here any minute," Hiram said. Blood was smeared on the leg of his khaki pants. "Somebody might of heard the shots."

Railroad pulled himself out from under the hood. "Onliest thing we got to worry about now, Hiram, is how we get this radiator to stop leaking. You find a tire iron and straighten out this here fan. Bobby Lee, you get the belt off'n the other car."

It took longer than the half hour Hiram had estimated to get the people's Studebaker back on the road. By the time they did it was twilight, and the red-dirt road was cast in the shadows of the pinewoods. They pushed the stolen Hudson they'd been driving off into the trees and got into the Studebaker.

Railroad gripped the wheel of the car and they bounced down the dirt road toward the main highway. Hat pushed back on his head, Hiram went through the dead man's wallet, while in the back seat Bobby Lee had the cat on his lap and was scratching it under the chin. "Kitty-kitty-kitty-kitty-kitty," he murmured.

"Sixty-eight dollars," Hiram said. "With the twenty-two from the wife's purse, that makes ninety bucks." He turned around and handed a wad of bills to Bobby Lee. "Get rid of that damn cat," he said. "Want me to hold yours for you?" he asked Railroad.

Railroad reached over, took the bills, and stuffed them into the pocket of the yellow shirt with bright blue parrots that had belonged to the husband who'd been driving the car. Bailey Boy, the grandmother had called him. Railroad's shoulder twinged.

The car shuddered; the wheels had been knocked out of kilter when it rolled. If he tried pushing past fifty, it would shake itself right off the road. Railroad felt the warm weight of his pistol inside his belt, against his belly. Bobby Lee hummed tunelessly in the back seat. Hiram was quiet, fidgeting, looking out at the dark trees. He tugged his battered coat out of the vent window, tried to shake some of the wrinkles out of it. "You oughtn't to use a man's coat without saying to him," he grumbled.

Bobby Lee spoke up. "He didn't want the cat to get away."

Hiram sneezed. "Will you throw that damn animal out the damn window?"

"She never hurt you none," Bobby Lee said.

Railroad said nothing. He had always imagined that the world was slightly unreal, that he was meant to be the citizen of some other place. His mind was a box. Outside the box was that world of distraction, amusement, annoyance. Inside the box his real life went on, the struggle between what he knew and what he didn't know. He had a way of acting—polite, detached—because that way he wouldn't be bothered. When he was bothered, he got mad. When he got mad, bad things happened.

He had always been prey to remorse, but now he felt it more fully than he had since he was a boy. He hadn't paid enough attention. He'd pegged the old lady as a hypocrite and had gone back into his box, thinking her just another fool from that puppet world. But that moment of her touching him—she'd wanted to comfort him. And he shot her.

What was it the old woman had said? "You could be honest if you'd only try. . . . Think how wonderful it would be to settle down and live a comfortable life and not have to think about somebody chasing you all the time."

He knew she was only saying that to save her life. But that didn't mean it couldn't also be a message.

Outside the box, Hiram asked, "What was all that yammer yammer with the grandmother about Jesus? We doing all the killing while you yammer yammer."

"He did shoot the old lady," Bobby Lee said.

"And made us carry her off to the woods, when if he'd of waited she could of walked there like the others. We're the ones get blood on our clothes."

Railroad said quietly, "You don't like the way things are going, son?"

Hiram twitched against the seat like he was itchy between the shoulder blades. "I ain't sayin' that. I just want out of this state."

"We going to Atlanta. In Atlanta we can get lost."

"Gonna get me a girl!" Bobby Lee said.

"They got more cops in Atlanta than the rest of the state put together," Hiram said. "In Florida. . . ."

Without taking his eyes off the road, Railroad snapped his right hand across the bridge of Hiram's nose. Hiram jerked, more startled than hurt, and his hat tumbled off into the back seat.

Bobby Lee laughed, and handed Hiram his hat.

It was after 11:00 when they hit the outskirts of Atlanta. Railroad pulled into a diner, the Sweet Spot, red brick and an asbestos-shingled roof, the air smelling of cigarettes and pork barbecue. Hiram rubbed some dirt from the lot into the stain on his pants leg. Railroad unlocked the trunk and found the dead man's suitcase, full of clothes. He carried it in with them.

On the radio sitting on the shelf behind the counter, Kitty Wells sang "It Wasn't God Who Made Honky-Tonk Angels." Railroad studied the menu, front and back, and ordered biscuits and gravy. While they ate Bobby Lee ran on about girls, and Hiram sat sullenly smoking. Railroad could tell Hiram was getting ready to do something stupid. He didn't need either of them anymore. So after they finished eating, Railroad left the car keys on the table and took the suitcase into the men's room. He locked the door. He pulled his .38 out of his waistband, put it on the sink, and changed out of the too-tight dungarees into some of the dead husband's baggy trousers. He washed his face and hands. He cleaned his glasses on the tail of the parrot shirt, then tucked in the shirt. He stuck the .38 into the suitcase and came out again. Bobby Lee and Hiram were gone, and the car was no longer in the parking lot. The bill on the table, next to Hiram's still smoldering cigarette, was for six dollars and eighty cents.

Railroad sat in the booth drinking his coffee. In the window of the diner, near the door, a piece of cardboard had been taped up, saying, "WANTED: FRY COOK." When he was done with the coffee, he untaped the sign and headed to the register. After he paid the bill he handed the cashier the sign. "I'm your man," he said.

The cashier called the manager. "Mr. Cauthron, this man says he's a cook."

Mr. Cauthron was maybe thirty-five years old. His carrot red hair stood up in a pompadour like a rooster's comb, and a little belly swelled out over his belt. "What's your name?"

"Lloyd Bailey."

"Lloyd, what experience do you have?"

"I can cook anything on this here menu," Railroad said.

The manager took him back to the kitchen. "Stand aside, Shorty," the manager said to the tall black man at the griddle. "Fix me a Denver omelet," he said to Railroad.

Railroad washed his hands, put on an apron, broke two eggs into a bowl. He threw handfuls of chopped onion, green pepper, and diced ham into a skillet. When the onions were soft, he poured the beaten eggs over the ham and vegetables, added salt and cayenne pepper. When he slid the finished omelet onto a plate, the manager bent down over it as if he were inspecting the paint job on a used car. He straightened up. "Pay's thirty dollars a week. Be here at six in the morning."

Out in the lot Railroad set down his bag and looked around. Cicadas buzzed in the hot city night. Around the corner from the diner he'd noticed a big Victorian house with a sign on the porch, "Rooms for Rent." He was about to start walking when, out of the corner of his eye, he caught a movement by the trash barrel next to the chain link fence. He peered into the gloom and saw the cat trying to leap up to the top to get at the garbage. He went over, held out his hand. The cat didn't run; it sniffed him, butted its head against his hand.

He picked it up, cradled it under his arm, and carried it and the bag to the rooming house. Under dense oaks, it was a big tan clapboard mansion with green shutters and hanging baskets of begonias on the porch, and a green porch swing.

The thick oval leaded glass of the oak door was beveled around the edge, the brass of the handle dark with age.

The door was unlocked. His heart jumped a bit at the opportunity it presented; at the same time he wanted to warn the proprietor against such foolishness. Off to one side of the entrance was a little table with a doily, vase and dried flowers; on the other a sign beside a door said, "manager."

Railroad knocked. After a moment the door opened and a woman with the face of an angel opened it. She was not young, perhaps forty, with very white skin and blonde hair. She looked at him, smiled, saw the cat under his arm. "What a sweet animal," she said.

"I'd like a room," he said.

"I'm sorry. We don't cater to pets," the woman said, not unkindly.

"This here's no pet, Ma'm," Railroad said. "This here's my only friend in the world."

The landlady's name was Mrs. Graves. The room she rented him was twelve feet by twelve feet, with a single bed, a cherry veneer dresser, a wooden table and chair, a narrow closet, lace curtains on the window, and an old pineapple quilt on the bed. The air smelled sweet. On the wall opposite the bed was a picture in a dime store frame, of an empty rowboat floating in an angry gray ocean, the sky overcast, only a single shaft of sunlight in the distance from a sunset that was not in the picture.

The room cost ten dollars a week. Despite Mrs. Graves's rule against pets, like magic she took a shine to Railroad's cat. It was almost as if she'd rented the room to the cat, with Railroad along for the ride. After some consideration, he named the cat Pleasure. She was the most affectionate animal he had ever seen. She wanted to be with him, even when he ignored her. She made him feel wanted; she made him nervous. Railroad fashioned a cat door in the window of his room so that Pleasure could go out and in whenever she wanted, and not be confined to the room when Railroad was at work.

The only other residents of the boarding house were Louise Parker, a school teacher, and Charles Foster, a lingerie salesman. Mrs. Graves cleaned Railroad's room once a week, swept the floors, alternated the quilt every other week with a second one done in a rose pattern that he remembered from his childhood. He worked at the diner from six in the morning, when Maisie, the cashier, unlocked, until Shorty took over at three in the afternoon. The counter girl was Betsy, and Service, a Negro boy, bussed tables and washed dishes. Railroad told them to call him Bailey, and didn't talk much.

When he wasn't working, Railroad spent most of his time at the boarding house, or evenings in a small nearby park. Railroad would take the Bible from the drawer in the boarding house table, buy an afternoon newspaper, and carry them with him. Pleasure often followed him to the park. She would lunge after squirrels and shy away from dogs, hissing sideways. Cats liked to kill squirrels, and dogs liked to kill cats. But there was no sin in it. Pleasure would not go to hell, or heaven. Cats had no souls.

The world was full of stupid people like Bobby Lee and Hiram, who lied to themselves and killed without knowing why. Life was a prison. Turn to the right, it was a wall. Turn to the left, it was a wall. Look up it was a ceiling, look down it was a floor. And Railroad had taken out his imprisonment on others; he was not deceived in his own behavior.

Railroad did not believe in sin, but somehow he felt it. Still, he was not a dog or a cat, he was a man. *You're one of my own children.* There was no reason why he had to kill people. He only wished he'd never have to deal with any Hirams and Bobby Lees anymore. He gazed across the park at the Ipana toothpaste sign painted on the wall of the Piggly Wiggly. *Whiter than white.* Pleasure crouched at the end of the bench, her haunches twitching as she watched a finch hop across the sidewalk.

Railroad picked her up, rubbed his cheek against her whiskers. "Pleasure, I'll tell you what," he whispered. "Let's make us a deal. You save me from Bobby Lee and Hiram, and I'll never kill anybody again."

The cat looked at him with its clear yellow eyes.

Railroad sighed. He put the cat down. He leaned back on the bench and opened the newspaper. Beneath the fold on the front page he read,

ESCAPED CONVICTS KILLED IN WRECK

VALDOSTA—Two escaped convicts and an unidentified female passenger were killed Tuesday when the late model stolen automobile they were driving struck a bridge abutment while being pursued by State Police.

The deceased convicts, Hiram Leroy Burgett, 31, and Bobby Lee Ross, 21, escaped June 23 while being transported to the State Hospital for the Criminally Insane for psychological evaluation. A third escapee, Ronald Reuel Pickens, 47, is still at large.

The lunch rush was petering out. There were two people at the counter and four booths were occupied, and Railroad had set a BLT and an order of fried chicken with collards up on the shelf when Maisie came back into the kitchen and called the manager. "Police wants to talk to you, Mr. C."

Railroad peeked out from behind the row of hanging order slips. A man in a suit sat at the counter, sipping sweet tea. Cauthron went out to talk to him.

"Two castaways on a raft," Betsy called to Railroad.

The man spoke with Cauthron for a few minutes, showed him a photograph. Cauthron shook his head, nodded, shook his head again. They laughed. Railroad eyed the back door of the diner, but turned back to the grill. By the time he had the toast up and the eggs fried, the man was gone. Cauthron stepped back to his office without saying anything.

At the end of the shift he pulled Railroad aside. "Lloyd," he said. "I need to speak with you."

Railroad followed him into the cubbyhole he called his office. Cauthron sat behind the cluttered metal desk and picked up a letter from the top layer of trash. "I just got this here note from Social Security saying that number you gave is not valid." He looked up at Railroad, his china blue eyes unreadable.

Railroad took off his glasses and rubbed the bridge of his nose with his thumb and forefinger. He didn't say anything.

"I suppose it's just some mixup," Cauthron said. "Same as that business with the detective this afternoon. Don't you worry about it."

"Thank you, Mr. Cauthron."

"One other thing, before you go, Lloyd. Did I say your salary was thirty a week? I meant twenty-five. That okay with you?"

"Whatever you say, Mr. Cauthron."

"And I think, in order to encourage trade, we'll start opening at five. I'd like you to pick up the extra hour. Starting Monday."

Railroad nodded. "Is that all?"

"That's it, Lloyd." Cauthron seemed suddenly to enjoy calling Railroad "Lloyd," rolling the name over his tongue and watching for his reaction. "Thanks for being such a Christian employee."

Railroad went back to his room in the rooming house. Pleasure mewed for him, and when he sat on the bed, hopped into his lap. But Railroad just stared at the picture of the rowboat on the opposite wall. After a while the cat hopped onto the window sill and out through her door onto the roof.

Only a crazy person would use the knowledge that a man was a murderer in order to cheat that man out of his pay. How could he know that Railroad wouldn't kill him, or run away, or do both?

Lucky for Cauthron that Railroad had made his deal with Pleasure. But now he didn't know what to do. If the old lady's message was from God, then maybe this was his first test. Nobody said being good was supposed to be easy. Nobody said, just because Railroad was turning to good, everybody he met forever after would be good. Railroad had asked Pleasure to save him from Bobby Lee and Hiram, not Mr. Cauthron.

He needed guidance. He slid open the drawer of the table. Beside the Bible was his .38. He flipped open the cylinder, checked to see that all the chambers were loaded, then put it back into the drawer. He took out the Bible and opened it at random.

The first verse his eyes fell on was from Deuteronomy: "These you may eat of all that are in the waters: you may eat all that have fins and scales. And whatever does not have fins and scales you shall not eat."

There was a knock at the door. Railroad looked up. "Yes?"

"Mr. Bailey?" It was Mrs. Graves. "I thought you might like some tea."

Keeping his finger in the Bible to mark his page, Railroad got up and opened the door. Mrs. Graves stood there with a couple of tall glasses, beaded with sweat, on a tray.

"That's mighty kind of you, Miz Graves. Would you like to come in?"

"Thank you, Mr. Bailey." She set the tray down on the table, gave him a glass. It was like nectar. "Is it sweet enough?"

"It's perfect, ma'm."

She wore a yellow print dress with little flowers on it. Her every movement showed a calm he had not seen in a woman before, and her gray eyes exuded compassion, as if to say, I know who you are but that doesn't matter.

They sat down, he on the bed, she on the chair. She saw the Bible in his hand. "I find many words of comfort in the Bible."

"I can't say as I find much comfort in it, ma'm. Too many bloody deeds."

"But many acts of goodness."

"You said a true word."

"Sometimes I wish I could live in the world of goodness." She smiled. "But this world is good enough."

Did she really think that? "Since Eve ate the apple, ma'm, it's a world of good and evil. How can goodness make up for the bad? That's a mystery to me."

She sipped her tea. "Of course it's a mystery. That's the point."

"The point is, something's always after you, deserve it or not."

"What a sad thought, Mr. Bailey."

"Yes'm. From minute to minute, we fade away. Only way to get to heaven is to die."

After Mrs. Graves left he sat thinking about her beautiful face. Like an angel. Nice titties, too. He would marry her. He would settle down, like the grandmother said. But he would have to get an engagement ring. If he'd been thinking, he could have taken the grandmother's ring—but how was he supposed to know when he'd killed her that he was going to fall in love so soon?

He opened the dresser, felt among the dead man's clothes until he found the sock, pulled out his savings. It was only forty-three dollars.

The only help for it was to ask Pleasure. Railroad paced the room. It was a long time, and Railroad began to worry, before the cat came back. The cat slipped silently through her door, lay down on the table, simple as you please, in the wedge of sunlight coming in the window. Railroad got down on his knees, his face level with the table top. The cat went "Mrrph?" and raised its head. Railroad gazed into her steady eyes.

"Pleasure," he said. "I need to get an engagement ring, and I don't have enough money. Get one for me."

The cat watched him.

He waited for some sign. Nothing happened.

Then, like a dam bursting, a flood of confidence flowed into him. He knew what he would do.

The next morning he walked down to the Sweet Spot whistling. He spent much of his shift imagining when and how he would ask Mrs. Graves for her hand. Maybe on the porch swing, on Saturday night? Or at breakfast some morning? He could leave the ring next to his plate and she would find it, with his note, when clearing the table. Or he could come down to her room in the middle of the night, and he'd ram himself into her in the darkness, make her whimper, then lay the perfect diamond on her breast.

At the end of the shift he took a beefsteak from the diner's refrigerator as an offering to Pleasure. But when he entered his room the cat was not there. He left the meat wrapped in butcher paper in the kitchen downstairs, then went back up and changed into Bailey Boy's baggy suit. At the corner he took the bus downtown and walked into the first jewelry store he saw. He made the woman show him several diamond engagement rings. Then the phone rang, and when the woman went to answer it he pocketed a ring and walked out. No clerk in her right mind should be so careless, but it went exactly as he had imagined it. As easy as breathing.

That night he had a dream. He was alone with Mrs. Graves, and she was making love to him. But as he moved against her, he felt the skin of her full breast deflate and wrinkle beneath his hand, and he found he was making love to the dead grandmother, her face grinning the same vacant grin it had when Hiram and Bobby Lee hauled her into the woods.

Railroad woke in terror. Pleasure was sitting on his chest, her face an inch from his, purring loud as a diesel. He snatched the cat up in both hands and hurled her across the room. She hit the wall with a thump, then fell to the floor, claws skittering on the hardwood. She scuttled for the window, through the door onto the porch roof.

It took him ten minutes for his heart to slow down, and then he could not sleep.

Someone is always after you. That day in the diner, when Railroad was taking a break, sitting on a stool in front of the window fan sipping some ice water, Cauthron came out of the office and put his hand on his shoulder, the one that still hurt occasionally. "Hot work, ain't it boy?"

"Yessir." Railroad was ten or twelve years older than Cauthron.

"What is this world coming to?" Maisie said to nobody in particular. She had the newspaper open on the counter and was scanning the headlines. "You read what it says here about some man robbing a diamond ring right out from under the nose of the clerk at Merriam's Jewelry."

"I saw that already," Mr. Cauthron said. And after a moment, "White fellow, wasn't it?"

"It was," sighed Maisie. "Must be some trash from the backwoods. Some of those poor people have not had the benefit of a Christian upbringing."

"They'll catch him. Men like that always get caught." Cauthron leaned in the doorway of his office, arms crossed above his belly. "Maisie," Cauthron said. "Did I tell you Lloyd here is the best short order cook we've had in here since 1947? The best *white* short order cook."

"I heard you say that."

"I mean, makes you wonder where he was before he came here. Was he short order cooking all round Atlanta? Seems like we would of heard, don't it? Come to think, Lloyd never told me much about where he was before he showed up that day. He ever say much to you, Maisie?"

"Can't say as I recall."

"You can't recall because he hasn't. What you say, Lloyd? Why is that?"

"No time for conversation, Mr. Cauthron."

"No time for conversation? You carrying some resentment, Lloyd? We ain't paying you enough?"

"I didn't say that."

"Because, if you don't like it here, I'd be unhappy to lose the best white short order cook I had since 1947."

Railroad put down his empty glass and slipped on his paper hat. "I can't afford to lose this job. And, you don't mind my saying, Mr. Cauthron, you'd come to regret it if I was forced to leave."

"Weren't you listening, Lloyd? Isn't that what I just said?"

"Yes, you did. Now maybe we ought to quit bothering Maisie with our talk and get back to work."

"I like a man that enjoys his job," Cauthron said, slapping Railroad on the shoulder again. "I'd have to be suicidal to make a good worker like you leave. Do I look suicidal, Lloyd?"

"No, you don't look suicidal, Mr. Cauthron."

"I see Pleasure all the time going down the block to pick at the trash by the Sweet Spot," Mrs. Graves told him as they sat on the front porch swing that evening. "That cat could get hurt if you let it out so much. That is a busy street."

Foster had gone to a ball game, and Louise Parker was visiting her sister in Chattanooga, so they were alone. It was the opportunity Railroad had been waiting for.

"I don't want to keep her a prisoner," he said. The chain of the swing creaked as they rocked slowly back and forth. He could smell her lilac perfume. The curve of her thigh beneath her print dress caught the light from the front room coming through the window.

"You're a man who has spent much time alone, aren't you," she said. "So mysterious."

He had his hand in his pocket, the ring in his fingers. He hesitated. A couple walking down the sidewalk nodded at them. He couldn't do it out here, where the world might see. "Mrs. Graves, would you come up to my room? I have something I need to show you."

She did not hesitate. "I hope there's nothing wrong."

"No, ma'm. Just something I'd like to rearrange."

He opened the door for her and followed her up the stairs. The clock in the hall ticked loudly. He opened the door to his room and ushered her in, closed the door behind them. When she turned to face him he fell to his knees.

He held up the ring in both hands, his offering. "Miz Graves, I want you to marry me."

She looked at him kindly, her expression calm. The silence stretched. She reached out; he thought she was going to take the ring, but instead she touched his wrist. "I can't marry you, Mr. Bailey."

"Why not?"

"Why, I hardly know you."

Railroad felt dizzy. "You could some time."

"I'll never marry again, Mr. Bailey. It's not you."

Not him. It was never him, had never *been* him. His knees hurt from the hardwood floor. He looked at the ring, lowered his hands, clasped it in his fist. She moved her hand from his wrist to his shoulder, squeezed it. A knife of pain ran down his arm. Without standing, he punched Mrs. Graves in the stomach.

She gasped and fell back onto the bed. He was on her in a second, one hand over her mouth while he ripped her dress open from the neck. She struggled, and he pulled the pistol out from behind his back and held it to her head. She lay still.

"Don't you stop me, now," he muttered. He tugged his pants down and did what he wanted.

How ladylike it was of her to keep so silent.

Much later, lying on the bed, eyes dreamily focused on the light fixture in the center of the ceiling, it came to him what had bothered him about the grand-mother. She had ignored the fact that she was going to die. "She would of been a good woman, if it had been somebody there to shoot her every minute of her life," he'd told Bobby Lee. And that was true. But then, for that last moment, she *became* a good woman. The reason was that, once Railroad convinced her she was going to die, she could forget about it. In the end, when she reached out to him, there was no thought in her mind about death, about the fact that he had killed her son and daughter-in-law and grandchildren and was soon going to kill her. All she wanted was to comfort him. She didn't even care if he couldn't be comforted. She was living in that exact instant, with no memory of the past or regard for the future, out of the instinct of her soul and nothing else.

Like the cat. Pleasure lived that way all the time. The cat didn't know about Jesus' sacrifice, about angels and devils. That cat looked at him and saw what was there.

He raised himself on his elbows. Mrs. Graves lay very still beside him, her blond hair spread across the pineapple quilt. He felt her neck for a pulse.

It was dark night now: the whine of insects in the oaks outside the window, the rush of traffic on the cross street, drifted in on the hot air. Quietly, Railroad slipped out into the hall and down to Foster's room. He put his ear to the door and heard no sound. He came back to his own room, wrapped Mrs. Graves in the quilt and, as silently as he could, dragged her into his closet. He closed the door.

Railroad heard purring, and saw Pleasure sitting on the table, watching. "God damn you. God damn you to hell," he said to the cat, but before he could grab her, the calico had darted out the window.

He figured it out. The idea of marrying Mrs. Graves had been only a stage in the subtle revenge being taken on him by the dead grandmother, through the cat. The wishes Pleasure had granted were the bait, the nightmare had been a warning. But he hadn't listened.

He rubbed his sore shoulder. The old lady's gesture, like a mustard-seed, had grown to be a great crow-filled tree in Railroad's heart.

A good trick the devil had played on him. Now, no matter how he reformed himself, he could not get rid of what he had done.

It was hot and still, not a breath of air, as if the world were being smothered in a fever blanket. A milk-white sky. The kitchen of the Sweet Spot was hot as the furnace of Hell; beneath his shirt Railroad's sweat ran down to slick the warm pistol slid into his belt. Railroad was fixing a stack of buttermilk pancakes when the detective walked in.

The detective walked over to the counter and sat down on one of the stools. Maisie was not at the counter; she was probably in the ladies' room. The detective took a look around, then plucked a menu from behind the napkin holder in front of him and started reading. On the radio Hank Williams was singing "I'm So Lonesome I Could Cry."

Quietly, Railroad untied his apron and slipped out of the back door. In the alley near the trash barrels he looked out over the lot. He was about to hop the chain link fence when he saw Cauthron's car stopped at the light on the corner.

Railroad pulled out his pistol, crouched behind a barrel and aimed at the space in the lot where Cauthron usually parked. He felt something bump against his leg.

It was Pleasure. "Don't you cross me now," Railroad whispered, pushing the animal away.

The cat came back, put her front paws up on his thigh, purring.

"Damn you! You owe me, you little demon!" he hissed. He let the gun drop, looked down at the cat.

Pleasure looked up at him. "Miaow?"

"What do you want? You want me to stop, do you? Then make it go away. Make it so I never killed nobody."

Nothing happened. It was just a fucking animal. In a rage, he dropped the gun and seized the cat in both hands. She twisted in his grasp, hissing.

"You know what it's like to hurt in your heart?" Railroad tore open his shirt and pressed Pleasure against his chest. "Feel it! Feel it beating there!" Pleasure squirmed and clawed, hatching his chest with a web of scratches. "You owe me! You owe me!" Railroad was shouting now. "Make it go away!"

Pleasure finally twisted out of his grasp. The cat fell, rolled, and scurried away, running right under Cauthron's car as it pulled into the lot. With a little bump, the car's left front tire ran over her.

Cauthron jerked the car to a halt. Pleasure howled, still alive, writhing, trying to drag herself away on her front paws. Her back was broken. Railroad looked at the fence, looked back.

He ran over to Pleasure and knelt down. Cauthron got out of the car. Railroad tried to pick up the cat, but she hissed and bit him. Her sides fluttered with rapid breathing. Her eyes clouded. She rested her head on the gravel.

Railroad had trouble breathing. He looked up from his crouch to see that Maisie and some customers had come out of the diner. Among them was the detective.

"I didn't mean to do that, Lloyd," Cauthron said. "It just ran out in front of me." He paused a moment. "Jesus Christ, Lloyd, what happened to your chest?"

Railroad picked up the cat in his bloody hands. "Nobody ever gets away with nothing," he said. "I'm ready to go now."

"Go where?"

"Back to prison."

"What are you talking about?"

"Me and Hiram and Bobby Lee killed all those folks in the woods and took their car. This was their cat."

"What people?"

"Bailey Boy and his mother and his wife and his kids and his baby."

The detective pushed back his hat and scratched his head. "You all best come in here and we'll talk this thing over."

They went into the diner. Railroad would not let them take Pleasure from him until they gave him a corrugated cardboard box to put the body in. Maisie brought him a towel to wipe his hands, and Railroad told the detective, whose name was Vernon Scott Shaw, all about the State Hospital for the Criminally Insane, and the hearselike Hudson, and the family they'd murdered in the backwoods. Mostly he talked about the grandmother and the cat. Shaw sat there and listened soberly. At the end he folded up his notebook and said, "That's quite a story, Mr. Bailey. But we caught the people who did that killing, and it ain't you."

"What do you mean? I know what I done."

"Another thing, you don't think I'd know if there was some murderer loose from the penitentiary? There isn't anyone escaped."

"What were you doing in here last week, asking questions?"

"I was having myself some pancakes and coffee."

"I didn't make this up."

"So you say. But seems to me, Mr. Bailey, you been standing over a hot stove too long."

Railroad didn't say anything. He felt as if his heart was about to break.

Mr. Cauthron told him he might just as well take the morning off and get some rest. He would man the griddle himself. Railroad got unsteadily to his feet, took the box containing Pleasure's body, and tucked it under his arm. He walked out of the diner.

He went back to the boarding house. He climbed the steps. Mr. Foster was in the front room reading the newspaper. "Morning, Bailey," he said. "What you got there?"

"My cat got killed."

"No! Sorry to hear that."

"You seen Miz Graves this morning?" he asked.

"Not yet."

Railroad climbed the stairs, walked slowly down the hall to his room. He entered. Dust motes danced in the sunlight coming through the window. The ocean rowboat was no darker than it had been the day before. He set the dead cat down next to the Bible on the table. The pineapple quilt was no longer on the bed; now it was the rose. He reached into his pocket and felt the engagement ring.

The closet door was closed. He went to it, put his hand on the doorknob. He turned it and opened the door.

NEIL GAIMAN

―❧────────────────────────────❧―

Shoggoth's Old Peculiar

Neil Gaiman is the author of the dark urban fantasy novel Neverwhere, *the humorous novel* Good Omens (*with Terry Pratchett*), *the acclaimed* Sandman *comic book series, and the magical graphic novel* Stardust—*co-created with artist Charles Vess and reminiscent of the tales of Lord Dunsany. Gaiman has also published numerous works of short fiction, the brilliant children's book* The Day I Swapped My Dad for Two Goldfish, *and created the* Neverwhere *television miniseries for England's BBC. Born in England, Gaiman now lives with his wife and children in the American Midwest.*

Although Gaiman's best known for dark fantasy fiction, the following tale comes from the offbeat, humorous side of his oeuvre. It is reprinted from his new story collection, Smoke and Mirrors.

—T. W.

B enjamin Lassiter was coming to the unavoidable conclusion that the woman who had written *A Walking Tour of the British Coastline,* the book he was carrying in his backpack, had never been on a walking tour of any kind, and would probably not recognize the British coastline if it were to dance through her bedroom at the head of a marching band, singing "I'm the British Coastline" in a loud and cheerful voice while accompanying itself on the kazoo.

He had been following her advice for five days now and had little to show for it, except blisters and a backache. *All British seaside resorts contain a number of bed-and-breakfast establishments, who will be only too delighted to put you up in the "off-season"* was one such piece of advice. Ben had crossed it out and written in the margin beside it: *All British seaside resorts contain a handful of bed-and-breakfast establishments, the owners of which take off to Spain or Provence or somewhere on the last day of September, locking the doors behind them as they go.*

He had added a number of other marginal notes, too. Such as *Do not repeat not under any circumstances order fried eggs again in any roadside cafe* and *What is it with the fish-and-chips thing?* and *No they are not.* That last was written beside a paragraph which claimed that, if there was one thing that the inhabitants of scenic villages on the British coastline were pleased to see, it was a young American tourist on a walking tour.

For five hellish days, Ben had walked from village to village, had drunk sweet tea and instant coffee in cafeterias and cafes and stared out at gray rocky vistas and at the slate-colored sea, shivered under his two thick sweaters, got wet, and failed to see any of the sights that were promised.

Sitting in the bus shelter in which he had unrolled his sleeping bag one night, he had begun to translate key descriptive words: *charming* he decided, meant *nondescript; scenic* meant *ugly but with a nice view if the rain ever lets up; delightful* probably meant *We've never been here and don't know anyone who has.* He had also come to the conclusion that the more exotic the name of the village, the duller the village.

Thus it was that Ben Lassiter came, on the fifth day, somewhere north of Bootle, to the village of Innsmouth, which was rated neither *charming, scenic,* nor *delightful* in his guidebook. There were no descriptions of the rusting pier, nor the mounds of rotting lobster pots upon the pebbly beach.

On the seafront were three bed-and-breakfasts next to each other: Sea View, Mon Repose, and Shub Niggurath, each with a neon VACANCIES sign turned off in the window of the front parlor, each with a CLOSED FOR THE SEASON notice thumbtacked to the front door.

There were no cafes open on the seafront. The lone fish-and-chips shop had a CLOSED sign up. Ben waited outside for it to open as the gray afternoon light faded into dusk. Finally a small, slightly frog-faced woman came down the road, and she unlocked the door of the shop. Ben asked her when they would be open for business, and she looked at him, puzzled, and said, "It's Monday, dear. We're never open on Monday." Then she went into the fish-and-chips shop and locked the door behind her, leaving Ben cold and hungry on her doorstep.

Ben had been raised in a dry town in northern Texas: the only water was in backyard swimming pools, and the only way to travel was in an air-conditioned pickup truck. So the idea of walking, by the sea, in a country where they spoke English of a sort, had appealed to him. Ben's hometown was double dry: it prided itself on having banned alcohol thirty years before the rest of America leapt onto the Prohibition bandwagon, and on never having got off again; thus all Ben knew of pubs was that they were sinful places, like bars, only with cuter names. The author of *A Walking Tour of the British Coastline* had, however, suggested that pubs were good places to go to find local color and local information, that one should always "stand one's round," and that some of them sold food.

The Innsmouth pub was called *The Book of Dead Names* and the sign over the door informed Ben that the proprietor was one A. Al-Hazred, licensed to sell wines and spirits. Ben wondered if this meant that they would serve Indian food, which he had eaten on his arrival in Bootle and rather enjoyed. He paused at the signs directing him to the *Public Bar* or the *Saloon Bar*, wondering if British Public Bars were private like their Public Schools, and eventually, because it sounded more like something you would find in a Western, going into the Saloon Bar.

The Saloon Bar was almost empty. It smelled like last week's spilled beer and the day-before-yesterday's cigarette smoke. Behind the bar was a plump woman with bottle-blonde hair. Sitting in one corner were a couple of gentlemen wearing long gray raincoats and scarves. They were playing dominoes and sipping dark brown foam-topped beerish drinks from dimpled glass tankards.

Ben walked over to the bar. "Do you sell food here?"

The barmaid scratched the side of her nose for a moment, then admitted, grudgingly, that she could probably do him a ploughman's.

Ben had no idea what this meant and found himself, for the hundredth time, wishing that A *Walking Tour of the British Coastline* had an American-English phrase book in the back. "Is that food?" he asked.

She nodded.

"Okay. I'll have one of those."

"And to drink?"

"Coke, please."

"We haven't got any Coke."

"Pepsi, then."

"No Pepsi."

"Well, what do you have? Sprite? 7UP? Gatorade?"

She looked blanker than previously. Then she said, "I think there's a bottle or two of cherryade in the back."

"That'll be fine."

"It'll be five pounds and twenty pence, and I'll bring you over your ploughman's when it's ready."

Ben decided as he sat at a small and slightly sticky wooden table, drinking something fizzy that both looked and tasted a bright chemical red, that a ploughman's was probably a steak of some kind. He reached this conclusion, colored, he knew, by wishful thinking, from imagining rustic, possibly even bucolic, ploughmen leading their plump oxen through fresh-ploughed fields at sunset and because he could, by then, with equanimity and only a little help from others, have eaten an entire ox.

"Here you go. Ploughman's," said the barmaid, putting a plate down in front of him.

That a ploughman's turned out to be a rectangular slab of sharp-tasting cheese, a lettuce leaf, an undersized tomato with a thumbprint in it, a mound of something wet and brown that tasted like sour jam, and a small, hard, stale roll, came as a sad disappointment to Ben, who had already decided that the British treated food as some kind of punishment. He chewed the cheese and the lettuce leaf, and cursed every ploughman in England for choosing to dine upon such swill.

The gentlemen in gray raincoats, who had been sitting in the corner, finished their game of dominoes, picked up their drinks, and came and sat beside Ben. "What you drinkin'?" one of them asked, curiously.

"It's called cherryade," he told them. "It tastes like something from a chemical factory."

"Interesting you should say that," said the shorter of the two. "Interesting you should say that. Because I had a friend worked in a chemical factory and he *never drank cherryade.*" He paused dramatically and then took a sip of his brown drink. Ben waited for him to go on, but that appeared to be that; the conversation had stopped.

In an effort to appear polite, Ben asked, in his turn, "So, what are *you* guys drinking?"

The taller of the two strangers, who had been looking lugubrious, brightened up. "Why, that's exceedingly kind of you. Pint of Shoggoth's Old Peculiar for me, please."

"And for me, too," said his friend. "I could murder a Shoggoth's. 'Ere, I bet that would make a good advertising slogan. 'I could murder a Shoggoth's.' I should write to them and suggest it. I bet they'd be very glad of me suggestin' it."

Ben went over to the barmaid, planning to ask her for two pints of Shoggoth's Old Peculiar and a glass of water for himself, only to find she had already poured three pints of the dark beer. *Well,* he thought, *might as well be hung for a sheep as a lamb,* and he was certain it couldn't be worse than the cherryade. He took a sip. The beer had the kind of flavor which, he suspected, advertisers would describe as *full-bodied,* although if pressed they would have to admit that the body in question had been that of a goat.

He paid the barmaid and maneuvered his way back to his new friends.

"So. What you doin' in Innsmouth?" asked the taller of the two. "I suppose you're one of our American cousins, come to see the most famous of English villages."

"They named the one in America after this one, you know," said the smaller one.

"Is there an Innsmouth in the States?" asked Ben.

"I should say so," said the smaller man. "He wrote about it all the time. Him whose name we don't mention."

"I'm sorry?" said Ben.

The little man looked over his shoulder, then he hissed, very loudly, "H. P. Lovecraft!"

"I told you not to mention that name," said his friend, and he took a sip of the dark brown beer. "H. P. Lovecraft. H. P. bloody Lovecraft. H. bloody P. bloody Love bloody craft." He stopped to take a breath. "What did *he* know. Eh? I mean, what did he bloody know?"

Ben sipped his beer. The name was vaguely familiar; he remembered it from rummaging through the pile of old-style vinyl LPs in the back of his father's garage. "Weren't they a rock group?"

"Wasn't talkin' about any rock group. I mean the writer."

Ben shrugged. "I've never heard of him," he admitted. "I really mostly only read Westerns. And technical manuals."

The little man nudged his neighbor. "Here. Wilf. You hear that? He's never heard of him."

"Well. There's no harm in that. *I* used to read that Zane Grey," said the taller.

"Yes. Well. That's nothing to be proud of. This bloke—what did you say your name was?"

"Ben. Ben Lassiter. And you are . . . ?"

The little man smiled; he looked awfully like a frog, thought Ben. "I'm Seth," he said. "And my friend here is called Wilf."

"Charmed," said Wilf.

"Hi," said Ben.

"Frankly," said the little man, "I agree with you."

"You do?" said Ben, perplexed.

The little man nodded. "Yer. H. P. Lovecraft. I don't know what the fuss is about. He couldn't bloody write." He slurped his stout, then licked the foam from his lips with a long and flexible tongue. "I mean, for starters, you look at them words he used. *Eldritch.* You know what *eldritch* means?"

Ben shook his head. He seemed to be discussing literature with two strangers in an English pub while drinking beer. He wondered for a moment if he had become someone else, while he wasn't looking. The beer tasted less bad, the farther down the glass he went, and was beginning to erase the lingering aftertaste of the cherryade.

"*Eldritch.* Means weird. Peculiar. Bloody odd. That's what it means. I looked it up. In a dictionary. And *gibbous*?"

Ben shook his head again.

"*Gibbous* means the moon was nearly full. And what about that one he was always calling us, eh? Thing. Wossname. Starts with a *b*. Tip of me tongue . . ."

"Bastards?" suggested Wilf.

"Nah. Thing. You know. *Batrachian.* That's it. Means looked like frogs."

"Hang on," said Wilf. "I thought they was, like, a kind of camel."

Seth shook his head vigorously. "S'definitely frogs. Not camels. Frogs."

Wilf slurped his Shoggoth's. Ben sipped his, carefully, without pleasure.

"So?" said Ben.

"They've got two humps," interjected Wilf, the tall one.

"Frogs?" asked Ben.

"Nah. Batrachians. Whereas your average dromedary camel, he's only got one. It's for the long journey through the desert. That's what they eat."

"Frogs?" asked Ben.

"Camel humps." Wilf fixed Ben with one bulging yellow eye. "You listen to me, matey-me-lad. After you've been out in some trackless desert for three or four weeks, a plate of roasted camel hump starts looking particularly tasty."

Seth looked scornful. "You've never eaten a camel hump."

"I might have done," said Wilf.

"Yes, but you haven't. You've never even been in a desert."

"Well, let's say, just supposing I'd been on a pilgrimage to the Tomb of Nyarlathotep . . ."

"The black king of the ancients who shall come in the night from the east and you shall not know him, you mean?"

"Of course that's who I mean."

"Just checking."

"Stupid question, if you ask me."

"You could of meant someone else with the same name."

"Well, it's not exactly a common name, is it? Nyarlathotep. There's not exactly going to be two of them, are there? 'Hullo, my name's Nyarlathotep, what a coincidence meeting you here, funny them bein' two of us,' I don't exactly think so. Anyway, so I'm trudging through them trackless wastes, thinking to myself, I could murder a camel hump . . ."

"But you haven't, have you? You've never been out of Innsmouth harbor."

"Well . . . No."

"There." Seth looked at Ben triumphantly. Then he leaned over and whispered into Ben's ear, "He gets like this when he gets a few drinks into him, I'm afraid."

"I heard that," said Wilf.

"Good," said Seth. "Anyway. H. P. Lovecraft. He'd write one of his bloody sentences. Ahem. 'The gibbous moon hung low over the eldritch and batrachian inhabitants of squamous Dulwich.' What does he mean, eh? *What does he mean?* I'll tell you what he bloody means. What he bloody means is that the moon was nearly full, and everybody what lived in Dulwich was bloody peculiar frogs. That's what he means."

"What about the other thing you said?" asked Wilf.

"What?"

"*Squamous.* Wossat mean, then?"

Seth shrugged. "Haven't a clue," he admitted. "But he used it an awful lot." There was another pause.

"I'm a student," said Ben. "Gonna be a metallurgist." Somehow he had managed to finish the whole of his first pint of Shoggoth's Old Peculiar, which was, he realized, pleasantly shocked, his first alcoholic beverage. "What do you guys do?"

"We," said Wilf, "are acolytes."

"Of Great Cthulhu," said Seth proudly.

"Yeah?" said Ben. "And what exactly does that involve?"

"My shout," said Wilf. "Hang on." Wilf went over to the barmaid and came back with three more pints. "Well," he said, "what it involves is, technically speaking, not a lot right now. The acolytin' is not really what you might call laborious employment in the middle of its busy season. That is, of course, because of his bein' asleep. Well, not exactly *asleep.* More like, if you want to put a finer point on it, *dead.*"

" 'In his house at Sunken R'lyeh dead Cthulhu lies dreaming,' " interjected Seth. "Or, as the poet has it, 'That is not dead what can eternal lie—' "

" 'But in Strange Aeons—' " chanted Wilf.

"—and by *Strange* he means *bloody peculiar—*"

"Exactly. We are not talking your normal Aeons here at all."

" 'But in Strange Aeons even Death can die.' "

Ben was mildly surprised to find that he seemed to be drinking another full-bodied pint of Shoggoth's Old Peculiar. Somehow the taste of rank goat was less offensive on the second pint. He was also delighted to notice that he was no longer hungry, that his blistered feet had stopped hurting, and that his companions were charming, intelligent men whose names he was having difficulty in keeping apart. He did not have enough experience with alcohol to know that this was one of the symptoms of being on your second pint of Shoggoth's Old Peculiar.

"So right now," said Seth, or possibly Wilf, "the business is a bit light. Mostly consisting of waiting."

"And praying," said Wilf, if he wasn't Seth.

"And praying. But pretty soon now, that's all going to change."

"Yeah?" asked Ben. "How's that?"

"Well," confided the taller one. "Any day now, Great Cthulhu (currently impermanently deceased), who is our boss, will wake up in his undersea living-sort-of quarters."

"And then," said the shorter one, "he will stretch and yawn and get dressed—"

"Probably go to the toilet, I wouldn't be at all surprised."

"Maybe read the papers."

"—And having done all that, he will come out of the ocean depths and consume the world utterly."

Ben found this unspeakably funny. "Like a ploughman's," he said.

"Exactly. Exactly. Well put, the young American gentleman. Great Cthulhu will gobble the world up like a ploughman's lunch, leaving but only the lump of Branston pickle on the side of the plate."

"That's the brown stuff?" asked Ben. They assured him that it was, and he went up to the bar and brought them back another three pints of Shoggoth's Old Peculiar.

He could not remember much of the conversation that followed. He remembered finishing his pint, and his new friends inviting him on a walking tour of the village, pointing out the various sights to him "that's where we rent our videos, and that big building next door is the Nameless Temple of Unspeakable Gods and on Saturday mornings there's a jumble sale in the crypt . . ."

He explained to them his theory of the walking tour book and told them, emotionally, that Innsmouth was both *scenic* and *charming*. He told them that they were the best friends he had ever had and that Innsmouth was *delightful*.

The moon was nearly full, and in the pale moonlight both of his new friends did look remarkably like huge frogs. Or possibly camels.

The three of them walked to the end of the rusted pier, and Seth and/or Wilf pointed out to Ben the ruins of Sunken R'lyeh in the bay, visible in the moonlight, beneath the sea, and Ben was overcome by what he kept explaining was a sudden and unforeseen attack of seasickness and was violently and unendingly sick over the metal railings into the black sea below . . .

After that it all got a bit odd.

Ben Lassiter awoke on the cold hillside with his head pounding and a bad taste in his mouth. His head was resting on his backpack. There was rocky moorland on each side of him, and no sign of a road, and no sign of any village, scenic, charming, delightful, or even picturesque.

He stumbled and limped almost a mile to the nearest road and walked along it until he reached a petrol station.

They told him that there was no village anywhere locally named Innsmouth. No village with a pub called *The Book of Dead Names*. He told them about two men, named Wilf and Seth, and a friend of theirs, called Strange Ian, who was fast asleep somewhere, if he wasn't dead, under the sea. They told him that they didn't think much of American hippies who wandered about the countryside taking drugs, and that he'd probably feel better after a nice cup of tea and a tuna and cucumber sandwich, but that if he was dead set on wandering the country taking drugs, young Ernie who worked the afternoon shift would be all too happy to sell him a nice little bag of homegrown cannabis, if he could come back after lunch.

Ben pulled out his *A Walking Tour of the British Coastline* book and tried to find Innsmouth in it to prove to them that he had not dreamed it, but he was unable to locate the page it had been on—if ever it had been there at all. Most of one page, however, had been ripped out, roughly, about halfway through the book.

And then Ben telephoned a taxi, which took him to Bootle railway station, where he caught a train, which took him to Manchester, where he got on an airplane, which took him to Chicago, where he changed planes and flew to Dallas, where he got another plane going north, and he rented a car and went home.

He found the knowledge that he was over 600 miles away from the ocean very comforting; although, later in life, he moved to Nebraska to increase the distance from the sea: there were things he had seen, or thought he had seen, beneath the old pier that night that he would never be able to get out of his head. There were things that lurked beneath gray raincoats that man was not meant to know. *Squamous.* He did not need to look it up. He knew. They were *squamous.*

A couple of weeks after his return home Ben posted his annotated copy of *A Walking Tour of the British Coastline* to the author, care of her publisher, with an extensive letter containing a number of helpful suggestions for future editions. He also asked the author if she would send him a copy of the page that had been ripped from his guidebook, to set his mind at rest; but he was secretly relieved, as the days turned into months, and the months turned into years and then into decades, that she never replied.

LAWRENCE OSGOOD

Great Sedna

The legend of Sedna is one of the best known of all Eskimo folk tales. In the following story, Lawrence Osgood molds its basic ingredients into a chilling work of mythic fiction. "Great Sedna" is reprinted from Pleiades, *a literary journal published in Missouri, edited by R. M. Kinder.*

Osgood's previous work has been published in The Canadian Fiction Magazine, The London Magazine, Carleton Miscellany, *and other publications. His plays have been published in* New American Plays *and* New Theatre in America *and performed Off Broadway. He lives in Germantown, New York.*

—T. W.

Deep below the frozen Polar Sea, Sedna stirred. A seal had entered her roofless stone house and was lifting with its nose the black hair hanging like a curtain of seaweed around her. Brushing against her breasts and arms, it divided the matted strands with practiced nudgings of its soft snout, clearing them from her sleeping face. Then, as the parted hair began to settle again around her shoulders, undulating in the wake of the seal's flippers, it left her. Rising through the mass of other seals, walrus, schools of fish, and solitary whales floating motionless or circling lazily above the house, it swam away across the sandy basin set like a crater in the ocean floor with the house at its center and Sedna seated on her stone bench at the center of the house. Reaching the basin's rim, the seal crested it and disappeared beyond into the murky reaches of the Arctic seabed.

Half awake, Sedna raised her right hand to her head. The hand had no fingers, not even a thumb. Dreamily she shoved its blunt stump into her subsiding hair. A memory of fingers stirred in her arm.

On a pebbled beach at a place called Pangnittuuq, a twelve-year-old girl sat on a rock, her head tipped to one side as she combed the hair hanging down to her lap. The black strands glistened in the sunlight that danced on waves in the bay, and as she ran her ivory comb through it, the hair crackled like a fire of twigs. Behind her her father sat in front of a skin tent chipping at a stone point. Two young men, her brothers, squatted watching him. Her back to them all, the girl combed her hair and looked out over the water. She was dreaming of her lover.

A sleepy giggle rose from Sedna's belly and broke from her lips in a string of bubbles.

All that summer, kayaks had appeared around the head-lands of the bay and approached the beach. Coming from other camps along the coast, they were resolutely paddled by young men of marriageable age wearing their best sealskin anoraks. Holding their heads high, they briskly dug the blades of the paddles into the water first on one side then the other. Turning away but watching sideways through her hair, the girl pretended to pay no attention to them. But a smile might play around her lips when a kayak got close enough for its paddler to see the full fall of the glossy curtain that hid her face. The young men's eyes would widen in astonishment and their tongues dart into the corners of their mouths.

But when a kayak ground against the pebbles on the beach and a young man leaped out of it as nimbly as he could, she'd swing around. Throwing her hair back over her shoulder and arching her spine so her small breasts thrust against her caribou-skin dress, she'd give the young man a hard look. Many of them were ugly, but even the handsome ones were startled by that stare. They all dropped their eyes under it before straightening their shoulders and, raising their heads again, went up to her father's tent. Listening to their voices as they talked to him, she never failed to hear in their mumbled recitals of family connections or high-pitched boasting about hunting skills the effects of her challenging look and of the jittery lust for her the combing of her hair had started in them. That too made her smile. None of them was anything like the lover she was waiting for.

And when they strutted back to their kayaks, not daring to meet her eyes again, and climbed in and paddled away, sitting straight as stalks of grass and taking tremendous strokes in a last effort to impress her, she often laughed out loud at them.

That made her father angry.

"How come you do that?" he'd shout at her in Inuktun. "How come you're so bad? You laugh at that young man like that he never come back. You never want to marry no man? You think I'm going to hunt for you all your life? Useless girl!"

Then one windy day yet another kayak appeared around the point. Even at a distance the paddler looked different from the others. Sitting high in his kayak, he took strokes that were smoother and more powerful. She could see he was also wearing an anorak unlike the others'. It appeared to be made of bird skins with the feathers still on that, fluttering in the wind, made his whole upper body seem to quiver and vibrate. And there was something strange about his eyes.

Keeping the curtain of her hair parted with the fingers of one hand while she combed it with the other, the girl watched him approach. Arrogance and mastery were in the long strong strokes that broke the unruly surface of the water.

The girl felt a flush of warmth in her loins. She realized she was sweeping the comb through her hair in time with his paddling. She stopped, then after a moment resumed combing with slower, more deliberate strokes.

At a short distance from shore, the stranger rested his hands on the shaft of his double-bladed paddle and, letting the kayak drift, turned his head toward her. And she saw what was strange about his eyes. They were covered by sun-glare goggles, a strip of ivory with two slits in it. Why should he wear this protection? Goggles were for shielding eyes against snow blindness in the spring. No one wore them in the middle of summer. A leather thong held the oblong of white bone tightly against his head, and around the narrow slits in its polished surface she could see lines scratched with soot. Above this unseasonal attachment his forehead was long and sloping, and below it his cheekbones were high and set wide apart. His nose was sharp, his chin small, and the lips of his mouth were as thin as knifeblades. The girl had never seen such a man. When she dropped her eyes from his face, she saw that the fingers that gripped his paddle were long and bony and taut with sinews. Her own hands now lay in her lap.

The stranger began to sing. His voice was rasping and cut harshly through the soft summer air.

> My house has food,
> My bed is warm,
> My arms are strong,
> My reach is long.
> Girl who will not marry,
> Come with me.

She was on her feet before she knew it, the comb falling unheeded from her lap. (Later, her father would pick it up.) She ran to the water's edge. The man grounded the bow of his kayak on the beach, released the watertight skirt around his waist, reached for her hand, and pulled her onto the deck. Though his eyes remained hidden behind the ivory slits, she felt them on her as she knelt there. Then she crawled between his legs, and curled up under the translucent skin of the kayak's deck. The smell of his animal clothing was strong in the stuffy air and was mixed with another, unfamiliar smell. She felt the kayak slide backwards, turn, and pull ahead.

Through the pounding of the blood in her ears she heard her father's voice calling her name. It grew fainter. She closed her eyes and waited for the time to pass that would take her to her husband's home.

In her half sleep, a sigh slid from Sedna's lips and rose above her head in bubbles that burst one by one. Languidly, she opened and closed her naked thighs. Water slapped and caressed her skin. The girl had been happy with that husband. His house, a tent of caribou skins, was indeed always full of food and the bed in it soft and warm with animal furs. And he was a passionate lover.

When the man made love to her the first time, carrying her up to his tent from a rocky shore, her legs paralyzed by the long crouch in his kayak, she thought it was only haste that made him forget his ivory mask. She reached up to pull it off. But he seized her wrist in his clawlike fingers and, releasing it only when she cried out in pain, shook his head. Then he started moving inside her.

After that she never tried to remove the mask. He wore it all the time. She even made a fetish of the smooth oblong that hid his eyes, studying the lines and circles scratched on it and making up meanings for them. Sometimes, while he was inside her, she pulled his head down and licked the ivory with her tongue.

There were other tents along the rocky shore, where a breeze was always blowing, and the families in them visited and welcomed her and gave her what she needed in the way of domestic utensils—bone needles and a needlecase, a stone pot, a wooden stirrer, a new comb. It didn't seem to matter that she'd brought no possessions of her own.

In the waters over Sedna's roofless house, a school of fish flashed by among the sea mammals hovering there. A bowhead whale spun ponderously on the axis of its own body, as if taking sympathetic pleasure in the picture that floated before Sedna's closed eyes of busy tents, stone beach, calm ocean, endless sky, and passionate husband. Two seals watched her attentively.

The picture changed and Sedna whimpered in her sleep. The seals dropped into the house and circled her. The bowhead swam away.

One afternoon as he reached the climax of his lovemaking, her husband threw back his head—and the ivory mask slipped. The girl found herself staring into the red eyes of a seahawk. She screamed, and in that instant everything changed. Their tent was not a tent but a nest, the rocky shore not a shore but a cliff, and the site of their home not a beach but a ledge. The furs beneath her were not furs but fishskins, and the utensils scattered around her were not utensils but scraps of bone. The smell of rotten food clung to everything, and the nest of woven sticks was streaked with white excrement. She screamed again, and as she did her husband screamed too, his hooked beak opening wide to show a red, pointed tongue, his hot breath stinking, his fiery unhooded eyes staring at her without expression. Then his talons released her, and he rose away from the nest with a slow, steady beating of his wings.

At the base of the cliff, a wave broke against the rocks, and a gust of rising wind threw a spatter of salt spray into the girl's face.

The bird returned as the sun was setting. It dropped a fish into the nest and began to tear it with its beak. It tossed some pieces toward the girl. She shrank away, watching the bird savage the fish. That day she stopped eating.

The women from other families who'd welcomed her and given her some of their possessions were not women at all but other birds in the colony of nests built all around her on rocky ledges. Now they sometimes flew by mocking her in screeching voices before soaring away. The comb one had given her was the backbone of a fish. The girl stopped combing her hair. Soon it lost its luster and became matted, tangled, and sticky with ooze from the nest's putrefying litter.

As the girl grew weaker and thinner, her bird husband, its talons holding her down on the rotting fish skins, seized and penetrated her less often. It spent more and more time away. But when cramps doubled her over one morning, she was terrified they might mean she was with child. When the bird had made love to her while she still believed him human, she'd often imagined the children they'd have, seeing strong handsome boys and pretty girls. Now the thought of offspring terrified her. Curled in pain in a corner of the nest, she imagined monsters forming in her womb. It was only when the cramps became constant that she understood they were caused by hunger. She hoped they would kill her.

The bird's ivory mask, lying where it had fallen when it slipped from his eyes, gradually disappeared under a thickening layer of fish bones, fish heads, fish skins, and the bird's excrement.

When the cramps in her stomach finally subsided and she was still alive, visions began to appear to the girl and float before her eyes in the wide sky full of summer sun that still stretched to the far horizon of the sea. She saw the pebbled beach at her father's camp, saw his tent of caribou skins above the beach, saw her brothers braiding strips of walrus hide for rope, saw her father's dogs on their summer island leaping for meat scraps thrown from her father's boat, saw her father standing by the rock on the shore where she used to sit combing her hair, saw him holding the comb she'd dropped when she ran to the stranger's kayak.

Then one day, looking down from the nest, she saw her father's boat itself bobbing on small waves at the base of the cliff. He and her two brothers were waving at her, and their voices calling her name were carried to her by the wind. With no hesitation at all, not caring if what she saw was real or only another vision, the girl rolled sideways over the edge of the nest and fell toward the sea.

Sedna's sleepy eyes saw the girl falling, a mass of foul hair streaming above her head. When she splashed into the water and rose again to its surface, Sedna felt on her own arms the grip of her brothers' strong hands lifting her into the boat.

Lying on real furs, the girl snuggled into them. Her father gave her one quick look, and then all three men picked up their paddles. Bending toward the water, each on his own side of the boat, her brothers bowed their heads to their work while her father sculled vigorously in the stern. They ignored her, but she felt their indifference as the warrant of her safety. She let the rhythm of their steady, surging strokes rock her to sleep.

In the half sleep of Sedna's memory of sleeping, the sound of the seahawk's first cry came to her like a small scratch on the surface of the sky. But its second cry woke her up, and as she stared blindly at the wall of black stone across from her platform in the house at the bottom of the sea, wide-awake images rushed into her mind.

The bird swooped over her father's boat, cried as it rose to turn, swooped back, hovered with talons spread, cried again, and lifted away. Her father and brothers looked at each other and returned to their paddles. She stared wide-eyed at the sky. Then, starting from the distant cliffs like a spiral of smoke, she saw the whole colony of seahawks take to the air. They raced through the sky and with the whirring of a hundred wings swept over the boat, banked like one bird, rose, turned, and swooped again. The sound of their cries as they passed was deafening. And as more birds of every kind—gulls, guillemots, terns, auks, petrels, murres—joined them with each pass over the boat, their mass filled the sky and darkened the water. The boat bucked in the waves whipped up by their wings. The birds' cries grew louder.

Gusts of wind seized her brothers' hair and flattened their anoraks against their chests. Soon the waves were so big that no matter how far over the sides of the boat they reached, their paddles caught air as often as water. Her father tottered as his own paddle swept through the empty troughs of waves whose frothy crests now broke regularly over the gunwales. The skins around the girl grew wet and cold, but she hugged them to her. The din of the birds' mixed cries, the heat of their passing breath, and the musty smell of their feathers swept over the boat again and again on the rising and of their wings.

Suddenly her brothers dropped their paddles and, gripping the sides of the wallowing boat, looked at her father. His own hair blowing wildly above his head, he nodded. With one swift movement, the young men seized their sister and threw her into the sea.

A shudder ran through Sedna's body as the girl's body struck the water. But the girl struggled up, and just as two hawks dropped from the rushing cloud, their talons stretched to sink into her shoulders, she grabbed the boat. The birds veered away. She looked at her father. He met her gaze for one long moment and reached toward the floor of the boat. His hand came up holding a long knife. He brought it down hard on her fingers.

The girl fell back into the sea, and the first joints of her fingers fell with her.

As she came up again and the birds screamed overhead, she reached for the lurching boat and gripped its gunwale with her mutilated hands. But again her father brought down his knife. The boat rocked, and again the girl fell into the sea. And the second joints of her fingers fell with her. She reached out once more and lay her bleeding stumps across the gunwale. The knife came down again. And for the third time the girl fell into the sea, and the third and last joints of her fingers fell with her.

But her father's work was not yet finished. When she hooked her thumbs over the side of the boat, he chopped them off too. Then, as the multitude of birds rushed by once more, releasing their rage in a long cacophonous scream, the girl sank slowly into the dark waters of the Polar Sea.

When she was gone, the cloud of birds swept over the foundering boat a final time and then rose silently into the sky and dispersed. One bird still circled overhead, shrilling and crying. Then it too flew away.

Sunlight once more struck the boat and glittered on the heaving sea. Its waves subsided, and in the boat the father and his sons turned their backs on one another and bailed. When the boat was dry and the sea entirely calm again, they still didn't meet each other's eyes. Nor did they look at one another even once during the long paddle back to the place called Pangnittuuq.

The girl fell through the sea. But as she drifted down, her tangled hair floating like a banner of seaweed above her head, the water around her began to churn and boil as first the tips of her eight fingers and then the sixteen other severed joints and finally her thumbs, falling through the water beside her, changed as they fell into ringed seals and bearded seals and walruses and narwhals and, last, whales. By the time she reached the ocean floor, landing at the center of a roofless house of stone that was waiting for her there, the drowning girl had become Great Sedna and the children of her two hands were massed in schools around her.

SYLVIA BROWNRIGG

The Bird Chick

Sylvia Brownrigg grew up in Mountain View, California and Oxford, England. She received a degree in philosophy from Yale University, and now lives in London where she is a reviewer for the Guardian, *the* London Times Literary Supplement, *and* New York Newsday. *Her short stories have been published in* Short Circuits *and other anthologies.*

"The Bird Chick" is a wonderfully bizarre tale from Brownrigg's first collection, Ten Women Who Shook the World, *published in England.*

—*T. W.*

At first we thought all she did was feed them. You know, there's one in every town. Some lady with ruffled coats puffing her up, her gray hair tangled, a little arm diving deep into a crumb-lined plastic bag and then flinging them, bread-bits, at her sweet babies—the tattered brown ducks that greet her with greedy dark eyes and a flap-splattering of wings.

We thought she was one of those.

It was only later that we found out she'd been talking to them all along.

Admittedly, she was classier from the start than the other folks in that category. Younger, too. This was the 1960s, remember, when youth culture was everywhere and fashions went wild. A typical outfit for her—and she stood out in our park wearing this, to give you an idea of the plain sort of park that it was—consisted of thigh-high white boots and a brief purple miniskirt, a fluffy fake fur coat striped in skunk colors. She looked terrific in that outfit, to tell you the truth. People would have certainly noticed her and tried to talk to her, if she hadn't been so busy feeding the birds.

The fact is, most people get in the habit of ignoring people like that. That's just how it is in parks, which are controlled environments, of course, but never so controlled that you don't have to make your own decisions about who to avoid. I should know. I was going to the park quite regularly myself at that time, strolling along with my little ones, and I had to figure out for myself who made it into the 'hello' camp and who definitely didn't. Included on the yes-list were the clown man who protested about the eating of red meat (I thought he had a point, though vegetarianism still seemed kinky to me then); the nice pair of mothers who spoke in a brittle language from a cold country but who smiled so peaceably; the blue-suited policeman, who seemed always to daydream and was an unlikely crimestopper; and the long-haired young boys who in those days still kicked a football around, having not yet jellied their limbs with video games and drugs.

Not included on the hello list were the sinister characters who lurked behind trees. Sometimes you saw them or heard them, other times you just knew they were there. One was a blank white man who proclaimed with hungry pleasure about the end of the world. Another was a yo-yo obsessive, who always seemed on the brink of nervous collapse. Then there were those mysterious little children who appeared to be parentless—I knew I should take pity on them and give them chocolate or raisins but I couldn't bring myself to do it. Another in this sad, greetingless category, though it shames me now to say it, was the bird chick herself, that tall slender gal who spent her hours with flying things.

She had theatrical ambitions. This was how I later reconstructed her story— well, with the help of the magazine articles and documentaries about her that came later. She came from a family of dancers and declaimers, so she always had a sense of the value of spectacle. She'd once tried her hand at the path of convention—a month in the drama school, training how to bray like a donkey— before she realized that she had to cut loose from all that, that her style of performance could not be caged in in that way.

She set out for the park, where she felt there were still opportunities. Park performance was an undercanvassed medium, she felt, and as you know in this she was just ahead of the be-ins and happenings. In the park she saw a universe of potential audience, a small sampling of the cosmos: babies and mothers, couples, loners and dogs. Foreigners and locals. Teams gathered for unspecified sports. All of these she could speak to, she felt, once she had discovered the right dramatic language.

So while the rest of us wove our checkerboard paths through that great green and treed park, going through our routines, the bird chick made her home by the gray pond, developing her company.

That is, she talked to the birds.

She told them, in a bird dialect not known by many, that she needed them for her project. She explained to the ducks and the swans that they had unexplored talents. She flattered them, the way people do when they want something from others. She cooed over the swans' long necks, the purity of their oh-so-white feathers. She admired the colors on the teal ducks, claimed they were eye-catching and unusual. She applauded aloud, actually—she would have drawn stares except that in that environment, as I've mentioned, people chose rather to avoid trouble and look away—when some of the little mergansers bobbed their heads beneath the water, leaving their pointed behinds fluffing comically straight up. She acted as if she'd never seen that before—laughing riotously each time they did it. She sighed with exaggerated pleasure at the deep call-chirps of widgeons. And, of course, when the geese took flight, she couldn't say enough about her awe at their technique, the grace and originality of their pattern, the fluid way that they flew together, flapping in unison, while yet retaining the strength of their individual selves. She particularly admired that, she said, and felt that it would come in handy in what she wanted them all to work towards.

Because a theatrical production—she chose the sporting metaphor rather than the domestic one, because her own family was troubled and scattered and couldn't really provide a good role model for the birds—was like playing on a team. Everyone was important for their separate contributions; everyone had their moment to be appreciated for their particular talent. Like that occasion towards the end of a pop concert when the lead singer goes around and introduces the band, the bird chick promised each member of the troupe their chance in the spotlight, their time of recognition. At the same time—and she emphasized this point, because as she said she wouldn't get anywhere with a gaggle of primadonnas—everyone had to realize that *all* the contributions were important, and acknowledge the significance of everyone else's work. The thing fell apart if they didn't all work together. From the person who helped move props on stage to whoever was chosen to give the big, set speeches, everyone had a part to play, quite literally, in the great production. She didn't want to see any sulking or competitiveness. It was a team work, a love-in, a collective effort. It was perfect harmony, it was the real thing.

The birds bought it.

Who can blame them? Some say the birds were a little naïve in this all along, but I say, when you have a person with the charisma it was later clear that she had, leading you on to an unforeseen future—the chances are you'll agree to anything. Inspired by her confidence in you you'll place all your confidence in her; drawn in by her promises of all you can accomplish you'll promise her yet more, you'll lay your neck on the line for her, you'll give her your all. This is the great thing about leadership: with it you get people doing what they never thought they could. It should hardly be surprising that a few feathers get ruffled along the way.

Shakespeare in the Park, that was her ambition. By the time the spring hit that year, the rest of us—how very ordinary we'd started to look, you know, in our middle-length dresses and our plain pink makeup! How boring we'd started to feel next to this surge of creativity—we were beginning to catch on. You couldn't tell at first what was taking place out there, but out of the corner of your eye, that eye you used to turn away from her because you'd labeled her a crazy, you did start to notice some strange behavior among the waterfowl. They seemed to swim more in formation. They held their heads higher. When children proffered stale breadcrusts there was less feverish gratitude. The bird chick, in rehearsing them, had encouraged in them the beginnings of self-respect, which was bound to alter the way they dealt with everyone else in the park.

For the longest time we couldn't tell what was happening. It did seem that there was a lot of communication going on, and at certain times of the day—dawn and dusk mostly, when the park was all but empty—a flurry of activity jumbled its corners. As the reporting later made clear, they were practicing scenes then. I know it's hard to imagine how any of us could have been unaware of what was going on, but I'm trying to convey to you what it's like when you're first in the presence of something so new, something your thoughts don't yet have a name for. It was the 60s, of course, and that kept happening then: someone would come along with an idea that seemed so utterly astounding that when you first heard it, it sounded like gibberish. The moonwalk, the Xerox machine, swear words in poetry, long hair on the Beatles. All of it took some getting used to. Any of those things, the first time you heard about them, seemed highly unlikely. You can't totally blame us if what we heard first of all there were honkings and quacks.

It wasn't until the bird chick started publicizing that the buzz really started in among those of us who used the park regularly. The air sparked with curiosity, the mothers altered their gossip. Gone was the small chit-chat about walking developments and the best brand of cereal; instead when we saw each other we whispered, as if it were illegal or subversive, about the pink pamphlets we'd seen here and there. Shakespeare in the Park, they simply suggested, with Native Performers. Women's toilets, men's, teahouses, benches: the pamphlets were scattered around where they'd catch your eye, and written with enough vagueness that they nabbed your attention. We became eager to know what precisely was meant by the word 'native.' (Still people hadn't made the imaginative leap that would later seem obvious.) Even the people you'd normally avoid seemed worth talking to about the mystery. The yo-yoer stopped yo-yoing for the sake of discussion. I bribed small children with candies to find out what they'd heard. The religious preacher was struck mute by the mention of Shakespeare.

When the performances started they changed everything forever. That first evening, I'll never forget it. People had come from far and wide—I mean, including people who'd never set foot in the park before, people who barely understood what a park really was—to see this latest event. I guess the word had gotten round that there was something new in the park here, so even with the word 'Shakespeare' attached it seemed daring, near revolutionary. It might have been the word 'native' that got the long-haired people out. In those days there was a swell of interest in the oppression of such groups. T-shirts sporting political figures (Mao, Che Guevara) were visible in the crowd. Round Lennon glasses on faces blank but committed. Blonde-haired chicks, skinny and mini-skirted, who could have been clones of the bird chick herself. As I say, this wasn't our usual crowd in the park—most of us were so normal in our dress and beliefs. I know some of the other park-goers felt we'd been invaded and were resentful. For myself, I had the opposite reaction: I suddenly felt very self-conscious that I'd yet to make a contribution to the burgeoning counter-culture. My first daring act was to attend this performance.

It was *Hamlet*. Ambitious, I know. The bird chick didn't do things by halves. An easier choice would have been one of the comedies, or else a history that people didn't have too much invested in—*Julius Caesar*, say, one that people were already used to seeing in modern dress and the like. But the bird chick and company went straight for the jugular. 'To be or not to be' and 'Good night, sweet prince,' the lines everyone has an opinion on, a feeling for, the lines that everyone thrills to.

For that very reason it was in fact a good choice, because the lines were delivered in that bird dialect understood by so few. Since it was *Hamlet* the thing was quite followable. You understood that the white swan was Hamlet, shuddering with grief, self-doubt and intelligence; that a widgeon was Claudius, praying for redemption all too guiltily; a bright teal was Ophelia, drowning in loveliness. If the finer points of the Yorick speech were missed, the sheer bluntness of our mortality there was not: you felt a sober shiver pass through the audience as Hamlet remembered his old buddy and spoke poems over his skull.

Very little, you may be surprised to hear, failed to come across in the bird chick company's version. There were times I even thought I heard the bird equivalent of the sharper phrases I waited for—'honeying and making love over the nasty sty,' for example, or ' 'Tis an unweeded garden, that grows to seed; things rank and gross in nature possess it merely.' In the interval chatter I gathered that for some the blurred meanings made the play all the more poignant: they understood the broad honk and sweep of Hamlet's progression, while not being distracted by individual words. There was also something that struck at the hearts of the more politically minded, at seeing this most famous drama of great literature acted out by the dispossessed. This was one of those points that was bound to pass by an ordinary viewer like me. Though I can affirm that it was strangely stirring to hear the rhythms of the bard—even in translation—come out of the beak of a snow-feathered swan.

The rest of the story has become so famous that I feel my own contribution may as well end soon. What I thought might interest is an account by someone like me who knew the original environment that the scheme was first hatched in. Also someone who could testify without bias as to the effect on the birds. Because from where I sat that first night, those birds seemed to me to be uplifted by their performance. (As indeed we all were.) I am not any kind of poet but I can say that there was a color in their eyes that was the pride of accomplishment; that I've never seen wings beat with such purpose and glory; that, in fact, birds seemed to me that night wiser than humans, with deeper emotions and a better comprehension of the deep questions of life. That is how those birds seemed to me that night, and whatever happened later I believe what I saw was real.

Nowadays we know these stories so well, we can write them before the papers do. I'm older, I understand how it goes. In those days I was impressionable—very—and so when the bird chick rose to fast fame I thought it would last. I believed the reports that she had changed the face of theater forever; I believed the claim that she had invented a new language for drama. I appreciated the appreciation of her drawing into the center a marginalized group to perform, the description of her as a true revolutionary. (High praise in those days.) I had every reason to believe these things. After all, there was no question that she had changed *us*, the park-goers, with her work. We were all, I know, more charitable with each other after Shakespeare in the Park. More patient with each other's foibles. More tolerant of our private strangenesses and habits.

But someone was bound to come along to knock her down, once they'd gone to the trouble of setting her up. As you know, it was the charge of exploitation that did it. How nasty were those very same writers who'd so praised her at first. One month they were happily profiling the unusual stars of the play, the next throwing dim light on the so-called indignity of that casting. What had been the innovative raw style of the bird chick became the clichéd mannerisms of one born to oppress. People who called themselves champions of the birds came in to shut the thing down, claiming ridiculous wages and non-standard treatment. (How can you expect standards, I wondered, when the very point was to break them?) You know all this. You remember all that fuss, or have read about it since. You remember how the bird chick's life story went in reverse: from admirable swan to crude ugly duckling gone bankrupt, someone her once friendly colleagues were all too eager to chuck from the nest.

Towards the end, when she was such a controversial figure and I knew it might be valuable, I tried to secure the bird chick's autograph. That sounds crasser than I mean it. It wasn't just monetary. The bird chick and her troupe really had changed my life. I wore short skirts these days. I had dyed my hair brighter. I experimented with boots, and had a greater interest in art. All of that was because of her, though her time was waning. I wanted to touch her, if I could, to have some souvenir of her and also to convey to her what she'd meant to so many of us in the park.

By then she was avoiding the press. She was everything but shattered. She was looking a little scraggly, to tell you the truth, a little down on her luck. If I hadn't known better by then I'd have thought her disreputable.

She sat on a bench, talking in a low voice to the birds. From the same plastic bag she still scattered breadcrumbs—the very non-standard treatment complained about by those self-righteous warriors. (Where were they now? What did they really care for birds? They were off somewhere else, no doubt, fighting another battle that wasn't their own.) I told my children to wait for me and I approached the bird chick cautiously, not wanting to scare her. The autograph book shook in my hand. I'd never actually been this close to her before, what with avoiding her at first and then knowing she was inaccessible once she was famous. From close to, she was beautiful. A wrecked sternness in her features and a softness about the eyes: a face that could struggle, but knew love was the main thing. Something strangely human about her face; I think this surprised me. At this point I had perhaps thought she'd be birdlike.

I cleared my throat as I got close to her, but she didn't stop talking to them. Ducks, geese and swans, mergansers and widgeons, swam desultorily around in the pond there before her, occasionally nibbling on the soggy tossed crumbs. She spoke to them steadily, softly, in a tone of reassurance, a tone affectionate and kind.

And here's the strange thing. The unbelievable. As I came close to the bird chick, so close I could touch her, I discovered I could understand what it was she said to those birds. The barrier between myself and that strange tongue fell away, and I heard the low sweet goodbyes of a bunch of good friends. It was always like this, the bird chick said, at the end of a show. Everyone had to disperse. It was one of the tragedies and beauties of theater. The astonishment created was by nature impermanent. It couldn't last forever, and it couldn't be captured. It was a gift given to those who were there. And after the show was over, that once team—all right, that once family—did what such groups do, that is find their own separate way.

She cried as she said it. The bird chick. So loving of those birds, still so pure after everything. Not wanting to hurt them or chastise them with the course of events.

Stupidly, I still hoped for my autograph. I was getting ready to ask her. But the bird chick stood up then, not even noticing my presence. She dropped her plastic bag and held her arms out wide as if in embrace. Then, with one great dramatic movement, she flung her arms outwards, out towards the waterfowl, hoping to scatter them.

It was her last piece of directing. Like the faithful troupe they had become, they followed her instruction. Out where the great arc of her arms was, those birds flew up in a snow-mist gray cloud, a loud flutter of wings and the honks of their kind. In a slow immense trance they rose over the pond, still to my mind speaking Shakespeare and those lines of the ages.

I watched the miracle of their departing flight and felt a cold grip of sadness alongside my heart. It came to me that we might have to go on without them in our park. They seemed to be flying so far, so determined to leave.

I turned to the bird chick for comfort, no thoughts now of an autograph. I just wanted someone to talk to about the nature of the loss. Right then she seemed to me like anybody else in the park you might strike up some talk with.

But the bird chick was gone. She must have flown too. I don't know why it surprised me—from the start she'd been one to defy the conventions. It made sense that she'd follow her bold gambit into the sky.

MARK W. TIEDEMANN

Psyché

Mark W. Tiedemann's short fiction has been published in The Magazine of
Fantasy & Science Fiction, Asimov's, Sirens, *and other venues. He lives in
St. Louis, Missouri.*

*"Psyché" is a story inspired by Berthe Morisot's painting of the same title.
(The painting depicts a young woman gazing at herself, off-center, in a
mirror.) Morisot played a vibrant part in the French Impressionist movement,
and was married to Eugene Manet, brother of the more famous Edouard.
Tiedemann uses these facts to concoct a delicious historical fantasy about art,
vision, and the nature of the soul. It is reprinted from the December issue of*
The Magazine of Fantasy & Science Fiction.

—T. W., E. D.

The scar appealed to her. That and the clear, almost glasslike eyes. He
seemed to be looking at her through a broken window. Berthe blinked
and looked away. He would be a fascinating subject for a painting.

"Not myself," he said, his Dutch accent slowing his words.

"I understand that, Monsieur Van Helsing," Berthe said. "I don't do—I have
never done—a death mask. It's not something my technique is well suited to—"

"Yes, yes, I realize that. This new style . . . I confess I do not care for it myself,
but it has certain advantages which I believe will work to my purposes."

Berthe smiled tolerantly and looked out her window. Paris seemed drugged
under the searing August sun and the late hour's light layered the city with an
amber stickiness that blurred detail and nagged at her to go to her easel and
palette.

"Wouldn't a sculptor be better . . . ?"

"No. The subject would not, I think, be served by a too precise rendering."
He drew a deep breath and seemed to look inward. His forehead creased thoughtfully. "There was a fluidity to him in . . . before."

Berthe flexed her fingers and winced at the slight pain. She rubbed her right
hand gently.

"Rheumatism?"

She looked up, startled.

"I am a doctor," he explained, the ghost of a smile twisting the scar. "Is it bad?"

Berthe shrugged. "Painting is sometimes difficult, but usually only in the morning or during winter. It is nothing."

"I could prescribe—"

"No. No, thank you." She sighed again. "Your offer intrigues me, I admit, but not for the reasons you may think."

"I am prepared to offer a good commission—"

"Of course, I had no doubt, but—in truth, monsieur, I would do this for the promise that I am allowed to paint you."

He laughed, a dry exhalation that, for a moment, she thought would degenerate into a ragged cough. For the first time during the interview she saw an unguarded emotion—surprise, perhaps even disbelief—animate his face.

"You are not serious."

"I am, I assure you." She switched hands and rubbed her left. "One finds that one has painted everything after a time. Even if one has not, it seems so. Ennui is a disease of the inspired."

"Is it?"

"You have never been inspired, monsieur?"

"No. Only obsessed. One does not suffer ennui when one is obsessed." He waved his left hand vaguely around his face. "What is it you see?"

"I don't know. But I am inspired."

"Mmm. I am flattered."

"I haven't painted much in this year. My husband passed away in April—"

"I am sorry."

"—and many of my friends, as well, have died in the last few years. I feel . . . short of time."

"I understand that fully. I am myself not young."

She nodded. "We both are of an age when it is best to be occupied so that we do not dwell on such things overly much."

"There is, unfortunately, nothing left for me to dwell on. Only details. Small things that I feel are necessary to complete what is past."

"Like this death mask?"

"Like the death mask, yes. The subject occupied my attentions for many years."

"Well. You have my terms. I wish to paint you."

"Please, I will pay you as well—"

"I do not ask—"

He pulled his wallet from within his heavy black coat and thumbed out a sheaf of notes. British pounds, she observed. Sound currency. Everything about this man seemed solid in the extreme. He counted briefly, then laid the notes on the table beside him and looked up.

"I shall be honored to have you paint me, Mme. Morisot. However, if you decide not to afterward, I shall fully understand."

Preparing the canvas, mixing the temperas, cleaning the brushes—all these details comprised for Berthe the closest thing she had ever found to religious ritual. Even her wedding had been a thing to tolerate, a nuisance. She smiled, remembering what she told her brother afterward. "I went through this ceremony without the least pomp, in a plain dress and hat, like the old woman that I am and with no guests." Old woman. She was amused by that now. She had been thirty-three at the time she had married Eugene and thought she knew what age meant. Since Eugene's death she *did* know. It meant loneliness.

At least, she thought, I am not a burden to anyone. Money had never been difficult, her family had seen to that. Attention—specifically its absence—had always been a problem. People did not take the new art very seriously, even less so when done by a woman, but after Manet's death a sudden interest had caused a rise in everyone's fortunes. Her paintings sold at auction now and Degas, at least, had made sure she received her due. Her reputation, her position, always problematic in polite society, now carried weight.

A heavy pounding at her door broke the reverie. She wiped her hands and went to answer it. A wagon stood in the narrow lane and two workmen waited at its gate while a third stood at her door.

"Yes?"

"Uh, we have a delivery for Mme. Morisot," he said, doffing his soiled cap.

"That is I."

He thrust a notebook and pencil toward her. "The manifest, please."

She took the pencil and signed. He bowed awkwardly and gestured to the other two. They lowered the gate and pulled a crate from the wagon bed.

The crate was roughly three feet on a side. Berthe led them to her studio and indicated a place on the floor. The workmen glanced nervously at the canvases standing about, mostly half-finished works, muttered good-days to her, and hurried out. When she reached the door the wagon was already pulling away. Berthe watched it until it rounded a corner.

She shrugged and returned to the studio.

Berthe picked up her prybar and walked around the crate, studying it. She had not expected this. She chose a board and jammed the iron bar in. The nails came out easily, for which she was thankful. She lifted off the top. A vague, stale odor escaped and she wrinkled her nose. An envelope lay atop the straw stuffing.

"Mme. Morisot, Please forgive the impersonal nature of this procedure. I do not wish to distract you from any reactions which may prove important. Forgive me the macabre circumstance. Within is the subject. V.H."

She pulled out straw until she came to a canvas wrap. She found the loose ends and pulled. The object weighed less than five pounds. The fabric felt quite cold and she carried it quickly to a table near her easel. She went back to the crate and pulled the rest of the straw out. Finding nothing more hidden within, she looked at the canvas-wrapped object suspiciously.

She ignored the ill-ease which increased as she unwrapped the canvas. The last fold revealed a head.

Berthe stepped back. No eyes—the sockets were empty—and no hair. The cheeks were sunken on either side of a straight, lipless mouth. Its ivory whiteness lent it an abstract quality, like a cameo or a dream; it was marbled with fine bluish traceries. The straight nose ended in a slight hook, giving the whole an aristocratic aspect contrary to every other detail, which seemed ascetic, almost monkish. It stood on a short-stump of neck.

When she looked up the shadows had changed. Day had moved on. Berthe turned, mildly puzzled, her legs sore. She went to the kitchen and poured water. She drank thirstily, filled her cup again, then looked for something to eat. There was a plate of beef and cheese in her ice box. Seeing it, she realized that she was famished.

She had not eaten so much at one time since Eugene had died. Her daughter, Julie, would be pleased. Too bad she was away, in England. Berthe sat back from the kitchen table and stared at the ruin of the meal, amazed at herself.

Berthe returned to her studio. The light slanted in through the wide windows, shadowing the head so that it appeared aglow, a thin nimbus encircling the bald skull. Her temperas were partially dried. Irritated, she began to mix new. It was sunset before she finished and the light had taken on a filmy, indistinct quality, selectively illuminating partial details throughout the studio. She sighed and covered the head for the night.

She poured a glass of wine and went to her bedroom. She sat in the wing-backed chair beside her bed and sipped while staring out at the night sky. Berthe slept little anymore, less so with each passing year. Night had become more a companion than a release. She glanced at the unfinished letter to her daughter on her nightstand. Her fingers ached. It could wait for tomorrow.

When she slept she dreamed of painting. It had been a bold move to ask the doctor to pose—she had done few men outside her family—but she did not feel she had to worry about scandal at her age. She did wonder, though, why now, after all this time, she found herself drawn to do a portrait of a stranger.

Her body complained after sleeping the night in the chair. Berthe made tea, ate a little bread, and went to the studio. She uncovered the head and went to her easel. She threw away the dried paints and started over. Her wrists pulled and her fingers moved stiffly, but she willed her way through the preparations. She did not look at the head until she was ready to work.

The morning light was soft and gave her all the details unaccented by harsh shadows. She selected a piece of chalk and began sketching the outlines with quick semicircular strokes. She found herself referring to the head itself less and less as the shape developed. It became easier simply to concentrate on memory than to try to copy the features directly. Each time she looked at it, something was different, a line had been misplaced, a proportion had shifted. Once, in her youth, she had suffered a severe eye problem which, for a time, terrified her that it might be permanent. She rubbed her eyes now, the old fear tingling in her chest, along the back of her scalp.

Berthe tossed the chalk aside and stood. Her back twinged. She limped around the studio. It was well after noon and she found herself ravenously hungry again. After she ate, she looked at her sketch.

The lines were a muddle, like a bad map, chalk marks hacked and scrawled across each other around the vague outline of a head. Only the shape of the eye sockets was clear.

The light now slanting through the windows came directly in harsh and sharp. The front of the head was in shadow. The eyes—empty sockets, she reminded herself—did not look so blind now.

Berthe mounted another blank canvas and selected another piece of chalk.

Berthe dropped the pen and rubbed her fingers. The letter, half done, looked illegible.

"—I cannot complete the commission. For some reason beyond my comprehension I am unable to see the subject through my medium. I regret that I must—"

I regret that I must . . . what?

"I regret, Eugene, that I must tell you I do not love you." She looked around, startled. But it was her own voice, within her own head, nothing more. Ancient memories. She had not thought of those days since before Eugene had died.

The hill was cold that day and they huddled close to keep warm. Neither had thought to bring a wrap, only canvases and paints and a basket with wine and bread. Eugene brought that, he always did, a sharp reminder of his romanticism. And again he brought up the subject of marriage, a sharp reminder of his hopelessness.

"How could I have said no?" Berthe asked. "He was so earnest . . ."

But there had always been his brother, Edouard, taller, more urbane, by far the talented one. Berthe wanted to believe that she had not married Eugene because she could not have Edouard. She saw Eugene as a victim. Everyone around him, those he most wanted to be like, trapped him into an unachievable ambition. Berthe always wished to emancipate him, but found no way to free someone from a self that disappointed. In time she saw that such freedom would only dissolve him.

"I am not young," she had said.

"Nor am I. But we are friends. And. . . ."

And, of course. Always and. The hillside had been cold, but Eugene, reliable, mediocre Eugene, had brought wine and an offer of solace.

"Then perhaps yes."

Berthe wiped at her cheeks as if expecting to find tears. Her skin was dry. She looked at the letter and slowly crumpled it.

She propped the mirror where she could see it from her easel. "If art is a reflection of life," she mused while she worked, "then perhaps life is but a reflection of death. So I will paint a reflection of death." It made as little sense out loud as it did quietly conceived, but Berthe did not pause. She moved the table bearing the head against the edge of the table with the mirror, then turned the head to face into the mirror.

"Now I just wait for the light," she sighed, satisfied.

She sat down before her canvas. No sketch this time, she had decided. Her paints were ready, brushes stacked. Berthe adjusted herself for comfort and looked into the mirror.

She saw only her studio.

"Damn," she whispered, and got up. She adjusted the mirror and went back to her seat. The mirror reflected the edge of her easel. She leaned to the right and saw herself appear.

She stared at the head, then looked back into the mirror.

The light caught her forehead, the crests of her cheeks, the tip of her nose. Her hair, shadowed, seemed its original rich chestnut brown and for a moment Berthe felt as if she were gazing at a portrait of herself much younger. She rubbed her eyes and went around to shift the mirror again.

As she turned and looked down at the head, a cloud passed through the light, softening the harsh angles of the dead face. She could not imagine that this had ever been a handsome man. Compelling, certainly.

She sat down before her easel and looked into the mirror.

Empty.

She blew a harsh breath and glared at the head. "Damn you," she hissed, reached out, and, fingers pressed down on the top of its skull, turned it to face her. She jerked her fingers away and rubbed them. The head felt cold. Berthe chided herself. "The imagination is a dangerous pet," she said, flexed her fingers, and lifted a brush.

She painted methodically, stroke by stroke, shaping the head with absences. The shadows first, then the dark suggestions embedded in the shadows. Berthe hardly looked at the head, again finding it easier to work from snatches and memory than to try to peer closely at the object.

She completed the canvas as the last light of dusk faded. Her eyes burned and her back felt encased in stone. When she stood a hundred small pains crackled from her ankles up to her neck. She dropped the brush into the clay cup with the others.

The image was too dark now to appraise. She pressed her fingers into her kidneys, flexed gently. Her ears filled with a rush of blood. Let it wait till morning. She walked carefully to the kitchen.

Halfway through her dinner she realized that she had had no breakfast and no lunch. She ached from sitting rigidly before her easel all day.

She poured herself wine and went back to the studio. She stood in the doorway. On the opposite side, now shrouded in darkness, was a closet. Within she had stored all of Eugene's canvases, his sketchbooks, his easels. There were a few paintings they had even done together. Berthe had never allowed anyone to see them. She had always yearned for uniqueness, the recognition that she was her own self and not the shadow of another. The collaborations had been made in the same spirit as lovemaking—privately, intimate revelations—and, Berthe felt, their meaning would diminish from exhibition.

"Or are you just ashamed of him?"

Berthe frowned at the voice. Her own, true, but when had she started speaking out loud to herself? She looked out over the rest of the night-hidden studio.

The mirror glowed. Beyond, the wide windows let in a pale blue light that delicately dusted corners and edges and flat surfaces, jumbling the shapes into an alien landscape. The light from the mirror, though, seemed bluer, a bit brighter, as if giving back more than it received. An illusion, Berthe thought, and smiled at the twinge of inspiration. She stepped into the studio and picked her way to the easel.

She set down the wine and removed the finished canvas, setting it off to the left. The blue light lifted the pattern of paint from its surface in meaningless swirls. Berthe began humming quietly to herself as she mounted a blank board to the easel. She took a drink, settled herself, and lifted a brush. She felt giddy, as a child embarking on some forbidden adventure.

When she gazed at the mirror it did not surprise her to see a face gaze back at her, clear and still, waiting with an expression of amused tolerance.

"I am ready," she said to the image. "Be patient. These things take time."

The paints had begun to dry, but Berthe managed. The dim rectangle seemed unreal, as if it were no surface at all but a window, and the colors, whatever they were, did not flow onto it so much as into it to hang suspended against the depths.

It surprised her how quickly the work proceeded. She sang to herself happily as she painted. Her glass was empty when she set the brush down. She grunted and slid from the stool, plucked the glass from the table, and went to the kitchen.

She moved from room to room of the house, her steps unerring, studying the walls and the furnishings in the monochrome illumination. The moon, she thought, must be enormous tonight. She saw everything with the kind of clarity still spring water lends to objects underneath it, slightly magnified and wetly still.

"I have lived here," she said and paused, frowning to herself. There ought to be more to that sentence, she thought, but it seemed complete enough. She had lived here, for thirty years. She and Eugene. She and her work. She and her children, her friends, her dreams. Clients, plans, creditors, colleagues, arguments, laughter, love . . . regret.

"I regret, Eugene, that I must tell you I do not love you."

"I know. But I love you and that is enough."

"Is it?"

He shrugged, looking perfectly foolish in his nightshirt, pale ankles much too thin to support all his immanent hope. "You may borrow some of mine from time to time."

And there was the bed in which, together, they had lent each other what they could of affection, companionship, intent, and, from time to time, passion. Berthe came to believe that she was for Eugene little more than a mirror in which he saw his own feelings reflected back. She had tried to give him what she could but perhaps, in the end, even that had not been necessary. What do mirrors actually have of their own? Perhaps she might have found out with Edouard.

But Edouard had been a prism through which light bent onto his canvases. Whose soul would she have been reflecting with him?

The mirror still glowed in the studio. She shrugged and returned to her easel. There was still time to do another before the light faded.

Dawn drove her to bed. She slept fitfully for a few hours, then awoke to the blazing light of midmorning, her eyes slitted in pain. She went to her parlor and took down the heavy velvet curtains and put them up over the windows in her studio. She used old canvases to fill in the cracks where sunlight found a way in and, satisfied with the thick quality of the darkness, she went back to the easel.

Berthe wondered briefly at the certainty of her technique as she mixed new colors in the dark. She had learned over time not to question too much. Use the moment when it comes, Cassatt had told her, liberate the image before it escapes you. Her early work, Degas had said, had always relied too much on the intellect. Observation must not be inextricably joined to analysis. Then, when her eyes had threatened to fail, she had taken the advice to heart and had learned how to respond first, then understand later. Still, it was all mirrors, and mirrors never satisfied.

The reflections in this mirror, though, never stayed still. She dipped her brushes, carried the pigments to the canvas, filled the vacant planes. A flicker, a shift, a change in the quality of illumination, all demanded a new canvas.

Her belly knotted finally and she went to the kitchen. It was night again. She found half a loaf of bread, the open end hardening. She broke it off and dipped it in wine and ate. As her hunger eased she stared out the window. She had bought this house, it had always remained hers even after she married Eugene. He had never asked that it be any different. It would not be anyway, she realized, since with his death it would have reverted to her after all.

"What was it you felt in me?" she asked.

She drew a deep breath, luxuriating in the sensation. She had not worked this hard, this intently for years. With Eugene's death the desire had all but vanished.

"I did not love you, but I miss you . . ."

"It is enough."

Berthe turned, peering into the darkness of the studio. The only light came from the mirror. More . . . ? I am tired.

More.

Berthe opened her eyes slowly to the pounding on the door. She gazed up at the warmly lit ceiling of her bedroom, sleepily fascinated by the richness of color and the restful shifting of shadow from the trees outside her window. The pounding stopped and started again.

She rolled over. The myriad aches had melded into one general agony. Her head throbbed. She squinted at the window. A light breeze made the curtains dance gracefully.

Voices drifted up from below the window. Berthe sighed heavily and rubbed her eyes. The window was closer than the door, she decided, and pushed herself to her feet.

"Madame Morisot!"

Berthe leaned from the window and stared down at two men. One was broad-shouldered and dressed in workman's clothes with a worn, shapeless cap on his head, the other was a bit taller, distinguished, with a beard, dressed in a brown suit. Both men looked familiar, but for different reasons.

"Yes?" she said.

"Are you all right?" the distinguished man asked.

"Yes, yes, quite . . ." Then she recognized them. François delivered her foods from the market. She smiled at him. "I'll be right down. Forgive me, I've over-slept."

Berthe pulled on her robe, embarrassed then. They must, she thought, think I'm mad, leaning out the window like that. What time was it, anyway? Wincing at each step, she descended the stairs to the kitchen. Her legs threatened to cramp, as if on the previous day she had walked twenty miles. She pulled open the door and François looked immediately relieved. He came in with a box and went straight to her pantry.

"Monsieur," she said to the other gentleman.

"We grew concerned," he said. "Are you well?"

"I don't know . . . I have just . . . I am not quite awake yet, Monsieur. Forgive me . . ."

"Not at all, forgive me. I hope I have not interrupted . . . ?"

François went out and returned with another box. As he passed her Berthe saw a bunch of grapes and snatched them out. François did not seem to notice and continued to the ice box.

"I am afraid, Monsieur, I was unable to fulfill your request," she said around a mouthful.

He blinked, but otherwise his expression did not change.

"I expected word sooner, I admit," he said finally, "that you could not. But as the days passed I began to hope. May I see what you have?"

For a moment Berthe felt an intense urgency to refuse. Puzzled, she stood there eating her grapes, worrying at her feelings, until François cleared his throat.

"Should I bring more, Madame Morisot?" he asked when she looked at him. "You've eaten everything here."

"Is there enough wine?" she asked.

"Well, as much as you usually need for a week . . ." François seemed uneasy, embarrassed.

"If I need more I'll send for it, François. Thank you." She went to the cabinet where she kept her market money and counted out his payment, then added a couple livres.

François thanked her and backed out of the door. Berthe headed matter-of-factly toward the studio.

"Come, Monsieur."

Berthe stopped three steps into the studio. It was still dark, only the light from the hallway showing her a vague path through the stacked canvases.

"Goodness," he said.

She picked her way to the window and threw open the curtains. Light flooded the space, momentarily blinding her. She turned away, fingers to her eyes until they adjusted.

Across the room he stood near the door, his own eyes wide with a powerful checked astonishment. They were very clear, very pale, and she remembered then that she had wished to paint him.

Between them the studio was cluttered with canvases. One remained on her easel, but dozens filled the countertops, the desks, propped on the floor against table legs, walls, in the chairs and against stools. Berthe started counting them, stopped at thirty-three, and searched for the head.

"Ah," she said, realizing that the mirror blocked her view of it. She went around the opposite side of the easel, stepping over finished work stacked carelessly on the floor. How many had she done? Her fingers ached dully.

She stopped before the easel. On the board mounted there dark blues and greens whorled around a bold head, high brow below thick black hair that fell in a braid that draped over the right shoulder. Proud eyes stared out at the world from above high cheekbones. Bearded, strong, and somehow very old. A silver ring depended from his right ear. The entire effect was of imminent dynamism, as if he were about to leave the studio to tend to the conquest of a city or a country.

"I don't remember . . ." she began, then looked around at the other canvases. Men and women, different ages, different colors, different eras. Large panels and small cameo size works littered the studio. Many were plain people, unexceptional except for the antiquity of their clothes or the evident foreignness of their race or culture. A small clutch of them were more modern.

Her workplace was a wreck of used material. The remnants of paint and brushes, broken charcoals, rags piled on rags, attested to the quantity of work produced.

The mirror stood where it had since—when?

"What day is this, Monsieur?"

"Wednesday"

"The date?"

"The fifth, Madame."

"Ah."

"When I did not hear from you after six days I became concerned."

"Yes, of course."

"Eh . . . where is the head?"

"Right here—"

She pointed to an empty space before the mirror.

The gentleman touched the countertop and dusted his fingers through a thick layer of chalky residue. He looked at the mirror, then inquiringly at Berthe.

She shook her head, dismayed, and looked about at the stacks of canvases. "I could not *see* it clearly, so . . ."

"You painted its reflection," he said, nodding. "Of course. Sensible." He waved at the paintings. "And these?" When Berthe did not reply, he nodded again. "Vlad Tsepes was an individual of many parts. Not a simple subject."

"I apologize, Monsieur."

"May I ask for what?"

"I . . . did not produce what you requested."

"On the contrary. These are quite satisfactory."

Berthe saw him study the paintings, recognized the intent expression of someone who understands the work, feels the innate quality and power. She wanted to argue, wanted, above all, an explanation, but she did not wish to disturb his pleasure.

Suddenly he went directly to one small portrait and lifted it with his fingertips. "This one . . . we were friends, long ago. He was the first I knew of that had been taken. I had forgotten . . ." He looked up, eyes moist, and nodded. "All of them must be his victims." He set the painting down and turned away from her for a moment. "It is more than I expected," he said finally. He looked up. "Now, the matter of payment."

"For what, Monsieur?"

"For all of them." He waved at the portraits cluttering the studio.

"Are you serious?"

He nodded.

Berthe shook her head. She named a price and wondered immediately what she had said.

"Oh, no, that is much too low. I will write a draft for what I believe is appropriate."

"As you wish . . ."

She began gathering the paintings, stacking them according to size. After a time she thought she recognized the look they all shared in common. Relief. She had seen it only a few times in her life, and in each instance it had been Eugene who had shown it to her. Once when she had agreed to marry him, again when she actually gave her vows. And again the hour of his death, though then it had been overshadowed by weariness. In each portrait she saw that same expression, over and over, the look of someone who has been laboring in an impossible task that is now complete.

When she turned she saw it again in her client's face. He seemed now so relieved that for a moment she did not know him. He gave her a bank draft, drawn on a Dutch bank, and smiled.

At the end of the day he had hired a wagon and workmen to load the collection. He paid them and gave them instructions where to take the cargo.

"Thank you, Madame. You have exceeded my expectations." He hesitated, then asked. "Do you wish still to paint me?"

Berthe looked up and saw him reflected in the mirror. His eyes were in shadow, but there were highlights within, faint and disappointing.

"Yes, I would. But it does not have to be at once."

"Then I will take my leave. I shall come when you request me."

She nodded absently and he withdrew. Gazing into the now blank mirror she knew that she would not paint him. He did not need liberating anymore.

Her fingers twinged. She went to the door and saw his carriage moving off down the street. Dusk was coming. She went to the kitchen and ate some beef, drank some wine, slowly, watching the light grow dim.

Berthe stood in the midst of her studio. The canvases gone, it seemed much too large. She walked around the desks and counters, circling her easel. She stopped and looked down.

Below the easel stood one more canvas. She frowned. He had forgotten one. She sighed impatiently and stooped to pick it up. Her back ached dully as she lifted it to the table.

"Oh."

It was her original charcoal sketch of the head, made the first day. The lines smeared and darted, a confusing mass of conflicting intentions around two blank areas where the eyes ought to be. Just as well it was left behind.

She brushed off the thick dust from the counter and propped it up. A senseless map. The mirror caught her eye and, smiling, she turned the canvas to face it. By the time she had it positioned properly, evening stole the last of the light.

She could start in the morning. She made her way to the door.

Glancing back, she saw her windows, deep blue, and, in the center of the studio, the mirror glowed.

"Oh," she said, "just one more, then."

Berthe returned to her easel and lifted a brush. "Of course, you were once a victim, too."

CAROL ANN DUFFY

Mrs. Beast

Carol Ann Duffy lives in Manchester, England and has published five poetry collections—her most recent is The World's Wife. *She has received numerous awards, and has edited the poetry collections* I Wouldn't Thank You for a Valentine: Poems For Young Feminists *and* Stopping For Death: Poems For Death and Loss. *Duffy has had several plays produced in England, and has been visiting Poetry Fellow at Wake Forest University. She currently lectures in poetry at Manchester Metropolitan University.*

"Mrs. Beast" comes from The Poetry Review, *a journal published in London, England by the Poetry Society.*

—T. W.

These myths going round, these legends, fairytales,
I'll put them straight; so when you stare
into my face—Helen's face, Cleopatra's,
Queen of Sheba's, Juliet's—then, deeper,
gaze into my eyes—Nefertiti's, Mona Lisa's,
Garbo's eyes—think again. The Little Mermaid slit
her shining, silver tail in two, rubbed salt
into that stinking wound, got up and walked,
in agony, in fishnet tights, stood up and smiled, waltzed,
all for a Prince, a pretty boy, a charming one
who'd dump her in the end, chuck her, throw her overboard.
I could have told her—look, love, I should know,
they're bastards when they're Princes.
What you want to do is find yourself a Beast. The sex

is better. Myself, I came to the House of the Beast
no longer a girl, knowing my own mind,
my own gold stashed in the Bank,
my own black horse at the gates
ready to carry me off at one wrong word,
one false move, one dirty look.

But the Beast fell to his knees at the door
to kiss my glove with his mongrel lips—good—
showed by the tears in his bloodshot eyes
that he knew he was blessed—better—
didn't try to conceal his erection,
size of a mule's—best. And the Beast
watched me open, decant and quaff
a bottle of Chateau Margaux '54,
the year of my birth, before he lifted a paw.

I'll tell you more. Stripped to his muslin shirt
and his corduroys, he steamed in his pelt,
ugly as sin. He had the grunts, the groans, the yelps,
the breath of a goat. I had the language, girls.
The lady says Do this. Harder. The lady says
Do that. Faster. The lady says That's not where I meant.
At last it all made sense. The pig in my bed
was *invited*. And if his snout and trotters fouled
my damask sheets, why, then he'd wash them. Twice.
Meantime, here was his horrid leather tongue
to scour in between my toes. Here
were his hooked and yellowy claws to pick my nose,
if I wanted that. Or to scratch my back
till it bled. Here was his bullock's head
to sing off-key all night where I couldn't hear.
Here was a bit of him like a horse, a ram,
an ape, a wolf, a dog, a donkey, dragon, dinosaur.

Need I say more? On my Poker nights, the Beast
kept out of sight. We were a hard school, tough as fuck,
all of us beautiful and rich—the Woman
Who Married a Minotaur, Goldilocks, The Bride
Of The Bearded Lesbian, Frau Yellow Dwarf, et Moi.
I watched those wonderful women shuffle and deal—
Five and Seven Card Stud, Sidewinder, Hold 'Em, Draw—
I watched them bet and raise and call. One night,
a head-to-head between Frau Yellow Dwarf and Bearded's Bride
was over the biggest pot I'd seen in my puff.
The Frau had the Queen of Clubs on the baize
and Bearded the Queen of Spades. Final card. Queen each.
Frau Yellow raised. Bearded raised. Goldilocks' eyes
were glued to the pot as though porridge bubbled there.
The Minotaur's wife lit a stinking cheroot. Me,
I noticed the Frau's hand shook as she placed her chips.
Bearded raised her a final time, then stared,
stared so hard you felt your frock would melt
if she blinked. Some dykes are like that. Frau Yellow
swallowed hard, then called. Sure enough, Bearded flipped
her Aces over; diamonds, hearts, the public Ace of Spades.

And that was a lesson learnt by all of us—
The drop-dead gorgeous Bride of the Bearded Lesbian didn't bluff.

But behind each player stood a line of ghosts
unable to win. Eve. Aschputtel. Marilyn Monroe.
Rapunzel slashing wildly at her hair.
Bessie Smith unloved and down and out.
Bluebeard's wives, Henry VIII's, Snow White
cursing the day she left the seven dwarfs, Diana,
Princess of Wales. The sheepish Beast came in
with a tray of schnapps at the end of the game
and we stood for the toast—*Fay Wray*—
then tossed our fiery drinks to the back of our crimson throats.
Bad girls. Serious ladies. Mourning our dead.

So I was hard on the Beast, win or lose,
when I got upstairs, those tragic girls in my head,
turfing him out of bed; standing alone
on the balcony, the night so cold I could taste the stars
on the tip of my tongue. And I made a prayer—
thumbing my pearls, the tears of Mary, one by one,
like a rosary—words for the lost, the captive beautiful,
the wives, those less fortunate than we.
The moon was a hand-mirror breathed on by a Queen.
My breath was a chiffon scarf for an elegant ghost.
I turned to go back inside. Bring me the Beast for the night.
Bring me the wine-cellar key. Let the less-loving one be me.

JANE YOLEN

Become a Warrior

"Swords-and-sorcery" adventure fiction has been a staple of the fantasy genre since the days of the pulp magazines, and still accounts for the greatest number of genre book sales today. It has been under-represented in the pages of The Year's Best Fantasy and Horror *volumes, however, for while this kind of fiction can be quite entertaining, it is rare to find short works of "swords-and-sorcery" with a literary bent, particularly now that the masters of the form (Fritz Leiber, C. L. Moore, et al.) are no longer with us. These days the best "swords-and-sorcery" fiction is being written at novel length.*

When a writer of Jane Yolen's stature turns her hand to the form, however, one can expect an exceptional tale. "Become a Warrior" is rendered in the distinctive Yolen style which makes her stories read like classic folk tales that have been passed down through generations rather than newly crafted on the page. Dubbed by reviewers as "the Hans Christian Andersen of America," Yolen has published more than one hundred fifty books for children, teenagers, and adults; has won the World Fantasy Award; and is a twenty-five-year veteran of the Board of Directors of the Society of Children's Book Writers and Illustrators. Her magical novels for adults include Briar Rose, Sister Light, Sister Dark, White Jenna, *and* The One-Armed Queen. *She lives in western Massachusetts and St. Andrews, Scotland.*

"Become a Warrior" is reprinted from Warrior Princesses, *an anthology edited by Elizabeth Ann Scarborough and Martin H. Greenberg.*

—T. W.

Both the hunted and the hunter pray to God.

The moon hung like a bloody red ball over the silent battlefield. Only the shadows seemed to move. The men on the ground would never move again. And their women, sick with weeping, did not dare the field in the dark. It would be morning before they would come like crows to count their losses.

But on the edge of the field there was a sudden tiny movement, and it was no shadow. Something small was creeping to the muddy hem of the battleground.

Something knelt there, face shining with grief. A child, a girl, the youngest daughter of the king who had died that evening surrounded by all his sons.

The girl looked across the dark field and, like her mother, like her sisters, like her aunts, did not dare put foot on to the bloody ground. But then she looked up at the moon and thought she saw her father's face there. Not the father who lay with his innards spilled out into contorted hands. Not the one who had braided firesticks in his beard and charged into battle screaming. She thought she saw the father who had always sung her to sleep against the night terrors. The one who sat up with her when Great Graxyx haunted her dreams.

"I will do for you, Father, as you did for me," she whispered to the moon. She prayed to the goddess for the strength to accomplish what she had just promised.

Then foot by slow foot, she crept onto the field, searching in the red moon's light for the father who had fallen. She made slits of her eyes so she would not see the full horror around her. She breathed through her mouth so that she would not smell all the deaths. She never once thought of the Great Graxyx who lived—so she truly believed—in the black cave of her dressing room. Or any of the hundred and six gibbering children Graxyx had sired. She crept across the landscape made into a horror by the enemy hordes. All the dead men looked alike. She found her father by his boots.

She made her way up from the boots, past the gaping wound that had taken him from her, to his face which looked peaceful and familiar enough, except for the staring eyes. He had never stared like that. Rather his eyes had always been slotted, against the hot sun of the gods, against the lies of men. She closed his lids with trembling fingers and put her head down on his chest, where the stillness of the heart told her what she already knew.

And then she began to sing to him.

She sang of life, not death, and the small gods of new things. Of bees in the hive and birds on the summer wind. She sang of foxes denning and bears shrugging off winter. She sang of fish in the sparkling rivers and the first green uncurlings of fern in spring. She did not mention dying, blood, or wounds, or the awful stench of death. Her father already knew this well and did not need to be recalled to it.

And when she was done with her song, it was as if his corpse gave a great sigh, one last breath, though of course he was dead already half the night and made no sound at all. But she heard what she needed to hear.

By then it was morning and the crows came. The human crows as well as the black birds, poking and prying and feeding on the dead.

So she turned and went home and everyone wondered why she did not weep. But she had left her tears out on the battlefield.

She was seven years old.

Dogs bark, but the caravan goes on.

Before the men who had killed her father and who had killed her brothers could come to take all the women away to serve them, she had her maid cut her black hair as short as a boy's. The maid was a trembling sort, and the hair cut was ragged. But it would do.

She waited until the maid had turned around and leaned down to put away the shears. Then she put her arm around the woman and with a quick knife's cut across her throat killed her, before the woman could tell on her. It was a mercy, really, for she was old and ugly and would be used brutally by the soldiers before being slaughtered, probably in a slow and terrible manner. So her father had warned before he left for battle.

Then she went into the room of her youngest brother, dead in the field and lying by her father's right hand. In his great wooden chest she found a pair of trews that had probably been too small for him, but were nonetheless too long for her. With the still-bloody knife she sheared the legs of the trews a hand's width, rolled and sewed them with a quick seam. All the women of her house could sew well, even when it had to be done quickly. Even when it had to be done through half-closed eyes. Even when the hem was wet with blood. Even then.

When she put on the trews, they fit, though she had to pull the drawstring around the waist quite tight and tie the ribbands twice around her. She shrugged into one of her brother's shirts as well, tucking it down into the waistband. Then she slipped her bloody knife into the shirt sleeve. She wore her own riding boots, which could not be told from a boy's, for her brother's boots were many times too big for her.

Then she went out through the window her brother always used when he set out to court one of the young and pretty maids. She had watched him often enough though he had never known she was there, hiding beside the bed, a dark little figure as still as the night.

Climbing down the vine, hand over hand, was no great trouble either. She had done it before, following after him. Really, what a man and a maid did together was most interesting, if a bit odd. And certainly noisier than it needed to be.

She reached the ground in moments, crossed the garden, climbed over the outside wall by using a twisted tree as her ladder. When she dropped to the ground, she twisted her ankle a bit, but she made not the slightest whimper. She was a boy now. And she knew they did not cry.

In the west a cone of dark dust was rising up and advancing on the fortress, blotting out the sky. She knew it for the storm that many hooves make as horses race across the plains. The earth trembled beneath her feet. Behind her, in their rooms, the women had begun to wail. The sound was thin, like a gold filiment thrust into her breast. She plugged her ears that their cries could not recall her to her old life, for such was not her plan.

Circling around the stone skirting of the fortress, in the shadow so no one could see her, she started around toward the east. It was not a direction she knew. All she knew was that it was away from the horses of the enemy.

Once she glanced back at the fortress that had been the only home she had ever known. Her mother, her sisters, the other women stood on the battlements looking toward the west and the storm of riders. She could hear their wailing, could see the movement of their arms as they beat upon their breasts. She did not know if that were a plea or an invitation.

She did not look again.

To become a warrior, forget the past.

Three years she worked as a serving lad in a fortress not unlike her own but many days' travel away. She learned to clean and to carry, she learned to work after a night of little sleep. Her arms and legs grew strong. Three years she worked as the cook's boy. She learned to prepare geese and rabbit and bear for the pot, and learned which parts were salty, which sweet. She could tell good mushrooms from bad and which greens might make the toughest meat palatable.

And then she knew she could no longer disguise the fact that she was a girl for her body had begun to change in ways that would give her away. So she left the fortress, starting east once more, taking only her knife and a long loop of rope which she wound around her waist seven times.

She was many days hungry, many days cold, but she did not turn back. Fear is a great incentive.

She taught herself to throw the knife and hit what she aimed at. Hunger is a great teacher.

She climbed trees when she found them in order to sleep safe at night. The rope made such passages easier.

She was so long by herself, she almost forgot how to speak. But she never forgot how to sing. In her dreams she sang to her father on the battlefield. Her songs made him live again. Awake she knew the truth was otherwise. He was dead. The worms had taken him. His spirit was with the goddess, drinking milk from her great pap, milk that tasted like honey wine.

She did not dream of her mother or of her sisters or of any of the women in her father's fortress. If they died, it had been with little honor. If they still lived, it was with less.

So she came at last to a huge forest with oaks thick as a goddess' waist. Over all was a green canopy of leaves that scarcely let in the sun. Here were many streams, rivulets that ran cold and clear, torrents that crashed against rocks, and pools that were full of silver trout whose meat was sweet. She taught herself to fish and to swim, and it would be hard to say which gave her the greater pleasure. Here, too, were nests of birds, and that meant eggs. Ferns curled and then opened, and she knew how to steam them, using a basket made of willow strips and a fire from rubbing sticks against one another. She followed bees to their hives, squirrels to their hidden nuts, ducks to their watered beds.

She grew strong, and brown, and—though she did not know it—very beautiful.

Beauty is a danger, to women as well as to men. To warriors most of all. It steers them away from the path of killing. It softens the soul.

When you are in a tree, be a tree.

She was three years alone in the forest and grew to trust the sky, the earth, the river, the trees, the way she trusted her knife. They did not lie to her. They did not kill wantonly. They gave her shelter, food, courage. She did not remember her father except as some sort of warrior god, with staring eyes, looking as she had seen him last. She did not remember her mother or sisters or aunts at all.

It had been so long since she had spoken to anyone, it was as if she could not speak at all. She knew words, they were in her head, but not in her mouth, on her tongue, in her throat. Instead she made the sounds she heard every day— the grunt of boar, the whistle of duck, the trilling of thrush, the settled cooing of the wood pigeon on its nest.

If anyone had asked her if she was content, she would have nodded.

Content.

Not happy. Not satisfied. Not done with her life's work.

Content.

And then one early evening a new sound entered her domain. A drumming on the ground, from many miles away. A strange halloing, thin, insistent, whining. The voices of some new animal, packed like wolves, singing out together.

She trembled. She did not know why. She did not remember why. But to be safe from the thing that made her tremble, she climbed a tree, the great oak that was in the very center of her world.

She used the rope ladder she had made, and pulled the ladder up after. Then she shrank back against the trunk of the tree to wait. She tried to be the brown of the bark, the green of the leaves, and in this she almost succeeded.

It was in the first soft moments of dark, with the woods outlined in muzzy black, that the pack ran yapping, howling, belling into the clearing around the oak.

In that instant she remembered dogs.

There were twenty of them, some large, lanky grays; some stumpy browns with long muzzles; some stiff-legged spotted with pushed-in noses; some thick-coated; some smooth. Her father, the god of war, had had such a motley pack. He had hunted boar and stag and hare with such. They had found him bear and fox and wolf with ease.

Still, she did not know why the dog pack was here, circling her tree. Their jaws were raised so that she could see their iron teeth, could hear the tolling of her death with their long tongues.

She used the single word she could remember. She said it with great authority, with trembling.

"Avaunt!"

At the sound of her voice, the animals all sat down on their haunches to stare up at her, their own tongues silenced. Except for one, a rat terrier, small and springy and unable to be still. He raced back up the path toward the west like some small spy going to report to his master.

Love comes like a thief, stealing the heart's gold away.

It was in the deeper dark that the dogs' master came, with his men behind him, their horses' hooves thrumming the forest paths. They trampled the grass, the foxglove's pink bells and the purple florets of self-heal, the wine-colored burdock flowers and the sprays of yellow goldenrod equally under the horses' heavy feet. The woods were wounded by their passage. The grass did not spring back nor the flowers raise up again.

She heard them and began trembling anew as they thrashed their way across her green haven and into the very heart of the wood.

Ahead of them raced the little terrier, his tail flagging them on, till he led them right to the circle of dogs waiting patiently beneath her tree.

"Look, my lord, they have found something," said one man.

"Odd they should be so quiet," said another.

But the one they called lord dismounted, waded through the sea of dogs, and stood at the very foot of the oak, his feet crunching on the fallen acorns. He stared up, and up, and up through the green leaves and at first saw nothing but brown and green.

One of the large gray dogs stood, walked over to his side, raised its great muzzle to the tree, and howled.

The sound made her shiver anew.

"See, my lord, see—high up. There is a trembling in the foliage," one of the men cried.

"You fool," the lord cried, "that is no trembling of leaves. It is a girl. She is dressed all in brown and green. See how she makes the very tree shimmer." Though how he could see her so well in the dark, she was never to understand. "Come down, child, we will not harm you."

She did not come down. Not then. Not until the morning fully revealed her. And then, if she was to eat, if she was to relieve herself, she had to come down. So she did, dropping the rope ladder, and skinning down it quickly. She kept her knife tucked up in her waist, out where they could see it and be afraid.

They did not touch her but watched her every movement, like a pack of dogs. When she went to the river to drink, they watched. When she ate the bit of journeycake the lord offered her, they watched. And even when she relieved herself, the lord watched. He would let no one else look then, which she knew honored her, though she did not care.

And when after several days he thought he had tamed her, the lord took her on his horse before him and rode with her back to the far west where he lived. By then he loved her, and knew that she loved him in return, though she had yet to speak a word to him.

"But then, what have words to do with love," he whispered to her as they rode.

He guessed by her carriage, by the way her eyes met his, that she was a princess of some sort, only badly used. He loved her for the past which she could not speak of, for her courage which showed in her face, and for her beauty. He would have loved her for much less, having found her in the tree, for she was something out of a story, out of a prophecy, out of a dream.

"I loved you at once," he whispered. "When I knew you from the tree."

She did not answer. Love was not yet in her vocabulary. But she did not say the one word she could speak: *avaunt*. She did not want him to go.

When the cat wants to eat her kittens, she says they look like mice.

His father was not so quick to love her.

His mother, thankfully, was long dead.

She knew his father at once, by the way his eyes were slotted against the hot sun of the gods, against the lies of men. She knew him to be a king if only by that.

And when she recognized her mother and her sisters in his retinue, she knew who it was she faced. They did not know her, of course. She was no longer seven but nearly seventeen. Her life had browned her, bronzed her, made her into such steel as they had never known. She could have told them but she had only contempt for their lives. As they had contempt now for her, thinking her some drudge run off to the forest, some sinister throwling from a forgotten clan.

When the king gave his grudging permission for their marriage, when the prince's advisers set down in long scrolls what she should and should not have, she only smiled at them. It was a tree's smile, giving away not a bit of the bark.

She waited until the night of her wedding to the prince, when they were couched together, the servants a giggle outside their door. She waited until he had covered her face with kisses, when he had touched her in secret places that made her tremble, when he had brought blood between her legs. She waited until he had done all the things she had once watched her brother do to the maids, and she cried out with pleasure as she had heard them do. She waited until he was asleep, smiling happily in his dreams, because she did love him in her warrior way.

Then she took her knife and slit his throat, efficiently and without cruelty, as she would a deer for her dinner.

"You father killed my father," she whispered, soft as a love token in his ear as the knife carved a smile on his neck.

She stripped the bed of its bloody offering and handed it to the servants who thought it the effusions of the night. Then she walked down the hall to her father-in-law's room.

He was bedded with her mother, riding her like one old wave atop another.

"Here!" he cried as he realized someone was in the room. "You!" he said when he realized who it was.

Her mother looked at her with half opened eyes and, for the first time, saw who she really was, for she had her father's face, fierce and determined.

"No!" her mother cried. "Avaunt!" But it was a cry that was ten years late.

She killed the king with as much ease as she had killed his son, but she let the knife linger longer to give him a great deal of pain. Then she sliced off one of his ears and put it gently in her mother's hand.

In all this she had said not one word. But wearing the blood of the king on her gown, she walked out of the palace and back to the woods, though she was many days getting there.

No one tried to stop her, for no one saw her. She was a flower in the meadow, a rock by the roadside, a reed by the river, a tree in the forest.

And a warrior's mother by the spring of the year.

NORMAN PARTRIDGE

Blackbirds

Norman Partridge's short fiction has been published regularly in suspense, mystery, and horror magazines and anthologies. His first collection, Mr. Fox and Other Feral Tales *won the Bram Stoker Award and his second collection,* Bad Intentions, *was a World Fantasy Award nominee. He is the author of four novels:* Slippin' into Darkness, Saguaro Riptide, The Ten Ounce Siesta, *and* Wildest Dreams. *Partridge has worked in libraries and steel mills. He loves fifties rock 'n' roll, drive-in movies, and old paperbacks where the bad guys get away with murder.*

"Blackbirds" is the third story we've taken by Partridge for our series. The first two stories were both realistic, psychological horror stories about adults. "Blackbirds," originally published in Imagination Fully Dilated, *is equally effective, but in a somewhat different vein, featuring a young protagonist caught in a situation of extraordinary strangeness.*

—E. D.

On an August morning in the summer of 1960, a man dressed in black shattered the kitchen window at the Peterson home.

The house was empty. Major Peterson was at the base, writing a report on the importance of preparedness in the peacetime army. Mrs. Peterson was shopping for groceries. Their daughter Tracy was doing volunteer work at the local hospital.

Billy Peterson was the youngest member of the family. He was ten years old. Like the rest of his family, Billy was not at home when the man in black shattered the kitchen window.

Billy was pedaling his bicycle down Old MacMurray Road.

Billy was pedaling very fast.

Billy's Daisy BB gun was slung over his shoulder, and he was wearing a small army surplus backpack.

There were only a few things in the backpack.

For one, there was a blackbird's nest. In the nest were three eggs.

And there were two more things. Two items that just like the backpack, had once been the official property of the United States Army.

One was a canteen, which Billy had filled with gasoline siphoned from his father's lawnmower.

The other was a hand grenade.

The man in black had a pet of sorts. A blackbird which perched on his shoulder.

A blackbird with a BB hole in its chest.

But the bird did not seem inordinately bothered by the injury. No doubt it was well-trained. It did not make a single sound. Its head mirrored the movements of its master's, searching here and there as the man in black explored the empty house.

But in the view of the man in black, the house was not empty.

In his view, he was surrounded by the Peterson family.

In his view, they were all around him.

Mrs. Peterson's coffee cup stood abandoned on the kitchen counter, bearing a stain of frosted pink lipstick.

But the man in black passed it by.

The scent of Tracy's girlish perfume drew him to the upstairs bathroom. He touched her uncapped perfume bottle, touched the damp towel Tracy had abandoned on the floor, touched Tracy's soap, touched the heap of girlish clothes she had tossed in the laundry hamper.

And the man in black left the room.

He followed the track of Major Peterson's bare feet on plush new carpet until he came to the major's walk-in closet.

The closet held many uniforms. The man in black ran his fingers over these. When he was done, he did not leave the closet.

Instead, he bent low and spun the dial on a safe which Major Peterson had bought at Sears.

He spun the dial with a calm sense of surety.

The numbers clicked into place.

The man in black opened the door.

There were many valuable things within the safe.

But the hand grenade was gone.

The mouth of the cave gaped wide.

Billy knew that it was a mouth that could not speak.

Shivering, Billy stared at it. He did not want to look away.

He could not look away. That was what he had done just the other day. He'd been staring at the mouth of the cave, staring into that black mouth that could not utter a single word, when his buddy Gordon Rogers said something stupid.

And, just for a second, Billy looked away.

Just for a second. Just long enough to give Gordon Rogers a poke in the ribs.

And when Billy looked back, a man was standing at the mouth of the cave.

A man dressed all in black.

Billy swallowed hard, remembering.

He wished that Gordon were here.

Maybe, in a way, he was.

No. That wasn't right. Billy knew that he was all alone now. Gordon was gone—as good as dead, really. And no one stood at the mouth of the cave.

No one stood there dressed all in black.

No one said, "Don't you know that caves are dangerous?"

No Gordon to answer, "If caves are so dangerous, what're you doing in one?"

"Guess," was the single word the man in black whispered, but there was no one to whisper it.

No one but Billy.

He stared at the mouth full of nothing.

"You're a mining engineer," he guessed.

But no one shook his head, as the man in black had done.

"You're a spelunker," Billy said.

And no one laughed.

"If you want me to ask, I'll ask." Billy said. "What are you?"

"I am an army."

"An army?" Billy shook his head. "You're just one guy!"

"I am an army, all the same."

"From where, then? You don't look like a Ruskie."

"I am not from Russia."

"Then where are you from?"

The question hung in the air. The mouth of the cave yawned wide, but there was only silence.

The man in black was not here.

So he could not answer, "I am an army . . . from hell."

Being an army was an occupation fraught with hazards. Violence was often unavoidable. People lied. And reconnaissance reports were sometimes less than accurate.

For example—there was no hand grenade in Major Peterson's safe. Which meant that there was no shiny hand-grenade pin to be had.

But the man in black found many other attractive things in the Peterson house. Things that could be of use.

He found Tracy's jump rope. Tracy had abandoned it long ago, of course. But not so long ago as she might have wished.

In addition to these things, the man in black found a towel used by both parents. The towel was the color of skin, and it bore tell-tale smudges of Mrs. Peterson's foundation cream, and from it Mr. Peterson's hair seemed to sprout, for just this morning he had trimmed his moustache before departing for the base, and the bristling hairs had adhered to the towel.

The man in black bunched the towel between his large palms. Then he twisted it, as if wringing it out.

Bunched again. Twisted again.

He worked faster and faster. Strange shapes appeared in the material. Shapes vaguely recognizable, but only for a moment, and then they were gone.

A nose. An eyebrow.

A woman's cheek daubed with foundation cream.

A man's graying moustache.

The man in black smiled as he wrapped the baseball in the towel and snared it with the jump rope.

Then he wrung the towel again, quite viciously this time.

Almost sadistically.

Soon the towel began to bleed.

Blood spattered the carpet as the man in black crossed Mr. and Mrs. Peterson's bedroom.

Soon each and every drop had been wrung from the towel.

The man in black shattered the bedroom window.

No one noticed.

No one was home.

And the neighbors, the man thought with a wry smile, had flown.

Billy was about to unzip his U.S. Army surplus backpack when something moved within.

Billy gasped. The canvas material seemed to pulse before his eyes. He watched it, but he couldn't move.

Until he heard the sound.

A faint cracking. The same sound Billy heard every morning when his father tapped a spoon against his soft-boiled egg.

Billy knew he had to move quickly. He unzipped the backpack. He snatched at the nest made from Gordon Rogers' Slinky and Mrs. Rogers' measuring tape and Mr. Rogers' toupee.

He spilled three eggs from the nest.

Immediately, he spotted the crack in the biggest egg.

Another peck and it widened. Yet another peck and the crack was a hole.

One more peck and something pink showed through.

Something pink inside a blackbird's egg.

Something as pink as Mr. Rogers' bald head.

The hole in the egg was very tiny. Not nearly as large as the mouth of the cave. But the mouth of the cave was silent, and the hole in the egg was not.

"Billy," a voice whispered from within. "Don't . . . please, Billy. For God's sake don't . . ."

It was a tiny voice. Not like Mr. Rogers' voice at all.

Not really.

Another tiny tap, like father's spoon at the breakfast table.

A crack rippled across the surface of the second egg.

The smallest egg.

Gordon's egg.

"Billy. . . ."

Billy jerked the canteen out of the backpack and doused the nest and all three eggs with gasoline.

The box of safety matches was in his pocket.

Soon they were in his hand.

Soon the nest was a funeral pyre.

It crackled and crackled. Blood boiled in the eggshells and sizzled away to nothing. Mrs. Rogers' measuring tape and Mr. Rogers' toupee were crisped to fine ash, and soon all that remained of the nest was Gordon's charred and blackened Slinky, which didn't move at all.

Everything was quiet again.

———

The man in black screamed.

Sparks erupted from his shoulders and ignited the blackbird's feathers and the bird screeched and took wing and crashed to the ground in a flaming, twisted heap while the man watched in agony.

But he did not watch for long. Fiery tongues leapt from his trouser cuffs and licked at his ankles. He ripped off his burning coat and tossed it in the corner. Hurriedly, he worked at the metal buckle of his flaming belt, his fingers blistering at the touch of hot metal.

And then just that quickly the fire was gone, and he scooped his winged companion from the floor and smoothed its black feathers, and he knew that there had been no fire at all.

No. That wasn't quite accurate. There had been a fire. It had not been here, however. The fire had occurred elsewhere. The man in black and his winged companion were only being informed of it.

Reconnaissance. Sometimes it was unreliable, and sometimes it stuck a little close to home.

The man in black picked up his coat, absently plucked lint from the sleeve, and slipped it on. The blackbird regained its perch on his shoulder.

The man sighed. The boy was not stupid. That much was certain.

In point of fact, the boy was very smart. But Billy Peterson was not nearly smart enough to tangle with an army of one.

The simple truth of it was that Billy had appeared at the Rogers' household at a most inauspicious moment. He had seen the blackbird lay three eggs in a nest made from a Slinky, a measuring tape, and a man's toupee.

And he had heard the man in black utter words over that nest.

The same words the man now uttered over a nest made from a bath towel, and a baseball, and a length of jump rope.

A nest like a hundred others, all across town.

Billy stared at the blackened remains of the Rogers' nest. The eggs were cracked and open, like broken black cups. The things that had grown inside were dead. That was very good.

Billy loaded his BB gun. He did not feel like a murderer. Still, he felt he should take the scorched nest to the cemetery and bury it.

Maybe he should do that with the pink bird, too.

Billy had noticed the bird just this morning. He had watched it take flight from a nest on the Jefferson's roof, tiny veined wings fluttering.

The pink bird was hard to miss.

And the sounds it made. A series of shrill skreeghs.

Well, Billy had never seen a pink bird. Never heard one, either. Maybe it was a pet. Mr. Jefferson had a daughter who went to school with Billy. A sharp-tongued girl named Joleen who hated Billy. Maybe the bird belonged to her.

The pink bird came straight at Billy. It dive-bombed him, circled high and came at him again.

Usually Billy did not shoot at birds. Old bottles and cans were his favorite targets, maybe a discarded monster model now and then. But when the pink bird came at him a third time, he shot it out of the sky.

Wounded, the bird crashed to the ground. It beat about the dirt with one broken wing, unable to right itself.

Billy approached the bird cautiously, because now he recognized the sound of its skreegh. Now he recognized its words.

"Billy . . . Billy . . . help me—"

He nearly screamed. The pink bird was some kind of freak. He stared down at it. Angry blue eyes stared up at him. Human eyes.

The pink bird was not a bird at all.

It had no beak. Only a mouth.

"Billy . . . I need to get to the mine . . ."

The bird had Joleen's mouth . . . and Joleen's voice.

Though it was not really like Joleen's voice at all.

". . . the mine, Billy," the voice said. "I have to go. I have to fly . . . follow the trail . . . follow the others to the black river . . . find the home of the three-headed dog and . . ."

Billy was frightened. He wanted to run.

He did.

"Billy, you little—"

He ran faster. He outran the awful thing's words.

Billy ran all the way to Gordon's house. He did not notice the broken pane in the kitchen window. He burst into the house without thinking.

No one seemed to be home.

And then Billy heard a voice coming from upstairs.

The voice of the man in black.

The day before, Gordon had said that the man was only playing a prank to scare them away from the mine.

The man did not sound like he was playing a prank now. Gun in hand, Billy crept upstairs, following the man's voice. He could not understand everything the man said. At times the man whispered too low for Billy to hear. Other times he used words that Billy didn't understand.

But Billy understood most of the words he heard. Most importantly, he understood what a soul was.

He'd heard his parents talk about souls taking flight to heaven. He'd never heard them speak of souls taking flight to hell, the way the man in black did. Normally, Billy would have thought that such talk was a bunch of mumbo jumbo. But when Billy looked into Mr. and Mrs. Rogers' bedroom and saw the nest with the three hideous eggs and the big ugly blackbird perched over them, he was so frightened that he might have believed anything.

The bird saw Billy before the man did.

One quiet clack of its beak and the man in black turned to face the boy.

He smiled at Billy, winked at the bird.

"This boy is troublesome," the man said. "Kill him."

The bird's black wings flapped like torn shadows as it rose from the bed.

Billy pulled the trigger and a BB punched the creature hard in the chest.

The bird dropped to the bed.

The man in black screamed a harsh, "No!"

Before the word was out of the man's mouth, Billy had grabbed the nest. He charged downstairs and ran all the way home.

He noticed many strange things as he ran. He saw many broken windows in his very quiet neighborhood. He spotted many tangled nests resting on the roof-tops.

Each nest was a crazy quilt of everyday items. Clothes and ribbons, telephone cord and clothesline, sharpshooter medals won in battle and bits of dismembered dolls long buried in sandboxes and weatherbeaten cowboy hats worn by boys who rode wooden ponies. But one thing was the same—every nest that Billy saw cradled one blood red egg for every occupant of the house on which it perched.

Billy wondered what would happen when those eggs cracked open. He remembered the things the pink bird had said. "... the mine, Billy. I have to go. I have to fly ... follow the trail ... follow the others to the black river ... find the home of the three-headed dog and ..."

The mine ... a trail.

A black river and a three-headed dog.

A trail to hell.

And a pink bird. A creature that carried Joleen Jefferson's soul.

There was no nest on Billy's house. This was a good sign. Maybe it meant that it wasn't too late.

Billy got a few tubes of BB's from his room. Then he opened the safe and stole his father's hand grenade.

He pedaled to the mine, all the while telling himself that he was crazy. He didn't want to believe that there could be other things like the pink bird. But when the egg in his backpack started to crack, and when he heard another voice, the voice of Gordon's dad ...

Billy held tight to his BB gun.

He watched the skies. There were no birds at all.

He listened. Not a single chirp, or caw, or skreegh.

Billy managed a deep breath.

By the time he gulped it down, the sky was alive with sound.

The sky was a rich red scream.

Hidden by the surrounding forest, the man in black watched the cave.

The blackbird sat heavily on his shoulder. Sharp talons speared his flesh. The bird's blood dripped down its thin legs, between its talons, soaking the man's clothes, mixing with the blood that flowed from the puckered wounds it had torn in the man in black's flesh.

The man in black did not mind the pain. He was an army. Armies engaged in war. There was pain in any war.

There were also captives. They flew above the man's head now, following him to the cave. Hundreds of pink things born of the blackbird perched on the man's shoulder. Hundreds of them flapping overhead, screaming in fright as their blue-veined wings drove them toward a horror they would never escape.

Hundreds of souls bound for hell.

Hundreds of captives bound for a world of pain.

This was a small town. Nothing more than a trial run. The man in black would have liked a larger challenge.

Still, there was the boy to consider.

After all, he had wounded the blackbird.

And he still had his BB gun.

Yes, this was indeed a war.

In a war, there was pain. In a war, there were captives.

But there were also casualties.

Billy stood at the mouth of the cave. He fired the gun again and again and again. The pink things plummeted from the blue sky and crashed to the earth. Many of them screamed his name as they fell.

The voices were all at once familiar, yet unfamiliar just the same. Voices that had encouraged Billy and comforted him and taught him many things. His little league coach's voice, and his piano teacher's voice, and the voice of the man who sold the ice cream from the back of a battered truck on summer afternoons.

Not all of the pink things screamed his name. Many darted past him with only a flutter of leathery wings, while others shrieked miserably as they disappeared into the black pit.

Billy could not shoot all of them. He could only fire the gun so fast.

Tears burned his eyes and his aim was poor.

Still, Billy tried his best. But the mouth of the cave was open, open so very wide. The other day, the silence of the open mouth had bothered him. But now it did not. Now he understood it.

The mouth was not open to speak.

It was open to swallow.

Billy reloaded his gun and continued firing.

Soon he stopped crying.

Soon his BB's were gone, and the sky was a pink canvas of writhing, naked wings.

Soon the man in black strode through the dark trees that ringed the cave.

Billy watched the man smile. Overhead, the souls of Billy's friends and enemies and people he had never met and would never meet raced past him like some strange airborne river.

Billy dropped his rifle and raised his father's hand grenade.

The man in black's smile did not falter.

"I'll stop you." Billy screamed above the deafening pink scream. "I'll stop *them*. Don't you think I won't."

"And you'll do it all by yourself," the man said, still smiling.

Billy nodded.

The man chuckled. "Then you too are an army of one."

"Sure I am." Billy bristled at the man in black's mocking tone. "I am an army of one. Just ask your bird."

As if on cue the bloody creature tumbled from the man in black's shoulder and dropped lightly upon a blanket of small pink corpses.

Tiny bones crunched underfoot as the man crossed the pink blanket. But he never looked down. Not once.

Cool air rushed past Billy, sucked into the cave like a breath. He retreated into the darkness of the cave, a torrent of pink things choking past him overhead, the grenade gripped tightly in his hands.

The man in black was silhouetted against a pink sky, sunlight flashing through a thousand furious wings behind him, nothing on his shoulder at all. He said, "The time has come to discuss the terms of your surrender."

Billy pulled the pin from the grenade. "I'll see you in hell first."

"If that is the way of it," the man said, "then I imagine that you will."

The mouth of the cave was silent.

The man in black said not a word.

Words were useless in this land of shrieking souls.

The man looked to the trees. Dark, gnarled branches, heavy with tortured pink things.

Each one, waiting for him to move.

Each one, waiting to follow.

The man brushed dust from his dark clothes. Still, he did not rise from the rock on which he sat. The exploding grenade had torn the rock from the collapsing mouth of the cave like some great broken molar.

And now the mouth was closed.

The man in black's master would feast no more today.

But this knowledge did not trouble the man in black, for he knew well that there were many other caves in this land.

So he sat upon the broken rock, and he listened to the pink things screeching in the trees, and he watched the skies.

Soon enough they came. Four of them, flying from the west.

Three landed in the trees. Their screams sliced an awful counterpoint to the cries of their cursed brethren.

The fourth broke off and flew to the man in black, who raised a beckoning hand.

The creature landed on his shoulder, its small talon's scrabbling over his flesh for purchase.

The man in black stroked the tiny thing, for this creature was different from the others. Once, twice, his hand traveled its trembling body. Pink skin smooth under his fingertips . . . then black down . . . then stiff black feathers. . . .

The man smiled and closed his eyes.

In his mind's eye he glimpsed a brave boy framed by the ravenous mouth of a cave. And then the mouth closed, and swallowed, and the brave boy was gone, torn to shreds by granite teeth.

And now there was a blackbird perched on the man in black's shoulder.

"What are you?" the man asked.

The brave boy answered in a voice that was all at once familiar, yet unfamiliar just the same.

"I am an army."

NICK DiCHARIO

Carp Man

Since Nick DiChario published his first story in 1991 he has been nominated for the World Fantasy Award, the Hugo Award, and the John W. Campbell Award for Best New Writer. His science fiction, fantasy, and mystery stories have appeared in Universe, The Magazine of Fantasy & Science Fiction, SF Age, Crime Through Time, *and a number of other magazines and anthologies. He lives in Rochester, New York, where he is the assistant editor of* HazMat Review, *a semiannual literary journal.*

"Carp Man" is a poignantly fishy story from the pages of the Tampa Tribune's Fiction Quarterly, *edited by Rick Wilber.*

—*T. W.*

I'm really sorry about Rena," said Marilee Hunsacker, standing at the threshold of Leonard's office.

Leonard glanced at the row of sympathy cards lining his mahogany desktop. *With Sincerest Condolences*, from the employees of New York Consolidated Funds . . . *Our Warmest Wishes*, Jim and Nancy Springer . . . *Peace and Love In Your Hour of Need*, from the Sisters of God's Eternal Mercy . . .

Marilee pursed her mimosa-glossed lips and sighed through her nose, making a teapot noise. Leonard was reminded of Rena and her late-night herbal tea habit.

"A special person, your Rena," said Marilee. "One of the good ones."

"Simon & Garfunkel," Leonard replied, tapping his engraved Mont Blanc in time to the Muzak. He pointed to the ceiling where hidden speakers softly reverberated. "If you really concentrate, it's amazing how many songs you can get. 'Bridge Over Troubled Water.' Recognize it?"

"We're all concerned, Len," said Marilee.

"Don't worry, I'm swell."

"If you need to talk, just say the word."

"I'm swell," said Leonard, "really."

"Well, it's good to have you back at the office." She tugged on the lapels of her polyester blazer and momentarily lost her balance. Leonard was reminded of a bass jerked sideways by the sharp treble hooks of a fishing lure.

"Len, I was wondering, maybe you'd like to go to dinner, just the two of us. I remember when I lost Henry. I know how difficult it can be. We could talk. That's what friends are for. Saturday night? My treat. I insist. I'll make reservations at the club."

Leonard smiled. Slippery woman, this Marilee Hunsacker, like the fresh-water eels he used to tease in the shallows of the Genesee River, when he was a young carp. The good old days. He missed them much.

"Dinner," he said without commitment. Leonard hungered for the sour taste of a blood leech. What time was it? Paleozoic? Mesozoic? Cenozoic? He checked the gold quartz wristwatch he'd received for twenty-five years of distinguished service:

9:22 A.M. :23. :24. :25 . . .

When he glanced up, Marilee Hunsacker was gone.

His first day back at work after nursing his wife through to the end of her long illness, and all Leonard could do was watch each minute tick off the clock until it was time for him to go home.

Mr. Gordon Stuckey, Senior Account Executive for New York Consolidated Funds, scurried into Leonard's office first thing the next morning. He was an angular man with a wide, toothy grin—something, no doubt, in the Northern Pike family. Old Spice and coffee breath swirled past Leonard's nose. Mr. Stuckey's large palms landed with a loud slap on Leonard's shoulders.

"Hey, Lenny Boy, how's the bachelor life treating you?" Mr. Stuckey sat in a chair too short for his long legs.

Rena had been the only person to call Leonard, Leonard. He had lost a wife and a name on the same day. "Don't worry about me, Mr. Stuckey."

"Wouldn't dream of it—Gordy, call me Gordy."

Gordy's complexion reminded Leonard of the farina Rena used to eat, in those final days, when she couldn't keep down any other food.

Gordy leaned forward and cleared his throat. "In case you need a hand settling the wife's affairs, my brother-in-law is an attorney. He usually does a mailing off the obits, but I told him you were a personal friend of mine. He'll discount his rates if you mention my name. Here's his card." Leonard looked at it, remembering how Rena used to scold him for picking his teeth with business cards.

Gordy stood and straightened his necktie. "Into each life some rain must fall, some days must be dark and dreary."

"Longfellow!" Leonard noted happily. This was Gordy's favorite quote. He'd often used it in his pep talks to the staff when the numbers weren't looking so good, somehow turning Longfellow, it seemed to Leonard, into his personal little cheerleader. "*Buck up, Rena, old girl!*" Gordy would have proclaimed had he bothered to visit Rena in the hospice. "*Some days must be dark and dreary.*" Leonard imagined Rena smiling placidly, as she always did with strangers.

Mr. Stuckey backed away swiftly and evenly, as if he'd been sucked in by a whirlpool of shifting currents outside Leonard's office. The man had a nice smooth back-flow. Leonard looked for Gordy's pectoral fins.

The Muzak kicked into another barely recognizable song, but Leonard figured it out right away. "Name that tune," said Leonard, rising from his chair, following Gordy out of his office. "*Sea of Love*, Sam Cooke, *Sea of Love!*"

But Gordy was gone. He'd vanished into the sea of clicking-humming video terminals and personal computers; of grinding-whirring copiers, printers, and plotters; of rapping fingernails, ringing telephones, and garbled voices; of shadows darting, some dangerous, some frightened, through desks and cabinets and cubicle walls and transparent floor-to-ceiling barrier reefs.

Everyone at the coffee machine stared at him. "I'm swell," said Leonard, "perfectly swell." He backed into his office and bumped the door shut with his tail-fin. His belly groaned and trembled as if there were worms nesting inside his human paunch. For a moment he lost feeling in his knees and toes—

water—

   treading—

   treading water—

Leonard clutched the edge of his desk. Was he losing it? Losing what? His humanity? Without Rena's love to landlock him he felt the tug of the river and the ponds, of the starwort, the hornwort, the crowfoot, and the caddisfly larvae.

He remembered a night not long ago: "Come with me, Rena," he'd said. "We can be together in the river."

"Don't be silly, Leonard."

He'd darted into the kitchen, filled a Rubbermaid water basin with tap water, and brought it to her bedside. Entwining their fingers, he'd splashed their hands into the warm pool. "It's not a glamorous life, nosing around in the silt for worms and larvae and leeches and newts, but we carp are generally happy fish, strong, healthy. I've adapted to your way of life. I've sacrificed. You can try it my way. It's only fair. It's only reasonable. We carp don't suffer from the same diseases—"

"Leonard," she'd interrupted, "what are you talking about?"

"Our hands. *Look at them.* Can't you see the scales forming?" And they were! His scales larger, healthier, shinier, but that made sense, he being a natural carp. With his help Rena could do it, too, if she tried. *"Try*, Rena, please, for me."

"Stop it, Leonard. That's enough of that kind of talk." She'd pulled her hand free. Water dripped from her fingertips like tiny pearls. How perfect. How telling. Rena the pearl.

The memories of his life at sea came flooding back. He'd completely forgotten his heritage. That was Rena's fault. She'd swept him away with the force of a tidal wave. "There's nothing to be afraid of," he'd said. "We're more than fifteen-hundred species strong. We're from the *Ostariophysi* group, more advanced than the salmon and the trout. That's respectable. In the North people frown upon us, but in Europe and Asia we're highly regarded."

"Please, stop," Rena had wept. "I need to know you'll be all right when I'm gone. Please, Leonard, you'll be all right, won't you? Won't you?"

Payday.

Leonard bought a bagged lunch from the fat cafeteria lady and walked alone in the breezeless park. He found a secluded bench facing the Genesee River and unwrapped his tuna sandwich. He could feel the bright sun scorching his scalp.

In the distance, the tall, black Plexiglass exterior of City Hall reflected a dark documentary of Main Street, a filmstrip clogged with city buses and colorless street lights and human heads bobbing like ping-pong balls in a murky pond.

Leonard had tried his best not to think about life without Rena, tried to be "all right," just the way she had hoped, but, gosh, a funny thing happened when he tried not to think. He kept suffering these intrusive kinds of thoughts. Thoughts of eels and Marilee Hunsacker, water fleas and Mr. Stuckey, juicy red worms and Muzak, a highly malignant mucus-secreting tumor with rounded anaplastic cells and a globule of mucus in the cytoplasm—

Rena. It always came back to Rena.

Leonard remembered the first day he'd noticed her as she kicked and swam in the river. <Mother, Father,> he'd said, <I must go. I've fallen in love with her beautiful feet.>

<Follow the path of your heart,> they had answered, chasing a clan of water mites. <But when you are too long gone, come home to the river. It is unnatural for a carp to be a man.>

True enough. Man, Leonard realized with some discomfort, would always remain shut up inside his own mind—the genius and the practical thinker and the insane—creating his personal phantasms, his gods and demons and dreams and terrors, from the tiniest manifestation to Buddha's Universal Mind. Man. Isolated. Alone. Not so with *Cyprinus carpio.* They shared a collective consciousness. No one carp experienced a disaggregate thought. No one carp swam alone.

Leonard stared longingly at the river.

A horse trotted past, toting a policeman on its back. <Go on,> the horse whinnied. <What are you waiting for? You're a carp out of water.>

Leonard watched the mare's tail swish the air. He leaned over, took off his shoes and socks, then stood and removed his shirt and tie. He stepped to the bank of the river and unzipped his trousers.

A woman shouted from the footpath, "Hey, somebody stop that pervert!"

The policeman reined in his horse. "Step back from the river, fella!" he yelled, "and put your hands over your head where I can see 'em!" He jabbed his heels into the horse's flanks.

But the horse shied and reared and whinnied a fuss. <Hurry up,> nickered the mare, <before some idiot saves your life.>

Leonard dropped his drawers and dove into the river. A rush of wet heat engulfed him. Water clogged his open mouth. The undertow sucked him down deep beneath the dark green waves. Scales and fins sprouted. Skull and mandible cracked into snout. Heart and liver and spleen crushed in under air bladder. Operculum folded over gills. Ribs and sternum collapsed around a newly formed dorsal artery. No more scapula, no more hip bone, no more fingers or toes or penis or nose. Arm-less, leg-less, he worked his maxillaries and flicked his tail-fin.

He chased a tadpole that wiggled underneath him with more grace than fear, reminding him of Rena the first night and the last night they'd made love.

Rena.

She might have been an eon ago. She might have been yesterday.

And all of the other carp said . . .

—<Leonard, what swell memories you have>—!

DELIA SHERMAN

The Faerie Cony-catcher

Delia Sherman holds a Ph.D. in Renaissance Studies, a background that surely came in handy when creating "The Faerie Cony-catcher," a sparkling and delightfully bawdy Elizabethan fairy tale, reprinted from Sirens and Other Daemon Lovers.

Sherman is the author of the historical fantasy novels The Porcelain Dove *and* The Brazen Mirror, *as well as numerous works of short fiction and a forthcoming Young Adult novel,* The Freedom Maze. *She is a consulting editor for Tor Books, edits anthologies for various publishers, and is on the board of the Tiptree Award for genre works dealing with gender issues. Her story "The Fall of the Kings," co-written with Ellen Kushner and published in last year's volume of* The Year's Best Fantasy and Horror, *was a finalist for the World Fantasy Award. Sherman divides her time between homes in the Boston area and New York City.*

—T. W.

In London town, in the reign of good Queen Bess that was called Gloriana, there lived a young man named Nicholas Cantier. Now it came to pass that this Nick Cantier served out his term as apprentice jeweler and goldsmith under one Master Spilman, jeweler by appointment to the Queen's Grace herself, and was made journeyman of his guild. For that Nick was a clever young man, his master would have been glad for him to continue on where he was; yet Nick was not fain thereof, Master Spilman being as ill a master of men as he was a skilled master of his trade. And Nick bethought him thus besides: that London was like unto the boundless sea where Leviathan may dwell unnoted, save by such small fish as he may snap up to stay his mighty hunger: such small fish as Nicholas Cantier. Better that same small fish seek out some backwater in the provinces where, puffed up by city ways, he might perchance pass as a pike and snap up spratlings on his own account.

So thought Nick. And on a bright May morning, he packed up such tools as he might call his own—as a pitch block and a mallet, and some small steel chisels and punches and saw-blades and blank rings of copper—that he might make shift to earn his way to Oxford. So Nick put his tools in a pack, with clean hosen and a shirt and a pair of soft leather shoon, and that was all his worldly wealth strapped upon his back, saving only a jewel that he had designed and made himself to be his passport. This jewel was in the shape of a maid, her breasts and belly all one lucent pearl, her skirt and open jacket of bright enamel, and her fair face of silver burnished with gold. On her fantastic hair perched a tiny golden crown, and Nick had meant her for the Faerie Queen of Master Spenser's poem, fair Gloriana.

Upon this precious Gloriana did Nick's life and livelihood depend. Therefore, being a prudent lad in the main, and bethinking him of London's traps and dangers, Nick considered where he might bestow it that he fall not prey to those foists and rufflers who might take it from him by stealth or by force. The safest place, thought he, would be his cod-piece, where no man nor woman might meddle without his yard raise the alarm. Yet the jewel was large and cold and hard against those softer jewels that dwelt more commonly there, and so Nick bound it across his belly with a band of linen and took leave of his fellows and set out northwards to seek his fortune.

Now Nick Cantier was a lusty youth of nearly twenty, with a fine, open face and curls of nut-brown hair that sprang from his brow; yet notwithstanding his comely form, he was as much a virgin on that May morning as the Virgin Queen herself. For Master Spilman was the hardest of task-masters, and between his eagle eye and his adder cane and his arch-episcopal piety, his apprentices perforce lived out the terms of their bonds as chaste as Popish monks. On this the first day of his freedom, young Nick's eye roved hither and thither, touching here a slender waist and there a dimpled cheek, wondering what delights might not lie beneath this petticoat or that snowy kerchief. And so it was that a Setter came upon him unaware and sought to persuade him to drink a pot of ale together, having just found xii pence in a gutter and it being ill-luck to keep found money and Nick's face putting him in mind of his father's youngest son, dead of an ague this two year and more. Nick let him run on, through this excuse for scraping acquaintance and that, and when the hopeful Cony-catcher had rolled to a stop, like a cart at the foot of a hill, he said unto him,

"I see I must have a care to the cut of my coat, if rogues, taking me for a country cony, think me meet for skinning. Nay, I'll not drink with ye, nor play with ye neither, lest ye so ferret-claw me at cards that ye leave me as bare of money as an ape of a tail."

Upon hearing which, the Setter called down a murrain upon milk-fed pups who imagined themselves sly dogs, and withdrew into the company of two men appareled like honest and substantial citizens, whom Nicholas took to be the Setter's Verser and Barnacle, all ready to play their parts in cozening honest men out of all they carried, and a little more beside. And he bit his thumb at them and laughed and made his way through the streets of London, from Lombard Street to Clerkenwell in the northern liberties of the city, where the houses were set back from the road in gardens and fields and the taverns spilled out of doors in benches and stools, so that toss-pots might air their drunken heads.

'Twas coming on for noon by this time, and Nick's steps were slower than they had been, and his mind dwelt more on bread and ale than on cony-catchers and villains.

In this hungry, drowsy frame of mind, he passed an alehouse where his eye chanced to light upon a woman tricked up like a lady in a rich-guarded gown and a deep starched ruff. Catching his glance, she sent it back again saucily, with a wink and a roll of her shoulders that lifted her breasts like ships on a wave.

Nick gave her good speed, and she plucked him by the sleeve and said, "How now, my friend, you look wondrous down i' the mouth. What want you? Wine? Company?"—all with such a meaning look, such a waving of her skirts and a hoisting of her breasts that Nick's yard, fain to salute her, flew its scarlet colors in his cheeks.

"The truth is, Mistress, that I've walked far this day, and am sorely hungered."

"Hungered, is it?" She flirted her eyes at him, giving the word a dozen meanings not writ in any grammar. "Then shall feed thy hunger, aye, and sate thy thirst too, and that right speedily." And she led him in at the alehouse door to a little room within, where she closed the door and thrusting herself close up against him, busied her hands about his body and her lips about his mouth. As luck would have it, her breath was foul, and it blew upon Nick's heat, cooling him enough to recognize that her hands sought not his pleasure, but his purse, upon which he put her from him.

"Nay, mistress," he said, all flushed and panting. "Thy meat and drink are dear, if they cost me my purse."

Knowing by his words that she was discovered, she spent no time in denying her trade, but set up a caterwauling would wake the dead, calling upon one John to help her. But Nick, if not altogether wise, was quick and strong, and bolted from the vixen's den 'ere the dog-fox answered her call.

So running, Nick came shortly to the last few houses that clung to the outskirts of the city and stopped at a tavern to refresh him with honest meat and drink. And as he drank his ale and pondered his late escape, the image of his own foolishness dimmed and the image of the doxy's beauty grew more bright, until the one eclipsed the other quite, persuading him that any young man in whom the blood ran hot would have fallen in her trap, aye and been skinned, drawn, and roasted to a turn, as 'twere in very sooth, a long-eared cony. It was his own cleverness, he thought, that he had smoked her out and run away. So Nick, having persuaded himself that he was a sly dog after all, rose from the tavern and went to Hampstead Heath, which was the end of the world to him. And as he stepped over the world's edge and onto the northward road, his heart lifted for joy, and he sang right merrily as he strode along, as pleased with himself as the cock that imagineth his crowing bringeth the sun from the sea.

And so he walked and so he sang until by and by he came upon a country lass sat upon a stone. Heedful of his late lesson, he quickly cast his eye about him for signs of some high lawyer or ruffler lurking ready to spring the trap. But the lass sought noways to lure him, nor did she accost him, nor lift her dark head from contemplating her foot that was cocked up on her knee. Her gown of gray kersey was hiked up to her thigh and her sleeves rolled to her elbows, so that Nick could see her naked arms, sinewy and lean and nut-brown with sun, and her leg like dirty ivory.

"Gie ye good-den, fair maid," said he, and then could say no more, for when she raised her face to him, his breath stopped in his throat. It was not, perhaps, the fairest he'd seen, being gypsy-dark, with cheeks and nose that showed the bone. But her black eyes were wide and soft as a hind's and the curve of her mouth made as sweet a bow as Cupid's own.

"Good-den to thee," she answered him, low-voiced as a throstle. "Ye come at a good hour to my aid. For here is a thorn in my foot and I, for want of a pin, unable to have it out."

The next moment he knelt at her side; the moment after, her foot was in his hand. He found the thorn and winkled it out with the point of his knife while the lass clutched at his shoulder, hissing between her teeth as the splinter yielded, sighing as he wiped away the single ruby of blood with his kerchief and bound it round her foot.

"I thank thee, good youth," she said, leaning closer. "An thou wilt, I'll give thee such a reward for thy kindness as will give thee cause to thank me anon." She turned her hand to his neck, and stroked the bare flesh there, smiling in his face the while, her breath as sweet as an orchard in spring.

Nick felt his cheek burn hot above her hand and his heart grow large in his chest. This were luck indeed, and better than all the trulls in London. "Fair maid," he said, "I would not kiss thee beside a public road."

She laughed. "Lift me then and carry me to the hollow, hard by yonder hill, where we may embrace, if it pleaseth thee, without fear of meddling eye."

Nick's manhood rose then to inform him that it would please him well, observing which, the maiden held up her arms to him, and he lifted her, light as a faggot of sticks but soft and supple as Spanish leather withal, and bore her to a hollow under a hill that was round and green and warm in the May sun. And he lay her down and did off his pack and set it by her head, that he might keep it close to hand, rejoicing that his jewel was well-hid and not in his codpiece, and then he fell to kissing her lips and stroking her soft, soft throat. Her breasts were small as a child's under her gown; yet she moaned most womanly when he touched them, and writhed against him like a snake, and he made bold to pull up her petticoats to discover the treasure they hid. Coyly, she slapped his hand away once and again, yet never ceased to kiss and toy with open lip, the while her tongue like a darting fish urged him to unlace his codpiece that was grown wondrous tight. Seeing what he was about, she put her hand down to help him, so that he was like to perish e'er he spied out the gates of Heaven. Then, when he was all but sped, she pulled him headlong on top of her.

He was not home, though very near it as he thrust at her skirts bunched up between her thighs. Though his plunging breached not her cunny-burrow, it did breach the hill itself, and he and his gypsy-lass both tumbled arse-over-neck to lie broken-breathed in the midst of a great candle-lit hall upon a Turkey carpet, with skirts and legs and slippered feet standing in ranks upon it to his right hand and his left, and a gentle air stroking warm fingers across his naked arse. Nick shut his eyes, praying that this vision were merely the lively exhalation of his lust. And then a laugh like a golden bell fell upon his ear, and was hunted through a hundred mocking changes in a ring of melodious laughter, and he knew this to be sober reality, or something enough like it that he'd best ope his eyes and lace up his hose.

All this filled no more than the space of a breath, though it seemed to Nick an age of the world had passed before he'd succeeded in packing up his yard and scrambling to his feet to confront the owners of the skirts and the slippered feet and the bell-like laughter that yet pealed over his head. And in that age, the thought was planted and nurtured and harvested in full ripeness, that his hosts were of faerie-kind. He knew they were too fair to be human men and women, their skins white nacre, their hair spun sunlight or moonlight or fire bound back from their wide brows by fillets of precious stones not less hard and bright than their emerald or sapphire eyes. The women went bare-bosomed as Amazons, the living jewels of their perfect breasts coffered in open gowns of bright silk. The men wore jewels in their ears, and at their forks, fantastic cod-pieces in the shapes of cockerels and wolves and rams with curling horns. They were splendid beyond imagining, a masque to put the Queen's most magnificent Revels to shame.

As Nick stood in amaze, he heard the voice of his coy mistress say, " 'Twere well, Nicholas Cantier, if thou woulds't turn and make thy bow."

With a glare for she who had brought him to this pass, Nick turned him around to face a woman sat upon a throne. Even were she seated upon a joint-stool, he must have known her, for her breasts and face were more lucent and fair than pearl, her open jacket and skirt a glory of gem-stones, and upon her fantastic hair perched a gold crown, as like to the jewel in his bosom as twopence to a groat. Nick gaped like that same small fish his fancy had painted him erewhile, hooked and pulled gasping to land. Then his knees, wiser than his head, gave way to prostrate him at the royal feet of Elfland.

"Well, friend Nicholas," said the Faerie Queen. "Heartily are you welcome to our court. Raise him, Peasecod, and let him approach our throne."

Nick felt a tug on his elbow, and wrenched his dazzled eyes from the figure of the Faerie Queen to see his wanton lass bending over him. "To thy feet, my heart," she murmured. "And, as thou holdest dear thy soul, see that neither meat nor drink pass thy lips."

"Well, Peasecod?" asked the Queen, and there was that in her musical voice that propelled Nick to his feet and down the Turkey carpet to stand trembling before her.

"Be welcome," said the Queen again, "and take your ease. Peasecod, bring a stool and a cup for our guest, and let the musicians play and our court dance for his pleasure."

There followed an hour as strange as any madman might imagine or poet sing, when Nicholas Cantier sat upon a gilded stool at the knees of the Queen of Elfland and watched her court pace through their faerie measures. In his hand he held a golden cup crusted with gems, and the liquor within sent forth a savor of roses and apples that promised an immortal vintage. But as oft as he, half-fainting, lifted the cup, so often did a pair of fingers pinch him at the ankle, and so often did he look down to see the faerie lass Peasecod crouching at his feet with her skirts spread out to hide the motions of her hand. One she glanced up at him, her soft eyes drowned in tears like pansies in rain, and he knew that she was sorry for her part in luring him here.

When the dancing was over and done, the Queen of Elfland turned to Nick and said, "Good friend Nicholas, we would crave a boon of thee in return for this our fair entertainment."

At which Nick replied, "I am at your pleasure, Madam. Yet have I not taken any thing from you save words and laughter."

" 'Tis true, friend Nicholas, that thou hast scorned to drink our Faerie wine. And yet hast thou seen our faerie revels, that is a sight any poet in London would give his last breath to see."

"I am no poet, Madam, but a humble journeyman goldsmith."

"That too, is true. And for that thou art something better than humble at thy trade, I will do thee the honor of accepting that jewel in my image thou bearest bound against thy breast."

Then it seemed to Nick that the Lady might have his last breath after all, for his heart suspended himself in his throat. Wildly looked he upon Gloriana's face, fair and cold and eager as the trull's he had escaped erewhile, and then upon the court of Elfland that watched him as he were a monkey or a dancing bear. And at his feet, he saw the dark-haired lass Peasecod, set apart from the rest by her mean garments and her dusky skin, the only comfortable thing in all that discomfortable splendor. She smiled into his eyes, and made a little motion with her hand, like a fishwife who must chaffer by signs against the crowd's commotion. And Nicholas took courage at her sign, and fetched up a deep breath, and said:

"Fair Majesty, the jewel is but a shadow or counterfeit of your radiant beauty. And yet 'tis all my stock in trade. I cannot render all my wares to you, were I never so fain to do you pleasure."

The Queen of Elfland drew her delicate brows like kissing moths over her nose. "Beware, young Nicholas, how thou triest our good will. Were we minded, we might turn thee into a lizard or a slow-worm, and take thy jewel resistless."

"Pardon, dread Queen, but if you might take my jewel by force, you might have taken it ere now. I think I must give it you—or sell it you—by mine own unforced will."

A silence fell, ominous and dark as a thundercloud. All Elfland held its breath, awaiting the royal storm. Then the sun broke through again, the Faerie Queen smiled, and her watchful court murmured to one another, as those who watch a bout at swords will murmur when the less-skilled fencer maketh a lucky hit.

"Thou hast the right of it, friend Nicholas: We do confess it. Come, then. The Queen of Elfland will turn huswife, and chaffer with thee."

Nick clasped his arms about his knee and addressed the lady thus: "I will be frank with you, Serenity. My master, when he saw the jewel, advised me that I should not part withal for less than fifty golden crowns, and that not until I'd used it to buy a master goldsmith's good opinion and a place at his shop. Fifty-five crowns, then, will buy the jewel from me, and not a farthing less."

The Lady tapped her white hand on her knee. "Then thy master is a fool, or thou a rogue and liar. The bauble is worth no more than fifteen golden crowns. But for that we are a compassionate prince, and thy complaint being just, we will give thee twenty, and not a farthing more."

"Forty-five," said Nick. "I might sell it to Master Spenser for twice the sum, as a fair portrait of Gloriana, with a description of the faerie court, should he wish to write another book."

"Twenty-five," said the Queen. "Ungrateful wretch. 'Twas I sent the dream inspired the jewel."

"All the more reason to pay a fair price for it," said Nick. "Forty."

This shot struck in the gold. The Queen frowned and sighed and shook her head and said, "Thirty. And a warrant, signed by our own royal hand, naming thee jeweler by appointment to Gloriana, by cause of a pendant thou didst make at her behest."

It was a fair offer. Nick pondered a moment, saw Peasecod grinning up at him with open joy, her cheeks dusky red and her eyes alight, and said: "Done, my Queen, if only you will add thereto your attendant nymph, Peasecod, to be my companion."

At this Gloriana laughed aloud, and all the court of Elfland laughed with her, peal upon peal at the mortal's presumption. Peasecod alone of the bright throng did not laugh, but rose to stand by Nicholas' side and pressed his hand in hers. She was brown and wild as a young deer, and it seemed to Nick that the Queen of Elfland herself, in all her female glory of moony breasts and arching neck, was not so fair as this one slender, black-browed faerie maid.

When Gloriana had somewhat recovered her power of speech, she said: "Friend Nicholas, I thank thee; for I have not laughed so heartily this many a long day. Take thy faerie lover and thy faerie gold and thy faerie warrant and depart unharmed from hence. But for that thou hast dared to rob the Faerie Queen of this her servant, we lay this weird on thee, that if thou say thy Peasecod nay, at bed or at board for the space of four-and-twenty mortal hours, then thy gold shall turn to leaves, thy warrant to fifth, and thy lover to dumb stone."

At this, Peasecod's smile grew dim, and up spoke she and said, "Madam, this is too hard."

"Peace," said Gloriana, and Peasecod bowed her head. "Nicholas," said the Queen, "we commence to grow weary of this play. Give us the jewel and take thy price and go thy ways."

So Nick did off his doublet and his shirt and unwound the band of linen from about his waist and fetched out a little leathern purse and loosed its strings and tipped out into his hand the precious thing upon which he had expended all his love and his art. And loathe was he to part withal, the first-fruits of his labor.

"Thou shalt make another, my heart, and fairer yet than this," whispered Peasecod in his ear, and so he laid it into Elfland's royal hand, and bowed, and in that moment he was, in the hollow under the green hill, his pack at his feet, half-naked, shocked as by a lightning-bolt, and alone. Yet before he could draw breath to make his moan, Peasecod appeared beside him with his shirt and doublet on her arm, a pack at her back, and a heavy purse at her waist, that she detached and gave to him with his clothes. Fain would he have sealed his bargain then and there, but Peasecod begging prettily that they might seek more comfort than might be found on a tussock of grass, he could not say her nay. Nor did he regret his weird that gave her the whip hand in this, for the night drew on apace, and he found himself sore hungered and athirst, as though he'd been beneath the hill for longer than the hour he thought. And indeed 'twas a day and a night and a day again since he'd seen the faerie girl upon the heath, for time doth gallop with the faerie kind, who heed not its passing. And so Peasecod told him as they trudged northward in the gloaming, and picked him early berries to stay his present hunger, and found him clear water to stay thirst, so that he was inclined to think very well of his bargain, and of his own cleverness that had made it.

And so they walked until they came to a tavern, where Nick called for dinner and a chamber, all of the best, and pressed a golden noble into the host's palm, whereat the goodman stared and said such a coin would buy his whole house and all his ale, and still he'd not have coin to change it. And Nick, flushed with gold and lust, told him to keep all as a gift upon the giver's wedding-day. Whereat Peasecod blushed and cast down her eyes as any decent bride, though the goodman saw she wore no ring and her legs and feet were bare and dusty from the road. Yet he gave them of his best, both meat and drink, and put them to bed in his finest chamber, with a fire in the grate because gold is gold, and a rose on the pillow because he remembered what it was to be young.

The door being closed and latched, Nicholas took Peasecod in his arms and drank of her mouth as 'twere a well and he dying of thirst. And then he bore her to the bed and laid her down and began to unlace her gown that he might see her naked. But she said unto him, "Stay, Nicholas Cantier, and leave me my modesty yet a while. But do thou off thy clothes, and I vow thou shalt not lack for pleasure."

Then young Nick gnawed his lip and pondered in himself whether taking off her clothes by force would be saying her nay—some part of which showed in his face, for she took his hand to her mouth and tickled the palm with her tongue, all the while looking roguishly upon him, so that he smiled upon her and let her do her will, which was to strip his doublet and shirt from him, to run her fingers and her tongue across his chest, to lap and pinch at his nipples until he gasped, to stroke and tease him, and finally to release his rod and take it in her hand and then into her mouth. Poor Nick, who had never dreamed of such tricks, was like to die of ecstasy. He twisted his hands in her long hair as pleasure came upon him like an annealing fire, and then he lay spent, with Peasecod's head upon his bosom, and all her dark hair spread across his belly like a blanket of silk.

After a while she raised herself, and with great tenderness kissed him upon the mouth and said, "I have no regret of this bargain, my heart, whatever follows after."

And from his drowsy state he answered her, "Why, what should follow after but joy and content and perchance a babe to dandle upon my knee?"

She smiled and said, "What indeed? Come, discover me," and lay back upon the pillow and opened her arms to him.

For a little while, he was content to kiss and toy with lips and neck, and let her body be. But soon he tired of this game, the need once again growing upon him to uncover her secret places and to plumb their mysteries. He put his hand beneath her skirts, stroking her thigh that was smooth as pearl and quivered under his touch as it drew near to that mossy dell he had long dreamed of. With quickening breath, he felt springing hair, and then his fingers encountered an obstruction, a wand or rod, smooth as the thigh, but rigid, and burning hot. In his shock, he squeezed it, and Peasecod gave a moan, whereupon Nick would have withdrawn his hand, and that right speedily, had not his faerie lover gasped, "Wilt thou now nay-say me?"

Nick groaned and squeezed again. The rod he held pulsed, and his own yard stirred in ready sympathy. Nick raised himself on his elbow and looked down into Peasecod's face—wherein warred lust and fear, man and woman—and thought, not altogether clearly, upon his answer. Words might turn like snakes to bite their tails, and Nick was of no mind to be misunderstood. For answer then, he tightened his grip upon those fair and ruddy jewels that Peasecod brought to his marriage-portion, and so wrought with them that the eyes rolled back in his lover's head, and he expired upon a sigh. Yet rose he again at Nick's insistent kissing, and threw off his skirts and stays and his smock of fine linen to show his body, slender and hard as Nick's own, yet smooth and white as any lady's that bathes in ass's milk and honey. And so they sported night-long until the rising sun blew pure gold leaf upon their tumbled bed, where they lay entwined and, for the moment, spent.

"I were well-served if thou shoulds't cast me out, once the four-and-twenty hours are past," said Peasecod mournfully.

"And what would be the good of that?" asked Nick.

"More good than if I stayed with thee, a thing nor man nor woman, nor human nor faerie kind."

"As to the latter, I cannot tell, but as to the former, I say that thou art both, and I the richer for thy doubleness. Wait," said Nick, and scrambled from the bed and opened his pack and took out a blank ring of copper and his block of pitch and his small steel tools. And he worked the ring into the pitch and, within a brace of minutes, had incised upon it a peavine from which you might pick peas in season, so like nature was the work. And returning to the bed where Peasecod lay watching, slipped it upon his left hand.

Peasecod turned the ring upon his finger, wondering. "Thou dost not hate me, then, for that I tricked and cozened thee?"

Nick smiled and drew his hand down his lover's flank, taut ivory to his touch, and said, "There are some hours yet left, I think, to the term of my bond. Art thou so eager, love, to become dumb stone that thou must be asking me questions that beg to be answered 'No?' Know then, that I rejoice in being thy cony, and only wish that thou mayst catch me as often as may be, if all thy practices be as pleasant as this by which thou hast bound me to thee."

And so they rose and made their ways to Oxford town, where Nicholas made such wise use of his faerie gold and his faerie commission as to keep his faerie lover in comfort all the days of their lives.

ZAN ROSS

At The River of Crocodiles

Zan Ross is a poet and fiction writer who lives in Western Australia. Her work has appeared in most of the major literary magazines on her home continent and she has published one collection of poetry, B-Grade. She is currently working on a Ph.D. in cultural studies at Curtin University in WA.

The unusual poem that follows comes from Southerly, *a literary journal published in Sydney, Australia and edited by Elizabeth Webby.*

—T. W.

Let's say
a woman goes to the river,
a basket on her head full of clothes.
She is here to wash—flakes of skin,
semen, blood,
faeces, urine dried in the fibers.
She comes to this same place morning,
night, draws water to cook, bathe
on the bank of The River of Crocodiles.

She is small, like a child, her skin
soft as tropical earth, her hair in a
plait to her waist. She walks in the
sound of water over stones, to the
sound of her own heart, her hips
breaking open a rhythm of claw and
tail mudfalls. She washes with one
eye closed, slapping against a stone
hunched in the mud.

Let's say
He sees her come to the river, smells

her brittle bones, her softness to
the steel of his hide. Their need
the same—desire each morning,
each evening when she comes,   leaves
gifts, hopes   to lure
a child into her body.
He spirals toward her.   She turns,
one eye closed, then looks to the river.
He is gentle, mounts
her three, four times. Semen drips
onto rock, and he knows, she knows.

Let's say
six months later the mid-wife will not
come. Her husband must help her deliver.
She is ripe fruit, splits when
the child slides onto the earth in a fall
of grace, his partial hide scraping the
man's hands as he holds it.   She
lifts her head, is silent
at evidence so incontrovertible.

Let's say
a man goes down to the river.
He carries a woman who has just
given birth. He carries a mis-
shapen child.   He tosses the
woman into the water, holds her head
until she drowns, her long hair trailing
current. Face up, her body flows
toward the sea.

The mis-shapen child is pitched into the
current, but   swims away. The father rises from
The River of Crocodiles, closes
his mouth full of teeth on the man's torso,
pulls him under and rolls,   rolls.

Can you say
what we know about these people,
what you know about these people?
If
I am telling you the truth;   if
you believe my story,
they are dead.

Because they belonged to my village,
we no longer go to The River of Crocodiles to
swim, wash, conceive,   though
water is our solace in this too hot place,
the river   is our desire.

STEVEN MILLHAUSER

Clair de Lune

Pulitzer Prize winner Steven Millhauser is one of the very best fantasists of our day, although his novels and stories are generally published and reviewed as mainstream fiction. He is the author of Edwin Mullhouse, Portrait of a Romantic, From the Realm of Morpheus, In the Penny Arcade, The Barnum Museum, Little Kingdoms, *and* Martin Dressler, *all of which are highly recommended. He has won the World Fantasy Award, and has been honored by the American Academy of Arts and Letters. Millhauser lives in upstate New York and teaches at Skidmore College.*

The luminous story that follows comes from Millhauser's most recent collection, The Knife Thrower and Other Stories.

—T. W.

The summer I turned fifteen, I could no longer fall asleep. I would lie motionless on my back, in a perfect imitation of sleep, and imagine myself lying fast asleep with my head turned to one side and a tendon pushed up along the skin of my neck, but even as I watched myself lying there dead to the world I could hear the faint burr of my electric clock, a sharp creak in the attic—like a single footstep—a low rumbling hum that I knew was the sound of trucks rolling along the distant thruway. I could feel the collar of my pajama top touching my jaw. Through my trembling eyelids I sensed that the darkness of the night was not dark enough, and suddenly opening my eyes, as if to catch someone in my room, I'd see the moonlight streaming past the edges of the closed venetian blinds.

I could make out the lampshade and bent neck of the standing lamp, like a great drooping black sunflower. On the floor by a bookcase the white king and part of a black bishop glowed on the moon-striped chessboard. My room was filling up with moonlight. The darkness I longed for, the darkness that had once sheltered me, had been pushed into corners, where it lay in thick, furry lumps. I felt a heaviness in my chest, an oppression—I wanted to hide in the dark. Desperately I closed my eyes, imagining the blackness of a winter night: snow covered the silent streets, on the front porch the ice chopper stood leaning next to the black mailbox glinting with icicles, lines of snow lay along the crosspieces of telephone poles and the tops of metal street signs: and always through my eyelids I could feel the summer moonlight pushing back the dark.

One night I sat up in bed harshly and threw the covers off. My eyes burned from sleeplessness. I could no longer stand this nightly violation of the dark. I dressed quietly, tensely, since my parents' room stood on the other side of my two bookcases, then made my way along the hall and out into the living room. A stripe of moonlight lay across a couch cushion. On the music rack I could see a pattern of black notes on the moon-streaked pages of Debussy's "Second Arabesque," which my mother had left off practicing that evening. In a deep ashtray shaped like a shell the bowl of my father's pipe gleamed like a piece of obsidian.

At the front door I hesitated a moment, then stepped out into the warm summer night.

The sky surprised me. It was deep blue, the blue of a sorcerer's hat, of night skies in old Technicolor movies, of deep mountain lakes in Swiss countrysides pictured on old puzzle boxes. I remembered my father removing from a leather pouch in his camera bag a circle of silver and handing it to me, and when I held it up I saw through the dark blue glass a dark blue world the color of this night. Suddenly I stepped out of the shadow of the house into the whiteness of the moon. The moon was so bright I could not look at it, as if it were a night sun. The fierce whiteness seemed hot, but for some reason I thought of the glittering thick frost on the inside of the ice-cream freezer in a barely remembered store: the popsicles and ice-cream cups crusted in ice crystals, the cold air like steam.

I could smell low tide in the air and thought of heading for the beach, but I found myself walking the other way. For already I knew where I was going, knew and did not know where I was going, in the sorcerer-blue night where all things were changed, and as I passed the neighboring ranch houses I took in the chimney-shadows black and sharp across the roofs, the television antennas standing clean and hard against the blue night sky.

Soon the ranch houses gave way to small two-story houses, the smell of the tide was gone. The shadows of telephone wires showed clearly on the moon-washed streets. The wire-shadows looked like curved musical staves. On a brilliant white garage door the slanting, intricate shadow of a basketball net reminded me of the rigging on the wooden ship model I had built with my father, one childhood summer. I could not understand why no one was out on a night like this. Was I the only one who'd been drawn out of hiding and heaviness by the summer moon? In an open, empty garage I saw cans of moonlit paint on a shelf, an aluminum ladder hanging on hooks, folded lawn chairs. Under the big-leafed maples moonlight rippled across my hands.

Oh, I knew where I was going, didn't want to know where I was going, in the warm blue air with little flutters of coolness in it, little bursts of grass-smell and leaf-smell, of lilac and fresh tar.

At the center of town I cut through the back of the parking lot behind the bank, crossed Main Street, and continued on my way.

When the thruway underpass came into view, I saw the top halves of trucks rolling high up against the dark blue sky, and below them, framed by concrete walls and the slab of upper road, a darker and greener world: a beckoning world of winding roads and shuttered houses, a green blackness glimmering with yellow spots of streetlamps, white spots of moonlight.

As I passed under the high, trembling roadbed on my way to the older part of town, the dark walls, spattered with chalked letters, made me think of hulking creatures risen from the underworld, bearing on their shoulders the lanes of a celestial bowling alley.

On the other side of the underpass I glanced up at the nearly full moon. It was a little blurred on one side, but so hard and sharp on the other that it looked as if I could cut my finger on it.

When I next looked up, the moon was partly blocked by black-green oak leaves. I was walking under high trees beside neck-high hedges. A mailbox on a post looked like a loaf of bread. Shafts of moonlight slanted down like boards.

I turned onto a darker street, and after a while I stopped in front of a large house set back from the road.

And my idea, bred by the bold moon and the blue summer night, was suddenly clear to me: I would make my way around the house into the back yard, like a criminal. Maybe there would be a rope swing. Maybe she'd see me from an upper window. I had never visited her before, never walked home with her. What I felt was too hidden for that, too lost in dark, twisting tunnels. We were school friends, but our friendship had never stretched beyond the edges of school. Maybe I could leave some sign for her, something to show her that I'd come through the summer night, into her back yard.

I passed under one of the big tulip trees in the front yard and began walking along the side of the house. In a black windowpane I saw my sudden face. Somewhere I seemed to hear voices, and when I stepped around the back of the house into the full radiance of the moon, I saw four girls playing ball.

They were playing Wiffle ball in the brilliant moonlight, as though it were a summer's day. Sonja was batting. I knew the three other girls, all of them in my classes: Marcia, pitching; Jeanie, taking a lead off first; Bernice, in the outfield, a few steps away from me. In the moonlight they were wearing clothes I'd never seen before, dungarees and shorts and sweatshirts and boys' shirts, as if they were dressed up in a play about boys. Bernice had on a baseball cap and wore a jacket tied around her waist. In school they wore knee-length skirts and neatly ironed blouses, light summer dresses with leather belts. The girl-boys excited and disturbed me, as if I'd stumbled into some secret rite. Sonja, seeing me, burst out laughing. "Well look who's here," she said, in the slightly mocking tone that kept me wary and always joking. "Who is that tall stranger?" She stood holding the yellow Wiffle-ball bat on her shoulder, refusing to be surprised. "Come on, don't just stand there, you can catch." She was wearing dungarees rolled halfway up her calves, a floppy sweatshirt with the sleeves pushed up above the elbows, low white sneakers without socks. Her hair startled me: it was pulled back to show her ears. I remembered the hair falling brown-blond along one side of her face.

They all turned to me now, smiled and waved me toward them, and with a sharp little laugh I sauntered in, pushing back my hair with my fingers, thrusting my hands deep into my dungaree pockets.

Then I was standing behind home plate, catching, calling balls and strikes.

The girls took their game seriously, Sonja and Jeanie against Marcia and Bernice. Marcia had a sharp-breaking curveball that kept catching the corner of the upside-down pie tin. "Strike?" yelled Sonja. "My foot. It missed by a mile. Kill the umpire!" The flattened-back tops of her ears irritated me. Jeanie stood glaring at me, fists on hips. She wore an oversized boy's shirt longer than her shorts, so that she looked naked, as if she'd thrown a shirt over a pair of underpants— her tan legs gleamed in the moonlight, her blond ponytail bounced furiously with her slightest motion, and in the folds of her loose shirt her jumpy breasts, appearing and disappearing, made me think of balls of yarn. The girls swung hard, slid into paper-plate bases, threw like boys. They shouted "Hey hey!" and "Way to go!" After a while they let me play, each taking a turn at being umpire. As we played, it seemed to me that the girls were becoming unraveled: Marcia's lumberjack shirt was only partly tucked into her faded dungarees, wriggles of hair fell down along Jeanie's damp cheeks, Bernice, her braces glinting, flung off the jacket tied around her waist, one of Sonja's cuffs kept falling down. Marcia scooped up a grounder, whirled, and threw to me at second, Sonja was racing from first, suddenly she slid—and sitting there on the grass below me, leaning back on her elbows, her legs stretched out on both sides of my feet, a copper rivet gleaming on the pocket of her dungarees, a bit of zipper showing, a hank of hair hanging over one eyebrow, she glared up at me, cried "Safe by a mile!" and broke into wild laughter. Then Jeanie began to laugh, Marcia and Bernice burst out laughing, I felt something give way in my chest and I erupted in loud, releasing laughter, the laughter of childhood, until my ribs hurt and tears burned in my eyes—and again whoops and bursts of laughter, under the blue sky of the summer night.

Sonja stood up, pushed a fallen sleeve of her sweatshirt above her elbow, and said, "How about a Coke? I've about had it." She wiped her tan forearm across her damp forehead. We all followed her up the back steps into the moonlit kitchen. "Keep it down, guys," she whispered, raising her eyes to the ceiling, as she filled glasses with ice cubes, poured hissing, clinking sodas. The other girls went back outside with their glasses, where I could hear them talking through the open kitchen window. Sonja pushed herself up onto the counter next to the dishrack and I stood across from her, leaning back against the refrigerator.

I wanted to ask her whether they always played ball at night, or whether it was something that had happened only on this night, this dream-blue night, night of adventures and revelations—night of the impossible visit she hadn't asked me about. I wanted to hear her say that the blue night was the color of old puzzle boxes, that the world was a blue mystery, that lying awake in bed she'd imagined me coming through the night to her back yard, but she only sat on the counter, swinging her legs, drinking her soda, saying nothing.

A broken bar of moonlight lay across the dishrack, fell sharply along a door below the counter, bent halfway along the linoleum before stopping in shadow.

She sat across from me with her hands on the silver strip at the edge of the counter, swinging her legs in and out of moonlight. Her knees were pressed together, but her calves were parted, and one foot was half-turned toward the other. I could see her anklebones. Her dungarees were rolled into thick cuffs halfway up the calf, one slightly higher than the other. As her calves swung back against the counter, they became wider for a moment, before they swung out.

The gentle swinging, the widening and narrowing calves, the rolled-up cuffs, the rubbery ribs of the dishrack, the glimmer of window above the mesh of the screen, all this seemed to me as mysterious as the summer moonlight, which had driven me through the night to this kitchen, where it glittered on knives and forks sticking out of the silverware box at the end of the dishrack and on her calves, swinging back and forth.

Now and then Sonja picked up her glass and, leaning back her head, took a rattling drink of soda. I could see the column of her throat moving as she swallowed, and it seemed to me that although she was only sitting there, she was moving all over: her legs swung back and forth, her throat moved, her hands moved from the counter to the glass and back, and something seemed to come quivering up out of her, as if she'd swallowed a piece of burning-cool moonlight and were releasing it through her legs and fingertips.

Through the window screen I could see the moonlit grass of the back yard, the yellow plastic bat on the grass, a corner of shingled garage and a piece of purplish-blue night, and I could hear Marcia talking quietly, the faint rumble of trucks rolling through the sky, a sharp, clicking insect.

I felt bound in the dark blue spell of the kitchen, of the calves swinging back and forth, the glittering silverware, moonlight on linoleum, silence that seemed to be filling up with something like a stretching skin, somewhere a quivering, and I standing still, in the spell of it all, watchful. Her hands gripped the edge of the counter. Her calves moved back and forth under pressed-together knees. She was leaning forward at the waist, her eyes shone like black moonlight, there was a tension in her arms that I could feel in my own arms, a tension that rippled up into her throat, and suddenly she burst out laughing.

"What are you laughing at?" I said, startled, disappointed.

"Oh, nothing," she said, slipping down from the counter. "Everything. You, for example." She walked over to the screen door. "Let's call it a night, gang," she said, opening the door. The three girls were sitting on the steps.

Marcia, taking a deep breath, slowly stretched out her arms and arched her back; and as her lumberjack shirt flattened against her, she seemed to be lifting her breasts toward the blue night sky, the summer moon.

Then there were quick good nights and all three were walking across the lawn, turning out sight behind the garage.

"This way, my good man," Sonja said. Frowning, and putting a finger over her lips, she led me from the kitchen through the shadowy living room, where I caught bronze and glass gleams—the edge of the fire shovel, a lamp base, the black glass of the television screen. At the front door flanked by thin strips of glass she turned the knob and opened the wooden door, held open the screen door. Behind her a flight of carpeted stairs rose into darkness. "Fair Knight," she said, with a little mock curtsey, "farewell," and pushed me out the door. I saw her arm rise and felt her fingers touch my face. With a laugh she shut the door.

It had happened so quickly that I wasn't sure what it was that had happened. Somewhere between "farewell" and laughter a different thing had happened, an event from a higher, more hidden realm, something connected with the dark blue kitchen, the glittering silverware and swinging legs, the mystery of the blue summer night. It was as if, under the drifting-down light of the moon, under the white-blue light that kept soaking into things, dissolving the day-world, a new shape had been released.

I stood for a while in front of the darkened front door, as if waiting for it to turn into something else—a forest path, a fluttering curtain. Then I walked away from the house along red-black slabs of slate, looked back once over my shoulder at the dark windows, and turned onto the sidewalk under high oaks and elms.

I felt a new lightness in my chest, as if an impediment to breathing had been removed. It was a night of revelations, but I now saw that each particle of the night was equal to the others. The moonlit path of black notes on the page of the music book, the yellow bat lying on just those blades of grass, the precise tilt of each knife in the dishrack, Sonja's calves swinging in and out of moonlight, Marcia's slowly arching back, the hand rising toward my face, all this was as unique and unrepeatable as the history of an ancient kingdom. For I had wanted to take a little walk before going to bed, but I had stepped from my room into the first summer night, the only summer night.

Under the high trees the moonlight fell steadily. I could see it sifting down through the leaves. All night long it had fallen into backyards, on chimneys and stop signs, on the crosspieces of telephone poles and on sidewalks buckled by tree roots. Down through the leaves it was slowly sifting, sticking to the warm air, forming clumps in the leaf-shadows. I could feel the moonlight lying on my hands. A weariness came over me, a weariness trembling with exhilaration. I had the sensation that I was expanding, growing lighter. Under the branches the air was becoming denser with moonlight, I could scarcely push my way through. My feet seemed to be pressing down on thick, spongy air. I felt an odd buoyancy, and when I looked down I saw that I was walking a little above the sidewalk. I raised my foot and stepped higher. Then I began to climb the thick tangle of moonlight and shadow, slipping now and then, sinking a little, pulling myself up with the aid of branches, and soon I came out over the top of a tree into the clearness of the moon. Dark fields of blue air stretched away in every direction. I looked down at the moonlit leaves below, at the top of a streetlamp, at shafts of moonlight slanting like white ladders under the leaves. I walked carefully forward above the trees, taking light steps that sank deep, then climbed a little higher, till catching a breeze I felt myself borne away into the blue countries of the night.

JORGE LUIS BORGES

The Rose of Paracelsus

Translated from the Spanish by Andrew Harley

Argentine poet, essayist, and short story writer Jorge Luis Borges (1899–1986) spent many years at the center of the vibrant Latin American literary scene, and was arguably one of the most important writers of our century. His dreamlike imagery and use of symbolism influenced a generation of writers the world over. His award-winning works include Ficciones, Labyrinths, Dreamtigers, Dr. Brodie's Report, *and* The Book of Sand; *he also co-edited* The Book of Fantasy (*with Adolfo Bioy Casares and Silvina Ocampo*), *an anthology which brought magical Latin American fiction to a wider world readership.*

The following fantasia, "The Rose of Paracelsus," made its first English appearance in 1998, translated by Andrew Hurley in The New York Review of Books.

—T. W.

Down in his laboratory, to which the two rooms of the cellar had been given over, Paracelsus prayed to his God, his indeterminate God—any God—to send him a disciple.

Night was coming on. The guttering fire in the hearth threw irregular shadows into the room. Getting up to light the iron lamp was too much trouble. Paracelsus, weary from the day, grew absent, and the prayer was forgotten. Night had expunged the dusty retorts and the furnace when there came a knock at his door. Sleepily he got up, climbed the short spiral staircase, and opened one side of the double door. A stranger stepped inside. He too was very tired. Paracelsus gestured toward a bench; the other man sat down and waited. For a while, neither spoke.

The master was the first to speak.

"I recall faces from the West and faces from the East," he said, not without a certain formality, "yet yours I do not recall. Who are you, and what do you wish of me?"

"My name is of small concern," the other man replied. "I have journeyed three days and three nights to come into your house. I wish to become your disciple. I bring you all my possessions."

He brought forth a pouch and emptied its contents on the table. The coins were many, and they were of gold. He did this with his right hand. Paracelsus turned his back to light the lamp; when he turned around again, he saw that the man's left hand held a rose. The rose troubled him.

He leaned back, put the tips of his fingers together, and said:

"You think that I am capable of extracting the stone that turns all elements to gold, and yet you bring me gold. But it is not gold I seek, and if it is gold that interests you, you shall never be my disciple."

"Gold is of no interest to me," the other man replied. "These coins merely symbolize my desire to join you in your work. I want you to teach me the Art. I want to walk beside you on that path that leads to the Stone."

"The path *is* the Stone. The point of departure is the Stone. If these words are unclear to you, you have not yet begun to understand. Every step you take is the goal you seek." Paracelsus spoke the words slowly.

The other man looked at him with misgiving.

"But," he said, his voice changed, "is there, then, no goal?"

Paracelsus laughed.

"My detractors, who are no less numerous than imbecilic, say that there is not, and they call me an impostor. I believe they are mistaken, though it is possible that I am deluded. I know that there *is* a Path."

There was silence, and then the other man spoke.

"I am ready to walk that Path with you, even if we must walk for many years. Allow me to cross the desert. Allow me to glimpse, even from afar, the promised land, though the stars prevent me from setting foot upon it. All I ask is a proof before we begin the journey."

"When?" said Paracelsus uneasily.

"Now," said the disciple with brusque decisiveness.

They had begun their discourse in Latin; they now were speaking German.

The young man raised the rose into the air.

"You are famed," he said, "for being able to burn a rose to ashes and make it emerge again, by the magic of your art. Let me witness that prodigy. I ask that of you, and in return I will offer up my entire life."

"You are credulous," the master said. "I have no need of credulity; I demand belief."

The other man persisted.

"It is precisely because I am *not* credulous that I wish to see with my own eyes the annihilation and resurrection of the rose."

"You are credulous," he repeated. "You say that I can destroy it?"

"Any man has the power to destroy it," said the disciple.

"You are wrong," the master responded. "Do you truly believe that something may be turned to nothing? Do you believe that the first Adam in paradise was able to destroy a single flower, a single blade of grass?"

"We are not in paradise," the young man stubbornly replied. "Here, in the sublunary world, all things are mortal."

Paracelsus had risen to his feet.

"Where are we, then, if not in paradise?" he asked. "Do you believe that the deity is able to create a place that is not paradise? Do you believe that the Fall is something other than not realizing that we are in paradise?"

"A rose can be burned," the disciple said defiantly.

"There is still some fire there," said Paracelsus, pointing toward the hearth. "If you cast this rose into the embers, you would believe that it has been consumed, and that its ashes are real. I tell you that the rose is eternal, and that only its appearances may change. At a word from me, you would see it again."

"A word?" the disciple asked, puzzled. "The furnace is cold, and the retorts are covered with dust. What is it you would do to bring it back again?"

Paracelsus looked at him with sadness in his eyes.

"The furnace is cold," he nodded, "and the retorts are covered with dust. On this leg of my long journey I use other instruments."

"I dare not ask what they are," said the other man humbly, or astutely.

"I am speaking of that instrument used by the deity to create the heavens and the earth and the invisible paradise in which we exist, but which original sin hides from us. I am speaking of the Word, which is taught to us by the science of the Kabbalah."

"I ask you," the disciple coldly said, "if you might be so kind as to show me the disappearance and appearance of the rose. It matters not the slightest to me whether you work with alembics or with the Word."

Paracelsus studied for a moment; then he spoke:

"If I did what you ask, you would say that it was an appearance cast by magic upon your eyes. The miracle would not bring you the belief you seek. Put aside, then, the rose."

The young man looked at him, still suspicious. Then Paracelsus raised his voice.

"And besides, who are you to come into the house of a master and demand a miracle of him? What have you done to deserve such a gift?"

The other man, trembling, replied:

"I know I have done nothing. It is for the sake of the many years I will study in your shadow that I ask it of you—allow me to see the ashes and then the rose. I will ask nothing more. I will believe the witness of my eyes."

He snatched up the incarnate and incarnadine rose that Paracelsus had left lying on the table, and he threw it into the flames. Its color vanished, and all that remained was a pinch of ash. For one infinite moment, he awaited the words, and the miracle.

Paracelsus sat unmoving. He said with strange simplicity:

"All the physicians and all the pharmacists in Basel say I am a fraud. Perhaps they are right. There are the ashes that were the rose, and that shall be the rose no more."

The young man was ashamed. Paracelsus was a charlatan, or a mere visionary, and he, an intruder, had come through his door and forced him now to confess that his famed magic arts were false.

He knelt before the master and said:

"What I have done is unpardonable. I have lacked belief, which the Lord demands of all the faithful. Let me, then, continue to see ashes. I will come back again when I am stronger, and I will be your disciple, and at the end of the Path I will see the rose."

He spoke with genuine passion, but that passion was the pity he felt for the aged master—so venerated, so inveighed against, so renowned, and therefore so hollow. Who was he, Johannes Grisebach, to discover with sacrilegious hand that behind the mask was no one?

Leaving the gold coins would be an act of almsgiving to the poor. He picked them up again as he went out. Paracelsus accompanied him to the foot of the staircase and told him he would always be welcome in that house. Both men knew they would never see each other again.

Paracelsus was then alone. Before putting out the lamp and returning to his weary chair, he poured the delicate fistful of ashes from one hand into the concave other, and he whispered a single word. The rose appeared again.

PETER STRAUB

Mr. Clubb and Mr. Cuff

Peter Straub is an elegant storyteller who authored the novels Marriages, Under Venus, Julia, If You Could See Me Now, Ghost Story, Shadowland, Floating Dragon, The Talisman *(with Stephen King),* Koko, Mrs. God, Mystery, The Throat, *and* The Hellfire Club. *His shorter fiction has been collected in* Houses Without Doors, *and he has also published two books of poetry,* Open Air *and* Leeson Park and Belsize Square. *Straub is equally comfortable writing about supernatural and psychological horrors.*

"Mr. Clubb and Mr. Cuff" is a sinister and comic tour de force, which is why I chose to reprint it despite its novella length. It was originally published in the anthology Murder for Revenge.

—E. D.

1

I never intended to go astray, nor did I know what that meant. My journey began in an isolated hamlet notable for the piety of its inhabitants, and when I vowed to escape New Covenant I assumed that the values instilled within me there would forever be my guide. And so, with a depth of paradox I still only begin to comprehend, they have been. My journey, so triumphant, also so excruciating, is both *from* my native village and *of* it. For all its splendor, my life has been that of a child of New Covenant.

When in my limousine I scanned *The Wall Street Journal*, when in the private elevator I ascended to the rosewood-paneled office with harbor views, when in the partners' dining room I ordered squab on a mesclun bed from a prison-rescued waiter known to me alone as Charlie-Charlie, also when I navigated for my clients the complex waters of financial planning, above all when before her seduction by my enemy Graham Leeson I returned homeward to luxuriate in the attentions of my stunning Marguerite, when transported within the embraces of my wife, even then I carried within the frame houses dropped like after-thoughts down the streets of New Covenant, the stiff faces and suspicious eyes, the stony cordialities before and after services in the grim great Temple—the blank storefronts along Harmony Street—tattooed within me was the ugly, en-igmatic beauty of my birthplace. Therefore I believe that when I strayed, and stray I did, make no mistake, it was but to come home, for I claim that the two strange gentlemen who beckoned me into error were the night of its night, the dust of its dust. In the period of my life's greatest turmoil—the month of my exposure to Mr. Clubb and Mr. Cuff, "Private Detectives Extraordinaire," as their business card described them—in the midst of the uproar I felt that I saw *the contradictory dimensions of . . .*

of . . .

I felt I saw . . . had seen, had at least glimpsed . . . what a wiser man might call . . . try to imagine the sheer difficulty of actually writing these words . . . the Meaning of Tragedy. You smirk, I don't blame you, in your place I'd do the same, but I assure you I saw *something*.

I must sketch in the few details necessary to understand my story. A day's walk from New York State's Canadian border, New Covenant was (and still is, still is) a town of just under a thousand inhabitants united by the puritanical Protestantism of the Church of the New Covenant, whose founders had broken away from the even more puritanical Saints of the Covenant. (The Saints had proscribed sexual congress in the hope of hastening the Second Coming.) The village flourished during the end of the nineteenth century, and settled into its permanent form around 1920.

To wit: Temple Square, where the Temple of the New Covenant and its bell tower, flanked left and right by the Youth Bible Study Center and the Combined Boys and Girls Elementary and Middle School, dominate a modest greensward. Southerly stand the shop fronts of Harmony Street, the bank, also the modest placards indicating the locations of New Covenant's doctor, lawyer, and dentist; south of Harmony Street lie the two streets of frame houses sheltering the town's clerks and artisans, beyond these the farms of the rural faithful, beyond the farmland deep forest. North of Temple Square is Scripture Street, two blocks lined with the residences of the reverend and his Board of Brethren, the afore-mentioned doctor, dentist, and lawyer, the president and vice-president of the bank, also the families of some few wealthy converts devoted to Temple affairs. North of Scripture Street are more farms, then the resumption of the great forest in which our village described a sort of clearing.

My father was New Covenant's lawyer, and to Scripture Street was I born. Sundays I spent in the Youth Bible Study Center, weekdays in the Combined Boys and Girls Elementary and Middle School. New Covenant was my world, its people all I knew of the world. Three fourths of all mankind consisted of gaunt, bony, blond-haired individuals with chiseled features and blazing blue eyes, the men six feet or taller in height, the women some inches shorter—the remaining fourth being the Racketts, Mudges, and Blunts, our farm families, who after generations of intermarriage had coalesced into a tribe of squat, black-haired, gap-toothed, moon-faced males and females seldom taller than five feet four or five inches. Until I went to college I thought that all people were divided into the races of town and barn, fair and dark, the spotless and the mud spattered, the reverential and the sly.

Though Racketts, Mudges, and Blunts attended our school and worshiped in our Temple, though they were at least as prosperous as we in town save the converts in their mansions, we knew them tainted with an essential inferiority. Rather than intelligent they seemed *crafty*, rather than spiritual, *animal*. Both in classrooms and Temple, they sat together, watchful as dogs compelled for the nonce to be "good," now and again tilting their heads to pass a whispered comment. Despite Sunday baths and Sunday clothes, they bore an unerasable odor redolent of the barnyard. Their public self-effacement seemed to mask a peasant amusement, and when they separated into their wagons and other vehicles, they could be heard to share a peasant laughter.

I found this mysterious race unsettling, in fact profoundly annoying. At some level they frightened me—I found them compelling. Oppressed from my earliest days by life in New Covenant, I felt an inadmissible fascination for this secretive brood. Despite their inferiority, I wished to know what they knew. Locked deep within their shabbiness and shame I sensed the presence of a freedom I did not understand but found *thrilling*.

Because town never socialized with barn, our contacts were restricted to places of education, worship, and commerce. It would have been as unthinkable for me to take a seat beside Delbert Mudge or Charlie-Charlie Rackett in our fourth-grade classroom as for Delbert or Charlie-Charlie to invite me for an overnight in their farmhouse bedrooms. Did Delbert and Charlie-Charlie actually have bedrooms, where they slept alone in their own beds? I recall mornings when the atmosphere about Delbert and Charlie-Charlie suggested nights spent in close proximity to the pigpen, others when their worn dungarees exuded a freshness redolent of sunshine, wildflowers, and raspberries.

During recess an inviolable border separated the townies at the northern end of our play area from the barnies at the southern. Our play, superficially similar, demonstrated our essential differences, for we could not cast off the unconscious stiffness resulting from constant adult measurement of our spiritual worthiness. In contrast, the barnies did not play at playing but actually *played*, plunging back and forth across the grass, chortling over victories, grinning as they muttered what must have been jokes. (We were not adept at jokes.) When school closed at end of day, I tracked the homebound progress of Delbert, Charlie-Charlie, and clan with envious eyes and a divided heart.

Why should they have seemed in possession of a liberty I desired? After graduation from Middle School, we townies progressed to Shady Glen's Consolidated High, there to monitor ourselves and our fellows while encountering the temptations of the wider world, in some cases then advancing into colleges and universities. Having concluded their educations with the seventh grade's long division and *Hiawatha* recitations, the barnies one and all returned to their barns. Some few, some very few, of *us*, among whom I had determined early on to be numbered, left for good, thereafter to be celebrated, denounced, or mourned. One of *us*, Caleb Thurlow, violated every standard of caste and morality by marrying Munna Blunt and vanishing into barnie-world. A disgraced, disinherited pariah during my childhood, Thurlow's increasingly pronounced stoop and decreasing teeth terrifyingly mutated him into a blond, wasted barnie-parody on his furtive annual Christmas appearances at Temple. One of *them*, one only, my old classmate Charlie-Charlie Rackett, escaped his ordained destiny in our twentieth year by liberating a plow horse and Webley-Vickers pistol from the family farm to commit serial armed robbery upon Shady Glen's George Washington Inn, Town Square Feed & Grain, and Allsorts Emporium. Every witness to his crimes recognized what, if not who, he was, and Charlie-Charlie was apprehended while boarding the Albany train in the next village west. During the course of my own journey from and of New Covenant, I tracked Charlie-Charlie's gloomy progress through the way stations of the penal system until at last I could secure his release at a parole hearing with the offer of a respectable job in the financial planning industry.

I had by then established myself as absolute monarch of three floors in a Wall Street monolith. With my two junior partners, I enjoyed the services of a fleet of paralegals, interns, analysts, investigators, and secretaries. I had chosen these partners carefully, for as well as the usual expertise, skill, and dedication, I required other, less conventional qualities.

I had sniffed out intelligent but unimaginative men of some slight moral laziness; capable of cutting corners when they thought no one would notice; controlled drinkers and secret drug-takers: juniors with reason to be grateful for their positions. I wanted no *zealousness*. My employees were to be steadfastly incurious and able enough to handle their clients satisfactorily, at least with my paternal assistance.

My growing prominence had attracted the famous, the established, the notorious. Film stars and athletes, civic leaders, corporate pashas, and heirs to longstanding family fortunes regularly visited our offices, as did a number of conspicuously well-tailored gentlemen who had accumulated their wealth in a more colorful fashion. To these clients I suggested financial stratagems responsive to their labyrinthine needs. I had not schemed for their business. It simply *came to me*, willy-nilly, as our Temple held that salvation came to the elect. One May morning, a cryptic fellow in a pinstriped suit appeared in my office to pose a series of delicate questions. As soon as he opened his mouth, the cryptic fellow summoned irresistibly from memory a dour, squinting member of the Board of Brethren of New Covenant's Temple. I *knew* this man, and instantly I found the tone most acceptable to him. Tone is all to such people. After our interview he directed others of his kind to my office, and by December my business had tripled. Individually and universally these gentlemen pungently reminded me of the village I had long ago escaped, and I cherished my suspicious buccaneers even as I celebrated the distance between my moral life and theirs. While sheltering these self-justifying figures within elaborate trusts, while legitimizing subterranean floods of cash, I immersed myself within a familiar atmosphere of pious denial. Rebuking home, I *was* home.

Life had not yet taught me that revenge inexorably exacts its own revenge.

My researches eventually resulted in the hiring of the two junior partners known privately to me as Gilligan and the Captain. The first, a short, trim fellow with a comedian's rubber face and disheveled hair, brilliant with mutual funds but an ignoramus at estate planning, each morning worked so quietly as to become invisible. To Gilligan I had referred many of our actors and musicians, and those whose schedules permitted them to attend meetings before the lunch hour met their soft-spoken advisor in a dimly lighted office with curtained windows. After lunch, Gilligan tended toward the vibrant, the effusive, the extrovert. Red faced and sweating, he loosened his tie, turned on a powerful sound system, and ushered emaciated musicians with haystack hair into the atmosphere of a backstage party. Morning Gilligan spoke in whispers; Afternoon Gilligan batted our secretaries' shoulders as he bounced officeward down the corridors. I snapped him up as soon as one of my competitors let him go, and he proved a perfect complement to the Captain. Tall, plump, silver haired, this gentleman had come to me from a specialist in estates and trusts discomfited by his tendency to become pugnacious when outraged by a client's foul language, improper dress, or other offenses against good taste. Our tycoons and inheritors of family fortunes were in no danger of arousing the Captain's ire, and I myself handled the unshaven film stars' and heavy metallists' estate planning. Neither Gilligan nor the Captain had any contact with the cryptic gentlemen. Our office was an organism balanced in all its parts. Should any mutinous notions occur to my partners, my spy the devoted Charlie-Charlie Rackett, to them Charles the Perfect Waiter, every noon silently monitored their every utterance while replenishing Gilligan's wineglass. My marriage of two years seemed blissfully happy, my reputation and bank account flourished alike, and anticipated perhaps another decade of labor followed by luxurious retirement. I could not have been less prepared for the disaster to come.

Mine, as disasters do, began at home. I admit my contribution to the difficulties. While immersed in the demands of my profession, I had married a beautiful woman twenty years my junior. It was my understanding that Marguerite had knowingly entered into a contract under which she enjoyed the fruits of income and social position while postponing a deeper marital communication until I cashed in and quit the game, at which point she and I could travel at will, occupying grand hotel suites and staterooms while acquiring every adornment which struck her eye. How could an arrangement so harmonious have failed to satisfy her? Even now I feel the old rancor. Marguerite had come into our office as a faded singer who wished to invest the remaining proceeds from a five- or six-year-old "hit," and after an initial consultation Morning Gilligan whispered her down the corridor for my customary lecture on estate tax, trusts, so forth and so on—in her case, due to the modesty of the funds in question, mere show. (Since during their preliminary discussion she had casually employed the Anglo-Saxon monosyllable for excrement, Gilligan dared not subject her to the Captain.) He escorted her into my chambers, and I glanced up with the customary show of interest. You may imagine a thick bolt of lightning slicing through a double-glazed office window, sizzling across the width of a polished teak desk, and striking me in the heart.

Already I was lost. Thirty minutes later I violated my most sacred edict by inviting a female client to a dinner date. She accepted, damn her. Six months later, Marguerite and I were married, damn us both. I had attained everything for which I had abandoned New Covenant, and for twenty-three months I inhabited the paradise of fools.

I need say only that the usual dreary signals, matters like unexplained absences, mysterious telephone calls abruptly terminated upon my appearance, and visitations of a melancholic, distracted *daemon*, forced me to set one of our investigators on Marguerite's trail, resulting in the discovery that my wife had been two-backed-beasting it with my sole professional equal, the slick, the smooth Graham Leeson, to whom I, swollen with uxorious pride a year after our wedding day, had introduced her during a function at the Waldorf-Astoria Hotel. I know what happened. I don't need a map. Exactly as I had decided to win her at our first meeting, Graham Leeson vowed to steal Marguerite from me the instant he set his handsome blue eyes on her between the fifty-thousand-dollar tables on the Starlight Roof.

My enemy enjoyed a number of natural advantages. Older than she by but ten years to my twenty, at six-four three inches taller than I, this reptile had been blessed with a misleadingly winning Irish countenance and a full head of crinkly red-blond hair. (In contrast, my white tonsure accentuated the severity of the all-too-Cromwellian townie face.) I assumed her immune to such obvious charms, and I was wrong. I thought Marguerite could not fail to see the meagerness of Leeson's inner life, and I was wrong again. I suppose he exploited the inevitable temporary isolation of any-spouse to a man in my position. He must have played upon her grudges, spoken to her secret vanities. Cynically, I am sure, he encouraged the illusion that she was an "artist." He flattered, he very likely wheedled. By every shabby means at his disposal he had overwhelmed her, most crucially by screwing her brains out three times a week in a corporate suite at a Park Avenue hotel.

After I had examined the photographs and other records arrayed before me by the investigator, an attack of nausea brought my dizzied head to the edge of my desk; then rage stiffened my backbone and induced a moment of hysterical blindness. My marriage was dead, my wife a repulsive stranger. Vision returned a second or two later. The checkbook floated from the desk drawer, the Waterman pen glided into position between thumb and forefinger, and while a shadow's efficient hand inscribed a check for ten thousand dollars, a disembodied voice informed the hapless investigator that the only service required of him henceforth would be eternal silence.

For perhaps an hour I sat alone in my office, postponing appointments and refusing telephone calls. In the moments when I had tried to envision my rival, what came to mind was some surly drummer or guitarist from her past, easily intimidated and readily bought off. In such a case, I should have inclined toward mercy. Had Marguerite offered a sufficiently self-abasing apology, I would have slashed her clothing allowance in half, restricted her public appearances to the two or three most crucial charity events of the year and perhaps as many dinners at my side in the restaurants where one is "seen," and ensured that the resultant mood of sackcloth and ashes prohibited any reversion to bad behavior by intermittent use of another investigator.

No question of mercy, now. Staring at the photographs of my life's former partner entangled with the man I detested most in the world, I shuddered with a combination of horror, despair, loathing, and—appallingly—an urgent spasm of sexual arousal. I unbuttoned my trousers, groaned in ecstatic torment, and helplessly ejaculated over the images on my desk. When I had recovered, weak-kneed and trembling I wiped away the evidence, fell into my chair, and picked up the telephone to request Charlie-Charlie Rackett's immediate presence in my office.

The cryptic gentlemen, experts in the nuances of retribution, might seem more obvious sources of assistance, but I could not afford obligations in that direction. Nor did I wish to expose my humiliation to clients for whom the issue of respect was all important. Devoted Charlie-Charlie's years in the jug had given him an extensive acquaintanceship among the dubious and irregular, and I had from time to time commandeered the services of one or another of his fellow yardbirds. My old companion sidled around my door and posted himself before me, all dignity on the outside, all curiosity within.

"I have been dealt a horrendous blow, Charlie-Charlie," I said, "and as soon as possible I wish to see one or two of the best."

Charlie-Charlie glanced at the folders. "You want serious people," he said, speaking in code. "Right?"

"I must have men who can be serious when seriousness is necessary," I said, replying in the same code.

While my lone surviving link to New Covenant struggled to understand this directive, it came to me that Charlie-Charlie had now become my only true confidant, and I bit down on an up-welling of fury. I realized that I had clamped shut my eyes, and opened them upon an uneasy Charlie-Charlie.

"You're sure," he said.

"Find them," I said, and, to restore some semblance of our conventional atmosphere asked, "The boys still okay?"

Telling me that the juniors remained content, he said, "Fat and happy. I'll find what you want, but it'll take a couple of days."

I nodded, and he was gone.

For the remainder of the day I turned in an inadequate impersonation of the executive who usually sat behind my desk and, after putting off the moment as long as reasonably possible, buried the awful files in a bottom drawer and returned to the town house I had purchased for my bride-to-be and which, I remembered with an unhappy pang, she had once in an uncharacteristic moment of cuteness called "our town home."

Since I had been too preoccupied to telephone wife, cook, or butler with the information that I would be late at the office, when I walked into our dining room the table had been laid with our china and silver, flowers arranged in the centerpiece, and in what I took to be a new dress, Marguerite glanced mildly up from her end of the table and murmured a greeting. Scarcely able to meet her eyes, I bent to bestow the usual homecoming kiss with a mixture of feeling more painful than I previously would have imagined myself capable. Some despicable portion of my being responded to her beauty with the old husbandly appreciation even as I went cold with the loathing I could not permit myself to show. I hated Marguerite for her treachery, her beauty for its falsity, myself for my susceptibility to what I knew was treacherous and false. Clumsily, my lips brushed the edge of an azure eye, and it came to me that she may well have been with Leeson while the investigator was displaying the images of her degradation. Through me coursed an involuntary tremor of revulsion with, strange to say, as its center a molten erotic core. Part of my extraordinary pain was the sense that I, too, had been contaminated: a layer of illusion had been peeled away, revealing monstrous blind groping slugs and maggots.

Having heard voices, Mr. Moncrieff, the butler I had employed upon the abrupt decision of the duke of Denbigh to cast off worldly ways and enter an order of Anglican monks, came through from the kitchen and awaited orders. His bland, courteous manner suggested, as usual, that he was making the best of having been shipwrecked on an island populated by illiterate savages. Marguerite said that she had been worried when I had not returned home at the customary time.

"I'm fine," I said. "No, I'm not fine. I feel unwell. Distinctly unwell. Grave difficulties at the office." With that I managed to make my way up the table to my chair, along the way signaling to Mr. Moncrieff that the Lord of the Savages wished him to bring in the predinner martini and then immediately begin serving whatever the cook had prepared. I took my seat at the head of the table, and Mr. Moncrieff removed the floral centerpiece of probing concern. This was false, false, false. Unable to meet her eyes, I raised mine to the row of Canalettos along the wall, then the intricacies of the plaster molding above the paintings, at last to the chandelier depending from the central rosette on the ceiling. More had changed than my relationship with my wife. The molding, the blossoming chandelier, even Canaletto's Venice resounded with a cold, selfish lovelessness.

Marguerite remarked that I seemed agitated.

"No, I am not," I said. The butler placed the ice-cold drink before me, and I snatched up the glass and drained half its contents. "Yes, I am agitated, terribly," I said. "The difficulties at the office are more far reaching than I intimated." I polished off the martini and tasted only glycerine. "It is a matter of betrayal and treachery, made all the more wounding by the closeness of my relationship with the traitor."

I lowered my eyes to measure the effect of this thrust to the vitals of the traitor in question. She was looking back at me with a flawless imitation of wifely concern. For a moment I doubted her unfaithfulness. Then the memory of the photographs in my bottom drawer once again brought crawling into view the slugs and maggots. "I am sickened unto rage," I said, "and my rage demands vengeance. Can you understand this?"

Mr. Moncrieff carried into the dining room the tureens of serving dishes containing whatever it was we were to eat that night, and my wife and I honored the silence which had become conventional during the presentation of our evening meal. When we were alone again, she nodded in affirmation.

I said, "I am grateful, for I value your opinions. I should like you to help me reach a difficult decision."

She thanked me in the simplest of terms.

"Consider this puzzle," I said. "Famously, vengeance is the Lord's, and therefore it is often imagined that vengeance exacted by anyone other is immoral. Yet if vengeance is the Lord's, then a mortal being who seeks it on his own behalf has engaged in a form of worship, even an alternate version of prayer. Many good Christians regularly pray for the establishment of justice, and what lies behind an act of vengeance but a desire for justice? God tells us that eternal torment awaits the wicked. He also demonstrates a pronounced affection for those who prove unwilling to let Him do all the work."

Marguerite expressed the opinion that justice was a fine thing indeed, and that a man such as myself would always labor in its behalf. She fell silent and regarded me with what on any night previous I would have seen as tender concern. Though I had not yet so informed her, she declared, the Benedict Arnold must have been one of my juniors, for no other employee could injure me so greatly. Which was the traitor?

"As yet I do not know," I said. "But once again I must be grateful for your grasp of my concerns. Soon I will put into position the bear traps which will result in the fiend's exposure. Unfortunately, my dear, this task will demand all of my energy over at least the next several days. Until the task is accomplished, it will be necessary for me to camp out in the _____ Hotel." I named the site of her assignations with Graham Leeson.

A subtle, momentary darkening of the eyes, her first genuine response of the evening, froze my heart as I set the bear trap into place. "I know, the _____'s vulgarity deepens with every passing week, but Gilligan's apartment is but a few doors north, the Captain's one block south. Once my investigators have installed their electronic devices, I shall be privy to every secret they possess. Might you not enjoy spending several days at Green Chimneys? The servants have the month off, but you might enjoy the solitude there more than you would being alone in town."

Green Chimneys, our country estate on a bluff above the Hudson River, lay two hours away. Marguerite's delight in the house had inspired me to construct on the grounds a fully equipped recording studio, where she typically spent days on end, trying out new "songs."

Charmingly, she thanked me for my consideration and said that she would enjoy a few days in seclusion at Green Chimneys. After I had exposed the traitor, I was to telephone her with the summons home. Accommodating on the surface, vile beneath, these words brought an anticipatory tinge of pleasure to her face, a delicate heightening of her beauty I would have, very likely *had*, misconstrued on earlier occasions. Any appetite I might have had disappeared before a visitation of nausea, and I announced myself exhausted. Marguerite intensified my discomfort by calling me her poor darling. I staggered to my bedroom, locked the door, threw off my clothes, and dropped into bed to endure a sleepless night.

I would never see my wife again.

2

Sometime after first light I had attained an uneasy slumber; finding it impossible to will myself out of bed on awakening, I relapsed into the same restless sleep. By the time I appeared within the dining room, Mr. Moncrieff, as well chilled as a good Chardonnay, informed me that madame had departed for the country some twenty minutes before. Despite the hour, did sir wish to breakfast? I consulted, trepidatiously, my wristwatch. It was ten-thirty: my unvarying practice was to arise at five-thirty, breakfast soon after, and arrive in my office well before seven. I rushed downstairs and, as soon as I slid into the backseat of the limousine, forbade awkward queries by pressing the button to raise the window between the driver and myself.

No such mechanism could shield me from Mrs. Rampage, my secretary, who thrust her head around the door a moment after I had expressed my desire for a hearty breakfast of poached eggs, bacon, and whole-wheat toast from the executive dining room. All calls and appointments were to be postponed or otherwise put off until the completion of my repast. Mrs. Rampage had informed me that two men without appointments had been awaiting my arrival since eight A.M. and asked if I would consent to see them immediately. I told her not to be absurd. The door to the outer world swung to admit her beseeching head. "Please," she said. "I don't know who they are, but they're *frightening* everybody."

This remark clarified all. Earlier than anticipated, Charlie-Charlie Rackett had deputized two men capable of seriousness when seriousness was called for. "I beg your pardon," I said. "Send them in."

Mrs. Rampage withdrew to lead into my sanctum two stout, stocky, short, dark-haired men. My spirits had taken wing the moment I beheld these fellows shouldering through the door, and I rose smiling to my feet. My secretary muttered an introduction, baffled as much by my cordiality as by her ignorance of my visitors' names.

"It is quite all right," I said. "All is in order, all is in train." New Covenant had just walked in.

Barnie-slyness, barnie-freedom, shone from their great round gap-toothed faces: in precisely the manner I remembered, these two suggested mocking peasant violence scantily disguised by an equally mocking impersonation of convention. Small wonder that they had intimidated Mrs. Rampage and her underlings, for their nearest exposure to a like phenomenon had been with our musicians, and when offstage they were pale, emaciated fellows of little physical vitality. Clothed in black suits, white shirts, and black neckties, holding their black derbies by their brims and turning their gappy smiles back and forth between Mrs. Rampage and myself, these barnies had evidently been loose in the world for some time. They were perfect for my task. *You will be irritated by their country manners, you will be annoyed by their native insubordination,* I told myself, *but you will never find men more suitable, so grant them what latitude they need.* I directed Mrs. Rampage to cancel all telephone calls and appointments for the next hour.

The door closed, and we were alone. Each of the black-suited darlings snapped a business card from his right jacket pocket and extended it to me with a twirl of the fingers. One card read:

MR. CLUBB AND MR. CUFF
Private Detectives Extraordinaire
Mr. Clubb

and the other:

MR. CLUBB AND MR. CUFF
Private Detectives Extraordinaire
Mr. Cuff

I inserted the cards into a pocket and expressed my delight at making their acquaintance.

"Becoming aware of your situation," said Mr. Clubb, "we preferred to report as quickly as we could."

"Entirely commendable," I said. "Will you gentlemen please sit down?"

"We prefer to stand," said Mr. Clubb.

"I trust you will not object if I again take my chair," I said, and did so. "To be honest, I am reluctant to describe the whole of my problem. It is a personal matter, therefore painful."

"It is a domestic matter," said Mr. Cuff.

I stared at him. He stared back with the sly imperturbability of his kind.

"Mr. Cuff," I said, "you have made a reasonable and, as it happens, an accurate supposition, but in the future you will please refrain from speculation."

"Pardon my plain way of speaking, sir, but I was not speculating," he said. "Marital disturbances are domestic by nature."

"All too domestic, one might say," put in Mr. Clubb. "In the sense of pertaining to the home. As we have so often observed, you find your greatest pain right smack-dab in the living room, as it were."

"Which is a somewhat politer fashion of naming another room altogether." Mr. Cuff appeared to suppress a surge of barnie-glee.

Alarmingly, Charlie-Charlie had passed along altogether too much information, especially since the information in question should not have been in his possession. For an awful moment I imagined that the dismissed investigator had spoken to Charlie-Charlie. The man may have broadcast my disgrace to every person encountered on his final journey out of my office, inside the public elevator, thereafter even to the shoeshine "boys" and cup-rattling vermin lining the streets. It occurred to me that I might be forced to have the man silenced. Symmetry would then demand the silencing of valuable Charlie-Charlie. The inevitable next step would resemble a full-scale massacre.

My faith in Charlie-Charlie banished these fantasies by suggesting an alternate scenario and enabled me to endure the next utterance.

Mr. Clubb said, "Which in plainer terms would be to say the bedroom."

After speaking to my faithful spy, the Private Detectives Extraordinaire had taken the initiative by acting as if *already employed* and following Marguerite to her afternoon assignation at the _____ Hotel. Here, already, was the insubordination I had foreseen, but instead of the expected annoyance I felt a thoroughgoing gratitude for the two men leaning slightly toward me, their animal senses alert to every nuance of my response. That they had come to my office armed with the essential secret absolved me from embarrassing explanations; blessedly, the hideous photographs would remain concealed in the bottom drawer.

"Gentlemen," I said, "I applaud your initiative."

They stood at ease. "Then we have an understanding," said Mr. Clubb. "At various times, various matters come to our attention. At these times we prefer to conduct ourselves according to the wishes of our employer, regardless of difficulty."

"Agreed," I said. "However, from this point forward I must insist—"

A rap at the door cut short my admonition. Mrs. Rampage brought in a coffeepot and cup, a plate beneath a silver cover, a rack with four slices of toast, two jam pots, silverware, a linen napkin, and a glass of water, and came to a halt some five or six feet short of the barnies. A sinfully arousing smell of butter and bacon emanated from the tray. Mrs. Rampage deliberated between placing my breakfast on the table to her left or venturing into proximity to my guests by bringing the tray to my desk. I gestured her forward, and she tacked wide to port and homed in on the desk. "All is in order, all is in train," I said. She nodded and backed out—literally walked backwards until she reached the door, groped for the knob, and vanished.

I removed the cover from the plate containing two poached eggs in a cup-sized bowl, four crisp rashers of bacon, and a mound of home-fried potatoes all the more welcome for being a surprise gift from our chef.

"And now, fellows, with your leave I shall—"

For the second time my sentence was cut off in midflow. A thick barnie-hand closed upon the handle of the coffeepot and proceeded to fill the cup. Mr. Clubb transported my coffee to his lips, smacked appreciatively at the taste, then took up a toast slice and plunged it like a dagger into my eggcup, releasing a thick yellow suppuration. He crunched the dripping toast between his teeth.

At that moment, when mere annoyance passed into dumbfounded ire, I might have sent them packing despite my earlier resolution, for Mr. Clubb's violation of my breakfast was as good as an announcement that he and his partner respected none of the conventional boundaries and would indulge in boorish, even disgusting behavior. I very nearly did send them packing, and both of them knew it. They awaited my reaction, whatever it should be. Then I understood that I was being tested, and half of my insight was that ordering them off would be a failure of imagination. I had asked Charlie-Charlie to send me serious men, not Boy Scouts, and in the rape of my breakfast were depths and dimensions of seriousness I had never suspected. In that instant of comprehension, I believe, I virtually knew all that was to come, down to the last detail, and gave a silent assent. My next insight was that the moment when I might have dismissed these fellows with a conviction of perfect rectitude had just passed, and with the sense of opening myself to unpredictable adventures I turned to Mr. Cuff. He lifted a rasher from my plate, folded it within a slice of toast, and displayed the result.

"Here are our methods in action," he said. "We prefer not to go hungry while you gorge yourself, speaking freely, for the one reason that all of this stuff represents what you ate every morning when you were a kid." Leaving me to digest this shapeless utterance, he bit into his impromptu sandwich and sent golden-brown crumbs showering to the carpet.

"For as the important, abstemious man you are now," said Mr. Clubb, "what do you eat in the mornings?"

"Toast and coffee," I said. "That's about it."

"But in childhood?"

"Eggs," I said. "Scrambled or fried, mainly. And bacon. Home fries too." Every fatty, cholesterol-crammed ounce of which, I forbore to add, had been delivered by barnie-hands directly from barnie-farms. I looked at the rigid bacon, the glistening potatoes, the mess in the eggcup. My stomach lurched.

"We prefer," Mr. Clubb said, "that you follow your true preferences instead of muddying mind and stomach by gobbling this crap in search of an inner peace which never existed in the first-place, if you can be honest with yourself." He leaned over the desk and picked up the plate. His partner snatched a second piece of bacon and wrapped it within a second slice of toast. Mr. Clubb began working on the eggs, and Mr. Cuff grabbed a handful of home-fried potatoes. Mr. Clubb dropped the empty eggcup, finished his coffee, refilled the cup, and handed it to Mr. Cuff, who had just finished licking the residue of fried potato from his free hand.

I removed the third slice of toast from the rack. Forking home fries into his mouth, Mr. Clubb winked at me. I bit into the toast and considered the two little pots of jam, greengage, I think, and rosehip. Mr. Clubb waggled a finger. I contented myself with the last of the toast. After a while I drank from the glass of water. All in all I felt reasonably satisfied and, but for the deprivation of my customary cup of coffee, content with my decision. I glanced in some irritation at Mr. Cuff. He drained his cup, then tilted into it the third and final measure from the pot and offered it to me. "Thank you," I said. Mr. Cuff picked up the pot of greengage jam and sucked out its contents, loudly. Mr. Clubb did the same with the rosehip. They sent their tongues into the corners of the jam pots and cleaned out whatever adhered to the sides. Mr. Cuff burped. Over-lappingly, Mr. Clubb burped.

"Now, that is what I call by the name of breakfast, Mr. Clubb," said Mr. Cuff. "Are we in agreement?"

"Deeply," said Mr. Clubb. "That is what I call by the name of breakfast now, what I have called by the name of breakfast in the past, and what I shall continue to call by that sweet name on every morning in the future." He turned to me and took his time, sucking first one tooth, then another. "Our morning meal, sir, consists of that simple fare with which we begin the day, except when in all good faith we wind up sitting in a waiting room with our stomachs growling because our future client has chosen to skulk in late for work." He inhaled. "Which was for the same exact reason which brought him to our attention in the first place and for which we went without in order to offer him our assistance. Which is, begging your pardon, sir, the other reason for which you ordered a breakfast you would ordinarily rather starve than eat, and all I ask before we get down to the business at hand is that you might begin to entertain the possibility that simple men like ourselves might possibly understand a thing or two."

"I see that you are faithful fellows," I began.

"Faithful as dogs," broke in Mr. Clubb.

"And that you understand my position," I continued.

"Down to its smallest particulars," he interrupted again. "We are on a long journey."

"And so it follows," I pressed on, "that you must also understand that no further initiatives may be taken without my express consent."

These last words seemed to raise a disturbing echo, of what I could not say, but an echo nonetheless, and my ultimatum failed to achieve the desired effect. Mr. Clubb smiled and said, "We intend to follow your inmost desires with the faithfulness, as I have said, of trusted dogs, for one of our sacred duties is that of bringing these to fulfillment, as evidenced, begging your pardon, sir, in the matter of the breakfast our actions spared you from gobbling up and sickening yourself with. Before you protest, sir, please let me put to you the question of you how you think you would be feeling right now if you had eaten that greasy stuff all by yourself?"

The straightforward truth announced itself and demanded utterance. "Poisoned," I said. After a second's pause, I added, "Disgusted."

"Yes, for you are a better man than you know. Imagine the situation. Allow yourself to picture what would have transpired had Mr. Cuff and myself not acted on your behalf. As your heart throbbed and your veins groaned, you would have taken in that while you were stuffing yourself the two of us stood hungry before you. You would have remembered that good woman informing you that we had patiently awaited your arrival since eight this morning, and at that point, sir, you would have experienced a self-disgust which would forever have tainted our relationship. From that point forth, sir, you would have been incapable of receiving the full benefits of our services."

I stared at the twinkling barnie. "Are you saying that if I had eaten my breakfast you would have refused to work for me?"

"You did eat your breakfast. The rest was ours."

This statement was so literally true that I burst into laughter and said, "Then I must thank you for saving me from myself. Now that you may accept employment, please inform me of the rates for your services."

"We have no rates," said Mr. Clubb.

"We prefer to leave compensation to the client," said Mr. Cuff.

This was crafty even by barnie-standards, but I knew a countermove. "What is the greatest sum you have ever been awarded for a single job?"

"Six hundred thousand dollars," said Mr. Clubb.

"And the smallest?"

"Nothing, zero, *nada*, zilch," said the same gentleman.

"And your feelings as to the disparity?"

"None," said Mr. Clubb. "What we are given is the correct amount. When the time comes, you shall know the sum to the penny."

To myself I said, *So I shall, and it shall be nothing*; to them, "We must devise a method by which I may pass along suggestions as I monitor your ongoing progress. Our future consultations should take place in anonymous public places on the order of street corners, public parks, diners, and the like. I must never be seen in your office."

"You must not, you could not," said Mr. Clubb. "We would prefer to install ourselves here within the privacy and seclusion of your own beautiful office."

"Here?" He had once again succeeded in dumbfounding me.

"Our installation within the client's work space proves so advantageous as to overcome all initial objections," said Mr. Cuff. "And in this case, sir, we would occupy but the single corner behind me where the table stands against the window. We would come and go by means of your private elevator, exercise our natural functions in your private bathroom, and have our simple meals sent in from your kitchen. You would suffer no interference or awkwardness in the course of your business. So we prefer to do our job here, where we can do it best."

"You prefer to move in with me," I said, giving equal weight to every word.

"Prefer it to declining the offer of our help, thereby forcing you, sir, to seek the aid of less reliable individuals."

Several factors, first among them being the combination of delay, difficulty, and risk involved in finding replacements for the pair before me, led me to give further thought to this absurdity. Charlie-Charlie, a fellow of wide acquaintance among society's shadow-side, had sent me his best. Any others would be inferior. It was true that Mr. Clubb and Mr. Cuff could enter and leave my office unseen, granting us a greater degree of security possible in diners and public parks. There remained an insuperable problem.

"All you say may be true, but my partners and clients alike enter this office daily. How do I explain the presence of two strangers?"

"That is easily done, Mr. Cuff, is it not?" said Mr. Clubb.

"Indeed it is," said his partner. "Our experience has given us two infallible and complementary methods. The first of these is the installation of a screen to shield us from the view of those who visit this office."

I said, "You intend to hide behind a screen."

"During those periods when it is necessary for us to be on-site."

"Are you and Mr. Clubb capable of perfect silence? Do you never shuffle your feet, do you never cough?"

"You could justify our presence within these sacrosanct confines by the single manner most calculated to draw over Mr. Clubb and myself a blanket of respectable, anonymous impersonality."

"You wish to be introduced as my lawyers?" I asked.

"I invite you to consider a word," said Mr. Cuff. "Hold it steadily in your mind. Remark the inviolability which distinguishes those it identifies, measure its effect upon those who hear it. The word of which I speak, sir, is this: *consultant*."

I opened my mouth to object and found I could not.

Every profession occasionally must draw upon the resources of impartial experts—consultants. Every institution of every kind has known the visitations of persons answerable only to the top and given access to all departments—consultants. Consultants are *supposed* to be invisible. Again I opened my mouth, this time to say, "Gentlemen, we are in business." I picked up my telephone and asked Mrs. Rampage to order immediate delivery from Bloomingdale's of an ornamental screen and then to remove the breakfast tray.

Eyes agleam with approval, Mr. Clubb and Mr. Cuff stepped forward to shake my hand.

"We are in business," said Mr. Clubb.

"Which is by way of saying," said Mr. Cuff, "jointly dedicated to a sacred purpose."

Mrs. Rampage entered, circled to the side of my desk, and gave my visitors a glance of deep-dyed wariness. Mr. Clubb and Mr. Cuff clasped their hands before them and looked heavenward. "About the screen," she said. "Bloomingdale's wants to know if you would prefer one six feet high in a black and red Chinese pattern or one ten feet high, Art Deco, in ochres, teals, and taupes."

My barnies nodded together at the heavens. "The latter, please, Mrs. Rampage," I said. "Have it delivered this afternoon, regardless of cost, and place it beside the table for the use of these gentlemen, Mr. Clubb and Mr. Cuff, highly regarded consultants to the financial industry. That table shall be their command post."

"Consultants," she said. "Oh."

The barnies dipped their heads. Much relaxed, Mrs. Rampage asked if I expected great changes in the future.

"We shall see," I said. "I wish you to extend every cooperation to these gentlemen. I need not remind you, I know, that change is the first law of life."

She disappeared, no doubt on a beeline for her telephone.

Mr. Clubb stretched his arms above his head. "The preliminaries are out of the way, and we can move to the job at hand. You, sir, have been most *exceedingly*, most *grievously* wronged. Do I overstate?"

"You do not," I said.

"Would I overstate to assert that you have been injured, that you have suffered a devastating wound?"

"No, you would not," I responded, with some heat.

Mr. Clubb settled a broad haunch upon the surface of my desk. His face had taken on a grave, sweet serenity. "You seek redress. Redress, sir, is a *correction*, but it is nothing more. You imagine that it restores a lost balance, but it does nothing of the kind. A crack has appeared on the earth's surface, causing widespread loss of life. From all sides are heard the cries of the wounded and dying. It is as though the earth itself has suffered an injury akin to yours, is it not?"

He had expressed a feeling I had not known to be mine until that moment, and my voice trembled as I said, "It is exactly."

"Exactly," he said. "For that reason I said *correction* rather than *restoration*. Restoration is never possible. Change is the first law of life."

"Yes, of course," I said, trying to get down to brass tacks.

Mr. Clubb hitched his buttock more comprehensively onto the desk. "What will happen will indeed happen, but we prefer our clients to acknowledge from the first that, apart from human desires being a deep and messy business, outcomes are full of surprises. If you choose to repay one disaster with an equal and opposite disaster, we would reply, in our country fashion, there's a calf that won't suck milk."

I said, "I know I can't pay my wife back in kind, how could I?"

"Once we begin," he said, "we cannot undo our actions."

"Why should I want them undone?" I asked.

Mr. Clubb drew up his legs and sat cross-legged before me. Mr. Cuff placed a meaty hand on my shoulder. "I suppose there is no dispute," said Mr. Clubb, "that the injury you seek to redress is the adulterous behavior of your spouse."

Mr. Cuff's hand tightened on my shoulder.

"You wish that my partner and myself punish your spouse."

"I didn't hire you to read her bedtime stories," I said.

Mr. Cuff twice smacked my shoulder, painfully, in what I took to be approval.

"Are we assuming that her punishment is to be of a physical nature?" asked Mr. Clubb. His partner gave my shoulder another all-too-hearty squeeze.

"What other kind is there?" I asked, pulling away from Mr. Cuff's hand.

The hand closed on me again, and Mr. Clubb said, "Punishment of a mental or psychological nature. We could, for example, torment her with mysterious telephone calls and anonymous letters. We could use any of a hundred devices to make it impossible for her to sleep. Threatening incidents could be staged so often as to put her in a permanent state of terror."

"I want physical punishment," I said.

"That is our constant preference," he said. "Results are swifter and more conclusive when physical punishment is used. But again, we have a wide spectrum from which to choose. Are we looking for mild physical pain, real suffering, or something in between, on the order of, say, broken arms or legs?"

I thought of the change in Marguerite's eyes when I named the _____ Hotel. "Real suffering."

Another bone-crunching blow to my shoulder from Mr. Cuff and a wide, gappy smile from Mr. Clubb greeted this remark. "You, sir, are our favorite type of client," said Mr. Clubb. "A fellow who knows what he wants and is unafraid to put it into words. This suffering, now, did you wish it in brief or extended form?"

"Extended," I said. "I must say that I appreciate your thoughtfulness in consulting with me like this. I was not quite sure what I wanted of you when first I requested your services, but you have helped me become perfectly clear about it."

"That is our function," he said. "Now, sir. The extended form of real suffering permits two different conclusions, gradual cessation or termination. Which is your preference?"

I opened my mouth and closed it. I opened it again and stared at the ceiling. Did I want these men to murder my wife? No. Yes. No. Yes, but only after making sure that the unfaithful trollop understood exactly why she had to die. No, surely an extended term of excruciating torture would restore the world to proper balance. Yet I wanted the witch dead. But then I would be ordering these barnies to kill her. "At the moment I cannot make that decision," I said. Irresistibly, my eyes found the bottom drawer containing the file of obscene photographs. "I'll let you know my decision after we have begun."

Mr. Cuff dropped his hand, and Mr. Clubb nodded with exaggerated, perhaps ironic, slowness. "And what of your rival, the seducer, sir? Do we have any wishes in regard to that gentleman, sir?"

The way these fellows could sharpen one's thinking was truly remarkable. "I most certainly do," I said. "What she gets, he gets. Fair is fair."

"Indeed, sir," said Mr. Clubb, "and, if you will permit me, sir, only fair is fair. And fairness demands that before we go any deeper into the particulars of the case we must examine the evidence as presented to yourself, and when I speak of fairness, sir, I refer to fairness particularly to yourself, for only the evidence seen by your own eyes can permit us to view this matter through them."

Again, I looked helplessly down at the bottom drawer. "That will not be necessary. You will find my wife at our country estate, Green . . ."

My voice trailed off as Mr. Cuff's hand ground into my shoulder while he bent down and opened the drawer.

"Begging to differ," said Mr. Clubb, "but we are now and again in a better position than the client to determine what is necessary. Remember, sir, that while shame unshared is toxic to the soul, shame shared is the beginning of health. Besides, it only hurts for a little while."

Mr. Cuff drew the file from the drawer.

"My partner will concur that your inmost wish is that we examine the evidence," said Mr. Clubb. "Else you would not have signaled its location. We would prefer to have your explicit command to do so, but in the absence of explicit, implicit serves just about as well."

I gave an impatient, ambiguous wave of the hand, a gesture they cheerfully misunderstood.

"Then all is. . . . how do you put it, sir? 'All is . . .' "

"All is in order, all is in train," I muttered.

"Just so. We have ever found it beneficial to establish a common language with our clients, in order to conduct ourselves within terms enhanced by their constant usage in the dialogue between us." He took the file from Mr. Cuff's hands. "We shall examine the contents of this folder at the table across the room. After the examination has been completed, my partner and I shall deliberate. And then, sir, we shall return for further instructions."

They strolled across the office and took adjoining chairs on the near side of the table, presenting me with two identical, wide, black-clothed backs. Their hats went to either side, the file between them. Attempting unsuccessfully to look away, I lifted my receiver and asked my secretary who, if anyone, had called in the interim and what appointments had been made for the morning.

Mr. Clubb opened the folder and leaned forward to inspect the topmost photograph.

My secretary informed me that Marguerite had telephoned from the road with an inquiry concerning my health. Mr. Clubb's back and shoulders trembled with what I assumed was the shock of disgust. One of the scions was due at two P.M., and at four a cryptic gentleman would arrive. By their works shall ye know them, and Mrs. Rampage proved herself a diligent soul by asking if I wished her to place a call to Green Chimneys at three o'clock. Mr. Clubb thrust a photograph in front of Mr. Cuff. "I think not," I said. "Anything else?" She told me that Gilligan had expressed a desire to see me privately—meaning, without the Captain—sometime during the morning. A murmur came from the table. "Gilligan can wait," I said, and the murmur, expressive, I had thought, of dismay and sympathy, rose in volume and revealed itself as amusement.

They were chuckling—even chortling!

I replaced the telephone and said, "Gentlemen, please, your laughter is insupportable." The potential effect of this remark was undone by its being lost within a surge of coarse laughter. I believe that something else was at that moment lost . . . some dimension of my soul . . . an element akin to pride . . . akin to dignity . . . but whether the loss was for good or ill, then I could not say. For some time, in fact an impossibly lengthy time, they found cause for laughter in the wretched photographs. My occasional attempts to silence them went unheard as they passed the dread photographs back and forth, discarding some instantly and to others returning for a second, even a third, even a fourth and fifth, perusal.

And then at last the barnies reared back, uttered a few nostalgic chirrups of laughter, and returned the photographs to the folder. They were still twitching with remembered laughter, still flicking happy tears from their eyes, as they sauntered grinning back across the office and tossed the file onto my desk. "Ah, me, sir, a delightful experience," said Mr. Clubb. "Nature in all her lusty romantic splendor, one might say. Remarkably stimulating, I could add. Correct, sir?"

"I hadn't expected you fellows to be stimulated to mirth," I grumbled, ramming the foul thing into the drawer and out of view.

"Laughter is merely a portion of the stimulation to which I refer," he said. "Unless my sense of smell has led me astray, a thing I fancy it has yet to do, you could not but feel another sort of arousal altogether before these pictures, am I right?"

I refused to respond to this sally but feared that I felt the blood rising to my cheeks. Here they were again, the slugs and maggots.

"We are all brothers under the skin," said Mr. Clubb. "Remember my words. Shame unshared poisons the soul. And besides, it only hurts for a little while."

Now I could not respond. What was the "it" which hurt only for a little while—the pain of cuckoldry, the mystery of my shameful response to the photographs, or the horror of the barnies knowing what I had done?

"You will find it helpful, sir, to repeat after me: *It only hurts for a little while.*"

"It only hurts for a little while," I said, and the naive phrase reminded me that they were only barnies after all.

"Spoken like a child," Mr. Clubb most annoyingly said, "in, as it were, the tones and accents of purest innocence," and then righted matters by asking where Marguerite might be found. Had I not mentioned a country place named Green . . . ?

"Green Chimneys," I said, shaking off the unpleasant impression which the preceding few seconds had made upon me. "You will find it at the end of _____ Lane, turning off _____ Street just north of the town of _____. The four green chimneys easily visible above the hedge along _____ Lane are your landmark, though as it is the only building in sight you can hardly mistake it for another. My wife left our place in the city just after ten this morning, so she should be getting there"—I looked at my watch—"in thirty to forty-five minutes. She will unlock the front gate, but she will not relock it once she has passed through, for she never does. The woman does not have the self-preservation of a sparrow. Once she has entered the estate, she will travel up the drive and open the door of the garage with an electronic device. This door, I assure you, will remain open, and the door she will take into the house will not be locked."

"But there are maids and cooks and laundresses and boot-boys and suchlike to consider," said Mr. Cuff. "Plus a majordomo to conduct the entire orchestra and go around rattling the doors to make sure they're locked. Unless all of these parties are to be absent on account of the annual holiday."

"The servants have the month off," I said.

"A most suggestive consideration," said Mr. Clubb. "You possess a devilish clever mind, sir."

"Perhaps," I said, grateful for the restoration of the proper balance. "Marguerite will have stopped along the way for groceries and other essentials, so she will first carry the bags into the kitchen, which is the first room to the right off the corridor from the garage. Then I suppose she will take the staircase up to her bed-room and air it out." I took pen and paper from my topmost drawer and sketched the layout of the house as I spoke. "She may go around to the library, the morning room, and the drawing room, opening the shutters and a few windows. Somewhere during this process, she is likely to use the telephone. After that, she will leave the house by the rear entrance and take the path along the top of the bluff to a long, low building which looks like this."

I drew in the well-known outlines of the studio in its nest of trees on the bluff above the Hudson. "It is a recording studio I had built for her convenience. She may well plan to spend the entire afternoon inside it, and you will know if she is there by the lights." Then I could see Marguerite smiling to herself as she fitted her key into the lock on the studio door, see her let herself in and reach automatically for the light switch, and a wave of emotion rendered me speechless.

Mr. Clubb rescued me by asking, "It is your feeling, sir, that when the lady stops to use the telephone she will be placing a call to that energetic gentleman?"

"Yes, of course," I said, only barely refraining from adding *you dolt*. "She will seize the earliest opportunity to inform him of their good fortune."

He nodded with the extravagant caution I was startled to recognize from my own dealings with backward clients. "Let us pause to see all round the matter, sir. Will the lady wish to leave a suspicious entry in your telephone records? Isn't it more likely that the person she telephones will be you, sir? The call to the athletic gentleman will already have been placed, according to my way of seeing things, either from the roadside or the telephone in the grocery where you have her stop to pick up her essentials."

Though disliking these references to Leeson's physical condition, I admitted that he might have a point.

"So, in that case, sir, and I know that a mind as quick as yours has already overtaken mine, you would want to express yourself with the utmost cordiality when the missus calls again, so as not to tip your hand in even the slightest way. But that, I'm sure, goes without saying, after all you have been through, sir."

Without bothering to acknowledge this, I said, "Shouldn't you fellows really be leaving? No sense in wasting time, after all."

"Precisely why we shall wait here until the end of the day," said Mr. Clubb. "In cases of this unhappy sort, we find it more effective to deal with both parties at once, acting in concert when they are in prime condition to be taken by surprise. The gentleman is liable to leave his place of work at the end of the day, which implies to me that he is unlikely to appear at your lovely country place at any time before seven this evening, or, which is more likely, eight. At this time of the year, there is still enough light at nine o'clock to enable us to conceal our vehicle on the grounds, enter the house, and begin our business. At eleven o'clock, sir, we shall call with our initial report and request additional instructions."

I asked the fellow if he meant to idle away the entire afternoon in my office while I conducted my business.

"Mr. Cuff and I are never idle, sir. While you conduct your business, we will be doing the same, laying out our plans, refining our strategies, choosing our methods and the order of their use."

"Oh, all right," I said, "but I trust you'll be quiet about it."

At that moment, Mrs. Rampage buzzed to say that Gilligan was before her, requesting to see me immediately, proof that bush telegraph is a more efficient means of spreading information than any newspaper. I told her to send him in, and a second later the Morning Gilligan, pale of face, dark hair tousled but not as yet completely wild, came treading softly toward my desk. He pretended to be surprised that I had visitors and pantomimed an apology which incorporated the suggestion that he depart and return later. "No, no," I said, "I am delighted to see you, for this gives me the opportunity to introduce you to our new consultants, who will be working closely with me for a time."

Gilligan swallowed, glanced at me with the deepest suspicion, and extended his hand as I made the introductions. "I regret that I am unfamiliar with your work, gentlemen," he said. "Might I ask the name of your firm? Is it Locust, Bleaney, Burns, or Charter, Carter, Maxton, and Coltrane?"

By naming the two most prominent consultancies in our industry, Gilligan was assessing the thinness of the ice beneath his feet: LBB specialized in investments, CCM and C in estates and trusts. If my visitors worked for the former, he would suspect that a guillotine hung above his neck; if the latter, the Captain was liable for the chop. "Neither," I said. "Mr. Clubb and Mr. Cuff are the directors of their own concern, which covers every aspect of the trade with such tactful professionalism that it is known to but the few for whom they will consent to work."

"Excellent," Gilligan whispered, gazing in some puzzlement at the map and floor plan atop my desk. "Tip-top."

"When their findings are given to me, they shall be given to all. In the meantime, I would prefer that you say as little as possible about the matter. Though change is a law of life, we wish to avoid unneccessary alarm."

"You know that you can depend on my silence," said Morning Gilligan, and it was true, I did know that. I also knew that his alter ego, Afternoon Gilligan, would babble the news to everyone who had not already heard it from Mrs. Rampage. By six P.M., our entire industry would be pondering the information that I had called in a consultancy team of such rarefied accomplishments *that they chose to remain unknown but to the very few.* None of my colleagues could dare admit to an ignorance of Clubb and Cuff, and my reputation, already great, would increase exponentially.

To distract him from the floor plan of Green Chimneys and the rough map of my estate, I said, "I assume some business brought you here, Gilligan."

"Oh! Yes—of course," he said, and with a trace of embarrassment brought to my attention the pretext for his being there, the ominous plunge in value of an overseas fund in which we had advised one of his musicians to invest. Should we recommend selling the fund before more money was lost, or was it wisest to hold on? Only a minute was required to decide that the musician should retain his share of the fund until next quarter, when we anticipated a general improvement, but both Gilligan and I were aware that this recommendation could easily have been handled by telephone, and soon he was moving toward the door, smiling at the barnies in a pathetic display of false confidence.

The telephone rang a moment after the detectives had returned to the table. Mr. Clubb said, "Your wife, sir. Remember: the utmost cordiality." Here was false confidence, I thought, of an entirely different sort. I picked up the receiver to hear Mrs. Rampage tell me that my wife was on the line.

What followed was a banal conversation of the utmost *duplicity.* Marguerite pretended that my sudden departure from the dinner table and my late arrival at the office had caused her to fear for my health. I pretended that all was well, apart from a slight indigestion. Had the drive up been peaceful? Yes, the highways had been surprisingly empty. How was the house? A little musty, but otherwise fine. She had never quite realized, she said, how very large Green Chimneys was until she walked around in it, knowing she was going to be there alone. Had she been out to the studio? No, but she was looking forward to getting a lot of work done over the next three or four days and thought she would be working every night, as well. (Implicit in this remark was the information that I should be unable to reach her, the studio being without a telephone.) After a moment of awkward silence, she said, "I suppose it is too early for you to have identified your traitor." It was, I said, but the process would begin that evening. "I'm so sorry you have to go through this," she said. "I know how painful the discovery was for you, and I can only begin to imagine how angry you must be, but I hope you will be merciful. No amount of punishment can undo the damage, and if you try to exact retribution you will only injure yourself. The man is going to lose his job and his reputation. Isn't that punishment enough?" After a few meaningless pleasantries the conversation had clearly come to an end, although we still had yet to say good-bye. Then an odd thing happened to me. I nearly said, *Lock all the doors and windows tonight and let no one in.* I nearly said, *You are in grave danger and must come home.* With these words rising in my throat, I looked across the room at Mr. Clubb and Mr. Cuff, and Mr. Clubb winked at me. I heard myself bidding Marguerite farewell, and then heard her hang up her telephone.

"Well done, sir," said Mr. Clubb. "To aid Mr. Cuff and myself in the preparation of our inventory, can you tell us if you keep certain staples at Green Chimneys?"

"Staples?" I said, thinking he was referring to foodstuffs.

"Rope?" he asked. "Tools, especially pliers, hammers, and screwdrivers? A good saw? A variety of knives? Are there by any chance firearms?"

"No firearms," I said. "I believe all the other items you mention can be found in the house."

"Rope and tool chest in the basement, knives in the kitchen?"

"Yes," I said, "precisely." I had not ordered these barnies to murder my wife, I reminded myself, I had drawn back from that precipice. By the time I went into the executive dining room for my luncheon, I felt sufficiently restored to give Charlie-Charlie that ancient symbol of approval, the thumbs-up sign.

3

When I returned to my office the screen had been set in place, shielding from view the detectives in their preparations but in no way muffling the rumble of comments and laughter they brought to the task. "Gentlemen," I said in a voice loud enough to be heard behind the screen—a most unsuitable affair decorated with a pattern of alternating ocean liners, martini glasses, champagne bottles, and cigarettes—"you must modulate your voices, as I have business to conduct here as well as you." There came a somewhat softer rumble of acquiescence. I took my seat to discover my bottom desk drawer pulled out, the folder absent. Another roar of laughter jerked me once again to my feet.

I came around the side of the screen and stopped short. The table lay concealed beneath drifts and mounds of yellow legal paper covered with lists of words and drawings of stick figures in varying stages of dismemberment. Strewn through the yellow pages were the photographs, loosely divided into those in which either Marguerite or Graham Leeson provided the principal focus. Crude genitalia had been drawn, without reference to either party's actual gender, over and atop both of them. Aghast, I leaned over and began gathering up the defaced photographs. "I must insist . . ." I said. "I really must insist, you know . . ."

Mr. Clubb immobilized my wrist with one hand and extracted the photographs with the other. "We prefer to work in our time-honored fashion," he said. "Our methods may be unusual, but they are ours. But before you take up the afternoon's occupations, sir, can you tell us if items on the handcuff order might be found in the house?"

"No," I said. Mr. Cuff pulled a yellow page before him and wrote *handcuffs*. "Chains?" asked Mr. Clubb.

"No chains," I said, and Mr. Cuff added *chains* to his list.

"That is all for the moment," said Mr. Clubb, and released me.

I took a step backwards and messaged my wrist, which stung as if from rope burn. "You speak of your methods," I said, "and I understand that you have them. But what can be the purpose of defacing my photographs in this grotesque fashion?"

"Sir," said Mr. Clubb in a stern, teacherly voice, "where you speak of defacing, we use the term *enhancement*. Enhancement is a tool we find vital to the method known by the name of Visualization."

I retired defeated to my desk. At five minutes before two, Mrs. Rampage informed me that the Captain and his scion, a thirty-year-old inheritor of a great family fortune named Mr. Chester Montfort d'M____, awaited my pleasure. Putting Mrs. Rampage on hold, I called out, "Please do give me absolute quiet, now. A client is on his way in."

First to appear was the Captain, his tall, rotund form as alert as a pointer's in a grouse field as he led in the taller, inexpressibly languid figure of Mr. Chester Montfort d'M____, a person marked in every inch of his being by great ease, humor, and stupidity. The Captain froze to gape horrified at the screen, but Montfort d'M____ continued round him to shake my hand and say, "Have to tell you, I like that thingamabob over there immensely. Reminds me of a similar thingamabob at the Beeswax Club a few years ago, whole flocks of girls used to come tumbling out. Don't suppose we're in for any unicycles and trumpets today, eh?"

The combination of the raffish screen and our client's unbridled memories brought a dangerous flush to the Captain's face, and I hastened to explain the presence of top-level consultants who preferred to pitch tent on-site, as it were, hence the installation of a screen, all the above in the service of, well, *service*, an all-important quality we . . .

"By Kitchener's mustache," said the Captain. "I remember the Beeswax Club. Don't suppose I'll ever forget the night Little Billy Pegleg jumped up and . . ." The color darkened on his cheeks, and he closed his mouth.

From behind the screen, I heard Mr. Clubb say, "Visualize *this*." Mr. Cuff chuckled.

The Captain recovered himself and turned his sternest glare upon me. "Superb idea, consultants. A white-glove inspection tightens up any ship." His veiled glance toward the screen indicated that he had known of the presence of our "consultants" but, unlike Gilligan, had restrained himself from thrusting into my office until given legitimate reason. "That being the case, is it still quite proper that these people remain while we discuss Mr. Montfort d'M____'s confidential affairs?"

"Quite proper, I assure you," I said. "The consultants and I prefer to work in an atmosphere of complete cooperation. Indeed, this arrangement is a condition of their accepting our firm as their client."

"Indeed," said the Captain.

"Top of the tree, are they?" said Mr. Montfort d'M____. "Except no less of you fellows. Fearful competence. *Terrifying* competence."

Mr. Cuff's voice could be heard saying, "Okay, visualize *this*." Mr. Clubb uttered a high-pitched giggle.

"Enjoy their work," said Mr. Montfort d'M____.

"Shall we?" I gestured to their chairs. As a young man whose assets equaled four or five billion dollars (depending on the condition of the stock market, the value of real estate in half a dozen cities around the world, global warming, forest fires, and the like) our client was a catnip to the ladies, three of whom he had previously married and divorced after siring a child upon each, resulting in a great interlocking complexity of trusts, agreements, and contracts, all of which had to be reexamined on the occasion of his forthcoming wedding to a fourth young woman, named like her predecessors after a semiprecious stone. Due to the perspicacity of the Captain and myself, each new nuptial altered the terms of those previous so as to maintain our client's liability at an unvarying level. Our computers had enabled us to generate the documents well before his arrival, and all Mr. Montfort d'M____ had to do was listen to the revised terms and sign the papers, a task which generally induced a slumberous state except for those moments when a prized asset was in transition.

"Hold on, boys," he said ten minutes into our explanations, "You mean Opal has to give the racehorses to Garnet, and in return she gets the teak plantation from Turquoise, who turns around and gives Opal the ski resort in Aspen? Opal is crazy about those horses, and Turquoise just built a house."

I explained that his second wife could easily afford the purchase of a new stable with the income from the plantation, and his third would keep her new house. He bent to the task of scratching his signature on the form. A roar of laughter erupted behind the screen. The Captain glanced sideways in displeasure, and our client looked at me, blinking. "Now to the secondary trusts," I said. "As you will recall, three years ago—"

My words were cut short by the appearance of a chuckling Mr. Clubb clamping an unlighted cigar in his mouth, a legal pad in his hand, as he came toward us. The Captain and Mr. Montfort d'M____ goggled at him, and Mr. Clubb nodded. "Begging your pardon, sir, but some queries cannot wait. Pickax, sir? Dental floss? Awl?"

"No, yes, no," I said, and then introduced him to the other two men. The Captain appeared stunned, Mr. Montfort d'M____ cheerfully puzzled.

"We would prefer the existence of an attic," said Mr. Clubb.

"An attic exists," I said.

"I must admit my confusion," said the Captain. "Why is a consultant asking about awls and attics? What is dental floss to a consultant?"

"For the nonce, Captain," I said, "these gentlemen and I must communicate in a form of cipher or code, of which these are examples, but soon—"

"Plug your blowhole, Captain," broke in Mr. Clubb. "At the moment you are as useful as wind in an outhouse, always hoping you will excuse my simple way of expressing myself."

Sputtering, the Captain rose to his feet, his face rosier by far than during his involuntary reminiscence of what Little Billy Pegleg had done one night at the Beeswax Club.

"Steady on," I said, fearful of the heights of choler to which indignation could bring my portly, white-haired, but still powerful junior.

"Not on your life," bellowed the Captain. "I cannot brook . . . cannot tolerate . . . If this ill-mannered dwarf imagines excuse is possible after . . ." He raised a fist. Mr. Clubb said, "Pish tosh," and placed a hand on the nape of the Captain's neck. Instantly, the Captain's eyes rolled up, the color drained from his face, and he dropped like a sack into his chair.

"Hole in one," marveled Mr. Montfort d'M____. "World class. Old boy isn't dead, is he?"

The Captain exhaled uncertainly and licked his lips.

"With my apologies for the unpleasantness," said Mr. Clubb, "I have only two more queries at this juncture. Might we locate bedding in the aforesaid attic, and have you an implement such as a match or a lighter?"

"There are several old mattresses and bedframes in the attic," I said, "but as to matches, surely you do not . . ."

Understanding the request better than I, Mr. Montfort d'M____ extended a golden lighter and applied an inch of flame to the tip of Mr. Clubb's cigar. "Didn't think that part was code," he said. "Rules have changed? Smoking allowed?"

"From time to time during the workday my colleague and I prefer to smoke," said Mr. Clubb, expelling a reeking miasma across the desk. I had always found tobacco nauseating in its every form, and in all parts of our building smoking had, of course, long been prohibited.

"Three cheers, my man, plus three more after that," said Mr. Montfort d'M____, extracting a ridged case from an inside pocket, an absurdly phallic cigar from the case. "I prefer to smoke, too, you know, especially during these deadly conferences about who gets the pincushions and who gets the snuffboxes. Believe I'll join you in a corona." He submitted the object to a circumcision, *snick-snick*, and to my horror set it alight. "Ashtray?" I dumped paper clips from a crystal oyster shell and slid it toward him. "Mr. Clubb, is it?, Mr. Clubb, you are a fellow of wonderful accomplishments, still can't get over that marvelous whopbopaloobop on the Captain, and I'd like to ask if we could get together some evening, cigars-and-cognac kind of thing."

"We prefer to undertake one matter at a time," said Mr. Clubb. Mr. Cuff appeared beside the screen. He, too, was lighting up eight or nine inches of brown rope. "However, we welcome your appreciation and would be delighted to swap tales of derring-do at a later date."

"Very, very cool," said Mr. Montfort d'M____, "especially if you could teach me how to do the whopbopaloobop."

"This is a world full of hidden knowledge," Mr. Clubb said. "My partner and I have chosen as our sacred task the transmission of that knowledge."

"Amen," said Mr. Cuff.

Mr. Clubb bowed to my awed client and sauntered off. The Captain shook himself, rubbed his eyes, and took in the client's cigar. "My goodness," he said. "I believe . . . I can't imagine . . . heavens, is smoking permitted again? What a blessing." With that, he fumbled a cigarette from his shirt pocket, accepted a light from Mr. Montfort d'M____, and sucked in the fumes. Until that moment I had not known that the Captain was an addict of nicotine.

For the remainder of the hour a coiling layer of smoke like a low-lying cloud established itself beneath the ceiling and increased in density as it grew toward the floor while we extracted Mr. Montfort d'M____'s careless signature on the transfers and assignments. Now and again the Captain displaced one of a perpetual chain of cigarettes from his mouth to remark upon the peculiar pain in his neck. Finally I was able to send client and junior partner on their way with those words of final benediction, "All is in order, all is in train," freeing me at last to stride about my office flapping a copy of *Institutional Investor* at the cloud, a remedy our fixed windows made more symbolic than actual. The barnies further defeated the effort by wafting ceaseless billows of cigar effluvia over the screen, but as they seemed to be conducting their business in a conventionally businesslike manner I made no objection and retired in defeat to my desk for the preparations necessitated by the arrival in an hour of my next client, Mr. Arthur "This Building Is Condemned" C____; the most cryptic of all the cryptic gentlemen.

So deeply was I immersed in these preparations that only a polite cough and the supplication of "Begging your pardon, sir," brought to my awareness the presence of Mr. Clubb and Mr. Cuff before my desk. "What is it now?" I asked.

"We are, sir, in need of creature comforts," said Mr. Clubb. "Long hours of work have left us exceeding dry in the region of the mouth and throat, and the pressing sensation of thirst has made it impossible for us to maintain the concentration required to do our best."

"Meaning a drink would be greatly appreciated, sir," said Mr. Cuff.

"Of course, of course," I said. "You should have spoken earlier. I'll have Mrs. Rampage bring in a couple of bottles of water. We have San Pellegrino and Evian. Which would you prefer?"

With a smile almost menacing in its intensity, Mr. Cuff said, "We prefer drinks when we drink. *Drink* drinks, if you take my meaning."

"For the sake of the refreshment found in them," said Mr. Clubb, ignoring my obvious dismay. "I speak of refreshment in its every aspect, from relief to the parched tongue, taste to the ready palate, warmth to the inner man, and to the highest of refreshments, that of the mind and soul. We prefer bottles of gin and bourbon, and while any decent gargle would be gratefully received, we have, like all men who partake of grape and grain, our favorite tipples. Mr. Cuff is partial to J. W. Dant bourbon, and I enjoy a glass of Bombay gin. A bucket of ice would not go amiss, and I could say the same for a case of ice-cold Old Bohemia beer. As a chaser."

"You consider it a good idea to consume, alcohol before embarking on"—I sought for the correct phrase—"a mission so delicate?"

"We consider it an essential prelude. Alcohol inspires the mind and awakens the imagination. A fool dulls both by overindulgence, but up to that point, which is a highly individual matter, there is only enhancement. Through history, alcohol has been known for its sacred properties, and the both of us know during the sacrament of Holy Communion, priests and reverends happily serve as bartenders, passing out free drinks to all comers, children included."

"Besides that," I said after a pause, "I suppose you would prefer not to be compelled to quit my employment after we have made such strides together."

"We are on a great journey," he said.

I placed the order with Mrs. Rampage, and fifteen minutes later into my domain entered two ill-dressed youths laden with the requested liquors and a metal bucket in which the necks of beer bottles protruded from a bed of ice. I tipped the louts a dollar apiece, which they accepted with boorish lack of grace. Mrs. Rampage took in this activity with none of the revulsion for the polluted air and spirituous liquids I had anticipated.

The louts slouched away through the door she held open for them; the chuckling barnies disappeared from view with their refreshments; and, after fixing me for a moment of silence, her eyes alight with an expression I had never before observed in them, Mrs. Rampage ventured the amazing opinion that the recent relaxation of formalities should prove beneficial to the firm as a whole and added that, were Mr. Clubb and Mr. Cuff responsible for the reformation, they had already justified their reputation and would assuredly enhance my own.

"You believe so," I said, noting with momentarily delayed satisfaction that the effects of Afternoon Gilligan's indiscretions had already begun to declare themselves.

Employing the tactful verbal formula for *I wish to speak exactly half my mind and no more*, Mrs. Rampage said, "May I be frank, sir?"

"I depend on you to do no less," I said.

Her carriage and face at that moment became what I can only describe as girlish—years seemed to drop away from her. "I don't want to say too much, sir, and I hope you know how much everyone understands what a privilege it is to be a part of this firm." Like the Captain, but more attractively, she blushed. "Honest, I really mean that. Everybody knows that we're one of the two or three companies best at what we do."

"Thank you," I said.

"That's why I feel I can talk like this," said my ever-less-recognizable Mrs. Rampage. "Until today, everybody thought if they acted like themselves, the way they really were, you'd fire them right away. Because, and maybe I shouldn't say this, maybe I'm way out of line, sir, but it's because you always seem, well, so proper you could never forgive a person for not being as dignified as you are. Like the Captain is a heavy smoker and everybody knows it's not supposed to be permitted in this building, but a lot of companies here let their top people smoke in their offices as long as they're discreet because it shows they appreciate those people, and that's nice because it shows if you get to the top you can be appreciated, too, but here the Captain has to go all the way to the elevator and stand outside with the file clerks if he wants a cigarette. And in every other company I know the partners and important clients sometimes have a drink together and nobody thinks they're committing a terrible sin. You're a religious man, sir, we look up to you so much, but I think you're going to find that people will respect you even more once it gets out that you loosened the rules a little bit." She gave me a look in which I read that she feared having spoken too freely. "I just wanted to say that I think you're doing the right thing, sir."

What she was saying, of course, was that I was widely regarded as pompous, remote, and out of touch. "I had not known that my employees regarded me as a religious man," I said.

"Oh, we all do," she said with almost touching earnestness. "Because of the hymns."

"The hymns?"

"The ones you hum to yourself when you're working."

"Do I, indeed? Which ones?"

" 'Jesus Loves Me,' 'The Old Rugged Cross,' 'Abide With Me,' and 'Amazing Grace,' mostly. Sometimes 'Onward, Christian Soldiers.' "

Here, with a vengeance, were Temple Square and Scripture Street! Here was the Youth Bible Study Center, where the child-me had hours on end sung these same hymns during our Sunday school sessions! I did not know what to make of the new knowledge that I hummed them to myself at my desk, but it was some consolation that this unconscious habit had at least partially humanized me to my staff.

"You didn't know you did that? Oh, sir, that's so *cute!*"

Sounds of merriment from the far side of the office rescued Mrs. Rampage from the fear that this time she had truly overstepped the bounds, and she made a rapid exit. I stared after her for a moment, at first unsure how deeply I ought regret a situation in which my secretary found it possible to describe myself and my habits as *cute*, then resolving that it probably was, or eventually would be, all for the best. "All is in order, all is in train," I said to myself. "It only hurts for a little while." With that, I took my seat once more to continue delving into the elaborations of Mr. "This Building Is Condemned" C____'s financial life.

Another clink of bottle against glass and ripple of laughter brought with them the long-delayed recognition that this particular client would never consent to the presence of unknown "consultants." Unless the barnies could be removed for at least an hour, I should face the immediate loss of a substantial portion of my business.

"Fellows," I cried, "come up here now. We must address a most serious problem."

Glasses in hand, cigars nestled into the corners of their mouths, Mr. Clubb and Mr. Cuff sauntered into view. Once I had explained the issue in the most general terms, the detectives readily agreed to absent themselves for the required period. Where might they install themselves? "My bathroom," I said. "It has a small library attached, with a desk, a work table, leather chairs and sofa, a billiard table, a large-screen cable television set, and a bar. Since you have not yet had your luncheon, you may wish to order whatever you like from the kitchen."

Five minutes later, bottles, glasses, hats, and mounds of paper arranged on the bathroom table, the bucket of beer beside it, I exited through the concealed door to the right of my desk as Mr. Clubb ordered up from my doubtless astounded chef a meal of chicken wings french fries, onion rings, and T-bone steaks, medium well. With plenty of time to spare, I immersed myself again in details, only to be brought up short by the recognition that I was humming, none too quietly, that most innocent of hymns, "Jesus Loves Me." And then, precisely at the appointed hour, Mrs. Rampage informed me of the arrival of my client and his associates, and I bade her bring them through.

A sly, slow-moving whale encased in an exquisite double-breasted black pin-stripe, Mr. "This Building Is Condemned" C____ advanced into my office with his customary hauteur and offered me the customary nod of the head while his three "associates" formed a human breakwater in the center of the room. Regal to the core, he affected not to notice Mrs. Rampage sliding a black leather chair out of the middle distance and around the side of the desk until it was in position, at which point he sat himself in it without looking down. Then he inclined his slablike head and raised a small, pallid hand. One of the "associates" promptly moved to open the door for Mrs. Rampage's departure. At this signal, I sat down, and the two remaining henchmen separated themselves by a distance of perhaps eight feet. The third closed the door and stationed himself by his general's right shoulder. These formalities completed, my client shifted his close-set obsidian eyes to mine and said, "You well?"

"Very well, thank you," I replied according to ancient formula. "And you?"

"Good," he said. "But things could still be better." This, too, followed long-established formula, but his next words were a startling deviation. He took in the stationary cloud and the corpse of Montfort d'M____'s cigar rising like a monolith from the reef of cigarette butts in the crystal shell, and, with the first genuine smile I had ever seen on his pockmarked, small-featured face, said, "I can't believe it, but one thing just got better already. You eased up on the stupid no-smoking rule which is poisoning this city, good for you."

"It seemed," I said, "a concrete way in which to demonstrate our appreciation for the smokers among those clients we most respect." When dealing with the cryptic gentlemen, one must not fail to offer intervallic allusions to the spontaneous respect in which they are held.

"Deacon," he said, employing the sobriquet he had given me on our first meeting, "you being one of a kind at your job, the respect you speak of is mutual, and besides that, all surprises should be as pleasant as this." With that, he snapped his fingers at the laden shell, and as he produced a ridged case similar to but more capacious than Mr. Montfort d'M____'s, the man at his shoulder whisked the impromptu ashtray from the desk, deposited its contents in the *pouhelle*, and repositioned it at a point on the desk precisely equidistant from us. My client opened the case to expose the six cylinders contained within, removed one, and proffered the remaining five to me. "Be my guest, Deacon," he said. "Money can't buy better Havanas."

"Your gesture is much appreciated," I said. "However, with all due respect, at the moment I shall choose not to partake."

Distinct as a scar, a vertical crease of displeasure appeared on my client's forehead, and the ridged case and its five inhabitants advanced an inch toward my nose. "Deacon, you want me to smoke alone?" asked Mr. "This Building Is Condemned" C____ "This here, if you were ever lucky enough to find it at your local cigar store, which that lucky believe me you wouldn't be, is absolutely the best of the best, straight from me to you as what you could term a symbol of the cooperation and respect between us, and at the commencement of our business today it would please me greatly if you would do me the honor of joining me in a smoke."

As they say, or, more accurately, as they used to say, needs must when the devil drives, or words to that effect. "Forgive me," I said, and drew one of the fecal things from the case. "I assure you, the honor is all mine."

Mr. "This Building Is Condemned" C____ snipped the rounded end from his cigar, plugged the remainder in the center of his mouth, then subjected mine to the same operation. His henchmen proffered a lighter, Mr. "This Building Is Condemned" C____ bent forward and surrounded himself with clouds of smoke, in the manner of Bela Lugosi materializing before the brides of Dracula. The henchmen moved the flame toward me, and for the first time in my life I inserted into my mouth an object which seemed as large around as the handle of a baseball bat, brought it to the dancing flame, and drew in that burning smoke from which so many other men before me had derived pleasure.

Legend and common sense alike dictated that I should sputter and cough in an attempt to rid myself of the noxious substance. Nausea was in the cards, also dizziness. It is true that I suffered a degree of initial discomfort, as if my tongue had been lightly singed or seared, and the sheer unfamiliarity of the experience—the thickness of the tobacco tube, the texture of the smoke, as dense as chocolate—led me to fear for my well-being. Yet, despite the not altogether unpleasant tingling on the upper surface of my tongue, I expelled my first mouthful of cigar smoke with the sense of having sampled a taste every bit as delightful as the first sip of a properly made martini. The thug whisked away the flame, and I drew in another mouthful, leaned back, and released a wondrous quantity of smoke. Of a surprising smoothness, in some sense almost cool rather than hot, the delightful taste defined itself as heather, loam, morel mushrooms, venison, and some distinctive spice akin to coriander. I repeated the process, with results even more pleasurable—this time I tasted a hint of black butter sauce. "I can truthfully say," I told my client, "that never have I met a cigar as fine as this one."

"You bet you haven't," said Mr. "This Building Is Condemned" C____, and on the spot presented me with three more of the precious objects. With that, we turned to the tidal waves of cash and the interlocking corporate shells, each protecting another series of interconnected shells which concealed yet another, like Chinese boxes.

The cryptic gentlemen one and all appreciated certain ceremonies, such as the appearance of espresso coffee in thimble-sized porcelain cups and an accompanying assortment of *biscotti* at the halfway point of our meditations. Matters of business being forbidden while coffee and cookies were dispatched, the conversation generally turned to the conundrums posed by family life. Since I had no family to speak of, and, like most of his kind, Mr. "This Building Is Condemned" C____ was richly endowed with grandparents, parents, uncles, aunts, sons, daughters, nephews, nieces, and grandchildren, these remarks on the genealogical tapestry tended to be monologuic in nature, my role in them limited to nods and grunts. Required as they were more often by the business of the cryptic gentlemen than was the case in other trades or professions, funerals were another ongoing topic. Taking tiny sips of his espresso and equally maidenish nibbles from his favorite sweetmeats (Hydrox and Milano), my client favored me with the expected praises of his son, Arthur junior (Harvard graduate school, English Lit.), lamentations over his daughter, Fidelia (thrice married, never wisely), hymns to his grandchildren (Cyrus, Thor, and Hermione, respectively, the genius, the dreamer, and the despot), and then proceeded to link his two unfailing themes by recalling the unhappy behavior of Arthur junior at the funeral of my client's uncle and a principal figure in his family's rise to an imperial eminence, Mr. Vincente "Waffles" C____.

The anecdote called for the beheading and ignition of another magnificent stogie, and I greedily followed suit.

"Arthur junior's got his head screwed on right, and he's got the right kinda family values," said my client. "Straight A's all through school, married a stand-up dame with money of her own, three great kids, makes a man proud. Hard worker. Got his head in a book morning to night, human-encyclopedia-type guy, up there at Harvard, those professors, they love him. Kid knows how you're supposed to act, right?"

I nodded and filled my mouth with another fragrant draft.

"So he comes to my uncle Vincente's funeral all by himself, which troubles me. On top of it doesn't show the proper respect to old Waffles, who was one hell of a man, there's guys still pissing blood on account of they looked at him wrong forty years ago, on top a that, I don't have the good feeling I get from taking his family around to my friends and associates and saying, so look here, this here is Arthur junior, my Harvard guy, plus his wife, Hunter, whose ancestors I think got here even before that rabble on the *Mayflower*, plus his three kids— Cyrus, little bastard's even smarter than his dad, Thor, the one's got his head in the clouds, which is okay because we need people like that, too, and Hermione, who you can tell just by looking at her she's mean as a snake and is gonna wind up running the world someday. So I say, Arthur junior, what the hell happened, everybody else get killed in a train wreck or something? He says, No, Dad, they just didn't wanna come, these big family funerals, they make 'em feel funny, they don't like having their pictures taken so they show up on the six o'clock news. Didn't wanna come, I say back, what kinda shit is that, you shoulda made 'em come, and if anyone took their pictures when they didn't want, we can take care of that, no trouble at all. I go on like this, I even say, what good is Harvard and all those books if they don't make you any smarter than this, and finally Arthur junior's mother tells me, Put a cork in it, you're not exactly helping the situation here.

"So what happens then? Insteada being smart like I should, I go nuts on account of I'm the guy who pays the bills, that Harvard up there pulls in the money better than any casino I ever saw, and you want to find a real good criminal, get some Boston WASP in a bow tie, and all of a sudden nobody listens to me! I'm seeing red in a big way here, Deacon, this is my uncle Vincente's funeral, and insteada backing me up his mother is telling me I'm not *helping*. I yell, You want to help? Then go up there and bring back his wife and kids, or I'll send Carlo and Tommy to do it. All of a sudden I'm so mad I'm thinking these people are insulting me, how can they think they can get away with that, people who insult me don't do it twice—and then I hear what I'm thinking, and I do what she said and put a cork in it, but it's too late, I went way over the top and we all know it.

"Arthur junior takes off, and his mother won't talk to me for the whole rest of the day. Only thing I'm happy about is I didn't blow up where anyone else could see it. Deacon, I know you're the type guy wouldn't dream of threatening his family, but if the time ever comes, do yourself a favor and light up a Havana instead."

"I'm sure that is excellent advice," I said.

"Don't let the thought cross your mind. Anyhow, you know what they say, it only hurts for a little while, which is true as far as it goes, and I calmed down. Uncle Vincente's funeral was beautiful. You woulda thought the pope died. When the people are going out to the limousines, Arthur junior is sitting in a chair at the back of the church reading a book. Put that in your pocket, I say, wanta do homework, do it in the car. He tells me it isn't homework, but he puts it in his pocket and we go out to the cemetery. His mother looks out the window the whole time we're driving to the cemetery, and the kid starts reading again. So I ask what the hell is it, this book he can't put down? He tells me, but it's like he's speaking some foreign language, only word I understand is *the* which happens a lot when your kid reads a lot of fancy books, half the titles make no sense to an ordinary person. Okay, we're out there in Queens, goddamn graveyard the size of Newark, FBI and reporters all over the place, and I'm thinking maybe Arthur junior wasn't wrong after all, Hunter probably hates having the FBI take her picture, and besides that little Hermione probably woulda mugged one of 'em and stole his wallet. So I tell Arthur junior I'm sorry about what happened. I didn't really think you were going to put me in the same grave as Uncle Waffles, he says, the Harvard smartass. When it's all over, we get back in the car, and out comes the book again. We get home, and he disappears. We have a lot of people over, food, wine, politicians, old-timers from Brownsville, Chicago people, Detroit people, L.A. people, movie directors, cops, actors I never heard of, priests, bishops, the guy from the Cardinal. Everybody's asking me, Where's Arthur junior? I go upstairs to find out. He's in his old room, and he's still reading that book. I say, Arthur junior, people are asking about you, I think it would be nice if you mingled with our guests. I'll be right down, he says, I just finished what I was reading. Here, take a look, you might enjoy it. He gives me the book and goes out of the room. So I'm wondering—what the hell *is* this, anyhow? I take it to the bedroom, toss it on the table. About ten-thirty, eleven, that night, everybody's gone, kid's on the shuttle back to Boston, house is cleaned up, enough food in the refrigerator to feed the whole bunch all over again, I go up to bed. Arthur junior's mother still isn't talking to me, so I get in and pick up the book. Herman Melville is the name of the guy, and I see that the story the kid was reading is called 'Bartleby the Scrivener.' So I decide I'll try it. What the hell, right? You're an educated guy, you ever read that story?"

"A long time ago," I said. "A bit . . . *odd,* isn't it?"

"Odd? That's the most terrible story I ever read in my whole life! This dud gets a job in a law office and decides he doesn't want to work. Does he get fired? He does not. This is a story? You hire a guy who won't do the job, what do you do, pamper the asshole? At the end, the dud ups and disappears and you find out he used to work in the dead letter office. Is there a point here? The next day I call up Arthur junior, say, could he explain to me please what the hell that story is supposed to mean? Dad, he says, it means what it says. Deacon, I just about pulled the plug on Harvard right then and there. I never went to any college, but I do know that nothing means what it says, not on this planet."

This reflection was accurate when applied to the documents on my desk, for each had been encoded in a systematic fashion which rendered their literal contents deliberately misleading. Another code had informed both of my recent conversations with Marguerite. "Fiction is best left to real life," I said.

"Someone shoulda told that to Herman Melville," said Mr. Arthur "This Building Is Condemned" C____.

Mrs. Rampage buzzed me to advise that I was running behind schedule and inquire about removing the coffee things. I invited her to gather up the debris. A door behind me opened, and I assumed that my secretary had responded to my request with an alacrity remarkable even in her. The first sign of my error was the behavior of the three other men in the room, until this moment no more animated than marble statues. The thug at my client's side stepped forward to stand behind me, and his fellows moved to the front of my desk. "What the hell is this shit?" said the client, because of the man in front of him unable to see Mr. Clubb and Mr. Cuff. Holding a pad bearing one of his many lists, Mr. Clubb gazed in mild surprise at the giants flanking my desk and said, "I apologize for the intrusion, sir, but our understanding was that your appointment would be over in an hour, and by my simple way of reckoning you should be free to answer a query as to steam irons."

"What the hell *is* this shit?" said my client, repeating his original question with a slight tonal variation expressive of gathering dismay.

I attempted to salvage matters by saying, "Please allow me to explain the interruption. I have employed these men as consultants, and as they prefer to work in my office, a condition I, of course, could not permit during our business meeting, I temporarily relocated them in my washroom, outfitted with a library adequate to their needs."

"Fit for a king, in my opinion," said Mr. Clubb.

At that moment the other door into my office, to the left of my desk, opened to admit Mrs. Rampage, and my client's guardians inserted their hands into their suit jackets and separated with the speed and precision of a dance team.

"Oh, my," said Mrs. Rampage. "*Excuse* me. Should I come back later?"

"Not on your life, my darling," said Mr. Clubb. "Temporary misunderstanding of the false-alarm sort. Please allow us to enjoy the delightful spectacle of your feminine charms."

Before my wondering eyes, Mrs. Rampage curtseyed and hastened to my desk to gather up the wreckage.

I looked toward my client and observed a detail of striking peculiarity, that although his half-consumed cigar remained between his lips, four inches of cylindrical ash had deposited a gray smear on his necktie before coming to rest on the shelf of his belly. He was staring straight ahead with eyes grown to the size of quarters. His face had become the color of raw pie crust.

Mr. Clubb said, "Respectful greetings, sir."

The client gargled and turned upon me a look of unvarnished horror.

Mr. Clubb said, "Apologies to all." Mrs. Rampage had already bolted. From unseen regions came the sound of a closing door.

Mr. "This Building Is Condemned" C____ blinked twice, bringing his eyes to something like their normal dimensions. With an uncertain hand but gently, as if it were a tiny but much-loved baby, he placed his cigar in the crystal shell. He cleared his throat; he looked at the ceiling. "Deacon," he said, gazing upward. "Gotta run. My next appointment musta slipped my mind. What happens when you start to gab. I'll be in touch about this stuff." He stood, dislodging the ashen cylinder to the carpet, and motioned his gangsters to the outer office.

4

Of course at the earliest opportunity I interrogated both of my detectives about this turn of events, and while they moved their mountains of paper, bottles, buckets, glasses, hand-drawn maps, and other impedimenta back behind the screen, I continued the questioning. No, they averred, the gentleman at my desk was not a gentleman whom previously they had been privileged to look upon, acquaint themselves with, or encounter in any way whatsoever. They had never been employed in any capacity by the gentleman. Mr. Clubb observed that the unknown gentleman had been wearing a conspicuously handsome and well-tailored suit.

"That is his custom," I said.

"And I believe he smokes, sir, a noble high order of cigar," said Mr. Clubb with a glance at my breast pocket. "Which would be the sort of item unfairly beyond the dreams of honest laborers such as ourselves."

"I trust that you will permit me," I said with a sigh, "to offer you the pleasure of two of the same." No sooner had the offer been accepted, the barnies back behind their screen, than I buzzed Mrs. Rampage with the request to summon by instant delivery from the most distinguished cigar merchant in the city a box of his finest. "Good for you, boss!" whooped the new Mrs. Rampage.

I spent the remainder of the afternoon brooding upon the reaction of Mr. Arthur "This Building Is Condemned" C____ to my "consultants." I could not but imagine that his hasty departure boded ill for our relationship. I had seen terror on his face, and he knew that I knew what I had seen. An understanding of this sort is fatal to that nuance-play critical alike to high-level churchmen and their outlaw counterparts, and I had to confront the possibility that my client's departure had been of a permanent nature. Where Mr. "This Building Is Condemned" C____ went, his colleagues of lesser rank, Mr. Tommy "I Believe in Rainbows" B____, Mr. Anthony "Moonlight Becomes You" M____, Mr. Bobby "Total Eclipse" G____, and their fellow archbishops, cardinals, and papal nuncios would assuredly follow. Before the close of the day, I would send a comforting fax informing Mr. "This Building Is Condemned" C____ that the consultants had been summarily released from employment. I would be telling only a "white" or provisional untruth, for Mr. Clubb and Mr. Cuff's task would surely be completed long before my client's return. All was in order, all was in train and, as if to put the seal upon the matter, Mrs. Rampage buzzed to inquire if she might come through with the box of cigars. Speaking in a breathy timbre I had never before heard from anyone save Marguerite in the earliest, most blissful days of our marriage, Mrs. Rampage added that she had some surprises for me too. "By this point," I said, "I expect no less." Mrs. Rampage *giggled*.

The surprises, in the event, were of a satisfying practicality. The good woman had wisely sought the advice of Mr. Montfort d'M____, who, after recommending a suitably aristocratic cigar emporium and a favorite cigar, had purchased for me a rosewood humidor, a double-bladed cigar cutter, and a lighter of antique design. As soon as Mrs. Rampage had been instructed to compose a note of gratitude embellished in whatever fashion she saw fit, I arrayed all but one of the cigars in the humidor, decapitated that one, and set it alight. Beneath a faint touch of fruitiness like the aroma of a blossoming pear tree, I met in successive layers the tastes of black olives, aged Gouda cheese, pine needles, new leather, miso soup, either sorghum or brown sugar, burning peat, library paste, and myrtle leaves. The long finish intriguingly combined Bible paper and sunflower seeds. Mr. Montfort d'M____ had chosen well, though I regretted the absence of black butter sauce.

Feeling comradely, I strolled across my office towards the merriment emanating from the far side of the screen. A superior cigar, even if devoid of black butter sauce, should be complemented by a worthy liquor, and in the light of what was to transpire during the evening I considered a snifter of Mr. Clubb's Bombay gin not inappropriate. "Fellows," I said, tactfully announcing my presence, "are preparations nearly completed?"

"That, sir, they are," said one or another of the pair.

"Welcome news," I said, and stepped around the screen. "But I must be assured—"

I had expected disorder, but nothing approaching the chaos before me. It was as if the detritus of New York City's half-dozen filthiest living quarters had been scooped up, shaken, and dumped into my office. Heaps of ash, bottles, shoals of papers, books with stained covers and broken spines, battered furniture, broken glass, refuse I could not identify, refuse I could not even *see* undulated from the base of the screen, around and over the table, heaping itself into landfill-like piles here and there, and washed against the plate-glass windows. A jagged five-foot opening gaped in a smashed pane. Their derbies perched on their heads, islanded in their chairs, Mr. Clubb and Mr. Cuff leaned back, feet up on what must have been the table.

"You'll join us in a drink, sir," said Mr. Clubb, "by the way of wishing us success and adding to the pleasure of that handsome smoke." He extended a stout leg and kicked rubble from a chair. I sat down. Mr. Clubb plucked an unclean glass from the morass and filled it with Dutch gin or genever from one of the minaret-shaped stone flagons I had observed upon my infrequent layovers in Amsterdam, the Netherlands. Mrs. Rampage had been variously employed during the barnies' sequestration. Then I wondered if Mrs. Rampage might not have shown signs of intoxication during our last encounter.

"I thought you drank Bombay," I said.

"Variety is, as they say, life's condiment," said Mr. Clubb, and handed me the glass.

I said, "You have made yourselves quite at home."

"I thank you for your restraint," said Mr. Clubb. "In which sentiment my partner agrees, am I correct, Mr. Cuff?"

"Entirely," said Mr. Cuff. "But I wager you a C-note to a see-gar that a word or two of reassurance is in order."

"How right that man is," said Mr. Clubb. "He has a genius for the truth I have never known to fail him. Sir, you enter our work space to come upon the slovenly, the careless, the unseemly, and your response, which we comprehend in every particular, is to recoil. My wish is that you take a moment to remember these two essentials: one, we have, as aforesaid, our methods which are ours alone, and two, having appeared fresh on the scene, you see it worse than it is. By morning tomorrow, the cleaning staff shall have done its work."

"I suppose you have been Visualizing," I said, and quaffed genever.

"Mr. Cuff and I," he said, "prefer to minimize the risk of accidents, surprises, and such by the method of rehearsing our, as you might say, performances. These poor sticks, sir, are easily replaced, but our work, once under way, demands completion and cannot be duplicated, redone, or undone."

I recalled the all-important guarantee. "I remember your words," I said, "and

I must be assured that you remember mine. I did not request termination. During the course of the day my feelings on the matter have intensified. Termination, if by that term you meant—"

"Termination is termination," said Mr. Clubb.

"Extermination," I said. "Cessation of life due to external forces. It is not my wish, it is unacceptable, and I have even been thinking that I overstated the degree of physical punishment appropriate in this matter."

" 'Appropriate?' " said Mr. Clubb. "When it comes to desire, *appropriate* is a concept without meaning. In the sacred realm of desire, *appropriate*, being meaningless, does not exist. We speak of your inmost wishes, sir, and desire is an extremely *thingy* sort of thing."

I looked at the hole in the window, the broken bits of furniture and ruined books. "I think," I said, "that permanent injury is all I wish. Something on the order of blindness or the loss of a hand."

Mr. Clubb favored me with a glance of humorous irony. "It goes, sir, as it goes, which brings to mind that we have but an hour more, a period of time to be splendidly improved by a superior Double Corona such as the fine example in your hand."

"Forgive me," I said. "And might I then request . . . ?" I extended the nearly empty glass, and Mr. Clubb refilled it. Each received a cigar, and I lingered at my desk for the required term, sipping genever and pretending to work until I heard sounds of movement. Mr. Clubb and Mr. Cuff approached. "So you are off," I said.

"It is, sir, to be a long and busy night," said Mr. Clubb. "If you take my meaning."

With a sigh I opened the humidor. They reached in, snatched a handful of cigars apiece, and deployed them into various pockets. "Details at eleven," said Mr. Clubb.

A few seconds after their departure, Mrs. Rampage informed me that she would be bringing through a fax communication just received.

The fax had been sent me by Chartwell, Munster, and Stout, a legal firm with but a single client, Mr. Arthur "This Building Is Condemned" C____. Chartwell, Munster, and Stout regretted the necessity to inform me that their client wished to seek advice other than my own in his financial affairs. A sheaf of documents binding me to silence as to all matters concerning the client would arrive for my signature the following day. All records, papers, computer discs, and other data were to be referred posthaste to their offices. I had forgotten to send my intended note of client-saving reassurance.

5

What an abyss of shame I must now describe, at every turn what humiliation. It was at most five minutes past six P.M. when I learned of the desertion of my most valuable client, a turn of events certain to lead to the loss of his cryptic fellows and some forty percent of our annual business. Gloomily I consumed my glass of Dutch gin without noticing that I had already far exceeded my tolerance. I ventured behind the screen and succeeded in unearthing another stone flagon, poured another measure, and gulped it down while attempting to demonstrate numerically that (a) the anticipated drop in annual profit could not be as severe as feared, and (b) if it were, the business could continue as before, without reductions in salary, staff, and benefits. Despite ingenious feats of juggling, the numbers denied (a) and mocked (b), suggesting that I should be fortunate to retain, not lose, forty percent of present business. I lowered my head to the desk and tried to regulate my breathing. When I heard myself rendering an off-key version of "Abide With Me," I acknowledged that it was time to go home, got to my feet, and made the unfortunate decision to exit through the general offices on the theory that a survey of my presumably empty realm might suggest the sites of pending amputations.

I tucked the flagon under my elbow, pocketed the five or six cigars remaining in the humidor, and passed through Mrs. Rampage's chamber. Hearing the abrasive music of the cleaners' radios, I moved with exaggerated care down the corridor, darkened but for the light spilling from an open door thirty feet before me. Now and again, finding myself unable to avoid striking my shoulder against the wall, I took a medicinal swallow of genever. I drew up to the open door and realized that I had come to Gilligan's quarters. The abrasive music emanated from his sound system. *We'll get rid of that, for starters,* I said to myself, and straightened up for a dignified navigation past his doorway. At the crucial moment I glanced within to observe my jacketless junior partner sprawled, tie undone, on his sofa beside a scrawny ruffian with a quiff of lime-green hair and attired for some reason in a skintight costume involving zebra stripes and many chains and zippers. Disreputable creatures male and female occupied themselves in the background. Gilligan shifted his head, began to smile, and at the sight of me turned to stone.

"Calm down, Gilligan," I said, striving for an impression of sober paternal authority. I had recalled that my junior had scheduled a late appointment with his most successful musician, a singer whose band sold millions of records year in and year out despite the absurdity of their name, the Dog Turds or the Rectal Valves, something of that sort. My calculations had indicated that Gilligan's client, whose name I recalled as Cyril Futch, would soon become crucial to the maintenance of my firm, and as the beaky little rooster coldly took me in I thought to impress upon him the regard in which he was held by his chosen financial planning institution. "There is, I assure you, no need for alarm, no, certainly not, and in fact, Gilligan, you know, I should be honored to seize this opportunity of making the acquaintance of your guest, whom it is our pleasure to assist and advise and whatever."

Gilligan reverted to flesh and blood during the course of this utterance, which I delivered gravely, taking care to enunciate each syllable clearly in spite of the difficulty I was having with my tongue. He noted the bottle nestled into my elbow and the lighted cigar in the fingers of my right hand, a matter of which until that moment I had been imperfectly aware. "Hey, I guess the smoking lamp is lit," I said. "Stupid rule anyhow. How about a little drink on the boss?"

Gilligan lurched to his feet and came reeling toward me.

All that followed is a montage of discontinuous imagery. I recall Cyril Futch propping me up as I communicated our devotion to the safeguarding of his wealth, also his dogged insistence that his name was actually Simon Gulch or Sidney Much or something similar before he sent me toppling onto the sofa; I see an odd little fellow with a tattooed head and a name like Pus (there was a person named

Pus in attendance, though he may not have been the one) accepting one of my cigars and eating it; I remember inhaling from smirking Gilligan's cigarette and drinking from a bottle with a small white worm lying dead at its bottom and snuffling up a white powder recommended by a female Turd or Valve; I remember singing "The Old Rugged Cross" in a state of partial undress. I told a face brilliantly lacquered with makeup that I was "getting a feel" for "this music." A female Turd or Valve, not the one who had recommended the powder but one in a permanent state of hilarity I found endearing, assisted me into my limousine and on the homeward journey experimented with its many buttons and controls. Atop the town-house steps, she removed the key from my fumbling hand gleefully to insert it into the lock. The rest is welcome darkness.

<h1 style="text-align:center">6</h1>

A form of consciousness returned with a slap to my face, the muffled screams of the woman beside me, a bowler-hatted head thrusting into view and growling, "The shower for you, you damned idiot." As a second assailant whisked her away, the woman, whom I thought to be Marguerite, wailed. I struggled against the man gripping my shoulders, and he squeezed the nape of my neck.

When next I opened my eyes, I was naked and quivering beneath an onslaught of cold water within the marble confines of my shower cabinet. Charlie-Charlie Rackett leaned against the open door of the cabinet and regarded me with ill-disguised impatience. "I'm freezing, Charlie-Charlie," I said. "Turn off the water."

Charlie-Charlie thrust an arm into the cabinet and became Mr. Clubb. "I'll warm it up, but I want you sober," he said. I drew myself up into a ball.

Then I was on my feet and moaning while I massaged my forehead. "Bath time all done now," called Mr. Clubb. "Turn off the wa-wa." I did as instructed. The door opened, and a bath towel unfurled over my left shoulder.

Side by side on the bedroom sofa dimly illuminated by the lamp, Mr. Clubb and Mr. Cuff observed my progress toward the bed. A black leather satchel stood on the floor between them. "Gentlemen," I said, "although I cannot presently find words to account for the condition in which you found me, I trust that your good nature will enable you to overlook . . . or ignore . . . whatever it was that I must have done . . . I cannot quite recall the circumstances."

"The young woman has been sent away," said Mr. Clubb, "and you need never fear any trouble from that direction, sir."

"The young woman?" I asked, and remembered a hyperactive figure playing with the controls in the back of the limousine. This opened up a fragmentary memory of the scene in Gilligan's office, and I moaned aloud.

"None too clean, but pretty enough in a ragamuffin way," said Mr. Clubb. "The type denied a proper education in social graces. Rough about the edges. Intemperate in language. A stranger to discipline."

I groaned—to have introduced such a creature to my house!

"A stranger to honesty, too, sir, if you'll permit me," said Mr. Cuff. "It's addiction turns them into thieves. Give them half a chance, they'll steal the brass handles off their mother's coffins."

"Addiction?" I said. "Addiction to what?"

"Everything, from the look of the bint," said Mr. Cuff. "Before Mr. Clubb and I sent her on her way, we retrieved these items doubtless belonging to you, sir." While walking toward me he removed from his pockets the following articles: my wristwatch, gold cuff links, wallet, the lighter of antique design given me by Mr. Montfort d'M____, likewise the cigar cutter, and the last of the cigars I had purchased that day. "I thank you most gratefully," I said, slipping the watch on my wrist and all else save the cigar into the pockets of my robe. It was, I noted, just past four o'clock in the morning. The cigar I handed back to him with the words "Please accept this as a token of my gratitude."

"Gratefully accepted," he said. Mr. Cuff bit off the end, spat it onto the carpet, and set the cigar alight, producing a nauseating quantity of fumes.

"Perhaps," I said, "we might postpone our discussion until I have had time to recover from my ill-advised behavior. Let us reconvene at . . ." A short period was spent pressing my hands to my eyes while rocking back and forth. "Four this afternoon?"

"Everything in its own time is a principle we hold dear," said Mr. Clubb. "And this is the time for you to down aspirin and Alka-Seltzer, and for your loyal assistants to relish the hearty breakfasts the thought of which sets our stomachs to growling. A man of stature and accomplishment like yourself ought to be able to overcome the effects of too much booze and attend to business, on top of the simple matter of getting his flunkies out of bed so they can whip up the bacon and eggs."

"Because a man such as that, sir, keeps ever in mind that business faces the task at hand, no matter how lousy it may be," said Mr. Cuff.

"The old world is in flames," said Mr. Clubb, "and the new one is just being born. Pick up the phone."

"All right," I said, "but Mr. Moncrieff is going to *hate* this. He worked for the duke of Denbigh, and he's a terrible snob."

"All butlers are snobs," said Mr. Clubb. "Three fried eggs apiece, likewise six rashers of bacon, home fries, toast, hot coffee, and for the sake of digestion a bottle of your best cognac."

Mr. Moncrieff picked up his telephone, listened to my orders, and informed me in a small, cold voice that he would speak to the cook. "Would this repast be for the young lady and yourself, sir?" he asked.

With a wave of guilty shame which intensified my nausea, I realized that Mr. Moncrieff had observed my unsuitable young companion accompanying me upstairs to the bedroom. "No, it would not," I said. "The young lady, a client of mine, was kind enough to assist me when I was taken ill. The meal is for two meal guests." Unwelcome memory returned the spectacle of a scrawny girl pulling my ears and screeching that a useless old fart like me didn't deserve her band's business.

"The phone," said Mr. Clubb. Dazedly I extended the receiver.

"Moncrieff, old man," he said, "amazing good luck, running into you again. Do you remember that trouble the duke had with Colonel Fletcher and the diary? . . . Yes, this is Mr. Clubb, and it's delightful to hear your voice again. . . . He's here, too, couldn't do anything without him. . . . I'll tell him. . . . Much the way things went with the duke, yes, and we'll need the usual supplies. . . . Glad to hear it. . . . The dining room in half an hour." He handed the telephone back to me and said to Mr. Cuff, "He's looking forward to the pinochle, and there's a first-rate Pétrus in the cellar he knows you're going to enjoy."

I had purchased six cases of 1928 Château Pétrus at an auction some years before and was holding it while its already immense value doubled, then tripled, until perhaps a decade hence, when I would sell it for ten times its original cost.

"A good drop of wine sets a man right up," said Mr. Cuff. "Stuff was meant to be drunk, wasn't it?"

"You know Mr. Moncrieff?" I asked. "You worked for the duke?"

"We ply our humble trade irrespective of nationality and borders," said Mr. Clubb. "Go where we are needed, is our motto. We have fond memories of the good old duke, who showed himself to be quite a fun-loving, spirited fellow, sir, once you got past the crust, as it were. Generous too."

"He gave until it hurt," said Mr. Cuff. "The old gentleman cried like a baby when we left."

"Cried a good deal before that too," said Mr. Clubb. "In our experience, high-spirited fellows spend a deal more tears than your gloomy customers."

"I do not suppose you shall see any tears from me," I said. The brief look which passed between them reminded me of the complicitous glance I had once seen fly like a live spark between two of their New Covenant forebears, one gripping the hind legs of a pig, the other its front legs and a knife, in the moment before the knife opened the pig's throat and an arc of blood threw itself high into the air. "I shall heed your advice," I said, "and locate my analgesics." I got on my feet and moved slowly to the bathroom. "As a matter of curiosity," I said, "might I ask if you have classified me into the high-spirited category, or into the other?"

"You are a man of middling spirit," said Mr. Clubb. I opened my mouth to protest, and he went on. "But something may be made of you yet."

I disappeared into the bathroom. *I have endured these moon-faced yokels long enough*, I told myself, *hear their story, feed the bastards, then kick them out.*

In a condition more nearly approaching my usual self, I brushed my teeth and splashed water on my face before returning to the bedroom. I placed myself with a reasonable degree of executive command in a wing chair, folded my pinstriped robe about me, inserted my feet into velvet slippers, and said, "Things got a bit out of hand, and I thank you for dealing with my young client, a person with whom, in spite of appearances, I have a professional relationship only. Now we may turn to our real business. I trust you found my wife and Leeson at Green Chimneys. Please give me an account of what followed. I await your report."

"Things got a bit out of hand," said Mr. Clubb. "Which is a way of describing something that can happen to us all, and for which no one can be blamed. Especially Mr. Cuff and myself, who are always careful to say right smack at the beginning, as we did with you, sir, what ought to be so obvious as not need saying at all, that our work brings about permanent changes which can never be undone. Especially in the cases when we specify a time to make our initial report and the client disappoints us at the said time. When we are let down by our client, we must go forward and complete the job to our highest standards with no rancor or ill-will, knowing that there are many reasonable explanations of a man's inability to get to a telephone."

"I don't know what you mean by this self-serving double-talk," I said. "We had no arrangement of that sort, and your effrontery forces me to conclude that you failed in your task."

Mr. Clubb gave me the grimmest possible suggestion of a smile. "One of the reasons for a man's failure to get to a telephone is a lapse of memory. You have forgotten my informing you that I would give you my initial report at eleven. At precisely eleven o'clock I called, to no avail. I waited through twenty rings, sir, before I abandoned the effort. If I had waited through a hundred, sir, the result would have been the same, on account of your decision to put yourself into a state where you would have had trouble remembering your own name."

"That is a blatant lie," I said, then remembered. The fellow had in fact mentioned in passing something about reporting to me at that hour, which must have been approximately the time when I was regaling the Turds or Valves with "The Old Rugged Cross." My face grew pink. "Forgive me," I said. "I am in error, it is just as you say."

"A manly admission, sir, but as for forgiveness, we extended that quantity from the git-go," said Mr. Clubb. "We are your servants, and your wishes are our sacred charge."

"That's the whole ball of wax in a nutshell," said Mr. Cuff, giving a fond glance to the final inch of his cigar. He dropped the stub onto my carpet and ground it beneath his shoe. "Food and drink to the fibers, sir," he said.

"Speaking of which," said Mr. Clubb. "We will continue our report in the dining room, so as to dig into the feast ordered up by that wondrous villain, Reggie Moncrieff."

Until that moment I believe that it had never quite occurred to me that my butler possessed, like other men, a Christian name.

7

"A great design directs us," said Mr. Clubb, expelling morsels of his cud. "We poor wanderers, you and me and Mr. Cuff and the milkman, too, only see the little portion right in front of us. Half the time we don't even see that in the right way. For sure we don't have a Chinaman's chance of understanding it. But the design is ever present, sir, a truth I bring to your attention for the sake of the comfort in it. Toast, Mr. Cuff."

"Comfort is a matter cherished by all parts of a man," said Mr. Cuff, handing his partner the rack of toasted bread. "Most particularly that part known as his soul, which feeds upon the nutrient adversity."

I was seated at the head of the table and flanked by Mr. Clubb and Mr. Cuff. The salvers and tureens before us overflowed, for Mr. Moncrieff, who after embracing each barnie in turn and then entering into a kind of conference or huddle, had summoned from the kitchen a meal far surpassing their requests. Besides several dozen eggs and perhaps two packages of bacon, he had arranged a mixed grill of kidneys, lamb's livers and lamb chops, and strip steaks, as well as vats of oatmeal and a pasty concoction he described as "kedgeree—as the old duke fancied it."

Sickened by the odors of the food, also by the mush visible in my companions' mouths, I tried once more to extract their report. "I don't believe in the grand design," I said, "and I already face more adversity than my soul could find useful. Tell me what happened at the house."

"No mere house, sir," said Mr. Clubb. "Even as we approached along _____ Lane, Mr. Cuff and I could not fail to respond to its magnificence."

"Were my drawings of use?" I asked.

"They were invaluable." Mr. Cuff speared a lamb chop and raised it to his mouth. "We proceeded through the rear door into your spacious kitchen or scullery. Wherein we observed evidence of two persons having enjoyed a dinner enhanced by a fine wine and finished with a noble champagne."

"Aha," I said.

"By means of your guidance, Mr. Cuff and I located the lovely staircase and made our way to the lady's chamber. We effected an entry of the most praiseworthy silence, if I may say so."

"That entry was worth a medal," said Mr. Cuff.

"Two figures lay slumbering upon the bed. In a blamelessly professional manner we approached, Mr. Cuff on one side, I on the other. In the fashion your client of this morning called the whopbopaloobop, we rendered the parties in question even more unconscious than previous, thereby giving ourselves a good fifteen minutes for the disposition of instruments. We take pride in being careful workers, sir, and like all honest craftsmen we respect our tools. We bound and gagged both parties in timely fashion. Is the male party distinguished by an athletic past?" Suddenly alight with barnieish glee, Mr. Clubb raised his eyebrows and washed down the last of his chop with a mouthful of cognac.

"Not to my knowledge," I said. "I believe he plays a little racquetball and squash, that kind of thing."

He and Mr. Cuff experienced a moment of mirth. "More like weight lifting or football, is my guess," he said. "Strength and stamina. To a remarkable degree."

"Not to mention considerable speed," said Mr. Cuff with the air of one indulging a tender reminisence.

"Are you telling me that he got away?" I asked.

"No one gets away," said Mr. Clubb. "That, sir, is Gospel. But you may imagine our surprise when for the first time in the history of our *consultancy*"—and here he chuckled—"a gentleman of the civilian persuasion managed to break his bonds and free himself of his ropes whilst Mr. Cuff and I were engaged in the preliminaries."

"Naked as jaybirds," said Mr. Cuff, wiping with a greasy hand a tear of amusement from one eye. "Bare as newborn lambie-pies. There I was, heating up the steam iron I'd just fetched from the kitchen, sir, along with a selection of knives I came across in exactly the spot you described, most grateful I was, too, squatting on my haunches without a care in the world and feeling the first merry tingle of excitement in my little soldier—"

"What?" I said. "You were naked? And what's this about your little soldier?"

"Hush," said Mr. Clubb, his eyes glittering. "Nakedness is a precaution against fouling our clothing with blood and other bodily products, and men like Mr. Cuff and myself take pleasure in the exercise of our skills. In us, the inner and the outer man are one and the same."

"Are they, now?" I said, marveling at the irrelevance of this last remark. It then occurred to me that the remark might have been relevant after all—most unhappily so.

"At all times," said Mr. Cuff, amused by my having missed the point. "If you wish to hear our report, sir, reticence will be helpful."

I gestured for him to go on with the story.

"As said before, I was squatting in my birthday suit by the knives and the steam iron, not a care in the world, when I heard from behind me the patter of little feet. *Hello*, I say to myself, *what's this*? and when I look over my shoulder here is your man, bearing down on me like a steam engine. Being as he is one of your big, strapping fellows, sir, it was a sight to behold, not to mention the unexpected circumstances. I took a moment to glance in the direction of Mr. Clubb, who was busily occupied in another quarter, which was, to put it plain and simple, the bed."

Mr. Clubb chortled and said, "By way of being in the line of duty."

"So in a way of speaking I was in the position of having to settle this fellow before he became a trial to us in the performance of our duties. He was getting ready to tackle me, sir, which was what put us in mind of football being in his previous life, tackle the life out of me before he rescued the lady, and I got hold of one of the knives. Then, you see, when he came flying at me that way all I had to do was give him a good jab in at the bottom of the throat, a matter which puts the fear of God into the bravest fellow. It concentrates all their attention, and after that they might as well belittle puppies for all the harm they're likely to do. Well, this boy was one for the books, because for the first time in I don't know how many similar efforts, a hundred—"

"I'd say double at least, to be accurate," said Mr. Clubb.

"—in at least a hundred, anyhow, avoiding immodesty, I underestimated the speed and agility of the lad and, instead of planting my weapon at the base of his neck, stuck him in the side, a manner of wound which in the case of your really *aggressive* attacker, who you come across in about one out of twenty, is about as effective as a slap with a powder puff. Still, I put him off his stride, a welcome sign to me that he had gone a bit loosey-goosey over the years. Then, sir, the advantage was mine, and I seized it with a grateful heart. I spun him over, dumped him on the floor and straddled his chest. At which point I thought to settle him down for the evening by taking hold of a cleaver and cutting off his right hand with one good blow.

"Ninety-nine times out of a hundred, sir, chopping off a hand will take the starch right out of a man. He settled down pretty well.

It's the shock, you see, shock takes the mind that way, and because the stump was bleeding like a bastard, excuse the language, I did him the favor of cauterizing the wound with the steam iron because it was good and hot, and it you sear a wound there's no way that bugger can bleed anymore. I mean, the *problem is solved*, and that's a fact."

"It has been proved a thousand times over," said Mr. Clubb.

"Shock being a healer," said Mr. Cuff. "Shock being a balm like salt water to the human body, yet if you have too much of either, the body gives up the ghost. After I seared the wound, it looked to me like he and his body got together and voted to take the next bus to what is generally considered a better world."

He held up an index finger and stared into my eyes while forking kidneys into his mouth. "This, sir, is a *process*. A *process* can't happen all at once, and every reasonable precaution was taken. Mr. Clubb and I do not have, nor ever have had, the reputation for carelessness in our undertakings."

"And never shall," said Mr. Clubb. He washed down whatever was in his mouth with half a glass of cognac.

"Despite the *process* under way," said Mr. Cuff, "the gentleman's left wrist was bound tightly to the stump. Rope was again attached to the acres of the chest and legs, a gag went back into his mouth, and besides all that I had the pleasure of whapping my hammer once and once only on the region of his temple, for the purpose of keeping him out of action until we were ready for him in case he was not boarding the bus. I took a moment to turn him over and gratify my little soldier, which I trust was in no way exceeding our agreement, sir." He granted me a look of the purest innocence.

"Continue," I said, "although you must grant that your tale is utterly without verification."

"Sir," said Mr. Clubb, "we know one another better than that." He bent over so far that his head disappeared beneath the table, and I heard the undoing of a clasp. Resurfacing, he placed between us on the table an object wrapped in one of the towels Marguerite had purchased for Green Chimneys. "If verification is your desire, and I intend no reflection, sir, for a man in your line of business has grown out of the habit of taking a fellow at his word, here you have wrapped up like a birthday present the finest verification of this portion of our tale to be found in all the world."

"And yours to keep, if you're taken that way," said Mr. Cuff.

I had no doubts whatsoever concerning the nature of the trophy set before me, and therefore I deliberately composed myself before pulling away the folds of toweling. Yet for all my preparations the spectacle of the actual trophy itself affected me more greatly than I would have thought possible, and at the very center of the nausea rising within me I experienced the first faint stirrings of my enlightenment. *Poor man*, I thought, *poor mankind.*

I refolded the material over the crablike thing and said, "Thank you. I meant to imply no reservations concerning your veracity."

"Beautifully said, sir, and much appreciated. Men like ourselves, honest at every point, have found that persons in the habit of duplicity often cannot understand the truth. Liars are the bane of our existence. And yet, such is the nature of this funny old world, we'd be out of business without them."

Mr. Cuff smiled up at the chandelier in rueful appreciation of the world's contradictions. "When I replaced him on the bed, Mr. Clubb went hither and yon, collecting the remainder of the tools for the job at hand—"

"When you say you replaced him on the bed," I broke in, "is it your meaning—"

"Your meaning might differ from mine, sir, and mine, being that of a fellow raised without the benefits of a literary education, may be simpler than yours. But bear in mind that every guild has its legacy of customs and traditions which no serious practitioner can ignore without thumbing his nose at all he holds dear. For those brought up into our trade, physical punishment of a female subject invariably begins with the act most associated in the feminine mind with humiliation of the most rigorous sort. With males the same is generally true. Neglect this step, and you lose an advantage which can never be regained. It is the foundation without which the structure cannot stand, and the foundation must be set in place even when conditions make the job distasteful, which is no picnic, take my word for it." He shook his head and fell silent.

"We could tell you stories to curl your hair," said Mr. Clubb. "Matter for another day. It was on the order of nine-thirty when our materials had been assembled, the preliminaries taken care of, and business could begin in earnest. This is a moment, sir, ever cherished by professionals such as ourselves. It is of an eternal freshness. You are on the brink of testing yourself against your past achievements and those of masters gone before. Your skill, your imagination, your timing and resolve, will be called upon to work together with your hard-earned knowledge of the human body, because it is a question of being able to sense when to press on and when to hold back, of, I can say, having that instinct for the right technique at the right time you can build up only through experience. During this moment you hope that the subject, your partner in the most intimate relationship which can exist between two people, owns the spiritual resolve and physical capacity to inspire your best work. The subject is our instrument, and the nature of the instrument is vital. Faced with an out-of-tune, broken-down piano, even the greatest virtuoso is up shit creek without a paddle. Sometimes, sir, our work has left us tasting ashes for weeks on end, and when you're tasting ashes in your mouth you have trouble remembering the grand design and your wee part in that majestical pattern."

As if to supplant the taste in question and without benefit of knife and fork, Mr. Clubb bit off a generous portion of steak and moistened it with a gulp of cognac. Chewing with loud smacks of the lips and tongue, he thrust a spoon into the kedgeree and began moodily slapping it onto his plate while seeming for the first time to notice the Canalettos on the walls.

"We started off, sir, as well as we ever have," said Mr. Cuff, "and better than most times. The fingernails was a thing of rare beauty, sir, the fingernails was prime. And the hair was on the same transcendant level."

"The fingernails?" I asked. "The hair?"

"Prime," said Mr. Clubb with a melancholy spray of food. "If they could be done better, which they could not, I should like to be there as to applaud with my own hands."

I looked at Mr. Cuff, and he said, "The fingernails and the hair might appear to be your traditional steps two and three, but they are in actual fact steps one and two, the first procedure being more like basic groundwork than part of the performance work itself. Doing the fingernails and the hair tells you an immense quantity about the subject's pain level, style of resistance, and aggression/passivity balance, and that information, sir, is your virtual Bible once you go past step four or five."

"How many steps are there?" I asked.

"A novice would tell you fifteen," said Mr. Cuff. "A competent journeyman would say twenty. Men such as us know there to be at least a hundred, but in their various combinations and refinements they come out into the thousands. At the basic or kindergarten level, they are, after the first two: foot soles; teeth; fingers and toes; tongue; nipples; rectum; genital area; electrification; general piercing; specific piercing; small amputation; damage to inner organs; eyes, minor; eyes; major; large amputation; local flaying; and so forth."

At mention of *tongue*, Mr. Clubb had shoved a spoonful of kedgeree into his mouth and scowled at the two paintings directly across from him. At *electrification*, he had thrust himself out of his chair and crossed behind me to scrutinize them more closely. While Mr. Cuff continued my education, he twisted in his chair to observe his partner's actions, and I did the same.

After *and so forth*, Mr. Cuff fell silent. The two of us watched Mr. Clubb moving back and forth in evident agitation between the two large paintings. He settled at last before a depiction of a regatta on the Grand Canal and took two deep breaths. Then he raised his spoon like a dagger and drove it into the painting to slice beneath a handsome ship, come up at its bow, and continue cutting until he had deleted the ship from the painting. "Now that, sir, is local flaying," he said. He moved to the next picture, which gave a view of the Piazetta. In seconds he had sliced all the canvas from the frame. "And that, sir, is what is meant by general flaying." He crumpled the canvas in his hands, threw it to the ground, and stamped on it.

"He is not quite himself," said Mr. Cuff.

"Oh, but I am, I am myself to an alarming degree, I am," said Mr. Clubb. He tromped back to the table and bent beneath it. Instead of the second folded towel I had anticipated, he produced his satchel and used it to sweep away the plates and serving dishes in front of him. He reached within and slapped down beside me the towel I had expected. "Open it," he said. I unfolded the towel. "Are these not, to the last particular, what you requested, sir?"

It was, to the last particular, what I requested. Marguerite had not thought to remove her wedding band before her assignation, and her . . . I cannot describe the other but to say that it lay like the egg perhaps of some small sandbird in the familiar palm. Another portion of my eventual enlightenment moved into place within me, and I thought: *Here we are, this is all of us, this crab and this egg*. I bent over and vomited beside my chair. When I had finished, I grabbed the cognac bottle and swallowed greedily, twice. The liquor burned down my throat, struck my stomach like a branding iron, and rebounded. I leaned sideways and, with a dizzied spasm of throat and guts, expelled another reeking contribution to the mess on the carpet.

"It is a Roman conclusion to a meal, sir," said Mr. Cuff.

Mr. Moncrieff opened the kitchen door and peeked in. He observed the mutilated paintings and the two objects nested in the striped towel and watched me wipe a string of vomit from my mouth. He withdrew for a moment and reappeared holding a tall can of ground coffee, wordlessly sprinkled its contents over the evidence of my distress, and vanished back into the kitchen. From even the depths of my wretchedness I marveled at the perfection of this display of butler decorum.

I draped the toweling over the crab and the egg. "You are conscientious fellows," I said.

"Conscientious to a fault, sir," said Mr. Cuff, not without a touch of kindness. "For a person in the normal way of living cannot begin to comprehend the actual meaning of that term, nor is he liable to understand the fierce requirements it puts on a man's head. And so it comes about that persons in the normal way of living try to back out long after backing out is possible, even though we explain exactly what is going to happen at the very beginning. They listen, but they do not hear, and it's the rare civilian who has the common sense to know that if you stand in a fire you must be burned. And if you turn the world upside down, you're standing on your head with everybody else."

"Or," said Mr. Clubb, calming his own fires with another deep draught of cognac, "as the Golden Rule has it, what do you do is sooner or later done back to you."

Although I was still one who listened but could not hear, a tingle of premonition went up my spine. "Please go on with your report," I said.

"The responses of the subject were all one could wish," said Mr. Clubb. "I could go so far as to say that her responses were a thing of beauty. A subject who can render you one magnificent scream after another while maintaining a basic self-possession and not breaking down is a subject highly attuned to her own pain, sir, and one to be cherished. You see, there comes a moment when they understand that they are changed for good, they have passed over the border into another realm from which there is no return, and some of them can't handle it and turn, you might say, to mush. With some it happens right at the foundation stage, a sad disappointment because thereafter all the rest of the work could be done by the crudest apprentice. It takes some at the nipples stage, and at the genital stage quite a few more. Most of them comprehend irreversibility during the piercings, and by the stage of small amputation ninety percent have shown you what they are made of. The lady did not come to the point until we had begun the eye work, and she passed with flying colors, sir. But it was then the male upped and put his foot in it."

"And eye work is delicate going," said Mr. Cuff. "Requiring two men, if you want it done even close to right. But I couldn't have turned my back on the fellow for more than a minute and a half."

"Less," said Mr. Clubb. "And him lying there in the corner meek as a baby. No fight left in him at all, you would have said. You would have said, that fellow there is not going to risk so much as opening his eyes until he's made to do it."

"But up he gets, without a rope on him, sir," said Mr. Cuff, "which you would have said was far beyond the powers of a fellow who had recently lost a hand."

"Up he gets and on he comes," said Mr. Clubb. "In defiance of all of Nature's mighty laws. Before I know what's what, he has his good arm around Mr. Cuff's neck and is earnestly trying to snap that neck while beating Mr. Cuff about the head with his stump, a situation which compels me to set aside the task at hand and take up a knife and ram it into his back and sides a fair old number of times. The next thing I know, he's on *me*, and it's up to Mr. Cuff to peel him off and set him on the floor."

"And then, you see, your concentration is gone," said Mr. Cuff. "After something like that, you might as well be starting all over again at the beginning. Imagine if you are playing a piano about as well as ever you did in your life, and along comes another piano with blood in its eye and jumps on your back. It was pitiful, that's all I can say about it. But I got the fellow down and jabbed him here and there until he was still, and then I got the one item we count on as a surefire last resort for incapacitation."

"What is that item?" I asked.

"Dental floss," said Mr. Clubb. "Dental floss cannot be overestimated as a particular in our line of work. It is the razor wire of everyday life, and fishing line cannot hold a candle to it, for fishing line is dull, but dental floss is both *dull* and
sharp. It has a hundred uses, and a book should be written on the subject."

"What do you do with it?" I asked.

"It is applied to a male subject," he said. "Applied artfully and in a manner
perfected only over years of experience. The application is of a lovely *subtlety*.
During the process, the subject must be in a helpless, preferably an unconscious,
position. When the subject regains the first fuzzy inklings of consciousness, he
is aware of no more than a vague discomfort like unto a form of numb tingling,
similar to when a foot has gone asleep. In a wonderfully short period of time,
that discomfort builds up itself, ascending to mild pain, real pain, *severe* pain,
and then outright agony. And then it goes past agony. The final stage is a mystical condition I don't think there is a word for which, but it close resembles
ecstasy. Hallucinations are common. Out-of-body experiences are common. We
have seen men speak in tongues, even when tongues were strictly speaking organs
they no longer possessed. We have seen wonders, Mr. Cuff and I."

"That we have," said Mr. Cuff. "The ordinary civilian sort of fellow can be a
miracle, sir."

"Of which the person in question was one, to be sure," said Mr. Clubb. "But
he has to be said to be in a category all by himself, a man in a million, you
could put it, which is the cause of my mentioning the grand design ever a
mystery to us who glimpse but a part of the whole. You see, the fellow refused
to play by the time-honored rules. He was in an awesome degree of suffering
and torment, sir, but he would not do us the favor to lie down and quit."

"The mind was not right," said Mr. Cuff. "Where the proper mind goes to
the spiritual, sir, as just described, this was that one mind in *ten* million, I'd
estimate, which moves to the animal at the reptile level. If you cut off the head
of a venomous reptile and detach it from the body, that head will still attempt
to strike. So it was with our boy. Bleeding from a dozen wounds. Minus one
hand. Seriously concussed. The dental floss murdering all possibility of thought.
Every nerve in his body howling like a banshee. Yet up he comes with his eyes
red and the foam dripping from his mouth. We put him down again, and I did
what I hate, because it takes all feeling away from the body along with the motor
capacity, and cracked his spine right at the base of the head. Or would have, if
his spine had been a normal thing instead of solid steel in a thick india-rubber
case. Which is what put us in mind of weight lifting, sir, an activity resulting
in such development about the top of the spine you need a hacksaw to get even
close to it."

"We were already behind schedule," said Mr. Clubb, "and with the time required to get back into the proper frame of mind, we had at least seven or eight
hours of work ahead of us. And you had to double that, because while we could
knock the fellow out, he wouldn't have the decency to stay out more than a few
minutes at a time. The natural thing, him being only the secondary subject, would
have been to kill him outright so we could get on with the real job, but improving
our working conditions by that fashion would require an amendment to our contract. Which comes under the heading of Instructions from the Client."

"And it was eleven o'clock," said Mr. Cuff.

"The exact time scheduled for our conference," said Mr. Clubb. "My partner was forced to clobber the fellow into senselessness, how many times was it, Mr. Cuff, while I prayed for our client to do us the grace of answering his phone during twenty rings?"

"Three times, Mr. Clubb, three times exactly," said Mr. Cuff. "The blow each time more powerful than the last, which combining with his having a skull made of granite led to a painful swelling of my hand."

"The dilemma stared us in the face," said Mr. Clubb. "Client unreachable. Impeded in the performance of our duties. State of mind, very foul. In such a pickle, we could do naught but obey the instructions given us by our hearts. *Remove the gentleman's head*, I told my partner, *and take care not to be bitten once it's off*. Mr. Cuff took up an ax. Some haste was called for, the fellow just beginning to stir again. Mr. Cuff moved into position. Then from the bed, where all had been lovely silence but for soft moans and whimpers, we hear a god-awful yowling ruckus of the most desperate and importunate protest. It was a sort to melt the heart, sir. Were we not experienced professionals who enjoy pride in our work, I believe we might have been persuaded almost to grant the fellow mercy, despite his being a pest of the first water. But now those heart-melting screeches reach the ears of the pest and rouse him into movement just at the moment Mr. Cuff lowers the boom, so to speak."

"Which was an unfortunate bit of business," said Mr. Cuff. "Causing me to catch him in the shoulder, causing him to rear up, causing me to lose my footing what with all the blood on the floor, then causing a tussle for possession of the ax and myself suffering several kicks to the breadbasket. I'll tell you, sir, we did a good piece of work when we took off his hand, for without the nuisance of a stump really being useful only for leverage, there's no telling what that fellow might have done. As it was, I had the devil's own time getting the ax free and clear, and once I had done, any chance of making a neat, clean job of it was long gone. It was a slaughter and an act of butchery with not a bit of finesse or sophistication to it, and I have to tell you, such a thing is both an embarrassment and an outrage to men like ourselves. Turning a subject into hamburger by means of an ax is a violation of all our training, and it is not why we went into this business."

"No, of course not, you are more like artists than I had imagined," I said. "But in spite of your embarrassment, I suppose you went back to work on . . . on the female subject."

"We are not *like* artists," said Mr. Clubb, "we *are* artists, and we know how to set our feelings aside and address our chosen medium of expression with a pure and patient attention. In spite of which we discovered the final and insurmountable frustration of the evening, and that discovery put paid to all our hopes."

"If you discovered that Marguerite had escaped," I said, "I believe I might almost, after all you have said, be—"

Glowering, Mr. Clubb held up his hand. "I beg you not to insult us, sir, as we have endured enough misery for one day. The subject had escaped, all right, but not in the simple sense of your meaning. She had escaped for all eternity, in the sense that her soul had taken leave of her body, and flown to those realms at whose nature we can only make our poor, ignorant guesses."

"She died?" I asked. "In other words, in direct contradiction of my instructions, you two fools killed her. You love to talk about your expertise, but you went too far, and she died at your hands. I want you incompetents to leave my house immediately. Begone. Depart. This minute."

Mr. Clubb and Mr. Cuff looked into each other's eyes, and in that moment of private communication I saw an encompassing and universal sorrow which utterly turned the tables on me: before I was made to understand how it was possible, I saw that the only fool present was myself. And yet the sorrow included all three of us, and more besides.

"The subject died, but we did not kill her," said Mr. Clubb. "We did not go, nor have we ever gone, too far. The subject chose to die. The subject's death was an act of suicidal will. Can you hear me? While you are listening, sir, is it possible, sir, for you to open your ears and hear what I am saying? She who might have been in all of our long experience the noblest, most courageous subject we ever will have the good fortune to be given witnessed the clumsy murder of her lover and decided to surrender her life."

"Quick as a shot," said Mr. Cuff. "The simple truth, sir, is that otherwise we could have kept her alive for about a year."

"And it would have been a rare privilege to do so," said Mr. Clubb. "It is time for you to face facts, sir."

"I am facing them about as well as one could," I said. "Please tell me where you disposed of the bodies."

"Within the house," said Mr. Clubb. Before I could protest, he said, "Under the wretched circumstances, sir, including the continuing unavailability of the client and the enormity of the personal and professional letdown felt by my partner and myself, we saw no choice but to dispose of the house along with the telltale remains."

"Dispose of Green Chimneys?" I said, aghast. "How could you dispose of Green Chimneys?"

"Reluctantly, sir," said Mr. Clubb. "With heavy hearts and an equal anger. With also the same degree of professional unhappiness experienced previous. In workaday terms, by means of combustion. Fire, sir, is a substance like shock and salt water, a healer and a cleanser, though more drastic."

"But Green Chimneys has not been healed," I said. "Nor has my wife."

"You are a man of wit, sir, and have provided Mr. Cuff and myself many moments of precious amusement. True, Green Chimneys has not been healed, but cleansed it has been, root and branch. And you hired us to punish your wife, not heal her, and punish her we did, as well as possible under very trying circumstances indeed."

"Which circumstances include our feeling that the job ended before its time," said Mr. Cuff. "Which circumstances is one we cannot bear."

"I regret your disappointment," I said, "but I cannot accept that it was necessary to burn down my magnificent house."

"Twenty, even fifteen years ago, it would not have been," said Mr. Clubb. "Nowadays, however, that contemptible alchemy known as Police Science has fattened itself up into such a gross and distorted breed of sorcery that a single drop of blood can be detected even after you scrub and scour until your arms hurt. It has reached the hideous point that if a constable without a thing in his head but the desire to imprison honest fellows employed in an ancient trade finds two hairs at what is supposed to be a crime scene, he waddles along to the laboratory and instantly a loathsome sort of wizard is popping out to tell him that those same two hairs are from the heads of Mr. Clubb and Mr. Cuff, and I exaggerate, I know, sir, but not by much."

"And if they do not have our names, sir," said Mr. Cuff, "which they do not and I pray never will, they ever after have our particulars, to be placed in a great universal file against the day when they *might* have our names, so as to look back into that cruel file and commit the monstrosity of unfairly increasing the charges against us. It is a malignant business, and all sensible precautions must be taken."

"A thousand times I have expressed the conviction," said Mr. Clubb, "that an ancient art ought not be against the law, nor its practitioners described as criminals. Is there even a name for our so-called crime? There is not. GBH they call it, sir, for Grievous Bodily Harm, or, even worse, Assault. We do not Assault. We induce, we instruct, we instill. Properly speaking, these cannot be crimes, and those who do them cannot be criminals. Now I have said it a thousand times and one."

"All right," I said, attempting to speed this appalling conference to its end, "you have described the evening's unhappy events. I appreciate your reasons for burning down my splendid property. You have enjoyed a lavish meal. All remaining is the matter of your remuneration, which demands considerable thought. This night has left me exhausted, and after all your efforts, you, too, must be in need of rest. Communicate with me, please, in a day or two, gentlemen, by whatever means you choose. I wish to be alone with my thoughts. Mr. Moncrieff will show you out."

The maddening barnies met this plea with impassive stares and stoic silence, and I renewed my silent vow to give them nothing—not a penny. For all their pretensions, they had accomplished naught but the death of my wife and the destruction of my country house. Rising to my feet with more difficulty than anticipated, I said, "Thank you for your efforts on my behalf."

Once again, the glance which passed between them implied that I had failed to grasp the essentials of our situation.

"Your thanks are gratefully accepted," said Mr. Cuff, "thought, dispute it as you may, they are premature, as you know in your soul. This morning we embarked upon a journey of which we have yet more miles to go. In consequence, we prefer not to leave. Also, setting aside the question of your continuing education, which if we do not address will haunt us all forever, residing here with you for a sensible period out of sight is the best protection from law enforcement we three could ask for."

"No," I said, "I have had enough of your education, and I need no protection from officers of the law. Please, gentlemen, allow me to return to my bed. You may take the rest of the cognac with you as a token of my regard."

"Give it a moment's reflection, sir," said Mr. Clubb. "You have announced the presence of high-grade consultants and introduced these same to staff and clients both. Hours later, your spouse meets her tragic end in a conflagration destroying your upstate manor. On the very same night also occurs the disappearance of your greatest competitor, a person certain to be identified before long by a hotel employee as a fellow not unknown to the late spouse. Can you think it wise to have the high-grade consultants vanish right away?"

I did reflect, then said, "You have a point. It will be best if you continue to make an appearance in the office for a time. However, the proposal that you stay here is ridiculous." A wild hope, utterly irrational in the face of the grisly evidence, came to me in the guise of doubt. "If Green Chimneys has been destroyed by fire, I should have been informed long ago. I am a respected figure in the town of _____, personally acquainted with its chief of police, Wendall Nash. Why has he not called me?"

"Oh, sir, my goodness," said Mr. Clubb, shaking his head and smiling inwardly at my folly, "for many reasons. A small town is a beast slow to move. The available men have been struggling throughout the night to rescue even a jot or tittle portion of your house. They will fail, they have failed already, but the effort will keep them busy past dawn. Wendall Nash will not wish to ruin your night's sleep until he can make a full report." He glanced at his wristwatch. "In fact, if I am not mistaken . . ." He tilted his head, closed his eyes, and raised an index finger. The telephone in the kitchen began to trill.

"He has done it a thousand times, sir," said Mr. Cuff, "and I have yet to see him strike out."

Mr. Moncrieff brought the instrument through from the kitchen, said, "For you, sir," and placed the receiver in my waiting hand. I uttered the conventional greeting, longing to hear the voice of anyone but . . .

"Wendall Nash, sir," came the chief's raspy, high-pitched drawl. "Calling from up here in _____ I hate to tell you this, but I have some awful bad news. Your place Green Chimneys started burning sometime around midnight last night, and every man jack we had got put on the job and the boys worked like dogs to save what they could, but sometimes you can't win no matter what you do. Me personally, I feel terrible about this, but, tell you the truth, I never saw a fire like it. We nearly lost two men, but it looks like they're going to come out of it okay. The rest of our boys are still out there trying to save the few trees you got left."

"Dreadful," I said. "Please permit me to speak to my wife."

A speaking silence followed. "The missus is not with you, sir? You're saying she was inside there?"

"My wife left for Green Chimneys this morning. I spoke to her there in the afternoon. She intended to work in her studio, a separate building at some distance from the house, and it is her custom to sleep in the studio when working late." Saying these things to Wendall Nash, I felt almost as though I were creating an alternative world, another town of _____ and another Green Chimneys, where another Marguerite had busied herself in the studio, and there gone to bed to sleep through the commotion. "Have you checked the studio? You are certain to find her there."

"Well, I have to say we didn't, sir," he said. "The fire took that little building pretty good, too, but the walls are still standing and you can tell what used to be what, furnishing-wise and equipment-wise. If she was inside it, we'd of found her."

"Then she got out in time," I said, and instantly it was the truth: the other Marguerite had escaped the blaze and now stood, numb with shock and wrapped in a blanket, unrecognized amidst the voyeuristic crowd always drawn to disasters.

"It's possible, but she hasn't turned up yet, and we've been talking to everybody at the site. Could she have left with one of the staff?"

"All the help is on vacation," I said. "She was alone."

"Uh-huh," he said. "Can you think of anyone with a serious grudge against you? Any enemies? Because this was not a natural-type fire, sir. Someone set it, and he knew what he was doing. Anyone come to mind?"

"No," I said. "I have rivals, but no enemies. Check the hospitals and anything else you can think of, Wendall, and I'll be there as soon as I can."

"You can take your time, sir," he said. "I sure hope we find her, and by late this afternoon we'll be able to go through the ashes." He said he would give me a call if anything turned up in the meantime.

"Please, Wendall," I said, and began to cry. Muttering a consolation I did not quite catch, Mr. Moncrieff vanished with the telephone in another matchless display of butler politesse.

"The practice of hoping for what you know you cannot have is a worthy spiritual exercise," said Mr. Clubb. "It brings home the vanity of vanity."

"I beg you, leave me," I said, still crying. "In all decency."

"Decency lays heavy obligations on us all," said Mr. Clubb. "And no job is decently done until it is done completely. Would you care for help in getting back to the bedroom? We are ready to proceed."

I extended a shaky arm, and he assisted me through the corridors. Two cots had been set up in my room, and a neat array of instruments—"staples"—formed two rows across the bottom of the bed. Mr. Clubb and Mr. Cuff positioned my head on the pillows and began to disrobe.

8

Ten hours later, the silent chauffeur aided me in my exit from the limousine and clasped my left arm as I limped toward the uniformed men and official vehicles on the far side of the open gate. Blackened sticks which had been trees protruded from the blasted earth, and the stench of wet ash saturated the air. Wendall Nash separated from the other men, approached, and noted without comment my garb of gray Homburg hat, pearl-gray cashmere topcoat, heavy gloves, woolen charcoal-gray pinstriped suit, sunglasses, and Malacca walking stick. It was the afternoon of a midsummer day in the upper eighties. Then he looked more closely at my face. "Are you, uh, are you sure you're all right, sir?"

"In a manner of speaking," I said, and saw him blink at the oozing gap left in the wake of an incisor. "I slipped at the top of a marble staircase and tumbled down all forty-six steps, resulting in massive bangs and bruises, considerable physical weakness, and the persistent sensation of being uncomfortably cold. No broken bones, at least nothing major." Over his shoulder I stared at four isolated brick towers rising from an immense black hole in the ground, all that remained of Green Chimneys. "Is there news of my wife?"

"I'm afraid, sir, that—" Nash placed a hand on my shoulder, causing me to stifle a sharp outcry. "I'm sorry, sir. Shouldn't you be in the hospital? Did your doctors say you could come all this way?"

"Knowing my feelings in this matter, the doctors insisted I make the journey." Deep within the black cavity, men in bulky orange spacesuits and space helmets were sifting through the sodden ashes, now and then dropping unrecognizable nuggets into heavy bags of the same color. "I gather that you have news for me, Wendall," I said.

"Unhappy news, sir," he said. "The garage went up with the rest of the house, but we found some bits and pieces of your wife's little car. This here was one incredible hot fire, sir, and by hot I mean *hot*, and whoever set it was no garden-variety firebug."

"You found evidence of the automobile," I said. "I assume you also found evidence of the woman who owned it."

"They came across some bone fragments, plus a small portion of a skeleton," he said. "This whole big house came down on her, sir. These boys are experts at their job, and they don't hold out hope for coming across a whole lot more. So if your wife was the only person inside . . ."

"I see, yes, I understand," I said, staying on my feet only with the support of the Malacca cane. "How horrid, how hideous, that it should all be true, that our lives should prove such a *littleness*. . . ."

"I'm sure that's true, sir, and that wife of yours was a, was what I have to call a special kind of person who gave pleasure to us all, and I hope you know that we all wish things could of turned out different, the same as you."

For a moment I imagined that he was talking about her recordings. And then, immediately, I understood that he was laboring to express the pleasure he and the others had taken in what they, no less then Mr. Clubb and Mr. Cuff but much, much more than I, had perceived as her essential character.

"Oh, Wendall," I said into the teeth of my sorrow, "it is not possible, not ever, for things to turn out different."

He refrained from patting my shoulder and sent me back to the rigors of my education.

9

A month—four weeks—thirty days—seven hundred and twenty hours—forty-three thousand, two hundred minutes—two million, five hundred and ninety-two thousand seconds—did I spend under the care of Mr. Clubb and Mr. Cuff, and I believe I proved in the end to be a modestly, moderately, middlingly satisfying subject, a matter in which I take an immodest and immoderate pride. "You are little in comparison to the lady, sir," Mr. Clubb once told me while deep in his ministrations, "but no one could say that you are nothing." I, who had countless times put the lie to the declaration that they should never see me cry, wept tears of gratitude. We ascended through the fifteen stages known to the novice, the journeyman's further five, and passed, with the frequent repetitions and backward glances appropriate for the slower pupil, into the artist's upper eighty, infinitely expandable by grace of the refinements of his art. We had the little soldiers. We had *dental floss*. During each of those forty-three thousand, two hundred minutes, throughout all two million and nearly six hundred thousand seconds, it was always deepest night. We made our way through perpetual darkness, and the utmost darkness, of the utmost night yielded an infinity of textural variation, cold, slick dampness to velvety softness to leaping flame, for it was true that no one could say I was nothing.

Because I was not nothing, I glimpsed the Meaning of Tragedy.

Each Tuesday and Friday of these four sunless weeks, my consultants and guides lovingly bathed and dressed my wounds, arrayed me in my warmest clothes (for I never after ceased to feel the blast of arctic wind against my flesh), and escorted me to my office, where I was presumed much reduced by grief as well as certain household accidents attributed to grief.

On the first of these Tuesdays, a flushed-looking Mrs. Rampage offered her consolations and presented me with the morning newspapers, an inch-thick pile of faxes, two inches of legal documents, and a tray filled with official-looking letters. The newspapers described the fire and eulogized Marguerite; the increasingly threatening faxes declared Chartwell, Munster, and Stout's intention to ruin me professionally and personally in the face of my continuing refusal to return the accompanying documents along with all records having reference to their client; the documents were those in question; the letters, produced by the various legal firms representing all my other cryptic gentlemen, deplored the (unspecified) circumstances necessitating their clients' universal desire for change in re financial management. These lawyers also desired all relevant records, discs, et cetera, et cetera, urgently. Mr. Clubb and Mr. Cuff roistered behind their screen. I signed the documents in a shaky hand and requested Mrs. Rampage to have these delivered with the desired records to Chartwell, Munster, and Stout. "And dispatch all these other records too," I said, handing her the letters. "I am now going in for my lunch."

Tottering toward the executive dining room, now and then I glanced into smoke-filled offices to observe my much-altered underlings. Some of them appeared, after a fashion, to be working. Several were reading paperback novels, which might be construed as work of a kind. One of the Captain's assistants was unsuccessfully lofting paper airplanes toward his wastepaper basket. Gilligan's secretary lay asleep on her office couch, and a records clerk lay sleeping on the file-room floor. In the dining room, Charlie-Charlie Rackett hurried forward to assist me to my accustomed chair. Gilligan and the Captain gave me sullen looks from their usual lunchtime station, an unaccustomed bottle of Scotch whiskey between them. Charlie-Charlie lowered me into my seat and said, "Terrible news about your wife, sir."

"More terrible than you know," I said.

Gilligan took a gulp of whiskey and displayed his middle finger, I gathered to me rather than Charlie-Charlie.

"Afternoonish," I said.

"Very much so, sir," said Charlie-Charlie, and bent closer to the brim of the Homburg and my ear. "About that little request you made the other day. The right men aren't nearly so easy to find as they used to be, sir, but I'm still on the job."

My laughter startled him. "No squab today, Charlie-Charlie. Just bring me a bowl of tomato soup."

I had partaken of no more than two or three delicious mouthfuls when Gilligan lurched up beside me. "Look here," he said, "it's too bad about your wife and everything, I really mean it, honest, but that drunken act you put on in my office cost me my biggest client, not to forget that you took his girlfriend home with you."

"In that case," I said, "I have no further need of your services. Pack your things and be out of here by three o'clock."

He listed to one side and straightened himself up. "You can't mean that."

"I can and do," I said. "Your part in the grand design at work in the universe no longer has any connection with my own."

"You must be as crazy as you look," he said, and unsteadily departed.

I returned to my office and gently lowered myself into my seat. After I had removed my gloves and accomplished some minor repair work to the tips of my fingers with the tape and gauze pads thoughtfully inserted by the detectives into the pockets of my coat, I slowly drew the left glove over my fingers and became aware of feminine giggles amidst the coarser sounds of male amusement behind the screen. I coughed into the glove and heard a tiny shriek. Soon, though not immediately, a blushing Mrs. Rampage emerged from cover, patting her hair and adjusting her skirt. "Sir, I'm so sorry, I didn't expect . . ." She was staring at my right hand, which had not as yet been inserted into its glove.

"Lawn-mower accident," I said. "Mr. Gilligan has been released, and I should like you to prepare the necessary papers. Also, I want to see all of our operating figures for the past year, as significant changes have been dictated by the grand design at work in the universe."

Mrs. Rampage flew from the room, and for the next several hours, as for nearly every remaining hour I spent at my desk on the Tuesday and Thursdays thereafter, I addressed with a carefree spirit the details involved in shrinking the staff to the smallest number possible and turning the entire business over to the Captain. Graham Leeson's abrupt disappearance greatly occupied the newspapers, and when not occupied as described I read that my archrival and competitor had been a notorious Don Juan, i.e., a compulsive womanizer, a flaw in his otherwise immaculate character held by some to have played a substantive role in his sudden absence. As Mr. Clubb had predicted, a clerk at the _____ Hotel revealed Leeson's sessions with my late wife, and for a time professional and amateur gossipmongers alike speculated that he had caused the disastrous fire. This came to nothing. Before the month had ended, Leeson sightings were reported in Monaco, the Swiss Alps, and Argentina, locations accommodating to sportsmen—after four years of varsity football at the University of Southern California, Leeson had won an Olympic silver medal in weight lifting while earning his MBA at Wharton.

In the limousine at the end of each day, Mr. Clubb and Mr. Cuff braced me in happy anticipation of the lessons to come as we sped back through illusory sunlight toward the real darkness.

10 The Meaning of Tragedy

Everything, from the designs of the laughing gods down to the lowliest cells in the human digestive tract, is changing all the time, every particle of being large and small is eternally in motion, but this simple truism, so transparent on its surface, evokes immediate headache and stupefaction when applied to itself, not unlike the sentence "Every word that comes out of my mouth is a bald-faced lie." The gods are ever laughing while we are always clutching our heads and looking for a soft place to lie down, and what I glimpsed in my momentary glimpses of the meaning of tragedy preceding, during, and after the experience of *dental floss* was so composed of paradox that I can state it only in cloud or vapor form, as:

The meaning of tragedy is: *All is in order, all is in train.*
The meaning of tragedy is: *It only hurts for a little while.*
The meaning of tragedy is: *Change is the first law of life.*

11

So it took place that one day their task was done, their lives and mine were to move forward into separate areas of the grand design, and all that was left before preparing my own departure was to stand, bundled up against the nonexistent arctic wind, on the bottom step and wave farewell with my remaining hand while shedding buckets and bathtubs of tears with my remaining eye. Chaplinesque in their black suits and bowlers, Mr. Clubb and Mr. Cuff ambled cheerily toward the glittering avenue and my bank, where arrangements had been made for the transfer into their hands of all but a small portion of my private fortune by my private banker, virtually his final act in that capacity. At the distant corner, Mr. Clubb and Mr. Cuff, by then only tiny figures blurred by my tears, turned, ostensibly to bid farewell, actually, as I knew, to watch as I mounted my steps and went back within the house, and with a salute I honored this last painful agreement between us.

A more pronounced version of the office's metamorphosis had taken place inside my town house, but with the relative ease practice gives even to one whose step is halting, whose progress is interrupted by frequent pauses for breath and the passing of certain shooting pains, I skirted the mounds of rubble, the dangerous loose tiles and more dangerous open holes in the floor, the regions submerged underwater, and toiled up the resilient staircase, moved with infinite care across the boards bridging the former landing, and made my way into the former kitchen, where broken pipes and limp wires protruding from the lathe marked the sites of those appliances rendered pointless by the gradual disappearance of the household staff. (In a voice choked with feeling, Mr. Moncrieff, Reggie Moncrieff, Reggie, the last to go, had informed me that his last month in my service had been "as fine as my days with the duke, sir, every bit as noble as ever it was with that excellent old gentleman.") The remaining cupboard yielded a flagon of genever, a tumbler, and a Montecristo torpedo, and with the tumbler filled and the cigar alight I hobbled through the devastated corridors toward my bed, there to gather my strength for the ardors of the coming day.

In good time, I arose to observe the final appointments of the life soon to be abandoned. It is possible to do up one's shoelaces and knot one's necktie as neatly with a single hand as with two, and shirt buttons eventually become a breeze. Into my traveling bag I folded a few modest essentials atop the flagon and the cigar box, and into a pad of shirts nestled the black Lucite cube prepared at my request by my instructor-guides and containing, mingled with the ashes of the satchel and its contents, the few bony nuggets rescued from Green Chimneys. The traveling bag accompanied me first to my lawyer's office, where I signed papers making over the wreckage of the town house to the European gentleman who had purchased it sight unseen as a "fixer-upper" for a fraction of its (considerably reduced) value. Next I visited the melancholy banker and withdrew the pittance remaining in my accounts. And then, glad of heart and free of all unnecessary encumbrance, I took my place in the sidewalk queue to await transportation by means of a kindly kneeling bus to the great terminus where I should employ the ticket reassuringly lodged within my breast pocket.

Long before the arrival of the bus, a handsome limousine crawled past in the traffic, and glancing idly within, I observed Mr. Chester Montfort d'M____ smoothing the air with a languid gesture while in conversation with the two stout, bowler-hatted men on his either side. Soon, doubtless, he would begin his instructions in the whopbopaloobop.

12

What is a pittance in a great city may be a modest fortune in a hamlet, and a returned prodigal might be welcomed far in excess of his true deserts. I entered New Covenant quietly, unobtrusively, with the humility of a new convert uncertain of his station, inwardly rejoicing to see all unchanged from the days of my youth. When I purchased a dignified but unshowy house on Scripture Street, I announced only that I had known the village in my childhood, had traveled far, and now in my retirement wished no more than to immerse myself in the life of the community, exercising my skills only inasmuch as they might be requested of an elderly invalid. How well the aged invalid had known the village, how far and to what end had he traveled, and the nature of his skills remained unspecified. Had I not attended daily services at the Temple, the rest of my days might have passed in pleasant anonymity and frequent perusals of a little book I had obtained at the terminus, for while my surname was so deeply of New Covenant that it could be read on a dozen headstones in the Temple graveyard, I had fled so early in life and so long ago that my individual identity had been entirely forgotten. New Covenant is curious—intensely curious—but it does not wish to pry. One fact and one only led to the metaphoric slaughter of the fatted calf and the prodigal's elevation. On the day when, some five or six months after his installation on Scripture Street, the afflicted newcomer's faithful Temple attendance was rewarded with an invitation to read the Lesson for the Day, Matthew 5:43—48, seated amidst numerous offspring and offspring's offspring in the barnie-pews for the first time since an unhappy tumble from a hayloft was Delbert Mudge.

My old classmate had weathered into a white-haired, sturdy replica of his own grandfather, and although his hips still gave him considerable difficulty his mind had suffered no comparable stiffening. Delbert knew my name as well as his own, and though he could not connect it to the wizened old party counseling him from the lectern to embrace his enemies, the old party's face and voice so clearly evoked the deceased lawyer who had been my father that he recognized me before I had spoken the whole of the initial verse. The grand design once again could be seen at its mysterious work: unknown to me, my entirely selfish efforts on behalf of Charlie-Charlie Rackett, my representation to his parole board and his subsequent hiring as my spy, had been noted by all of the barnie-world. I, a child of Scripture Street, had become a hero to generations of barnies! After hugging me at the conclusion of the fateful service, Delbert Mudge implored my assistance in the resolution of a fiscal imbroglio which threatened his family's cohesion. I, of course, assented, with the condition that my services should be free of charge. The Mudge imbroglio proved elementary, and soon I was performing similar services for other barnie clans. After listening to a half-dozen accounts of my miracles while setting broken barnie-bones, New Covenant's physician visited my Scripture Street habitation under cover of night, was prescribed the solution to his uncomplicated problem, and sang my praises to his fellow townies. Within a year, by which time all New Covenant had become aware of my "tragedy" and consequent "reawakening," I was managing the Temple's funds as well as those of barn and town. Three years later, our reverend having in his ninety-first year, as the Racketts and Mudges put it, "woke up dead," I submitted by popular acclaim to appointment in his place.

Daily, I assume the honored place assigned me. Ceremonious vestments assure that my patchwork scars remain unseen. The Lucite box and its relics are interred deep within the sacred ground beneath the Temple where I must one day join my predecessors—some bony fragments of Graham Leeson reside there, too, mingled with Marguerite's more numerous specks and nuggets. Eye patch elegantly in place, I lean forward upon the Malacca cane, and while flourishing the stump of my right hand as if in demonstration, with my ruined tongue whisper what I know none shall understand, the homily beginning, *It only* . . . To this I append in silent exhalation the two words concluding that little book brought to my attention by an agreeable murderer and purchased at the great grand station long ago, these: *Ah, humanity!*

MICHAEL BLUMLEIN

Revenge

Michael Blumlein returns to the pages of The Year's Best Fantasy and Horror *with a tale of magical realism that is strikingly original and literally haunting. Blumlein, a doctor who lives and practices in the San Francisco Bay Area, is the author of two novels,* XY *and* The Movement of Mountains, *and one story collection,* The Brains of Rats. *His short fiction has been published in* Omni, Interzone, *and other magazines, as well as in the adult fairy tale anthology* Black Swan, White Raven. *"Revenge" is reprinted from the April issue of* The Magazine of Fantasy & Science Fiction.

—T. W.

The burial took place at Our Lady of Tears in Colma, and Luis stayed until the others had gone, until the diminutive grave was filled and tamped with dirt and the grave-diggers had shouldered their shovels and gone on to dig elsewhere. He stayed until he was alone, and so it was that he alone saw the child ascend. Barely a week old when she died, she looked slightly older now, a child of perhaps three months of age, driven by hunger and other primal urges and forced to look outside herself for help. Her eyes wandered this way and that, unfocused, it seemed, uncensoring, until at last they fixed on her father. She seemed to recognize him. Her face, which up to that moment had been a minor chaos of muscle contraction and relaxation, became still.

Luis was mesmerized. Emotion left him. He waited for her to speak.

She told him she had died too soon. She blamed the doctor. "The blood is on his hands, Father."

Luis believed the same. "What should I do?"

"Blood for blood," she said.

Luis nodded. This, too, he believed. "How?" he asked.

"Man to man. And do not wait too long. The sooner the better."

Luis, who had been floundering since her death, agreed. He was happy at last for a way to channel his grief, and with more hope than he had felt in many days, he rejoined his wife Rosa, who was being comforted by her family. At his arrival she took his hand, which was cold, and by that, and the look on his face, she knew immediately what was in his heart. Despairing, she beseeched him otherwise. She begged him, she kissed his hand, she pressed his palm to her heart. But Luis could not be moved. His hand stayed cold, and Rosa, foreseeing another tragedy, broke down in fresh tears. Dutifully, Luis took her in his arms. One of her sisters muttered a blessing. An aunt, wringing a tear-stained handkerchief, invoked the love of God. Someone keened.

A week later, Rosa tried to reason with her husband. "I have spoken with a lawyer," she told him after the boys were in bed. "He wants to meet with us."

"I have no interest in lawyers," replied Luis.

"He asks for no money. He just wants to talk."

"I have nothing to say."

"He wants to help us, Luis. He says there are grounds for a strong case."

"Grounds, he means, for him to get rich."

"He knows of another baby who died at this doctor's hands. We are not the first. The lawyer says the doctor could be charged with negligence."

"Rosa," said Luis. "Look at us. Who are we to accuse a doctor?"

"Not us. The lawyer. He would do the talking. He's a smart man, Luis. He asked questions that made me think. Questions, he said, they should have asked in the hospital. I trust him."

Luis was silent. He had no time for lawyers, no trust in anyone but himself. Man to man, she had said. An eye for an eye. It was his duty. On the other hand, he did not want to cause his wife unnecessary grief.

"Then go to him," he said. "Talk to this lawyer."

"Yes?"

"By all means. Please. We must do what is right."

Luis by nature was not a violent man. Before the death of his daughter, he was tender with his wife and gentle with his children. And even after, the violence he planned did not spill beyond its target. He didn't yell at the kids or bark at his wife, didn't lose his temper at work or with friends. If anything, he seemed more docile than usual, except to Rosa, who knew him best. She worried, but she also held out hope that with time his wounds would heal.

Luis owned a machete from his days as a field hand in Mexico. He had used it to cut wood, clear brush and on occasion kill a chicken for dinner. It had an ebony handle that he polished and a steel blade he kept sharp. Three weeks after his daughter's death, he left in the morning as usual, but instead of going to work, he drove to the medical building where Dr. Admonson had his obstetrics practice. He wore a white button-down shirt, pressed pants and cowboy boots. His hair was slicked down and parted, his mustache neatly trimmed. He carried the machete loosely in his left hand, drawing curious glances from passersby, none of whom took it upon himself to comment. At the medical building he rode the elevator to the third floor, where he exited with two youngish women and an elderly man. Dr. Admonson's office was at the end of the corridor on the left. The waiting room, whose pastel walls were hung with watercolors of flowers and idyllic landscapes, was full of women. Some were at term; some were just getting started; one or two suckled newborns. Luis was the only man in the room. He was also the only person carrying a machete.

He found an empty place on a couch next to a woman with a toddler in her lap and took a seat. A hush fell in the room as everyone took note of him. He stared at the floor. The toddler, drawn by the gleaming machete, squirmed away from her mother and went for the blade. Luis quickly blocked her way and shook his finger in remonstrance. An instant later, her mother snatched her back. A nurse in a starched white lab coat opened an interior door and called the name of a patient. The two of them disappeared inside, at which point Luis got up and tapped on the receptionist's frosted window. It slid open.

"May I help you?"

"I want to see the doctor."

The receptionist was a woman in her sixties with silver blue hair and glasses that magnified her eyes. She sat at a low desk from whose vantage point the machete was hidden.

"Are you here with someone?" she asked.

He shook his head.

"Do you have an appointment?"

"He delivered my baby. I want to talk to him."

She pushed her glasses up the bridge of her nose and peered at Luis. "Pertaining to what?"

"My baby," he repeated. "Maria Elena Hermosilla Rodriguez."

Dr. Admonson had a number of patients named Rodriguez, but the receptionist kept up with the mothers, not the babies. The name was not familiar to her. She looked at her appointment book.

"I have an opening tomorrow at two."

Luis stared at her blankly. He was not prepared to negotiate.

"Two tomorrow?" she repeated.

"Today," he said.

"We're very busy today."

This met with no reply, and the receptionist, a retired retail clerk with passing knowledge of the vagaries of human behavior, deemed it an inopportune time to persevere. She rechecked her book.

"All right. I'll try to squeeze you in. You'll have to wait though."

Luis nodded and returned to his seat. Several more patients were called by the nurse, while others entered the office to take their places. He was troubled. He loved women of all ages and types, but most of all, he loved women who were carrying new life. Pregnancy was a miracle and a sacrament to him, a time for women to be honored, protected and loved especially hard. How could he kill the doctor without creating panic among them? Even behind closed doors they would hear him hacking away, they would smell the blood and suffer. Then the burden of guilt would be on him.

The nurse appeared at her door and called his name. Slowly, he stood, machete in hand, hacking edge out, tip to the floor. He was caught between duty and love, between command and conscience. The nurse took a step toward him. He shrank back. She took another. She said his name.

He fled.

Two days later, at Mass, Maria Elena visited him again. She was dressed in Mary Janes and a pink crinoline skirt and wore a bow in her hair. She had some questions, chiefly why her father had not done what he had promised.

"I cannot kill a man like an animal," Luis replied with downcast eyes. "That would make me an animal too."

"An eye for an eye," said Maria Elena. "That was our agreement."

"I beg your forgiveness, little one, but I cannot."

She looked at him in such a way that he felt guilty of being less than a man. Then her expression changed.

"Another way perhaps."

Luis brightened. "Yes. Anything but cold-blooded murder."

"The doctors are smart. The doctors and the lawyers. Smart and powerful. We must be cunning. And patient. We must plan carefully."

This was a relief to Luis, who did not want a repeat of the debacle with the machete. The thought of what he had nearly inflicted on those innocent women filled him with shame.

"Do you have an idea?" he asked.

Maria Elena did, but she wasn't saying, not just yet. Instead, she gave him an enigmatic smile, and for a moment he got a glimpse of her as a young woman. She had an uncanny resemblance to someone he knew, and then it dawned on him that that someone was himself, that his daughter now looked just as he might have looked had he been born female. Long lashes, dark eyes, broad cheeks and lips. Hair the color of coal. Skin like clay. It was unsettling. The girl had something up her sleeve, and suddenly, he wasn't sure he wanted to know what.

He was sitting in a pew at the back of the church. From the pulpit the priest gave the call to prayer. Reflexively, Luis fell to his knees and clasped his hands together. Organ music filled the air, then the choir began to sing. Maria Elena joined in, her voice soulful and sweet. It eased her father's heart to hear her sing. Here especially, in the bosom of the Lord. What did he possibly have to fear?

A week later, he shaved his mustache and made an appointment to see the doctor. He gave his name as Luis Flores and neither the receptionist nor the nurse recognized him. He was ushered uneventfully into the doctor's office, and fifteen minutes later, Dr. Admonson swept in. He was a rangy man in his early fifties with silver hair, liquid blue eyes and a disarming smile. He shook Luis's hand, glanced at his chart, which was blank, then sat opposite him at his desk.

"What can I do for you, Mr. Flores?"

Luis had rehearsed what to say, but the sight of the doctor unnerved him. Suddenly, he was back at the hospital, with all the attendant feelings of helplessness, panic and despair. Rosa's bag of waters had broken six weeks ahead of time, in itself not a terrible tragedy, except that labor had not followed. The baby could have been delivered by Caesarean section, but Dr. Admonson had said no, he wanted to give it as much time as possible to mature inside its mother, whom he put in the hospital at bed rest and visited daily, monitoring her for signs of infection or fetal distress. None occurred, and Rosa and Luis waited, a week, then two, then three. Their anxiety mounted, and repeatedly, they questioned the doctor about the wisdom of waiting so long. Repeatedly, he reassured them. And finally labor arrived, and the child was breech, and instead of doing a Caesarean section and bringing it out safely through Rosa's belly, Dr. Admonson, who decried unnecessary surgery, elected a vaginal delivery, during which the baby's head got stuck, so that forceps had to be used. Luis remembered the clink of metal as the blades were engaged, the beads of sweat on the doctor's forehead, his strained words behind the green surgical mask. And then the tugging of his daughter through the birth canal, the gentle but insistent pressure that had inadvertently broken her neck, so that instead of kicking and wailing at delivery, she had come out limp and blue. And then the bleeding on the brain that followed, and her being rushed to intensive care and put on a respirator and other machines to keep her alive. And how after a week—when she couldn't survive on her own—the machines were turned off, and she was allowed to die. And Rosa's tears, and from her breasts the rivers of warm milk. And his own tears, and his rage, and his vow of revenge.

Dr. Admonson bridged his fingers and awaited a reply to his question. It was rare but not unheard of that a man came to him alone, a husband without a wife, a beau without his belle, looking for advice. Often, like this man, they were shy. Usually this meant that the reason for coming involved questions of fertility. What they thought of as their manhood. He tried again.

"What brings you in today, Mr. Flores?"

"I need help," Luis muttered, which was manifestly true. It was also what Maria Elena had told him to say.

"In what way?" Admonson asked.

Luis stared into his hands. The plan, such as it was, had been to ask for help and then to receive it, in this way insinuating himself, however tangentially, into the doctor's life, thus buying time to plot his revenge. The plan's weakness was that, beyond this vague request for help, he had nothing more to say.

"Mr. Flores?"

Luis attempted to elaborate. "I need a doctor."

"Of course. But as you must be aware, I am an obstetrician. On occasion, a gynecologist. This means I take care of women. Is there a woman involved somehow in this? A problem at home? Elsewhere? I have no moral agenda, Mr. Flores, and frankly, there are few things that either surprise or offend me. But you have to help out. You have to speak your mind."

Luis shrunk from the doctor's ease of delivery, his fluid command of the situation. His purpose in coming, ill-defined to begin with, drained from him completely. He felt as he had as an immigrant boy fresh from the farm, when the English-speaking school teacher had upbraided him in a language he did not understand. His mind went blank. He picked at a piece of skin in his palm and at length muttered an apology and got up to go. He looked for his hat, but he had left it at home. What could he have been thinking, he wondered, to have come without his hat?

To his surprise, Maria Elena was not cross. She understood how lacking he was in cunning, how disinclined to subterfuge and deception. Patiently, she worked with him, built up his courage, rehearsed what to say. When in these practice sessions he faltered, she reminded him of the doctor's offense, appealing to his pride and sense of justice. For maximum effect, she sometimes appeared to him as she had at the moment of her birth, head grotesquely ballooned with blood, body limp as a rag. At other times she used a different tactic, coming to him as a girl, or a young woman, splendid in appearance, vivacious and full of promise. In this way she reminded him what had been cut short. The flower that had been denied its bloom. She was diligent in fanning the flames of his deprivation and discontent.

Two weeks later, wearing a bolo tie and white cowboy shirt with mother-of-pearl snaps, Luis returned to the doctor. He apologized for his previous behavior. He admitted it was not easy saying what he had come to say.

"And what is that?"

"I want you to be my doctor."

Admonson regarded him. "But why?"

Luis faltered.

Admonson became impatient. "I don't see how I can."

"By saying yes."

"And what will I do for you? What is it that you need?"

It was a difficult question, and Luis waited for Maria Elena's help, which she had promised. Moments later, she materialized, wearing a peasant blouse embroidered with finches and other colorful birds. Her hair was wound in a thick braid and her face painted with makeup. She slid behind him on the chair and eased him forward, until he was perched on the edge. She pushed his knees together in a feminine way and folded his hands demurely in his lap. She bowed his head ever so slightly, in deference to the doctor's position of superiority. She added a faint sibilance to his voice.

"I put myself in your hands, Doctor."

It didn't take a genius to get the message. Nor, once it registered, was it hard to understand why the man insisted on being so vague and indirect. Admonson chided himself. He took pride in his ability to read people, and it irked him when he couldn't. He had been misled by the man's attire, his cowboy boots and starched shirts. By his calloused hands and yes, his Mexican background. The only men posing as women he had ever seen, and these from a distance, were white and anything but shy. He asked if Luis had spoken with anyone else regarding this matter.

"No, Doctor."

"There are specialty clinics, you know. People with more experience than I have. To tell the truth, I have none at all. You would be my first, my only, patient."

Luis inclined his head to signify he took this as a compliment.

"I really shouldn't," said Admonson, who was, despite himself, intrigued. "Apart from a basic standard of care, it's a question of common sense. Simply put, you'd be better served by an expert in the field."

"Please, Doctor."

Admonson resisted. "I could give you a referral."

Flatter him, whispered Maria Elena. Appeal to his skill. His reputation.

"You know how to treat women," said Luis. "You're the best there is. Everyone says."

Admonson demurred.

Luis insisted. "I beg of you."

"I couldn't," said Admonson.

Tell him the truth, Maria Elena enjoined. That your fate is in his hands.

"My fate is in your hands," said Luis.

"I hardly believe that," replied Admonson, flattered nonetheless.

Luis inclined his head, gave a chesty sigh and slowly stood, striking a posture midway between disappointment and defeat. "I am sorry then. I should not have come. I should not have bothered you."

He turned to go and had his hand on the door, when Admonson called him back.

"If I consent to be your doctor in this, I'll need your full cooperation. You understand that."

"Yes, Doctor."

"And you're willing to accept the risks. Psychological, emotional, physical. Whatever. You'll sign a document to that effect."

"Yes."

Admonson weighed the situation one last time. Something didn't seem quite right, but he was not one to back down from a challenge. He could always change his mind later.

"All right. You're willing, I'm willing." He motioned to the chair Luis had recently vacated. "Have a seat. We might as well get started."

Thereafter, his questions became blunt and sexually explicit. Luis's cheeks burned with embarrassment, and he would have run from the room had Maria Elena not been there to help out. She did the talking: it was shocking some of the things she said. But she made no apology. It was necessary, she told her father. If he wanted his revenge, this was the way.

And so it was that Luis Flores, formerly Rodriguez, began his daily doses of estrogen, putting his trust in the hands of the man whose hands had caused his greatest grief. Maria Elena appeared frequently the first few months of his treatment to encourage him and insure he kept his appointments with Dr. Admonson for his monthly injections. She was with him when, at the doctor's insistence, he took the battery of psychological tests to determine his personality profile, his mental stability and adjustment potential. She helped him brave the furtive curiosity of the pharmacist who dispensed his medication, and she stayed with him through the bouts of nausea caused by the pills. She did not explain the specifics of her plan for revenge. She had, in fact, little at all to say about the future. When Luis asked, she was either vague or else told him to be patient, so that eventually he stopped asking. He gave himself up to the treatments and did what he could to ingratiate himself to Admonson. As time passed, Maria Elena came less often, until, at length, for reasons known only to herself, she stopped her visits altogether.

Not long after, Rosa came across his bottle of pills. She had done the laundry and was piling his underwear in the top drawer of the bureau when she felt something in the toe of one of his socks. Normally, she would not have given in to curiosity, but under the circumstances, which included an increasingly moody and uncommunicative husband and a marriage on the verge of collapse, she felt justified in investigating. The bottle, which had no label, was half full. The pills were small, oval and white, with a line down the center and a number embossed above the line. She recognized them as the same pills her mother had been taking ever since her ovaries and womb had been removed. This puzzled and alarmed her.

That night, after the children were in bed, she confronted her husband. She accused him of having an extra-marital affair, which the pills were somehow connected to. She lost her temper and screamed at him. This was most unusual.

Humiliated at being discovered and stung by her accusation of infidelity, Luis was speechless. He had not considered the effect of his clandestine behavior on his wife, had not thought of much else but his own wounds since his daughter's death. He had never intended to hurt anyone but the doctor. Certainly not Rosa. If anything, he had assumed that her suffering, like his, would be placated by revenge. Once the shock of her accusation passed, he vehemently denied having an affair. Lamely, he tried pretending the pills were for someone else. This only made matters worse, so that finally, he told his wife the truth. The pills were his. Then he told a lie.

"They're an aphrodisiac."

Rosa found this hard to believe.

"I want another child," he said.

She frowned. "You've hardly touched me since the tragedy. It's hard to make babies without touching."

His mind had been full of other things, he wanted to say, but he was afraid to tell her what. So he said nothing.

"You blame me for her death," said Rosa.

"No. I blame the doctor." He hesitated. "Forgive me, but sometimes I also blame God."

Rosa was not surprised. "I worry for you, Luis. In church I pray for your bitterness to end."

"I pray also," he said.

"For what do you pray?"

He looked down.

"I am your wife," Rosa reminded him. "Please, show me your face."

With an effort Luis lifted his head and met her eyes. They were dark and steady and inviting of trust. The eyes of a woman, he thought, the eyes of a mother. He wanted to be like her, worthy of trust. Like the women he had sat with in the doctor's waiting room. New mothers, expectant mothers, women inextricably bound to life.

"I pray for another chance," he said.

Rosa was touched, and her face softened. Then something came over her. Rarely the initiator in matters of sex for fear of offending her husband's manhood, she cast fear aside and reached out and touched Luis's cheek with her fingertips. She stroked his skin, the wings of his nose, his lips. He responded by kissing her palm, then embracing her. It was their first such contact in weeks, and the joy of it kept them from letting go, until finally Luis freed an arm to turn off the light. He was anxious to put his wife's mind at ease, eager to show his love further. Fleetingly, it crossed his mind that, hope beyond hope, they might even conceive a child.

High hope, deep despair. When the time came, he could not harden enough to enter Rosa, much less plant the seed. They tried one thing after another, they sweated and toiled, but success eluded them, and finally, they gave up. It was an embarrassment to both of them, an admission of troubles deeper than they imagined. It was a long time before they tried again.

In the months that followed other changes befell their relationship. As his breasts swelled, Luis took to dressing and undressing in private, so that Rosa would not see. Once or twice a week he took a pill he had gotten from the doctor to get rid of the excess water and feeling of bloatedness the hormones caused. On these days he was in and out of the bathroom so many times at work that his boss started to complain. Fearful for his job, Luis took to taking the pills at night, so that instead of missing time at work, he missed sleep. This made him cantankerous and moody. He became subject to fits of temper, and once, to the fear and amazement of his wife and children, he actually broke down in tears. When he recounted this embarrassing episode to Admonson, who was, ironically, the only person in this time of distress he felt capable of confiding in, the doctor explained that it was probably the medicine at work. Women were often temperamental when their hormones were surging.

"Am I a woman now?" asked Luis, displaying a naiveté that worried Admonson.

"No," he replied. "You're a man on hormones. You're far from being a woman."

Luis wasn't so sure. If he were a man, he would have killed this so-called doctor long ago.

"Am I a homosexual?" he asked.

Admonson regarded him. "What do you think you are?"

"I'm following orders."

"Not mine," Admonson was quick to reply.

Luis would not meet his eyes.

"I'm getting a funny feeling here," Admonson said. "Like you're not sure about the way things are going. You're not happy. Maybe we should put things on hold for right now."

"On hold?"

"Stop the medicine. Re-think what we're doing here."

"I'm doing what I'm supposed to," replied Luis.

"You said you're following orders. Whose?"

Luis scolded himself for saying too much. This doctor was cagey. He made you think you could trust him, made you almost like him, then he turned the tables, killing your baby, betraying your trust. A person had to be careful.

"My orders," said Luis. "I'm doing this for myself."

"That's the way it has to be. It has to come from you. From inside. It has to be what you want. What you truly think you are."

Admonson was winging it. By rights he shouldn't have taken the case at all, but curiosity had pushed his hand and now vanity kept him from letting go. He had done some reading and talked to a few colleagues. As long as the treatment was merely a matter of prescribing hormones, it was reversible and relatively safe. He hadn't decided what he would do once they tackled the issue of surgery. As a physician he was as well-acquainted as anyone with the subtleties of the female form, but he had absolutely no experience at all in molding that form from one of the opposite sex. The knowledge of what he would have to cut was actually rather unsettling. He asked Luis if he had given any thought to the matter.

Crafty, thought Luis. Trying to scare me off. He sensed the doctor's trepidation, which made him glad.

"Sometimes I feel like I'm burning up," he said, thinking the news of this might worry the doctor further. "Like there's a fire in my skin. A fever."

"Hot flashes," said Admonson.

Luis frowned.

"The hormones," he explained. "I did warn you."

"I don't like it."

"What's to like? No one said it was easy becoming a woman. Maybe if you grew your hair long. Learned to use a little makeup. A little lipstick." He reached for a framed photograph that sat on the corner of his desk and held it out to Luis. "My wife. She spends half an hour every morning at the mirror. And again in the evening, if we're going out. It's work being a woman. It takes commitment." He paused, grinned. "But then if you're lucky, you get a man like me."

Luis felt simultaneously humiliated and confused. For want of a reply he looked at the photograph of Admonson's wife, a delicately boned, elegant-looking woman in her forties. He wondered what she did to stand up to her husband. And, conversely, what attracted her to him.

"I have no wish to get a man," he said quietly.

Admonson pondered this, shrugged. "No. Of course not. You're married." He took back the picture. "My wife and I have been together twenty-two years. She's a real trooper. A diamond in the rough. Don't know what I'd do without her." He glanced at Luis. "You haven't spoken of your own wife lately. What does she make of all this?"

Luis stiffened. The thought of Rosa made him defensive. "There are no arguments in our family. Whatever I am, I am still the head of the house."

"It's a man's world," agreed Admonson. "Are you sure you want to give it up?"

Luis had never considered it. True, his thirst for revenge had been hottest early on, before he had begun his treatments. He had changed, was changing, but whatever he ultimately became, he expected to be able to call back his former self on demand.

"I give up nothing," he said.

"Ah. A feminist."

Luis frowned. "Women are the salt of the earth. The ones who love. I don't understand you. How can a doctor of women not like women?"

"I have great respect for women," replied Admonson. "I'm not sure I could ever get through labor as they do. Or have children cling like little monkeys to my breast. Or suffer mood swings every month when I'm about to menstruate." He shook his head at the marvel of it all. "Women are amazing creations. They deserve all the credit in the world. They wake me at night, they get me going in the morning, I'm with them all day. My life revolves around women. How can I not like them?"

He returned his wife's photograph to its spot on his desk, then added, "And they pay the bills. What more could a man ask?"

Luis churned inside. He was no match for this doctor, who parried and twisted everything he said. Revenge, it was clear, would not come in the form of words. He stood up.

"I'll take my shot now."

"Of course." Admonson, ever the gentleman, left his chair and extended his hand. "It's been good chatting. And don't worry. We'll take this thing one step at a time. I'll see you in a month."

That night Luis had a dream. A nightmare rather, against which he fought and flailed, twisting the sheets, throwing off the pillow, straining the plastic buttons on his pajama top until, stretched to the breaking point, they popped off. When he woke, drenched in sweat, the overhead light in the bedroom was on, because Rosa, hearing him cry out, had feared that something was wrong. Upon seeing his naked torso, with the rounded breasts and pink nipples of a young woman, she knew that she was right. She had let things go on too long. Her husband had passed beyond help, at least beyond hers. She muttered a prayer, crossed herself and spent the remainder of the night on the living room couch. The following morning, children in tow, she moved out.

Luis was grief-stricken and full of remorse. He vowed to stop the treatments. But each time he tried, he failed. On three separate occasions he made a point of tossing the bottle of pills in the garbage only to find them back in his sock, or in his hand, a fresh tablet on his tongue, or tumbling down his throat to his stomach to work its magic. He called to cancel his monthly doctor's appointment, but when the receptionist came on, the line inexplicably went dead. He called again and did cancel, but when the day came, he went anyway. He was in the grip of something he couldn't control, and he suspected his daughter's hand in it, even though it had been months since she had bothered to pay him a visit. He wondered where it was all leading. More than anything, he prayed that it would soon end.

Three days after leaving, Rosa returned to the apartment to pick up some clothes, expecting her husband to be at work. But, bereft at his family's departure, Luis had called in sick. The meeting between them was awkward in the extreme. Rosa tried to get in and out without talking, but, driven to the brink by her husband's relentless apologies and entreaties to return, she lost control, bursting out in a torrent of questions, none of which he was able to answer to her satisfaction. Was he sick? she asked. No, he replied, not sick. Crazy? No, not crazy either. He was afraid to tell her about Maria Elena, not because she wouldn't believe the child might visit but because she wouldn't believe she would be so cruel and ruthless as to orchestrate her own revenge. Rosa would assume he was either lying or possessed; so he said nothing.

Given so little to work with, Rosa had no choice. If Luis wasn't willing to trust her, she couldn't very well trust him. She needed to look out for herself and the children, and thus stood firm in her decision to separate. It was, she felt, her duty as a mother.

Luis was heartbroken, though he couldn't honestly blame her. He shared his wife's belief in motherhood as a sacred trust, and he made her promise to keep herself and the children safe. For his part he promised that all the trouble would soon be over. This made Rosa cry, and Luis hugged her. I love you, he murmured. She squeezed him. I love you too.

He insisted she and the children have the apartment. He would find something else, a room somewhere, a studio. When the dust settled a little, they would talk again.

He took a room in a cheap hotel and a week later moved to a flat occupied by a practical-minded widow from Guadalajara who shared a bedroom with her mother and disabled daughter and rented out two others to make ends meet. Luis got a clean room with a bureau, a wooden armchair, a throw rug and a window overlooking an alley. Across the hall from him was the other boarder, a laconic Salvadorean gentleman in his sixties, who liked to drink alone. Relationships in the household were cordial but circumscribed. Luis left early for work, returned late and kept to himself. He sent the bulk of his paycheck to Rosa. What little he had left went to the doctor, the medication and the occasional thrift-store shirt or sweater to accommodate his new shape. For fear of running into Rosa and the children he stopped going to church, although he continued to pray, sometimes feverishly, in his room. He had not seen Maria Elena for months and worried that she had forsaken him. He longed for her reassurance and sense of purpose. Her wits and determination. He prayed that she return, and at the same time he prayed for Rosa, whom he missed dearly, and for the children, whom he loved beyond measure. And he prayed for himself, because, of everyone, he needed it most of all.

As the anniversary of Maria Elena's death approached, he started to unravel. The rage and sorrow and despair he had kept inside seemed all to bubble up at once. He missed work. He holed up in his room. When the date came for his monthly visit to the doctor, it was all he could do to struggle into some clothes and get out the door.

Admonson seemed pleased to see him. He asked if there was anything new to report.

"I'm being poisoned," said Luis.

Admonson became instantly alert. "What do you mean?"

"I'm suffering. She has left me. She must think I am worthless. Beneath contempt. Yet I do this for her."

"For whom?"

"My daughter. My beloved Maria Elena." He fingered the wooden cross he had taken to wearing around his neck.

Admonson did not conceal his alarm. "What daughter? What poison?"

Luis felt close to bursting. There was a letter opener on the doctor's desk. He could kill him now. Kill him, then kill himself. Be done with it.

A voice suggested he hold off a minute.

Luis almost wept with relief. It was Maria Elena, and though he couldn't see her, he knew she was close by. Leave the doctor, she said. Leave him now and come to me. The time has arrived. Come to me.

Luis trembled with joy. Without another word he fled the doctor's office, fled the waiting room full of mothers and infants, fled the medical building and headed for the streets. All that day and all the next the voice followed him. It called to him in the wind off the hills and the steam rising from sidewalk grates, in the electric buzz of trolley wires and the squeal of car brakes. It sang to him in the hiss of his shower and the flush of his toilet, in the fog and rain and rising sun. He listened in rapture, he who had been so forlorn. He begged to see her face.

But Maria Elena chose not to show herself. Instead, she kept repeating the same half-dozen words over and over, until Luis grabbed his ears and cried for her to stop. She did not, and this made him angry. He scolded her, father to daughter, occasioning his landlady, who happened to be nearby, to ask who he was talking to.

"Maria Elena," he replied.

She cocked an eye.

"My dead daughter," he explained.

The woman crossed herself and went away, but the next day, with apologies for the inconvenience, gave Luis his notice. Two days later he was out on the street and driven to distraction by his daughter's relentless chatter. Her words had ceased being words, and the drone had become impossible to bear. In desperation he made his way to his old apartment, arriving at the door just as Rosa was on the way out. She was dressed in black.

"I was wondering if you'd come," she said.

"Forgive me. I'm half crazy. I could think of nowhere else."

"Do you need a ride?"

"I need help."

This she could believe, and though her husband's urgent manner and disheveled appearance made her wary, she was not dead in the heart. She took his arm. "Come. We'll go together."

It was the anniversary of their daughter's death. Rosa drove to the cemetery, where they were joined by other members of the family, including their two sons, who came with an aunt. Luis wept to see them again, wept to see Rosa, wept anew when the prayer for Maria Elena was given. The girl stopped chattering long enough for him to hear. The force of her silence was overwhelming. He felt light as a cloud. When the prayer ended, she appeared to him for the last time.

She came as a mature woman and exuded a sense of contentment and imminent satisfaction. Luis could not understand why. Apart from a year of waiting, he had done nothing to avenge her death. At best, he had only marginally insinuated himself into the doctor's life, and to what effect? The doctor was not suffering. Far from it. He seemed to have the upper hand at every turn.

It was August, and a fog-driven wind cut through Luis's clothing. He hugged himself and blew into his hands, but the chill, like a tide, crept inward. Like something from the grave, it made him tremble. The feeling of weightlessness vanished. Suddenly, he was cold. And frightened. He thought his time had come to die.

Maria Elena hovered a foot or two above the grave. Her feet were planted in air, her legs slightly spread, her arms akimbo. Her expression was resolute, yet there was a certain playfulness in her eyes.

The wind picked up, tossing Luis's hair across his face. He heard laughter, then noticed that a bird now perched on Maria Elena's outstretched finger. A sparrow. In its beak it held a seed.

Maria Elena had hair the color of coal. Eyes that matched the polished ebony of her father's machete. Lips the flesh of saints. When she smiled, her face burst to life and the sparrow took flight, circling once in a halo around her head and once around the grave. Then, straight as an arrow, it headed for Luis.

Afterwards, he would remember a parting kiss. An inner quickening. A warmth. The bird vanished inside him, and moments later his precious daughter, his treasure, Maria Elena Hermosilla Rodriguez, was gone.

They named her Angelica. At her birth nine months later Dr. Admonson used a modified Caesarean section. Perhaps this was because he had been chastened by past failures with natural childbirth. Perhaps because, despite an exhaustive search, he had failed to locate the mother's vagina. Whatever the reason, he exercised the physician's prerogative to usurp Mother Nature in favor of a surgical delivery. The C-section served another purpose as well: it allowed him to look inside Luis to see just what the hell was going on.

What he saw was not so different from what he always saw: a term infant attached by a cord and placenta to a source of nutrition, in this case the blood-engorged wall of Luis's lower intestine. After removing the baby and severing the cord, he took a sample of the attachment site for further study. He looked around for anything else out of the ordinary and finding nothing, sewed his patient up. Then he went to talk to the press.

Rosa, who was not present at the birth, met her husband and new daughter in the recovery room. Luis's impregnation, which to many had come as a shock and embarrassment, was to her a miracle, the answer, if slightly outlandish, to her prayers. She was as thrilled as any new parent. More, perhaps, because she had just landed a new job she would have hated to leave, even for a month or two. Now she wouldn't have to, and at the same time she could have the joy of a new face, a new spirit in the family. It was as close to Heaven in mortal flesh as she could imagine. She felt deeply blessed.

Luis was still recovering from the anesthetic when she entered the room. He didn't completely recognize her, but she kissed him anyway and held his hand while he slept. The baby was wrapped in a flannel receiving blanket and tucked in a bassinet next to his bed. When she started to cry, Rosa instinctively picked her up. She cradled her in her arms and held her to her chest, but the child's wailing only grew louder. Finally, Luis opened his eyes. He motioned to his wife.

"Give her to me," he said feebly.

Rosa complied. "She's hungry."

Luis pulled his gown aside and placed the child at his breast. She rooted a few moments before latching on. Luis felt an instant of pain, then the milk started to flow. It was an incredible sensation. He thought of all the things that might have happened, all the things that did. Who was he, he wondered, to deserve such a miracle? The Devil had been inside him. Now the Devil had turned to light.

He transferred the baby to his other breast, where she promptly fell asleep. Luis soon followed, and what he dreamed he did not remember, and when he woke was ravenous, and ate a meal that was quite enough, said the astonished nurse, for two grown people, or even, God forbid, three.

HOLLY PRADO

The Tall, Upheaving One

Holly Prado grew up in Nebraska and Michigan, and now lives in Los Angeles, where she reviews poetry and fiction for the Los Angeles Times. *Her poetry has been published in* The Paris Review, The Kenyon Review, Rolling Stone, *and other magazines, in numerous anthologies, and is included on the CD* Word Rituals.

"The Tall, Upheaving One" is part of a mytho-poetic sequence in Esperanza: Poems for Orpheus, *Prado's seventh book. Orpheus was the Greek god of inspiration, as well as the renowned musician who lost his wife, Euridice, to the Underworld. "The singing of Orpheus," writes Prado, "lifted trees from the earth to dance; drew wild animals, tamed, to him; enchanted even Hades and Persephone, the King and Queen of Souls in the Underworld. This was the Orpheus his ancient Greek followers could turn to not as a national god with public powers but as one whose influence could be felt individually in curative ways."*

—T. W.

The cypress that I pray to:
it can fly.   nothing is a single
species.   we're made of bark, then
avalanche.   Orpheus can make us anything,

can make us god's own door.   cypress
or oak or black: to be accepted there,
across the boundary, as when I leave the house
this morning, walking—nothing painful
in my legs.   I tell misunderstanding,
"this is our last year together," then,
I see, just up the street, that planets
are our bodies; their mouths slam through
my wrists.   I was a child who practiced
jumping from the top of anything right
into the air.   music was a swirl of vines
and leaves that left my throat.

I'm calling.   and I'm waiting.
and I'm called to.

this black, the pure unknown which finds its way
exactly like the song you can't get rid of,
the one I start with now and won't give up.
the god, obsessed with worship that is memorized,
abiding, until the prayer itself moves inside
out, converts these worlds of sliding rock to fragrance.

I'm calling and I'm calling and I'm called.

PATRICIA A. MCKILLIP

❧ ⸻⸻⸻⸻⸻⸻⸻⸻⸻⸻⸻⸻⸻⸻⸻⸻ ☙

Oak Hill

Patricia A. McKillip is the World Fantasy Award–winning author of The Forgotten Beasts of Eld, The Riddlemaster Trilogy, The Book of Atrix Wolfe, Winter Rose, Song for the Basilisk, *and many other novels, beautifully crafted and utterly magical. She has also written short fiction published in various anthologies and often reprinted in* The Year's Best Fantasy and Horror.

This year she's back with "Oak Hill," a story which is something of a departure. "Oak Hill" is an urban fantasy tale set on the streets of Bordertown, an imaginary city in a series of books created for teenage readers. You needn't be familiar with the series, however, to slip under the spell of McKillip's distinctive prose—evoking the angst of adolescence with an almost painful clarity.

McKillip lives in the Catskill Mountains of New York State.

—T. W.

Maris wrote in her book:

"Dear Book, You are my record and my witness of the magic I learn in Bordertown. I have chosen you because you are silver and green, which seem to me magic colors, though I don't know why. Anyway, as soon as I learn some spells I will write them in you. As soon as I find Bordertown." Squatting on the dusty road, the blank book on her knee, she looked up at a distant growl of gears. She stuck her thumb out, hopefully. A woman in a pickup with a front seat full of what looked like the brawling body parts of fourteen children, all under six, gave Maris a haggard look and left her in a cloud of gold. Maris blinked dust out of her eyes, and picked up her pen again, which was also silver, with a green plume. "I hope to get there soon. That woman did not look as though she knew the way, nor does this road look like it knows the way to anything but worn-out farms and diners. But. You never know. That, I believe, is the first rule of magic."

She stopped there, pleased, and put the book and pen into her backpack.

Much later, after an endless ride in a slow truck towing a full hay-wagon that kept wanting to ramble off by itself into the fields, she sat in a diner at a truck stop just off the interstate and alternately chewed french fries and the end of her pen as she wrote. It was quite late; the nearest city, she guessed from the newspapers in the racks, seemed to be Oak Hill. From the size of the newspaper, there was a lot of it. "Bordertown could be there. It could be anywhere," she wrote. "Which is just as well, since I have no idea where I am. Did I cross a state line in that hay-wagon? Anyway, it gives me some place to go toward. Oak Hill. It sounds magical, a great city within an ancient forest of oak overlooking the world." She paused, seeing it instead of the lights flashing in the dark along the interstate, instead of trucks grinding and snorting their way to the ranks of fuel pumps beside the diner. "But possibly it has no more to do with oaks than Los Angeles has to do with angels. Expect the unexpected. Which is another rule of magic. Except in this case, I think the expected is more—"

"You want something besides fries, hon?" the waitress asked her. The waitress was tall and big-boned, with a heavy, placid face and skin as clear and smooth as silk. Yes, Maris said silently, intensely, I want your skin. Your beautiful milky skin. I will give you anything for that.

"No," she said aloud. "Just another coke, please."

The waitress hovered. "It's kind of late, isn't it? For you to be out here by yourself?"

"My parents are over at the motel," Maris said glibly, "watching TV."

"Oh."

"I got hungry."

"Oh." She shifted weight, her expression unchanging. "Good thing you brought your backpack with you, to keep it safe. Never know about parents."

"It has my secrets in it," Maris explained. "I'm going to learn magic." That, she learned early, always made people fidget, forget to ask questions, find something interesting in the stuffed deer head, or the clock across the room. Another thing was her face, which made them uncomfortable, especially when she painted stars over the chronic mega-zits that built up like cinder cones over a smoldering beneath the surface. Her eyes were too close together, and a watery grey; her nose had grown a roller-coaster bump in the middle of it; her long hair, once white-blonde, had changed the past year or so into a murky, indeterminate shade between ash and mud. She had taken to dressing out of thrift shops to distract attention from her hopeless face: worn velvets, big hats with fake pearl necklaces looped along the brim, sequined tops that made her glitter like tinfoil on a bright day, long, tattered skirts of rich, warm colors that made her look mysterious, a gypsy, a fortune-teller, a woman who knew secrets she might part with for the right gift. Her mother said she looked like an explosion at a Halloween party. "People like you for yourself," her mother said. "Not what you look like. I mean—You know what I mean. Anyway. I love you."

The waitress seemed unfazed by magic; the word glanced off her benign expression without a ripple, as if it were something kids did, like dyeing their hair green, and then grew out of. "Well," she said. "I guess they'll know where to find you when they miss you."

"Nobody knows where to find me," Maris wrote a day or three days or a year later, her back against a cement wall, as if she had been driven there by the overwhelming noise of the city. Her fingers holding the pen were cold; she had been cold since she got to the city, though people slept outside without blankets, and the thin light passed through a windless shimmering of heat and dust. It made writing difficult, but at least the fear stayed in her fingers; so far it hadn't gone to her head. She paused to stare at a group of people on the other side of the street. They had just come out of a club; they wore black leather, black beads, black feathers in their long, pale, rippling hair. Their sunshades were tinted silver; they stared back at Maris out of insect eyes, and then began to laugh. She pushed back against the wall, as if she could make herself invisible. "Oak Hill has no oaks. Oak Hill has no trees. The truck driver said he knew where I should go, and he stopped in the middle of all this and said this is it. This is what? I asked. He said, This is the end of the line. I got out and he kept going. If this is the end of the line, then why did he keep going? You don't understand, I said. I am going to Bordertown to learn magic. This isn't Bordertown. This isn't where I want to go. And he said, Take a look at that. All I saw were some white-haired kids on fancy bikes. He said, Keep out of their way, and find a place to stay with your own kind; that's all I can tell you. Then I got out and he kept going." She paused again, watched a pair of bikers shouting at one another, both with one thigh-high leather boot dropped for balance in four inches of water pooling over a clogged drain, as they argued about who had splashed who. She returned her attention to her book. "This is not at all what I expected the unexpected to be like."

A shadow fell over her. She looked up into the most beautiful face she had ever seen.

Later, when she had time to think again, she wondered which she had seen first: the beauty that transfixed her and changed the way she thought about the word, so that it stretched itself, in an instant, to embrace even the noisy, unfeeling, vain and swaggering opposite sex; or, as her eyes rose instinctively to see her own reflection in his expression, the terrifying malevolence in his eyes.

She jumped, a faint squeak escaping her; she felt her shoulder blades hit the wall. "You," he said explosively.

She made another strangled noise.

"Get out of here. Find your own kind. If you have one. There must be some place for small, white mice to scutter together in this town. You are taking up space in my eyes that I require for other purposes, such as reading the graffiti on the wall behind you."

She stared at him, stunned by hatred, as if he had walked across the chaotic street just to slap her for existing. She recognized him then, by his thigh-high boots: one of the bikers who had been arguing in the puddle. His satin shirt, the same silvery-grey as his eyes, had a tide-line of water and dirt on the front. She wondered if he had eaten the other biker, or just froze him to death with his eyes.

She caught her breath suddenly, dizzily. I am here, she thought. This is the place. "You," she said, scarcely hearing herself. "You are not human."

He spat, just missing her shoe. "Why am I still seeing you?" he wondered.

"I came here because of you."

He was seeing her then, where before he had seen only what he was not. His eyes narrowed dangerously. "You are not worth the chase, ugly little mouse," he said softly. "You are not worth breath. But I will give you ten. Five breaths of terror, and five of flight, before I summon a pack of ferrets to catch the mouse. They like to play with mice, and there are very few places here to hide. One."

"I came here to learn magic."

He blinked, perhaps hoping she would disappear. "Two."

"I have a book to write the spells in." She showed him. "And a pen." She was babbling, she knew, wasting breath, but if he was all the magic she met in Bordertown, then he was all she had. "I'm not running away from anything, or anyone, and you're right, I am ugly, but that's not why I want to learn—"

"Three."

"So since you can't stand the sight of me, maybe there's someone you know who is blind, maybe, or doesn't care—And it's not even for me," she added desperately.

"Four."

"I mean, it's not so I can turn myself beautiful or something, at least I don't think it is, it's just that—"

"Five."

"It's what I want. How can I say what I want when I don't even know what magic is? The word for it is all I know, and you know all the rest. Teach me."

He was so still she didn't hear him breathe. Then he said very softly, "Run."

For a moment, they both wondered if she would. Then she heard the word itself, clear and simple, as if he had handed her a pebble. He had given her five more breaths; he had given her more than that; maybe the danger was not from him. Maybe he was teaching her the first step: How to listen. Or maybe, she thought as she hugged book and backpack to herself and scrambled to her feet, it was a word of advice, something to do with the sudden roar of bikes around the corner. She whirled, then turned back to look at him. "Thank you," she said, and saw his look of utter astonishment. Then she ran down the street, smelling the clogged drain, oil spills, exhaust, hearing laughter around her, burning like the hazy light. Dragons bellowed at her heels, followed her around corners, down alleys where rats and startled cats scurried for safety. She risked a single glance backward, out of curiosity, and found more of him, though younger, lithe and feral, their wild hair white as dandelion seed, their faces, like his, doors that opened and slammed at once, so that she could only glimpse something they would never let her enter. Their hatred was unambiguous and relentless. They would not let her go; they followed her through crowds and up steps, into abandoned buildings and out again, whooping and calling, barking like dogs, crying a name now and then, until they until finally tired of playing, and on a busy street, where pedestrians, laughing and cursing, leaped out of their way, one shot forward among the crush to ride beside her.

He caught her arm; sobbing, her hair catching in her eyes, she tried to pull away. "Get on!" the biker hissed, and Maris, stumbling over her hem, tried desperately to see. The voice was a woman's. "Hurry!"

She had lost her backpack in some alley; but she still clutched her book and pen; even now, trying to hoist herself onto a moving bike, she refused to drop them. The bike picked up speed; hair flicking into Maris' eyes and mouth was dark. She spat it out, tightening her hold, the book and pen crammed between them. It was a long time before the voices of dragons behind them became the beat of her heart.

Later, under the light of a single bare bulb hanging down from a scruffy ceiling, she wrote, "Dear Book, I don't know where I am." She paused, hugging herself, staring down at the book. Her skirt was ripped, her feet blistered and bleeding from running in vintage patent leather shoes; her hair and face were grubby, her hands skinned from where she had slipped on garbage in an alley and skidded on cobblestones. She picked up the pen again, though it hurt to write. "You are all I have left of the other world. I lost everything else. This house is swarming with people. Most of them are my age. They came for so many reasons. Some of them are too scared of what they ran from to talk. Some of them are too angry. The house was an apartment building once, I think. There are stairs running everywhere. But a lot of the walls were torn down. Or maybe they just fell down. You can see plumbing pipes, and water stains all over. They gave me something to eat, and told me never, never go into that part of town again. But how can I not? I asked them where to go to learn magic. They just laughed. He didn't laugh. Trueblood. That's what they said he was. Elf. Beautiful and dangerous to humans. But he has something I want."

She paused again, glimpsing his face among the scattered, terrifying memories of the afternoon. Had he warned her about the bikers? Or had he called them? She wrote again, slowly, "I'll have to disguise myself somehow to go back there. They know my face."

The mysterious comings and goings in the house, she learned as days passed, had simple explanations; there was some order to the constant movement, the replacement of faces. Many of the kids had jobs; they played in bands, or made things to sell, like jewelry, or dyed clothes, out of what they found thrown out in the streets, or in cardboard boxes at thrift shops. Things filtered down to them from places that gave Maris a glimpse of a world beyond the bleak, crumbling buildings. Some—odd, bright feathers, dried leaves—hinted of the wood that Maris had guessed must be only a ghost, a memory of oak among the streets. Other things spoke of wealth: rich fabrics, tarnished rings, beads and buttons tossed casually away that bore elaborate carvings, or strange, woven designs, or even faces, sometimes, that seemed not quite human. "Where did you get this?" she asked constantly. "Where did this come from? What is this?" The answers were always vague, unsatisfying, and accompanied by the baffled expression that Maris seemed to inspire in people.

"Nobody understands why you're here," a girl who made colorful shirts out of scraps told her one day.

"I came to learn magic," Maris said; it seemed simple enough, and she had said it a hundred times.

"Why? Because of something that happened to you? Because of someone?" Maris gazed at her, baffled herself, then thought she understood.

"You mean because of the way I look? Because I'm ugly? Things happened to me because of that, and that's why I ran away to learn magic?"

"You're not—" the girl stopped, and started again. "No one that just comes here for—" She stopped again. "I mean—"

Maris scratched her head, wondered absently if she had fleas. "Maybe," she suggested, "I could understand what you mean if you tell me why you're here."

The girl's face, whose beauty she seemed always trying to deny, slammed shut like a door, the way the elven faces had, against Maris. Then, as she studied

Maris's face, with its churning skin and angelfish eyes, Maris saw her open again, slowly, to show Maris things she kept hidden behind her eyes: fear, loathing, hope.

"You're not afraid," she said abruptly. "You're not afraid of—what you left behind. That's what makes you different."

Maris peered at her, between strands of untidy hair. "Maybe you could explain," she said tentatively. "Maybe you could tell me your name."

They sat for a long time on the bare mattress where Elaine sewed swatches of gaudy fabric into a sleeve while she talked. At supper, an endless parade wandered at will through the kitchen, most of it standing up to eat before parts broke off and disappeared, to be replaced by others, rattling crockery, sucking in stew, grunting to one another while they chewed. Maris, who helped cook, took a closer look at the faces around her. For days, they had seemed indistinguishable, all pale and thin, secretive, giving her strangers' stares if they looked at her at all. Few of them knew her name, though someone had given her a nickname. She had been called a lot of things, most of them having to do with fast food, or small, burrowing animals. But this one surprised her. Teacher, they called her, because she was always asking unanswerable questions. Teach.

Tonight she separated their faces, picked out things from their expressions, their eyes, put words to them: furtive, belligerent, sick, angry, scared. All of them were scared, she realized slowly. Even the ones who ignited at a skewed look, a word pitched wrong. They hit with their eyes, their fists, their voices. Nothing could come close to them; they were scared the worst.

"Dear Book," she wrote after supper. "I could not believe the things Elaine told me. She showed me her scars. She said I could not, no, there was no way, but I finally persuaded her: she is going to dye my hair with her cloth dyes, which she says are made of natural things, like nuts and berries. She knows someone who knows someone who finds those things and makes the dyes. She said she'd think about my face, which is easy to forget, but hard not to recognize, especially with all the living constellations on it. She told me not to talk about myself like that. Why shouldn't I? Everyone else does. Besides, that way I get to laugh first. She didn't understand that. Anyway, she knows someone else who makes masks out of feathers and painted cloth, but so far she's balking over that. She thinks it's too dangerous. But so is magic. I didn't know that before, but I know it now."

She woke in the dark, that night, hearing strange music. The house was pitch-black, as if the power had gone out again; a single streetlight, as yet unbroken, gave her an obscure perspective of shadowy stairs and corners as she moved through the house. The music drew her down, down, like a child's hand, innocent and coaxing, saying: Come look at this flower, come look at this pebble, this nut. She followed it without thinking, barefoot, her eyes barely open, trailing the torn lace of an old, sleeveless flapper's dress she wore to bed. Before she had gotten up, the moment she had heard the music, she had reached for her book and pen; she carried them without realizing it, without wondering what she would do with them on an empty city street in the middle of the night.

The door squealed when she opened it, but no one in the house called out. The gritty sidewalk was still warm. She saw no one playing anywhere; the music might have come from someone piping on the moon. She yawned, trying to open her eyes, see more clearly. It comes from the streets, she thought, entranced. All the water pipes and cables underground are playing themselves. The electricity is singing. She felt the vibrations through her feet, heard the music find its way into her blood. Then she heard herself humming random, unpredictable notes, like the patter of light rain. The city flowed away from her eyes in a sea-wave, a cluttered grey tumble of buildings and streets, with lamp lights spinning like starfish among them. It paused, and rolled toward her again, green this time and golden-brown, smelling not of stone but of earth.

She stood on the oak hill, surrounded by a vast wood. The trees were huge, old, towering over her, even while she saw through them into the distances they claimed. I am queen of the hill, she thought dreamily. Where is my face? She bent, still humming, and began to gather fallen leaves.

She found the oak leaves, the next morning, inside the pages of her book.

She shook them out slowly, staring. Around her she heard the heavy thump of feet finding the floor, a tea kettle shrieking in the kitchen, somebody running up a scale on an electric guitar, somebody else yelling in protest. She shifted a leaf, fitted one over another, another against them. Her skin prickled suddenly. She picked up the pen, wrote unsteadily on a blank page: "Thank you."

She borrowed thread from Elaine, to patch a skirt, she said, and spent the morning sewing leaves into a crude mask. The eye holes were tricky; they kept slipping away, no matter how much thread she used. Finally she threatened them with scissors if they did not let her see, and leaves opened under her needle to let the city in.

She tore a ribbon from her skirt to tie it with, and slid it back into her book. Elaine, sewing with feverish concentration on her mattress, scarcely looked up from her own work as Maris dropped the thread beside her. She grunted, and pushed a jar with her dirty, delicate bare foot towards Maris. "That dye I promised you."

"What color?"

Elaine shrugged. "Something. I'm not sure. It'll find its color from your hair."

It found no color at all, apparently, Maris saw when her hair dried. I look like I've been frightened to death, she thought, trying to flatten a silvery crackling cloud of spider web. All the mirrors in the house were cracked, warped, distressed. Like all the faces in them, she thought, wandering from one to another, trying to get a clearer image of herself. She gave up finally, and borrowed clothes to go outside: a pair of torn jeans, a black T-shirt that said, "Yosemite National Park. Feed the wildlife in you." She went barefoot in case she had to run.

She was lost before she turned three corners. The ominous, sagging buildings all looked alike; strangers jostled her without seeing her. The city stank like an unwashed, unfed animal; it wailed and growled incessantly. There seemed no magic anywhere, nor any possibility of magic, ever in mortal time. There were no leaves anywhere, only stone and shadow and light too harsh to see through. Maris opened her book, found the mask quickly. She tied it on and breathed again. In disguise, she thought, you can be anyone. Anything. Then, chilled, she remembered what she was carrying.

But they don't have to be mine, she thought an instant later. I found them in the street. Someone must have dropped them, someone too much in a hurry to stop. She tangled the pen into the tangle of silver on her head, let the green plume dangle over her shoulder, and tucked the book under her arm. He hadn't noticed the closed book, probably, only the open book before she began to run.

Her skin prickled as she thought of him, part fear, part anticipation. How can I persuade him? she asked the book. Maybe I should give him something. If I ever find him again. If he even lets me talk before he calls the ferrets. Anyway, I don't have anything he would want. I don't even have anything he would want to look at.

Or is he expecting me?

She let the city pull her into itself, drifted with it deeper into its unknown heart.

Gradually she realized that people were staring at her, avoiding her, parting to let her pass, even those who wore fine, scrolled blades like pendants around their necks and masked their eyes with darkness. She was used to hastily averted eyes, even to the sudden silence that she seemed to inspire, at least among humans, before she passed and they thought she couldn't hear their jokes behind her back. But these were the ferrets, wild, magical creatures who had chased her, barking, through the streets; now they were stepping out of her way, their faces carefully expressionless. Can't they tell? she wondered. Can't they see? It's only me behind a mask of dying leaves and a T-shirt from Yosemite. They couldn't, apparently. She walked taller, took a longer, sweeping stride through them, refusing to think about what would happen when they did find out that it was only her.

She saw him finally, coming toward her down the sidewalk, and she stopped. He saw her at the same time; his face hardened. But it had masked itself against fear, she saw in wonder, not against her. He stepped around her carefully, hoping, it seemed, that she had not stopped for him. But she turned, looking up at him as he passed, holding his eyes, until he took a futile half-step, trapped in her gaze, and finally stood still.

He whispered, "Who are you?"

She swallowed sudden dryness, decided simply to answer his question. "Maris."

"Who do you want?"

"You."

He drew breath slowly. His skin was so pale it could not grow any whiter, but she saw the tension along his jaw. "What do you want from me?"

She swallowed again, feeling the closed book under her elbow pushing hard against her ribs, wondering how much power the mask she wore held over him, wondering if she had the courage to say what she wanted to say. But how else would she know who she was, in that moment, in his eyes? She answered finally, carefully, "I want you to say yes. To anything I ask."

"Yes."

"Good." She lifted her hand, pushed the mask up so that he could see her marred, sweaty human face. "Teach me magic."

He stared at her silently a moment longer. Then a shudder rippled through him, pushed words out. "Who are you?"

She opened her mouth, then stared back at him, suddenly perplexed. Maris, she had started to say, but she did not recognize this Maris, who had stopped a Trueblood in his tracks and made him ask her for her name. "I don't know," she said slowly, still astonished that he was not summoning his ferrets furiously out of gutter drains and broken windows. "Who are you afraid of?"

She heard his breath again; his face lost some of its rigidity. "I could not see your eyes," he said softly. "Or your face. Only leaves. You looked at me out of leaves as old as our world, and said you had come for me. Until now, I thought I was afraid of nothing." He paused again. "I seem to be afraid of you. Where did you get the leaves?"

"In a dream."

He nodded, unsurprised. "And you came back here to look for me. You aren't afraid of me, even after I drove you out of here."

Oh, yes, I am, she thought. Oh, yes. I would be just as afraid of the lightning bolt I caught in my hand. But I am the Maris who can catch a lightning bolt and still be alive and talking to it. "Why did the forest let me dream about it? Why did it give me leaves?"

He shook his head. "I have dreamed of it. But it has never let me take anything away with me." He touched the leaves above her eyes gently, tentatively. Then he asked, unexpectedly, "What happened to your hair?"

"It went white."

Again he nodded; such things happened, she guessed, in the old forest. "You look more like one of us."

"I was trying to disguise myself, so you wouldn't recognize me and chase me away again."

He shrugged slightly. "It wouldn't have mattered; all humans look alike to me. I would never have recognized you without the leaves."

"But you didn't know—"

"I recognized the magic in you," he said simply.

She felt her clenched hold on the book, on herself, loosen a little. Standing on the crowded, burning street with him, human in a place where borders merged, worlds touched and might explode or sing at any moment, she suddenly felt safe. "Then you will teach me."

His brows lifted slightly, ruefully; he looked for a moment almost human. "I said yes."

"Dear Book," she wrote in fear and triumph that night, on her stained mattress, while the old building stirred noisily around her. Sounds of hurrying boots and arguments cluttered the air; someone played a raucous ballad on a guitar; someone else played, very faintly, an older ballad on a pipe. "Today I did my first magic. I made one of the Trueblood see my human face and say my name. Maybe that's why we all have come here, with our scars and our secret faces. We want the ancient magic to recognize us. To welcome us home." She paused. Her pen descended, hesitated at a word, wrote again finally. "I'll write to my mother tomorrow. This is hardest for me to say. She was right."

CHRISTOPHER HARMAN

Jackdaw Jack

Christopher Harman was born in Chorley, Lancashire, England. After living and working in the Blackpool area for ten years he now lives in Preston, Lancashire and works in public libraries. In his spare time he enjoys horror and science fiction films, modern classical music, hill walking, and local history. Although he was a fan of Tolkien, C. S. Lewis, and Ursula K. Le Guin during his teens, he developed a preference for horror and supernatural fiction. The writers who have made the biggest impression on him are M. R. James and Ramsey Campbell.

He began writing on a cold, wet November afternoon in 1991 and since then his stories have been published in All Hallows, *the* Doppelganger Broadsheet, *and* The Year's Best Fantasy and Horror.

Harman is a master at creating menace out of seemingly ordinary English country life. Last year, his story "In the Fields" was picked for our eleventh annual volume. "Jackdaw Jack" was originally published in Ghosts & Scholars 26.

—E. D.

It was the wind suddenly prising at the row of windows high above the shelves that roused Karen Vaunce from her usual mid-afternoon stupor. She shook herself and stared into the microfilm reader screen that was a sunlit view onto an older world. Determined to concentrate, she was already looking past the scrawl of the census enumerator and into the reflected reference library, idly intent on two figures behind the glass doors. She recognised them when they entered, their voices dropping only a little as the librarian eyed them owlishly and other heads bobbed up. Karen smiled to herself, recalling their bemused faces in the pub the previous evening, when she'd told them how she was spending her remaining free weeks before college in September.

Pulling up a chair, Linda produced a snare-drum rattle. "How can you stand it? It's like a morgue, this place," she said, unbuttoning her red leatherette coat.

"It was till you arrived," Karen said, laying down her pen and stretching. One of the window panes creaked in sympathy. Graham turned from showing his chewing mouth to the librarian. "If any of my descendants start researching me I'll haunt them."

"What makes you think you're going to have any descendants, Graham?" Linda said his name with sarcastic emphasis, but her look was sly, encouraging. Graham chewed vigorously around a grin and started flicking her hair. Karen could smell the oil that patched his overalls. Beginning to feel excluded, she asked him why he wasn't at the garage.

"Test driving a BMW," he said, looking impressed with himself.

"Like all over Colmorden, he's testing it," Linda said, her eyes bright and wicked. At her invitation to join them, Karen cast a rueful glance at the screen as if she hadn't already decided to quit for the day. "Might as well," she said. Stowing away her notes, she felt she'd achieved something. She'd found her grandmother's grandfather and his two brothers, though Gran had mentioned only one. With their parents, William and Ivy Singleton, they were a neat family unit living in Grobbey in 1851. Karen twisted the motorised lever and flying names were like stacked ridges of trembling grey cloud. The noise should have precluded talk, but Linda persisted as she opened a Mars Bar. Reflected in the reader screen, the librarian looked up from her desk. "What?" Karen almost shouted. The librarian was rising—a slow jack-in-the-box.

"Somebody's watching." Linda's voice rang theatrically, because the film had snagged somewhere between the reels. Peering, pulling gently, Karen was aware of a buttress of sunlight with a dark shape at its source in one of the high windows. She jumped as the film freed itself and rattled on. Of course—a momentary power cut. But Linda was tapping her shoulder, smirking as she pointed a thick finger of chocolate at the window.

A head and shoulders, edges faded by an aureole of sunlight like shards of ice. Someone wearing a cape? Waving?

"Window cleaner? I dunno," Karen muttered, self-conscious, convinced the figure was gesturing at her and everyone knew it.

The film slow hand-clapped on one reel. Karen pulled it off and fitted it into its box. Glancing up again, she saw that there was nobody there, but as if it had been affronted by their stares, the window abruptly clattered open on the hinge running along its base. Noises nosed in: cars, car horns, a dog barking and a sound that had Karen watching the rushing clouds as if they really could be rubbing together like millions of wind-tormented leaves. Graham was at the door, calling out, "Are we going or what?"

Outside, the wind had dropped to a breeze. The metallic pink BMW stood at the curb. Karen sat behind Linda, and Graham swung the vehicle into the traffic, then turned off into a street of peeling terraces. Away from the town centre he drove with uncharacteristic caution, but this wasn't his rust-scabbed Cortina, and in these streets there were few to impress. Beyond allotments, white smoke, confused by the wind, spread like foliage over two factory chimneys. At Linda's insistence, Graham turned back for the centre of town. In the High Street, they were hemmed in by traffic as shoppers, perhaps expecting rain, dodged around them. The interior of the car had more style and comfort than Karen was used to at home in Coniston Street. She wondered if it was the tinted glass that created the effect of a shadow swooping low, again and again, over the car.

Graham left Karen and Linda outside Lewis's. Inside, Linda wandered to a counter where a girl was demonstrating make-up. Karen ate in the café upstairs, then stood outside at the bus-stop. The four o'clock queue wound back on itself twice. Gran's face appeared, thin, vague-eyed, reproachful, amidst Karen's uncharitable thoughts on pensioners who had all day to shop, then grumbled at peak hour queues. When the bus arrived, all the seats were taken and those standing in the aisle were not about to alight. She trudged back to the library.

When she arrived home soon after seven, her father was adjusting his peaked cap before the hallway mirror.

"Your Aunt Marie rang. Your Gran had a bit of a turn this afternoon."

Karen stood indecisively. Gran had been unwell for weeks, and Karen was unsure how to express more than a general concern. "Oh, right," she said.

"Marie thought it's be best if you went around another night."

"No problem," Karen said absently. She dropped her bag and went upstairs to run a bath. It was a relief when her father called up and the front door slammed: he was still unused to abandoning her for his new night-shift job guarding a warehouse full of electrical goods.

She returned downstairs and left the remains of a chicken casserole twirling in the microwave. In the living room she got out her notes, not sure what was unsettling her until the hum of the oven ceased and uncovered the continual swish of heavy traffic on wet roads. But no—that couldn't be right; the rain had held off and, besides, at this hour the main road at the end of the street no longer streamed with commuter traffic. It was more like trees in motion, she decided; not that there were many near here, but for a few spindly specimens in wire skirts that the vandals had overlooked. It was fatigue, of course; the aural equivalent of spots before the eyes.

Karen switched on the television and turned up the volume, then scanned through the names she'd noted down at the library. There were a few here she'd like to have presented to Gran tonight in exchange for the stories behind them. A sheet slipped to the carpet. Penciled names were faded caterpillars on a sparse web, but even Aunt Marie would be impressed when it was finished—not that a family tree was ever truly finished. In her mind's eye, the colours of the angular branches, fruited with names, were accentuated by the gaudy paraphernalia of an overlit quiz show on the television.

That night she dreamed of the tree until she'd drained it of its rainbow colours, leaving it a stark black thing. But in the moments before she awoke the next morning, dense masses of foliage were growing on the branches, smothering the names.

The dream had faded by lunchtime when Karen caught the bus into town. Watery sunlight exposed the bleak, blanched concrete of the bus station, where, in a corner, a single-decker waited. The driver looked delighted to see her, but just as delighted by the shoppers who rapidly filled the bus after her. By the time it had left the suburbs of Colmorden, Karen was the sole passenger again.

The sky was grey. Sporadic drops made splattered insect shapes on the windows, distorting the fields. Six miles out, the trees began. Light smeared through the dull green canopy over the bus. More light gathered ahead, then they were out of the trees for a moment—time enough to see a tower and then a long roof shape come into view as the road curved. Karen leant into the window, intent on an indistinct shape that lifted from the roof before disappearing behind the tower. Trees again, and she was glancing from side to side at white-washed cottages and sober red-brick dwellings clothed in creeper, through which burglar alarms poked pinched grey faces. A moment later, the road fed into a wide green.

Alighting from the bus, Karen squinted a moment beneath a grey, yet radiant, sky; black dots hovered until a succession of blinks shifted them jerkily over the trees. As she crossed the green, the wind tugged at her, shook the crimson-flowered rhododendrons threateningly before a dark gabled house by the church.

She pressed the doorbell and watched two men in hard hats moving obscurely on scaffolding against the church tower. "Can I help you?" A dark wing flexed—a wing of tarpaulin from the church roof. "Excuse me. Ex . . ." Karen turned as the words registered.

The priest riffled through a diary as fat and black as a Bible as she introduced herself, careful to mention the time of the appointment. At last he clapped a hand to his forehead. "Of course," he said. "I'm sorry—I've been expecting someone else."

Sorry to disappoint you, Karen thought as he led her to a room as bare as a cell. There was a large picture window with a table before it piled with parish registers.

The church filled the view from the window. As she worked, Karen glanced up occasionally to note how far its shadow had advanced towards her on the grass. By three-thirty, the shadow was with her in the room. Her shoulder ached from writing. The two workmen sat high on a girder, their legs dangling. The younger one raised his mug to her. Karen smiled, more to herself than at him, in the dimly lit room. She got up to switch the light on, then opened a can of lemonade. She was staring dreamily at the fireplace, aware of a dry rustle from the chimney, when an abrupt penetrating tap startled her. Turning back to the window, she had the odd impression that a shape had hung just below the upper frame before pulling up and out of sight. That must have been a movement made by one of the workmen who'd now finished their tea-break. The middle-aged man was folding his tabloid as the younger one shook his flask over the chasm of shadow flanking the nave. Half an hour later, Karen saw they had been joined by two others in white overalls. The workmen watched from a respectful distance as the newcomers, moving with ponderous caution, picked out objects from a rectangular hole in the roof before placing them in a container like an extra-large hold-all.

By early evening, two registers remained, but Karen had tired of the relentless succession of births and deaths, the interminable entrances and exits that made her own life seem fleeting. She packed her notebooks away and stepped into the hallway. The priest was on the telephone trying to interrupt vociferous squeaks. Seeing Karen, he raised his eyes questioningly and pointed at the front door. She nodded and he smiled and raised a hand. Karen let herself out, wondering if she'd been blessed.

From the bus-stop, her eyes constantly strayed to the church. Seen almost end-on, it was a great darkened doorway into the woods. The gravestones reminded her that she'd intended to examine the inscriptions. Another day, perhaps. She shivered, willing the bus to hurry. As the wind strengthened, the woods moved with a languorous power. A painful creaking had her spinning to face the cottages behind her. Above them, within the swirling leafage, a package of darkness remained motionless. If it was a perched figure, had it called to her? The voice came again, almost blown away by the wind. She turned back to find a white transit van had pulled up. The driver's window framed the small, neat features of the younger of the two workmen. He didn't appear to mind asking her a third time.

Hurrying around the front of the van, Karen found his workmate holding open the passenger door, then she was inside, relieved as he slammed the door on insistent creakings and flappings like sails.

"I saw you with those big books," the driver said, as the back doors were opened and his partner climbed in effortfully. Karen explained, in an indifferent tone, adding, "It's for my Grandma really—she's always on about the past."

The van entered the trees. Karen watched the wing mirror let go of the lights of the village.

"Sounds like hard work to me," the driver said.

"It's easier than what you're doing—I'm scared of heights."

A voice at her shoulder. "Not just heights to be scared of, is there, Andy? Want to hear something really scary?"

"Go on, Eric—tell her," Andy said with amused resignation.

Eric's rough, round face hovered between them. "There's three of us normally, but yesterday this one," he tapped Andy's shoulder, "was at Colmorden College doing his day release, so there's just me and Brian. So it's afternoon tea-break. I stop no matter what—but not our Brian. He'd been wittering on about hearing scratching sounds under a section of the church roof. Well, I couldn't hear nowt so I left him to it. Anyway, a few minutes later this wind came up sudden. It made a right mess and Brian was shouting blue murder—well, crying, more like. When I got to him he was flat on his back, eyes on stalks, and he was pointing. And I looked and I saw this big black shape dipping into the trees behind the church . . ."

"A loose sheet of tarpaulin—that's my theory," Andy interjected. Karen couldn't be certain in the darkness if he'd given her a reassuring wink. Eric went on:

"Well, whatever he saw or I saw, them bones were real enough. Brian had hefted up some roof slates and there was a space inside about three feet deep—full of 'em, it was."

"Did you see the forensic blokes up there?" Andy asked matter-of-factly.

The trees wearied her. It was as if the van were suspended over the hub of two immense revolving dark wheels. They were silent until the woods ended at an invisible fence, and the fields raced off beneath a vault of blue and grey cloud. Only the horizon was clear. Karen wished Eric had less to say for himself, but she listened to his anecdotes, smiled when Andy smiled, shared with him the occasional colluding glance.

Outside the house in the Coniston Street, she stood at the van window. It was more than cold air that made her thanks a little breathless.

"Any time," Andy said, reaching across the passenger seat to hand her a card.

Running up the drive, it was too dark for Karen to read the words until the halogen lamp over the door came on as if for the new act of a play. Next to "Colmorden Building Services" was a scribbled name and telephone number.

It wasn't too late to visit Gran, but she'd ring first. Aunt Marie answered and Karen wistfully recalled a time when her grandmother had been well enough to look after herself.

"Hi—it's Karen. How's Gran?"

There was a drawing in of breath. "Recovering. I think it was a reaction to these new tablets she's taking."

"I found out a few more things," Karen said, clutching Andy's card.

"Oh, yes." Aunt Marie sounded circumspect.

Recounting a few names, Karen heard her voice entering a void until one name prompted an interruption.

"You'd better keep Harold Singleton under your hat when you see her. He's the one that's supposed to have seen the Jackdaw Jack. Your Gran woke up yesterday afternoon yelling her head off that Jack had escaped."

Karen took a breath, her mind clutching at elusive memories, but Aunt Marie was already explaining testily. "You must have heard it when you were little. It's an old Grobbey tale told to get kids up to bed."

Had someone called out in the background?

"I'd better let you go now, Karen—that's your Gran."

Karen went to bed early that night, and found herself in the van again.

"You don't know my name yet," she says.

"No—but I know who you are."

It's so dark she's no longer sure it is Andy. Regular brushing of foliage against the roof of the van sounds purposeful, and that whirring in the back where Eric sits silent, unseen. . . . She pulls at the door and the wind screams, the trees tumble like immense engines. She can't see the woods that she spends the rest of the night wandering.

The following afternoon, Karen bought some large-print romances for Gran in the library book-sale, then she trudged up the wide marble staircase to the reference library. Seeing the microfilm reader free a leaden weight shifted inside her.

More names, *dramatis-personae* bereft of a play. She'd persevered for an hour when a yawn made her jaw ache. Her eyes watered and names in the 1871 census ran. She looked away from the screen briefly. A tramp stared blankly into the *Investors Chronicle*. A head-scarfs woman struggling with a crossword puzzle was almost hidden behind turreted encyclopedia The librarian was in low voiced discussion with a man in a a business suit. The hum of the microfilm reader was a patient one-note lullaby that dropped a tone when she returned her gaze unwillingly to the screen. A name leapt forward from the background that looked the colour and texture of old skin, and behind her eyes appeared a vision of lightning over night time woodland trees close-packed as cauliflower heads.

"Whitaker, Jack. Roofer."

A metallic screeching made her skin crawl. Karen saw reflected in the screen the raised lid of the map cabinet. The librarian was hauling out huge, yellowing Ordnance Survey maps for the man in the suit. Was an odour, like old, fusty dishcloths, emanating from the maps? Karen scribbled the name into her notebook. Glancing up, she thought at first someone had switch off the microfilm reader, but it was a shadow shed from behind that filled the screen. The smell was worse; she grimaced as her head swam. It had to be the tramp and he was standing behind her. She'd remonstrate with the librarian—that'd teach him; but he must have sensed her irritation because he was withdrawing. Bowing her head to her notes, Karen felt an urge to tear them up. And something troubled her; she'd seen the figure stalking off to the exit but hadn't heard the click of the security system. She twisted in her seat. Two desks away, in his usual place, the tramp puckered his lips at her as he scratched audibly beneath his upraised chin.

When she arrived home, her father had gone to work. She scanned the roof-scape from her room. Her eyes smarted. Returning on the bus, spots had moved in her peripheral vision, and she'd developed the notion that one had kept pace, hopping, half flying at a distance. Even now, on the choppy black waves of distant roofs, a group of chimneys seemed to alternately dilate and narrow. She rubbed her eyes and tried to sort out the day's findings. She'd felt too jaded to be methodical. Dates were missing; her handwriting would have made the census enumerator blush. She recalled the photocopy and the ill-tempered satisfaction it had given her to ask the librarian for "something on Grobbey" a minute before the library closed. The woman evidently hadn't forgiven her for the episode in the library with Linda and Graham. In a back room, filing cabinet drawers had slammed before the librarian emerged with a booklet from which Karen photocopied two facing pages. There was a drawing of a church dwarfed by a furious scribble of trees. Karen read:

"Grobbey lacks the boggarts and piskies of other Lancashire villages but in the Roofer, alias Jackdaw Jack, it has its own home-grown demon."

She realised she was hungry and went down to the kitchen. She read as she ate.

"Following a gale which appeared from nowhere on February 18th, 1868, seemingly to vent its fury on Grobbey alone, one Jack Whitaker appeared just as mysteriously. His offer to repair the storm-damaged roof of St Cuthbert's was accepted by Fr William McPhee and thereafter he stayed on as handyman. Whitaker was a sharp featured, wiry fellow often to be found holding forth in local inns where somehow he contrived to reveal little about his past. Witty, a little cruel, it took little persuasion for him to prick the pomposity of local worthies with imitations of uncanny accuracy. He charmed old ladies and was seldom without a young one on his arm. There had always been whispers, and when some of these same girls disappeared, the whispers multiplied. Someone said they'd seen a group of raggedly black-clad figures cavorting on the church roof. It was rumoured that traces of blood and feathers had been found on the altar. A woman said she'd been waylaid by Whitaker on Grobbey green: she'd patiently acquiesced in his affectionate face-pulling at her child in its pram—until she realised the tongue he waggled was a large worm.

"Soon after this incident, Whitaker vanished. This was proof enough for some that the girls' fates were linked with his, though in what way nobody could be certain. A search party set forth for the woods, there to find Whitaker's cottage abandoned. Shortly before sunset, the party discovered one Harold Singleton, inebriated and incoherent. An incorrigible ne'er-do-well, he was already on a charge for poaching on Crown lands. They'd expected a tale, but the one he offered had them peering up at the trees. Singleton claimed he'd been followed by something high within them, and sensing it draw closer, he'd panicked and aimed his shotgun. It misfired, and buckshot sprayed wide. A wind emerged, tossing the foliage, and he'd glimpsed Whitaker screaming as his peculiarly gloved hands had clasped his eyes. A voluminous black garment had flapped frenziedly around him and it seemed the very wood was an extension of him. Singleton swore that, notwithstanding the fact Whitaker was injured, as likely as not blinded, he maintained his elevated position and was moving in the general direction of Grobbey.

"There was no further sighting of the fugitive, but nevertheless, two days later, the Bishop of Blackburn ordered an exorcism to banish whatever might linger in the village. Others said the ceremony was undertaken to bind Whitaker inside the church, into some cranny of which, known only to himself, he had hidden."

Karen folded the photocopy again and again and threw it into the kitchen bin. It was understandable for Gran to want to forget her grandfather's wayward brother, especially if he was connected to a story like that. Of course, details had been elaborated over the years, and one of the main players was a drunkard, so why did it trouble her? She found herself searching urgently in her pockets for Andy's card.

He must not have returned from work, but after listening to the chirruping ring for longer than she could bear, Karen slammed the receiver with mingled feelings of anxiety and betrayal.

She rang Linda, and the ringing tone was persisting stubbornly when the doorbell sounded. Karen rushed into the hallway. In the glass panel of the front door, she thought for a moment that black flames flicked in a halo of sodium light, but, opening the door, she found Linda in a black leather jacket. At the kerb, the driver's window of the Cortina was a square mouth bawling rock music. Inside, coaxing the dregs from an upturned can, Graham looked like he was singing into a microphone. Real friends for all their limitations, Karen thought, asking Linda to give her five minutes. Rum and Coke? Yes—two or three of those would do nicely. In her room, she brushed her hair to a shine. Squinting at herself in the mirror, her eyes were blue-shadowed hollows, but she prided herself on applying eye shadow more effectively than Linda had done tonight.

Graham drove by the pub in the next street, then past Chaplin's where students congregated. As they sped along wider, leafier avenues at the edge of town, Karen asked where they were going. Linda squirmed round in her seat, her face flushed. In the windscreen, fields gathered around the last street lamps.

"Go on—guess," she said.

"Not Grobbey?" Karen said sullenly, convinced her presence was an alcohol-prompted afterthought.

"It's a nice little place, Grobbey," Graham countered. "You can introduce us to some of your relatives."

Linda giggled, then continued giggling at nothing. They began to goad each other playfully; to Karen the previous day seemed as remote and full of possibilities as childhood. Twenty minutes later the woods took them before releasing them onto Grobbey green.

Graham circled the green slowly, eyeing the houses like a prospective burglar. The church was a slab of shadow, then they were passing the pub with cars parked before its lights in a curving fan of colour. Linda was whispering in Graham's ear, and Karen realised they weren't going to stop. Two figures stood in the pub doorway. Karen knocked and waved in frantic, happy recognition. She was sure Andy had seen her, though he'd only time to look startled as the car accelerated, heading for the road that would return them to Colmorden.

It wasn't spite. They'd simply forgotten her. Linda was nuzzling Graham's neck. Karen slumped against her window, resigned. She hadn't noticed until now that it was windy again. The trees in turmoil reminded her of volatile crowds in silent films. She felt calm until the car jolted before coming to a halt. Linda was laughing as she undid her seat belt, then she was opening her door. Cold air pushed in heedless of Karen's dismay. Graham turned the radio on, but the clamour of wind wouldn't let her hear it. Pushing at his door, the wind yanked it wide for him. He reached back into the car five shadowed fingers. "Five minutes," he shouted.

"Bastards!" Karen said, watching them move off in the headlight beams, the wind buffeting them as they leaned against each other.

Spread like wings, the doors shuddered feebly and, after she'd climbed into the front seat, it took all her strength to wrench them closed. She wished she could turn off the rushing and creaking outside as easily as the hiss coming from the radio. Wait, just wait, she told herself.

She sensed five minutes becoming more like ten. Pressing the indicator stalk, she despaired of the pitiful piping that emerged. Foliage advancing and withdrawing on the car soon made waiting a worse option, but she had to force herself to stand outside and call out. After a moment, she let the wind push her forward within the headlight beams. They'd lit her for yards further than she'd have expected when she stopped and called out again. The dark gaps between the trees ahead were yawning mouths. She turned back and a wall of trees faced her. The breath caught in her throat. It was the moon that had been lighting her way, and now, as if irritated at her discovery, it rolled behind the clouds.

A car door slammed. They wouldn't leave her—they wouldn't. She ran towards the sound, stumbled at another, fell. Her hands felt sticky where they'd hit the ground but there wasn't time to think about that. A scream had her running again, almost immediately overjoyed at light filtering between boughs. It was the road. There was a white van; its headlights illuminated Graham's car pointing into the woods and still unoccupied. Karen ran to the passenger window of the van where Eric scowled.

"What's going on? You looked terrified waving at us like that. Then we drive past and see the car with nobody in it. He's a worrier, Andy—he's gone to search for you."

"Which way?"

Pointing, Eric looked unnerved. Karen ran, ignoring his protests. She felt in control now and, calling Andy's name, it surprised her that there was no answer.

After only a few yards, the woods had surrounded her. Shifting moonlight made the trees seem to march. She sensed a circling motion and turned with it, fearfully, There was a scream that fled through the woods, wind-carried. She ran back, but the road evaded her. The trees ended, but it was a clearing.

"Karen." Thank God, thank God. It was Andy, but where? She went forward, turning as she sensed a greater movement circling the clearing—closing in.

"Here. Climb up. It's not safe."

He was in a tree. She even knew which one, though she couldn't see him. She could have laughed.

It was huge and old. Branches spread almost from floor level, and it was an easy stride from a lower to a higher one, from where she stared up into a shifting sky of foliage. "Andy?" She'd have been content to stay there but for a crashing of branches approaching the clearing, and Andy's oddly even-toned demand. "Higher—hurry." Someone tumbled into the moonlight. Then it was as if the trees expelled a clump of shadow that caught up the first figure and bore it onwards and up into the trees at the far side. A scream echoed as if the perimeter of the clearing was stone. Unable to move, Karen hugged a bough. If Andy had seen what she'd witnessed, would he sound as collected? One word emerged from the darkness above—"Higher."

At every side, sweeping wing motions of foliage opened great skewed windows onto the other trees. Only a glimpse, but had she seen a pair of figures on a branch? She twisted. In another direction, another pair of shapes, and there was no mistake this time. Barely distinguishable from the shuddering leafage that surrounded it, a figure stood on a branch. Leaning against it, a seated shape kicked feebly. When the standing figure stooped down to its companion, Karen was already glancing away, distracted by sounds of foliage giving way above her. She was trembling violently as if the wind had made her a creature of branches and leaves. She reached a foot down for the lower bough but failed to meet it. The scene in the other tree replayed behind her eyes. The expression on the face of the kicking figure had been unique in her experience, but the face itself had been familiar enough for her to know that whoever it was making its way down to her, it was not Andy. The lower bough might have dissolved in darkness, but widening her eyes for a sight of it only sharpened her recall of the head lolling back, the mouth gaping like a chick's craving grubs, the beaked face pecking down—once, twice.

She was letting go, stepping out into darkness, when hands gripped her shoulders.

"Careful." With the voice came a foul odour, enveloping her. She shouted raggedly, kicked, flailed, but the grasp only tightened. And she fought just as hard the conviction that the hands weren't hands at all, and the raucous, cajoling voice nothing like Andy's nor any other she'd ever heard, when it said:

"Karen—look up, look up, look up."

SARAH CORBETT

Dark Moon

Sarah Corbett was born in 1970 and raised in north Wales. She took a degree at the University of Leeds, then traveled extensively before recently completing a master's degree in Creative Writing at the University of East Anglia. The Red Wardrobe *is her first book, for which she won an Eric Gregory Award and was shortlisted for the Forward Poetry Prize (Best First Collection) and the T. S. Eliot Prize.*

"Dark Moon" comes from The Red Wardrobe, *and was also printed in the July 16, 1998 edition of the British newspaper,* The Independent.

—T. W.

This is the dark me—
twisted body of hawthorn,
the latent witching of that tree,
its black muscle harming itself
but growing old, and ugly face
proud to be ugly,
a sneer at beautiful things.

Prepare yourself,
I may bud and burst—
a veiled hag, a trick of spring
that watches inwards, turns
and turns a hallowed magic
from my harsh skin,
my spiked and flowering hands.

ELLEN KUSHNER

The Death of the Duke

Ellen Kushner is the host, writer, and co-producer of "Sound & Spirit," a national weekly radio program exploring mythology, spirituality, and music from around the world. She is also the author of the novels Swordspoint *and* Thomas the Rhymer *(winner of the World Fantasy and Mythopoeic Awards), as well as the editor of the anthologies* Basilisk *and* Horns of Elfland. *In addition, she has written numerous works of short fiction and children's books.*

"The Death of the Duke," first published in Starlight 2, *is an elegantly penned story set in the imaginary city of Riverside, in a world deliciously reminiscent of the tales of Dorothy Dunnett and Georgette Heyer. For fans of* Swordspoint, *the events of this story take place some forty years after the close of that novel. Kushner is currently at work on a new Riverside novel in collaboration with Delia Sherman.*

—T. W.

The Duke was an old man, and his young wife had never known him when his hair grew dark and heavy, and lay across the breasts of his many lovers like a mantle.

She was a foreigner, and so she did not understand, when he'd come home to his city to die, and the nursing of him through his final illness began to tax her strength, why his relations were so concerned to help her in the choosing of a manservant to attend him.

"Let him be pretty," said gentle Anne with a blush.

"But not *too* pretty." Sharp Katherine flashed her a look.

"By all means," the young wife said, "why not let him be as pretty as may be, if it will please my husband, so long as he is strong and careful?"

And since neither one would answer her, nor even look at her nor at each other, she chose a lovely young man whose name was Anselm. She did not know how badly he had wanted the job.

Anselm had a steady hand and clear eyes. He could fold linen and pour medicine, slip a shirt on and off with a minimum of fuss, and wield a razor quickly and efficiently. The Duke insisted on being presentable at all times, although he was no longer able to go anywhere. In his youth, the Duke's cuffs had foamed with lace, breaking like waves over the backs of his hands. His hands had been thin then, but they were thinner now.

Now the old Duke lay in the bed he had not lain in for twenty years, in the house he had built, furnished and decorated and then abandoned. In a time when today's young lovers were not yet born, the Duke had left his city and his rights and his duties to follow his lover, the first and oldest and best, to a far island where they might live at last for love, although the word was never spoken.

Sitting by him on the bed, his young wife said to the Duke, "There was an old woman outside, waiting for me in the doorway of your house. She took me by the wrist; quite strong, her fingers. 'Is he in there?' she asked me. 'Is he? They say he's come back home. They say that he is in there dying.'"

The Duke's smile had always been thin as a whip. "I hope you told her they were right."

His wife pressed his hand. She loved him helplessly and entirely. She was to be the last of his loves. Knowing it comforted her only a little; sometimes, not at all.

"Go and dress," he told her. "It will take you longer than you think to dress for the sort of party you are going to tonight."

She hated to leave him. "My maid can lace me up in no time."

"There's still your hair, and the jewels and the shoes. . . . You'll be surprised."

"I want to stay with you." She snuggled into the bony hollow of his shoulder. "Suppose you're hungry, or the pain starts up again?"

"Anselm will bring me what I need." The Duke twined his fingers in her hair, stroking her scalp. "Besides, I want to see if they fitted it properly."

"I don't care. I'm sure it's a beautiful gown; you chose it."

The stroking stilled. "You *must* care. They must learn to know you, and to respect you."

She said, "At home, no one could respect a wife who left her husband to go to a party when he was—when he was ill."

"Well, things are different here. I told you they would be."

It was true. But she would come with him. Five years ago, she had married a stranger, a man wandering her island half-crazed with the loss of his lover, the oldest and the best. In her village, she was past the age of being wed. But it was only that she had been waiting for him: a man who saw her when he looked at her. He surprised her with her own desires, and how they could be satisfied.

That he had once been a duke in a foreign country was a surprise he'd saved for the end. The rings on his hands, which he'd never removed, not even in his grief, he wanted to return to his family himself. She had begged to come with him on this final journey, although they both knew that it would end with him leaving her there alone. She wanted to see his people, to visit the places he had known; to hear him remember them there. She wanted his child to be born in the house of his fathers.

The last jewel was set in place on his wife's gown, the last curl pinned, the last flower arranged to suit the Duke's discerning eye. Exotic and stylish, livid and bright, the Duke's foreign wife went off in the carriage in a clatter of hooves and outriders, a blazon of flambeaux.

Candles were lit by the Duke's bed. Anselm sat quietly in a shadowed corner of the room.

"My wife," the Duke said, his eyes shut, white face against white pillow, "was the daughter of a great physician. He taught her all he knew, passed on to her his philtres and potions. She was justly proud, and healed a king with them. She loved a boy, a nobleman, but he was haughty, and did not return her love, nor could she could make him. There are no philtres for that, whatever anyone may tell you." His own laugh made him catch his breath in pain. "Nor for this. It vexes her. And me."

Anselm said, "I wish it could be otherwise."

The Duke said dryly, "You're very kind. So do I. I suppose, being old, I should be graceful about it, and pretend not to mind much. But I have never lived to gratify others."

"No," said the lovely servant, whose loveliness went unnoticed. The Duke's eyelids were thin, almost blue, stretched over his eyes. His mouth was stiff with pain. "You caused some trouble in your time."

The taut face softened for a moment. "I did."

Anselm approached him with a drink poured into a silver cup. The cup was engraved with the Duke's family crest, a swan. There was no telling how old it was.

The Duke was tall, long-boned. There was not much flesh left on him and his skin was dry and parchment-thin. Anselm held him while he took for the drink. It was like holding the mirror of a shadow: light instead of dark, edged instead of flat.

"Thank you," said the Duke. "That ought to help, for awhile. I will sleep, I think. When she comes home, I want to hear what happened at the party. Something is bound to have, her first time out."

"You want to cause some trouble now, do you?" his servant gently teased.

The thin lips smiled. "Maybe." Then, "No. Not now. What would be the use?"

"What was the use then?"

"I wanted . . . to be amused."

Closer now, the planes of his own face gilded by candlelight, Anselm said, "Men died for you."

"Not for me. For him."

"He killed them for you."

"Yesss . . ." a long breath of satisfaction.

Anselm leaned closer. "And you remember. I know you do. You were there. You saw it all. How they were good, but he was the best." His strong hand was dark against the linen sheet. "There is no swordsman like him now."

"But there never was." The Duke's voice was stretched so thin that Anselm, bending close, must hold his breath to hear. "There never was anyone like him."

"And will not be again, I think." Anselm said as softly, and as much to himself. "Never."

The Duke lay back, his color gone, and the pillow engulfed him, welcoming him back to his new world, the world of brief strengths and long weaknesses.

Still glittering with finery, and the kiss of wine and rich company, the Duke's wife returned to him, to find out whether he slept, or whether he waited for her in the darkness.

From the huge bed his thin, dry voice said, "You smell of revelry."

She struck a light, revealing herself in splendor. The flowers were only a little withered at her breast. Despite the scratch of lace and the weight of gold, she settled herself beside him on the bed. "Ah! That's good, now I no longer need to be held up." She sighed as he slowly unlaced her stays. "I pretended—" She stopped, then went on, shyly, determined not to be afraid of him, "I told myself they are your hands, keeping my back straight before them all."

He chuckled. "And were people so hard on you?"

"They *stare* so! It is not polite. And they say things I do not understand. About each other, about you . . ."

"What about me?"

"I don't know. I don't understand it. Empty, pointless things that are supposed to mean more than they say. How you must find the city changed, and old friends gone."

"All true. I hope you were not too bored."

She pinched his shoulder. "Now you sound like them! No, I was not bored. I even got a compliment. An old man with diamonds and bad teeth said I was a great improvement on your first wife. He had very poor color—liver, I should think," she added hurriedly, having spoken of something she had intended not to.

"Yes," her husband said, impervious. "They can forgive me a foreigner better than they can an actress. Or maybe I finally merit pity, not censure, because I am sicker than any of them would like to be. Maybe that's all it is." His ruminations gave way to a story, more disjointed than he intended, a tale of past insult, of revenge. A lover spurned, the Duke's first wife publicly hissed; a young man's anger and the answer of money and steel. Blood and no healing, only scars closing over a dirty wound.

These were not stories that she had heard before, on the sunny island where they had been wed among the bees' hum and the thyme. They did not even describe a man she knew.

Lying undressed in the dark, next to his thin and burning body, she wondered for the first time if they had been right to come here to this place of his past.

His hand moved, half-aware, to her shoulder blade, cupping it like a breast. Her whole body flushed with memory. She desired him suddenly, wanted her strong lover back. But she knew the disease, she knew its course, and clenched her heart around the knowledge that that would not happen. All that had passed between their bodies was done, now, and was growing in her belly. In the future it would comfort her, but not now.

"People do not forget," he said. She'd thought he was asleep, his breathing was so quiet.

"You," she said tenderly. "They do not forget you."

"Not me. Themselves. I was important only for what I made them feel. Remember that." His fingers tightened on her, urgent and unalluring. "And do not trust anyone from my past. They have no cause to love me."

"I love you."

A little later, he sighed in his sleep, and spoke the name of his first wife, while he held her. She felt her heart twist and turn over, close to the child she carried, so that there was room for little inside her but pain and love.

Physicians hoping to make their fame and fortunes came to bleed him.

"There isn't enough left of me as is," said the Duke. He sent his wife down to chase them all away, knowing it would give her satisfaction to have someone else to be angry with.

Anselm was shaving him, gently and carefully. "In the old days," Anselm said, "you would have had them skewered."

The Duke did not even smile. "No. He did not kill unarmed men. There was no challenge in it."

"How did you find challenges for him? Did you have a good eye?"

Now the old lips quirked. "You know—I must have. I never thought of it. But there was a certain kind of bully I delighted in provoking: the swaggering cocksure idiot who pushed everyone out of the way, and beat up on the girl who worked to keep him in funds. That sort generally carried a sword."

"And would you know now?" Anselm busied himself with cleaning the brushes. "Would you know a decent swordsman if you saw one—by the swagger, say, or by the stance?"

"Only," said the Duke, "if he were being particularly annoying. May I see that?"

When Anselm offered the brush for inspection, close, so the weak eyes could focus on it, the Duke closed his fingers around the young man's wrist. His touch was paper-dry. Anselm kept his arm steady, although his eyelids trembled, a fringe of dark lashes surrounding blue eyes so dark as to be almost violet.

"You have a good wrist," the Duke observed. "When do you practice?"

"In my room." Anselm swallowed. His skin was burning where the bony fingers barely touched it.

"Have you killed anyone?"

"No—not yet."

"They don't kill much, nowadays, I hear. Demonstration bouts, a little blood on the sleeve."

The Duke's wife came in at the door without knocking, full of her achievement. But the Duke held his servant's wrist for one moment more, and looked at his face, and saw that he was beautiful.

Visitors sometimes were allowed, although not the ones who promised a miracle cure. The pain came and went; the Duke took to asking his wife two and three times a day whether there were enough poppy juice in the house laid by. The medicine made his mind wander, so that he talked with ghosts, and she learned more of his past than sometimes she wanted to hear. When visitors came, people who were still alive, she often sat quietly in a corner of the room, willing herself invisible, to learn more. Other old men, more robust than her husband, she still found not half as beautiful. She wondered how he ever could have touched them, and tried to imagine them young and blooming.

Lord Sansome came to gloat, her husband said, or maybe to apologize; either way, it would be amusing to see what time had done with him. She thought admitting such a man unwise, but he made a nice change from the ghosts.

Sansome had bad teeth and a poor color, but he took the glass of wine that Anselm offered. The nobleman approved the young servant up and down. He settled by the bed with his gold-headed stick upright between his knees.

The Duke watched his visitor through half-lidded eyes; he was tired, but wanted no drugs until he'd gone.

Sansome uttered no commonplaces, nor was he offered any. And so there was silence until the Duke said, "Whatever you are thinking is probably true. Thank you for coming. It is prodigious kind."

His foreign wife didn't know what *prodigious* meant. It sounded like an insult; she readied herself for action. But Lord Sansome continued to sit.

The Duke closed his eyes but kept on talking: "I do not think that I am going to die while you sit there. Though I know it would please you greatly."

Across the room, Anselm made a noise that in a less well-bred servant would have been a snort. He busied himself with the brushes, so that all they could hear was their *hush-hush-hush* as he cleaned.

At last, Sansome spoke. "I thought you gone years ago. No one knew where you were. I thought you'd died of a broken heart."

"It mended."

"You told me you didn't have one."

"Wishful thinking. I see that yours beats on."

"Oh, yes." Sansome's thick-veined hands opened and closed on the gold ball of his stick. "Mine does. Though we never know what's around the corner, do we?"

"I believe I do."

"Perhaps something may yet surprise you." Unexpectedly, Lord Sansome smiled warmly at the Duke's manservant. Anselm looked annoyed.

"He's good with a blade," Sansome observed.

"You've had the pleasure?"

"Once or twice. A nice, close shave."

"Oh." The old Duke laughed, and kept on laughing at a joke no one else could see, until his breath drew in pain, and wife and servant shut him off from view while they held and gave him drink to ease him.

When Lord Sansome was gone, "People do not forget," the Duke said dreamily. "I think this pleases me. Or why would I have come back?"

"My references came from somewhere." Anselm was curt with the Duke, who had been goading him with revelations. They were alone together. "I never would have gotten in to you without them. Your family checked; and I do know how to valet. Now tell me again. Tell me about how he held his hands."

"They were never empty. He was always doing something: gripping bars to strengthen his wrists, squeezing balls, tossing a knife . . . and other things." The Duke smiled most annoyingly to himself. Anselm was coming to know that smile, and knew that there was no coaxing out of the Duke whatever memories it hid.

The old man's face clouded, and he began to swear, inelegantly, with pain. Anselm wiped his sweating face with a cold cloth, and kept on this way until the Duke could speak again: "As an adventure, this is beginning to pall. Life grows dull when all I have to wonder about is how long my shirt will stay dry, and whether I am going to swallow soup or vomit it up. I would say, let's have it over and done with, but my wife will not like that. Of course," he bared his teeth in a painful grin, "she doesn't like me in this condition, either. There really is no pleasing some people."

"You must take comfort in the child that is to come."

"Not really. That was only to please my wife. I do not want posterity. I was a great disappointment to my parents."

Anselm shrugged. "Aren't we all?"

"But when I am dead, it will keep her from doing something stupid. That is important."

Anselm was good at catching hints. "Shall I fetch your lady?"

"No." The Duke's hand was cold on his. "Let us talk."

"I'm not like you," Anselm said hopelessly. "Words are not my tools. All I can do is ask questions. You are the one who knows things, sir, not I. What I want to know, even you cannot show me."

"Annoying for you," the sick man said; "since sometimes I do see him, yet—in the corners of the room. But it's only the drugs, since he never answers when I speak."

"He was the greatest swordsman who ever lived. If taking drugs would let me see him, I'd do it." Anselm paced the room, his measured valet's demeanor given way to an athlete's ardent stride. "I wonder, sometimes, if there is any point even in trying. He took his secrets with him. If only I could have watched how he did what he did!" The sick man made no reply. "You were there. You saw. What did you see? Can't you tell me? What did you see?"

The Duke slowly smiled, his vision turned inward. "It was beautiful; not like this. He killed them quickly, with one blow, straight to the heart."

"How?" Anselm demanded, fists clenched. "No one offers his heart to the sword."

With every one of his fighter's senses, he felt the Duke's regard full upon him, unclouded by dream or pain. It drew him back to the bed, as though to close with an opponent, or a partner.

"No one?" the Duke whispered. Anselm knelt to hear him. "Not no one, boy."

The Duke's hand drifted down into his dark and springy hair.

Anselm said, "You are a terrible man." He seized the fingers, tangled in his hair with his own, and pulled them through his curls down to his mouth.

Lying by him in the dark, the Duke's wife said, "I have seen so many women through childbirth, I should be more afraid. But I am not. I know this will be a good child. I hope that you will see him."

His hand was on her gently rounded belly. "I hope he will not be too unhappy."

"As you were?" she answered sadly. "No, my darling. This one will know that he is loved, I promise you!" She gripped his fragile hand; fading, like the rest of him, even in the dark. "And he will know all about his father, that I promise, too."

"No," the man said; "not if it makes him unhappy."

"He will be happy."

"You promise that, do you?" She heard his smile. "Will you take him back to the island, then, to run with the goats?"

"Certainly not!" Sometimes the things he assumed amazed her. "He will stay here, with his family. He must be raised in your city, among people who know you."

"I think he would be more happy on the island." The Duke sighed. "I wish I could go back there, after, and rest on a hill above the sea. But I suppose it is impossible."

In a small voice she said, "I suppose it is. Where will you go, then?"

"I shall lie in the Stone City: ranks and ranks of tombs like houses, with all my ancestors, my family—that should please your sense of decorum. They are not the company I would have chosen, but I suppose I will not care then."

"I will bring him there. To visit you."

He pulled his hand away. "By no means. I forbid it."

"But I want him to know you."

"If you insist on telling the child stories about me, do it somewhere nice, with a fire, and bread and milk . . ." She had given him poppy syrup; soon he would sleep. "I hope he will be beautiful. Not like me. Beautiful as you are. As *he* was."

Some of the time, he spoke of people she did not know. But she knew this one well, this loved ghost from his past, the beautiful, the rare, first love and best. She willed her breath to evenness, her arms to softness. A memory, nothing, against a living child.

"I wanted him to kill me. Years ago. But he never got round to it."

"Hush, love, hush."

"No, but he promised! And so I hold him to it. In the end he failed me, he left me. But he will come for me. Long ago he promised to come for me. He is my death."

She held him tightly to her, hoping he was too far gone to notice her sobbing breath, and the tears that fell on both their skins.

Lord Sansome did not come again, though he sent the Duke's bodyservant, Anselm, a gift of money.

"What will you spend it on?" the Duke inquired; "swords or sweethearts?"

His servant frowned. "I feel I should return it. It isn't right for me to take what I do not intend to earn."

"Oh, re-eally?" Weariness drew out the old man's drawl. "But surely my old friend can be nothing but pleased that you care for me so thoroughly? It is his right to tip you if he wishes."

Anselm drew back. "Do you want to be shaved or don't you?"

"Is anyone expected?"

"No one but Her Ladyship, and that not until noon."

"She will not mind. The way I look, I mean. Put that thing down, Anselm. It is the wrong blade for you. Lord Sansome doesn't know it, but I do. I do."

The hours when he knew her grew farther apart. At last, she was uncovering every thing that he had kept from her—promises to his first wife, quarrels with his lovers, games with his sister—she heard a young man's voice, disputing with a tutor, and murmuring provocation so sweet it could only be to his old lover, the first and best. Did she give him more poppy than she should, to keep the voices coming, and to shield him from the pain? She tried, but in the end she had to fail, as even love could not appease the author of the play that he was in. He did not eat, he barely spoke. The old tart who had known him young came back to the door. His lady would not let her in to see him now, but, seeking her own comfort, went down to sit a moment with this relic of his past.

In the shadowed room, the Duke's patient servant waited.

The old Duke opened his eyes wide and looked at him.

"Oh," he said. "I didn't think it would be now."

"When else?" said the swordsman. "I promised, didn't I?"

"You did. I thought you had forgotten."

"No. Not this."

"I always wanted you to."

"Of course you did. But that wasn't the time."

"How bright it is! Do it quickly. I'm afraid of pain."

The other end of the bright blade laughed. "You can't breathe properly. You can't even feel your feet. This will be quick. Open your arms, now."

"Oh," said the old Duke again; "I knew you'd come."

JUDY BUDNITZ

Hershel

Judy Budnitz is a cartoonist for The Village Voice, *and a young writer whose work has appeared in* The Paris Review, Story, Glimmer Train, *and the anthology* 25 and Under. *She grew up in Atlanta, graduated from Harvard in 1995, and is currently getting her master's degree in creative writing at New York University. Her first collection,* Flying Leap *was published when she was twenty-four years old, and is a pure delight. The following tender fable, "Hershel," comes from its pages.*

—T. W.

When I was your age, back in the old country, they didn't make babies the way they do now. Back then people didn't dirty their hands in the business; they went to the baby-maker instead.

These days, these young people, they all want to do it themselves; they'd buy the do-it-yourself kit if there were such a thing. They don't trust anybody else to do it for them. And most of them aren't any good at it—baby making requires skill and training. These modern babies they turn out today, some of them are all wrong, and the parents keep them anyway. That's why the world's all mixed up these days. I haven't seen a baby in the last twenty years that could hold a candle to Hershel's.

Who was Hershel? He was the baby-maker in our village. He did wonderful work. People came for miles around to buy his babies. He was a good man, never cheated customers. They bought babies by the pound back then, and Hershel always gave them exactly what they wanted, not an ounce more or less.

Most people got one at about six and a half to seven pounds. A baby was a large purchase; people saved for years to buy one. Sometimes a very poor couple would buy a small one. Hershel didn't recommend this; the small ones were scrawny and underdone and often died. He made no guarantees. Once the baby left his hands, that was it. You couldn't bring it back.

Hershel seldom left his workshop. He rose with the cocks and worked all day. When the stars came out, you could see in his window the orange glow of a candle as he tinkered away far into the night. People had to come to the workshop to place their orders. It was a large stone building in the middle of the village and it looked like a bakery, with large ovens and chimneys like fingers pointing at the sky, puffing out white smoke and a sweet yeasty smell.

Sometimes a woman came alone to order her baby. More often she made it a big occasion, with most of the family tagging along. As Hershel emerged from the steam to greet her, the woman would say, Hershel, make me a baby. And Hershel would nod and say, God willing.

And then he would take the grease pencil from behind his ear and begin to make notes. A boy or a girl this time? he would say. How large? What color? And the woman might say, Brown curls, please, and a nose like my sister Sarah's, and a special mole in a special place so that I will always know she is mine. Hershel would write it all down and say, No guarantees, remember, no returns.

The parents would give him the money, and nine months later to the day, the baby would be finished. Sometimes it was what they had ordered. More often it wasn't. But it didn't matter, because Hershel's babies were such wondrous things that people fell in love with them instantly and forgot the specifications they had made. The woman cradling her new baby in her arms would say, Oh, I *did* want a boy after all, and I *did* want black hair, not brown, and *look* at his little nose like a sideways potato! Thank you, thank you, Hershel.

And Hershel would blush and stare at the floor and say, It is the hand of God. Whether he was being modest or whether it was an excuse for his mistakes, I do not know. I only know how wonderful the babies were, how fresh and new and perfect as he wrapped them up and handed them over the counter to the parents.

Once the babies passed over the counter, Hershel washed his hands of them. He said he was not responsible for how they turned out. He said once, I only make the outsides. The parents make the insides. I make only the seed. If they cultivate it, then it will flourish.

Did he ever miss the babies once they were gone? We often wondered. Hershel had no wife, no children of his own. His work occupied all of his time. He lived in a little room in the back of his workshop, empty save a bed and a table and a prayer book. He was not an old man, though he stooped and shuffled like one. His eyes were unreadable behind the thick glasses.

He was not secretive or mysterious about his work. He was fair to customers, never cheating them by filling their babies with water to seem heavier, as I have heard crooked baby-makers do. Hershel allowed anyone to come into his workshop to watch him work. During my childhood I spent many hours there, watching. The other boys came, too, and the girl named Alina. We felt more at home there than any other place.

The place was lush and steamy. The babies were sensitive and needed warmth to grow. Hershel began by making dough. He stirred together powders and liquids in a big wooden bowl, carefully testing its consistency. We did not know what went into the dough and could not ask, for as he mixed and poured, Hershel chanted prayers, one after another in a torrent, sometimes with his eyes closed.

When the dough was golden pink and about the consistency of an earlobe (Hershel once let us touch the dough, making us wash our hands first), Hershel then began to knead it. This was wonderful to watch. Though a slight man, Hershel had thick muscular arms built up over years of kneading. We watched the dough somersault and dance, and the ropes of muscles stood out on his arms and the sweat ran down his cheek, and we boys looked at one another and said, *That's* what I want to be when I grow up.

Then Hershel placed the dough in a bowl and covered it and left it to rise. When it grew to twice its size, he punched it down again. Twice he did this. Then he rolled up his sleeves, wiped his glasses, and began the most wonderful part. With his strong, sensitive hands, he began to shape the dough into a baby, chanting prayers all the while. As he shaped the head and neck and belly, he prayed for the things he could not shape: the heart and the mind and the soul. He caressed arms and legs into shape, he twisted fingers and toes and patted cheeks into place. Soon the complete body lay before him, dusted with flour. Except for the ears, which he had left as buds. They would uncurl and bloom during the baking.

Then he would slide the baby on its back into the oven. The ovens were clean and white and were kept at exactly 98.6 degrees all year round. The babies shifted and bubbled as they baked, rocking about on their backs. Some stretched; others curled up. Hershel checked them conscientiously but did not disturb them. After nine months (he kept careful records) he would draw them out either by the head or the feet. Nothing could compare to the sight of a new baby fresh from the oven, crisp at the fingernails, crying from the cold as Hershel held him aloft, checking for any mistakes in his handiwork.

I am Hershel's work. That probably explains why I've turned out so well.

Hershel claimed to have no bond to us. He said he had merely prepared us for our rightful parents, just a step along the way. Nevertheless, we were all attracted to him. As children we brought him gifts: a flower, a drawing. Once I brought him a bird, frozen, cupped in my mittens. A pet for you, Hershel. Put him in the oven, bring him back! I said. He shook his head sadly.

When we were older, my friends and I supplied him with firewood for the great ovens. We invited him to our homes for holiday meals. He seldom accepted. He was a solitary man. Sometimes, though, we would glimpse him in the window, looking up from his prayer book to watch us tumbling in the snow.

Hershel never picked favorites. But secretly I hoped that he had liked me (even a little bit) more than the others, that he had blessed me with an extra stroke, a pinch, a little more attention than the others, in the making. I'm sure the others hoped the same thing, too: that Hershel had given them something special, an extra ingredient.

I thought, sometimes, that he watched me more than the others.

As I grew older, I began to look forward to the time when Hershel would make a child for me. But then the trouble came. We did not know then that it was a mere hint of what was to come.

The girl named Alina, she was beautiful. She was about my age, with hair to her waist and shining eyes. Hershel had made her, and I sometimes thought jealously that perhaps *she* was a favorite, for how could she be so beautiful if he had not worked longer on her and given her some extra spice?

As children we had played together. She had been daring, quick on her feet, skipping along the top rails of fences or turning cartwheels. Now that she was older she had to wear long skirts and cover her hair, but she was the same laughing red-lipped Alina dancing about on her long new legs, gypsyish and wild.

I dreamed of her. We all did. I remember waking in the night to hear my younger brother whisper *Alina!* in his sleep. He was only fifteen and still a boy. I lay awake, burning with jealousy over the fact that she could be dancing in another's head.

And then—I don't remember how it happened, how the man first saw her. Perhaps he was out hunting for sport and came through our village. Perhaps Alina was in the city visiting her relatives and he saw her there. Where doesn't matter. The man took one look at her and wanted her for his own.

It all happened so quickly. How could she refuse? He was a wealthy landowner with connections in the government. Her family was poor. He had ice-blue eyes and a set of iron teeth. He was very powerful. He owned everything. She had no choice really.

Then again, he was rich. He was powerful. He may have been handsome. So . . . she married. I do not know if she wished it or not. But she was gone and we all missed her. The clouds came down, the snow fell, and the sky did not clear. We suffered terrible nightmares.

And then we heard stories. We heard that he was cruel. That he left her alone for days. That he beat her. That he did not love her as a man loves a woman, but as a man loves a horse that is beautiful and good to ride. As the stories trickled out to us, we suffered for her.

Then suddenly she came back, wearing a long coat and a veil over her face. She did not go home to her parents. She went instead to Hershel's workshop. She burst in from the cold, dropped a heavy, clinking bundle on the counter, and said, Hershel, make me a man.

She looked at him and she knew he would not refuse. She saw that, like the rest of us, he loved her. But he could not act on his love because he was almost a father to her, and he could not love a daughter as a husband. And yet still he loved, and he dreamed, and his dreams spread to all the men and boys he had ever made, so that they all woke in the night with a chorus of *Alina!*

How did she know it? Perhaps suffering had sharpened her eyes. Perhaps Hershel had given her something extra that let her know his thoughts. She said, Make me a man. And he silently nodded.

She pushed the bundle toward him and said, Two hundred pounds' worth; I will be back in nine months.

She looked hard at him, her face chiseled sharp by desperation, and he longed to press again the cheek he had once pressed into shape. But she was gone.

Hershel rolled up his sleeves and began. He refused other orders and worked only on Alina's man. He worked for days in a frenzy, without eating or sleeping or praying. All his love for Alina and all his years of experience he poured into the colossal mound of dough. He kneaded it, wrestled with it, massaged it, the sweat rolling unchecked down his face and dripping in the dough. The massive body took shape beneath his hands. He labored over the face, carving out nostrils with his fingernails. When he was finished, the man was over six and a half feet tall. I don't know how he got it into the oven.

When Alina returned, she looked more ravaged than before. Again she wore the veil. Again she went directly to Hershel's workshop. Wordlessly, Hershel led forth the man. Alina stared.

He was a giant, and smooth and beautiful as a piece of Roman statuary.

Hershel had no clothes to fit him, so the man stood wrapped in a sheet. The eyes were iridescent, like fish scales. Each muscle bulged firm and strong, and they lay together snugly like bricks forming a wall. Hershel had even drawn the lines in his palms promising long life and happiness.

Alina did not thank Hershel. She merely took the giant by the hand and led him into the night. Hershel dusted his floured hands against his apron and closed his eyes. He saw again her face as it had been a moment before, eyes lit up with joy. That moment, he thought, that look, it was worth any price. If he couldn't love her, Hershel thought, then at least she could be loved by something made by his hands.

I wish I could have told him that he had made *me*, and I could have loved her, too.

The news of what happened next, in the great house in the city, traveled back to us quickly. Such news always does.

Alina quietly led the man to her bedroom in the house of her husband. Her husband, she thought, was away. But the husband came upon them, the two of them, in the bed together, late in the night.

Alina was not frightened at first. Her husband was a slight man, and no match for her giant.

But her man lay unmoving, breathing deep and slow. The husband thundered closer and rolled his colorless eyes and shouted threats and obscenities. Alina then clutched at the man, called to him, tried to rouse him—but still he lay sleeping like a slab. And as she screamed and pounded on him and forcibly turned his face to her, she sobbed and cursed Hershel, for she saw in her hands the wide-eyed, uncomprehending smile of a newborn. And then her husband cut them both down with his sword.

That was the end of Hershel. As soon as he heard the news he closed his doors. The ovens went cold. And he disappeared without saying good-bye to all his children. We followed his footprints in the snow, but they stopped abruptly, like a sentence interrupted. We could not find him.

We grieved. The whole village did. For Hershel. For Alina. For the hundreds of beautiful unborn children that had been taken from us.

And we became frightened, for we learned that the other baby-makers in the surrounding villages were also disappearing, closing up their shops and leaving, or suffering strange accidents, or just *gone* suddenly, with food going cold on the table and the chair tipped over backward and the window broken. What about our *children?* we cried, but it was only the beginning, only a hint of the larger tide turning and building and washing over us, the days and years of blackness, of madness that you would not believe if I told you.

Afterward your grandmother and I had to make your father by ourselves. It was an awkward, newfangled thing for us. But I think he turned out all right. And then your father and mother, they managed pretty well with you. Your ears did not turn out quite as well as mine, I think. But they are good ears. They listen well.

RAY VUKCEVICH

By the Time We Get to Uranus

Ray Vukcevich has published fiction in The Magazine of Fantasy & Science Fiction, Asimov's Science Fiction, The Quarterly, Pulphouse, Rosebud, The Urbanite, Aboriginal SF, Twist of the Tale, *and other magazines and anthologies. His first novel,* The Man of Maybe Half-a-Dozen Faces, *is forthcoming from St. Martin's Press. Vukcevich lives in Oregon and writes that "in my other job, I'm a research programmer for a couple of university brain labs."*

"By the Time We Get to Uranus" is an unusual, surrealistic story inspired by an unusual, surrealistic painting. The tale comes from the small press anthology Imagination Fully Dilated, *a collection of original fiction based on the evocative art of Alan M. Clark.* Imagination Fully Dilated *was published by Cemetery Dance Publications, Baltimore, and edited by Alan M. Clark and Elizabeth Engstrom.*

—T. W.

Molly had come down with suit in the springtime. What had been a rare and puzzling skin condition a year ago was now an epidemic. People developed space suits and then they floated off the planet. They usually grabbed whatever stuff was nearby as they left. Molly and Jack weren't much concerned with a cure; there would be no cure for years, if ever. Too late. Sooner or later Jack would be suiting up himself, and that was the problem they were having such trouble talking about. They'd both be going, but they wouldn't be going together.

Jack didn't think Molly's overshoes were fooling anyone. The suit always started with your feet. Everyone knew that. People see a pretty blond woman in a loose red, green, and yellow flowered blouse and big rubber galoshes, they know her skin's got to be going silver, turning to suit, could be halfway up to her butt, you couldn't tell with those relaxed-fit jeans she's wearing.

"Everyone's looking at me," Molly said. "I feel like I'm wearing clown shoes."

"No they aren't," Jack said. A lie. "Why don't you sit down here, and I'll go see what we have to do about getting on the plane."

They were flying out of LAX on the way home from a visit with her mother. Molly had told him she needed the trip to say good-bye to everyone else she loved. It had been hard, but they'd done it, and now they were going home to Oregon. Jack came back with the boarding passes and sat down beside her.

"Everyone was gray," she said.

"What?"

"Mom," she said. "You. The neighbors. Everyone. The color of fear is gray. You all try not to show it." She squeezed his hand.

He didn't know what to say. Maybe everyone had been gray. Maybe in some strange way it was the best they could do in sympathy with Molly who was turning silver from the ground up.

She turned her head away but not before he saw the slow tears. He leaned in and kissed her on the cheek.

"I'm sorry," she said.

"Never mind." He gave her his handkerchief. Say something. Say something. "Seeing your father's trains was pretty neat."

She gave him a weak smile and hugged her canvas bag to her chest. She'd taken one of her father's miniature locomotives, Ol' Engine Number Nine. She'd spent so many happy childhood hours watching her father's trains go around and around and listening to his stories. Molly had been in college when he died. Her mother had left the trains as they were—the track and station and all the little people and cows and, of course, the box cars and locomotives, the Pullman cars, the dining cars, flatbeds and tank cars. The setup was like a shrine, and it embarrassed them both a little, but neither suggested they should box the trains up and put them in storage.

Now Molly would take her favorite locomotive with her when she left the planet.

Boarding for flight 967 to Portland was announced. First class first and folks with babies. Or if you're willing to admit you need some help. They waited.

Then they got on, and he took the window seat. Molly would want to get up. They sat silently waiting for takeoff. He wished she'd look through the in-flight magazine. He wished he could think of something funny or cheerful to say. He looked out the window. They took off.

Flying in the sunshine at last, Jack saw a wondrous sight, but stopped himself before he could point it out to her—a flock of people in space suits rising up through the smog. They looked as if they'd all been tossed out of a bar together. Tumbling, rolling, twisting. Some hugging their knees. Others stretched out in that optimistic flying superhero posture you so often saw on TV. Others turning head over heels. Cartwheels. And one couple holding hands. How had they managed that?

Oh, look, he almost said, but remembered instead the last flock they'd seen rising. The three of them, Molly, her mother Beth, and Jack, had been drinking ice tea in the glass box that was Beth's balcony overlooking downtown Tarzana. None of them saying much. Being gray, he supposed. Then suited figures rose from somewhere in the urban jumble below. He could see they were not all taking off from the same spot, but they roughly converged without touching before they got very high.

"Why do you suppose that happens?" he asked.

"What?" Beth said.

Molly didn't seem to be paying attention.

"The way they always seem to come together as they leave," Jack said. "You always see groups."

"Actually, if you watch long enough," Beth said, "you see lots of them going alone." She glanced over at Molly who Jack could now tell from her rigid posture and the red flush around ears had been paying attention after all. Beth took her hand. "I'm sorry, Sweetie."

"There's got to be some way to delay it," Jack said. Maybe if they just got it out in the open. How could you solve a problem if you couldn't even talk about it? "Some way for you to wait for me."

"There's not," Molly said.

"How do you know?"

"There was this thing on prisoners, Jack," Beth said. "On TV."

"What about prisoners?"

"Well, when it's time for them to go, you know, leave this Earth, they have to let them out."

"What happens if they don't let them out?"

Beth looked away. "You don't want to know."

Molly threw her napkin down on the table. "That's just it," she said. "He really does want to know. Everything about this whole business interests him deeply." She pushed away from the table and hurried back inside.

And now on the plane home he watched the flock of suited figures until the plane moved above and beyond them. "Maybe we could stay higher than you need to be until I can catch up," he said.

"What do you mean?" She didn't turn her head to look at him.

"I mean we could hire a plane and fly really high, higher than you'll need to be while I catch up."

"Right." She rolled her head toward him and gave him a tired look. "Maybe we can get the air force to refuel us." She turned away again.

Okay, it was a stupid idea. He was slowly learning to keep his ideas to himself until he'd ironed the wrinkles out of them, but it wasn't easy. Way back when their marriage was young, he'd told her one of the things that made him so crazy in love with her was that he felt free to say stupid things to her. Losing that was hard.

They had gotten rid of Sparky the golden retriever because they were afraid he would jump up on Molly and tear her suit. It would have been nice to come home and be greeted by the animal who had never really been anything but a big puppy. The doghouse with the long leash they hooked Sparky to when they got tired of him jumping up on the French doors begging to get in remained in the backyard.

At the kitchen table with his morning coffee, Jack looked out at the doghouse and leash and thought that he should move them to the garage, but he thought that every morning. Molly sat in her furry pink robe slouched over a bowl of cereal. He didn't think she was really eating it.

He picked up the paper again. "Hey, listen to this," he said. "Blah blah blah and on the question of why you get air and pressure and temperature control, not to mention food, water, and waste disposal, the answer is that the good stuff comes from one parallel universe and the bad stuff gets dumped into another."

"I like the one about how we're the cheap fish that god put on Earth to condition the tank," Molly said, "and now we're being pulled off so he can put in a more exotic and interesting species."

Jack lowered the paper. "You really don't care how it all works, do you."

"I really don't care, Jack," she said.

The last time they'd made love, he had joked and called her Barbarella in her silver thigh-high boots. She hit him and laughed, hugged him and cried softly on his chest.

Okay, so how about this? Jack is entirely in his head now, discussing his new idea with a mental construct that looks just like today's Molly but listens like the old Molly. He might even be asleep at his desk where he was still going over sources on suiting when she wandered off to bed.

We make a small cut. Who knows what's under there? Don't you want to know? If it's really skin, it'll heal. It won't hurt. You said so yourself.

But what if it doesn't heal, Jack? What if there is still a tear and I'm leaking in space. I can't be leaking in space.

That's another thing, he says, just how do you, how do we, well, take a leak in space?

All the comforts of home, Jack.

Maybe I'll make the cut when I have a suit of my own.

Don't do it, Jack.

Just a little cut. There just above your knee.

Bright red blood rises from the razor sharp slice in the silver fabric.

"Jack."

"Hmm?"

"Jack, please."

Jack jerked up from the desk and looked up at her standing in the doorway of his office. Backlighted from the living room, she seemed to be nude. At least on top.

"What is it?" He got to his feet and came around his desk. There had been something desperate in her tone.

She took his hand and put it on her stomach. "Look here." He could see the very top of the light patch of pubic hair and then silver. He touched the seam lightly. It felt like a cold scar.

"And here." She moved his hand to the top of her left hip. Silver fingers of suit fabric spread into the small of her back. Molly's space pants were complete.

"My guess is a catheter," she said. "Now will you shut up about it?"

The suit had crept up her abdomen to just below her breasts.

"It's possible," he said, "that our universe has touched another somehow and the very different physical rules of the two universes have gotten all jumbled together."

"That must be it," Molly said.

"Or maybe everyone over here with a suit has a double without a suit over there, and somehow what's happening here has metaphorical significance over there."

Molly rolled her eyes, turned and headed for the door.

"Look here," he said quietly, finally giving up on working his way up to it.

Something in his tone stopped her. "What is it, Jack?"

He had his shoe off and his foot in his lap. She approached and dropped down on her knees in front of him. He pulled the big toe of his right foot away from the others. "There," he said, "can you see it?"

A patch of suit.

"I'm so sorry, Jack," she said. She hugged his foot to her cheek and then kissed his toes.

Plan B was a shortwave radio. A ham rig. Transmitter, receiver—the works. He didn't bother with a license. If everything else failed, maybe he could at least stay in touch with her until she drifted out of range.

It turned out Jack was not the only one with such a plan. The guy at the radio place told him he was lucky he hadn't waited another week or he might not have been able to pick what he wanted right off the shelves.

"How will I know where to tune in?" Jack asked.

"Suit communication happens on two frequencies," the clerk said in a tone implying Jack had either been living in the wilderness or was an idiot.

"And those are?"

"HF One and HF Two."

"I don't see anything like that on the dial," Jack said.

"You wouldn't," the clerk said. "I'm talking about Holy Frequency One and Holy Frequency Two. No one knows why God needs two."

Jack pushed his credit card across the counter and glanced at the door to make sure he was clear to make a break for it if necessary. "Do you suppose you could give me the actual numbers?"

The clerk ran Jack's card through the machine. "Sign here," he said.

Jack signed. The clerk took the pen back and wrote the holy frequencies on Jack's receipt.

"Thank you." Jack picked up his boxes. He supposed he had been aware, in some detached way, of the world going crazy around him, but he had been entirely zeroed in on Molly. He hurried home to her.

"There's got to be a way to slow you down," he said. "Or speed me up. I simply cannot accept the scenario where I'm drifting along through space behind you just out of radio range until we get to Uranus."

"Urine nus," she said. "You pronounce it like we all pee."

"You say urine nus," he sang. "And I say your anus."

He'd made her smile. It felt wonderful.

"So why Uranus?" she said.

"I read where someone worked it all out," he said. "The speed we'll be traveling, everything. There's a window. People leaving during this window will just cross the orbit of Uranus in time to be captured by the gravity of the gas giant."

"And what about the people who left before or leave later?"

"They go to Saturn," he said, "or maybe Neptune. Who knows? Some might miss planets altogether."

"And does this genius say why the gravity of Uranus and the other planets will be working any better than the gravity of Earth?"

"It just will be, that's all," Jack said. "What I want to talk about is figuring out a way to go together." He took her hand. "If I miss Uranus, Molly, I could go to Pluto."

Her suit would cover her shoulders soon. He still had only boots and pants not up to his knees.

"I'm already feeling light, Jack." She squeezed his hand. "I don't want to spend these last few days working on a problem we can't solve."

"But . . ."

"I can't feel you," she said. She pulled his hand up to her face. "Touch me here. I want to feel your skin."

"Maybe I could buy an ordinary space suit," Jack said. "And put it on and hold onto you. We both shoot into space and when my skin suit is finished, I just throw away the store-bought one?"

Molly had gotten her helmet that morning. Jack's pants weren't even done yet.

Now she snatched Ol' Engine Number Nine from the kitchen table. "Hold me," she said. "I think something's happening."

He pulled her in close, still muttering nonsense about his latest plan. Her faceplate snapped into place. The sound startled him and he nearly jumped away from her, but then he saw the fear in her eyes behind the glass and held on tight. She went weightless in his arms.

Then she was more than weightless. He could feel her tugging to get higher. He was having trouble holding her down. She slipped away from him and her head bounced lightly against the ceiling. She drifted toward the French doors. He grabbed her foot.

She dragged him toward the doors.

"It hurts." She might have been shouting, but her voice was muffled. "I need to go up, Jack."

"Not yet!"

She parted the French doors with both hands, threw them open wide, and dragged him out into the backyard. He took giant steps, dream leaps, as she pulled him off the ground. He would have to let her go.

Then he saw Sparky's leash. He got a good grip on her ankle with one hand and stretched down for the leash. The grass had grown up around it. Had it been that long? Just a few more inches. No, he couldn't reach it. Desperately he hopped toward the doghouse. The force pulling her into space was getting stronger. He would have only one more chance.

He got to the doghouse in another two big leaps and hooked his foot into the door and pulled down with his leg. He got the other foot hooked in, too, and pulled with both legs. Molly came down. Jack reached down with one hand and grabbed Sparky's leash. He maneuvered it through his fingers until he found the end. Her pull was very strong now. If he didn't get her tied down in just the next few moments, he would lose her.

He looped the leash around her ankle and his other hand. He pulled himself closer and took the leash in his teeth. Then with his free hand and his teeth, he tied a clumsy knot. It wouldn't hold, but it wouldn't have to hold long. He let go of her leg and grabbed the leash with both hands and secured the knot.

Jack fell back onto the ground and Molly shot off for space. He heard her cry out when the leash stopped her with a snap. She floated above the backyard like a tethered balloon. He thought crazily that the neighbors would think this was some kind of advertising gimmick. What would they think he was selling?

When he noticed the doghouse lifting off the ground, he grabbed and secured the other end of Sparky's leash to a water spout and left Molly tethered and moving one arm slowly up and down like she was pointing at something. She seemed bigger, bulging. He needed to talk with her.

The shortwave rig was in his office. He had thought she'd already be out of sight by the time he used it. He would be in his office surrounded by his books. He would read her things. They would talk. She would tell him what she saw. Now he needed the radio in the backyard. She was right there. He couldn't just go into his his office where he could not see her.

Molly hung motionless now at the end of the leash, and it was like looking down at her dangling from a cliff rather than stretching up toward space.

"Molly!" He yelled. No response.

Jack ran into the kitchen and got the long black extension cord they used to power the stereo when they had backyard parties. He hauled the radio gear out of his office and set it up on a TV tray and plugged it in.

He pulled up a chair and put on the big earphones. He pulled the microphone in its black plastic stand in close and turned the dial to Holy Frequency One. "Molly? Come in, Molly. Can you hear me, Molly? Come in."

Nothing.

He tried Holy Frequency Two.

Still nothing.

If God did speak now, Jack would have to tell Him to get off the air. He needed to talk to Molly.

He stood up and yanked on the leash trying to get her attention. After maybe a dozen tugs, he saw her bend her head down to face the ground. The effort seemed monumental. He waved his arms at her and jumped up and down.

"Is your radio on?" he shouted and pointed at his ears. "Your radio!"

He sat back down in front of his microphone and put the earphones on again.

He found her on Holy Frequency Two.

"Molly!"

"Jack," she gasped. "My foot. I think the pull is getting so hard it will pull my foot off. The prisoners. Remember? Flattened sticky goo on the ceiling. Did mother describe it to you? I think you'll have to let me go, Jack."

She gasped in pain again and dropped Ol' Engine Number Nine. The miniature locomotive bounced onto the lawn.

"Oh, no, Jack."

Jack leaned over and picked it up. He stood up and lobbed it back up at her. She snatched at it, but it slipped through her fingers and fell again.

"This can't be happening," he shouted into the microphone. "It can't be real. The pieces don't fit together quite right. There are too many loose ends! Nothing is working right. There must be something else to try. I can figure it out. Wait, Molly. Just hold on a little longer."

He grabbed the train and threw it up at her.

She missed it again.

"Oh, cut me loose, Jack," she said. "Just cut me loose."

Then she screamed. She seemed to be elongating like a victim on the rack in an old movie, and he couldn't stand the sound of her pain. He ripped off the earphones and ran to the end of the leash.

For an endless moment he couldn't get it untied and didn't know what to do. Then he took a deep breath, took out his Swiss Army knife and carefully opened the big blade.

He cut the leash.

Molly shot into the air.

Jack scrambled back to his earphones. ". . . love you, Jack."

And then she was gone.

Jack made careful preparations for his own departure. He would take her train, of course, but he also had a few other supplies. A flashlight for one thing. If you were going to be floating through the deep darkness to Uranus, you'd want to be able to shine a light around and see what was what. The Collected Works. And a small fire extinguisher.

"By the time we get to Uranus, there'll be all this junk floating everywhere." The Earth was a big wet blue marble, and he was already talking to himself. "All the stuff people grabbed when they floated away. We'll need to assign clean up crews to pick it all up. Or maybe we can just rearrange it. Who knows maybe someday there will be so much you can see the rings of Uranus from Earth not that there will be anyone on Earth by that time. But you know what I mean."

"Do you know how far away Uranus is?" Not Jack. A voice on his suit radio.

"Well, now that I can no longer touch it . . ."

Hoots. Jeeze Louise. Who is this joker?

Then he saw them. Suited figures scattered around him, the closest waving his arms like a mechanical man maybe a hundred yards away, the sun gleaming in his faceplate.

"My name is Jack," he said, "and like all of you, I'm on my way to Uranus."

"I think we're too late for Uranus," someone said.

"So, here we are zooming along at what? Maybe a hundred miles an hour?" someone else said.

"Oh, surely much faster than that."

"Do you have any idea of how long it would take to get to Uranus, Jack?"

"I really don't think I want to know that," Jack said.

He got a firm grip in Ol' Engine Number Nine, switched on his flashlight, and activated the fire extinguisher which increased his velocity considerably.

KELLY LINK

The Specialist's Hat

Kelly Link lives in Boston and works in a bookstore. She won the 1998 James Tiptree, Jr. Award for her short story, "Travels with the Snow Queen." Edgewood Press will be publishing a collection of her short stories in 1999.

Link says of "The Specialist's Hat": "This story came from three places. One was a house that one of my father's friends described where as a child he rode his bicycle around the enormous attic. The second was an outdoor exhibit of folklore in Raleigh, North Carolina where I read about the snake whiskey. I've adapted it only a little for this story. The third place is the Peabody Museum in Cambridge, Massachusetts, where I read the passage about the specialist's hat. This passage was stuck up on a wall beside an empty exhibit case. I copied it down. On subsequent visits I have not been able to find the hat, the exhibit case, or the particular quotation. Again, for the purposes of the story, I have altered the passage."

The story was originally published in the December issue of the webzine, Event Horizon: science fiction, fantasy, horror.

—E. D., T. W.

"When you're Dead," Samantha says, "you don't have to brush your teeth."

"When you're Dead," Claire says, "you live in a box, and it's always dark, but you're not ever afraid."

Claire and Samantha are identical twins. Their combined age is twenty years, four months, and six days. Claire is better at being Dead than Samantha.

The babysitter yawns, covering up her mouth with a long white hand. "I said to brush your teeth and that it's time for bed," she says. She sits cross-legged on the flowered bedspread between them. She has been teaching them a card game called Pounce, which involves three decks of cards, one for each of them. Samantha's deck is missing the Jack of Spades and the Two of Hearts, and Claire keeps on cheating. The babysitter wins anyway. There are still flecks of dried shaving cream and toilet paper on her arms. It is hard to tell how old she is— at first they thought she must be a grownup, but now she hardly looks older than them. Samantha has forgotten the babysitter's name.

Claire's face is stubborn. "When you're Dead," she says, "you stay up all night long."

"When you're dead," the babysitter snaps, "it's always very cold and damp, and you have to be very, very quiet or else the Specialist will get you."

"This house is haunted," Claire says.

"I know it is," the babysitter says. "I used to live here."

> Something is creeping up the stairs,
> Something is standing outside the door,
> Something is sobbing, sobbing in the dark;
> Something is sighing across the floor.

Claire and Samantha are spending the summer with their father, in the house called Eight Chimneys. Their mother is dead. She has been dead for exactly 282 days.

Their father is writing a history of Eight Chimneys, and of the poet, Charles Cheatham Rash, who lived here at the turn of the century, and who ran away to sea when he was thirteen, and returned when he was thirty-eight. He married, fathered a child, wrote three volumes of bad, obscure poetry, and an even worse and more obscure novel, *The One Who Is Watching Me Through the Window*, before disappearing again in 1907, this time for good. Samantha and Claire's father says that some of the poetry is actually quite readable, and at least the novel isn't very long.

When Samantha asked him why he was writing about Rash, he replied that no one else had, and why didn't she and Samantha go play outside. When she pointed out that she *was* Samantha, he just scowled and said how could he be expected to tell them apart when they both wore blue jeans and flannel shirts, and why couldn't one of them dress all in green and the other pink?

Claire and Samantha prefer to play inside. Eight Chimneys is as big as a castle, but dustier and darker than Samantha imagines a castle would be. The house is open to the public, and during the day people—families—driving along the Blue Ridge Parkway will stop to tour the grounds and the first story; the third story belongs to Claire and Samantha. Sometimes they play explorers, and sometimes they follow the caretaker as he gives tours to visitors. After a few weeks, they have memorized his lecture, and they mouth it along with him. They help him sell postcards and copies of Rash's poetry to the tourist families who come into the little gift shop. When the mothers smile at them, and say how sweet they are, they stare back and don't say anything at all. The dim light in the house makes the mothers look pale and flickery and tired. They leave Eight Chimneys, mothers and families, looking not quite as real as they did before they paid their admissions, and of course Claire and Samantha will never see them again, so maybe they aren't real. Better to stay inside the house, they want to tell the families, and if you must leave, then go straight to your cars.

The caretaker says the woods aren't safe.

Their father stays in the library on the second story all morning, typing, and in the afternoon he takes long walks. He takes his pocket recorder along with him, and a hip flask of Old Kentucky, but not Samantha and Claire.

The caretaker of Eight Chimneys is Mr. Coeslak. His left leg is noticeably shorter than his right. Short black hairs grow out of his ears and his nostrils, and there is no hair at all on top of his head, but he's given Samantha and Claire permission to explore the whole of the house. It was Mr. Coeslak who told them that there are copperheads in the woods, and that the house is haunted. He says they are all, ghosts and snakes, a pretty bad-tempered lot, and Samantha and Claire should stick to the marked trails, and stay out of the attic.

Mr. Coeslak can tell the twins apart, even if their father can't; Claire's eyes are grey, like a cat's fur, he says, but Samantha's are *gray* like the ocean when it has been raining.

Samantha and Claire went walking in the woods on the second day that they were at Eight Chimneys. They saw something. Samantha thought it was a woman, but Claire said it was a snake. The staircase that goes up to the attic has been locked. They peeked through the keyhole, but it was too dark to see anything.

> *And so he had a wife, and they say she was real pretty. There was another man who wanted to go with her, and first she wouldn't, because she was afraid of her husband, and then she did. Her husband found out, and they say he killed a snake and got some of this snake's blood and put it in some whiskey and gave it to her. He had learned this from an island man who had been on a ship with him. And in about six months snakes created in her and they got between her meat and the skin. And they say you could just see them running up and down her legs. They say she was just hollow to the top of her body, and it kept on like that till she died. Now my daddy said he saw it.*
>
> —An Oral History of Eight Chimneys

Eight Chimneys is over two hundred years old. It is named for the eight chimneys which are each big enough that Samantha and Claire can both fit in one fireplace. The chimneys are red brick, and on each floor there are eight fireplaces, making a total of twenty-four. Samantha imagines the chimney stacks stretching like stout red tree trunks, all the way up through the slate roof of the house. Beside each fireplace is a heavy black firedog, and a set of wrought iron pokers shaped like snakes. Claire and Samantha pretend to duel with the snake-pokers before the fireplace in their bedroom on the third floor. Wind rises up the back of the chimney. When they stick their faces in, they can feel the air rushing damply upward, like a river. The flue smells old and sooty and wet, like stones from a river.

Their bedroom was once the nursery. They sleep together in a poster bed which resembles a ship with four masts. It smells of mothballs. Charles Cheatham Rash slept here when he was a little boy, and also his daughter. She disappeared when her father did. It might have been gambling debts. They may have moved to New Orleans. She was fourteen years old, Mr. Coeslak said. What was her name, Claire asked. What happened to her mother, Samantha wanted to know. Mr. Coeslak closed his eyes in an almost wink. Mrs. Rash had died the year before her husband and daughter disappeared, he said, of a mysterious wasting disease. He can't remember the name of the poor little girl, he said.

Eight Chimneys has exactly 100 windows, all still with the original wavery panes of hand-blown glass. With so many windows, Samantha thinks, Eight

Chimneys should always be full of light, but instead the trees press close against the house, so that the rooms on the first and second story—even the third-story rooms—are green and dim, as if Samantha and Claire are underwater. This is the light that makes the tourists into ghosts. In the morning, and again towards evening, a fog settles in around the house. Sometimes it is grey like Claire's eyes, and sometimes it is more gray, like Samantha's.

> I met a woman in the wood,
> Her lips were two red snakes.
> She smiled at me, her eyes lewd
> And burning like a fire.

A few nights ago, the wind was sighing in the nursery chimney. Their father had already tucked them in, and turned off the light. Claire dared Samantha to stick her head into the fireplace, in the dark, and so she did. The cold, wet air licked at her face, and it almost sounded like voices talking low, muttering. She couldn't quite make out what they were saying.

Their father has been drinking steadily since they arrived at Eight Chimneys. He never mentions their mother. One evening they heard him shouting in the library, and when they came downstairs, there was a large sticky stain on the desk, where a glass of whiskey had been knocked over. It was looking at me, he said, through the window. It had orange eyes.

Samantha and Claire refrained from pointing out that the library is on the second story.

At night, their father's breath has been sweet from drinking, and he is spending more and more time in the woods, and less in the library. At dinner, usually hot dogs and baked beans from a can, which they eat off of paper plates in the first floor dining room, beneath the Austrian chandelier (which has exactly 632 leaded crystals shaped like teardrops), their father recites the poetry of Charles Cheatham Rash, which neither Samantha nor Claire cares for.

He has been reading the ship diaries which Rash kept, and he says that he has discovered proof in them that Rash's most famous poem, *The Specialist's Hat*, is not a poem at all, and in any case, Rash didn't write it. It is something that one of the men on the whaler used to say, to conjure up a whale. Rash simply copied it down and stuck an end on it and said it was his.

The man was from Mulatuppu, which is a place neither Samantha nor Claire has ever heard of. Their father says that the man was supposed to be some sort of magician, but he drowned shortly before Rash came back to Eight Chimneys. Their father says that the other sailors wanted to throw the magician's chest overboard, but Rash persuaded them to let him keep it until he could be put ashore, with the chest, off the coast of North Carolina.

> The specialist's hat makes a noise like an agouti;
> The specialist's hat makes a noise like a collared peccary;
> The specialist's hat makes a noise like a white-lipped peccary;
> The specialist's hat makes a noise like a tapir;
> The specialist's hat makes a noise like a rabbit;
> The specialist's hat makes a noise like a squirrel;

The specialist's hat makes a noise like a curassow;
The specialist's hat moans like a whale in the water;
The specialist's hat moans like the wind in my wife's hair;
The specialist's hat makes a noise like a snake
I have hung the hat of the specialist upon my wall.

The reason that Claire and Samantha have a babysitter is that their father met a woman in the woods. He is going to meet her, tonight, and they are going to have a picnic supper and look at the stars. This is the time of year when the Perseids can be seen, falling across the sky on clear nights. Their father said that he has been walking with the woman every afternoon. She is a distant relation of Rash, and besides, he said, he needs a night off, and some grownup conversation.

Mr. Coeslak won't stay in the house after dark, but he agreed to find someone to look after Samantha and Claire. Then their father couldn't find Mr. Coeslak, but the babysitter showed up precisely at seven o'clock. The babysitter, whose name neither twin quite caught, wears a blue cotton dress with short floaty sleeves. Both Samantha and Claire think she is pretty in an old-fashioned sort of way.

They were in the library with their father, looking up Multatuppu in the red leather atlas, when she arrived. She didn't knock on the front door, she simply walked in, and up the stairs, as if she knew where to find them.

Their father kissed them goodbye, a hasty smack, told them to be good and he would take them into town on the weekend to see the Disney film. They went to the window to watch as he walked out of the house and into the woods. Already it was getting dark, and there were fireflies, tiny yellow-hot sparks in the air. When their father had quite disappeared into the trees, they turned around and stared at the babysitter instead. She raised one eyebrow. "Well," she said. "What sort of games do you like to play?"

Widdershins around the chimneys,
once, twice, again.
The spokes click like a clock on the bicycle;
they tick down the days of the life of a man.

First they played Go Fish, and then they played Crazy Eights, and then they made the babysitter into a mummy by putting shaving cream from their father's bathroom on her arms and legs, and wrapping her in toilet paper. She is the best babysitter they have ever had.

At nine-thirty, she tried to put them to bed. Neither Claire nor Samantha wanted to go to bed, so they began to play the Dead game. The Dead game is a let's pretend that they have been playing every day for 274 days now, but never in front of their father or any other adult. When they are Dead, they are allowed to do anything they want to. They can even fly, by jumping off the nursery beds, and just waving their arms. Someday this will work, if they practice hard enough.

The Dead game has three rules.

One. Numbers are significant. The twins keep a list of important numbers in a green address book that belonged to their mother. Mr. Coeslak's tour has been a good source of significant amounts and tallies: they are writing a tragical history of numbers.

Two. The twins don't play the Dead game in front of grownups. They have been summing up the babysitter, and have decided that she doesn't count. They tell her the rules.

Three is the best and most important rule. When you are Dead, you don't have to be afraid of anything. Samantha and Claire aren't sure who the Specialist is, but they aren't afraid of him.

To become Dead, they hold their breath while counting to 35, which is as high as their mother got, not counting a few days.

"You never lived here," Claire says. "Mr. Coeslak lives here."

"Not at night," says the babysitter. "This was my bedroom when I was little."

"Really?" Samantha says. Claire says, "Prove it."

The babysitter gives Samantha and Claire a look, as if she is measuring them: how old; how smart; how brave; how tall. Then she nods. The wind is in the flue, and in the dim nursery light they can see the little strands of fog seeping out of the fireplace. "Go stand in the chimney," she instructs them. "Stick your hand as far up as you can, and there is a little hole on the left side, with a key in it."

Samantha looks at Claire, who says, "Go ahead." Claire is fifteen minutes and some few uncounted seconds older than Samantha, and therefore gets to tell Samantha what to do. Samantha remembers the muttering voices, and then reminds herself that she is Dead. She goes over to the fireplace and ducks inside.

When Samantha stands up in the chimney, she can only see the very edge of the room. She can see the fringe of the mothy blue rug, and one bed leg, and beside it, Claire's foot, swinging back and forth like a metronome. Claire's shoelace has come undone, and there is a Band-Aid on her ankle. It all looks very pleasant and peaceful from inside the chimney, like a dream, and for a moment, she almost wishes she didn't have to be Dead. But it's safer, really. She sticks her left hand up as far as she can reach, trailing it along the crumbly wall, until she feels an indentation. She thinks about spiders and severed fingers, and rusty razorblades, and then she reaches inside. She keeps her eyes lowered, focused on the corner of the room, and Claire's twitchy foot.

Inside the hole, there is a tiny cold key, its teeth facing outward. She pulls it out, and ducks back into the room. "She wasn't lying," she tells Claire.

"Of course I wasn't lying," the babysitter says. "When you're Dead, you're not allowed to tell lies."

"Unless you want to," Claire says.

> Dreary and dreadful beats the sea at the shore.
> Ghastly and dripping is the mist at my door.
> The clock in the hall is chiming one, two, three, four.
> The morning comes not, no, never, no more.

Samantha and Claire have gone to camp for three weeks every summer since they were seven. This year their father didn't ask them if they wanted to go back, and after discussing it, they decided that it was just as well. They didn't want to have to explain to all their friends how they were half-orphans now.

They are used to being envied, because they are identical twins. They don't want to be pitiful.

It has not even been a year, but Samantha realizes that she is forgetting what her mother looked like. Not her mother's face so much as the way she smelled, which was something like grass, and something like Chanel No. 5, and like something else too. She can't remember whether her mother had gray eyes, like her, or grey eyes, like Claire. She doesn't dream about her mother anymore, but she does dream about Prince Charming, a bay whom she once rode in the horse show at her camp. In the dream, Prince Charming did not smell like a horse at all. He smelled like Chanel No. 5. When she is Dead, she can have all the horses she wants, and they all smell like Chanel No. 5.

"Where does the key go to?" Samantha says.

The babysitter holds out her hand. "To the attic. You don't really need it, but taking the stairs is easier than the chimney. At least the first time."

"Aren't you going to make us go to bed?" Claire says.

The babysitter ignores Claire. "My father used to lock me in the attic when I was little, but I didn't mind. There was a bicycle up there and I used to ride it around and around the chimneys until my mother let me out again. Do you know how to ride a bicycle?"

"Of course," Claire says.

"If you ride fast enough, the Specialist can't catch you."

"What's the Specialist?" Samantha says. Bicycles are okay, but horses can go faster.

"The Specialist wears a hat," says the babysitter. "The hat makes noises."

She doesn't say anything else.

> When you're dead, the grass is greener
> Over your grave. The wind is keener.
> Your eyes sink in, your flesh decays. You
> Grow accustomed to slowness; expect delays.

The attic is somehow bigger and lonelier than Samantha and Claire thought it would be. The babysitter's key opens the locked door at the end of the hallway, revealing a narrow set of stairs. She waves them ahead and upwards.

It isn't as dark in the attic as they had imagined. The oaks that block the light and make the first three stories so dim and green and mysterious during the day, don't reach all the way up. Extravagant moonlight, dusty and pale, streams in the angled dormer windows. It lights the length of the attic, which is wide enough to hold a softball game in, and lined with trunks where Samantha imagines people could sit, could be hiding and watching. The ceiling slopes down, impaled upon the eight thick-waisted chimney stacks. The chimneys seem too alive, somehow, to be contained in this empty, neglected place; they thrust almost angrily through the roof and attic floor. In the moonlight, they look like they are breathing. "They're so beautiful," she says.

"Which chimney is the nursery chimney?" Claire says.

The babysitter points to the nearest righthand stack. "That one," she says. "It runs up through the ballroom on the first floor, the library, the nursery."

Hanging from a nail on the nursery chimney is a long, black object. It looks lumpy and heavy, as if it were full of things. The babysitter takes it down, twirls it on her finger. There are holes in the black thing, and it whistles mournfully as she spins it. "The Specialist's hat," she says.

"That doesn't look like a hat," says Claire. "It doesn't look like anything at all." She goes to look through the boxes and trunks that are stacked against the far wall.

"It's a special hat," the babysitter says. "It's not supposed to look like anything. But it can sound like anything you can imagine. My father made it."

"Our father writes books," Samantha says.

"My father did too." The babysitter hangs the hat back on the nail. It curls blackly against the chimney. Samantha stares at it. It nickers at her. "He was a bad poet, but he was worse at magic."

Last summer, Samantha wished more than anything that she could have a horse. She thought she would have given up anything for one—even being a twin was not as good as having a horse. She still doesn't have a horse, but she doesn't have a mother either, and she can't help wondering if it's her fault. The hat nickers again, or maybe it is the wind in the chimney.

"What happened to him?" Claire asks.

"After he made the hat, the Specialist came and took him away. I hid in the nursery chimney while it was looking for him, and it didn't find me."

"Weren't you scared?"

There is a clattering, shivering, clicking noise. Claire has found the babysitter's bike and is dragging it towards them by the handlebars. The babysitter shrugs. "Rule number three," she says.

Claire snatches the hat off the nail. "I'm the Specialist!" she says, putting the hat on her head. It falls over her eyes, the floppy shapeless brim sewn with little asymmetrical buttons that flash and catch at the moonlight like teeth. Samantha looks again, and sees that they are teeth. Without counting, she suddenly knows that there are exactly fifty-two teeth on the hat, and that they are the teeth of agoutis, of curassows, of white-lipped peccaries, and of the wife of Charles Cheatham Rash. The chimneys are moaning, and Claire's voice booms hollowly beneath the hat. "Run away, or I'll catch you and eat you!"

Samantha and the babysitter run away, laughing, as Claire mounts the rusty, noisy bicycle and pedals madly after them. She rings the bicycle bell as she rides, and the Specialist's hat bobs up and down on her head. It spits like a cat. The bell is shrill and thin, and the bike wails and shrieks. It leans first towards the right, and then to the left. Claire's knobby knees stick out on either side like makeshift counterweights.

Claire weaves in and out between the chimneys, chasing Samantha and the babysitter. Samantha is slow, turning to look behind. As Claire approaches, she keeps one hand on the handlebars, and stretches the other hand out towards Samantha. Just as she is about to grab Samantha, the babysitter turns back and plucks the hat off Claire's head.

"Shit!" the babysitter says, and drops it. There is a drop of blood forming on the fleshy part of the babysitter's hand, black in the moonlight, where the Specialist's hat has bitten her.

Claire dismounts, giggling. Samantha watches as the Specialist's hat rolls away.

It gathers speed, veering across the attic floor, and disappears, thumping down the stairs. "Go get it," Claire says. "You can be the Specialist this time."

"No," the babysitter says, sucking at her palm. "It's time for bed."

When they go down the stairs, there is no sign of the Specialist's hat. They brush their teeth, climb into the ship-bed, and pull the covers up to their necks. The babysitter sits between their feet. "When you're Dead," Samantha says, "do you still get tired and have to go to sleep? Do you have dreams?"

"When you're Dead," the babysitter says, "everything's a lot easier. You don't have to do anything that you don't want to. You don't have to have a name, you don't have to remember. You don't even have to breathe."

She shows them exactly what she means.

When she has time to think about it (and now she has all the time in the world to think), Samantha realizes, with a small pang, that she is now stuck, indefinitely between ten and eleven years old, stuck with Claire and the babysitter. She considers this. The number 10 is pleasing and round, like a beach ball, but all in all, it hasn't been an easy year. She wonders what 11 would have been like. Sharper, like needles, maybe. She has chosen to be Dead instead. She hopes that she's made the right decision. She wonders if her mother would have decided to be Dead, instead of dead, if she could have.

Last year, they were learning fractions in school when her mother died. Fractions remind Samantha of herds of wild horses, piebalds and pintos and palominos. There are so many of them, and they are, well, fractious and unruly. Just when you think you have one under control, it throws up its head and tosses you off. Claire's favorite number is 4, which she says is a tall, skinny boy. Samantha doesn't care for boys that much. She likes numbers. Take the number 8, for instance, which can be more than one thing at once. Looked at one way, 8 looks like a bent woman with curvy hair. But if you lay it down on its side, it looks like a snake curled with its tail in its mouth. This is sort of like the difference between being Dead and being dead. Maybe when Samantha is tired of one, she will try the other.

On the lawn, under the oak trees, she hears someone calling her name. Samantha climbs out of bed and goes to the nursery window. She looks out through the wavy glass. It's Mr. Coeslak. "Samantha, Claire!" he calls up to her. "Are you all right? Is your father there?" Samantha can almost see the moonlight shining through him. "They're always locking me in the tool room," he says. "Are you there, Samantha? Claire? Girls?"

The babysitter comes and stands beside Samantha. The babysitter puts her finger to her lip. Claire's eyes glitter at them from the dark bed. Samantha doesn't say anything, but she waves at Mr. Coeslak. The babysitter waves too. Maybe he can see them waving, because after a little while, he stops shouting and goes away. "Be careful," the babysitter says. "*He'll* be coming soon. It will be coming soon."

She takes Samantha's hand, and leads her back to the bed, where Claire is waiting. They sit and wait. Time passes, but they don't get tired, they don't get any older.

Who's there?
Just air.

The front door opens on the first floor, and Samantha, Claire, and the baby-sitter can hear someone creeping, creeping up the stairs. "Be quiet," the baby-sitter says. "It's the Specialist."

Samantha and Claire are quiet. The nursery is dark and the wind crackles like a fire in the fireplace.

"Claire, Samantha, Samantha, Claire?" The Specialist's voice is blurry and wet. It sounds like their father's voice, but that's because the hat can imitate any noise, any voice. "Are you still awake?"

"Quick," the babysitter says. "It's time to go up to the attic and hide."

Claire and Samantha slip out from under the covers and dress quickly and silently. They follow her. Without speech, without breathing, she pulls them into the safety of the chimney. It is too dark to see, but they understand the babysitter perfectly when she mouths the word, Up. She goes first, so they can see where the fingerholds are, the bricks that jut out for their feet. Then Claire. Samantha watches her sister's foot ascend like smoke, the shoelace still untied.

"Claire? Samantha? Goddammit, you're scaring me. Where are you?" The Specialist is standing just outside the half-open door. "Samantha? I think I've been bitten by something. I think I've been bitten by a goddamn snake." Samantha hesitates for only a second. Then she is climbing up, up the nursery chimney.

CHARLES DE LINT

Twa Corbies

"Twa Corbies," like much of de Lint's work, is a tale of modern mythic fiction which draws upon Native Canadian legends as well as Celtic lore and the myths of other North American immigrant groups. The story is set in the imaginary city of Newford, which exists somewhere (we never know quite where) in Canada or the northern United States. The story's narrator is Jilly Coppercorn, a young woman from previous Newford tales whose artistic vocation allows her to see the ghosts in Newford shadows and the First People (the animal-people of Native lore) who haunt its darkest streets. The title of the story comes from a traditional, and rather macabre, Scottish ballad. "Twa Corbies" was originally published in Australia in Twenty 3: A Miscellany *(edited by Anna Hepworth, Simon Oxwell, and Grant Watson), and reprinted in de Lint's most recent collection,* Moonlight and Vines.*

Charles de Lint is the author of numerous works, including the Newford novels* Memory and Dream, Trader, *and* Someplace to Be Flying. *He lives in Ottawa, Ontario with his wife, MaryAnn Harris.*

—T. W.

As I was walkin' all alane I heard twa corbies makin' mane . . . —from "Twa Corbies." Scots traditional

1

Gerda couldn't sleep again. She stood by the upright piano, wedding picture in hand, marveling at how impossibly young she and Jan had been. Why, they were little more than children. Imagine making so serious a commitment at such an age, raising a family and all.

Her insomnia had become a regular visitor over the past few years—often her only one. The older she got, the less sleep she seemed to need. She went to bed late, got up early, and the only weariness she carried through her waking hours was in her heart. A loneliness that was stronger some nights than others. But on those nights, the old four-poster double bed felt too big for her. All that extra room spread over the map of the quilt like unknown territories, encroaching on her ability to relax, even with the cats lolling across the hills and vales of the bed's expanse.

It hadn't always been that way. When Jan was still alive—before the children were born, and after they'd moved out to accept the responsibility of their own lives—she and Jan could spend the whole day in bed, passing the time with long conversations and silly little jokes, sharing tea and biscuits while they read the paper, making slow and sweet love. . . .

She sighed. But Jan was long gone and she was an old woman with only her cats and piano to keep her company now. This late at night, the piano could offer her no comfort—it wouldn't be fair to her neighbors. The building was like her, old and worn. The sound of the piano would carry no matter how softly she played. But the cats . . .

One of them was twining in and out against her legs now—Swarte Meg, the youngest of the three. She was just a year old, black as the night sky, as gangly and unruly as a pumpkin vine. Unlike the other two, she still craved regular attention and loved to be carried around in Gerda's arms. It made even the simplest of tasks difficult to attend to, but there was nothing in Gerda's life that required haste anymore.

Replacing the wedding picture on the top of the piano, she picked Swarte Meg up and moved over to the window that provided her with a view of the small, cobblestoned square outside.

By day there was always someone to watch. Mothers and nannies with their children, sitting on the bench and chatting with each other while their charges slept in prams. Old men smoking cigarettes, pouring coffee for each other out of a thermos, playing checkers and dominoes. Neighborhood gossips standing by the river wall, exaggerating their news to give it the desired impact. Tourists wandering into the square and looking confused, having wandered too far from the more commercial streets.

By this time of night, all that changed. Now the small square was left to fend for itself. It seemed diminished, shadows pooling deep against the buildings, held back only by the solitary street lamp that rose up behind the wrought-iron bench at its base.

Except . . .

Gerda leaned closer to the windowpane.

What was this . . . ?

2

Sophie's always telling me to pace myself. The trouble is, when I get absorbed in a piece, I can spend whole days in front of the canvas, barely stopping to eat or rest until the day's work is done. My best times, though, are early in the morning and late at night—morning for the light, the late hours for the silence. The phone doesn't ring, no one knocks on your door. I usually seem to finish a piece at night. I know I have to see it again in the morning light, so to stop myself from fiddling with it, I go out walking—anywhere, really.

When the work's gone well, I can feel a deep thrumming build up inside me and I wouldn't be able to sleep if I wanted to, doesn't matter how tired I might be. What I need then is for the quiet streets of the city and the swell of the dark night above them to pull me out of myself and my painting. To render calm to my quickened pulse. Walking puts a peace in my soul that I desperately need after having had my nose up close to a canvas for far too long.

Any part of the city will do, but Old Market's the best. I love it here, especially at this time of night. There's a stillness in the air and even the houses and shops seem to be holding their breath. All I can hear is the sound of my boots on the cobblestones. One day I'm going to move into one of the old brick buildings that line these streets—it doesn't matter which one, I love them all. As much for where they are, I suppose, as for what they are.

Because Old Market's a funny place. It's right downtown, but when you step into its narrow, cobblestoned streets, it's like you've stepped back in time, to an older, other place. The rhythms are different here. The sound of traffic seems to disappear far more quickly than should be physically possible. The air tastes cleaner and it still carries hints of baking bread, Indonesian spices, cabbage soups, fish, and sausages long after midnight.

On a night like this I don't even bother to change. I just go out in my paint-stained clothes, the scent of my turps and linseed trailing along behind me. I don't worry about how I look because there's no one to see me. By now, all the cafés are closed up and except for the odd cat, everybody's in bed, or checking out the nightlife downtown. Or almost everybody.

I hear the sound of their wings first—loud in the stillness. Then I see them, a pair of large crows that swoop down out of the sky to dart down a street no wider than an alleyway, just ahead of me.

I didn't think crows were nocturnal, but then they're a confusing sort of animal at the best of times. Just consider all the superstitions associated with them. Good luck, bad luck—it's hard to work them all out.

Some say that seeing a crow heralds a death.

Some say a death brings crows so that they can ferry us on from this world to the next.

Some say it just means there's a change coming.

And then there's that old rhyme. One for sorrow, two for mirth . . .

It gets so you don't know what to think when you see one. But I do know it's definitely oh so odd to see them at this time of night. I can't help but follow in their wake. I don't even have to consider it, I just go, the quickened scuff of my boots not quite loud enough to envelop the sound of their wings.

The crows lead me through the winding streets, past the closed shops and cafés, past the houses with their hidden gardens and occasional walkways overhead that join separate buildings, one to the other, until we're deep in Old Market, following a steadily narrowing lane that finally opens out onto a small town square.

I know this place. Christy used to come here and write sometimes, though I don't think he's done it for a while. And he's certainly not here tonight.

The square is surrounded on three sides by tall brick buildings leaning against each other, cobblestones underfoot. There's an old-fashioned streetlight in the center of the square with a wrought-iron bench underneath, facing the river. On the far side of the river I can barely see Butler Common, the wooded hills beyond its lawns, and on the tops of the hills, a constellation of twinkling house lights.

By the bench is an overturned shopping cart with all sorts of junk spilling out of it. I can make out bundles of clothes, bottles and cans, plastic shopping bags filled with who knows what, but what holds my gaze is the man lying beside the cart. I've seen him before, cadging spare change, pushing that cart of his. He looks bigger than he probably is because of the layers of baggy clothes, though I remember him as being portly anyway. He's got a touque on his head and he's wearing fingerless gloves and mismatched shoes. His hairline is receding, but he still has plenty of long, dirty blonde hair. His stubble is just this side of an actual beard, greyer than his hair. He's lying face-up, staring at the sky.

At first I think he's sleeping, then I think he's collapsed there. It's when I see the ghost that I realize he's dead.

The ghost is sitting on the edge of the cart—an insubstantial version of the prone figure, but this one is wearing a rough sort of armor instead of those layers of raggedy clothes. A boiled leather breastplate over a rough sort of tunic, leggings and leather boots. From his belt hangs an empty scabbard. Not big enough for a broadsword, but not small either.

I start forward, only I've forgotten the crows. The flap of their descending wings draws my gaze up and then I can't hold onto the idea of the dead man and his ghost anymore, because somewhere between the moment of their final descent and landing, the pair change from crows into girls.

They're not quite children, but they don't have adult physiques either. I'm just over five feet, but they're shorter and even slighter of build. Their skin is the color of coffee with a dash of milk, their hair an unruly lawn of blue-black spikes, their faces triangular in shape with large green eyes and sharp features. I can't tell them apart and decide they must be twins, even dressing the same in black combat boots, black leggings, and black oversized raggedy sweaters that seem to be made of feathers. They look, for all the world, like a pair of . . .

"Crow girls," I hear myself say in a voice that's barely a whisper.

I lower myself down onto the cobblestones and sit with my back against the brick wall of the house behind me. This is a piece of magic, one of those moments when the lines between what is and what might be blur like smudged charcoal. Pentimento. You can still see the shapes of the preliminary sketch, but now there are all sorts of other things hovering and crowding at the edges of what you initially drew.

I remember how I started thinking about superstitions when I first saw these two girls as crows. How there are so many odd tales and folk beliefs surrounding crows and other black birds, what seeing one, or two, or three might mean. I can't think of one that says anything about seeing them flying at night. Or what to do when you stumble upon a pair of them that can take human form and hold a conversation with a dead man. . . .

One of the girls perches by the head of the corpse and begins to play with its hair, braiding it. The other sits cross-legged on the ground beside her twin and gives her attention to the ghost.

"I was a knight once," the ghost says.

"We remember," one of the girls tells him.

"I'm going to be a knight again."

The girl braiding the corpse's hair looks up at the ghost. "They might not have knights where you're going."

"Do you know that?"

"We don't know anything," the first girl says. She makes a steeple with her hands and looks at him above it. "We just are."

"Tell us about the King's Court again," her twin says.

The ghost gives a slow nod of his head. "It was the greatest court in all the land. . . ."

I close my eyes and lean my head back against the wall of the building I'm sitting against, the bricks pulling at the tangles of my hair. The ghost's voice holds me spellbound and takes me back, in my mind's eye, to an older time.

"It was such a tall building, the tallest in all the land, and the King's chambers were at the very top. When you looked out the window, all creation lay before you."

I start out visualizing one of the office buildings downtown, but the more I listen, the less my mind's eye can hold the image. What starts out as a tall, modern office skyscraper slowly drifts apart into mist, reforms into a classic castle on top of a steep hill with a town spread out along the slopes at its base. At first I see it only from the outside, but then I begin to imagine a large room inside and I fill it with details. I see a hooded hawk on a perch by one window. Tapestries hang from the walls. A king sits on his throne at the head of a long table around which are numerous knights, dressed the same as the ghost. The ghost is there, too. He's younger, taller, his back is straighter. Hounds lounge on the floor.

In Old Market, the dead man talks of tourneys and fairs, of border skirmishes and hunting for boar and pheasant in woods so old and deep we can't imagine their like anymore. And as he speaks, I can see those tourneys and country fairs, the knights and their ladies, small groups of armed men skirmishing in a moorland, the ghost saying farewell to his lady and riding into a forest with his hawk on his arm and his hound trotting beside his horse.

Still, I can't help but hear under the one story he tells, another story. One of cocktail parties and high-rise offices, stocks and mergers, of drops in the market and job losses, alcohol and divorce. He's managed to recast the tragedy of his life into a story from an old picture book. King Arthur. Prince Valiant. The man who lost his job, his wife, and his family, who ended up dying, homeless and alone on the streets where he lived, is an errant knight in the story he tells.

I know this, but I can't see it. Like the crow girls, I'm swallowed by the fairy tale.

The dead man tells now of that day's hunting in the forests near the castle. How his horse is startled by an owl and rears back, throwing him into a steep crevice where he cracks his head on a stone outcrop. The hawk flies from his wrist as he falls, the laces of its hood catching on a branch and tugging off its hood. The hound comes down to investigate, licks his face, then lies down beside him.

When night falls, the horse and hound emerge from the forest. Alone. They approach the King's castle, the hawk flying overhead. And there, the ghost tells us, while his own corpse lies at the bottom of the crevice, his lady stands with another man's arm around her shoulders.

"And then," the ghost says, "the corbies came for their dinner and what baubles they could find."

I open my eyes and blink, startled for a moment to find myself still in Old Market. The scene before me hasn't changed. One of the crow girls has cut off the corpse's braid and now she's rummaging through the items spilled from the shopping cart.

"That's us," the other girl says. "We were the corbies. Did we eat you?"

"What sort of baubles?" her companion wants to know. She holds up a Crackerjack ring that she's found among the litter of the ghost's belongings. "You mean like this?"

The ghost doesn't reply. He stands up and the crow girls scramble to their feet as well.

"It's time for me to go," he says.

"Can I have this?" the crow girl holding the Crackerjack ring asks.

The other girl looks at the ring that's now on her twin's finger. "Can I have one, too?"

The first girl hands her twin the braid of hair that she's cut from the corpse.

After his first decisive statement, the ghost now stands there looking lost.

"But I don't know where to go," he says.

The crow girls return their attention to him.

"We can show you," the one holding the braid tells him.

Her twin nods. "We've been there before."

I watch them as they each take one of his hands and walk with him toward the river. When they reach the low wall, the girls become crows again, flying on either side of the dead man's ghostly figure as he steps through the wall and continues to walk, up into the sky. For one long moment the impossible image holds, then they all disappear. Ghost, crow girls, all.

I sit there for a while longer before I finally manage to stand up and walk over to the shopping cart. I bend down and touch the corpse's throat, two fingers against the carotid artery, searching for a pulse. There isn't any.

I look around and see a face peering down at me from a second-floor window. It's an old woman and I realize I saw her earlier, that she's been there all along. I walk toward her house and knock on the door.

It seems to take forever for anyone to answer, but finally a light comes on in the hall and the door opens. The old woman I saw upstairs is standing there, looking at me.

"Do you have a phone?" I ask. "I need to call 911."

3

What a night it had been, Gerda thought.

She stood on her front steps with the rather self-contained young woman who'd introduced herself as Jilly, not quite certain what to do, what was expected at a time such as this. At least the police had finally gone away, taking that poor homeless man's body with them, though they had left behind his shopping cart and the scatter of his belongings that had been strewn about it.

"I saw you watching from the window," Jilly said. "You saw it all, but you didn't say anything about the crow girls."

Gerda smiled. "Crow girls. I like that. It suits them."

"Why didn't you say anything?"

"I didn't think they'd believe me." She paused for a moment, then added, "Why don't you come in and have a cup of tea?"

"I'd like that."

Gerda knew that her kitchen was clean, but terribly old-fashioned. She didn't know what her guest would think of it. The wooden kitchen table and chairs were the same ones she and Jan had bought when they'd first moved in, more years past than she cared to remember. A drip had put a rusty stain on the porcelain of her sink that simply couldn't be cleaned. The stove and fridge were both circa 1950—bulky, with rounded corners. There was a long wooden counter along one wall with lots of cupboards and shelves above and below it, all loaded with various kitchen accoutrements and knickknacks. The window over the sink was hung with lacy curtains, the sill a jungle of potted plants.

But Jilly seemed delighted by her surroundings. While Gerda started the makings for tea, putting the kettle on the stove, teacups on the table, she got milk from the fridge and brought the sugar bowl to the table.

"Did you know him?" Gerda asked.

She took her Brown Betty teapot down from the shelf. It was rarely used anymore. With so few visitors, she usually made her tea in the cup now.

"The man who died," she added.

"Not personally. But I've seen him around—on the streets. I think his name was Hamish. Or at least that's what people called him."

"The poor man."

Jilly nodded. "It's funny. You forget that everyone's got their own movie running through their heads. He'd pretty much hit rock bottom here, in the world we all share, but the whole time, in his own mind, he was living the life of a questing knight. Who's to say which was more real?"

When the water began to boil, Gerda poured some into the pot to warm it up. Emptying the pot into the sink, she dropped in a pair of teabags and filled the pot, bringing it to the table to steep. She sat down across from her guest, smoothing down her skirt. The cats finally came in to have a look at the company, Swarte Meg first, slipping under the table and up onto Gerda's lap. The other two watched from the doorway.

"Did . . . we really see what I think we saw?" Gerda asked after a moment's hesitation.

Jilly smiled. "Crow girls and a ghost?"

"Yes. Were they real, or did we imagine them?"

"I'm not sure it's important to ask if they were real or not."

"Whyever not?" Gerda said. "It would be such a comfort to know for certain that some part of us goes on."

To know there was a chance one could be joined once more with those who had gone on before. But she left that unsaid.

Jilly leaned her elbow on the table, chin on her hand, and looked toward the window, but was obviously seeing beyond the plants and the view on the far side of the glass panes, her gaze drawn to something that lay in an unseen distance.

"I think we already know that," she finally said.

"I suppose."

Jilly returned her attention to Gerda.

"You know," she said. "I've seen those crow girls before, too—just as girls, not as crows—but I keep forgetting about them, the way the world forgets about people like Hamish." She sat up straighter. "Think how dull we'd believe the world to be without them to remind us. . . ."

Gerda waited a moment, watching her guest's gaze take on that dreamy distant look once more.

"Remind us of what?" she asked after a moment.

Jilly smiled again. "That anything is possible."

Gerda thought about that. Her own gaze went to the window. Outside she caught a glimpse of two crows, flying across the city skyline. She stroked Swarte Meg's soft black fur and gave a slow nod. After what she had seen tonight she could believe it, that anything was possible.

She remembered her husband Jan—not as he'd been in those last years before the illness had taken him, but before that. When they were still young. When they had just married and all the world and life lay ahead of them. That was how she wanted it to be when she finally joined him again.

If anything was possible, then that was how she would have it be.

TERRY DOWLING

Jenny Come to Play

*Terry Dowling is one of Australia's most respected and internationally
acclaimed writers of science fiction, fantasy, and horror. He is the author of
the novels* Rynosseros, Blue Tyson, Twilight, *and* Wormwood, *and his short
fiction is collected in* The Man Who Lost Red *and* An Intimate Knowledge
of the Night. *He has edited* Mortal Fire *(with Doctor Van Ikin) and* Best
Australian Science Fiction. *Dowling's short fiction has been chosen for* The
Year's Best Australian Science Fiction and Fantasy, The Year's Best Fantasy
and Horror, *and* The Year's Best Horror *and he has won nine Ditmar Awards,
two Readercon Awards, and two Aurealis Awards.*

"Jenny Come to Play," was published in Aurealis *25/26 in late December
1998 and won the 1998 Aurealis Award for Best Horror Short Story. It was
chosen for* The Year's Best Australian Science Fiction and Fantasy: Volume
2. *The story, not for the faint of heart, comes from Dowling's seven-part novel,*
Blackwater Days, *recently published by Eidolon Publications.*

—E. D.

When Dan Truswell learned from the activities coordinator, soon after
2 P.M. that Wednesday afternoon, that Julie Haniver was sitting catatonic in the hospital library, he took it as a routine shut-down by
the slim, nervous young woman, paged Hans and Carla, and left them
to deal with it.

It was when Peter Rait knocked at his door less than two minutes later and
said Dan had to come see Julie, talk to Julie, that Dan decided to check on her
himself. Peter was one of Blackwater's star 'attractions', an amiable, likeable
schizophrenic who had an uncanny knack for reading his fellow inmates. When
Peter showed worry, it was usually worth worrying about.

Dan locked his office and accompanied Peter around to the library in the Prior
Wing.

"What does Phil say?" Dan asked his frowning companion, knowing how Peter
and his schizoid friend, Phillip Crow, made a fascinating double-act.

Peter shrugged, which was more exasperating than it ought to have been. Phil
hadn't expressed an opinion this time. That meant Peter had reacted on his

own, which was even more amazing. Then again, he'd shown Julie a lot of attention in the four months she'd been at Blackwater.

Dan trusted Peter's insights enough to let him be there when they entered the library. Hans and Carla were already with Denise, the activities coordinator, but hadn't yet approached the girl sitting by the corner window, looking out at the fine spring afternoon. When Dan indicated Peter, they nodded and stayed at the desk. They knew Peter was good at getting through to Julie.

Dan crossed the room, sat near the petite, olive-skinned young woman with the short black hair and very pretty elfin features. Peter stood to one side.

"Julie?" Dan said gently. "Can you hear me, Julie?"

The young woman showed no sign of having heard. She sat absolutely still, gazing out the window, her eyes unfocused, watching yet watching nothing.

"Ask her who she's looking out for," Peter said, with uncommon directness.

"Peter, let me handle this."

But it was as if Peter hadn't heard. "Ask her, Doctor Dan. Ask who she's watching for!"

"Peter! That's enough!"

His tone at least made Julie blink.

"Ask her about Jackie!" Peter said, his parting shot because Carla was there then to lead him away.

But it was Peter suggesting it, and it *was* Julie—this withdrawn, shy, young woman who'd turned up one day back in June and signed herself in, without any identity but her name, no next of kin she could give, no family, no memories (she claimed) to help them build a past, the backgrounds of heredity and environment that had produced her.

"Julie, are you waiting for someone?"

Still the eyes gazed out at the grounds, broke into the emptiness and infinities of reverie before ever reaching the sunny lawns and trees.

"Julie, who is Jackie?"

Julie blinked once, twice. The eyes grabbed, locked into focus. She turned to face him, gave a nervous, embarrassed smile.

"Are you okay now?" Dan asked.

She nodded, ventured another tentative smile, noticed Peter and the others over by the desk.

Normally Dan would've left it to Carla at this point, but Peter going solo kept him there.

"Julie, who is Jackie?"

Julie frowned, sighed and looked directly at him.

"Jackie's my sister."

"Really? You never said you had a sister." Dan held back the rush of questions that were immediately there. There might be no sister at all, just an imaginary one, a convenient fiction. It hadn't surfaced during the hypnotherapy sessions. Nor did he want to move over to the armchairs or to an interview room. The view out the library window was probably part of it. She'd been watching for this "sister" most likely.

"Tell me about Jackie."

"It's why I'm here."

"Jackie wanted you here?" Dan truly expected her to have forgotten how she came to be at Blackwater, to say that this sister had been the one who'd committed her, part of a familiar enough persecution-and-betrayal scenario. Julie's answer surprised him only by its opposite tack, not its content.

"No. I came here to escape Jackie. I thought she wouldn't be able to find me here."

"Ah, I see," Dan said, kindly. He'd heard this sequence of events many times too. Only the look of intense concern on Peter's face when Dan glanced round at the others kept him with her. "And have you seen her out there, Julie?"

"She's coming today. I thought it'd be last night but it will be today."

"How do you know?"

"Jackie always leaves things."

"Oh, like what? What sort of things?"

"Just things. Signs."

"You've seen these signs? What are they?"

When Julie didn't answer, Dan tried again. "But she wouldn't come from out there, would she, Julie? She'd come in by the front gate."

The young woman frowned, studied the grounds with renewed concentration. The emotion in her eyes could have been terror, panic, utter dread. (Phobos and Deimos, the twin moons of insanity—one of Peter's lines.) Not for a moment did Dan see it as guile, the sort of cunning so many paranoid schizophrenics affected. This woman seemed truly terrified.

"Julie?" he said, both to keep her with him and to comfort her.

"She won't give up. She'll keep looking."

"Yes, well, we'll keep an eye out for her too."

Dan almost fell off his chair when she turned and grabbed his arms.

"Don't tell her I'm here!" She spat the words at him, eyes wide, face twisted by fear.

"You're safe here, Julie," Dan managed, and by then Carla was there, soothing her, urging her up, Hans assisting, leading her off to her room, leaving Denise by the desk and Peter desperately wanting to follow, to do something. He came over to Dan.

"She's really scared of her sister," Peter said, as if it hadn't been obvious. "We have to protect her. Keep her hidden."

"There may not be a sister," Dan said, wondering as always why he bothered to tell Peter Rait these things.

"There is and there isn't," Peter said, frowning with what seemed to be both puzzlement and concern. "But Julie's right. Jackie does leave things."

This was where Peter Rait was at his brilliant, entertainment-value best. It was just that Phillip Crow wasn't with him, making it unprecedented, almost as disturbing in a way as Julie's outburst.

"Oh? What sort of things?"

"Last week a piece of cloth tied to that pine over there." He pointed out the window. "Last night she would've put something closer to let Julie know she's coming."

"What sort of thing?"

Peter shrugged. "Something closer. Maybe not visible from the library window, but sharing a connection, yeah. Can I go sit with her?"

"She's resting now. You can see her later. Go and wait for her in the Games Room."

Peter nodded, then smiled as if grasping some secret strategy Dan had suggested. "Right. The play's the thing, isn't it?"

Dan said nothing. From long experience he knew enough just to watch him go.

What Dan did do when he reached his office again was go over Julie Haniver's file, reacquainting himself with what little they had. She'd admitted herself on June 4, uncertain of her age but probably around 22 to 24, had been diagnosed as stressed and exhausted, subject to unspecified feelings of persecution, anxiety attacks, even catatonic withdrawal, real or feigned. Though testing initially as a disorganised personality, she'd responded well to treatment and was usually calm and controlled. She could have been a case of nervous exhaustion following prolonged drug abuse, but her initial physical showed none of the attendant signs of that, no signs of harm at all apart from a nasty childhood or early adolescent scar above the hip on her right side. The distinctive, double hand-sized patch of keloid ridges and welts may have been from an accident involving fire or acid, possibly was the result of extreme parental or sibling abuse. That might explain the disordered, dissociated behavior: the anxiety of residual trauma. Someone named Jackie may have been responsible. Friend, relative or carer, who could say?

But nothing else in the file. Just ID shots and dated close-ups of the wound for the usual information, legal and insurance reasons. If it hadn't been for the scar and the memory loss (alleged, never proven) with its significant implications, Julie Haniver could have been discharged.

The more Dan considered it, the more she did seem like someone who might feign a mental disorder to be in a safe place. It certainly happened from time to time.

But the scar. Raw and brutal-looking. An acid burn? The result of a very clumsy, even amateur, medical procedure?

It was the photographs of the scar (and remembering Peter Rait's concern) that made Dan go out onto the terrace and walk round the outside of the building to the library windows in the Prior Wing. There was nothing tied to the low bushes or the pilasters of the terrace balustrade, but just below the window near where Julie had been sitting, there was a small stack of stones—maybe ten in all, just piled atop one another and collapsed in against the wall.

Dan immediately thought of Peter, yet knew that he would never knowingly interfere with a fellow inmate's treatment. There seemed to be only three explanations: it was coincidence—someone had just happened to leave a construct in that spot; or Peter had done it to confirm Jackie's existence for this newfound friend who desperately needed to believe she did exist; or Jackie was indeed out there.

Dan left the stones where they were and returned to his office. No sooner had he put Julie's file away than, like Fate on his heels, Angela phoned to say a Ms Jackie Haniver was waiting in Reception to see him about her sister.

Though Dan would have preferred to collect his thoughts, take time to consider the rush of events, he felt a real curiosity, even a sense of urgency about the whole business. He told Angela to have one of the staff bring Ms Haniver through at once. There were often days when Blackwater's well-established routines came undone in spectacular, sometimes alarming, usually comical ways, but this time Dan felt an uncommon pressure, as if the "briars of unreason" (as Peter Rait and Phillip Crow put it) were indeed taking over the garden.

Less then ten minutes after discovering the pile of stones, he was sitting in his office across from what seemed to be Julie's identical twin. The young woman wore a smart blue suit, was well groomed and carefully made up, and appeared very composed about the whole matter, radiating a charm and poise well beyond her years.

"You understand, Dr Truswell, that I've been looking for Julie for quite some time. I can't make her come back with me, I know, even were you to allow it, but naturally I do feel responsible for her care and safety."

"And we're naturally very glad to see you, Ms Haniver. We've had so little to go on where Julie's concerned."

"Please. Call me Jackie. And it's Perfini, not Haniver. That's a name Julie's been using. I used it at Reception because I knew it would identify me to you. I have certified copies of Julie's birth documentation here. You can keep the photocopies." Dan scanned them when she passed them over, passed back the originals. " 'Haniver' was a family *nom de guerre* or *nom de theatre*. Can I see my sister?"

"I'd like you to," Dan said, making notes on the writing pad in front of him. "But not right away. We have to deal with your appearance in terms of Julie's needs. She said she didn't *want* you to know she was here, and seems highly agitated at the thought of you finding her. Letting you see her could well seem like a betrayal. Forgive how this sounds but Julie's well-being must come first. You can help us prepare her for meeting you. Help us to get her to ask for you."

"I have to take your word for all this, don't I? That she's agitated? That she doesn't want to see me?"

"I'm afraid so. If you have doubts, there are legal procedures we can suggest. You can bring legal representation to our next meeting. Outside experts can verify admission and diagnostic protocols . . ."

Jackie Perfini smiled and raised a hand. "Unnecessary, Doctor. I accept what you're telling me. I'm just surprised and hurt about this. Of course I accept your professional judgement. But what are the chances of her being released into my care? The legalities?"

"Again, that will depend on her recovery. You're probably aware that once someone is committed, or commits themselves as Julie has, they can only be discharged when a qualified person deems their condition satisfactory."

"Julie must be that, surely. She's dreamy and distracted and withdrawn, but hardly crazy. I'm surprised she's so upset, and amazed to think she might have committed herself just to be away from us."

"Who is us, Jackie?"

"Our father died last year. I meant our sister, Jenny, and me."

"Your mother?"

"Died soon after Julie and Jenny were born."

"You and Julie look identical."

Jackie smiled. "Dr Truswell, I think you're interrogating me. In a moment you'll be asking if I have a scar of my left side just above the hip."

"Do you?"

"I'm afraid not. I'm eighteen months older than Julie and Jenny. We do look alike, I know, but Julie and Jenny were born conjoined. Congenitally united, as they say."

"Jackie, Siamese twins not sharing vital organs or major skeletal features are usually separated as soon after birth as is safely possible. That's a nasty scar. A bad separation procedure."

"Bad 'procedure'! God, I love these terms! It was butchery! It's a wonder they survived. Dr Truswell, my family emigrated from Sicily. Lots of faith in the old ways. Lots of family honour. Lots of shame in having deformed children. Julie and Jenny were born there."

"It wasn't a hospital birth."

"Correct. But it's more complex, more tragic for them than that. Our father, the bastard, had more than a passing interest in teratology."

"Teratology? Monsters?"

"Don't look so amazed, Doctor. It's more common than most of us think. Alonzo was fascinated with the old *Wunderkammern*—the 'wonder-cabinets' and 'cases of curiosities', so famous and popular in the 16th and 17th centuries, that became the private collections and eventually the public museums. He had a modest but growing collection of oddities, a museum of his own, a sort of travelling show."

Dan couldn't believe what he was hearing. "He *left* them joined?"

Jackie Perfini nodded. "A shameful and hideous thing, I know. He had them wet-nursed by an aunt, then took them to be part of his own *Wunderkammer*. A living exhibit. But then Alonzo Perfini was a selfish and domineering man. A persuasive and charming man when he needed to be. An atheist and occultist. A would-be mystic and entrepreneur. His heroes were Giovanni Batista Belzoni, Elias Ashmole and the Dutchman, Dr Frederic Ruysch. These twins had caused his wife to die, he liked to believe, though it wasn't true. Maria was already very ill. Here he was with his great love of monsters, having become the father of two. Or one, depending on your viewpoint. It was destiny, something that suggested a mystical purpose. He was much taken with the notion of things being joined. The alchemical union of opposites."

"Hardly opposites, Jackie."

"Nevertheless, he left them joined to grow up like that."

"Until when?"

"Till just after puberty. They were barely thirteen. They persuaded a second cousin who was an intern to perform the 'procedure', as you call it."

"Without your father's consent?"

"Of course. He was furious."

Dan was still trying to follow the reality which had brought Julie, Jenny and Jackie to this point in their lives. "Where were you when this happened, Jackie?"

"I was with the show for a while as an infant, then Alonzo left me with some of Maria's relatives in a village outside Palermo before he took his troupe north. Eventually they sent me to Australia and I was raised by aunts in Melbourne. I was told my father had gone off travelling, grieving for the loss of his wife and baby."

"Baby?"

"No one knew it was twins then. The story was that it was a stillborn boy. Maria was so sick, probably even she did not know the truth. They even had a funeral—it was all a mockery. When the girls were old enough, he added them to his show, had documents falsified saying they shared vital organs and had to stay joined. Even the girls grew up believing it. I didn't meet them until they came to Australia six years ago."

"Where's Jenny now?"

"Down in Sydney, safe and happy enough. Even more shy than Julie. But missing Julie terribly."

"Can you bring her here?"

"I tried to get her to come. She wouldn't. No offence, Dr Truswell, but she thought this place would be too much like the *Perfini Chamber of Wonders* and his travelling *Wonder Show*. She's had enough of imprisonment and disordered minds and being regarded as a curiosity. Part of one."

Dan understood her reservations. "Still, seeing her might help Julie's recovery considerably."

"My feelings exactly. But I've lived with this, Dr Truswell. I know only too well how Jenny feels. Until Julie went missing back in June, we all had a relatively quiet life together."

"A normal life, Jackie?"

"Normal enough. Jenny was seeing someone, a young man. I could give you his number next time I visit. Julie was starting to go out more."

Dan made a few more points on his notepad. "It's difficult to know what to do. Despite what you tell me, Julie was terrified at the prospect of your coming here."

Jackie Perfini smiled. "And she would've told you I leave things, signs that I'm following her. She's done that before. Left signs, I mean."

"She does it herself?"

"I'm afraid so. It's something she did during their time in the show. At first it was just a book or a stone or a flower, but then she started making things out of folded paper, clay . . ."

"Like piling up stones or tying strips of cloth to trees."

"That sort of thing, yes. But it's just a game. She'll still come into our rooms at home and leave things. It's not serious, is it?"

"Of course not. But in her stressed condition she's made it part of her perception of you, I'm afraid. She believes you're the one doing it."

Jackie frowned, then sighed and smiled. "Well, so long as she's safe. That's the main thing now. I respect her decision to come here, though I can hardly say I'm happy about it. I'd be grateful if you'd talk to Julie about all this. See if you can get her to come home. She's had a hard life."

"Jackie, how did you find her here?"

"I called hospitals, hostels, Lifeline, drop-in centres, places like that. Had the police looking for a while. You probably got a call here. Then Jenny suggested I try looking for her under the name 'Haniver', an alias they used in the show."

"I see. Well, I'd still like to meet Jenny. I think it's very important."

"Yes, well that's up to Julie and Jenny, isn't it?"

"I think it would probably be beneficial for both of them."

"I agree. So you speak to Julie and I'll speak to Jenny."

"How can we reach you?"

"Best I call you. I'm still deciding where to stay in the area. I can't be away from Jenny for too long."

"Can you give me a number where I can at least call Jenny?"

"Later, Dr Truswell. I'll need to clear this with Jenny first."

It was exasperating, even infuriating, though Dan was by no means a stranger to the byzantine nature of family affairs. Institutions like Blackwater attracted the end-products of crisis and despair, with the added pressures of inheritance complications and human rights issues. Jackie Perfini was giving him as much and as little as he was giving her.

"Then please call soon. We need to settle things for Julie's sake."

"All our sakes, Doctor. But Julie's and Jenny's most of all, yes. They had and still have a special connection. Jenny doesn't say much about it, but she's deeply troubled when Julie is away."

So how must she be feeling now? Dan wondered. *Who's minding her?*

Dan shook the young woman's hand when she stood and offered it, feeling more frustrated than he could remember. He wanted to ask more about her father's travelling show, where it went, what occurred during those crucial years, wanted to ask about her own life. But now it was *quid pro quo* and the smartly dressed young woman was heading to the door.

As soon as Jackie left him at Reception, Dan had Hans note the make and colour of her car, then placed an immediate call to Jay Wendt over in Everton.

"Jay? Dan Truswell. I need Wendt Investigations do me an urgent favour. There'll be a—" Hans said a few words from the front door. "—white '94 Laser coming down the highway towards town in about ten minutes. Victorian number plate. Young female driver. Blue suit; short black hair. I need a local destination for her."

To Dan's relief, Jay was able to oblige. He replaced the receiver and leant back in his chair, told himself it was the most he could do other than talk to Julie, try to get her side of Jackie's story, find out more about Jenny from her. Later, he'd phone Harry Badman down in Sydney, see if there was any background on the names Perfini or Haniver in the CIB database.

But now he had rounds to do, counselling to give, bits of his own fraying world to bring to order. He was half an hour at it, busily trying his best to keep his thoughts off Julie's catatonia and Jackie Perfini's sudden appearance—the whole disturbing, strangely compelling sequence of events—when he was called to the phone.

"Dan, it's Jay. I'm halfway down the Putty Road. Your subject has left the Hunter Valley altogether."

"She didn't stay local?"

"She's heading for Sydney, I'd say. Flat out too. You want me to stay on this?"

"Jay, I really need you to. This woman is the sister of a patient. We might need a destination in a hurry."

"Then I'll call a pal of mine in Windsor. Stephanie Ashburn. She can pick it up there and I'll come back. She's good, Dan. Don't worry. If necessary, I'll get someone from Parramatta to get out there as well. There'll be other traffic but we might need to leap-frog the closer she gets to home."

"Sounds like quite an operation."

"Just like the big kids do. I'll do a trace on the registration too and call when I've got something, okay?"

"Thanks, Jay."

There was no way he could return to his rounds. At 3:50 he paged Carla and asked her to bring Julie Haniver to his office as soon as possible.

When the girl was ushered in and given an armchair opposite Dan's near the french doors, she looked calm enough, though she never took her eyes off Dan for a moment, obviously expecting some fears to be confirmed.

Dan thanked her for coming and opened his notepad. He'd already decided to play it straight with her. When Carla had gone, he didn't hesitate.

"Jackie was here, Julie."

"I know."

"How do you know?"

"Peter told me."

Dammit. Peter Rait had far too much liberty, Dan decided, then retracted it. Peter had never been the enemy before, probably wasn't now. Though he'd never acted on his own before either.

"She already knew you were here, Julie. We didn't tell her."

"Peter told me that too, Doctor Dan. It's okay. I shouldn't have used the name Haniver. It was an old show name."

Thank God. Dan settled back. Julie seemed uncommonly composed and alert now, very focused indeed.

"She told me about Jenny. About the Perfini Wonder Show. About your father and his interests."

Julie nodded slightly, as if expecting it. "He couldn't help himself. Jenny keeps saying it. He couldn't help the things he did."

"Well, maybe so, Julie. But we need to know more about it. What can you tell us?" *Now that Jackie's been here*. Dan didn't need to add.

"We didn't have to be joined. It was only cartilage and muscle. Alonzo knew some doctors interested in *Wunderkammern*. They faked X-rays of the Lugli twins from Padua. Alonzo showed the authorities false X-rays. Jenny and I never knew."

"How did you find out?"

"It just became too much. What he did. We kept away from Italy, certainly from Sicily. Our first names were changed. We used the name Haniver. It's an in-joke. But we found we had a cousin interning in Frankfurt when we were there. When Alonzo had food poisoning and was taken in for tests, Carlo came and got us from the carnival and took us to visit. We sometimes did go out with Papa and his friends. We could walk well enough to look like we were closely arm in arm. Carlo didn't take us straight to Papa's ward. He did some X-rays of us. We didn't have to stay joined."

"Did Carlo go to the authorities?"

"Not then. It was a family thing, you see. He got two friends to help. Alonzo was away. They did the operation in our wagon."

"They *what*? That's burn scarring you've got, Julie. Interns with access to X-

ray equipment and hospital facilities would hardly use acid or resort to cauter-
ising wounds with flame. Do you actually remember the operation?"

There seemed a dreamlike quality between them now, almost as if her words
were being recited from some false memory. "No. Jenny told me about it. I've
forgotten a lot of things."

"Jenny wouldn't lie to you." He had to be so careful.

"Never. Jenny is my dearest friend. She's in my song. I'm in hers."

"Your song? I don't follow."

There was much more animation in Julie's features now. She was smiling
again. "When we were young, it was our private game. We'd sing it."

"Please sing it now, Julie. Would you?"

Julie smiled and did so, in a light, clear voice.

"When will Jenny come to play?
When will Jenny come to stay?
Jenny's never somewhere else,
Jenny's here with me, myself."

"Thank you, Julie. I take it as an honour."

"Jenny would sing 'Julie'; I'd sing 'Jenny'. We thought we'd have one another
forever. We didn't know we could be apart. We never expected it."

"You miss that, don't you, Julie?"

"Sometimes desperately, Doctor Dan. It was all there was. You made it your
world every conscious moment. Washing. Going to the toilet. Even pretending
to be alone by turning away from each other. Playing at separation. But I grew
to hate it too. Because of Alonzo. What he did. And once Carlo showed us we
were probably separable. It wasn't the same. It wasn't a necessity any longer.
More like an oversight."

"So why don't you remember?"

"I was ill or something. 'Highly strung', they said. With bad headaches. I had
to be sedated a lot. I remember that."

Dan leant back in his chair, made himself lean back, stay calm. He could no
longer be sure what was truth or fiction. Perhaps he did need Peter Rait's view
on this.

"Julie, after the operation, what happened to Carlo?"

"Carlo? I've put so much out of my mind, Doctor Dan, I don't know. Carlo
just disappeared. Alonzo was furious. Humiliated. He tried to convince us the
separation *had* been riskier than Carlo said, that he never wanted to take the
chance, even claimed that he'd been misled by unscrupulous members of his
Wunderkammer group."

"Julie, what do you mean Carlo disappeared?"

"We never saw him again. I never did. Perhaps he ran away. Alonzo said what
Carlo had done had shamed him, made him a laughing stock before his peers."

The story was changing again. "His peers, not his family. Who were they
again?"

"Others who owned *Wunderkammern* and traded exhibits with him. We never
went back to Palermo. Alonzo finally sold off his collection and brought us to
Australia."

"Did he do that in a hurry?"

"Not for three years. But then it all happened so quickly."

"What name did you use in Melbourne?"

"The show name. Haniver. He didn't want to use Perfini. He preferred the Flemish name, said it advertised his field of interests better."

"Oh? How so?"

Julie shrugged. "I don't know. Perhaps others interested in wonder-cabinets would recognise the name."

"Right. Julie, you seem to be recalling quite a bit now. Can you give me your address and phone number in Sydney?"

"Didn't Jackie?"

"No, she didn't."

"She was protecting Jenny."

"But you trust me. Can you give me your home address or phone number?"

"Doctor Dan, please understand. I need to protect Jenny too."

Which possibly explained the lies. Dan studied the earnest face, lacking only make-up to be identical to Jackie's. Something *was* dramatically different now. If not for Jackie's visit lending an element of credibility to the whole thing, Dan wouldn't have believed any of it. He still couldn't help but feel it was some kind of hoax, or at least that layers of deception were at work, being employed to conceal what little truth there was. It was almost as if Julie had done a quick change, had managed a conspiracy so she could play both parts. Yet more than ever he had to accept the prevailing situation, not fight it, not force it.

"Julie, you believe we're genuinely trying to help you? That we want you and Jenny to be safe?"

"Of course I do."

"You and Jackie both want to protect Jenny. Jackie says that she's with Jenny down in Sydney, is that correct?"

"Yes."

"Yet you didn't want Jackie to find you."

"That's right."

"Can you explain that? Knowing Jackie is living with Jenny, knowing that Jenny misses you terribly, why would you run away from them?"

"I don't know. I just don't know."

"Please try, Julie. Why did you run away from Jenny?"

"I ran away from Jackie!"

"Why? Why would you do that? Why would you do that to Jenny as well?"

"I just don't know."

"Do you want to know?"

"What?"

"Would you like me to help you find out why you're here?"

There were only frowns now, bewilderment and uncertainty crimping her forehead, her confusion drawing out into its inevitable edge of panic. He could see it pulling at her eyes.

"H—how?"

"You remember our hypnotherapy sessions, Julie. Now Jackie's found you, I'd like to use hypnosis again. See what we can learn."

What is true, Dan told himself.

"Hypnotise me? Now?"

"That's right. We did it before, remember? It might help a lot."

"You'll find out where Jenny is."

"Not if I promise *not* to ask you that, Julie. Do you trust me about that?"

Before she could answer, the phone rang. Dan excused himself, crossed to his desk and answered it.

"Hello?"

"Is that Dan Truswell?" a woman's voice asked.

"It is."

"Dr Truswell, I'm Stephanie Ashburn, a friend of Jay Wendts. I've followed the subject to a Dalloway Road address in Horsley Park. That's outside Blacktown, near Fairfield. It's semi-rural. Lots of open fields and market gardens."

"I think I know it, Stephanie. Go on."

"I've just arrived. That's 72 Dalloway Road."

"Describe the location, please."

"Large-enough property, maybe three hectares. Just an ordinary fibro cottage, a few big trees."

"Any sheds or garages?"

"There's a very large, corrugated iron shed set away to the right of the house. It's seen better days but it's sturdy enough. I'd say about thirty metres by fifteen, about four metres high."

"Where did the car pull up?"

"Outside the shed."

"Not the house?"

"Right. No lights visible, but the shed has no windows on the two sides I can see. No signs of activity. What should I do?"

"You're not too obvious?"

"I'm quite a ways from the place."

"Okay. Stephanie, phone Jay and tell him where you are. I'd appreciate it if you could stay there till one of us calls."

"Let me give you my number here."

Dan wrote it down and hung up. Then, as he turned from the desk, he saw a small paper object sitting among his files. It was an origami figure of—what else?—two humans joined at back or front. But dropped there by which sister—Julie or Jackie? He couldn't know. When had either had the chance? Jackie as she left? Julie as she came in?

Without touching it, he turned back to the armchairs by the long windows, now golden with late afternoon light.

"The hypnosis, Julie. What do you say?"

She looked up at him, wide-eyed, clearly troubled by the prospect. "Can Peter be here?"

Dan didn't flinch, didn't blink or hesitate. "If you want. I know he'd like to be."

Julie nodded. Dan returned to his desk, paged Carla and asked her to send Peter round to his office. By the time he arrived, Dan had his recorder set up and a chair positioned slightly behind Julie's so their guest would be out of direct sight. Peter took it with a smile and a nod, for all the world like a colleague here to observe an interesting procedure. Dan couldn't help smiling back, then set the recorder going and began.

"Peter, Julie and I decided we'd try some more hypnotherapy and thought you'd like to join us. You'll observe the usual courtesies, I know."

Peter nodded. "As silent as the Moon," he said. "Not a bird, nor the mewings of the baby stoat."

Baby stoat? Was he quoting? Dan could never be sure. But Peter settled back quietly, his eyes fixed attentively on Julie for a moment, then closed in his usual contemplative manner.

Dan positioned himself, began the relaxation recital. Julie visibly settled in her chair, actually seemed glad to give in to Dan's suggestions. Within a few minutes she had lapsed into the trance.

"Julie, tell me about the Perfini Wonder Show."

"Wonder-cabinet," Julie murmured, plumbing the years.

"Yes, the Perfini wonder-cabinet. The *Wunderkammer*. Tell me about it."

"We travelled through Europe," Julie said. "Papa took us through so many different countries. Not the big cities all that often, and not all the towns. He knew where to go. The special fairs. The right estates."

"I'm sure. When did he first start showing you and Jenny?"

Julie didn't hesitate; Jenny was such a powerful reality for her. "When we were five. We were the special exhibit. He saved us till last."

"Did you enjoy it?"

"We loved it. We loved the attention then."

"Then? Not later?"

"Later it was different."

"How much later?"

"When we had turned ten. It was different, then."

"How was it different?"

Julie frowned and didn't answer. Her left cheek spasmed—a nervous tic. Behind her right shoulder, Peter Rait's eyes opened wide as if in some shared sympathetic alarm, then closed again. He was trying to behave.

"Julie," Dan repeated gently. "How was it different?"

Julie was resisting, was even shaking her head a little. There was conflict, something she didn't want to face. Dan was about to put a new question when Peter broke trust and, eyes still closed, asked a question of his own.

"All the best wonder shows have a secret room, Julie. A special room. What happened in the secret room?"

Dan was furious but said nothing. Like Jenny, Peter was a powerful force in Julie's life. *She* had wanted him there.

Tears were rolling down Julie's cheeks when she answered. "It was where Papa took us."

Dan stayed silent. Let Peter ask it.

"To do what? What happened there, Julie?"

"He showed us undressed. He let them touch us." Despair had tightened her throat. The words were pinched, broken with sobbing now.

"He molested you? Both of you?"

Dan found they were his questions, coarsely, heavy-handedly, almost cruelly put, as direct as Peter always was; though here he was, without Phillip, coherent and focused and helping *without* Phillip Crow! The briars of unreason were blooming indeed.

Julie blinked away more tears, nodded.

Dan might not have persisted. Peter did.

"But it was your father! How could it happen?"

"We resisted. They held us down. Sometimes they tied our hands. Put rags in our mouths. We had no choice."

Dan intervened. "What about your visit to the hospital? Carlo doing the X-rays? What about your separation?"

"Carlo didn't do the separation. Carlo became a fine pair of wings. We did some of it ourselves, Jenny and me."

"What?" Dan said and, unsure of what he had heard, went back. "Carlo became what?"

But Julie was locked onto Peter's earlier question. "Papa said it was what many collectors did. Became teratophiles. There were codes, passwords, that let them into the secret rooms all over Europe. They all had them—the travelling shows and respectable homes. There were special fairs. There still are. It isn't new. The practice has been going on for centuries."

Dan composed himself. "But Carlo tried to help."

"He tried. But Papa caught him. Made him into a fine pair of wings."

There it was again, but Dan didn't bring it up then. "So how were you separated? If Carlo didn't do it?"

"One of the Papa's guests in Frankfurt was a surgeon. Papa let him visit us alone. He felt very guilty after he had been with us. He took pity on us, told Jenny and me it was just a lot of muscle joining us. No arteries, nothing vital. There'd be blood, he said, quite a lot, but he told us what he'd have to do, said he'd bring the necessary instruments and drugs."

Despite the bizarre experiences of Dan's own life, it all sounded like so much fabrication again, a tall tale growing larger and more improbable by the minute: first Carlo, now this Frankfurt surgeon. Carlo becoming a nice pair of wings.

But then, like a spectre at the feast, or more a mind-reader in a high-class nightclub act, Peter was there.

"Julie, this is very important. Doctor Dan and I are finding this hard to accept. You must help us. Your Papa let this surgeon bring a bag of things into the secret room?"

"A lot of them brought bags and cases. Teratophiles are like paraphiles everywhere. Some brought masks and hoods, special costumes and things to use on us. Their cameras. Papa trusted and liked this man. Xavier Pangborn was as great an admirer of Frederic Ruysch as Papa was. Only when the pain became too much, and we were crying out, did Papa break in. He and Dr Pangborn had a terrible fight." Julie winced at the memory. Her cheek spasmed. "Jenny was in so much pain. She passed out. I had to finish the job before I passed out too."

Finish the job!

Dan made himself stay calm, focused. Things did happen violently, strangely, in life; people were capable of the most extraordinary things, acts of courage and strength—incredible perversion too—a mix of the courageous and the outra-geous that did make it seem that orthodoxy and consensus were always some-where else in human affairs.

"What happened to Xavier Pangborn?" Dan asked, warning Peter with a look.

"We awoke in a house with Dr Pangborn and women we didn't know tending to us. Alonzo was downstairs, furious, so very angry, but also very afraid that Pangborn would tell the authorities and so was trying to be civil. The same shame and guilt that had made Pangborn help us had also led him to destroy all incriminating papers and exhibits of his own. Now he was a pillar of belated virtue. He said he'd have contacts keep an eye on us. Alonzo would never be sure who he meant and so actually made the best of the situation. He eventually sold off his own collection and brought us down to Australia."

"So you were reunited with Jackie."

Julie frowned. "It was more like meeting her for the first time, really. Jenny and I were too young to remember her with the show."

"She became very taken with Jenny. Why is that, Julie?"

"Jenny has always been shy and fragile. The trauma of what those men did, the results of the separation—she took it all so much harder than I did. One of us had to cope. One of us had to be stronger."

"But Jackie came looking for you, too, Julie. Jackie cares enough for you to have searched for you."

Julie's mouth was a grim line. Her frown crushed her brow with the intensity of suffering, not merely concentration.

They should stop soon. But there was still so much to learn and Julie was so responsive, so lucid like this. He'd never have expected it. Dan decided to avoid further mention of Jackie; that was the harming stressor here.

"How did Alonzo earn his living in Melbourne, Julie?"

The frown went away; her mouth softened. "He had contacts there—keepers of *Wunderkammern* like himself. One of them gave him a job as assistant curator in a local museum."

"With a secret room, no doubt." Dan couldn't help himself.

Julie took it as a question. "I suppose. It was a large public museum. There are always parts the public doesn't see."

That the brotherhood of cabinet-keepers kept secret, Dan decided.

"How did he treat you?"

"Well, from then on. We were with family. He found his interests elsewhere. And Xavier Pangborn came to see us."

"Pangborn did?"

"He was in Australia lecturing at ANU and Monash. One evening he stopped by. That was before he went missing."

"Went missing?" It was going wild again.

"It was a terrible thing. His wife was with him. There was a big search. It was in all the papers."

Did Alonzo kill him? Dan wanted to ask, but somehow knew Julie would have no idea. If her story were true—this terrible, elaborate, improbable tale—she had every reason to want to put it out of mind. He was probably going too far now. But Jackie had disturbed him; the case of this mysterious young woman sitting before him had opened out, blossomed amazingly. There were too many facts but not enough certainties.

It didn't stop Peter.

"Julie, what did you mean Alonzo made Carlo into a nice pair of wings?"

"Peter!"

"She isn't under, Doctor Dan. She's pretending to be in a trance!"

Dan was affronted, amazed yet convinced all at once. He hadn't wanted to believe it, but of course she was pretending; it had let her deal with experiences too difficult to face otherwise. But the illusion had to be preserved. He had to try to save it.

"Peter, listen very carefully. Trust my professional judgment here. I know for a fact Julie *is* under, and she's going to answer your question right now to prove it. Julie, please answer Peter's question."

Dan again leant forward slightly, urging the young woman with his body language to continue with the vital pretence.

And the words came in the same calm tone she had been using at the outset.

"Alonzo made monsters in the old way. Many keepers of *Wunderkammern* did. You know, fitting bat wings to the bodies of lizards, then carefully drying them to make dragons. Adding a human foetus' arms to the body of a skate. Sticking horns onto monkey skulls. The first platypus taken to Europe was regarded as such a fake. They tried to pull the beak off. Carlo was killed and dried, flayed and 'leathered'. His skin was used for wings."

Wilder and wilder, Dan thought. This couldn't go on. Julie improvising; Peter playing the role of a conspirator in some charade. Though Jackie *had* been real. She *had* been.

"Ask her about her surname," Peter prompted, leaning forward as well, playing his part, though he looked more concerned than ever. "Haniver."

"Haniver?" Dan echoed, but the phone rang. He crossed to his desk, grabbed the receiver. "Hello?"

"Dan, it's Jay. Stephanie's not answering her mobile. She was going to do a lost motorist routine, knocking at the door, asking for directions. So she may have switched it off."

Dan kept him voice low and matter-of-fact. "Is there a problem?"

"Not necessarily. But it wasn't our arrangement. Whenever there's risk—what we call a 'nasty'—we leave our mobiles on."

"What about your back-up from Parramatra?"

"Dan, there was enough traffic going into Horsley Park for Stephanie not to stand out. I called Rick and let him go. Oh, and incidentally, the Laser is registered to a Laura Barraclough in Melbourne and hasn't been reported stolen. I'd say it's on loan."

"Okay. Jay, I'm probably overreacting badly but there's an edge to this I don't like at all. If Stephanie's run up against Jackie she may be in trouble."

"But Jackie isn't the patient."

"Correct. Like I said, she's a patient's sister and seems pretty unstable. Let me know the moment Stephanie calls in."

"Done. What do we do in the meantime?"

"You've got the number in Dalloway Road?"

"Yes."

"Call in favours, Jay. See if you can get a local squad car round there."

"You really do suspect foul play?"

"They won't find anything," Julie said from her chair by the windows.

"Hold it a moment, Jay," Dan said, turning to face her. "What do you mean?"

Julie's face was like a golden mask in the last of the sunlight. "The house at 72 is a trap. It's what's called a 'false door' in Egyptology, what the teratophile cabinet owners call a blind to throw off undesirables. But it's a trap house. Jackie will have taken Stephanie to meet Alonzo and Xavier."

"But they're dead!"

"Yes. But she knows it'll bring me back."

More and more the briars were coiling up.

"Julie, you've got to help me. You've got to explain clearly what's going on!"

"Jackie's changed the rules. She's always been concerned with connection, bringing things together, but now she's harming Jenny."

That was Alonzo with the connection thing, not Jackie! Julie was changing her story again.

"We're going to bring the police in on this," Dan said. "Listen, Jay . . ."

But Julie's words brought him up short. "You'll never find the house if you do."

"What?"

"If you or your friend there call the police, Doctor Dan, I swear I'll go catatonic and you'll get nothing. Jackie will never call again. Jenny will die. Stephanie may already be dead."

"What then?"

"You get this Jay friend of yours to drive us down to Sydney. I'll take you to the house. Then you can call your police friends."

"I can't do that, Julie."

"But you know you will anyway. I've got to save Jenny, Doctor Dan. It has to be this way. I know Jackie."

Stephanie never called in; her phone remained switched off. The Fairfield police found her car outside 72, found the house deserted, its lights operated by timers, found the shed locked but empty inside when they forced the lock.

This came to them in Jay's Nissan Patrol as they plunged down the Putty Road, Jay driving, Julie next to him, Dan in the back waiting for Harry Badman to return his calls.

Neither Dan nor Jay was surprised when, at 6:20, they turned into Walgrove Road and headed for Horsley Park. Of course the trap house and the real one would be close enough for convenience.

"Tell us about Alonzo and Xavier Pangborn, Julie," Dan said. "How they can be involved."

"You'll see."

Dan refused to give up. "I think I might be a better friend to Jenny than you are right now."

Julie turned in her seat to look at him. "What do you mean?"

"You're doing this because you want to help Jenny."

"Yes! Save Jenny!" Still she faced him, half-turned, eyes glittering in the dim interior.

"Why am *I* doing it?"

"Because you want to know what's going on. Because of his friend." She indicated Jay. "Stephanie."

"More than that. You know it's more than that."

"What then?"

"You want to help Jenny. But I want to help Jenny *and* Julie. Because Jenny needs to have Julie safe too, doesn't she? It can't be all right unless you're both safe."

"Yes." It was a ghostly, feeling-charged affirmation, said with a new and different emotion. She believed him, was accepting what he said. Perhaps he was earning the truth from her.

"Tell me how Alonzo and Xavier are involved!"

And Julie told them as they did 110ks along Walgrove Road.

"Both men were interested in joining opposites, in bringing things together, the old alchemical quest. Alonzo left us joined. Xavier used us because we were. The prize of Xavier's collection, probably genuine, was two joined bodies."

"Congenitally joined?"

"Oh no, Doctor Dan. An ancient Roman punishment was to tie the condemned to a corpse, back to back or face to face, then leave you. If you weren't lucky enough to die from shock, your body was poisoned by the rotting cadaver. Necrosis took over. Xavier had acquired the preserved remains of such a wretch left like this in a cell in ancient Syria long ago. Preserved by desert heat and aridity. The bodies were unearthed in the 1700s, reached Amsterdam in the 1830s, finally made it into Xavier's collection just before we were born. The same year."

Dan thought he understood. "Xavier acquired the double corpses. Alonzo then fathered conjoined daughters not long after. He couldn't resist. He left you like that as a gesture, a living symbol of Xavier's exhibit."

"Yes." It was breathed rather than said. "That was partly the reason. He also enjoyed the notion for itself."

"Then the separation . . ."

"Was motivated by genuine compassion from Xavier, we believe, by outrage at something they'd done as competitive, obsessive, heartless, younger men, not just to spite a rival."

"Then . . ." And again Dan understood. "When Xavier went missing . . ."

"Yes. Alonzo avenged himself in the appropriate way. Xavier ended his days in a cellar face to face with a corpse."

"How do you know this?"

"Jackie told me."

"*Jackie!* How does she know?"

"She became Alonzo's favourite when he came to Australia. He needed to gloat. He showed her what he'd done."

"Showed her! My God!"

They turned off Walgrove Road onto Horsley Drive, then Julie directed them right into Walworth and along the crests of the low hills, the road winding its way past isolated houses with cheerily lit windows, past long intervening outlooks and swales where the land rolled away in darkened vistas, marked only by occasional, far-off, twinkling points of light: touches of civilisation and sanity.

Enough touches, for other things were out there as well. The residues of madness and obsession.

"Lots of room out here, Doctor Dan," Julie said, as if answering him. "Lots of houses and sheds few people ever get to see inside of."

Lots of opportunities for secret lives, Dan thought. "What will Jackie do, Julie?"

"I don't know, Doctor Dan. But I think she wants to harm me and Jenny."

"She said she cared for Jenny. For you too."

"Sometimes she does. But she scared me. I had to leave."

You left Jenny! Dan couldn't accept that. "Julie, was Jenny already dead when you ran away?"

And is Jackie waiting to join the two of you—Xavier-like—back together? Face to face? To reunite you at last?

"Not when I left. But Jackie loves Jenny. She wouldn't harm her."

"She might to get at you. People do it all the time. Harm what they love."

"Not Jenny!" Julie said as if desperately needing to believe it. "Turn here!"

There was a street sign Dan didn't have time to read or even ask about because, almost immediately, Julie was telling Jay to pull over in front of a large open field. No, not a field; a drab fibro house sat at the end of a driveway, a single light showing dimly from what seemed to be the living room. To the right of the house was a large, corrugated iron shed, just like the one Stephanie had described for the place on Dalloway Road, about thirty metres by fifteen, four metres or so high, with no visible windows and none of the double doors you'd expect for housing large vehicles in such a structure.

"There." Julie pointed, indicating the shed and the solitary door they could see on its northwestern corner.

Jay reached for his car-phone.

"Don't!" Julie said, in a voice that actually startled Dan, so different it was to anything he'd ever heard from her. "Please! She will harm Jenny! And Stephanie! She probably doesn't know we're here yet!"

Jay switched off the engine. "Lives are at risk, Julie."

"They certainly will be if we don't follow her system."

"System?" Jay asked before Dan could.

"That's a *Wunderkammer* there," Julie answered. "She will have prepared it for us."

Again Jay reached for the phone. "Someone has to know. No one's going in there . . ."

Dan gripped his shoulder. "Jay, it probably does have to be this way. What's the layout, Julie?"

"She will have changed it. It's the House of Iitoi, most likely. From the Hopi legend. The maze pattern you see all over the Southwestern USA. The Arizonan labyrinth with Death at the centre. Your journey through the maze to Death at the centre is the journey through life . . ."

"Julie!" Dan said, still gripping Jay's shoulder, knowing how carefully this had to be played. "Tell us what to expect."

"There's usually an entry corridor going round the perimeter, leading inwards. There'll be photographs, exhibits to arouse interest, *vanitas mundi* tableaux . . ."

"*Vanitas* what?" Jay asked.

"Displays," Dan said. "Vitrines containing exhibits. Go on, Julie."

"Definitely a maze."

"With traps? Shortcuts? You've been in there. You've seen it."

"I can't say. She will have changed it, Doctor Dan. But she wants me in there with Jenny. She won't risk harming me."

"Give us the address here, Julie," Dan said. "As we go in, Jay phones the police. No one goes anywhere till that's done."

"But *as* we go in," Julie said. "I have to be in there. Promise. Both of you."

Dan did at once. Jay hesitated, furious, then grudgingly did so, as if such oaths could hold true just by being given. There was danger here, and madness, though fortunately Jay, like Dan, recognised an essential process at work, saw that any show of force could not guarantee the safety of lives within. But a trail of crumbs had to be left for the cavalry, even if it was to be after the event. Everything on Jackie's terms, *if* they decided to go in.

"Lot 6, Jellicoe Road," Julie told them, opening her door and getting out, with Dan right behind her, determined to stay close.

Jay did too, slipping his gun into the inside pocket of his wind-jacket, his mobile in his left hand. "I want to check the address," he said, and rushed off into the night. They could hear his footsteps along the road.

"He'll call the police," Julie said, taking Dan's arm and leading him up the driveway, angling towards the shed. "We need to continue without him."

"We can't do that, Julie. His friend is in there. He deserves to be here too."

"Don't you see, Doctor Dan? If we make this difficult for Jackie, she'll make it difficult for us. He can follow. Please."

Dan tried to think it through, calculate what was to be lost or gained.

But the door was suddenly there and it opened easily when Julie turned the handle and, almost before he knew it, they were in the long 1.2 metre-wide passageway that stretched out before them, roofed and walled with sheet iron, wooden-floored, lit by single frosted bulbs every seven metres or so. The building's outer wall had been corrugated iron, but its interior was faced with sheet iron, suggesting a double wall, probably with insulating batts in between. On the inner wall of the passage were framed photographs—first, of the original eponymous twins, Chang and Eng, and of other famous conjoined siblings, then of a whole series of renowned 'freaks' and hoaxes. Hanging from the roofbeams, casting eerie shadows and set turning in the warm close air by Dan and Julie entering the corridor, were the shrivelled remains of false monsters. Dan saw a winged, serpent-like thing the red of old blood, then a grimacing homunculus— no doubt a late-development foetus, its wizened features and oversized hands probably added by some experienced teratologist. Other dim shapes swung and spiralled further down the passageway.

From even further off, deeper within the structure, came music—the faintest strains of Prokofiev, if Dan wasn't mistaken—which lent a disturbing, too-discordantly civilised edge to the whole thing, but also gave a sense of direction and destination, some kind of centre to all this.

Julie went on ahead, leaving Dan to follow. They had to complete the circuit, it seemed, follow the passage the length of the shed's long southern side, turn left along its eastern end. There were more sheet metal walls, naked bulbs, photos in dusty frames, shrivelled shapes turning overhead, then another turn left down the long northern side.

Now the photos were different. Now the pictures were of Julie and Jenny, their story told in graphic, pathetic detail: showing them first as infants, cute and normal-looking in matching outfits; then as happy little girls in identical smiling poses; then as pre-pubescent youngsters suddenly displayed naked and joined by their short 'bridge' of flesh—just the two of them alone initially, staring wide-eyed in confusion and alarm, then attended by as many as seven figures in dark business suits, though more often one or two and always male it seemed, all but the girls masked, appropriately, with dominoes or grotesque animal and demon masks, lacquered and snouted as if denizens from a Venetian Carnivale. Sometimes the girls were shackled; other times they simply huddled together, hiding their nude or half-dressed state.

Then it changed again. Dan saw images even more blatantly sexual, and more and more often, one of the twins was shown with her hands fastened behind her and her mouth taped, while the other received the attentions of some visitor or other with what seemed increasing abandon.

"Julie," Dan said, whispered in the close air, his first words in that terrible place. "You're the one restrained, aren't you?"

Julie nodded, not turning, sobbing. "She enjoyed it! The bitch actually enjoyed it, can you believe that? I was always raped, but she *liked it!*"

"Jenny did? But you said Jenny and you . . ."

"Not Jenny!" she cried, sobbing bitterly now, still pressing ahead, still not looking round. "Not *Jenny!*"

"That's Jackie?" Dan's gaze flicked from image to image and knew it was. "But Jackie spoke of Jenny too . . ."

He didn't need to go on, certainly didn't need to speak what Julie so painfully knew. It was what Peter Rait had said about there being a sister. *There is and there isn't.*

There was no Jenny.

They'd both lost a sister, had both changed too much to be what they once were for each other; yet both had vivid, profoundly affecting memories of a loved one who *was* another part of them, *was* the perfect friend and sibling.

Julie didn't see her in Jackie. Jackie couldn't find her in Julie.

They'd lost each other, couldn't be it for one another, had become too different, too definitely separate; yet out of trauma, betrayal, terrible loss, had invented the one point at which they *could* connect. Preserving something of the lost intimacy, some kind of way back.

As a schoolboy in Reardon, Dan remembered that his kindergarten teacher had made a Wendy House at the back of the classroom, named, no doubt, after Peter Pan and Wendy—a house where the children played at being grown-ups. This was a Jenny House—everything in it a shrine to what Julie and Jackie had made between them. But playing at grown-ups. What chance had they?

Dan saw how it was. Hurrying along after Julie, rushing past those frightful images, he understood the terrible dilemma. Jackie wanted to unite with her version of Jenny—which only Julie could provide. Of course she'd wanted her back. Julie wanted to unite with *her* version of Jenny as well, but *not* with Jackie! That paradox, that crisis of opposites, had made Julie flee; the opposite pendulum swing had brought her back again into the same irreconcilable crisis.

There was only one way the sisters could ever be joined that would let them *both* join with Jenny. Peter had probably known more about it in his incredible way, had wanted Dan to ask about their pseudonym. Haniver. Now there wasn't time. Now there was only the terrible danger.

"Julie, we must go back!" he cried, grabbing at her arm, but she pulled away. Dan hurried forward, went to grab at her again, but then the lights went out and a tremendous snaring weight fell on him from above. He could hear a far-off pounding as he sank to the floor.

Perhaps he lost consciousness for a few moments, Dan couldn't be sure. He found himself trying to put the world back together, found himself fighting with the weight oppressing him when the lights came on again, saw he was wrestling with a coil of heavy rope triggered to drop from above. The driving beat he could hear was probably Jay pounding at the *locked* entry door (for Jackie would have locked it behind them).

Dan finally freed himself from the tangle and stood. There was no sign of Julie, of course: nothing ahead but the passage, the stuffy dimness and turning constructs, more pictures on the walls.

There *were* traps. There *were* shortcuts and secret panels. Julie had been snatched away.

The pounding stopped. The Prokofiev was back and other sounds: far-off scuffling, thumps against the iron, muffled cries.

Dan pounded the walls a moment, crying their names, then rushed along the corridor, his footsteps ringing on the wooden floor, his hands slapping the iron. He had to get to the centre, to wherever Jackie had Julie. And Stephanie, if she were even still alive.

There was a crash and the building shuddered. Dan ignored it, continued running, bringing wind to the dead air.

Again, the building shook to an impact, a shuddering crash, this time followed by a wrenching sound.

It was Jay! Jay was ramming his four-wheel drive into the building, trying to force a way in. And again the structure shook. Beams creaked. Pictures fell and iron sheets were sprung on their uprights.

Dan wrenched one sheet away, actually pried it free and brought it clattering down, then stepped into an inner part of the corridor. One stage closer.

Again Jay rammed the building. Beams groaned, dust settled, more metal sheeting warped out from the timber. Tearing his fingers, Dan wrenched another section of wall free, revealed another inner coil of the maze. There couldn't be many more. He ran on, slewing into the walls when Jay rammed the structure a fifth time, making headway surely.

Then Dan could hear voices raised in anger, accusation, women's voices shouting; made out actual words.

"Jenny doesn't love you!"

"Jenny doesn't love *you*!"

He stopped to listen.

"Do it! Go on! I dare you!"

"Not with you! With her!"

He ran, plunging round the circuit, trying to get into wherever it was. And again the building resounded to a blow, this time followed by a shuddering crash as more outer structural supports gave way.

Dan rounded the next corner, crashed into a locked door and went spinning back, stunned by the impact.

"Julie!" he cried. "Jackie, let me in!"

Again Jay rammed the building. It was solidly made, but never meant for this sort of battering. Something had to be giving.

"He'll do it!" a voice beyond the door cried—Julie or Jackie, Dan couldn't tell. "He will!"

And dazed, bloodied, pushing against the door, Dan thought they meant Jay.

When the door gave way and Dan toppled into the large central room, he saw in a glance a host of disparate things: the old-style record player, the specimen tables and cases of exhibits, the clustering of shapes dangling from the roof-beams; saw the girls lying naked and joined in the shallow pit in the middle of the floor, yes, glued together front to front with the tubes of instant glue lying near them, Julie's hands tied behind her back; saw too what he had set in motion by pushing back the door: the big tub of acid even now tipping onto them.

He'll do it!

The screams and thrashing about were hideous and mercifully short, and there was drumming, a relentless drumming that wasn't the blood rushing through Dan's heart and temples, that was suddenly Jay bursting into the room, eyes wide, gun drawn.

They stood in the dreadful quiet, in a near-silence of sizzling and dripping that faded even as they watched, faded to the lowest, faintest mewing of despair.

"Where's Steph?" Jay said.

"Listen!" Dan told him.

"Where is she?"

"Listen, dammit!"

And they heard it again: a dismal far-off wail, a dull thumping.

"Where's that coming from?" Jay demanded.

"There's always a secret room," Dan said, remembering what Peter had said to Julie. "Try over there, but stay clear of the pit. That's acid."

They circled the central depression where the bodies lay contorted and, yes, virtually indistinguishable now, went to one of the dimly lit corners. The mewing was louder, the dull thumping more distinct.

They discovered a catch near the ceiling, another sunk into the wooden floor, and fumbled at them, Dan with bloody fingers, Jay clumsy with desperation, but finally pulled back the panel to reveal a room lit by its single bulb.

Stephanie was on the floor, naked, gagged, strapped between the dried corpses of Alonzo and Xavier, their shrivelled heads and faces jammed against hers, their groins pressing close, front and back. Though clearly exhausted, she was jerking the hideous construct as best she could, eyes wide with sheer terror and a hysteria very close to madness.

Jackie had used false street signs, so it took the police and ambulances a while to find them at Lot 3 Dinsmoor Road. And it took hours of Dan and Jay answering questions at the local police station to explain just what it was that had occurred, and why. Thankfully, Harry Badman phoned in at last and vouched for them, added his verifications to those already provided by Blackwater, but it wasn't until 2 A.M. that Dan and Jay reached Everton again. Knowing how some things needed to be anchored in the mundane as soon as possible, Dan had Barbara, Mark and Carla 'debrief' them for almost another hour before sending Jay off home.

The next morning, Dan wasn't at all surprised to find Peter Rait sitting at the corner window in the library where he'd found Julie—could it be?—less than twenty-four hours before.

"I should've asked you about the name," Dan said. "Haniver."

Peter nodded and smiled. "You should have, yes. Though it couldn't have ended any other way."

"Tell me about it now."

"There used to be quite a thriving market in monsters. Many were made in Antwerp, a Flemish seaport on the Scheldt the French called Anvers. A 'Jenny Haniver' was the name they gave to such merchandise."

"These false monsters?"

"Yes, Doctor Dan. False dreams, in a way. Imitations of wonder some needed to believe in so much. The sisters knew what they were making."

"They died for it, Peter."

"Yes, but it's closure, isn't it? They had already lost one another, were getting further and further apart."

"Their *Wunderkammer* was a death-trap."

"Ah, but then, Doctor Dan, that's like the world itself. The best of them always are."

ILAN STAVANS

Blimunda

Translated from the Spanish by Harry Morales

1998 was a year full of ghost tales in American literary journals, many by Hispanic writers. The brief, strange, memorable story that follows is one of the best of them, beautifully translated by Harry Morales.

   Ilan Stavans teaches at Amherst College. His books include The Hispanic Condition, The One-Handed Pianist and Other Stories, *and* The Oxford Book of Jewish Stories. *He has been nominated for the National Book Critics Circle Award and is the recipient of a Guggenheim Fellowship and the Latino Literature Prize, among other honors. "Blimunda" is reprinted from* AGNI, *published in Boston and edited by Askold Melnyczuk.*

—*T. W.*

for L. H.

Greco lived in Heinlopo, a major commercial shrimp fishing port, and was the owner of several boats, each of them containing two large, strong nets. He would contract day laborers who would leave at dawn to go fishing and would return in the late afternoon to gather and deposit shrimps into small barrels and later clean the nets. Greco had a daughter named Blimunda. Because she was beautiful and intelligent, Blimunda managed to convince her father to enroll her in a convent in Huatusco City. She spent seven years there, educating herself and becoming a young lady. By the time she left the convent, she had earned such a reputation that every handsome man in Heinlopo desired her. As a result, Greco quickly arranged for her to marry Lafcadio Reyes, the son of an associate of his. Blimunda learned to love Lafcadio, living together for another seven years, and eventually having a son. But when their son was three or four years old, Blimunda caught pneumonia and died.

   On the night of Blimunda's wake, her son ran into the room where all of the mourners were congregating and said: "Something strange is happening near the nets, behind the house. Mother is there, watching." Everyone thought the boy was talking nonsense. But they all ran out of the room anyway and saw that Blimunda's ghost was actually pinned up against an old, cracked wall. She was wearing a beautiful white tunic and her eyes were pointedly fixed on an indiscriminate spot on the ground.

The mourners became frightened. Blimunda's body was resting, shrouded, in a coffin inside the house, but her spirit was outside, entranced and pensive. Greco, who was already an old man at the time, much against his own will, tried to drive it away with a stick. He was unsuccessful and the ghost continued to show no fear. The neighbors, stirred by the news, arrived at the wall and couldn't believe what they saw: one neighbor throwing rocks at it, which passed right through Blimunda, while someone else had a crucifix out and was courageously using it as a shield while muttering commands at it to go away, like one does to an evil force.

The next day the body was buried in a cemetery fifteen kilometers away into the mainland, in the Valle del Conejo. The townspeople thought that by moving the body away from Heinlopo and burying it far away, they would solve the problem. But no, Blimunda's spirit remained pinned up against the wall, watching.

There were two reactions in town: out of fear, most of Greco's neighbors left Heinlopo and headed for the capital. They argued that her ghost would bring others. To them, once a place had been possessed, it would remain satanic forever. The second reaction came from Blimunda's relatives and friends, who treated her naturally. Even though they wouldn't come too close because they noticed her spirit seemed somewhat nervous, they would go shrimp fishing just the same, without a care in the world, mindful that a ghost can be allowed to generate fear but it shouldn't take away one's livelihood.

In the meantime, all the remaining neighborhood children—Blimunda and Lafcadio's son amongst them—would cry whenever they saw the ghost, no matter how many times they were exposed to it. But nothing changed: it continued to be pinned up against the wall, day and night, with her eyes fixed on the ground.

Cabalists, magicians, therapists, and priests arrived in Heinlopo, followed by two politicians from Paranagua, who had decided to come when they learned that mass fear was motivating the townspeople to slowly desert the beaches of Heinlopo. That's also when Plinio, Blimunda's cousin, made it home. He immediately met with Lafcadio, who told him about what had happened. When he learned after an absence of many years, that his dear childhood companion had died, his heart started beating fast.

So he went to have a tête-à-tête with the ghost. Blimunda seemed young, serene, and her hair was flowing freely, her white tunic absorbing the light of the sun and the moon. Even then her fixed eyes projected her intelligence.

"What did she say before she died?" Plinio asked later.

"Nothing, really," replied Lafcadio.

Actually, she had mumbled a few syllables, but her fever and chills had drowned them out.

"She appears nervous to me," Plinio added.

He went to her house and then up to her bedroom where he noticed that Lafcadio had removed all the tools, clothing, photographs, and household goods which reminded him of Blimunda, thereby erasing her from his life. He looked all over the room, from top to bottom, and then later searched the other rooms and closets. He was looking for something, but didn't know what. During his search he came across old postcards, a pair of pajamas that Uncle Baltazar had worn during his stay in Texas, old fishing nets which weren't used anymore, trophies, and decorated medals. But the search was in vain.

As Plinio was leaving the house that night, he noticed something strange: Blimunda's ghost wasn't where it always was. The wall was bare, and a radiance remained in the area. Suddenly, he turned around and noticed one of the boats was missing. He looked out at the sea and saw that Blimunda's ghost had thrown the oars overboard and was sitting in the boat, looking at him from somewhere in the open sea.

"What are you waiting for?" he shouted at it.

Although she was far away, Plinio could see her smiling. But no answer came.

A storm was threatening from high above. He continued to observe the ghost for a while, then later returned to Lafcadio's house and went to sleep.

The next morning, he saw Blimunda's ghost again, pinned up against the wall with her eyes fixed at a right angle with the ground. Her radiance had now disappeared and she could hardly be seen. A non-believer would certainly not have been able to confirm that there was actually a ghost there, floating in the corner, near the fishing nets. But her shining, relaxed smile made her a pleasant entity to behold.

Plinio walked up to the ghost and intuitively started to scratch the wall and dig into the ground with his foot. Although his hands were hurting, he could see her smooth, clear smile in the background. He felt good: he was doing something right. After much digging in the ground, he finally reached bottom and found a chest hidden in the dirt. A treasure. When he looked up and noticed Blimunda's ghost trembling, he got scared and decided to bury the chest again. Because after all, he knew that such secrets should not be revealed during the day. Plinio then took off his shirt and pants and went swimming in the sea. He swam for three hours or more and afterwards went home to sleep.

He woke up at midnight, feeling sleepless. He got up and without knowing why, went to Lafcadio's room and said good-bye. His uncle hardly seemed to notice, though. He did the same with Blimunda's son, then returned to his room, packed his clothes, made his way to the room housing the fishing nets and left the house with the ghost walking directly behind him.

Plinio cast his bags aside near the peeling wall and proceeded to dig up the chest. He opened it up and saw that it contained a notebook, a wristwatch with a crown that was disintegrating from old age, an amulet, and two letters.

"Go in peace," he said to Blimunda. "No one will read the contents of these letters or this notebook . . . except me."

The ghost opened its mouth as if wanting to say something but nothing came out.

Plinio read the material: beautiful, genuine correspondence and a diary of an impossible and passionate love. When he finished, he saw the ghost at the beach, waiting for him in a launch. Plinio walked towards it and climbed into the boat.

They sailed away—nowhere in particular, just far, far away. While sailing, he lit a match and burned the material. He deposited the ashes in the chest, locked it, and threw it into the sea. He noticed how the ghost's shadow started to submerge and then finally sink into the sea, its bubbles hypnotizing him. Blimunda, finally at rest, had disappeared.

Plinio then sailed back to Heinlopo in order to tell Greco the news and summon the townspeople back home.

CHANA BLOCH

Mrs. Dumpty

Chana Bloch has published three books of poems: The Secrets of the Tribe, The Past Keeps Changing, *and* Mrs. Dumpty *(selected by Donald Hall for the 1998 Felix Pollak Prize in poetry). Bloch's translations include the biblical* Song of Songs *and works by modern Israeli poets. Among her awards are two fellowships from the National Endowment for the Arts and one from the National Endowment for the Humanities. Bloch lives in Berkeley, California and is W. M. Keck Professor of English Literature and Director of the Creative Writing Program at Mills College in Oakland.*

Bloch's most recent collection, Mrs. Dumpty, *is a memoir-in-verse about the dissolution of the author's long and loving marriage as a result of her husband's mental illness. The following short but powerful poem, making deft use of imagery from a classic fantasy rhyme, comes from that collection. It was also published in the August 24 and 31 issues of* The New Yorker *magazine.*

—*T. W.*

The last time the doctors gave up,
I put the pieces together
and bought him a blue wool jacket, a shirt,
and a tie with scribbles of magenta,
brown buckle shoes. I dressed him
and sat him down
with a hankie in his pocket, folded into points.
Then a shell knit slowly
over his sad starched heart.

He'd laugh and dangle his long legs and call out,
What a fall that was!
And I'd sing the refrain,
What a fall!

And now he's at my door again, begging
in that leaky voice,
and I start wiping the smear
from his broken face.

A. S. BYATT

Cold

British author A. S. Byatt won the Booker Prize for her glorious novel
Possession—a literary mystery with a fairy tale at its heart. She is also the
author of The Virgin in the Garden, Still Life, The Tower of Babel *and (of*
particular note to fantasy readers) The Djinn in the Nightingale's Eye, *among*
other highly acclaimed works. Her magical novella Angels and Insects *was*
made into a feature film of the same title. Byatt, who is also a literary critic
and college lecturer, lives in London.

Byatt's interest in fairy tale themes is evident in her body of work, and in
the following story. "Cold" is set in the lands of Once Upon a Time—but is
certainly no children's tale. This exquisite story comes from the author's most
recent collection, Elementals: Stories of Fire and Ice.

—T. W.

In a temperate kingdom, in the midst of a landmass, with great meandering rivers but no seashores, with deciduous forests, and grassy plains, a princess was born on a blue summer day. She was eagerly awaited, although she was the thirteenth child, for the first twelve royal children were all princes, and her mother longed for gentleness and softness, whilst her powerful father longed for delicacy and beauty. She was born after a long labour, which lasted a day and a night, just as the sun began to colour the sky, but before it had warmed the earth. She was born, like most babies, squashed and livid, with a slicked cap of thick black hair. She was slight enough, but perfectly shaped, and when the nurses had washed off her protective waxy crust the blood began to run red and rapid, to the tips of her fine fingers and under the blue of her lips. She had a fine, transparent skin, so the blush of blood was fiery and rosy; when her hair was washed, it sprang into a soft, black fur. She was pronounced—and was—beautiful. Her exhausted mother, whose own blood began to stir faster again as the child was laid on her breast, said she should be named 'Fiammarosa,' a name that just came into her head at that moment, as a perfect description. Her father came in, and picked her up in her new rosy shawl, holding the tiny creature clasped in his two huge hands, with her little red legs waving, and her composed pink face yawning perfectly above his thumbs. He was, like his father before him, like all the kings of that country, a large, strong, golden-bearded, deep-voiced, smiling man, a good soldier who avoided conflict, a good huntsman who never killed heaps and droves of creatures, but enjoyed the difficulty of the chase, the dark of the forests, the rush of the rivers. When he saw his daughter, he fell in love with her vulnerable fragility, as fathers do. No one shall ever hurt you, he said to the little creature, whose wavering hand brushed against the soft curls of his beard, whose fingers touched his warm lips. No one. He kissed his wife's damp brow, and she smiled.

When Fiammarosa was a few months old, the sooty first hair, as it does, came out in wisps and strands, collecting on her white lawn pillows. In its place, slowly and strongly, grew pale golden hair, so pale it shone silver when the light was in it, though it could be sunny-yellow seen against scalp, or brow, or, as it grew, on her narrow neck. As she drank in her mother's milk, she became milky; the flush faded as though it had never been, and the child's skin became softly pale, like white rose petals. Her bones were very fine, and the baby chubbiness all children assume before they move was only fleeting in her; she had sharp cheekbones, and a fine nose and chin, long, fine, sharp fingers and toes, even as an infant. Her eyes, under white brows and pearly eyelids, retained that dark, deep colour that is no colour, that in the newborn we call blue. The baby, said the nurse, was like fine bone china. She looked breakable. She behaved as though she herself thought she was fragile, moving little, and with a cautious carefulness. As she grew, and learned to crawl, and to walk, she grew thinner and whiter. The doctors pronounced her 'delicate.' She must be kept warm, they said, and rest frequently. She must be fed well, on nourishing things, things that would fill her out—she must drink concentrated soups, full of meat juices and rich with vegetables, she must have creams and zabagliones, fresh fruits and nourishing custards. This regime had a certain success. The white limbs filled out, the child's cheeks rounded over those edged bones, she acquired a pretty pout and faint dimples on her little fists. But with the milky flesh came languor. Her pale head dropped on its pale stalk. The gold hair lay flat and gleaming, unmoving like the surface of a still liquid. She walked at the right age, spoke at the right age, was docile and learned good manners without fuss. She had a habit of yawning, opening her shell-pink lips to show a row of perfect, gleaming, tiny white teeth, and a rosy tongue and gullet. She learned to put out a limp hand in front of this involuntary grimace, which had an aspect of intense laziness, and another aspect, her mother once thought, of a perfectly silent howl or cry.

Never was a young girl more loved. Her parents loved her, her nurses loved her, her twelve brothers, from the young men to the little boys, loved her, and tried to think of ways to please her, and to bring roses to the pale cheeks and a smile to the soft mouth. In spring weather, well-wrapped in lambswool shawls and fur bonnets, she was driven out in a little carriage, in which she lolled amongst soft cushions, staring indifferently at the trees and the sky. She had her own little rose-garden, with a pool full of rosy fish in green deeps, and a swing on which, in the warmest, brightest weather, her brothers pushed her gently to and fro, whilst she leaned her face on the cool chains and looked down at the grass.

Picnics were brought out to this garden, and Fiammarosa reclined on a grassy slope, swathed in soft muslins, with a wide straw hat tied under her chin with pink ribbons, to protect her from sunburn. It was discovered that she had a taste for water-ices, flavoured with blackberry and raspberry, and for chilled slices of watermelon. These delicacies brought a fleeting smile to her normally expressionless face. She liked to lie on the grassy bank and watch her brothers play badminton, but any suggestion, as she grew older, that she might join in brought on an attack of yawning, a drooping, a retreat to the darkened rooms of the palace. Her brothers brought her presents; she was unimpressed by parakeets and kittens, but became curiously attached to a little silver hand-mirror, engraved with twining roses, from her eldest brother.

Her tutor loved her, too. He was a brilliant young man, destined to be a professor, who was writing a great history of the kingdom from its remotest beginnings, and had not wanted the court appointment at all. He loved her not despite, but because of, her lethargy. He was sorry for her. There were days when, for no reason he could discern, she was able to sit upright and concentrate, infrequent days when she suddenly surprised him with a page of elegant calculations, or an opinion as piercingly clever as it was unexpected, on a poem or a drawing he was discussing with her. She was no fool, Fiammarosa, but there was no life in her, most of the time. She yawned. She drooped. He would leave their study to fetch a book, and return to find the white head dropped onto the circle of the milky arms on the table, a picture of lassitude and boredom, or, just possibly, of despair. He asked her, on one of these days, if she felt ill, and she said, no, why should she?, directing at him a blank, gentle, questioning look. I feel much as usual, she said. Much as I always feel. She spoke, he thought, with a desperate patience. He closed the window, to keep out the draught.

During her early years, the earth went through one of its periodic coolings. Autumn came earlier and earlier, the rose leaves were blown about the enclosed garden, there was a nip in the air in late summer, and snow on the ground before the turn of the year. The palace people redoubled their efforts to protect the princess, installing velvet curtains and bed-hangings. On very cold nights, they lit a fire in the pretty fireplace in her bedroom, so that the coloured streamers of reflected flames chased each other across the carved ceiling, and moved in the soft hangings on the walls. Fiammarosa was now at the edge of girlhood, almost a woman, and her dreams troubled her. She dreamed of dark blue spaces, in which she travelled, without moving a muscle, at high speeds above black and white fields and forests. In her dreams she heard the wind coil, howling, round the outside walls, and its shriek woke her, so that she heard with her ears what she had dreamed in her skull. The wind spoke with many voices, soft and shrill, rushing and eddying. Fiammarosa wanted to see it. She felt stifled in her soft blankets, in her lambswool gown. She went to the window, and dragged open the curtain. Behind it, her breath, the breath of the room, had frozen into white and glistening feathers and flowers on the glass, into illusory, disproportionate rivers with tributaries and frozen falls. Through these transparent, watery forms she could see the lawns and bushes, under snow, and the long tips of icicles poured down from the eaves above her. She put her cheek against the frozen tracery, and felt a bite, a burn, that was both painful and intensely pleasurable.

Her soft skin adhered, ever so slightly, to the ice. Her eyes took in the rounded forms of the lawns under snow, the dark blue shadows across it, the glitter where the light from her window sliced it, and the paler glitter where the moonlight touched the surface. And her body came alive with the desire to lie out there, on that whiteness, face-to-face with it, fingertips and toes pushing into the soft crystals. The whole of her short, cosseted history was against her; she drew back from the glass, telling herself that although the snow blanket looked soft and pretty it was dangerous and threatening; its attraction was an illusion of the glass.

But all the next day, she was possessed by this image of her own naked body, stretched on a couch of snow. And the next night, when the palace was dark and silent, she put on a flowered silk wrap, covered with summer poppies, and crept down the stairs, to see if there was a way out into the garden. But all the doors she could find were locked, and barred, and she was discovered by a patrolling guardsman, to whom she said with a tentative smile that she had come down because she was hungry. He was not to know that she always had sweet biscuits by her bed. So he took her to the kitchen, and poured a glass of milk for her in the larder, and found her some white bread and jam, which she nibbled, still smiling at him, as she questioned him about his work, the places where the keys were kept, the times of his patrols.

When she followed him into the larder, as he ladled milk from a great stone jar in the light of a candle, she felt cold rise from the stone floor, and pour from the thick walls, and sing outside the open grated window. The guard begged her to go into the kitchen—'You will catch your death in this draught,' he said— but the Princess was stretching her fingers to touch the eddying air.

She thanked him prettily, and went back to her hot little room where, after a moment's thought, she took her wrought-iron poker and broke up the banked coals of her fire, feeling faint as she hung over it, with the smoke and the bright sparks, but happy, as the life went out of the coals, the reds burned darker, and were replaced by fine white ash, like the snow. Then she took off her gown, and rolled open the nest of bedclothes, and pulled back the great curtains—it was not possible to open the window—and lay back, feeling the sweat of her efforts cool delectably in the crevices of her skin.

The next night she reconnoitred the corridors and cupboards, and the night after that she went down in the small hours, and took a small key from a hook, a key that unlocked a minor side-door, that led to the kitchen-garden, which was now, like everywhere else, under deep snow, the taller herbs stiffly draggled, the tufted ones humped under white, the black branches brittle with the white coating frozen along their upper edges. It was full moon. Everything was black and white and silver. The princess crept in her slippers between the beds of herbs, and then bent down impulsively and pulled off the slippers. The cold snow on the soles of her feet gave her the sense of bliss that most humans associate with warm frills of water at the edge of summer seas, with sifted sand, with sunny stone. She ran faster. Her blood hummed. Her pale hair floated in the wind of her own movement in the still night. She went under an arch and out through a long ride, running lightly under dark, white-encrusted boughs, into what in summer was a meadow. She did not know why she did what she did next. She had always been decorous and docile. Her body was full of an electric charge, a thrill, from an intense cold. She threw off her silk wrap, and her creamy woollen nightgown, and lay for a moment, as she had imagined lying, with her naked skin on the cold white sheet. She did not sink; the crust was icy and solid. All along her body, in her knees, her thighs, her small round belly, her pointed breasts, the soft inner skin of her arms, she felt an intense version of that paradoxical burn she had received from the touch of the frosted window. The snow did not numb Fiammarosa; it pricked and hummed and brought her, intensely, to life. When her front was quite chilled, she turned over on her back, and lay there, safe inside the form of her own faint impression on the untouched surface. She stared up, at the great moon with its slaty shadows on its white-gold disc, and the huge fields of scattered, clustered, far-flung glittering wheeling stars in the deep darkness, white on midnight, and she was, for the first time in her life, happy. This is who I am, the cold princess thought to herself, wriggling for sheer pleasure in the snow-dust, this is what I want. And when she was quite cold, and completely alive and crackling with energy, she rose to her feet, and began a strange, leaping dance, pointing sharp fingers at the moon, tossing her long mane of silver hair, sparkling with ice-crystals, circling and bending and finally turning cartwheels under the wheeling sky. She could feel the cold penetrating her surfaces, all over, insistent and relentless. She even thought that some people might have thought that this was painful. But for her, it was bliss. She went in with the dawn, and lived through the day in an alert, suspended, dreaming state, waiting for the deep dark, and another excursion into the cold.

Night after night, now, she went and danced in the snowfield. The deep frost held and she began to be able to carry some of her cold energy back into her daily work. At the same time, she began to notice changes in her body. She was growing thinner, rapidly—the milky softness induced by her early regime was replaced with a slender, sharp, bony beauty. And one night, as she moved, she found that her whole body was encased in a transparent, crackling skin of ice, that broke into spiderweb-fine veined sheets as she danced, and then reformed. The sensation of this double skin was delicious. She had frozen eyelashes and saw the world through an ice-lens; her tossing hair made a brittle and musical sound, for each hair was coated and frozen. The faint sounds of shivering and splintering and clashing made a kind of whispered music as she danced on. In the daytime now, she could barely keep awake, and her night-time skin persisted patchily in odd places, at the nape of her neck, around her wrists, like bracelets. She tried to sit by the window, in her lessons, and also tried surreptitiously to open it, to let in the cold wind, when Hugh, her tutor, was briefly out of the room. And then, one day, she came down, rubbing frost out of her eyelashes with rustling knuckles, and found the window wide open, Hugh wrapped in a furred jacket, and a great book open on the table.

'Today,' said Hugh, 'we are going to read the history of your ancestor, King Beriman, who made an expedition to the kingdoms beyond the mountains, in the frozen North, and came back with an icewoman.'

Fiammarosa considered Hugh.

'Why?' she said, putting her white head on one side, and looking at him with sharp, pale blue eyes between the stiff lashes.

'I'll show you,' said Hugh, taking her to the open window. 'Look at the snow on the lawns, in the rose-garden.'

And there, lightly imprinted, preserved by the frost, were the tracks of fine bare feet, running lightly, skipping, eddying, dancing.

Fiammarosa did not blush; her whiteness became whiter, the ice-skin thicker. She was alive in the cold air of the window.

'Have you been watching me?'

'Only from the window,' said Hugh, 'to see that you came to no harm. You can see that the only footprints are fine, and elegant, and naked. If I had followed you I should have left tracks.'

'I see,' said Fiammarosa.

'And,' said Hugh, 'I have been watching you since you were a little girl, and I recognise happiness and health when I see it.'

'Tell me about the icewoman.'

'Her name was Fror. She was given by her father, as a pledge for a truce between the ice-people and King Beriman. The chronicles describe her as wondrously fair and slender, and they say also that King Beriman loved her distractedly, and that she did not return his love. They say she showed an ill will, liked to haunt caverns and rivers and refused to learn the language of this kingdom. They say she danced by moonlight, on the longest night, and that there were those in the kingdom who believed she was a witch, who had enchanted the King. She was seen, dancing naked, with three white hares, which were thought to be creatures of witchcraft, under the moon, and was imprisoned in the cells under the palace. There she gave birth to a son, who was taken from her, and given to his father. And the priests wanted to burn the icewoman, "to melt her stubbornness and punish her stiffness," but the King would not allow it.

'Then one day, three northmen came riding to the gate of the castle, tall men with axes on white horses, and said they had come "to take back our woman to her own air." No one knew how they had been summoned: the priests said that it was by witchcraft that she had called to them from her stone cell. It may have been. It seems clear that there was a threat of war if the woman was not relinquished. So she was fetched out, and "wrapped in a cloak to cover her thinness and decay" and told she could ride away with her kinsmen. The chronicler says she did not ask to see her husband or her tiny son, but "cold and unfeeling as she had come" mounted behind one of the northmen and they turned and rode away together.

'And King Beriman died not long after, of a broken heart or of witchcraft, and his brother reigned until Leonin was old enough to be crowned. The chronicler says that Leonin made a "warm-blooded and warm-hearted" ruler, as though the blood of his forefathers ran true in him, and the "frozen lymph" of his maternal stock was melted away to nothing.

'But I believe that after generations, a lost face, a lost being, can find a form again.'

'You think I am an icewoman.'

'I think you carry the inheritance of that northern princess. I think also that her nature was much misunderstood, and that what appeared to be kindness was extreme cruelty—paradoxically, probably her life was preserved by what appeared to be the cruelest act of those who held her here, the imprisonment in cold stone walls, the thin prison dress, the bare diet.'

'I felt that in my bones, listening to your story.'

'It is *your* story, Princess. And you too are framed for cold. You must live—when the thaw comes—in cool places. There are ice-houses in the palace gardens—we must build more, and stock them with blocks of ice, before the snow melts.'

Fiammarosa smiled at Hugh with her sharp mouth. She said:

'You have read my desires. All through my childhood I was barely alive. I felt constantly that I must collapse, vanish, fall into a faint, stifle. Out there, in the cold, I am a living being.'

'I know.'

'You choose your words very tactfully, Hugh. You told me I was "framed for cold." That is a statement of natural philosophy, and time. It may be that I have ice in my veins, like the icewoman, or something that boils and steams at normal temperatures, and flows busily in deep frost. But you did not tell me I had a cold nature. The icewoman did not look back at her husband and son. Perhaps she was cold in her soul, as well as in her veins?'

'That is for you to say. It is so long ago, the tale of the icewoman. Maybe she saw King Beriman only as a captor and conqueror? Maybe she loved someone else, in the North, in the snow? Maybe she felt as you feel, on a summer's day, barely there, yawning for faintness, moving in shadows.'

'How do you know how I feel, Hugh?'

'I watch you. I study you. I love you.'

Fiammarosa noticed, in her cool mind, that she did not love Hugh, whatever love was.

She wondered whether this was a loss, or a gain. She was inclined to think, on balance, that it was a gain. She had been so much loved, as a little child, and all that heaping of anxious love had simply made her feel ill and exhausted. There was more life in coldness. In solitude. Inside a crackling skin of protective ice that was also a sensuous delight.

After this clarification, even when the thaw came, and the snow ran away, and fell in damp, crashing masses from the roof and the branches, Fiammarosa's life was better. Hugh convinced the King and Queen that their daughter needed to be cold to survive, and the ingenuity that had been put into keeping her warm and muffled was diverted, on his suggestion, into the construction of ice-houses, and cool bedrooms with stone walls on the north side of the palace. The new Fiammarosa was full of spiky life. She made little gardens of mountain snow-plants around her ice-retreats, which stood like so many summer-houses in the woods and the gardens. No one accused her of witchcraft—this was a later age—but there was perhaps a little less love for this coldly shining, fiercely energetic, sharp being than there had been for the milky girl in her rosy cushions. She studied snow-crystals and ice formations under a magnifying glass, in the winter, and studied the forms of her wintry flowers and mosses in the summer. She became an artist—all princesses are compelled to be artists, they must spin, or draw, or embroider, and she had always dutifully done so, producing heaps of cushions and walls of good-enough drawings. She hated 'good enough' but had had to be content with it. Now she began to weave tapestries, with silver threads and ice-blue threads, with night violets and cool primroses, which mixed the geometric forms of the snow-crystals with the delicate forms of the moss and rosettes of petals, and produced shimmering, intricate tapestries that were much more than 'good enough,' that were unlike anything seen before in that land. She became an assiduous correspondent, writing to gardeners and natural philosophers, to spinners of threads and weavers all over the world. She was happy, and in the winter, when the world froze again under an iron-grey sky, she was ecstatic.

Princesses, also, are expected to marry. They are expected to marry for dynastic reasons, to cement an alliance, to placate a powerful rival, to bear royal heirs. They are, in the old stories, gifts and rewards, handed over by their loving fathers to heroes and adventurers who must undergo trials, or save people. It would appear, Fiammarosa had thought as a young girl, reading both histories and wonder tales, that princesses are commodities. But also, in the same histories and tales, it can be seen that this is not so. Princesses are captious and clever choosers. They tempt and test their suitors, they sit like spiders inside walls adorned with the skulls of the unsuccessful, they require superhuman feats of strength and cunning from their suitors, and are not above helping out, or weeping over, those who appeal to their hearts. They follow their chosen lovers through rough deserts, and ocean tempests, they ride on the wings of the north wind and enlist the help of ants and eagles, trout and mice, hares and ducks, to rescue these suddenly helpless husbands from the clutches of scheming witches, or ogre-kings. They do have, in real life, the power to reject and some power to choose. They are wooed. She had considered her own cold heart in this context and had thought that she would do better, ideally, to remain unmarried. She was too happy alone to make a good bride. She could not think out a course of action entirely but had vaguely decided upon a course of prevarication and intimidation, if suitors presented themselves. For their own sakes, as much as for her own. She was sorry, in the abstract—she thought a great deal in the abstract, it suited her—for anyone who should love her, or think it a good idea to love her. She did not believe she was truly lovable. Besides her parents, and her brothers, whose love was automatic and unseeing, the only person who truly loved her was Hugh. And her cold eye, and her cold mind, had measured the gulf between what Hugh felt for her and what she felt for him. She tried never to let it show; she was grateful, his company was comfortable to her. But both he and she were intelligent beings, and both knew how things stood.

The King had his own ideas, which he believed were wise and subtle, about all this. He believed his daughter needed to marry more than most women. He believed she needed to be softened and opened to the world, that she had inherited from the unsatisfactory icewoman a dangerous, brittle edge which would hurt her more than anyone else. He believed it would be good for his daughter to be melted smooth, though he did not, in his thinking, push this metaphor too far. He had a mental image of an icicle running with water, not of an absent icicle and a warm, formless pool. He thought the sensible thing would be to marry this cold creature to a prince from the icelands from which the original Fror had been snatched by King Beriman, and he sent letters to Prince Boris, beyond the mountains, with a sample of his daughter's weaving, and a painting of her white beauty, her fine bones, blue eyes and cool gold hair. He was a great believer in protocol, and protocol had always, at these times, meant that the picture and the invitation must go to many princes, and not only one. There must be a feast, and something of a competition. What happened customarily was that the Princess's portrait would go simultaneously (allowing for the vagaries of horses and camels, galleons and mule trains) to many eligible princes. The princes, in turn, on receiving the portrait, would return gifts, sumptuous gifts, striking gifts, to the king, to be given to the Princess. And if she found them acceptable (or if her father did), then the princes would make the journey in person, and the Princess, in person, would make her choice. In this way, the King offended none of his proud neighbours, leaving the choice to the whim, or the aesthetic inclination, of the young woman herself. Of course, if there were any pressing reason why one alliance was more desirable than another, most fathers would enlighten their daughters, and some would exhort or threaten. In the case of Fiammarosa none of this applied. Her father wished her to marry for her own good, and he wished her to marry Prince Boris simply because his kingdom was cold and full of icebergs and glaciers, where she would be at home. But he did not say this, for he knew that women are perverse.

The portraits, the letters, dispersed through the known world. After a time, the presents began to return. A small golden envoy from the East brought a silken robe, flame-coloured, embroidered with peacocks, light as air. A rope of pearls, black, rose, and luminous pale ones, the size of larks' eggs, came from an island kingdom, and a three-dimensional carved chess game, all in different jades, with little staircases and turrets edged with gold, came from a tiny country between two deserts. There were heaps of gold and silver plates, a leopard in a cage, which sickened and died, a harp, a miniature pony, and an illuminated treatise on necromancy. The King and Queen watched Fiammarosa as she gravely thanked the messengers. She appeared to be interested in the mechanism of an Orcalian musical box, but only *scientifically* interested, so to speak. Then Prince Boris's envoy arrived, a tall fair man with a gold beard and two gold plaits, riding a hairy, flea-bitten warhorse, and followed by packhorses with great pine chests. He opened these with a flourish, and brought out a robe of silver fox-fur, an extraordinary bonnet, hung with the black-tipped tails of ermine stoats, and a whalebone box, polished like a new tooth, containing a necklace of bears' claws threaded on a silver chain. The Princess put her thin hands, involuntarily, to her slender throat. The envoy said that the necklace had been worn by Prince Boris's mother, and by her mother before her. He was clad in fleeces and wore a huge circular fur hat coming down over his ears. Fiammarosa said that the gifts were magnificent. She said this so gracefully that her mother looked to see if some ancestral inkling in her responded to bears' claws. There was no colour at all in her lips, or in her cheeks, but with her that could be a sign of pleasure— she whitened, where other women blushed. The King thought to himself that a man and his gifts were not the same thing. He thought that the narrow neck would have a barbaric beauty, circled by the polished sharp claws, but he did not wish to see it.

The last envoy declared that he was not the last envoy, having been parted from his fellows on their dangerous voyage. They had travelled separately, so that one at least of them might arrive with his gift. Prince Sasan, he said, had been much moved by the Princess's portrait. She was the woman he had seen in his dreams, said the envoy, lyrically. The Princess, whose dreams entertained no visitors, only white spaces, wheeling birds and snowflakes, smiled composedly, without warmth. The envoy's gift took a long time to unwrap. It was packed in straw, and fine leather, and silk. When it was revealed, it appeared at first sight to be a rough block of ice. Then, slowly, it was seen to be a glass palace, within the ice, so to speak, as hallucinatory turrets and chambers, fantastic carvings and pillars, revealed themselves in the ice and snow of mountain peaks. But once the eye had learned to read the irregularities of the surface, the magnifications and the tunnels within the block, it was seen to be a most cunningly wrought and regularly shaped transparent castle, within whose shining walls corridors ran into fretted chambers, staircases (with carved balustrades) mounted and descended in spirals and curves, in which thrones and pompous curtained beds stood in glistening cubicles, in which miraculous fine curtains of translucent glass floated between archways in still space. The glass castle was large enough for the centre to be hidden from the eye, though all the wide landings, the narrow passages, the doors and gangways, directed the eye to where the thickness of the transparent glass itself resisted penetration. Fiammarosa touched its cool surface with a cool finger. She was entranced by the skill of the layering. It was all done in a crystal-clear glass, with a green-blue tinge to it in places, and a different green-blue conferred simply by thickness itself. The eye looked through, and through, and in. Light went through, and through, and in. Solid walls of light glittered and, seen through their substance, trapped light hung in bright rooms like bubbles. There was one other colour, in all the perspectives of blue, green, and clear. From the dense, invisible centre little tongues of rosy flame (made of glass) ran along the corridors, mounted, gleaming, in the stairwells and hallways, threaded like ribbons round galleries, separated, and joined again as flames do, round pillars and gates. Behind a curtain of blue, a thread of rose and flame shone and twisted. The Princess walked round, and back, looking in. 'It is an image of my master's heart,' said the lyrical envoy. 'It is a poetic image of his empty life, which awaits the delicate warmth of the Princess Fiammarosa in every chamber. He has been set on fire by his vision of the portrait of the Princess.'

The envoy was a sallow young man, with liquid brown eyes. The bluff King and the careful Queen were not impressed by his rhetoric. The Princess went on walking round the glass block, staring in. It was not clear that she had heard his latest remarks.

The second envoy from Prince Sasan arrived a few days later, dusty and travel-worn, another sallow man with brown eyes. His gift was dome-shaped. He too, as he unwrapped it, spoke lyrically of the contents. He did not appear to be speaking to a script; lyricism appeared to spring naturally to the lips of the Sasanians. His gift, he said, was an image, a metaphor, a symbol, for the sweetness and light, the summer world which the thought of the Princess had created in the mind of his master.

The second gift was also made of glass. It was a beehive, a transparent, shining form constructed of layers of hexagonal cells, full of white glass grubs, and amber-coloured glass honey. Over the surface of the cells crawled, and in the solid atmosphere hung and floated, wonderfully wrought insects, with furry bodies, veined wings, huge eyes, and fine antennae. They even carried bags of golden pollen on their black, thread-glass legs. Around the hive were glass flowers with petals of crumpled and gleaming yellow glass, with crowns of fine stamens, with blue bells and fine-throated purple hoods. A fat bee was half-buried in the heart of a spotted snapdragon. Another uncoiled a proboscis and sipped the heart of a campanula. So, said the lyrical envoy, was the heart of his master touched by the warm thought of the Princess, so was love seeded, and sweetness garnered, in the garden of his heart. Hugh thought that this might be too much for his austere pupil, but she was not listening. She had laid her cool cheek against the cool glass dome, as if to catch the soundless hum of the immobile spun-glass wings.

The third envoy arrived bloodied and incoherent. He had been set upon by bandits and had been forced to hide his package in a hollow tree, from which he had retrieved it, late at night. He unpacked it before the court, murmuring incoherently, 'So delicate, I shall be tortured, never forgiven, has harm come to it?' His package was in two parts, tall and cylindrical, fat and spherical. Out of the cylindrical part came a tall glass stem, and a series of fine, fine, glass rods, olive-green, amber, white, which he built, breathing heavily, into an extraordinarily complex web of branches and twigs. It was large—the height, maybe, of a two-year-old child. Folded into his inner garments he had a plan of the intervals of the sprouting of the branches. The assembly took a long time—the Queen suggested that they go and take refreshment and leave the poor, anxious man to complete his labour unobserved and in peace, but Fiammarosa was entranced. She watched each slender stem find its place, breathing quietly, staring intently. The spherical parcel proved to contain a pleroma of small spherical parcels, all nestling together, from which the envoy took a whole world of flowers, fruit, twining creepers, little birds, frost-forms and ice-forms. Part of the tree he hung with buds, tight and bursting, mossy and glistening, rosy and sooty-black. Then he hung blossoms of every kind, apple and cherry, magnolia and catkins, hypericum and chestnut candles. Then he added, radiating between all these, the fruits, oranges and lemons, silver pears and golden apples, rich plums and damsons, ruddy pomegranates and clustered translucent crimson berries and grapes with the bloom on them. Each tiny element was in itself an example of virtuoso glass-making. When he had hung the flowers and the fruit, he perched the birds, a red cardinal, a white dove, a black-capped rosy-breasted bull-finch, a blue Australian wren, an iridescent king-fisher, a blackbird with a gold beak, and in the centre, on the crest of the branches, a bird of paradise with golden eyes in its midnight tail, and a crest of flame. Then he hung winter on the remaining branches, decorating sharp black twigs with filigree leaf skeletons, flounces of snow, and sharp icicles, catching the light and making rainbows in the air. This, he said breathlessly, was his master's world as it would be if the Princess consented to be his wife, a paradise state with all seasons in one, and the tree of life flowering and fruiting perpetually. There is bleak winter, too, said the Princess, setting an icicle in motion. The envoy looked soulfully at her and said that the essential sap of trees lived through the frost, and so it was with the tree of life, of which this was only an image.

The Princess did not leave the tree for the rest of the day. Look, she said to Hugh, at the rich patterning of the colours, look at the way the light shines in the globes of the fruit, the seeds of the pomegranate, the petals of the flowers. Look at the beetles in the clefts of the trunk, like tiny jewels, look at the feathers in the spun-glass tail of the bird. What kind of a man would have made this?

'Not a prince, a craftsman,' said Hugh, a little jealous. 'A prince, merely finds the best man, and pays him. A prince, at most, makes the metaphor, and the craftsman carries it out.'

'I make my own weaving,' said the Princess. 'I design and I weave my own work. It is possible that a prince made the castle, the hive and the tree.'

'It is possible,' said Hugh. 'A prince with a taste for extravagant metaphor.'

'Would you prefer a necklace of bears' claws,' asked the icewoman, 'if you were a woman? Would you?'

'A man and his gifts are two things,' said Hugh. 'And glass is not ice.'

'What do you mean?' asked the Princess. But Hugh would say no more.

The princes arrived, after a month or two, in person. Five had made the journey, Prince Boris, the plump dusky prince who had sent the pearls, the precise, silk-robed prince who had sent the silk robe, the curly, booted and spurred prince who had sent the chess game, and Prince Sasan, who arrived last, having travelled furthest. Prince Boris, the King thought, was a fine figure of a man, strong like an oak-tree, with golden plaits and a golden beard. His pale-blue eyes were icy pools, but there were wrinkles of laughter in their corners. Prince Sasan rode up on a fine-boned, delicate horse, black as soot, and trembling with nerves. He insisted on seeing to its stabling himself, though he was accompanied by a mea-gre retinue of squires with the same sallow skins and huge brown eyes as the envoys. His own hair was black, like his horse, and hung, fine and dry and very straight, in a dark fringe, and a dark curtain, ending at his shoulders. He was a small man, a little shorter than Fiammarosa, but his shoulders were powerful. His face was narrow and his skin dark gold. His nose was sharp and arched, his brows black lines, his lashes long and dark over dark eyes, deeper-set than the envoys'. Prince Boris had a healthy laugh, but Prince Sasan was cat-like and silent. He made his bows, and spoke his greetings, and then appeared content to watch events as though he was the audience, not the actor. He took Fiam-marosa's hand in his thin hand, when he met her, and lifted it to his lips, which were thin and dry. 'Enchanted,' said Prince Sasan. 'Delighted,' said the ice-woman, coolly. That was all.

The visits were the occasion of much diplomacy and various energetic rides and hunting expeditions, on which, since it was high summer, the Princess did not join the company. In the evenings, there were feasts, and musical entertain-ments. The island prince had brought two porcelain-skinned ladies who played exquisite tinkling tunes on xylophones. The curly prince had a minstrel with a harp, and Prince Boris had two huntsmen who played a rousing, and bloodcurdling, duet on hunting-horns. The Princess was sitting between Boris and the curly prince, and had been hearing tales of the long winters, the Northern Lights, the floating icebergs. Prince Sasan beckoned his squire, who unwrapped a long black pipe, with a reed mouthpiece, from a scarlet silk cloth. This he handed to the Prince, who set it to his own lips, and blew one or two tentative notes, reedy, plangent, to set the pitch. 'I based this music,' he said, looking down at the table, 'on the songs of the goat-herds.' He began to play. It was music unlike anything they had ever heard. Long, long, wavering breaths, with pure notes chasing each other through them; long calls which rose and rose, trembled and danced on the air, fell, whispered, and vanished. Circlings of answering phrases, flights, bird-cries, rest. The Princess's mind was full of water frozen in mid-fall, or finding a narrow channel between ribs and arches of ice. When the strange piping came to an end, everyone complimented the Prince on his playing.

Hugh said, 'I have never heard such long phrases ride on one breath.'
'I have good lungs,' said Prince Sasan. 'Glass-blower's lungs.'
'The glass is your own work?' said the Princess.
'Of course it is,' said Prince Sasan.
The Princess said that it was very beautiful. Prince Sasan said:
'My country is not rich, though it is full of space, and I think it is beautiful. I cannot give you precious stones. My country is largely desert: we have an abundance only of sand, and glass-blowing is one of our ancient crafts. All Sasanian princes are glass-blowers. The secrets are handed on from generation to generation.'
'I did not know glass was made from sand,' said the Princess. 'It resembles frozen water.'
'It is sand, melted and fused,' said Prince Sasan. His eyes were cast down.
'In a furnace of flames,' said Hugh, impulsively. 'It is melted and fused in a furnace of flames.'
The Princess trembled slightly. Prince Sasan lifted his gaze, and his black look met her blue one. There were candles between them, and she saw golden flames reflected in his dark eyes, whilst he saw white flames in her clear ones. She knew she should look away, and did not. Prince Sasan said:
'I have come to ask you to be my wife, and to come with me to my land of sand-dunes and green sea-waves and shores. Now I have seen you, I—'
He did not finish the sentence.
Prince Boris said that deserts were monotonous and hot. He said he was sure the Princess would prefer mountains and forests and rushing cold winds.
The Princess trembled a little more. Prince Sasan made a deprecating gesture with his thin hand, and stared into his plate, which contained sliced peaches, in red wine, on a nest of crushed ice.
'I will come with you to the desert,' said the Princess. 'I will come with you to the desert, and learn about glass-blowing.'
'I am glad of that,' said Prince Sasan. 'For I do not know how I should have gone on, if you had not.'
And amidst the mild uproar caused by the departure from protocol, and the very real panic and fear of the King and Queen and Hugh, the two of them sat and looked steadily across the table at the reflected flames in each other's eyes.

Once it became clear that the Princess's mind was made up, those who loved her stopped arguing, and the wedding took place. Fiammarosa asked Hugh to come to with her to her new home, and he answered that he could not. He could not live in a hot climate, he told her, with his very first note of sharpness. Fiammarosa was glittering, restless and brittle with love. Hugh saw that she could not see him, that she saw only the absent Sasan, that dark, secret face imposed on his own open one. And he did not know, he added, having set his course, how she herself would survive. Love changes people, Fiammarosa told him in a small voice. Human beings are adaptable, said the icewoman. If I use my intelligence, and my willpower, she said, I shall be able to live there; I shall certainly die if I cannot be with the man on whom my heart is set. He will melt you into a puddle, Hugh told her, but only silently, and in his mind. She had never been so beautiful as she was in her wedding gown, white as snow, with lace like frost-crystals, with a sash blue as thick ice, and her pale face sharp with happiness and desire in the folds of transparent veiling.

The young pair spent the first week of their marriage in her old home, before setting out on the long journey to her new one. All eyes were on them, each day, as they came down from their bed-chamber to join the company. The housemaids whispered of happily bloodstained sheets—much rumpled, they added, most vigorously disturbed. The Queen observed to the King that the lovers had eyes only for each other, and he observed, a little sorrowfully, that this was indeed so. His daughter's sharp face grew sharper, and her eyes grew bluer and clearer; she could be seen to sense the presence of the dark Sasan behind her head, across a room, through a door. He moved quietly, like a cat, the southern prince, speaking little, and touching no one, except his wife. He could hardly prevent himself from touching her body, all over, in front of everyone, Hugh commented to himself, watching the flicker of the fine fingers down her back as the Prince bent to bestow an unnecessary kiss of greeting after a half-hour absence. Hugh noticed also that there were faint rosy marks on the Princess's skin, as though it had been scored, or lashed. Flushed lines in the hollow of her neck, inside her forearm where the sleeve fell away. He wanted to ask if she was hurt, and once opened his mouth to do so, and closed it again when he saw that she was not listening to him, that she was staring over his shoulder at a door where a moment later Sasan himself was to appear. If she was hurt, Hugh knew, because he knew her, she was also happy.

Fiammarosa's honeymoon nights were indeed a fantastic mixture of pleasure and pain. She and her husband, in a social way, were intensely shy with each other. They said little, and what they said was of the most conventional kind: Fiammarosa at least heard her own clear voice, from miles away, like that of a polite stranger sharing the room in which their two silent selves simmered with passion. And Sasan, whose dark eyes never left hers when they were silent, looked down at the sheets or out of the window when he spoke, and she knew in her heart that his unfinished, whispered sentences sounded as odd to him as her silver platitudes did to her. But when he touched her, his warm, dry fingers spoke to her skin, and when she touched his nakedness she was laughing and crying at once with delight over his golden warmth, his secret softness, the hard, fine arch of his bones. An icewoman's sensations are different from those of other women, but Fiammarosa could not know how different, for she had no standards of comparison; she could not name the agonising bliss that took possession of her. Ice burns, and it is hard to the warm-skinned to distinguish one sensation, fire, from the other, frost. Touching Sasan's heat was like and unlike the thrill of ice. Ordinary women melt, or believe themselves to be melting, to be running away like avalanches or rivers at the height of passion, and this, too, Fiammarosa experienced with a difference, as though her whole being was becoming liquid except for some central icicle, which was running with waterdrops that threatened to melt that too, to nothing. And at the height of her bliss she desired to take the last step, to nothing, to nowhere, and the next moment cried out in fear of annihilation. The fine brown fingers prised open the pale-blue eyelids. 'Are you there?' asked the soft whisper. 'Where are you?' and she sighed, and returned.

When the morning light came into the room it found them curled together in a nest of red and white sheets. It revealed also marks, all over the pale cool skin: handprints round the narrow waist, sliding impressions from delicate strokes, like weals, raised rosy discs where his lips had rested lightly. He cried out, when he saw her, that he had hurt her. No, she said, she was part icewoman, it was her nature, she had an icewoman's skin that responded to every touch by blossoming red. Sasan still stared, and repeated, I have hurt you. No, no, said Fiammarosa, they are the marks of pleasure, pure pleasure. I shall cover them up, for only we ourselves should see our happiness.

But inside her a little melted pool of water slopped and swayed where she had been solid and shining.

The journey to the new country was long and arduous. Fiammarosa wrapped herself in a white hooded cloak, to reflect the sunlight away from her, and wore less and less inside it, as they rode south, through dark forests, and out onto grassy plains. They embarked, in a port where neither of them spoke the language, in the Sasanian boat that had been waiting for them, and sailed for weeks across the sea, in breezy weather, in a sudden storm, through two days and nights of glassy calm. Sasan enjoyed the voyage. He had a bucket with a glass bottom which he would let down into the green water to watch the creatures that floated and swam in the depth. He wore no more than a wrap round his narrow hips, and during the calm, he went overboard and swam around and under the boat, calling out to Fiammarosa, who sat swathed in white, wilting a little, on the deck, and answered breathlessly. He would bring glasses and buckets of the sea water on deck, and study the bubbles and ripples. He liked also to look at the sleek sea-surface in the moonlight, the gloss on the little swellings and subsidings, the tracks of phosphorescence. Fiammarosa was happier in the moonlight. It was cooler. She sat in a thin gown in the night air and smiled as her husband displayed his drawings and discoveries of translucency and reflection. He played his strange flute, and she listened, rapt. They sailed on. Every day was a little warmer. Every day the air was a little thicker, a little hotter.

When they came to the major port of Sasania, which was also its capital city, they were welcomed into the harbour by a flotilla of small boats bearing drummers and flautists, singers and cymbal-clashers. Fiammarosa nearly fell, when her foot touched land; the stone of the harbour-steps was burning to the touch, and the sun was huge and glaring in a cobalt-blue sky with no clouds and no movement of air. She made a joke about the earth moving, after the movement of the waves, but the thought she had was that her temperate summers, with their bright flowers and birdsong, had no connection to this hot blue arch in which a few kites wheeled, slowly. The people had prepared a curtained litter for their delicate new queen, and so she was able to subside, panting, onto cushions, wondering if she would survive.

The palace was white and glistening, as though it was moulded from sugar. It had domes and towers, plain and blind and geometrically simple and beautiful. It was designed to keep out the sun, and inside it was a geometric maze of cool corridors, tiled in coloured glass, lit only by narrow slits of windows, which were glazed in beautiful colours, garnet, emerald, sapphire, which cast bright flames of coloured light on the floors. It was a little like a beehive, and inside its central dome a woven lattice-work of coloured light was spun by tiny loopholes and slits in the surface, shifting and changing as the sun moved in the dark bright sky outside. Optimism returned to Fiammarosa when she saw these dark corridors, these dim spaces. Icewomen like bright light, bright cold light, off-white; and darkness and confinement oppress them. But the molten heat outside oppressed her more. And there was so much in the palace to delight her senses. There was fruit on glass dishes, pearly and iridescent, smoky amber, translucent rose and indigo. There were meditative flute-players dropping strings of sound all day into the still air from little stools under the loopholes on the turns of the stairs. There were wonderful white jugs of latticino work, with frivolous frilled lips, containing pomegranate juices or lemonade, or swaying dark wine. Her own apartment had a circular window of stained glass, a white rose, fold on fold, on a peacock-blue ground. Within the heavy doors hung curtains of tiny glass beads of every conceivable colour, shimmering and twinkling. Round the walls were candleholders, all different, a bronze glass chimney, an amethyst dish full of floating squat candles, a candelabra dripping with glass icicles. And her loom was there, ready for her, and a basket of wools in all the subtle shades she loved.

In the long days that followed, Fiammarosa found that her husband worked hard, and was no sedentary or sportive prince. Sasania was, he told her, a poor country. The people lived on fish which they caught in the sea, and vegetables irrigated in little plots from the river whose mouth had formed the harbour of the city. Beyond the city, and a few other towns on the coastal strip, Sasan told her, there was nothing but desert—he described dunes and oases, sandstorms and dancing mirages with the passion of a lover describing the woman he loved. Ah, the space of the bare sand, under the sun, under the stars, said Sasan. The taste of dates, of water from deep cool wells. The brilliance of the shimmering unreal cities in the distance, which had given him many ideas for cityscapes and fantastic palaces of glass. Fiammarosa stretched her imagination to conceive what he was describing, and could not. She connected the distant shimmering to her imaginations of lost glaciers and untrodden snowfields. Sasan explained, enthusiastically (they were talking more easily now, though still like two tentative children, not the man and woman whose bodies tangled and fought at night)—Sasan explained the connection of the desert with the glass, which Sasania despatched in trading ships and caravans to the corners of the known world. Glass, Sasan said, was made of the things which they had in abundance—the sand of the desert, three parts, lime, and soda which they made from the wracks, or seaweeds, which clung to the rocks round their coasts. The most difficult, the most precious part, he said, was the wood, which was needed both for the furnaces and for potash. The coastal woods of the country all belonged to the King, and were cared for by rangers. Glass, according to legend, had been found by the first Prince Sasan, who had been no more than an itinerant merchant with a camel train, and had found some lumps and slivers of shining stuff in the cinders of his fire on the seashore. And yet another Sasan had discovered how to blow the molten glass into transparent bottles and bowls, and yet another had discovered how to fuse different colours onto each other. In our country, Sasan said to his wife, princes are glassmakers and glassmakers are princes, and the line of artists runs true in the line of kings.

Every day he brought back from his dark workroom gifts for his bride. He brought crystal balls full of the fused scraps of coloured canes left over from his day's lamp-work. Once, Fiammarosa ventured to the mouth of the cavern where he worked, and peered in. Men stripped to their waists and pouring sweat were feeding the great furnaces, or bending over hot lamps, working on tiny scraps of molten glass with magnifying glasses and sharp tweezers. Others were turning the sullen, cooling red glass with large metal pincers on clattering wheels, and one had a long tube raised to his mouth like a trumpet of doom, blowing his breath into the flaming, molten gob at the end of it which flared and smoked, orange and scarlet, and swelled and swelled. Its hot liquid bursting put the pale princess in mind of the ferocity of her love-making and she opened her mouth, in pleasure and pain, to take in such a blast of hot, sparking wind, that she fell back, and could barely stagger to her room. After that, she spent the long hot days lying on her bed, breathing slowly. Sasan came in the cool of the evening; she took pleasure, then, in food, candle-flames, transparency and shadows. Then they made love. She put it to herself that she was delighting in extremity; that she was living a life pared down to extreme sensations. Dying is an ancient metaphor for the bliss of love, and Fiammarosa died a little, daily. But she was also dying in cold fact. Or in warm fact, to be more precise. She thought she was learning to live for love and beauty, through the power of the will. She was to find that in the end these things are subject to the weather—the weather in the world, and the tourbillons and sluggish meanders of the blood and lymph under the skin.

There was another, growing reason for the sickness against which she threw all her forces. When she understood this, she had a moment of despair and wrote to Hugh, begging him to reconsider his decision. I am not well, she wrote, and the days, as you knew they would be, are long and hot, and I am driven by necessity to languish in inactivity in the dark. I believe I am with child, dear Hugh, and am afraid, in this strange place amongst these strange people, however kind and loving they are. I need your cool head, your wisdom; I need our conversations about history and science. I am *not unhappy*, but I am not well, and I need your counsel, your familiar voice, your good sense. You foresaw that it would be hard—the heat, I mean, the merciless sun, and the confinement which is my only alternative. Could you, best of friends, at least come on a visit?

She despatched this letter, along with her regular letter to her parents, and almost at once regretted it, at least partly. It was a sign of weakness, an appeal for help she should not need. It was as though, by writing down her moment of weakness and discontent, she had made it into a thing, unavoidable. She felt herself becoming weaker and fought against a more and more powerful demon of discontent. Sasan was making her a series of delicate latticino vases. The first was pencil-slender, and took one rose. It was white. The next was cloudy, tinged with pink, and curved slightly outwards. The third was pinker and rounder, the fourth blushed rosy and had a fine blown bowl beneath its narrow neck. When the series of nine was completed, cherry-pink, rose-red, clear-red, deep crimson and almost black with a fiery heart, he arranged them on the table in front of her, and she saw that they were women, each more proudly swollen, with delicate white arms. She smiled, and kissed him, and ignored the fiery choking in her throat.

The next day a letter came from Hugh. It had crossed with her own—she could by no means yet expect an answer. It began with the hope that she would, far away as she was, share his joy, at least in spirit. He had married Hortense, the chamberlain's daughter, and was living in a state of comfort and contentment he had never imagined or hoped for.

There followed, in a riddling form, the only love-letter Fiammarosa had ever had from Hugh. I cannot, he said, hope to live at the extremes of experience, as you can. No one who has ever seen you dance on the untrodden snow, or gather ice-flowers from bare branches, will ever be entirely able to forget this perfect beauty and live with what is pleasant and daily. I see now, said Hugh, that extreme desires extreme, and that beings of pure fire and pure ice may know delights we ordinary mortals must glimpse and forgo. I cannot live in any of your worlds, Princess, and I am happy in my new house, with my pretty woman, who loves me, and my good chair and sprouting garden. But I shall never be *quite* contented, Princess, because I saw you dance in the snow, and the sight took away the possibility of my settling into this life. Be happy in your way, at the furthest edge, and remember, when you can, Hugh, who would be quite happy in his—if he had never seen you.

Fiammarosa wept over this letter. She thought he would not have written so, if it was not meant to be his last letter. She thought, her own letter would cause him pain, and possibly cause him to despise her, that she could so easily and peremptorily summon him, when things were hard. And then she began to weep, because he was not there, and would not come, and she was alone and sick in a strange land, where even the cool air in the dark corridors was warm enough to melt her a little, like a caress given to a snow figure. When she had wept some time, she stood up, and began to walk somewhat drunkenly through the long halls and out across a courtyard full of bright, dazzling air in which the heat currents could be seen to boil up and weave their sinuous way down, and up again, like dry fountains. She went slowly and bravely, straight across, not seeking the shadow of the walls, and went into the huge, echoing, cave-like place where Sasan and his men were at work. Dimly, dazzled, she saw the half-naked men, the spinning cocoons, like blazing tulips, on the end of the pontils, the iron tweezers. Sasan was sitting at a bench, his dark face illuminated by the red-hot glow from a still-molten sphere of glass he was smoothing and turning. Beside him, another sphere was turning brown, like a dying leaf. One hand to her belly, Fiammarosa advanced into the heat and darkness. As she reached Sasan, one of the men, his arms and shoulders running with sweat, his brow dripping, swung open the door of the furnace. Fiammarosa had time to see shelves of forms, red and gold, transparent and burning, before the great sun-like rose of heat and light hit her, and she saw darkness and felt dreadful pain. She was melting, she thought in confusion, as she fell, slowly, slowly, bending and crumpling in the blast, becoming hot and liquid, a white scrap, moaning in a sea of red blood, lit by flames. Sasan was at her side in an instant, his sweat and tears dripping onto the white, cold little face. Before she lost consciousness Fiammarosa heard his small voice, in her head. 'There will be another child, one who would never otherwise have lived; you must think of *that* child.' And then, all was black. There was even an illusion of cold, of shivering.

After the loss of the child, Fiammarosa was ill for a long time. Women covered her brow with cloths soaked in ice-water, changing them assiduously. She lay in the cool and the dark, drifting in and out of a minimal life. Sasan was there, often, sitting silently by her bed. Once, she saw him packing the nine glasses he had made for her in wood-shavings. With care, she recovered, at least enough to become much as she had been in her early days as a girl in her own country, milky, limp and listless. She rose very late, and sat in her chamber, sipping juice, and making no move to weave, or to read, or to write. After some months, she began to think she had lost her husband's love. He did not come to her bedroom, ever again, after the bloody happening in the furnace-room. He did not speak of this, or explain it, and she could not. She felt she had become a milk-jelly, a blancmange, a form of a woman, tasteless and unappetising. Because of her metabolism, grief made her fleshier and slower. She wept over the plump rolls of creamy fat around her eyelids, over the bland expanse of her cheeks. Sasan went away on long journeys, and did not say where he was going, or when he would return. She could not write to Hugh, and could not confide in her dark, beautiful attendants. She turned her white face to the dark blue wall, wrapped her soft arms round her body, and wished to die.

Sasan returned suddenly from one of his journeys. It was autumn, or would have been, if there had been any other season than immutable high summer in that land. He came to his wife, and told her to make ready for a journey. They were going to make a journey together, to the interior of his country, he told her, across the desert. Fiammarosa stirred a little in her lethargy.

'I am an icewoman, Sasan,' she said, flatly. 'I cannot survive a journey in the desert.'

'We will travel by night,' he replied. 'We will make shelters for you, in the heat of the day. You will be pleasantly surprised, I trust. Deserts are cold at night. I think you may find it tolerable.'

So they set out, one evening, from the gate of the walled city, as the first star rose in the velvet blue sky. They travelled in a long train of camels and horses.

Fiammarosa set out in a litter, slung between mules. As the night deepened, and the fields and the sparse woodlands were left behind, she snuffed a rush of cool air, very pure, coming in from stone and sand, where there was no life, no humidity, no decay. Something lost stirred in her. Sasan rode past, and looked in on her. He told her that they were coming to the dunes, and beyond the first dunes was the true desert. Fiammarosa said she felt well enough to ride beside him, if she might. But he said, not yet, and rode away, in a cloud of dust, white in the moonlight.

And so began a long journey, a journey that took weeks, always by night, under a moon that grew from a pared crescent to a huge silver globe as they travelled. The days were terrible, although Fiammarosa was sheltered by ingenious tents, fanned by servants, cooled with precious water. The nights were clear, empty, and cold. After the first days, Sasan would come for her at dusk, and help her onto a horse, riding beside her, wrapped in a great camel-hair cloak. Fiammarosa shed her layers of protective veiling and rode in a pair of wide white trousers and a flowing shift, feeling the delicious cold run over her skin, bringing it to life, bringing power. She did not ask where they were going. She did not even wonder why he still did not come to her bed, for the heat of the day made everything, beyond mere survival, impossible. But he spoke to her of the hot desert, of how it was his place. These are the things I am made of, he said, grains of burning sand, and breath of air, and the blaze of light. Like glass. Only here do we see with such clarity. Fiammarosa stared out, sometimes, at the sand as it shimmered in the molten sunlight, and at her husband standing there in the pure heat and emptiness, bathing himself in it. Sometimes, when she looked, there were mirages. Sand and stones appeared to be great lagoons of clear water, great rivers of ice with ice-floes, great forests of conifers. They could have lived together happily, she reflected, by day and night, in these vanishing frozen palaces shining in the hot desert, which became more and more liquid and vanished in strips. But the mirages came and went, and Sasan stood, staring intently at hot emptiness, and Fiammarosa breathed the night air in the cooling sand and plains.

Sometimes, on the horizon, through the rippling glassy air, Fiammarosa saw a mirage which resembled a series of mountain peaks, crowned with white streaks of snow, or feathers of cloud. As they progressed, this vision became more and more steady, less and less shimmering and dissolving. She understood that the mountains were solid, and that their caravan was moving towards them. Those, said Sasan, when she asked, are the Mountains of the Moon. My country has a flat coast, a vast space of desert, and a mountain range which forms the limit of the kingdom. They are barren, inhospitable mountains; not much lives up there; a few eagles, a few rabbits, a kind of ptarmigan. In the past, we were forbidden to go there. It was thought the mountains were the homes of demons. But I have travelled there, many times. He did not say why he was taking Fiammarosa there, and she did not ask.

They came to the foothills, which were all loose scree, and stunted thorn trees. There was a winding narrow path, almost cut into the hills, and they climbed up, and up, partly by day now, for the beasts of burden needed to see their way. Fiammarosa stared upwards with parted lips at the snow on the distant peaks beyond them, as her flesh clung to her damp clothes in the heat. And then suddenly, round a rock, came the entrance to a wide tunnel in the mountainside. They lit torches and lanterns, and went in. Behind them the daylight diminished to a great O and then to a pinprick. It was cooler inside the stone, but not comfortable, for it was airless, and the sense of the weight of the stone above was oppressive. They were travelling inwards and upwards, inwards and upwards, trudging steadily, breathing quietly. And they came, in time, to a great timbered door, on massive hinges. And Sasan put his mouth to a hole beside the keyhole, and blew softly, and everyone could hear a clear musical note, echoed and echoed again, tossed from bell to bell of some unseen carillon. Then the door swung open, lightly and easily, and they went into a place like nowhere Fiammarosa had ever seen.

It was a palace built of glass in the heart of the mountain. They were in a forest of tall glass tubes with branching arms, arranged in colonnades, thickets, circular balustrades. There was a delicate sound in the air, of glass bells, tubular bells, distant waterfalls, or so it seemed. All the glass pillars were hollow, and were filled with columns of liquid—wine-coloured, sapphire, amber, emerald and quicksilver. If you touched the finer ones, the liquid shot up, and then steadied. Other columns held floating glass bubbles, in water, rising and falling, each with a golden numbered weight hanging from its balloon. In the dark antechambers, fantastic candles flowered in glass buds, or shimmered behind shades of figured glass set on ledges and crevices. As they moved onwards through the glass stems, all infinitesimally in motion, they came to a very high chamber miraculously lit by daylight through clear glass in a high funnelled window, far, far above their heads. Here, too, the strange pipes rose upwards, some of them formed like rose bushes, some like carved pillars, some fantastically twined with glass grapes on glass vines. And in this room, there were real waterfalls, sheets of cold water dropping over great slabs of glass, like ice-floes, into glassy pools where it ran away into hidden channels, water falling in sheer fine spray from the rock itself into a huge glass basin, midnight-blue and full of dancing cobalt lights, with a rainbow fountain rising to meet the dancing, descending mare's-tail. All the miracles of invention that glittered and glimmered and trembled could not be taken in at one glance. But Fiammarosa took in one thing. The air was cold.

By water, by stone, by ice from the mountain top, the air had been chilled to a temperature in which her icewoman's blood stirred to life and her eyes shone.

Sasan showed her further miracles. He showed her her bedchamber, cut into the rock, with its own high porthole window, shaped like a many-coloured rose and with real snow resting on it, far above, so that the light was grainy. Her bed was surrounded by curtains of spun glass, with white birds, snow birds, snow-flowers and snow-crystals woven into them. She had her own cooling waterfall, with a controlling gate, to make it more, or less, and her own forest of glass trees, with their visible phloem rising and falling. Sasan explained to her the uses of these beautiful inventions, which measured, he said, the weight, the heat, the changes of the ocean of elementary air in which they moved. The rising and falling glass bubbles, each filled to a different weight, measured the heat of the column of water that supported them. The quicksilver columns, in the fine tubes within tubes, were made by immersing the end of the tube in a vessel of mercury, and stopping it with a finger, and then letting the column of quicksilver find its level, at which point the weight of the air could be read off the height of the column in the tube. And this column, he said, varied, with the vapours, the winds, the clouds in the outer atmosphere, with the height above the sea, or the depth of the cavern. You may measure such things also with alcohol, which can be coloured for effect. Fiammarosa had never seen him so animated, nor heard him speak so long. He showed her yet another instrument, which measured the wetness of the incumbent air with the beard of an oat or, in other cases, with a stretched hair. And he had made a system of vents and pulleys, channels and pipes, taps and cisterns, which brought the mountain snow and the deep mountain springs in greater and lesser force into the place, as the barometers and thermometers and hygrometers indicated a need to adjust the air and the temperature. With all these devices, Sasan said, he had made an artificial world, in which he hoped his wife could live, and could breathe, and could be herself, for he could neither bear to keep her in the hot sunny city, nor could he bear to lose her. And Fiammarosa embraced him amongst the sighing spun glass and the whispering water. She could be happy, she said, in all this practical beauty. But what would they live on? How could they survive, on glass, and stone, and water? And Sasan laughed, and took her by the hand, and showed her great chambers in the rock where all sorts of plants were growing, under windows which had been cut to let in the sun, and glazed to adjust his warmth, and where runnels of water ran between fruit trees and seedlings, pumpkin plants and herbs. There was even a cave for a flock of goats, hardy and silky, who went out to graze on the meagre pastures and came in at night. He himself must come and go, Sasan said, for he had his work, and his land to look to. But she would be safe here, she could breathe, she could live in her own way, or almost, he said, looking anxiously at her. And she assured him that she would be more than happy there. 'We can make air, water, light, into something both of us can live in,' said Sasan. 'All I know, and some things I have had to invent, has gone into building this place for you.'

But the best was to come. When it was night, and the whole place was sleeping, with its cold air currents moving lazily between the glass stems, Sasan came to Fiammarosa's room, carrying a lamp, and a narrow package, and said, 'Come with me.' So she followed him, and he led her to a rocky stairway that went up, and round, and up, and round, until it opened on the side of the mountain itself, above the snow-line. Fiammarosa stepped out under a black velvet sky, full of burning cold silver stars, like globes of mercury, onto a field of untouched snow, such as she had never thought to see again. And she took off her slippers and stepped out onto the sparkling crust, feeling the delicious crackle beneath her toes, the soft sinking, the voluptuous cold. Sasan opened his packet, which contained the strange flute he had played when he wooed her. He looked at his wife, and began to play, a lilting, swaying tune that ran away over the snowfields and whispered into the edges of silence. And Fiammarosa took off her dress, and her shawls and her petticoat, stood naked in the snow, shook out her pale hair and began to dance. As she danced, a whirling white shape, her skin of ice-crystals, that she had believed she would never feel again, began to form along her veins, over her breasts, humming round her navel. She was lissom and sparkling, she was cold to the bone and full of life. The moon glossed the snow with gold and silver. When, finally, Sasan stopped playing, the icewoman darted over to him, laughing with delight, and discovered that his lips and fingers were blue with cold; he had stopped because he could play no more. So she rubbed his hands with her cold hands, and kissed his mouth with her cold lips, and with friction and passion brought his blood back to some movement. They went back to the bedchamber with the spun-glass curtains, and opened and closed a few channels and conduits, and lay down to make love in a mixture of currents of air, first warm, then cooling, which brought both of them to life.

In a year, or so, twin children were born, a dark boy, who resembled his mother at birth, and became, like her, pale and golden, and a pale, flower-like girl, whose first days were white and hairless, but who grew a mane of dark hair like her father's and had a glass-blower's, flute-player's mouth. And if Fiammarosa was sometimes lonely in her glass palace, and sometimes wished both that Sasan would come more often, and that she could roam amongst fjords and ice-fells, this was not unusual, for no one has everything they can desire. But she was resourceful and hopeful, and made a study of the vegetation of the Sasanian snow-line, and a further study of which plants could thrive in mountain air under glass windows, and corresponded—at long intervals—with authorities all over the world on these matters. Her greatest discovery was a sweet blueberry, that grew in the snow, but in the glass garden became twice the size, and almost as delicate in flavour.

Honorable Mentions: 1998

Acaster, Linda D., "The Lake," *Dark Horizons* 37.

Adams, John Luther, "The Place Where You Go to Listen," *The North American Review*, Vol. 283, #2.

Addison, Linda A., "Fiery Oracle" (poem), *White Knuckles* 8.

Adrian, Chris, "The Sum of Our Parts," *Ploughshares*, Winter 1998.

Aniolowski, Scott David, "Mr. Bauble's Bag," *Horrors! 365 Scary Stories*.

Anzalone, A. L., "The Kiss," *The Urbanite* 10.

Ardai, Charles, "Kyushu's Disguise," *Noirotica 2: Pulp Friction*.

Arnzen, Michael, "Immaterial Girl," *Imagination Fully Dilated*.

Asher, Neal L., "Alternative Hospital," *Kimota* 8.

Asplund, Russell, "The Rabbi and the Sorcerer," *Alfred Hitchcock's Mystery Magazine*, Oct.

Astley, Mark, "Women's Trouble," *Psychotrope* 6.

Attard, Karen, "Extracts From a Chronicle," *Eidolon* 25/26.

Bailey, Dale, "Night of the Fireflies," *The Magazine of Fantasy & Science Fiction*, Jan.

Barker, Trey R., "Embrace the Flesh," *Night Terrors* 7.

———, "Head," *Talebones* 10.

———, "Stones in the Passway," *Epitaph* 4.

Barr, Nevada, "Ione," *Mary Higgins Clark Mystery Magazine*, Summer.

Barton, Antigone, "More People Like Me," *AHMM* Jan.

Behnke, Thomas, "Insomnia" (poem), *Talebones* 12.

Benderson, Bruce, "Old World Manners," *Brothers of the Night*.

Bennett, Nancy, "John's Tale," *All Hallows* 19.

Berliner, Janet, "Amazing Grace: A 'Legs' Cleveland Musical Production," *More Monsters from Memphis*.

Bernard, Kenneth, "Fish Eye," *Salmagundi*, Fall.

Bestwick, Simon, "The Elms," *Enigmatic Tales* 2, Sep.

———, "The Foot of the Garden," *Enigmatic Tales* 1.

Bigelow, Gary, "Quilts," *Sisters of Internment*.

Bisson, Terry, "Incident at Oak Ridge," *F&SF*, July.

Blaylock, James P., "The Old Curiosity Shop," *F&SF*, Feb.

Blevins, Tippi N., "A Month of Bleeding," *The Kiss of Death*.

Block, Lawrence, "Like a Bone in the Throat," *Murder for Revenge*.

———, "Three in the Side Pocket," *Hot Blood X*.

Bohnhoff, Maya Kaathryn, "Who Have No Eyes," *Interzone* 134.

Borges, Jorge Luis, "Shakespeare's Memory," translated from the Spanish by Andrew Hurley, *The New Yorker*, March 13.

Boston, Bruce, "Confessions of a Body Thief" (poem), *Broadside*.

———, "The Humpback and the Changeling" (poem), *Mythic Delirium*.

Bowes, Richard, "Diana in the Spring," *F&SF*, Aug.

———, "So Many Miles to the Heart of a Child," *F&SF*, Apr.

Braly, David, "The Rut," *AHMM*, Apr.

Brandon, Paul, "The Marsh Runners," *Dreaming Down-Under*.

Braunbeck, Gary A., "Adhumbria," *The Conspiracy Files*.

———, "Erosion Road," *Horrors! 365 Scary Stories*.

———, "Iphigenia," *Dark Whispers*.

Brenchley, Chaz, "The Day I Gave up Smoking," *Cemetery Dance* 29.

———, "The Keys to D'Esperance," (chapbook).

———, "Murder at the Red House," *Blood Waters*.

Brite, Poppy Z., "Are You Loathsome Tonight?," *Are You Loathsome Tonight?*

———, "Monday's Special," Ibid.

Brown, Simon, "Love and Paris," *Eidolon* 25/26.

———, "With Clouds at our Feet," *Dreaming Down-Under*.

Bruchman, Denise M., "Fate's Exile," *Imagination Fully Dilated*.

Bryant, Edward, "Ashes on Her Lips," *Sirens and other Daemon Lovers*.

Budnitz, Judy, "Got Spirit," *Flying Leap*.

Burke, John, "Handfast," *The Ex Files*.

Butlin, Ron, "A Stranger's House," *The Third Alternative* 18.

Cabrera, Lydia, "Daddy Turtle and Daddy Tiger," translated from the Spanish by Susan Bassnett, *The Voice of the Turtle*.

Cadger, Rick, "Heart of the Machine," *Dark Horizons* 37.

Cadigan, Pat, "Witnessing the Millennium," *Disco 2000*.

Campbell, Ramsey, "Never to be Heard," *Imagination Fully Dilated*.

———, "The Other Names," *Interzone* 137.

———, "Ra*e," *Ghosts and Grisly Things*.

———, "Twice by Fire," *The Crow: Shattered Lives & Broken Dreams*.

Carr, Michael, "In the Trembling," *Gothic.net*, Sep.

Carradice, Phil, "The Isle of Avalon," *The Mammoth Book of Arthurian Legends*.

Carson, Ciaran, "They Seek Him There" (poem), *Chicago Review*, Vol. 44, Nov. 3/4.

Cary, Madeleine, "Red-Eye," *Interzone* 131.

Cave, Hugh, "Right of Way," *Night Terrors* 6.

Chandra, G. S. Sharat, "Demon," *Sari of the Gods*.

Chapman, Stepan, "The Medic," *Maverick Press* 12.

Chizmar, Richard T., "The Man with X-Ray Eyes," *The UFO Files*.

———, "Monsters," *Horrors! 365 Scary Stories*.

Christian, M., "One After Another," *Noirotica 2: Pulp Friction*.

Clairday, Robynn, "Afraid of the Water," *Peridot Books*, Summer.

Clark, Lee, "The Assassination of Emil Butha," *Mindmares*, Spring.

Clegg, Douglas, "265 and Heaven," *Imagination Fully Dilated*.

Clinton, Robert, "Serpentine," *The American Voice* 46.

Coates, Deborah, "The Queen of Mars," *Between the Darkness and the Fire: Imaginative Fiction from the Internet*.

Cohen, Lisa R., "Innamorata," *Realms of Fantasy*, Dec.

Colagna, Allison, "Crystal Blue," *Enigmatic Tales* 1–2.

Congreve, William, "Boy," *Epiphanies of Blood*.

_____, "The Death of Heroes" (novella), Ibid.

_____, "The Maker of Loaded Dice," *Infinitas Bookshop*.

_____, Conover, David, "In Living Color (A Denouement)," *Imagination Fully Dilated*.

Constantine, Storm, "My Lady of the Hearth," *Sirens and other Daemon Lovers*.

Contos, Maria, "The Necklace," *Roadworks* 2.

Cornelison, J. Garrett, "A Rape of Gomorrah" (poem), *Frisson* 9, Spring.

Coulter, Lynn B., "The Singing Thing," *F&SF*, Jan.

Cowdrey, Albert E., "White Magic," *F&SF*, Mar.

Crawford, Dan, "Dead Certainties," *Not One of Us* 20.

Crofts, Terry, "The Legend of Flannan Isle," *All Hallows* 19.

Cromby, Andrew, "The Fireman of Bentley Wood," *Nasty Piece of Work* 7.

Crowther, Peter, "Front-Page McGuffin and the Greatest Story Never Told," *Black Cats and Broken Mirrors*.

_____, "Fugue on a G-String," (chapbook).

_____, "The Space Between the Lines," *Imagination Fully Dilated*.

D'Ammassa, Don, "Cat Eyes," *Night Terrors* 7.

_____, "Leave Me Alone," *Night Terrors* 6.

_____, "Scylla and Charybdis," *In the Shadow of the Gargoyle*.

Dann, Jack, "Spirit Dog," *The Crow: Shattered Lives & Broken Dreams*.

Davidson, Avram, and Swanwick, Michael, "Vergil Magus: King Without Country," *Asimov's Science Fiction*, July.

Davis, Carol Anne, "The Ghosts of Bees," *Fresh Blood* 2.

Davis, John, "Fifth Step," *Imagination Fully Dilated*.

Dedman, Stephen, "A Single Shadow," *Interzone* 131.

de Lint, Charles, "China Doll," *The Crow: Shattered Lives & Broken Dreams*.

_____, "If I Close My Eyes Forever," *Moonlight and Vines*.

_____, "In the Quiet After Midnight" *Olympus*.

_____, "The Pennyman," *Black Cats and Broken Mirrors*.

_____, "Second Chances," Triskell Press chapbook.

_____, "Sweetgrass & City Streets" (poem), *Moonlight and Vines*.

Deering, Valerie, "Some" (poem), *Dangerous Dames*.

Denton, Bradley, "Blackburn Bakes Cookies," *One Day Closer to Death*.

Devereaux, Robert, "Pine Supine," *Horrors! 356 Scary Stories*.

DeVita, Randy, "Collections," *White Knuckles* 8.

Dixit, Shikhar, "Suits," *Gathering Darkness*, June.

_____, "Theirs is the Language of Muffled Voices," *Mindmares*, Spring.

Doctorow, Cory, "Jaime Spanglish in the Nile," *On Spec*, Winter.

Donati, Stefano, "So Much to Answer For," *Not One of Us* 19.

Dowling, Terry, "Downloading," *Event Horizon*, Oct.

Dozois, Gardner and Swanwick, Michael, "Ancestral Voices" (novella), *Asimov's SF*, Aug.

Duchamp, L. Timmel, "Portrait of the Artist as a Middle-aged Woman," *Leviathan Two*.

Duffy, Steve, "The Close at Chadminster," *The Night Comes On*.

_____, "Ex Libris," Ibid.

_____, "Figures on a Hillside," Ibid.

_____, "The Lady of the Flowers," *Ghosts & Scholars* 27.

———, "The Night Comes On," *The Night Comes On.*

———, "On the Dunes," *All Hallows,* 17.

———, "One Over," *The Night Comes On.*

———, "The Ossuary," Ibid.

———, "Out of the Water, Out of the Sea," Ibid.

———, "The Return Journey," Ibid.

———, "Tidesend," Ibid.

Duncan, Andy, "The Premature Burials," *Gothic.net.*

Duncker, Patricia, "The Arrival Matters," *Monsieur Shoushana's Lemon Trees.*

Dyer, Lawrence, "Colonies," *Interzone* 138.

Edghill, India, "Bisclavret," *Marion Zimmer Bradley's Fantasy Magazine,* 38.

———, "Maiden Phoenix," *MZBFM* 35.

Egan, Doris, "The Sweet of Bitter Bark and Burning Clove," *Sirens and Other Daemon Lovers.*

Eisenstein, Phyllis, "The Island in the Lake," *F&SF,* Dec.

Ellis, Dave, "Blood from a Stone," *Peeping Tom* 29.

Emery, Lorin, "Hallowed Ground," *The Vampire's Crypt,* Spring.

Engstrom, Elizabeth, "One Fine Day on the River Styx," *Imagination Fully Dilated.*

———, "Renewing the Option," *The UFO Files.*

Etchemendy, Nancy, "Double Silver Truth," *F&SF,* June.

Evenson, Brian, "Body," *Fetish.*

Fairchild, Michelle and Fairchild, Jeannine Renee, "Sweet Little Death," *Noirotica 2: Pulp Friction.*

Farrant, M. A. C., "Closing Time at Barbie's Boutique," *What's True, Darling.*

Ferguson, Andrew C., "Shades of Burke and Hare at the Jekyll and Hyde," *All Hallows* 19.

Ferrenz, Barbara J., "Burb Vamp," *Horrors! 365 Scary Stories.*

Files, Gemma, "Bottle of Smoke," *Demon Sex.*

———, "Torch Song," *Transversions* 8/9.

Finch, Paul, "Daddy was a Space Alien," *Nasty Piece of Work* 7.

———, "Enemies at the Door," *The Third Alternative* 16.

Ford, Michael, "Imogean," *Eureka Literary Magazine,* Spring.

Foster, Alan Dean, "Procrastination," *The Crow: Shattered Lives & Broken Dreams.*

Fowler, Christopher, "The Cages," *Personal Demons.*

———, "Five Star," Ibid.

———, "Learning to Let Go," Ibid.

———, "Normal Life," *Dark Terrors 4.*

———, "Still Life," *Personal Demons.*

Fowler, Karen Joy, "Go Back," *Black Glass.*

Frahm, Leanne, "Rain Season," *Eidolon* 27.

Freireich, Valerie J., "Stepmother," *Weird Tales* 313.

Friesner, Esther M., "Brown Dust," *Starlight 2.*

———, "In the Realm of Dragons," *Asimov's SF,* Feb.

Frost, Gregory, "How Meersh the Bedeviler Lost His Toes," *Asimov's SF,* Sep.

G, Amelia, "Blowfish," *Eros ex Machina.*

Gagliani, William D., "Until Hell Calls Our Names," *More Monsters from Memphis.*

Gaiman, Neil, "Desert Wind" (poem), *Smoke and Mirrors.*

———, "How Do You Think It Feels?" *In the Shadow of the Gargoyle.*

———, "Looking for the Girl," *Demon Sex.*

———, "Tastings," *Sirens and Other Daemon Lovers.*

———, "The Wedding Present," *Dark Terrors 4*.

Gallagher, Stephen, "The Boy Who Talked to Animals," *Peeping Tom* 29.

Gardner, C. A., "In Our Boxes," *Gothic.net*, July.

Garland, Mark A., "Harvest Moon," *Fields of Blood*.

George, Stephen R., "The Rescue," *Deadbolt Magazine* Vol. 1, No. 1.

Geston, Marks, "The Allies," *F&SF*, May.

Gioseffi, Daniela, "The Music of Mirrors," *Prairie Schooner*, Summer.

Gish, Robert Franklin, "Seeing the Elephant," *Dreams of Ouivira*.

Glass, Alexander, "A Bottleful of Shadows," *The Third Alternative* 17.

——— "The Mark of the Butterfly," *The Third Alternative* 18.

Goldstein, Lisa, "The Game this Year," *Asimov's SF*, Dec.

Gomez, Jewelle, "Lynx and Strand," *Don't Explain*.

Gorodischer, Angélica, "The End of a Dynasty," translated from the Spanish by Ursula K. Le Guin, *Starlight 2*.

Gould, Jason, "Kiss Me With Your Jackal Lips," *The Third Alternative* 15.

Graham, John, "The Dean of Gravity," *Between*.

Grant, Charles L., "The Soft Sound of Wings," *In the Shadow of the Gargoyle*.

Gresham, Stephen, "The Saint, The Satyr, and the Snakehole," *Hot Blood X*.

Griffin, Larry D., "Bacchus with the Boys" (poem), *The Oyster Review* Web site.

Griffin, Marnie Scofidio, "The Swans," *The Urbanite* 10.

Griffin, Peni R., "Fata," *Realms of Fantasy*, Feb.

Grimwood, Terry, "Demons and Demons," *Peeping Tom* 32.

Hardison, Janet, "Attrition," *Lore* 9.

Hays, Jess, "Matins," *The Vampire's Crypt*, Spring.

Higgins, Stephen, "The Waiting Tree," *Aurealis* 22.

Hinojosa, Francisco, "The Creation," translated from the Spanish by Kurt Hollander, *Hectic Ethics*.

Hodge, Brian, "As Above, So Below," (novella), *Fallen Idols*.

———, "Cenotaph," *In the Shadow of the Gargoyle*.

———, "Crime Movies," *Noirotica 2: Pulp Friction*.

———, "Desert Shoreline," *Horrors! 365 Scary Stories*.

———, "Empathy," *Hot Blood X*.

Hoffman, Nina Kiriki, "Caretaking," *Black Cats and Broken Mirrors*.

———, "Gone to Heaven Shouting," *F&SF*, Jan.

———, "Sweet Nothings," *F&SF*, Aug.

Holder, Nancy, "Appetite," *Hot Blood X*.

———, "The Ladies' Room," *The Conspiracy Files*.

———, "Little Dedo," *In the Shadow of the Gargoyle*.

Holmquest, C. L., "Live and Death," *Dark Annie* 1.

Hood, Daniel, "Scipio," *More Amazing Stories*.

Hood, Robert, "Tamed," *Dreaming Down-Under*.

Houarner, Gerard Daniel, "My Kind of Woman," *Nasty Piece of Work*, 9.

———, "Our Lady of the Jars," *Epitaph* 4.

Howell, Brian, "Head of a Girl," *Neonlit: Time Out Book of New Writing* Vol. 1.

Hughes, Rhys, "In the Margins," *Roadworks* 2.

Ikezawa, Natsuki, "Revenant," translated from the Japanese by Dennis Keene, *Still Lives*.

Indick, Ben P., "A Flash of Silver," *Horrors! 365 Scary Stories*.

Jackson, Shelley, "Cancer," *Fence*, Spring.

————, "Jominy, (An Art History)," *Fetish*.

Jacob, Charlee, "Legion," *Going Postal*.

————, "Soft Snares," *More Monsters from Memphis*.

————, "Co-Authoring the Delirium" (poem), *Mythic Delirium*.

Jacobs, Harvey, "Goobers," *F&SF*, July.

Jacobs, Mark, "The Liberation of Little Heaven," *American Literary Review* Web site, Fall.

Jakeman, Jane, "Neon," *Ghosts & Scholars* 26.

————, "River," *All Hallows* 18.

Jakubowski, Maxim, "Wearing Her Don't-Talk-to-Me-Face," *Eros ex Machina*.

James, Evelyn, "Dancing With Alligators" (poem), *The Georgia Review*, Vol. LII, No. 1.

Jonas, Gary, "Broken Spirits," *Curse of the Magazine Killers*. 127

————, "La Cenerentola," *Interzone* 136.

Kanar, Bryn, "Four of a Kind," *Cemetery Dance* 29.

Keleman, Aubri, "The Moon from Estonia" (poem), *The Malahat Review* 124.

Kelly, Michael, "Killing the Rat," *The Literary Journal*, June.

Kenworthy, Christopher, "The Clear," *Event Horizon*, Jan.

Kernaghan, Eileen, "Wild Things" (poem), *On Spec*, Fall.

Ketchum, Jack, "Amid the Walking Wounded," *The UFO Files*.

————, "The Exit at Toledo Blade Boulevard," *The Exit at Toledo Blade Boulevard*.

————, "Firedance," *Imagination Fully Dilated*.

————, "The Visitor," *The Exit at Toledo Blade Boulevard*.

————, "When the Penny Drops," *The Exit at Toledo Blade Boulevard/Cemetery Dance* 29.

————, "Winter Child," *The Exit at Toledo Blade Boulevard*.

Kiernan, Caitlín R., "Breakfast in the House of the Rising Sun," *Noirotica 2: Pulp Friction*.

————, "Postcards from the King of Tides," *Candles for Elizabeth*.

————, "Superheroes," *Brothers of the Night*.

Kihn, Greg, "Olivia in the Graveyard with Pablo," *Hot Blood X*.

Kilworth, Garry, "Mirrors," *Sirens and Other Daemon Lovers*.

King, Ladonna, "Saint" (poem), *Not One of Us* 19.

Knudsen, Kerry, "Plaything," *Cyber-Psychos AOD* 8.

Koertge, Ronald, "Lazarus" (poem), *The Barcelona Review* Web site.

Koja, Kathe, "Reckoning," *Extremities*.

Krysl, Marilyn, "Eating God," *How to Accommodate Men*.

Kushner, Ellen, "Hot Water," *The Essential Bordertown*.

Lanata, Jorge, "Hide the Moon," translated from the Spanish by Asa Zatz, *Prospero's Mirror*.

Landis, Geoffrey A., "Snow," *Starlight 2*.

Lane, Joel, "The Country of Glass," *Dark Terrors 4*.

————, "Nowhere to Go," *Nasty Piece of Work* 10.

————, "Prison Ships," *The Third Alternative* 17.

————, "The Willow Pattern," *The Ex Files*.

Langford, David, "As Strange a Maze as E'er Men Trod," *Shakepearean Detectives: More Shake-spearean Whodunnits*.

Lannes, Roberta, "Mr Guidry's Head," *Dark Terrors 4*.

Lawrence, Stephen, "The Conversion of Anage," *Aurealis* 19.

Lawson, Chris, "Unborn Again," *Dreaming Down-Under*.

Lebbon, Tim, "The First Law" (novella), *Faith in the Flesh*.

————, "From Bad Flesh" (novella), Ibid.

Lee, Mary Soon, "Heron," *Transversions* 8/9.

———, "Roadside Stop," *Pirate Writings* 15.

———, "The Three Kingdoms," *Talebones* 12.

Lee Tanith, "I Bring You Forever," *Realms of Fantasy*, June.

———, "Jedella Ghost," *Interzone* 135.

———, "Yellow & Red," *Interzone* 132.

Leonard, Paul, "Riverrun," *The Third Alternative* 18.

Lepovetsky, Lisa, "The Big One," *Horrors! 365 Scary Stories*.

Lewis, D. F., "The Last Story in the Book," *Dark Horizons* 37.

———, "The Tszarina's Overcoat," *Flesh & Blood* 3.

Lifshin, Lyn, "Afterwards it was Like" (poem), *Frisson*, Winter 1997.

Lillie, Brent, "Split," *Eidolon* 27.

Link, Kelly, "Carnation, Lily, Lily, Rose," *Fence*, Fall.

Little, Bentley, "Life With Father," *Going Postal*.

———, "Playing with Fire," *Hot Blood X*.

Lockey, Paul, "Adventure Weekend," *Nasty Piece of Work* 7.

Lockley, Steve, "Always a Dancer," *Indigenous Fiction*, Aug.

Lopez, Barry, "Two Dogs at Rowena," *Off the Beaten Path: Stories of Place*.

MacIntyre, F. Gwynplaine, "Mother-of-All," *The Mammoth Book of Fairy Tales* (1997).

MacLeod, Catherine, "The Bone House," *On Spec*, Winter.

MacLeod, Ian B., "The Summer Isles," *Asimov's SF*, Oct/Nov.

Maguire, Gregory, "Beyond the Fringe," *A Glory of Unicorns*.

Malenky, Barbara, "Seasons," *Space & Time* 88.

Mann, Anthony, "Vault," *The Third Alternative* 18.

Margolin, Phillip, "Angie's Delight," *Murder for Revenge*.

Marshall III, Joseph, "Cozy by the Fire," *The Dance House: Stories from Rosebud*.

Massie, Elizabeth, "Thanks," *Lore* 9.

Masterton, Graham, "Anais," *Manitou Man: The Worlds of Graham Masterton*.

———, "Picnic at Lac du Sang," *Hot Blood X*.

———, "Saving Grace," *Manitou Man: The Worlds of Graham Masterton*.

Maynard, L. H. and Sims, M. P. N., "Moths," *Enigmatic Novellas* 1.

———, Sims "Veneer," *Black Rose* 2, July.

McAuley, Paul J., "Sea Change, with Monsters" (novella), *Asimov's SF*, Sep.

———, "The Secret of My Success," *Interzone* 131.

McGarry, Terry, "God of Exile," *Talebones* 12.

McGuire, D. A., "The Jet Stone," *AHMM*, Dec.

McMahon, Paul, "How Brando was Made," *The Darkest Thirst*.

McMullen, Sean, "Rule of the People," *Aurealis* 20/21.

McNaughton, Brian, "Fragment of a Diary Found on Ellesmere Island," *Horrors! 365 Scary Stories*.

———, "Interrupted Pilgrimage," Ibid.

———, "Lovelocks," Ibid.

Meikle, William, "Wee Robbie," *Kimota* 8.

Meno, Joe, "Drive," *Horrors! 365 Scary Stories*.

Miller, James, "Weak End," *Dark Terrors* 4.

Millhauser, Steven, "Beneath the Cellars of Our Town," *The Knife Thrower and Other Stories*.

Mingin, William, "Crush," *Tales of the Unanticipated* 19.

Monteleone, Thomas F., "Under Your Skin," *Imagination Fully Dilated*.

———, "A Mind is a Terrible Thing," *The Conspiracy Files*.

Moore, Judi, "Thumbs," *Interzone* 133.

Morlan, A. R. "The Time of the Bleeding Pumpkins," *Fields of Blood.*

Morlan, A. R. and Johnson, James B., ". . . Redeem my Soul From the Power of the Grave . . ." *Space & Time* 88.

Morrell, David, "Front Man," *Murder for Revenge.*

Mosiman, Billie Sue, "Love Lies Bleedin' " *The UFO Files.*

Mundt, Martin, "Fashion Victim," *Horrors! 365 Scary Stories.*

Murphy, Joe, "Insects and Desire," Ibid.

Murphy, Roberta, "Owl Noises," *The Third Alternative* 17.

Murray, Will, "Miss Hitchbone Reclaims Her Own," *Horrors! 365 Scary Stories.*

Navarro, Yvonne, "Cold Beneath the Vinegar Tree," *Imagination Fully Dilated.*

———, "Dad Brings a Deader Home," *Dark Whispers.*

Neilson, Robert, "Pin-Up," *Nasty Piece of Work* 7.

Newton, Kurt, "Live Among the Dream Merchants" (poem), *Terata: Anomalies of Literature.*

Nicholls, Mark, "What Come in Threes," *All Hallows* 17.

Nichols, Ian, "The Last Dance," *Dreaming Down-Under.*

Nichols, Lyn, "No Pain," *Horrors! 365 Scary Stories.*

Nicholson, Geoff, "Making Monsters," *Dark Terrors* 4.

Nicholson, Scott, "Haunted," *More Monsters from Memphis.*

Nickles, Tim, "Glisten and Beyond Herring," *The Ex Files.*

Nicoll, Gregory, "As Thousands Screamed," *Horrors! 365 Scary Stories.*

Oates, Joyce Carol, "The Collector of Hearts," *The Collector of Hearts.*

———, "Feral," *F&SF*, Sep.

———, "The Sons of Angus MacElster," *Conjunctions* 30.

O'Driscoll, Mike, "Dancing with Creation," *The Third Alternative* 15.

Olsen, Lance, "Family," *The Literary Review*, Fall.

O'Nan, Stewart, "The Departed," *Epoch*, Vol. 47, No. 1.

Osier, Jeffrey, "The Disembodied," *Dark Regions* 3.

Partridge, Norman, "Coyotes," *The Conspiracy Files.*

———, "Red Right Hand," (chapbook).

Paul, Chris, "Three Dogs Bark," *Odyssey* 3.

Pelan, John and Lee, Edward, "Stillborn," *Imagination Fully Dilated.*

Peterson, Geri, "The Grimm Truth" (poem), *The New Yorker*, Dec. 7.

peteso, "Little Angels," *Imagination Fully Dilated.*

Pflug, Ursula, "Stones," *Divine Realms.*

Piccirilli, Tom, "Cower Before Bobo," *Horrors! 365 Scary Stories.*

———, "From the Swamp Rot Rises My Baby's Dreams," Ibid.

———, "Go Back to the Church," *More Monsters from Memphis.*

———, "Thunders of the Captains, and the Shouting," *The Conspiracy Files.*

———, "Where the Martyred Flesh Knows Serenity," *The Third Alternative* 18.

Ping, Wang, "Crush," *Fetish.*

Piziks, Steven, "The Rose, the Rich Man and Mother Berchte," MZBFM 35.

Pollack, Rachel, "The Fool, the Stick, and the Princess," *F&SF*, Oct/Nov.

Pollard, J. A., "Jinn," *Going Postal.*

Post, Roy L., "Incident at Mile 51," *Going Postal.*

Powell, Padgett, "All Along the Watchtower," *Aliens of Affection.*

Priest, Christopher, "I, Haruspex," *The Third Alternative* 16.

Proulx, Annie, "The Half-Skinned Steer," *Off the Beaten Path: Stories of Place.*

Radeck, I. B., "The Knight's Tale and the Maiden's Tale" (poem), *Apples and Oranges, Oranges and Apples International Poetry Magazine* Web site.

Rathbone, Wendy, "An Immortal Valentine" (poem), *Dreams of Decadence* 6.

Reed, Kit, "On the Penal Colony," *F&SF*, Aug.

Reyes, Alfonso, "The Dinner," translated from the Spanish by Rick Francis, *Prospero's Mirror*.

Reynolds, Kay, "Good-bye to Singer Swann," *Horrors! 365 Scary Stories*.

Richter, Joan, "Recipe Secrets," *Ellery Queen's Mystery Magazine* Sept./Oct.

Riedel, Kate, "Whyte Laydie," *On Spec*, Spring.

Rios, Alberto, "Don Gustavo, Who Had a Hand for an Ear," *Prairie Schooner*, Summer.

Robertson, Miriam, "Road Kill," *Gravity's Angels*.

Robertson, William P., "The Sea" (poem), *Penny Dreadful* 7.

Roche, Thomas S., "Forgetaboutit," *Noirotica 2: Pulp Friction*.

Rodd, David, "Box Number," *All Hallows* 17.

Rodgers, Alan, "At the Bus Station," *Horrors! 365 Scary Stories*.

Rogers, Bruce Holland, "The Dead Boy at Your Window," *The North American Review*, Nov/Dec.

_____, "Thirteen Ways to Water," *Black Cats and Broken Mirrors*.

Rogers, L. K., "Plain Jane," *Flesh & Blood* 3.

Rooke, Leon, "Eustace Among the Gypsies," *The Antioch Review*, 1998.

Rosenman, John B., "Neighbors," *Going Postal*.

Rowe, Christopher, "Kin to Crows," *Realms of Fantasy*, June.

Royle, Nicholas, "Vicki Dreams," *Peeping Tom* 32.

Rubinstein, Gillian, "And Still the Birds Keep Circling," *Trapped!*

Russell, Jay, "Sullivan's Travails," *Dark Terrors* 4.

Russo, Patricia, "Holly," *Lore* 9.

Russo, Richard Paul, "Butterflies," *F&SF*, Aug.

Ryan, Patrick, "The Real Ones," *The Ontario Review* 49.

Saaveq, Pedro J., "Mordred on the Couch" (poem), *The New York Quarterly* 57.

Sallee, Wayne Allen, "Carrion Luggage," *Cyber-Psychos AOD* 8.

_____, "Don's Last Minute," *Horrors! 365 Scary Stories*.

_____, "It's Hell Waking Up," Ibid.

Sallis, James, "Old Time," *Realms of Fantasy*, Dec.

Salmonson, Jessica Amanda, "Collector of Rugs," *Horrors! 365 Scary Stories*.

_____, "The Ugly Unicorn," A *Glory of Unicorns*.

Sanchez, Magaly, "Catalina in the Afternoons," translated from the Spanish by Cindy Schuster, *Cubana: Contemporary Fiction by Cuban Women*.

Sandner, David and Weisman, Jacob, "Egyptian Motherlode," *Realms of Fantasy*, Apr.

Saunders, George, "Sea Oak," *The New Yorker* Dec. 28 and Jan. 4, 1999.

Savage, Felicity, "How Shannaro Tolkinson Lost and Found His Heart," *The Essential Bordertown*.

Schein, Lorraine, "Dream Pillow I," *Space & Time* 88.

Schimel, Lawrence, "Secret Societies," *Blood Lines*.

Schimel, Lawrence and Mosiman, Billie Sue, "The Scent of Magnolias," *Southern Blood*

Schonfeld, Yael, "Behind the Wheel," *Talebones* 12.

Schow, David J., "Gills," *Crypt Orchids*.

_____, "The Incredible True Facts in the Case," Ibid.

_____, "Petition," *Gothic.net*, Dec.

_____, Play adaptation of Robert Bloch's story "Final Performance," Ibid.

Schutz, Benjamin M., "Not Enough Monkeys," *EOMM*, Sep./Oct.

Schwader, Ann K., "Home Visitor," *Dreams of Decadence* 6.

Schweitzer, Darrell, "On the Last Night of the Festival of the Dead," *Weird Tales* 313.

———— "Seeking the Gifts of the Queen of Vengeance," *Odyssey* 2.

————, "A Servant of Satan," *Interzone* 136.

Shaw, Melissa Lee, "Heat" (poem), *Sirens and Other Daemon Lovers*.

Sherman, Delia, "Socks," *The Essential Bordertown*.

Sherman, Josepha, "The Cat Who Wasn't Black," *Black Cats and Broken Mirrors*.

Shirley, John, "Black Hole Sun, Won't You Come?," *Black Butterflies*.

————, "What Would You Do for Love?," Ibid.

Silva, David B., "The Night in Fog," (chapbook)

Silverberg, Robert, "Waiting for the End," *Asimov's SF*, Oct./Nov.

Silverman, Leah, "Always Been the Special One," *On Spec*, Fall.

Sinclair, Iain, "No More Yoga of the Night Club," *Fresh Blood* 2.

Singleton, Sarah, "Cassilago's Wife," *Interzone* 137.

Sinha-Morey, Bobbi, "Funeral Dance" (poem), *Talebones* 10.

Smith, D. K., "Bottomless," *Titanzine* Web site.

Snyder, Midori, "Dragon Child," *The Essential Bordertown*.

Somtow, S. P., "More Strange Than True," *Midsummer Night's Dreams*.

———— "Red as Jade" (novella), *The Crow: Shattered Lives & Broken Dreams*.

Springer, Nancy, "Frogged," *Black Cats and Broken Mirrors*.

————, "The Time of Her Life," *More Amazing Stories*.

Stableford, Brian, "O for a Fiery Gloom and Thee," *Sirens and Other Daemon Lovers*.

Steiber, Ellen, "Argentine," *The Essential Bordertown*.

————, "In the Season of Rains," *Sirens and Other Daemon Lovers*.

Stein, Bob, "Making It Right," *Horrors! 365 Scary Stories*.

Stevenson, Jennifer, "There Will Always Be Meat," *Fields of Blood*.

Straub, Peter, "Isn't it Romantic?" *Murder on the Run*.

Strieber, Whitley, "Desperate Dan," Ibid.

Studach, Stephen, "Dialogue with the Devil," *Penumbra*.

————, "Pain Demon," Ibid.

Swanwick, Michael, "Radiant Doors," *Asimov's SF*, Sep.

Swenson, Honna, "The Jesus Shrine," *Epitaph* 4.

Taylor, Lucy, "Dead Blue," *Imagination Fully Dilated*.

————, "The Hungry Hour," *The Mammoth Book of New Erotica*.

————, "Joy Ride," *Eros ex Machina*.

————, "Torch Song," *Noirotica 2: Pulp Friction*.

Tem, Melanie, "The Game," *Weird Tales* 313.

————, "Memento Mori," *Hot Blood X*.

————, "Sweet," *Going Postal*.

Tem, Steve and Melanie, "Lost," *Imagination Fully Dilated*.

Tem, Steve Rasnic, "The Cough," *Horrors! 365 Scary Stories*.

————, "Daytimer," Ibid.

————, "The Doll Thief," *The Third Alternative* 17.

————, "What Slips Away," *More Monsters From Memphis*.

Terry, Philip, "Do-It-Yourself Fable," *The North American Review*, Vol. 283, No. 1.

Tessier, Thomas, "Curing Hitler," *Dark Terrors* 4.

Thomas, Rob, "Sheep," *Trapped! Cages of Mind and Body*.

Thomas, Scott, "Sharp Medicine," *The Darklands Project*, Jan.

———, "Touched with Broken Clouds," *Penny Dreadful* 8, Autumn.

Timlett, Peter Valentine, "The Temptation of Launcelot," *The Mammoth Book of Arthurian Legends*.

Trommeshauser, Dietmar, "I Cry in White" (poem), *Transversions* 8/9.

Tuttle, Lisa, "My Pathology," *Dark Terrors* 4.

Vachss, Andrew, "Reaching Back," *Safe House: A Collection of the Blue*.

VanderMeer, Jeff, "Flight is for Those Who Have Not Crossed Over," *The Third Alternative* 17.

Waggoner, Tim, "All Fall Down," *Night Terrors* 6.

Wagoner, David, "The Four Fates" (poem), *The Southern Review*, Vol. 34, No. 4.

Walter, Victor, "A Bell for Rome," *New England Review*, Vol. 19, No. 1.

Walters, Christopher Lee, "The Renfields," *Weird Tales* 313.

Walton, Jo, "In Death's Dark Halls, A Dog Howls" (poem), *Dark Planet Poetry* Web site.

Ward, C. E., "Doctor's Orders," *Vengeful Ghosts*.

———, "Mirror Image," Ibid.

Ward, Cynthia, "Six-Guns of the Sierra Nevada," *Pulp Eternity* Volume 1.

Wargelin, Paul Victor, "Yours Truly, Charles A. Siringo," *Storyteller*, Winter.

Warren, Kaaron, "The Glass Woman," *Aurealis* 22.

Wass, Derek W., "The Talent Show," *Night Terrors* 6.

Watson, Ian, "The Bible in Blood," *Weird Tales* 313.

Webb, Don, "And the Woman Said," *Horrors! 365 Scary Stories*.

———, "Meeting the Messenger," *Realms of Fantasy*, June.

———, "Pagan Survival," *The Explanation*.

Wein, Elizabeth, "No Human Hands to Touch," *Sirens and Other Daemon Lovers*.

Weiner, Andrew, "The Disappearance Artist," *This Is the Year Zero*.

Westgard, Sten, "The Collector of Hands," *The Third Alternative* 18.

Whitbourn, John, "Another Place," *Binscombe Tales*.

———, "Binscombe Jihad," Ibid.

———, "Reggie Suntan," Ibid.

———, "Till Death do us Part," Ibid.

———, "A Video Nasty, or, The Sins of the Fathers," Ibid.

Willard, Willard, "The Ghosts of Ponce de Leon Park," *Crime Time* 2.2.

Williams, Conrad, "The Aspect," *The Third Alternative* 17.

———, "Consummation," *The Ex Files*.

———, "Eta," *Neonlit: Time Out Book of New Writing* 1.

———, "The Gallery," *The Third Alternative* 15.

———, "The Light that Passes Through You," *Sirens and Other Daemon Lovers*.

———, "The Suicide Pit," *Dark Terrors* 4.

Williams, Lisa, "Eve, After Eating" (poem), *Raritan Quarterly Review*.

Williams, Tess, "The Body Politic," *Dreaming Down-Under*.

Wiloch, Thomas, "Dr. Treacher's Asylum," *Epitaph* 4.

Wilson, Gahan, "The Cleft," *The Cleft and Other Odd Tales*.

Wilson, Robert Charles, "The Inner Inner City," *Realms of Fantasy*, Oct.

———, "Protocols of Consumption," *The UFO Files/Realms of Fantasy*, June.

Woodward, Simon, "Kisses by the Moth," *Nasty Piece of Work* 9.

Wormser, Baron, "Spirits of the Mall" (poem), *Michigan Quarterly Review*, Vol. 37, No. 4.

Yolen, Jane, "Green Ghosts," *Here There Be Ghosts*.

———, "It was the Hour" (poem), Ibid.

———, "Mandy," Ibid.

———, "Souls," Ibid.

Yolen, Jane and Harris, Robert, "Carrion Crows," *The Crow: Shattered Lives and Broken Dreams.*

Yumiko, Kurahashi, "The Witch Mask," *The Woman with the Flying Head.*

———, "The Trade," Ibid.

———, "The Woman with the Flying Head," Ibid.

The People Behind the Book

Horror editor ELLEN DATLOW was the fiction editor for *Omni* magazine and *Omni Online* for seventeen years. She is currently the editor of the online magazine *Event Horizon* (http://www.eventhorizon.com/sfzine/). She has edited numerous anthologies including *Alien Sex*, *Little Deaths*, *Lethal Kisses*, *Off Limits*, and *Sirens and other Daemon Lovers* (with Terri Windling). She has won five World Fantasy Awards for her editing. She lives in New York City.

Fantasy editor TERRI WINDLING has been an editor of fantasy literature for almost two decades, winning five World Fantasy Awards for her work. She has published more than twenty anthologies, including *The Armless Maiden* and *The Essential Bordertown* (with Delia Sherman). As a fiction writer, her books include *The Wood Wife* (winner of the Mythopoeic Award), and *The Moon Wife* (forthcoming). She also writes a regular column on folklore for *Realms of Fantasy* magazine. As a painter, she has exhibited in a number of museums across the U.S. and abroad. She divides her time between homes in Devon, England and Tucson, Arizona.

Packager JAMES FRENKEL edited Dell Books's science fiction and fantasy in the late 1970s and early 1980s, was the publisher of Bluejay Books in the 1980s, and has been a consulting editor for Tor Books for more than ten years. Along with KRISTOPHER O'HIGGINS and a legion of student interns, Frenkel edits, packages, and agents books in Madison, Wisconsin.

Media critic ED BRYANT is an award-winning writer of science fiction, fantasy, and horror. He has had short fiction published in numerous magazines and anthologies. He has won the Hugo Award for his fiction. His work also includes writing for television. He lives in Denver.

Comics critic SETH JOHNSON is a freelance writer who has written for newspapers and done work in the game industry. He lives in Madison, Wisconsin.

Artist THOMAS CANTY has won the World Fantasy Award for Best Artist. He has painted illustrations for innumerable books, ranging from fantasy and horror to suspense and thrillers. He is also an art director, and has designed many books and book jackets during a career that spans over twenty years. He has painted and designed the jacket/covers for every volume of *The Year's Best Fantasy and Horror*. He lives outside Boston.

Also available from St. Martin's Press

		Quantity	Price
The Year's Best Fantasy: Second Annual Collection ISBN: 0-312-03007-X (trade paperback)	($13.95)	_____	_____
The Year's Best Fantasy and Horror: Third Annual Collection ISBN: 0-312-04450-X (trade paperback)	($14.95)	_____	_____
The Year's Best Fantasy and Horror: Fourth Annual Collection ISBN: 0-312-06007-6 (trade paperback)	($15.95)	_____	_____
The Year's Best Fantasy and Horror: Fifth Annual Collection ISBN: 0-312-07888-9 (trade paperback)	($15.95)	_____	_____
The Year's Best Fantasy and Horror: Sixth Annual Collection ISBN: 0-312-09422-1 (trade paperback)	($16.95)	_____	_____
The Year's Best Fantasy and Horror: Seventh Annual Collection ISBN: 0-312-11102-9 (trade paperback)	($16.95)	_____	_____
The Year's Best Fantasy and Horror: Eighth Annual Collection ISBN: 0-312-13219-0 (trade paperback)	($16.95)	_____	_____
The Year's Best Fantasy and Horror: Ninth Annual Collection ISBN: 0-312-14450-4 (trade paperback)	($17.95)	_____	_____
The Year's Best Fantasy and Horror: Tenth Annual Collection ISBN: 0-312-15701-0 (trade paperback)	($17.95)	_____	_____
The Year's Best Fantasy and Horror: Eleventh Annual Collection ISBN: 0-312-19034-4 (trade paperback)	($17.95)	_____	_____
Writing Science Fiction and Fantasy ISBN: 0-312-08926-0 (trade paperback)	($9.95)	_____	_____

Postage & Handling:
(Books up to $12.00 - add $3.00; books up to $15.00 - add $3.50; books above $15.00 - add $4.00 — plus $1.00 for each additional book) 8% Sales Tax (New York State residents only)

Amount enclosed: _____

Name: _____

Address: _____

City: _____ State: _____ Zip: _____

Send this form (or a copy) with payment to:
Publishers Book & Audio, P.O. Box 070059, 5448 Arthur Kill Road, Staten Island, NY 10307.
Telephone (800) 288-2131. Please allow three weeks for delivery.
To place an order call: 1(888)330-8477 or Fax: 1(800)672-2054 • To reach a Customer Service Rep call:
1(888)330-8477 or Fax: 1(800)672-7540 • St. Martin's Press is a Pubnet Publisher • SAN 2002132